ROYAL
SCANDAL

ROYAL
SCANDAL

AIMÉE CARTER

DELACORTE PRESS

Text copyright © 2024 by Aimée Carter
Jacket art copyright © 2024 by Yordanka Poleganova

All rights reserved. Published in the United States by Delacorte Press,
an imprint of Random House Children's Books,
a division of Penguin Random House LLC, New York.

Delacorte Press is a registered trademark and the colophon
is a trademark of Penguin Random House LLC.

Visit us on the Web! GetUnderlined.com

Educators and librarians, for a variety of teaching tools,
visit us at RHTeachersLibrarians.com

Library of Congress Cataloging-in-Publication Data is available upon request.
ISBN 978-0-593-48593-4 (hardcover) — ISBN 978-0-593-48595-8 (ebook)

Printed in the United States of America
10 9 8 7 6 5 4 3 2 1
First Edition

TO MALCOLM

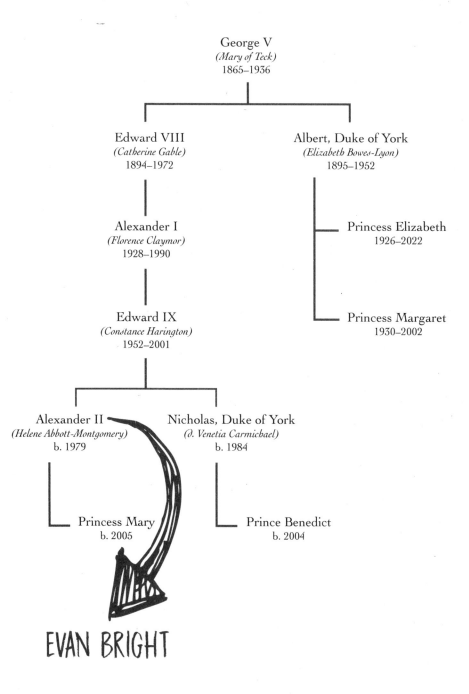

George V
(Mary of Teck)
1865–1936

Edward VIII
(Catherine Gable)
1894–1972

Albert, Duke of York
(Elizabeth Bowes-Lyon)
1895–1952

Alexander I
(Florence Claymor)
1928–1990

Princess Elizabeth
1926–2022

Edward IX
(Constance Harington)
1952–2001

Princess Margaret
1930–2002

Alexander II
(Helene Abbott-Montgomery)
b. 1979

Nicholas, Duke of York
(∂. Venetia Carmichael)
b. 1984

Princess Mary
b. 2005

Prince Benedict
b. 2004

EVAN BRIGHT

CHAPTER ONE

We at the *Regal Record* hope you've been good this year, because it seems like Saint Nicholas has come early for us all.

Despite rumours of a cancellation thanks to an untimely blizzard across the pond, the United Kingdom's notoriously naughty royal family will indeed be hosting a state banquet tonight for the president of the United States, Hope Park, and it promises to be chockful of chaos.

Under ordinary circumstances, this state visit would be noteworthy considering President Park is both the first woman and first Korean American to hold the highest office in the US. But, just like every other significant event as of late, this historic achievement has already been overshadowed by the most recent addition to the House of Windsor's royal family tree.

That's right—Evangeline Bright, the King's illegitimate American daughter, will be in attendance tonight, and given her past exploits, it's safe to assume she'll do something gratingly inept to steal the thunder—and the headlines—from those who've actually earned their place at the royal table.

In the five and a half months since Evangeline's tasteless and explosive BBC One interview detailing her own sordid behaviour that led directly to Jasper Cunningham's death—of which she was cleared of criminal charges, thanks to a reported backroom deal between Scotland Yard and the King's personal lawyers—the palace has seen fit to shove her down the throats of the British people at seemingly every turn. Hospital openings, charity appearances, even walkabouts typically reserved for legitimate members of the royal family—Evangeline has merrily joined in on all, resulting in a long list of missteps and blunders. Yet despite the efforts of the palace to make her palatable, it's becoming painfully clear that no amount of media and etiquette training can turn this American frog into a princess.

How much longer can the royal family's already-tattered reputation withstand the Bright blight? While we wait to see the fallout of tonight's state banquet and Evangeline's inevitable indiscretions, we at the *Regal Record* can only apologise yet again for revealing her identity this summer and unleashing this Pandora's box of mayhem and vexation on not only the entire country, but the world. One must own up to one's mistakes, and we deeply regret our part in this royal fiasco.

Let us hope that no one else ends up dead tonight.

—*The Regal Record,* 18 December 2023

"I'M WELL AWARE THAT BEING on time isn't a priority for you," says Tibby, clutching her phone like she's about to chuck it at my tiara. "But could you at least *pretend* to care that I'm about to lose my bloody job?"

I'm leaning against the wall in the long gallery of Windsor Castle, trying to keep my head upright as I fiddle with a strap on my stiletto. My gown isn't making it any easier, and as I set my foot down, the heel snags and comes dangerously close to ripping the shimmering burgundy fabric.

"It's my shoe," I mutter, untangling my hem. "One of the straps is loose."

Tibby arches an eyebrow as I test my weight again. Somehow, despite what has been an obscenely long day full of trivial appointments and last-minute fittings, Lady Tabitha Finch-Parker-Covington-Boyle's black pixie cut is still perfectly styled, and her tailored gray dress doesn't have a single piece of lint on it. Unfortunately for both of us, this superpower has yet to rub off on me in the six months she's been my personal secretary/babysitter, and no one is more aggrieved by my failure to develop a completely new personality than Tibby.

"I don't care if the heel's broken off and you're walking on your tiptoes," she says. "We *cannot* be late, Evan."

"We're not late." As I resume my march down the corridor, now with a noticeably uneven gait, I glance through the nearest window and into the dark courtyard beyond. A line of luxury vehicles snakes along the opposite wing of Windsor Castle, and royal footmen hoist umbrellas as tonight's guests exit their cars and step into the December downpour. "Okay, we're a little late, but—"

"There is no such thing as a 'little' late," says Tibby. "If His Majesty discovers you're missing, it'll be my neck on the block, not yours."

"He'll be too busy with the president to notice. Besides, they don't need me for the pictures, and I'm not escorting anyone inside."

"An unforgivable oversight," says Tibby irritably, as if this, too, is somehow my fault. "You're His Majesty's daughter, *and* you're American. You should be in the procession, preferably on the arm of a member of the president's family. Your absence will only start another wave of rumors in the press."

"I start rumors by breathing," I say. "Besides, it'd be an insult to pair me with anyone important."

Tibby sniffs. "Illegitimate or not, you're still of royal blood."

"Which is the only reason I'm part of this dog and pony show in the first place," I say. "That and the fact that the universe has a terrible sense of humor."

By the time we turn the corner and pass the royal family's private apartments, my scalp is throbbing. I reach up to adjust the Queen Florence tiara that's secured to my braided updo, but before my fingers can even graze the glittering headpiece, Tibby swats my hand away.

"Don't you dare," she says with more vehemence than usual. "Can you imagine the headlines if your tiara falls off in front of the Royal Rota? The metaphor alone—"

"The pins are digging in," I protest. "I think my scalp might actually be bleeding."

"Ignore it. The banquet won't last more than three or four hours."

"Three or four—" I gape at her. "Haven't you people ever heard of the Geneva Conventions?"

"You're royalty, darling," she says in the dismissive tone she always uses when I complain. "The Geneva Conventions don't apply."

I start to object, but before I can utter more than a single syllable, Tibby turns on her heel to face me, and I stumble to a halt.

"I understand you're uncomfortable, Evan," she says, her voice low and hurried. "I understand you'd rather not sit around for hours listening to a bunch of politicians make each other feel important. But this is the price you pay for being royal. This is the price you pay for living in a castle with a staff of hundreds to cater to your whims. You have every resource you could ever need, every opportunity you could ever dream of, and you are one of the most famous people in the world. You are privileged in a way damn few others are, and if you tell me one more time how uncomfortable your designer shoes and couture gown and priceless tiara are, I *will* throttle you."

For a long moment, we stare at each other in silence. She's

right, of course—every word of it—and I hate that six months ago, I would have throttled myself for acting like this, too.

"Sorry," I mumble, my cheeks growing warm. "I think I'm spending too much time around Maisie."

"Her Royal Highness's faults are no excuse for yours," says Tibby tartly, but at last she steps aside, and we continue down the hall toward the state apartments. "The people are watching you, Evan, and they deserve more than another ungrateful brat. Especially when you offer them hope that maybe their lives can become a fairy tale, too."

I snort. "Being accused of murder and having all my secrets exposed to the entire world counts as a fairy tale now?"

"Haven't you read the Brothers Grimm?" says Tibby. "Murder is practically a plot requirement. If we want any chance of making it in time, we'll have to go this way."

She ushers me into the royal family's private chapel—sacrilegious, I'm sure, though clearly the only sin Tibby's worried about is tardiness. She's moving so quickly now that I'm forced to do a strange skip to keep up, but when we finally reach the threshold of St. George's Hall, I stop in my tracks—and so does she.

While normally the vast hall is empty, save for the ever-present paintings, marble busts, and suits of armor that line the walls, a table that easily seats two hundred now stretches from one end to the other, covered in massive festive bouquets and more plates and utensils than I've ever seen. And because my life, while newly charmed, can never be fair, nearly all of tonight's guests are already inside as a fleet of footmen show them to their seats.

Tibby swears. "Keep your head up, but move quickly," she whispers, and this time I don't complain as we hurry to the nearest exit. Before we make it more than twenty feet, however, a woman at the end of the table gasps.

"Evangeline?" she says, her voice mercifully low. A few of her companions turn to look at me, too, and I smile and press my finger to my lips. Her shock quickly turns to conspiratorial amusement, and even though I'm not a princess—or even an official member of the royal family—she dips in a low curtsy.

A rising murmur follows Tibby and me now, and I do my best to walk properly in my uncooperative shoe, keenly aware of all the eyes on us. It's only sheer luck that I don't trip and fall on my face, and when we finally reach the nearest exit, Tibby all but yanks me through the doorway—

And straight into the middle of an explosion of camera flashes.

"Ah, Evangeline," says a deep voice as the door closes behind us. "I'm pleased you were able to make it."

His Majesty King Alexander II, monarch of the United Kingdom and Commonwealth, stands fifteen feet away in the opulent Grand Reception Room, his blue eyes fixed directly on me. While his slightly balding head is bare, his tuxedo is heavy with sashes and medals he never actually earned, and even though he's not especially tall or commanding, everything in the room seems to revolve around him like he's the only source of gravity.

Beside him stands a square-jawed woman I instantly recognize as President Park. They're posing for a cluster of photographers and members of the Royal Rota—the group of journalists whose only job is to cover the royal family—and both are still smiling widely even though every single camera is now pointed toward me.

Perfect.

Sorry, I mouth as a deep blush spreads across my face. I should curtsy, or at the very least dip my head in a show of respect. But as Tibby is so quick to lament, I'm not exactly a stickler for the rules, and as long as I have dual citizenship, I refuse to bow to anyone—even my endlessly patient father.

He doesn't seem to mind, and when he shoots me a wink before turning back to President Park, I know I'm forgiven for my unexpected entrance. By him, at least. Tibby is another story, and as she squeezes my arm in a supposed show of support, I'm sure it's only to measure how much acid she'll need to dissolve my body after she murders me for this.

As the photographers reluctantly return their attention to the main attraction, I slip into an empty corner and try to make myself as small as possible. Somehow, in the greatest show of self-restraint I've managed since arriving in England, I resist the urge to make sure my tiara hasn't slipped out of place. Given the number of pins currently digging into my scalp, it's undoubtedly right where I left it, but Tibby's earlier quip about headlines and a falling crown haunts me like a premonition I can't shake.

"And now our families," announces Alexander, and he gestures toward the other side of the room, where a small crowd is gathered. I spot two bobbing tiaras among the sea of suits and dresses, and finally Queen Helene appears with Princess Mary in tow.

Admittedly it doesn't take much to make me feel like an impostor most of the time, but one look at them, and I shrink even further into the metaphorical shadows. They're both stunning—the kind of gorgeous that only money can buy, with flawless porcelain skin, shiny hair, and blindingly white smiles. My statuesque stepmother is in a flowing ivory gown with her blond hair wrapped around the base of her glittering headpiece, and it's obvious why she's been declared the most beautiful woman in the world by multiple magazines. Everyone in the room is watching her—everyone except my father.

Maisie, my equally elegant half sister, wears a sapphire dress covered in crystals, but nothing outshines the intricate tiara perched above her strawberry-blond waves. There's something slightly off about her expression, though—something cold and a little stiff, but not so much that she's dragging down the mood. It could be anything, from the indignity of being in a color she doesn't love to an actual problem she has to ignore for a few hours in order to transform into Her Royal Highness Princess Mary, heir to the throne and the future Queen of the United Kingdom, and I make a mental note to ask if she's okay.

As they make their way across the room, they're accompanied by a clean-shaven man I recognize as President Park's husband and a teenage boy I can't place as easily. But there's no question who he is, not when he has the president's square jaw and her husband's lithe build.

When his mother was elected three years ago, Thaddeus Park was quiet, awkward, and best known for his love of Star Wars. Now, at eighteen, he has most *definitely* grown into that jaw. And those cheekbones. And those shoulders. I give myself five seconds to stare before I tear my eyes away, reminding myself that I have my own quiet and adorably awkward boyfriend who, less than thirty minutes ago, sent Tibby a text wishing me luck tonight, followed by a single x—which, apparently, he only ever uses with me.

Tibby lets out a low whistle as she also admires the view, and I elbow her in the side. "He's my age," I hiss. "Cougar."

"How old do you think I am?" says Tibby, aghast, and I shrug.

"Old enough to be my babysitter."

"I am not your *babysitter*," she says with familiar exasperation. "I am your private sec—"

"Miss Bright."

An older man with a short salt-and-pepper beard steps out of the crowd, and though he stands stiffly and with an air of formality, there's a twinkle of amusement in his eye.

"Mr. Jenkins," I say, biting back a grin. Even though I've known Jenkins longer than I've known almost anyone, I've never seen him in a tux before, and he also has an impressive set of medals—including the star worn by Knight Commanders of the Royal Victorian Order. I'll never catch up to what people like Tibby and my half sister have known practically from birth, but I feel some small sense of victory for recognizing this much. "I'm sorry we're late. It's not Tibby's fault—"

"Never mind that," he says with his usual gentle understanding. "His Majesty has requested that you join him and the Park family for these photographs."

I blink. Sure enough, when I glance over Jenkins's shoulder, my father is chuckling at something Mr. Park said, but his gaze quickly meets mine, and he tilts his head toward the others.

"Really?" I say in a low voice, but I already have my answer.

"You're sure it won't ruin the photo shoot? Or insult the first family?"

"Quite sure," says Jenkins, and he offers me his arm. "If you please."

Tibby prods me in the small of my back, and I loop my elbow around Jenkins's and do my best not to limp. Maybe kicking off my broken shoe wouldn't be the worst idea in the world, even if it means I'll lose at least four inches. But before I can weigh the pros and cons, Jenkins is handing me off to Alexander, and it's too late to do anything about it now.

"You look lovely," murmurs my father, kissing me on the cheek. "Why don't you and Maisie stand with Thaddeus?"

While I expect him and the president to be front and center, they both step aside and position the three of us in the middle, with Thaddeus Park towering over me and my half sister. And as he peers down at me, I swear he smirks.

"Nice to meet you," he says in an American accent that matches mine. I'm so used to hearing the seemingly endless varieties in the UK by now, however, that it sounds strangely alien to my ears. "I was hoping you'd be here."

"You were?" I say, taken aback. "Why?"

He chuckles, and while it's the kind of laugh that probably puts most people at ease, I bristle. "Isn't it obvious?"

"Not really," I say, and before he can explain—or formulate a witty comeback, which seems more his style—the official palace photographer clears his throat. The seven of us all face forward, and I smile, hoping like hell that my sudden spike of anxiety doesn't show on my face.

"A little closer, if you would, Your Majesties," says the photographer, and while this is clearly directed at my father and Helene, who could fit half a continent between them, Thaddeus shifts toward me, too.

It's a small movement—barely more than an inch or two—but instinctively I edge away, and that minor adjustment is too much for my shoe to bear. The strap snaps, and with a sharp jolt of pain in my ankle, I'm suddenly falling, dangerously close to taking the president down with me.

But then, like this is all some choreographed dance we've practiced together, Thaddeus catches me effortlessly, his arms strong and secure around me. I gasp, and as I slowly absorb what's happening, I realize I'm staring directly into his dark eyes.

Click.

A camera goes off, and then another, and another, until all I hear are the echoes of shutters and phones as seemingly every single photographer and member of the Royal Rota take our picture. With a self-satisfied grin, Thaddeus helps me back to my feet, his hand lingering on my bare arm for much longer than it should. And if there was any question of which photo the press will use for tomorrow's headlines, there isn't anymore.

Terrific.

CHAPTER TWO

KIT LAUGHS SO LOUDLY THAT I have to pull Tibby's phone away from my ear.

"Only you, Evan," he manages, and I can picture him shaking his head, his dark wavy hair nearly skimming his jaw now despite the number of times Helene has begged him to cut it. "Turning one of those stuffy banquets into a cheating scandal. I'm impressed."

"It's not funny," I say, shifting on the cushioned window seat in one of Windsor Castle's massive libraries. The room is almost completely devoid of light, and the floor-to-ceiling bookshelves loom eerily around me, but I can take a little spookiness as long as it comes with privacy. "Everyone's saying we've broken up—"

"Have we?" he says, still chuckling. "Did you meet the love of your life tonight, and you've rung to tell me you're kicking me to the curb?"

His voice is slightly muffled now, and I make a face. "Of course not. You're Googling the photos, aren't you?"

"Naturally," he says, and a beat later, he bursts into another fit of laughter. "He escorted you *and* Maisie into the banquet? Whose idea was that?"

"His," I groan. "Alexander thought it was chivalrous. Stop— I told you it was bad."

"On the contrary, this is the highlight of my week," says Kit, and I can hear him grinning. "The snap of him catching you is actually rather stunning. If I were the one you were gazing at so lovingly, I'd frame it."

My tiara bumps against the wall, and I wince, finally giving in and digging around for the offending bobby pins. "You're terrible to me."

"Indeed. I suppose I'll just have to make it up to you at Christmas, won't I?"

I straighten, pins forgotten. "You're coming to Sandringham? But I thought—"

"My parents decided to holiday in the Maldives," says Kit. "They offered to fly me out, too, but I can think of few methods of torture more painful than spending another two weeks alone with them. And away from you."

This makes me melt a little, but considering Kit has barely seen his parents in years, it also comes with a helping of guilt. "Isn't your mother excited to spend the holidays with you?"

"Maybe. But she and my father have plenty to work through on their own, and I'd only be a hindrance. Besides, we've done nothing but partake in awkward conversations and lingering silences since the end of term, and I think we're all rather weary of tiptoeing around each other at this point," he admits. "I'll visit her again in February for her birthday."

"Okay," I say, not sure whether to be disappointed for his mother or relieved I'll get to spend Christmas with him after all. "Maisie keeps talking about how much she hates Sandringham, but it sounds kind of magical, having a tree and family and actually celebrating."

"It is," says Kit, and I can tell from the sudden softness in his voice that we're both thinking the same thing. Ever since my grandmother died when I was eleven, I've spent Christmas at various boarding schools, surrounded by a smattering of teachers without families and classmates whose parents couldn't be bothered to bring them along on whatever glamorous vacation they'd planned. Twice I was the only person left behind, save for the headmistress, and all I remember about those weeks are loneliness and desperately wanting to see my mom.

This year will be different, I promise myself. This year, even though my mother will be in Virginia and I'll be an ocean away in a secluded English manor, I'll have Alexander, Maisie, and Kit there to cushion the blow. And I *will* have a good time.

"When are you supposed to arrive?" I say. "Maisie and I are taking a car there on Saturday—"

"Room for one more?"

I jump, nearly dropping Tibby's phone as a low voice floats toward me in the darkness. Standing in the doorway, silhouetted by light from the drawing room beyond, is Thaddeus Park, holding a plate and two flutes of what I think is champagne.

"What are you doing here?" I blurt, not caring how rude I must sound. "Didn't security stop you in the vestibule?"

"You mean that room with all the weapons and display cases?" He starts toward me, slow enough not to spill his contraband. "They did, but I seem to have found my way here anyway. This place is a maze, isn't it? Worse than the White House."

"You get used to it," I say, before I hear Kit's voice—distant and tinny now that I'm holding the phone by my knees. I hastily return it to my ear. "Sorry, what did you say?"

"Is that him?" says Kit. "Are you about to hang up on me for a clandestine rendezvous with your new lover?"

I make a face. "What *century* are you from?" I mutter, desperately hoping Thaddeus didn't hear that.

Kit chuckles. "Ring me later, or whenever Tibby's willing to part with her mobile again. Don't worry about the photographs, all right? It'll blow over."

I'm not so sure, but I say my goodbyes and stretch out my legs, refusing to make any room for Thaddeus on the window seat. He perches on a nearby chair instead, balancing the plate of cookies on a small accent table between us.

"Sorry," he says, but judging by his grin, he's really not. "Was that your boyfriend?"

"So you *do* know he exists," I say dryly, and despite my annoyance, I take one of the cookies from the stack. I don't touch the flute beside it, though, and Thaddeus doesn't seem bothered as he sips from his own. "Shouldn't you be enjoying the party?"

"You mean the self-congratulatory political networking event masquerading as a fancy ball? I'm good," he says, popping a cookie into his mouth and chewing thoughtfully. "It's not easy, is it? Having to be two people at once."

I frown mid-bite. "What are you talking about?"

He gives me a knowing look. "When my mom was a senator from Pennsylvania, I could be myself. But as soon as she ran for president, there was suddenly all of this pressure to be . . . *not* me. To be presentable at all times. To stop talking about the things that made me interesting. Everything I used to like about myself became too specific, too embarrassing, too controversial—"

"That last Star Wars trilogy really did divide the fandom, didn't it?" I say, and he chuckles.

"Joking aside, I've noticed it with you, too," he says. "From a distance, I mean. Not in a stalker way, but . . . it's hard not to follow your story, with how often you're in the headlines. And when you joined the royal family, you seemed like this . . . this beautiful, wild, willfully independent human, and no one could tell you who you were or what to do. And even when everyone accused you of murdering that dickweasel who assaulted you, and the papers broke the news about your mom's mental illness and what she did to you—"

"We're not talking about that," I say coldly, and he immediately holds up his hands in a mea culpa.

"Right—of course," he says hastily. "I just mean . . . you seemed indifferent to the noise. You were still *you*. But as soon as you stepped into the public eye and gave that interview, you became . . . polished. Predictable. You've done what's expected of you, the same way I have. And I don't know about you, but I miss the person I used to be."

This is alarmingly vulnerable, considering we just met, and a knot forms in the pit of my stomach. I don't *feel* any different. I still like the same music. I still read the same books. I still watch way too much Netflix in what little free time I have now, and I've even started to learn how to play the guitar—badly, admittedly, but it's still just for me. No one else.

I know exactly what Thaddeus is talking about, though, and I feel a stab of something unexpectedly powerful—wistfulness, maybe, or some kind of nostalgia I didn't know was there. Because I *am* two people now. Just as Maisie has to be Princess Mary, the graceful and beloved heir to the throne, I have to be Evangeline, the illegitimate daughter of the King, who's just grateful to be included. Even though Evan is the person I really am, the person I've always been, I can't be her anymore—at least not where a stranger could see me. And despite his jarring candor and overfamiliarity, Thaddeus Park is still very much a stranger.

"I don't think I've really changed," I say at last, keeping my voice mild as I avoid his stare and feign interest in my bracelet instead. There are only two charms on it—a music note that was a gift from a classmate, and a tiny tiara that Kit gave me for my birthday—and I roll the latter between my fingers. "I'm still me."

"And I'm still me, underneath the politics and the workouts and the curated wardrobe," says Thaddeus. "But we can't let the public know that, can we, Your Royal Highness?"

No, we can't. I let the tiara charm drop, more shaken than I want to admit that someone I met five minutes ago understands part of my life better than I do. "I'm not a princess," I say, grasping onto this instead of letting myself linger on the rest. "Didn't your handler tell you that?"

"But you're the King's daughter," he says, as if this somehow supersedes a thousand years of history and royal protocol.

"Illegitimate," I point out. "I'm a mutt in a family of purebreds, and I definitely don't have a title."

Thaddeus blinks. "Well, that's rude."

I let out a breathy laugh, because no one has actually said that before, even though it's probably true. I don't care about the title, not really—but I can't pretend not to care about the respect and legitimacy that would come with it. And that is *not* a conversation I want to have with anyone, let alone Thaddeus Park.

"You know," he says slowly, "princess or not, you and I could send the internet into a feeding frenzy, if we wanted to."

I raise an eyebrow. "I think we already have."

He shrugs. "That picture's too formal to be a showstopper. But if I post a selfie of us together, maybe of you kissing me on the cheek . . ."

He leans in closer, and even though it's probably an innocent move, my skin crawls as I jerk away, and every muscle in my body tenses, ready to bolt. My panic must show on my face, because Thaddeus straightens instantly, his eyes wide and his mouth gaping.

"Shit, I—that was creepy, I'm sorry," he says, and to his credit, he sounds genuinely contrite. "I just meant, you know . . . a cute picture. We could make finger hearts or funny faces. Something like that. Nothing suggestive or—I know you have a boyfriend, I didn't mean it like that—"

"I think Evangeline has had enough photographs of her taken tonight," says a voice from the doorway, and relief rushes through me as I look up to see Tibby standing there, hands on her hips and her expression deadly.

"Right," says Thaddeus sheepishly, and I'm on my feet before he can even shift his weight. "I really am sorry."

"It's okay," I say, even though it isn't. But that's not completely his fault. Jasper Cunningham is the real reason for my racing pulse, and why I'll never again feel safe with a boy I don't fully trust. "We're not allowed to take selfies in the royal residences anyway. It's a security thing."

"Oh." His face falls, and I'm halfway to Tibby by the time he stands. "It was truly an honor to meet you, Evangeline. If you're ever in the US and want to see the White House library . . ."

"I'll look you up," I say, even though I have absolutely no intention of doing so. As I reach Tibby, however, something tugs at me—some long-ingrained irrational need to make sure he, a stranger I'll probably never see again, doesn't feel bad about how this went. Or maybe the small connection we made is stronger than I think it is. And so, despite having every reason to march out of here without so much as a goodbye, I glance over my shoulder and add, "Maybe we can take that selfie there."

His grin returns, and Tibby loops her arm in mine as we disappear into the maze that is Windsor Castle.

CHAPTER THREE

@thaddeusapark Living it up like royalty at Windsor Castle tonight. Huge thanks to Their Majesties King Alexander and Queen Helene, Her Royal Highness Princess Mary, and my very special new expat friend . . . ☺

—Instagram user @thaddeusapark, below a selfie of Thaddeus Park in a tuxedo, the background dark and indistinct, and his left thumb and pointer finger pressed together to make a finger heart, 18 December 2023

"THADDEUS IS USING YOU, YOU know," says Tibby as we cross an empty state room with red fabric walls. Though it isn't dusty, it looks like it hasn't been used in years, and our footsteps sound hollow against the thin carpet.

"I sort of worked that out for myself," I say as she pulls on the frame of a giant ornate mirror, which swings open to reveal another lavish state room—this one with green walls, gilded furniture, and massive portraits hanging in gold frames. "Thanks for jumping in back there. I wasn't sure what he was going to do."

"He wouldn't have tried anything," she says, even though she can't possibly be certain. "He's the son of the American president, and surely someone's taught him manners. But you have ten times the number of followers he does, and he clearly wanted a candid photo to boost his own profile. May I have my mobile back now?"

I hand it over, even though I'm still hopeful Kit might call again. "Is it always going to be like this? Is everyone I meet going to want something from me?"

"Yes," says Tibby, and the word sinks to the pit of my stomach like a brick. "You might get lucky and meet the rare individual who's interested in you as a person, or who believes you can't offer them anything they don't already have, but most people are always going to want something from you. You simply have to be careful who you trust."

I sigh inwardly. A year ago, no one knew who I was, and only a handful of my classmates even bothered to talk to me on a semi-regular basis. Now millions of people follow an Instagram account I don't even personally use, and based on the endless sea of comments I saw the one and only time I explored Tibby's handiwork, a disconcerting number seem to think this means they know exactly who I am. And the thought of so many strangers having a fully formed opinion of me still makes me break out in a cold sweat.

We step into an area I recognize now—the antechamber to the Windsor throne room. I can hear the faint murmur of voices filtering in from the Waterloo Chamber beyond, and I stop beside a bust of one of the Georges. "Do I have to go back to the party? I have a headache, and I lost my shoes hours ago."

"Your shoes are on their way to the royal cobbler, where they'll either be fixed or burned to ash. I haven't decided yet. But you've done your time tonight," adds Tibby, angling away from the crowded ballroom and instead leading me toward the secret passageway into the throne room. "As long as you sit still long enough for a picture while the jeweler removes your tiara, we can return to your apartment now."

The throne room isn't completely empty, but I only have to smile and say a few words before we escape into the Grand Reception Room and the more restricted areas of Windsor Castle beyond. It's a relief to be away from all those curious stares, and I drop my aching shoulders as we head back toward the private apartments.

"Are you coming to Sandringham for Christmas?" I say, hiking up the hem of my gown so it doesn't drag on the floor. My bare feet are freezing, but I'm too worn-out to care.

"Sandringham?" says Tibby. "Why on earth would I spend Christmas there?"

"Queen Victoria's your ancestor, isn't she? Doesn't that make you family?"

"If anything more distant than first cousins was still considered *family*, half of England's aristocratic marriages wouldn't exist," she says. "I'm spending Christmas at our country home in Kent, and for the New Year, I'll be in the Seychelles."

"Oh." I don't expect her to work during the holidays, of course, but the thought of Tibby not being there to cram my schedule full of lessons and fittings and appearances for three whole weeks is both daunting and exhilarating. "I'll miss you."

She gives me a strange look, though there's a softness to it that's almost foreign on her sharp features. "I'll be back before you know it. And in the meantime, you'll get to learn how to hunt and ski, and you'll have plenty of empty hours to spend with Maisie."

"Absolutely none of those things sounds appealing," I say as we approach my apartment. "Kit's coming, though."

"Is he? Should I make sure certain necessities are added to your luggage?"

It takes me a beat to realize what she means, and my cheeks instantly grow hot. *"No,"* I say firmly. "We're not—*no.*"

"Better safe than sorry," she hums, pushing open the door. And while my face still burns, the fact that Tibby isn't treating me like I'm about to break—especially when everyone else in my life, Kit included, avoids the topic completely—almost makes up for the humiliating breach of privacy. *Almost.*

The royal jeweler appears in record time to take possession of the Queen Florence tiara, but Tibby makes him wait a solid ten minutes while she figures out the perfect angle for Instagram. Even though the tiara is technically mine—Queen Florence, my great-grandmother, willed it to me when I was a baby—it's kept in a vault somewhere, or maybe the Tower of London, where the Crown Jewels are guarded. Either way, I won't see it again until the next state banquet, or whatever future event requires me to wear a tiara, and despite my tender scalp, I'm sorry to see it go.

Tibby sticks around only long enough to make sure my dress is hung up properly, and as soon as she leaves, I wrap myself in a fuzzy blanket, flop onto the antique sofa, and open my laptop. Rather than scour British news sites—and possibly, by now, CNN and various popular celebrity blogs—for commentary about my supposed flirtation with Thaddeus, I open VidChat and click my mother's icon.

Two rings echo throughout my sitting room, which is surprisingly cozy tonight as a fire crackles beneath the elaborate mantelpiece, and suddenly my mother's smiling face appears on-screen. Her auburn curls are loose, a sure sign she's not in her studio for once, and I notice a large abstract landscape behind her—the one that hangs in her dining room.

"Evie! How did it go?" she says, and while sometimes she's distracted and agitated, especially when her doctors are adjusting her medication, tonight she's clear-eyed and fully focused on me. "I saw the photos online—you looked stunning."

I grimace. "It was fine, I guess. If you've seen the pictures, then you already know what happened."

"You mean when the president's son grabbed you?" she says. "What happened there?"

I explain everything, from my broken shoe to how late Tibby and I were, to my encounter with Thaddeus in the library, and by the time I'm through, my mother sighs.

"Missteps happen, Evie," she says. "Especially when you're in the public eye so often. You're all right, though? Your ankle is okay, and he didn't . . . ?"

I shake my head. "He didn't touch me, except to stop me from falling on my face. My ankle's a little sore, but it'll be fine. I just . . ." *It's not easy, is it? Having to be two people at once.* "I'm not good at being perfect all the time."

"No one is, sweetheart," she says. "And you haven't had much of a chance to practice, either. You'll get better at the details as you go."

I'm not sure I want to, though. But while my mother broke up with Alexander, the love of her life, to avoid becoming queen, she seems to derive no end of pride and pleasure from watching me take my place as his daughter, no matter how bad I am at it.

"You haven't seen anyone lurking near the house, have you?" I say after a beat, eager to change the subject. "Alexander said the palace is still getting daily questions about you from that reporter."

"The one who's writing a biography of me?" she says. "No, security hasn't seen anything suspicious, and neither have I. But a friend said she received a strange phone call asking about the family, so it's likely only a matter of time before he figures out where I am."

I scowl. "If anything happens—"

"I'll be sure to let your father know immediately," she says. "Though honestly, Evie, sometimes I wonder if it wouldn't be in my best interest to work with . . . what's his name?"

"Ryan," I say bitterly. "Ryan Crewes."

"Ryan Crewes," she echoes. "If he's going to write my story, I might as well have some say in it."

While she has a point, the events of my childhood don't exactly paint her in a positive light. I have no memory of it, but my mother was arrested for trying to drown me in a bathtub when I was four, in the midst of a psychotic break due to undiagnosed paranoid schizophrenia. In her own unwell mind, she was trying to protect me from my stepmother, Helene—who, as far as I know, hadn't actually threatened me. But my mother's mental illness lied to her constantly. It still does, on her bad days, even with medication and treatment. While I know the public will draw their own conclusions with or without the real story, I don't want to see her words twisted into something monstrous in order to sell more books. And I wouldn't put anything past Ryan Crewes or the other so-called royal biographers who've been circling us for months.

"Maybe you can work with someone you've handpicked," I suggest. In a few years, once the sensational headlines that ran for weeks over the summer have faded in public memory. "But for now—"

The sharp rap of knuckles on wood ricochets through my sitting room, and I jump, twisting around to glare at the offending door. My mother leans toward the camera, her frown deepening.

"Do you need to get that?" she says, and I shake my head.

"Whoever it is will go awa—"

The urgent knocks quickly turn into demanding thuds, and I hear a muffled voice through the wood.

"Evan, you better bloody be in there. I need to talk to you."

I groan inwardly. "Mom, it's Maisie," I say. Out of all the people in Windsor tonight, she's one of the few I can't ignore. "Could I—"

"Of course, sweetheart. I need to start dinner anyway," she says. "Call me back when you can."

After closing my laptop, I mutter a few deeply unkind things about my half sister as I throw off my blanket and climb to my feet. The fire crackles cheerfully, its warmth fighting the castle chill, and I yank open the door that leads into the hallway. "Whatever this is about, it better be—"

"The head of palace security cornered Daddy after dinner," says my sister as she sweeps into the room, the hem of her sapphire gown billowing behind her. "One of the protection officers stationed on the reserve in Kenya called. Benedict is missing."

It takes me a beat to fully absorb what she's saying, and I stare at her, stunned. "Wait—*what?*"

Maisie rolls her eyes. "Benedict," she says slowly, "our traitorous swine of a cousin, is gone. Absent. In the wind. Vanished—"

"I know what 'missing' means," I say in a strangled voice. "How did he slip past his protection officers? Wasn't the whole point of Alexander sending him to the reserve to keep an eye on him?" And to keep him away from Maisie and me. But five months and thousands of miles aren't enough to erase my memory of the look on Ben's face when he realized he was caught, and a shiver runs through me.

I'm going to destroy you.

His Royal Highness Prince Benedict of York was the first member of the family to treat me with any decency after I arrived in London, but he was also the one who leaked a video of me pushing Jasper Cunningham off a balcony after the sleazy asshole tried to rape me. The footage was edited, of course— Jasper and Ben had drugged my drink, and I couldn't even walk straight, let alone shove an athletic nineteen-year-old hard enough for him to fall to his death. But Ben made the entire world believe it was me, and even after untangling the truth, I still have no idea why.

"Uncle Nicholas is trying to track him down," says Maisie as she begins to pace with the energy of a restless raccoon. "But Benedict has plenty of friends, and he could be anywhere by now."

"We live in the twenty-first century. Someone *has* to know where he is," I argue, fighting the urge to pace, too.

"I've already scoured the gossip sites and social media," says Maisie. "There's no sign of him."

My hands start to sting, and with vague bewilderment, I

realize my nails have dug into my palms, causing eight dark red crescent marks in my pale skin. The color is nearly identical to the ink Ben used for the note he sent me shortly after he was shipped off to the reserve, and even though I haven't looked at it in months, I remember every word.

No matter where I am in the world, I still know your secrets. Enjoy this while it lasts.

"What are the odds he'll disappear for good and leave us alone?" I say, rubbing my hands together to soothe them.

"Exceptionally low, unless we're lucky and he's been eaten by a lion," says Maisie. "Benedict's never been one to take blows to his pride lightly, and I guarantee you he won't go quietly."

From anyone else, I'd take this dramatic proclamation with a grain of salt. But Maisie knows Ben better than anyone, and while she's prone to theatrics—something about being a princess, probably—I saw enough of Ben's dark side over the summer to believe her.

"Do you think he'll tell everyone what really happened?" I say, almost too afraid to suggest it. No use giving the universe any ideas, after all.

For a split second, I see a flicker of very real fear in Maisie's eyes. While there's nothing Ben can do to me that he hasn't already tried, he could still destroy Maisie's life with bone-chilling ease—because while I might not have been the one who pushed Jasper to his death, she was. And even though it was an accident, even though she was acting in self-defense, if the truth gets out—if Ben goes public with what really happened that night, and everything we did to cover it up—there's no telling what the fallout might be. But I do know, without a sliver of doubt, that it would be catastrophic—not just to me and Maisie, but to the entire royal family and the monarchy itself.

"He won't," she says at last, as if her stubbornness alone can make it so. "He has no way of proving it, not after we deleted the video."

"But he's third in line to the throne," I point out, though we're both keenly aware of that nasty little fact. "He has credibility on his side, and even if the palace denies it, some people will still believe him."

"Let them," she says coldly. "There are some who believe I died at birth and was replaced with another baby, you know, but their conspiracy theories are just that."

This is news to me—weird news, but still news—and I blink. "But this is true, Maisie. And if he somehow managed to copy the video—"

A ding echoes from inside her clutch, and without waiting for me to finish, she pulls out her phone. Her pinched expression grows even more haggard at the sight of whatever's on her screen, and she turns toward the door. "I can't stay. I only wanted to warn you."

"Thanks," I say dryly. "I'm sure the thought of Ben peeking through my window will lull me to sleep tonight."

Maisie gives me a withering look, though it's tempered by the way she tugs anxiously on one of her strawberry-blond waves. "Don't be daft. You have curtains."

"That's not—" I begin, but there's no point. I study her. "Are you okay?"

"What do you think?" she says waspishly, dropping her hand. "Not only has Benedict slipped his lead, but he's also got a massive vendetta against both of us, and we have no idea what he's going to try next. How could I possibly be—"

"I'm not talking about Ben," I say, glancing at her phone. "Have you heard from Gia since she got back from Spain?"

Instantly what little warmth lingers between us turns to ice. "I need to go," says Maisie. "If Benedict shows up at your window tonight, do let him know that I don't care if we share blood—I *will* turn the Tower back into a working prison if he puts even a toe out of line."

"Also a comforting thought," I mutter, but if Maisie hears me, she doesn't react. Instead, she yanks open the door and disappears into the hallway, leaving me on my own with the weight of every terrible thing Ben could do to us hanging over me, and the knowledge that whatever it is, he will relish the carnage.

CHAPTER FOUR

"Henrietta, in your twenty years covering the royal family, have you ever seen a state banquet quite like this?"

"It was certainly one for the books, though I must emphasize that the press isn't invited to the banquet itself, or the ball afterward. We're only invited for photographs and the occasional short interview before the festivities begin. The rest is a closely guarded secret."

"Even with the excitement of President Park visiting the UK for the first time, I don't imagine anything that happened behind closed doors could possibly outshine Evangeline's faux pas during the family photograph yesterday."

"She does have a knack for drawing attention, doesn't she? In her defence, it seems like this was due to a wardrobe malfunction rather than any desire to steal the spotlight, as she removed her heels immediately after the photographs were taken."

"You've been spending quite a bit of time on the subject of Evangeline as of late, haven't you?"

"I have, yes. She's lived a fascinating life so far, especially for someone who's only eighteen, and it's been a pleasure to learn more about her in my research for my new book, *Royal Rebel*—which will be released on Thursday, just in time for a last-minute Christmas gift for all the royal watchers in your life."

"Well, I'll certainly be putting it on my list. What would you say most surprised you over the course of your research?"

"A number of things, really. Evangeline may be famous worldwide now, a mere six months after joining the royal family, but very little is known about her life beforehand. As you've said, she does have a knack for drawing attention in rather scandalous ways, but I'd say the thing that surprised me most was her empathy."

"Her empathy?"

"She has a reputation for misbehaving, of course, after getting expelled from nine boarding schools in seven years. But the acts that led to these expulsions never seemed to be rooted in malice or destructive tendencies."

"Even the infamous arson mishap that resulted in her fleeing to England?"

"Especially that. According to her former maths instructor, he believes Evangeline set the fire to destroy the only evidence of her roommate's poor marks—which reportedly risked her future Ivy League education."

"Her roommate's? Not her own?"

"No, not her own. That's really the heart of the many examples of what makes Evangeline such a fascinating addition to the royal family—and, I believe, an asset to this country going forward. She's truly remarkable, and despite the occasional blunder, I feel very strongly that once she's had the chance to prove herself, we'll all agree that she's as much a royal jewel as Princess Mary."

—ITV News's interview with royal expert
Henrietta Smythe, 19 December 2023

THE DRIVE FROM WINDSOR CASTLE to Sandringham Estate, the privately owned country home of the royal family near the east coast of England, is almost three miserable hours long.

Maisie and I spend nearly every minute in silence, as I read a fantasy novel while she scrolls through her phone, hastily replying to every soft ding that echoes in the back of the Range Rover. I desperately want to ask if she's heard any news about Ben, but one look at the thundercloud that is her face, and I'm sure it isn't worth the risk. I might have made some less-than-stellar choices in my life, but even I know better than to test her right now.

I console myself with the fact that over the past five days, no sightings of Ben have been reported on social media, and no new rumors have surfaced about his supposed whereabouts. And while that doesn't mean he isn't still out there, it does, at least, imply that he's staying hidden. For now. And so, with the thought of an actual Christmas to look forward to, I focus on my book and do my best not to let Ben ruin this, too.

We're driving along a low stone wall that looks older than the United States when, for the first time in hours, Maisie looks up from her screen. Rather than say anything, however, she makes a strange sound that's halfway between a growl and a whistling teakettle, and she shoves her phone into her purse with such force that I'm surprised she doesn't throw it out the window instead.

"Everything okay?" I say mildly.

"Marvelous," she mutters, turning away from me to stare out at the bare trees. I consider leaving her be, since it's worked out well so far. But then, with as much stealth as possible when I'm sitting less than two feet away, her hand snakes up to brush her cheek, and I realize she's crying.

With a grimace, I close my book and slip it into the bag at my feet. "You don't have to tell me what's going on," I say. "But I'm here if you ever want to talk, all right?"

A muscle twitches in her jaw. "I'm fine," she says tightly, and I can hear the thickness in her voice now. "Have you checked Instagram recently?"

This is the last thing I expect her to say, and I frown. "Tibby handles that. I don't even have the password to my account."

"Of course you bloody don't," she mutters. "Thaddeus Park messaged me the other day."

"He did?" I say, suddenly dreading where this conversation is going. "I didn't know you two were friends."

"We're not." She finally looks at me, and although it's only for a split second, it's impossible not to notice how red her eyes are. "He asked for your number, and he wouldn't believe me when I said you haven't got a mobile."

I scowl. "Probably because he saw me using Tibby's. Did he say why he wanted it?"

"No, but it's not exactly hard to guess, is it?"

No, it's not. I lean my head back against the leather seat and sigh. I've never had a phone before—they weren't allowed at most of my boarding schools, and since my mother doesn't like using them, I've never seen the point—but this only reinforces my desire not to get one. "What else did he say?"

"The usual flattery and sycophancy," she says. "Though he's really not too terrible, all things consid—what on *earth* is going on?"

She's leaning forward now, craning her neck in a direction I can't see. Frowning, I shift closer to her, the kind of close that would normally have her up in arms, but instead she barely seems to notice. And as the car slows, I see why.

Up ahead, clustered around large and extravagant wrought-iron gates, is a crowd of about a dozen people holding signs made of poster board. And even though the temperature is well above freezing, they're clad in winter coats and hats, and every single one has a scarf wrapped around the lower half of their face, leaving only their eyes visible.

Our car slows, and the crowd turns toward us, thrusting their signs in the air. They look homemade, with different handwriting and colors, but they all hold the same sentiment.

ABOLISH THE MONARCHY

NO MORE FREELOADING

REVOLT AGAINST THE ROYALS

Unnerved, I shrink away from Maisie and back into my seat. "Is this normal?" I say, trying to pretend like the hint of fear in my voice has always been there.

"No," says Maisie quietly, and in the front passenger seat, our protection officer speaks quietly on his phone, his head swiveling as he takes in the crowd.

"Additional security is on their way," he says, glancing over his shoulder and through the clear partition at Maisie and me. But it's cold comfort as the protesters surround us, their mostly hidden faces inches from ours and separated only by glass.

None of them are shouting or hurling insults our way, though. They simply stare at us through the windows, and as the seconds tick by, I feel Maisie's hand wrap around mine.

"Don't look at them," she whispers. And even though every-thing in me wants—*needs*—to keep my eyes on the protesters, I tear my gaze away and focus on the back of our driver's head. He, too, is tense, and I notice that both men have unbuckled their seat belts.

Finally, after what feels like an hour but is probably no more than a minute or two, the gates open, and several security of-ficers join the fray, all holding batons. They hastily usher the crowd away from the car, and at last we continue forward. Before we make it to the safety of what must be Sandringham Estate, however, I glance out the window one more time, only to meet the menacing stare of a man in a teal scarf.

He doesn't speak—he doesn't even move—but that single look is enough, and a shiver runs down my spine. I hastily avert my eyes again, my fingers tightening around Maisie's. And even when we cross onto the private road and the gates swing shut, putting an ever-growing buffer between our Range Rover and the protesters, neither of us lets go.

CHAPTER FIVE

Maisie

Gia, we need to talk.

Gia

I think you've said enough.

Maisie

You're taking this all entirely the wrong way, you know.

Gia

Am I? How good to know that yet again, you're in the right, and I'm simply misunderstanding Her Royal Highness's intentions.

Maisie

We've just arrived at Sandringham. Will you please answer your bloody mobile when I call?

Gia

I'm with my family.

Maisie

Please. There were protesters waiting for us, and security wasn't prepared. It was terrifying.

Gia

Are you all right?

Maisie

No. I'm shaking.

Gia

Are you hurt? Did they attack you?

Maisie

No, but I really need to hear your voice right now.

Gia

I told you, I'm with my family, and I need some time. We'll speak after Christmas.

	Maisie
	But that's days away.

Gia

I need time to think. If you care for me at all, please respect that.

	Maisie
	That's not fair and you know it.
	Gia?
	Gia, please.
	Are you still coming to Klosters?

Gia

Only if you stop with this nonsense.

	Maisie
	I'm sorry.

Gia

I don't believe you.

	Maisie
	What do you want me to say? You know the position I'm in.

Gia

Of course I do. But you can't always be the priority, Maisie. Sometimes I get to be, too.

	Maisie
	You're always my priority.

Gia

Am I? Because I'm really not so sure.

*—Text message exchange between
Her Royal Highness the Princess Mary
and Lady Georgiana Greyville,
23 December 2023*

MY HEART IS STILL POUNDING by the time the car pulls up to the sprawling four-story mansion at the heart of Sandringham Estate. Under most circumstances, I'd be cracking a dry joke about Maisie's standard of living, or at the very least gawking at the warm brick-and-stone facade. But for now, it takes all I have to hide the tremble in my hands as I climb out of the Range Rover, grateful that my legs are still working.

"*This* is Sandringham House?" I say, trying to feign some semblance of normalcy even as my thoughts keep flashing back to the man in the teal scarf.

"Of course," says Maisie, whose phone is dinging again, and she barely looks up as she exits the vehicle. "What did you expect, a hovel?"

"A house," I say as I head for the double front doors, which stand open beneath an intricate stone awning. "I expected a house. Not—whatever this is."

"We're the royal family. We do not live in *houses*. Though I do hope Tibby packed your thermal underwear," adds Maisie, her eyes still glued to her phone as she breezes past me and into the entrance hall. "You can see your breath in the bedrooms at night."

Every detail of the foyer is exquisite, from the rich dark wood paneling to the polished marble floor and the festive garlands decorating the winding staircase, and despite the adrenaline still coursing through my system, I pause to drink it all in. It really is stunning, and I have absolutely no idea what Maisie's been complaining about for the past week.

In the middle of the hall, a stout man waits for us beside a strange brass contraption, and he bows as we approach. "Good afternoon, Your Royal Highness, Miss Bright. Welcome to Sandringham House."

"Thank you, Paul," says Maisie with surprising warmth. "I don't suppose you'll take a bribe this year, will you? I have . . ."

She digs through her purse and pulls out half a dozen candy bars. "A Dairy Milk, a Flake, a Double Decker, a Mars bar, a peppermint Aero . . ."

"Your Royal Highness is too kind," says Paul with a hint of a smile. "But I fear that my honor remains unimpeachable."

"I was afraid of that," says Maisie with a sigh, and without explanation, she toes off her shoes, shoves her coat into my arms, and sits down on the odd apparatus. As I watch, baffled, Paul fiddles with a metal slide that almost looks like—

"Is that a scale?" I blurt, and as soon as I say it, I'm sure I'm right. Maisie rolls her eyes, but Paul glances at me with patient amusement.

"Indeed," he says as he nudges a few of the markers over. "The tradition of the weigh-in dates back over a century, to Edward VII, who believed that weight gain meant his guests had enjoyed themselves. Thank you, Your Royal Highness," he adds, and Maisie hops off. "Miss Bright, if you would."

I blink, horrified. "Wait—I'm supposed to do it, too?"

"If I have to, then you certainly do," says Maisie as she steps back into her shoes.

While Paul records her weight in a heavy leather-bound book, a maid appears at my side, and she takes Maisie's coat from my arms and waits for mine. I hesitate, but this isn't the only odd royal tradition I've come up against since joining the family, and I doubt it'll be the last.

Maisie disappears, her heels clicking on the marble floor as Paul carefully measures my weight. I consider asking what it is, but after months of having the media scrutinize everything about me, including my dress size and the circumference of my arms, I decide I don't want to know. As soon as he gives me the all clear, I jump down and shove my feet back in my Doc Martens, twisting around to figure out where Maisie went.

"Did you see—" I begin, but before I can finish my question, the front doors fly open, revealing an older woman with long silver hair, a fur coat, and a small brown-and-white spaniel trotting at her heels. I've only met her once, but I could pick her out of a crowd of thousands.

Queen Constance, Alexander's mother—and my grandmother.

For what feels like the longest moment of an already infinite day, she and I stand fifteen feet apart, staring at each other like opponents about to fight to the death. Or at least that's how she's staring at *me*. I'm mostly just trying to stop myself from biting the inside of my cheek so hard that I draw blood.

I haven't seen her—and have barely heard a word about her—since she retreated to Balmoral, the royal family's Scottish castle, the day after I arrived in England. For the first time in fifty years, she missed Trooping the Colour and other summer traditions so she could protest my invitation into the family. Never mind that I'm her flesh and blood, or that I'm as much her grandchild as Maisie is. Constance hates me so completely that I'm positive she would rather live the rest of her life as a commoner than say a single decent word to me.

Sure enough, as soon as the maid takes her coat, Constance walks past me as if I'm not even there, pausing only for the absolute minimum amount of time it takes Paul to weigh her. "Is Her Royal Highness here?" she says in a clipped voice.

"Yes, Your Majesty," says Paul as he once again adjusts the

markers on the old-fashioned scale. "Her Majesty the Queen and His Royal Highness the Duke of York have also arrived. I believe they're enjoying the luncheon buffet in the dining room."

I keep my expression carefully neutral. Helene and Nicholas's affair isn't exactly a well-kept secret among the family, and no doubt the staff has known even longer, but I have no idea if Constance is aware that her daughter-in-law is sleeping with the wrong son—and has been for several years now, according to Alexander.

"Very well," says Constance, her voice impassive. With a sniff, she stands, not sparing me so much as a glance before disappearing through one of the large archways and into the corridor beyond. The dog lingers, staring up at me with liquid brown eyes, and I'm about to reach down and pet it when Constance's sharp voice cuts through the silence.

"Zaffre, *come.*"

Reluctantly the dog trots off, and I watch it go, doing my best not to take Constance's continued rejection personally. But even after all these months, it's still a losing battle.

"I'm sure Her Majesty is very busy," says Paul kindly, and I tear my gaze away from the archway and force a small smile.

"Probably has a massive pile of Christmas presents to wrap," I agree, even though I'm sure Constance has never wrapped a gift in her life. "Where should I . . . ?"

"The dining room is to the left, if you're hungry," says Paul. "We're only awaiting His Majesty now."

"Right," I say, my anxiety mounting. But then I realize the implication of what Paul's said, and hope sizzles through me like electricity. "Wait, does that mean Kit's here already? Lord Clarence, I mean—"

"I vastly prefer the first," says a low voice behind me, and I spin around so quickly that I nearly trip over my own feet.

There, standing at the bottom of the winding staircase, his smile warm and his dark wavy hair somehow even longer than it was during our last VidChat, is Kit.

I don't know which of us moves first, but two seconds later, his arms are around me, and my cheek is pressed to his shoulder as I hug him in return. He buries his face in my hair, his rib cage expanding beneath his soft sweater as he inhales, but there's something about the way he holds me that doesn't feel exactly right—something slightly desperate, maybe, with a hint of relief and fear.

The protesters at the gate—he must've passed them, too. I squeeze him a little tighter, hoping it's enough to reassure him that everything is fine. And as the seconds pass, the desperation fades, replaced by his usual calm and dependable demeanor.

"Missed you," I mumble, and when I tilt my head up, he's there, his nose a fraction of an inch from mine.

"I missed you, too," he says softly, for my ears only. And even though we're not alone, he brushes his lips against mine, and the nervous tension in my body melts away. "Are you hungry?"

"Starving," I admit, though I don't mention it's because I was too nervous to eat breakfast. I kiss him again before reluctantly letting him go. "But I think Constance already claimed the dining room."

Kit takes my hand, his fingers lacing through mine. "The dining room is big enough for both of you," he assures me. "If Her Majesty wants to avoid you, then she ought to be the one going out of her way, not you."

As we pass out of the entrance hall, I offer Paul a smile and a wave. To my surprise, he bows his head in return, and while it's a small gesture—and definitely something no one else in the family would notice—my cheeks grow warm with both gratitude and embarrassment.

On our meandering way to the dining room, Kit gives me the grand tour of the main floor, and we pause in each new space as I take it all in. Sandringham House isn't as ostentatious as Windsor Castle or Buckingham Palace, but it doesn't skimp on the finery, either. Or the fireplaces, or the crown molding, or the heraldry that seems to be everywhere, especially in a room Kit calls the saloon.

"Alexander usually invites the cousins here for Christmas," says Kit, his voice lower than usual as we explore a sizable white drawing room with a painting of a sky on the ceiling. "This year, however, it'll just be the immediate family."

"That'll be a barrel of laughs," I mutter. I've never met any of the other members of the royal family—the list of names that extends seemingly endlessly in the line of succession after Ben— but it would've been nice to have a few decoys to throw in front of Constance if she gets snippy.

"It won't be so bad," Kit assures me. "There are plenty of places to disappear if Constance or Aunt Helene step out of line."

"It's not just them I'm worried about," I say darkly, and he smirks.

"Ah, yes. Maisie's been in a mood lately, hasn't she?"

"Tell me about it," I say, relieved I'm not the only person who's noticed. "The drive up here was miserable. I think she's fighting with Gia."

"They have their spats," he says with a shrug. "Though they tend to make up fairly quickly."

"I think this one's worse than usual," I admit. "Has Rosie said anything?"

"Rosie?" he says, and I give him a pointed look.

"Don't pretend she doesn't text you practically every day. I know she likes you."

Kit looks sheepish, even though her crush is entirely one-sided. "It's not every day," he insists. "But it is whenever she can think of a good excuse. No, she hasn't said anything—and she would, if she knew something was going on."

We head down a long hallway now, and I catch a whiff of beef and gravy and fresh-baked bread. My stomach gurgles, but even hunger can't make my feet move any faster toward the inevitable cold war in the dining room. Kit doesn't seem especially eager to arrive, either, and I peer up at him, searching his grim expression for an explanation I know won't be there.

"Are you okay?" I say, and he blinks, as if I've snapped him out of a trance.

"Better than okay," he promises, ducking his head to kiss me again. "I haven't been this happy in months."

He doesn't look happy, though, not with the way his brow is slightly furrowed and his eyes look like they're in shadow. I hug his arm, but before I can press, Constance's sharp voice filters through a set of open double doors just down the corridor.

". . . stop this foolishness at *once.*" Somehow she sounds even more deadly than she looked in the entrance hall, and I fight the urge to drag Kit back the way we came. "I've no idea what you two expect will come of this. Certainly nothing good."

"I don't see how it's any of your business, Mother." Nicholas's voice isn't nearly as loud, but it's steady and unwavering, and it's clear this isn't the first time my uncle's had to deal with her demands.

"I'm the head of this family," she snaps. "That makes it entirely my business."

Kit and I stop at the doorway in time to see Helene's eyebrows rise so high they nearly touch her hairline. Though she and Nicholas are the only people seated at the long mahogany table, which is laden with crystal glasses, fine china, and festive decorations, the pair of them are practically perched on each other's laps. Constance stands stiffly near one of the windows, and I'm suddenly positive that she walked in on a scene she wasn't prepared for. Because she didn't know about their affair.

"On the contrary," says Helene, her voice as cool as the icy-blue walls, "Alexander is the head of this family now. And he's perfectly content with the situation."

Constance scoffs. "Alexander is the reason public opinion of the monarchy has plummeted, with the consequences of his actions still ricocheting through the headlines. He's already made us a laughingstock, and this"—she gestures toward Helene and Nicholas—"*this* will only further ensure our demise—"

"Demise, Mother?" says someone new over my shoulder. "Isn't that a trifle dramatic?"

I recognize my father's voice instantly, but when I twist around, I freeze, my heart in my throat. Lingering behind me in a cozy red sweater is Alexander, looking more relaxed than I've seen him in months. But he's not alone.

Standing to his right in the hallway, her auburn curls loose and her cheeks still pink from the December chill, is my mother.

CHAPTER SIX

The past cannot be cured.

—Queen Elizabeth (b. 1533, r. 1558–1603)

MY MOM IS HERE.

In England.

At Sandringham.

For Christmas.

These are the only coherent words my mind can form as I launch myself toward her, and she catches me in a tight hug. She feels stronger than the last time I saw her back in June, and I inhale her scent, my thoughts reeling.

My mom is here. In England. At Sandringham. For Christmas.

And so are Constance and Helene.

A knot of fear forms in the pit of my stomach, and I pull away enough to look at her. "What are you doing here?" I manage, my voice already ragged. "I thought you were staying in Virginia."

"We wanted to surprise you, Evie," she says, but she must sense my apprehension, because she peers at me uncertainly. "It's a good surprise, right?"

"The best," I say, and it is. I haven't spent Christmas with her since I was ten years old. But I can feel the white-hot stares watching us from the dining room, and all I can think about is how everyone at Sandringham knows the darkest details of the worst day of her life. And I'm absolutely sure some of them won't hesitate to use them against her.

"Ah, the epitome of propriety has arrived at last," says Helene from her seat at the table. "And I see he's brought a guest."

My mother releases me and turns her attention to the dining room, though her hand settles on my back, as if she isn't entirely ready to let go. While Helene looks impossibly smug as she leans even closer to Nicholas, Constance stands frozen beside the velvet curtains, seemingly rendered speechless by Alexander's audacity. That, at least, is one thing we have in common.

"Hello, Helene," says my mother as she steps into the room with my father at her side, both of them either oblivious to Constance or pointedly ignoring her. "It's good to see you."

"Likewise," says Helene, her honeyed voice oozing with insincerity. "You look well, Laura."

She fixes her blue eyes on my mother, and a shiver runs down my spine. My mom shouldn't be here. She shouldn't have to face Helene, who's the reason everyone in the world knows about her mental illness and the psychotic break that permanently altered our lives when I was four. My mother shouldn't have to be polite to a woman who's never shown her an ounce of compassion or empathy, and who sure as shit won't start now.

But my mom is a better human being than I'll ever be, and she smiles with warmth Helene doesn't deserve. "I *am* well, thank you," she says. "It's good to be back in England. Nicholas— you've grown up, haven't you?"

"It happens from time to time," says my uncle, and though he sounds genuinely friendly, he at least has the decency to look abashed. Good. While Helene was the one to tell the press about my mother's arrest and mental illness, all the details came straight from Nicholas—including the part about the bathtub.

But either my mom doesn't know or she doesn't hold grudges like Alexander and I do, and she flashes him a wide smile. "Alex told me you two are living together now," she says. "I'm thrilled for you."

Nicholas smiles self-consciously, and his arm tightens around Helene. "Thank you," he says. "All on the quiet, of course, but we're very hap—"

"You've brought *her* here? For Christmas?"

All at once, Constance seems to reanimate from her spot beside the window, and she fixes her livid stare on my father. Feeling like I've swallowed a lump of searing-cold metal, I tuck myself underneath my mom's arm, as if I can somehow shield her from whatever metaphorical daggers my grandmother is about to throw.

"Hello, Mother," says Alexander. "How lovely to finally see you again. No doubt you remember Laura."

Remember? I glance at my mom, who looks completely unfazed. In my mind, she and my royal relatives exist in two different worlds, completely separate from each other except for the bridge that is me and Alexander. But now that I'm standing here, face to face with the familiarity and contempt between the members of my unorthodox family, it's suddenly clear that the Venn diagram I've been picturing is much, much closer to a circle.

"Were you not content ruining my last Christmas with my late husband?" says Constance, every inch of her dripping with disdain as she glares at my mother. "Did you come to ruin this one, too?"

"If memory serves," says Alexander smoothly, "the tantrum you threw about hosting Laura—who, if you'll recall, was my fiancée at the time—was the reason Father was in a foul mood. *He* was pleased to welcome her into the family."

"Until you informed him that you intended on abdicating in order to marry your American harlot," snaps Constance. "That certainly put a dampener on the festivities, didn't it?"

"Only for you and Father," says Alexander, and he turns toward the long buffet set up against the wall. "Laura, you must be starving after your flight."

He picks up two plates, but Constance clearly isn't done with this conversation, and she steps closer to the table, her fingers curling around the back of an intricately carved chair.

"Will you and your *guest* be sharing a room again, then?" she says, her voice tight with barely contained spite. "Never mind that you're a married man."

"Helene and I are legally separated, Mother, as you damn well know," says Alexander with a hint of weariness now. "Must you make this difficult? Laura hasn't had the opportunity to celebrate Christmas with Evan in a very long time, and—"

"Which reminds me," interrupts Constance, as if an idea's just occurred to her. "Perhaps you'd prefer to use one of the other rooms this year, given the . . . amenities in your en suite."

Almost everyone in the room freezes at that—even Helene, whose wineglass is halfway to her lips. Only Kit and I glance at each other, both silently asking for an explanation. But I've never been here before, and Kit, no doubt, has never had a reason to explore my father's bathroom.

Oh.

Oh.

Rage washes over me, burning away my confusion until only cold clarity remains. I don't know exactly what Constance is talking about, but I recognize the shape of her verbal swipe— the insinuation that my mom can't be trusted anywhere near a bathtub without risking another *incident*. And just as Kit's hand touches my elbow, I slide away from him and toward the table, planting myself directly across from Constance.

"Do you remember the first time we met?" I say easily, even though my blood's boiling. "The day after I arrived at Windsor, before the investiture ceremony. I'm pretty sure I was wearing pajamas."

Constance simply stares at me, her expression turning to stone.

"You don't?" I say, keeping my voice casual. "Because I do. I remember every word you said to me. It's not every day my own grandma calls me a mangy stray at a dog show."

Behind me, I hear my mom inhale sharply, and Alexander sputters. "Mother?" he says, like Constance would ever confirm it to his face, but I keep going.

"You also said I was a mistake." I glance at Helene, who was the real wordsmith there. "One that should've been corrected in the womb. You're sure you don't remember?"

Silence. Kit's beside me again, solid and warm and no longer trying to stop me, and I feel my mother's hand on my shoulder, but I don't know her touch well enough to figure out what she's trying to say.

"Does anyone know the name of the reporter who wrote that unofficial biography of me?" I ask. "Henrietta something?"

"Henrietta Smythe," says Alexander, sounding only slightly strained. "She was a member of the Royal Rota for two decades."

"Right. Henrietta Smythe." I'm still holding Constance's clear blue gaze, and neither of us blinks. "Isn't there a chapter in the book about the day I arrived in England, and the twenty-four hours before my identity became public?"

To my surprise, it's Kit who replies. "There is," he says. "Though it's almost entirely fictionalized."

I tilt my head. "I know the book's already published, but do you think Henrietta Smythe might be interested in what really happened? For future editions, I mean."

"The royal family doesn't speak directly to our unofficial biographers," says Alexander, his voice stronger now. "It offers too much legitimacy to their occasionally extraordinary claims. But I'm certain we could arrange for a proxy to contact her, if you're serious. We've certainly done such things in the past."

Constance's flinty expression doesn't budge, but I can see the wrath in her eyes—the acknowledgment of my very real threat. And I know she knows I'm deadly serious.

"I'll think about it," I say at last. "Decide after the holidays."

"Of course," says Alexander. "We'll discuss it in the new year. Mother, have you eaten? Dinner won't be served until eight o'clock, and—"

Constance whirls around, and without another word, she

marches out of the dining room in a cloud of cashmere and contempt, her adorable spaniel trotting once again at her heels.

No one says anything for several long seconds, until the silence grows so heavy and awkward that it becomes unbearable. Both my father and Nicholas appear vaguely amused, while Helene finally takes that sip of her wine. But my mother looks . . . lost, maybe. Guarded, like Constance's blow landed, and she knows she has to protect herself from any further attacks. The rage returns, bubbling up inside me like lava, but just as I'm about to blurt out something to break the tension, Kit takes a single step toward my mother.

"Ms. Bright," he says warmly, as if the entire encounter with Constance never happened—as if the only strange part about this is the fact that he and my mother have never been introduced. "It's a pleasure to finally meet you."

"You must be Kit," she says, her wariness slowly fading. "You're even more handsome in person."

"And I can see where Evan gets her looks," says Kit, his cheeks pink. But as they slip into a comfortable exchange of pleasantries, Alexander takes my elbow, guiding me toward the buffet.

"Where is your sister?" he says as he starts to fill a plate, and I shrug.

"She ran off as soon as we got here."

"Right," he says with a hint of disappointment. "I suppose we'll do introductions later, then. Did you two pass by the, er . . . incident at the gate?"

"You mean the weirdly quiet protesters looking for any excuse to pull out a guillotine?" I say. "Yeah, we saw them. Why is my mom here?"

I lower my voice so it carries only between the two of us, and I can tell from the way Alexander's expression grows pinched that he understands exactly why I'm asking.

"Because she wants to be here," he says softly while he helps himself to the potatoes. "Because we would both like to spend Christmas together, as a family."

"They're going to eat her alive," I whisper. "That thing with Constance and the bathtub—"

"It will not happen again," says Alexander, moving on to the roasted chicken. "I promise. You've nothing to worry about, Evie—just relax and try to enjoy yourself, all right? You deserve it."

What I deserve is to know my mother is safe, both mentally and physically, but before I can spit that out between gritted teeth, Alexander heads back to her and hands her the plate. "Your favorites, if I recall. Let's sit, shall we?"

I remain beside the buffet as I watch them choose seats much too close to Helene and Nicholas, my jaw clenched so tightly that it aches. Kit joins me, wrapping his arm around my shoulders, and I lean into him.

"Would you like to go to the shops later?" he murmurs. "I need to buy your mum a gift."

This is obviously an attempt to distract me, but even though the idea of leaving my mother here makes me feel vaguely nauseated, he has a point. I have no idea if she received the present I sent to Virginia, and I can't stand the thought of her not having anything to open under the tree on Christmas. "Depends on whether Constance is on her way back to Balmoral yet," I mutter.

"Unlikely," he admits. "But your mum will be all right for a little while, Ev. Alexander has everything under control, and regardless of their verbal barbs, Constance and my aunt aren't ones to get their hands dirty."

"Maybe not," I say darkly. "But I am."

Kit presses a quick kiss to my temple, and despite my stewing, despite the omnipresent tension in the room and his grim mood, I swear I see him smirk.

CHAPTER SEVEN

'MAD MISTRESS' SPOTTED
AT SANDRINGHAM FOR CHRISTMAS

Laura Bright, mother of the King's illegitimate daughter, Evangeline, has joined the royal family for Christmas in Norfolk.

A woman identified as the infamous American mistress was photographed early this afternoon in a Range Rover driven by the King as they entered the grounds of Sandringham Estate. Though Buckingham Palace has refused to comment, an anonymous source close to the royals confirms that Bright, 43, made the trip from the United States specifically to spend the holiday with her daughter.

This is believed to be Bright's first visit to England since news of her affair with the King broke last summer. Traditionally, only members of the royal family are issued invitations to Sandringham, though exceptions have been made for both betrothed and former partners, including Venetia, Duchess of York, who divorced the Duke of York in 2006 but continues to join the royals for Christmas each year.

There has been no word as to whether either Bright will make an appearance on the walk to St Mary Magdalene Church, which the royal family famously attends for a service on Christmas morning.

—*The Daily Sun,* 23 December 2023

LATER THAT AFTERNOON, WHEN WE'VE miraculously made it through lunch without any bloodshed, my mother goes upstairs to take a nap, and Kit and I head into the village near Sandringham.

The protesters are gone now, either of their own volition or because security chased them away, but I'm still a ball of anxious energy as our driver navigates the narrow lanes that lead into town. All I can think about is the poison Constance could whisper in my mother's ear over the next week, and while I know my mom isn't fragile, if Constance finds the right combination of words, it could cause the kind of wound that'll never fully heal—which I'm sure is exactly her intention.

"It'll be all right," says Kit as the Range Rover winds through a village full of houses and businesses all built from the same red brick. "Your mother can hold her own, and Alexander will intervene if Constance tries anything else."

I want to believe him, but he's never seen my mom when her illness is winning, when her mind is playing tricks on her and she can't tell what's real. "I wish Constance would crawl back to her Scottish castle and let the rest of us enjoy the holiday," I mutter. "It'd be the greatest Christmas gift I've ever gotten."

Kit squeezes my fingers. "We'll just have to find a way to make the best of it."

Our eyes meet, and there's a hint of something in his gaze—something dark that adds gravity to his words, an unexpected solemnity that feels too heavy for the circumstances. I shift in my seat to face him. "Are you sure you're okay?"

"Positive," he says, but that darkness flickers again, even as he manages a faint smile. "It was a difficult term, that's all."

I'm not surprised. Kit's one of the most intelligent people I've ever met, but Oxford isn't exactly a walk in the park for anyone. "We'll take it easy this week," I promise. "Though I bet the Maldives is looking pretty good right now, compared to all this drama."

"On the contrary," he says, bringing our joined hands to his lips and kissing my knuckles. "There's nowhere else in the world I'd rather be. Or anyone else I'd rather be with."

As I rest my head on his shoulder, our driver parks in front of a shop on a quiet corner, which is only distinguishable from the rest of the town thanks to a faded pink sign that reads *Noble Norfolk Novelties*. While I can't tell what the shop sells, Kit seems to perk up when we climb out of the car.

"I think you'll like this place," he says as he pushes open the door, and a bell tinkles above us.

This place, as it turns out, is a strange hybrid of a bookstore, a gift shop, and an old-fashioned ice cream parlor. It's warm inside and smells like Christmas, and as I pause at the entrance, taking it all in, a woman with rosy cheeks bustles out from one of the aisles.

"Welcome," she says cheerfully. "How may I help you?"

"We're looking for a last-minute gift," says Kit as I examine a collection of jewelry beside the antique cash register. Some pieces are made of polished stones, while others show off flowers captured in resin or hand-painted earrings in the shape of tiny crowns.

"Anything in particular?" says the woman, but she must catch me eyeing the jewelry, because she adds, "All handmade by my daughter. Only fifteen and already so talented. Do you see anything you like, love?"

"It's all beautiful," I say, and as I glance up at her, recognition dawns on her round face. I smile politely, bracing myself for whatever's about to come, but other than her brief surprise, the only change to her expression is a faint hint of pity.

I touch a ring made of tiny pink stones fashioned into a miniature rose, and something subtle shifts inside me. She doesn't see me—she doesn't see a customer coming into her shop to buy a gift for an unexpected relative. She sees Evangeline, the King's illegitimate daughter, who has excellent posture and is always polite, who would never wear ripped leggings in public, and who everyone knows was sexually assaulted and accused of murder. Maybe in a decade or two, I'll have done enough for one of the worst moments of my life not to be the first thing everyone thinks of when I'm mentioned, but for now, I might as well have a neon sign above my head that screams *victim*.

"Is the ice cream parlor open?" says Kit as I pretend to focus on a pair of resin earrings.

"It is," says the woman, her voice an octave higher than before. "You *must* try our seasonal selections—they're like Christmas for your taste buds."

Mercifully the woman follows Kit to the other side of the shop, where the ice cream freezer is displayed beneath a chalkboard sign listing all the flavors, and I take the opportunity to duck into the crammed aisles. I'm not alone—a dark-haired personal protection officer trails after me with all the discretion of a lumbering grizzly bear—but I have a moment to realign myself and to become Evan again. On my first full day in England, during those precious few hours when I was still anonymous, Tibby warned me that if my identity was leaked, my life would never be the same. That I'd be stalked and hounded everywhere I went, and no matter what I accomplished, it would always be overshadowed by the accident of my birth.

She was mostly right, and despite her warning, I wasn't prepared for the level of scrutiny I've faced since. I'm still not, and even in this new place, far from Windsor and the crowds of London, I'm painfully aware that the world won't hesitate to turn on me if I even think about stepping out of line.

As I reach the back of the store, I turn the corner and stop suddenly. Two feet in front of me, on a rickety display that looks like it's balancing on willpower alone, are a dozen copies of Henrietta Smythe's new biography—complete with a black-and-white picture of my face on the cover. My cheeks grow hot as I glance around, and only once I'm sure this part of the shop is empty, I gingerly pick up the top copy and read the back.

The true story of Evangeline Bright, the secret American princess who's destined to take the royal world by storm.

"It's not a bad photo of you," says Kit softly behind me, and I jump. "Though I'm afraid that's the only good thing I can say about the book."

I wrinkle my nose and set it back down. "I can't believe you read it. Were you really that bored at your parents' place?"

He shrugs. "Maisie always asks me to read the unofficial biographies—she likes to know what they say, if only to prove them wrong. I assume that's a trait you two share. Chocolate candy cane with eggnog and evergreen swirl," he adds, offering me one of the cones in his hand.

I take it curiously and allow myself a cautious lick. To my surprise, the shopkeeper isn't wrong. It does taste like Christmas. "Weird," I mumble.

"The ice cream, or my reading habits?" says Kit as we leave the display behind and head down an aisle full of souvenirs and knickknacks.

"Both." I touch the spine of a purple leather-bound sketchbook, though when I start to slide it off the shelf, I realize it has a cartoon cat on the cover. "Do you think anyone's going to read it? The biography, I mean."

"I fear it's already a bestseller," he says, unearthing a wooden box that holds a miniature painting set, complete with five colors, two brushes, and several small canvases. "Don't worry—it's mostly fiction."

"That's exactly what I'm afraid of." I nod toward the box in his hand. "My mom would love that."

"Really?" says Kit. "I thought she'd have a dozen like it."

I shrug. "She always says there's no such thing as too much paint."

Kit holds on to the paint set as we move down the aisle, and we both pause the conversation to lick our cones. "It's really not as bad as it could be," he says, and it takes me a beat to realize he's talking about the biography, not the ice cream. "If anything, it's surprisingly kind toward you. She interviewed some of your schoolmates and a few people who claim to be family friends, but there's nothing terribly personal—"

"Kitters?"

We both look up at the same time. At the end of the aisle stands a girl not much older than me, with flaming-red hair and a smattering of freckles so adorable that I'm instantly jealous. Beside her is a brown-haired boy—man—roughly the same age, and though his expression looks like it's set in a permanent scowl, there's something inexplicably open about him.

"Aoife? Dylan?" says Kit, his voice tight with wariness I don't understand. "What are you doing here?"

"Good to see you, too, mate," says the boy—man—Dylan. He smiles, but even though I think he means it, it comes off as pained. "My gran lives here. Aoife's visiting for Christmas."

The redheaded girl nudges him affectionately, and I notice their clasped hands. "You must be Evangeline," she says to me. "I've heard so much about you."

"Wish I could say the same," I say, glancing at Kit. His lips are pursed, and he looks vaguely like a deer in headlights.

"Evangeline," he says in that polite, formal tone he only uses around other people. "This is Dylan and Aoife. Dylan and I were at Eton together, and now we're on the same course at Oxford, while Aoife's studying computer science."

This immediately piques my interest, considering I'll be studying the same in the autumn, but Aoife laughs before I can bring it up. "You make it sound like we all nod to each other as we pass in the hall," she says. "We're friends. Good friends, I'd say. Wouldn't you?" She looks at Dylan, who grunts in agreement.

"Had to carry his arse home from the pub a few times," he says, and Kit turns pink. He's mentioned going out with friends during our VidChat calls, but for the life of me, I can't remember him ever mentioning names. Or that he was close with anyone at Oxford.

"Complete exaggeration," Kit assures me with a forced smile. "If anything, I was the one keeping Dylan upright."

Aoife snorts. "Oh, no—*I'm* the one who had to tuck you both into bed," she teases before catching my eye. "Don't worry, it's all in good fun. Unlike Dylan and me, Kit's not a dosser."

I have absolutely no idea what that means, and I'm afraid to ask. Dylan must see my confusion, because he finally cracks a smile.

"She means he's a good lad," he says. "On the straight and narrow, as it were."

"*He's* actually at uni to study, rather than to poison his liver," she jokes. "And he talks about you all the bleedin' time. I don't know what kind of magic you've worked on him, but he's completely besotted."

Kit's blushing so hard now that he's practically scarlet. "Same magic you've worked on Dylan to get him to utter more than two words at a time," he says, but as he speaks, his phone chirps. He checks his screen, and his brow furrows. "I'm afraid we need to go."

"Bugger, really?" says Aoife, her shoulders slumping. "I was hoping you'd have time to grab a coffee. I've wanted to meet you for ages, Evangeline."

"We'll have to arrange something soon," mumbles Kit as he hastily types out a reply to whatever message he's received. I fight the urge to glance at his screen, sure he'll tell me eventually as long as this isn't a ruse to escape. "Evangeline, did you want to get something?"

I nod and take the box from under his arm. "You say good-bye, and I'll pay."

Kit doesn't argue, and considering he never lets me pay for a thing, that's how I know this isn't some kind of ploy to shake off his friends. I excuse myself and head for the register, where the shopkeeper is beaming at my return, and as I pull the rose ring from the velvet case, I hear footsteps behind me.

"I'm sorry if I came off a bit strong back there," says Aoife, pausing in front of the jewelry display. "Oh, these are grand."

"Her daughter made them," I say, and the shopkeeper winks.

"And you have nothing to apologize for. It's nice to meet some of Kit's friends. I don't really have many of my own here."

Aoife's easy grin returns as the shopkeeper rings me up. "Well, you can consider me one, then, if you'd like," she says, and there's a question there that I can't turn down—not politely, anyway. And definitely not as Evangeline.

"I would," I say, even though I'm not so sure. "You'll have to tell me more stories about Oxford."

She laughs again, any tension in her gone now. "I've got plenty of those, haven't I? Your Kit's a good lad. Brings out the best in us, or at least he tries, bless him."

He brings out the best in me, too, but I don't say that out loud. Kit and I've made more than our fair share of headlines since he took my hand at Wimbledon, and even though he and Aoife are friends, that's the kind of thing I want to—need to—keep private.

Once I pay for the gifts, Aoife and I head out onto the sidewalk together, still trailed by my personal protection officer. Kit and Dylan are waiting for us beside the Range Rover, and while they're chatting with the ease of two people who've known each other for years, Kit's posture is rigid, and his foot is tapping on the pavement to a fast and erratic beat.

"Evan," he says, too anxious to hide the impatience in his voice—or remember to call me Evangeline in front of his friends. "I'm afraid we really must go."

"No worries, mate," says Dylan, but Aoife's round eyes go a bit watery, and to my surprise, she catches me in a hug.

"Kit has my number," she says into my hair. "Stay in touch, yeah?"

"I will," I say, already feeling guilty for the lie. But I don't know how else to make a graceful exit, and it would take too long to explain that I don't have a phone. "It was really nice meeting you."

When she finally lets me go, she squeezes my free hand before latching onto Dylan's arm once more. Kit and I both pitch what's left of our ice cream, and I slide into the car, not sure whether I'm more relieved that's over or nervous about what comes next.

"They seem friendly," I say as soon as Kit joins me and closes the door. My protection officer climbs into the front seat beside the driver, and the car begins to move, leaving Dylan and Aoife behind. "Why did you never mention them?"

"Didn't I?" says Kit, even though I'm sure we both know he didn't. "I'll introduce you properly when you join us next year."

I eye him, not entirely sure how to take this gentle dismissal. But before I can press, he glances at his phone again, and while I know it's rude, I shift closer to him. "Who texted you?"

"Maisie," he says grimly, and he tilts his phone to show me. "It's a 9-9-9 text."

"A what?" I say, squinting at the screen. Sure enough, Maisie's texted a simple *999*, and despite Kit's three follow-up messages, she hasn't responded. "What does that mean?"

"It means there's an emergency," says Kit. "Like your American 9-1-1."

My heart stutters, and suddenly I feel like there's a block of ice in my stomach. "My mom," I say tightly. "If Constance did something—"

"You know how Maisie is," says Kit. "It could be anything. A lost shoe, a bit of friendly gossip she's blown out of proportion—"

"But she'd be answering you, then, right?" I say, silently willing the car to go faster. "If she hasn't said anything yet . . ."

I trail off, and Kit takes my hand, his thumb stroking my skin. But while we don't speak for the rest of the drive, my imagination more than makes up for our silence, and by the time we finally arrive at Sandringham House, I've already come up with a dozen different scenarios, each more devastating than the last.

A footman opens the door for us, and as Kit and I hurry inside, I notice Paul packing the antique scale into a cushioned crate. He bows his head in greeting, but before he speaks, a torrent of words rushes out of me.

"Is everything okay? Maisie sent Kit a text, and she said something's wrong, but we don't know what—"

"Do you know where Princess Mary is, Paul?" says Kit, far more calmly, as he slides my coat from my shoulders.

"Her Royal Highness is in the white drawing room with

Their Majesties and their guests," he says. "Should I let her know you've returned?"

I'm already striding across the entrance hall as Kit responds, "That won't be necessary," and his footsteps quickly catch up with mine. "Evan, whatever's going on, it can't be a true emergency if the staff hasn't been informed."

"You don't understand how bad things can get for my mom," I say, keeping my voice low as we round the corner. "If Constance or Helene went after her—"

"*Where* have you been?"

I skid to a stop, nearly plowing directly into my half sister as she paces the width of the corridor. Her face is flushed, her eyes are wild with panic, and she sidesteps me without a single dirty look—which is how I'm suddenly sure this isn't a false alarm.

"What's going on?" I say, ignoring her question. "Is my mom okay? What—"

"Your mother?" says Maisie, taken aback. "How on earth would I know? Is she here, too? Has the entire planet been invited and no one's bothered to tell me?"

Kit takes my hand again. "Evan's mother is here as Uncle Alexander's guest. What's happened? Why weren't you answering your mobile?"

"Mummy took it," says my half sister, tugging on a lock of her hair. "She's upset I missed lunch, or she was, but now—"

"*Maisie,*" I snap, and for once, she actually shuts up. "Why are we here? What's—"

A loud and vivacious laugh reverberates from the nearby drawing room, cutting me off. It's not my mother's, and it definitely doesn't sound like anything that could ever come out of

Helene's or Constance's mouth. But while I don't recognize it, Kit stiffens.

"Is that . . . ?" He trails off, and Maisie nods. "And did she bring . . . ?"

"Of course she bloody did."

Kit grits his teeth so hard that a muscle in his jaw jumps. "And Alexander's fine with it?"

"What do you think?" says Maisie witheringly, and Kit's scowl deepens. "But she has no idea, and Nicholas isn't saying a bloody word—"

"Are you two going to speak in code all night, or do I eventually get to find out what's going on?" I hiss, and both Maisie and Kit focus on me with very real fear in their eyes.

"Our aunt is here," says Maisie at last. "*Former* aunt. But she never seems to have received that particular message, because she shows up every bloody year, and—"

"*Who?*" I press. "Who are you talking about?"

More raucous laughter echoes from the drawing room, and as Maisie and Kit exchange yet another uncertain glance, I huff. Releasing Kit's hand, I creep toward the doorway until I can peek inside.

". . . and so I tell the sheik that of course it doesn't matter, it's only a Kokoschka, but he ought to be prepared to lose the Renoir auction, because my astrologer's assured me that Jupiter will be moving into my second house the day before—the *day* before!— and there's simply no way I can lose."

A blond woman lounges on a velvet sofa with her back to me, wineglass in hand as she gestures wildly. Nicholas perches beside her, though he leans into the armrest, putting as much space between them as possible. Constance sits unsmilingly in a chair nearby, and to my surprise, Alexander and Helene stand together by the fireplace, his expression stony and hers deeply troubled. It's the first time I've seen them go near each other voluntarily in months.

I'm about to pull back and ask who the blond is when she turns enough for me to see her profile, and even though I've never met her, I recognize her instantly. She's beautiful, in an overdone way that makes it clear she's fighting her real age. And while I never paid much attention to her growing up, it was impossible to miss the onslaught of skin-care ads, tell-alls, and talk show appearances that she still manages to book to this day.

Venetia, Duchess of York.

As everything Kit and Maisie said clicks like pieces of a puzzle I never should've solved, I notice that Alexander and Helene aren't watching Venetia. They're looking behind her, to the corner of the room I can't easily see.

Dread fills the pit of my stomach, and I inch forward to reveal the handsome blond boy leaning against the piano, perfectly at home in a room so full of tension that it seems to seep out of the walls. And as my blood turns to ice and my ears fill with static, his gaze shifts, and he looks directly at me.

Ben.

CHAPTER EIGHT

Has Prince Benedict of York finally returned to the UK?

Though Benedict has made a name for himself as a fixture in the London nightlife scene over the past year, he's been conspicuously missing in action since July. After weeks of questions from his loyal fans, Buckingham Palace finally released a statement in August announcing that the nineteen-year-old had decided to spend the rest of his summer—and the following autumn, putting off his acceptance to the University of St Andrews for another term—at an undisclosed wildlife sanctuary in Kenya. Though the prince has always been known for his love of animals, the trip was reportedly unannounced due to security concerns after the intense media scrutiny focused on the royal family over the summer.

But the third in line to the throne was spotted at Heathrow this morning with his mother, Venetia, Duchess of York, as the pair left the airport's private Windsor Suite. Are the prince and his mother expected at the reportedly ultra-low-key royal family gathering at Sandringham this year? The ex-wife of the Duke of York has never missed a Christmas, even in the midst of their contentious divorce, and it's no surprise that His Royal Highness has decided to make the arduous journey back for the holidays, given his close relationship with Princess Mary. After months apart, we've no doubt that their reunion will be full of good cheer.

—*The Regal Record,* 23 December 2023

I SPIN AROUND AND PRESS my back to the wall, my heart racing as a picture frame digs into my side.

Ben is here.

Ben knows *I'm* here.

And if he doesn't know about my mom yet, he will soon enough.

Maisie grabs my wrist and yanks me farther into the corridor, clear of the inhospitable drawing room and Ben's unnerving stare. "Did you see him?" she whispers.

I nod and do my best to swallow the panic rising in me like bile. "Why is he here? *How* is he here? I thought—"

"Ah, there you all are. I was beginning to wonder."

The three of us turn toward the drawing room together, and my insides churn for real this time, threatening to expel the ice cream I can still taste.

Ben stands in the doorway, his hands in the pockets of his navy blazer. He smiles like nothing ever happened, like we're one big, happy family reuniting for the holidays, and as his blue eyes settle on me, a shiver runs down my spine.

"Benedict," says Kit with more self-control than I've ever possessed in my life. "I was under the impression you weren't coming to Sandringham this year."

Ben shrugs. "Mummy insisted I join her. You know how she is," he adds with what I used to think was charming geniality. "Once she has her mind set on something, there's no talking her out of it."

"I'm sure you could've come up with an excuse," says Maisie, sugary venom dripping from every word. "Like maybe the fact that none of us wants you here. His Majesty hasn't forgotten what you did, and rest assured, neither have we."

Hurt flickers across his face, so real I almost feel sorry for him. But he's Ben. He's the one who tried to ruin my life—who could still ruin Maisie's with a single slip of the tongue—and even after all these months, I still have no idea why.

"I did some terrible things over the summer," he says. "Awful things I'll never be able to erase. And I know I don't deserve a second chance, but if you'd all be willing to indulge me for a moment . . . especially you, Evan."

He gestures toward the drawing room, where the adults are gathered. I shrink back, a sour taste in my mouth, but before I can refuse, Maisie cuts in.

"We don't need your fake apologies, Benedict. We need you to *leave.*"

"And I will," he says. "Right after Christmas. Please—this won't take long, and it'll save me from trying to explain the details of this whole mess to Mummy."

Inexplicably, this seems to be the thing that thaws Maisie's stubbornness, and she and Kit exchange a look I don't understand. "Fine," she snaps. "But in five minutes, we're all leaving."

"What?" I say, stunned she's given in so easily. Before I can properly protest, however, Maisie loops her arm in mine and yanks me forward, and it's all I can do to keep my balance as she drags me after Ben and into the white drawing room.

As soon as we step over the threshold—or, in my case, stumble and nearly face-plant on the rug—the hum of conversation falls silent, and all eyes are on us. I'm not surprised that Alexander's expression is a mixture of fury and concern, or that

Constance's and Helene's are impossible to read. But the worry written on Nicholas's face is disconcerting, and Venetia . . .

Venetia, Duchess of York, Ben's mother and Nicholas's ex-wife, is looking at me like we're standing outside a chocolate factory, and I'm her golden ticket in.

"Evangeline!" she cries, rising to her feet and crossing the room in her towering heels. "At last. It's *such* a pleasure, my darling."

I stand stock-still as she presses her lips to my cheeks in a double kiss, and when she looks me up and down, it takes everything I have not to wipe off the magenta lipstick stains she's undoubtedly left behind.

"Mummy," says Ben imploringly. "I have something I'd like to say to everyone."

"Oh, yes, button. Of course," says Venetia, and she winks at me like she knows exactly what's coming before bustling back to her seat.

Ben clears his throat, gazing solemnly around the room at each of us. "I appreciate your time, and I won't waste it," he begins. "It's no secret that over the summer, I was . . . less than my best self."

Maisie scoffs. "That's putting it mildly," she mutters, and while Ben must hear her, he doesn't look our way.

"I won't make excuses," continues Ben. "There are none, anyway, that could possibly justify my actions, particularly my treatment of Evangeline."

Though he says my name, he still doesn't give me more than a passing glance, and I'm not sure whether to be relieved or creeped out. Kit wraps his arm around my shoulders, as if he alone can stand between Ben and whatever words he's about to wield, and I let myself lean into him.

"As a member of this family—the royal family—it's easy to forget how isolated we are from the rest of the world," says Ben. "Not just physically, but emotionally, too. It's always been hard for me to let strangers in, and I'll admit, I struggled to accept Evan. The entire situation was . . . jarring, and with Jasper's death and the fallout that happened . . . well." He gives a perfect imitation of a self-loathing scowl. "It made me question everything important in my life, and I became a person I wasn't proud of.

"But my time in Kenya gave me the opportunity to open up," he adds. "To relax, to forget about the pressures of being royal, and to reexamine my priorities. Those months allowed me to reflect on what I was doing with my life and how I was conducting myself in the name of this family, and all I felt was shame. While I know nothing will ever make up for my abysmal behavior, these few days together are my chance to show you I've changed, and I'm asking you—*begging* you—to let me."

It's a moving speech, or at least I think it might be if anyone else were giving it. But all I feel is the cold, hard lump of anger and bewilderment settling in the pit of my stomach, and I glance around at the others, searching for—I don't know. Support, maybe. Comradery in thinking that Ben is full of shit.

Instead, Venetia is dabbing her eyes, as if Ben has just announced his nomination for sainthood. Nicholas looks reluctantly resigned, and while Constance's expression has barely changed, the corners of her mouth are angled the slightest bit upward, which is more of a smile than I've ever seen from her before. Even Helene is studying Ben like she's contemplating his request.

Only my father and Maisie look as disdainful as I feel. But rather than tell Ben to piss off, Alexander straightens to his full height, every bit a king now as he was with President Park.

"Your behavior wasn't only unacceptable, Benedict," he says with quiet hostility that's impossible to miss. "It was a threat to this family and to the monarchy itself."

"I know," says Ben, and I swear I see him gulp. "You have every right to throw me out in the cold and slam the door, Uncle Alexander, and I don't think anyone in this room would blame you."

Venetia sniffs, and it's clear she, at least, will fight to the death to protect her monster of a son. Alexander's gaze flickers toward her, but he refocuses on Ben almost immediately and considers him for an uncomfortably long moment.

"You may be my nephew," says Alexander, "but Evangeline is my daughter. And from this moment on, you will treat her with the respect to which she's fully entitled."

"Understood," says Ben, and this time, when he looks at me, it's more than just a glance. "I'm truly sorry, Evan, for every-thing. I should've welcomed you into the family with open arms, and instead . . ." He trails off, as if he's too ashamed of the details to recount them, and I narrow my eyes.

"Instead you tried to destroy my life," I say bitingly. "You told *everyone* about—"

"Trust, once broken, is impossible to mend completely," says Alexander suddenly, loud enough to drown me out. "By virtue of blood, Benedict, you'll always be family. But if you want to be part of this monarchy, too, then you need to prove you're willing to uphold the values of the crown. You need to earn your role and your titles and every privilege that comes with them, and there will be no more second chances. Is that understood?"

Ben nods, seemingly abashed, but I gape at my father, too stunned for words. After everything Ben did, after every lie, every threat, every betrayal, Alexander is letting him waltz right back into our lives like it was all nothing.

"No," I blurt with such force that I take an involuntary step forward. "You know what he did, Alexander. You all *know*—"

"Why don't we speak outside, Evan?" says my father calmly, like I'm the one who's being unreasonable. Like he hasn't just offered a lifeline to the person who leaked the video of Jasper trying to rape me, and who might still have evidence that Maisie was the one who really killed him.

"Is this some kind of joke?" I say incredulously as Alexander strides toward me. "Or is this just good old-fashioned nepotism, and we're expected to excuse any and all toxic behavior, so long as you were born into the right family?"

I look around the room, but while Maisie is glaring at Ben, she doesn't speak up. And as Alexander joins me and sets his hand on my elbow, I peer at Kit, expecting at least some level of support. But he won't even meet my eye.

This, more than anything—more than Constance's cold stare, more than Maisie's silence, even more than Alexander's gentle attempt to guide me toward the door—is what finally makes me move. With my jaw tight and my heart racing, I jerk away from my father and storm back into the hallway. I'm not sure where I'm going, but it doesn't matter, as long as it's as far from Ben and the rest of my callous family as possible.

I make it twenty feet before I hear hurried footsteps behind me, and yet again, Alexander's hand is on my arm. "Evie—"

"Don't *touch* me," I snarl, whirling around to face him so quickly that he nearly runs straight into me. He hastily raises his hands and takes a step back, like I'm some wild animal threatening to rip out a chunk of his flesh.

"Evangeline," he says in a measured tone that only incenses me further. "Why don't we discuss this privately—"

"Do you not remember what he did to me? To Maisie?" I say. "Are you seriously going to forgive him just because he spent ten minutes coming up with some speech about how much he's changed? Because he hasn't, you know. You don't do the kinds of things he did and then suddenly find your moral compass because you've petted a few elephants."

"I know," says Alexander quietly. "And I would very much appreciate the opportunity to speak to you behind closed doors."

This is such a strange request that the fire fueling my rage sputters, and I still. Both Kit and Maisie linger in the corridor behind him, only a few feet from the drawing room where everyone else is still gathered, and both of them look . . . grim. Angry, I think. Maybe even scared.

At last, even though I have no desire to hear whatever justification Alexander's come up with, I nod stiffly. He leads me a safe distance down the hallway and into the empty dining room, and with my hands balled into fists, I take up a position near the windows, my arms crossed and my posture rigid.

Alexander waits until both Maisie and Kit have joined us, and he closes the door with a soft *click*. "This has nothing to do with how we may or may not feel about Ben," he says at last, his voice low and serious. "This is about making sure Venetia never discovers the details."

I blink, not sure I'm hearing him right. "Venetia? *That's* who you're all worried about?"

"She has the biggest mouth in the history of this family," says Maisie bitterly. "Whenever the money's getting low, she writes a new book, milking her farce of a marriage to Uncle Nicholas for all it's worth. If she finds out what really happened over the summer, then the entire world will know before the week's out."

I frown. "But she must have some idea of what went down. Ben just apologized in front of her."

"And you'll note how he took care not to mention any specifics," says Alexander. "I suspect he's told Venetia that he was unkind toward you—a bit of a bully, perhaps, or a little too aloof. But nothing that can't be forgiven in time."

"So she doesn't know Ben leaked the video of me and Jasper?" I say. "Or that he drugged my drink, or threatened Maisie, or—"

"The rule of thumb to follow with Venetia," says Alexander, "is if the press doesn't know, then neither does she."

We stand in silence for a long moment as I process this, and slowly my temper ebbs. Not completely—I'll never *not* be angry about what Ben's put me through, or what he could still do to my sister, or what passes for acceptable in this supposed family. But at least it isn't directed at the three of them anymore.

I let my arms drop in a show of tentative peace, if not surrender. "If she's such a blabbermouth, then why not just kick both of them out now?"

"Because," says Alexander wearily, "we can't send either of them away without informing Venetia of all that's happened. And if Ben is whispering his version of events in her ear, and she runs to the press . . ."

He trails off, and I look between him and Maisie. "Then we'll deny it and tell the world about every despicable thing he's done," I say, baffled that this hasn't already occurred to them. "Wasn't that the whole reason I gave that interview? So Maisie has plausible deniability if Ben ever goes public or the recording ever resurfaces?"

Alexander grimaces. "Yes," he allows. "But . . ."

"But what?" I press, though no one says anything. "Maisie, back me up here."

She takes a deep breath, and even from across the room, I notice her hands are trembling. "Daddy's right," she says as Kit squeezes her elbow. "Venetia's widely seen as a credible source of insider information about our family. She embellishes from time to time, but she's never outright lied about our lives, and the public knows it."

I gape at her—at both of them. "You want Ben to stay?"

"Of course not," she snaps. Her eyes are red now, and despite the ferocity in her voice, she looks like she's about to cry. "I want him gone just as badly as you do. But Ben knows too much, and this *will* go poorly if we force them to leave."

"And you don't think it will if he sticks around?" I say, my own anger bubbling to the surface again as I turn back to

Alexander. "You're really okay with us all sleeping under the same roof?"

"No," he admits. "I've already instructed security to monitor Benedict at all times. But we'll have a better chance of controlling the narrative if he's here, where we can keep an eye on him. And, to be frank, I think more danger lies in what could—and likely would—happen if we banish him now. Not to mention the scandal it would cause."

I open and shut my mouth, momentarily speechless. "Is that what this is really about? You're going to let Ben get away with everything he did just to avoid another scandal?"

"I cannot disown him without reason—a very public reason," says my father and there's steel in his voice now. "I don't like this, either, Evan, but we're between a rock and a hard place, and certain choices must be made. Ben's entire future is wrapped up in this family, and in my allowing him to remain an active part of it. Now that we all know what he's capable of, he'll take care to earn back our trust. And until—unless—he does something truly dangerous, we must find a way to live with him."

My heart races, and I'm so furious that I can barely speak. "If something happens to one of us—to my mom—"

"Then I will destroy him," says Alexander calmly. "You have my word."

Maisie huffs. "We could just have him killed now and save everyone the trouble," she mutters.

"Only as a last resort," says Alexander, and I don't think he's joking.

But no matter what my father says, I know—from the look in Ben's eyes to the way he says my name to his charade of regret—that he isn't here to win us over. He didn't come back to beg forgiveness or to prove he loves us after all.

Ben is here for revenge. And I refuse to let him have it.

CHAPTER NINE

"Henrietta, would you say that it is unprecedented for the King to so blatantly flaunt his mistress at a royal family gathering?"

"In modern times, certainly, but historically, royal mistresses were extremely common and typically had a prominent place in the royal household. Anne Boleyn is likely the most famous example, though of course she eventually became the second wife of Henry VIII."

"And lost her head for it, as we all know. What about Wallis Simpson, as a more recent example?"

"As the Prince of Wales, Edward VIII certainly made no secret of his affair with Wallis Spencer—who later became Wallis Simpson—after meeting her in San Diego in 1920. This was before he married Catherine Gable in 1927, however, so he was really the third wheel of her first marriage."

"So it's been more than a century since any king has had a mistress?"

"It's been more than a century since any king was *caught* with a mistress. There have been whispers—particularly about Alexander I—for decades, but no woman was ever named."

"Until Laura Bright."

"Until Laura Bright, yes. Though while I will admit it does look rather dodgy, with His Majesty himself escorting Ms. Bright to Sandringham, one might speculate that she was joining her daughter, Evangeline, for Christmas, rather than coming as the King's plus-one."

"Is there any evidence that she and His Majesty may be resuming their affair?"

"It's anyone's guess, though to do so in such a public manner would be daring, to say the least. Especially with the Queen and Queen Mother present at Sandringham."

"I expect the royals are in for an awkward Christmas, wouldn't you say?"

"That's certainly putting it mildly."

—ITV News's interview with royal expert
Henrietta Smythe, 23 December 2023

BEN IS EVERYWHERE.

I have no idea how he does it, but for the rest of the afternoon, every time I venture into one of the common areas of Sandringham, he's there—lurking in a corner, perched on an out-of-the-way armchair, or seated on the opposite side of the room, rarely part of the conversation, but always watching. And usually watching me.

The rest of the family barely bats an eye, as if they've already forgotten the reason for his apology in the first place. Even Maisie seems to reluctantly accept his presence, though she, at least, never actively acknowledges his existence. Despite her unspoken support, however, the whole situation is so unnerving that once I make sure my mom is still sleeping off her jet lag, Kit and I sneak away to spend the evening on my bedroom sofa, up to our eyeballs in cheesy Christmas movies. I'm not in the right headspace to enjoy them, not with Ben skulking nearby. But Kit gets sniffly every time the inevitable happy ending rolls around, so I don't argue when he suggests yet another. At least one of us is having a good holiday.

Sometime in the middle of our marathon, we fall asleep on the couch together, and I wake in the gray morning light to the sound of indistinct whispers. They're faint at first, as if they're coming from the other side of the wall, but after a groggy moment, I realize they're murmuring my name.

"Evangeline."

"Evangeline."

"Evangeline."

The whispers repeat a dozen times over, each voice slightly different from the last. I must still be dreaming, or maybe this place is haunted, and a prickly sensation runs down my spine as I groan into Kit's chest. "Go *away.*"

"I will do no such thing," says an uppity voice, and I sit up like I really have just heard a ghost.

Maisie stands in the doorway, dressed in what I can only call British country chic—a fitted tweed jacket, tan pants, and brown boots so polished that they look wet. Her hair is braided and wrapped into a stylish-but-casual updo, and I shudder at the thought of what time she must've gotten up to make it all happen.

"You do know it's barely dawn, right?" I mumble as Kit stirs beside me. We're both fully dressed—which includes fluffy robes, bulky sweaters, and fuzzy socks, considering it's about two degrees above freezing in my room—but Maisie's eyebrows shoot up anyway.

"Pardon me for interrupting," she says, a note of amusement in her voice. "Did you not check your itinerary? We leave for the Christmas Eve hunt in thirty minutes."

"I don't kill innocent animals," I say, rubbing the sleep from my eyes.

"But you do eat them," she says, and I shrug, too tired to defend my hypocrisy. "It's all for tonight, you know. Edward IX had a thing about hunting game for the Christmas Eve feast himself, and it stuck. You don't have to shoot anything," she adds. "The route also offers several lovely views of the estate."

"I can see it just fine from my window." My neck is sore from lying on Kit all night, and I dig my fingers into the offending muscle. "Is everyone else going?"

Maisie sniffs. "Mummy shares your softhearted sentiments, and Venetia's always moaning about her manicure, but as far as I know, everyone else will be joining the hunting party."

"Including Ben?" I say, and her eyes narrow.

"I expect so. He has yet to miss a year."

If I was even remotely tempted to tag along, that immediately quells it. "If it's all the same to you, I'd rather not go anywhere near him while he's holding a deadly weapon."

Maisie scoffs. "I loathe Benedict as much as you do, but he wouldn't dare try anything. Not with so many witnesses."

"Still. Accidents happen, and I'd prefer not to give him an opening. You shouldn't, either, you know."

"He wouldn't dare risk giving Daddy a public reason to cut him off," she says, but underneath her dismissiveness, there's a note of fear that she can't hide entirely. "Benedict is nothing without this family, and he knows it. He may be a snake, and I certainly won't be taking him into my confidence anytime soon, but I'm perfectly safe around him. We both are, and I assure you, he'll be on his best behavior."

"Maybe," I mutter, though I don't know who she's trying to convince—me or herself. "His best behavior isn't exactly setting the bar high, you know."

With a sigh that makes it clear I'm the bane of Maisie's existence, she looks at Kit instead. "Will *you* be joining us this year?"

" 'Fraid not," he says as he sits up beside me. His hair is sticking out in every direction, and he futilely tries to comb his fingers through his wild waves. "I was thinking about giving Evan a tour of the gardens and the walking trails through the woods."

"At least she'll be getting *some* fresh air," mutters Maisie. "Whether you hunt or not, you're both expected at the Christmas party this evening—we'll be decorating the tree in the white drawing room, followed by a formal dinner and opening gifts. And," she adds pointedly, "the dress code is black-tie."

She eyes the cartoon reindeer on my socks with disdain, and without another word, she turns on her heel and marches out of the room, closing the door behind her.

As soon as she's gone, I lie back down in a huff and wiggle my freezing toes. "It's starting to feel like we're the only people actually trying to avoid Ben."

Kit settles on the sofa with me. "Everyone else is used to him, and it's easier to resume old patterns than establish new ones." He nuzzles my cheek. "Good morning."

"Good morning," I say, relaxing as he wraps his arms around me. "You stayed over."

"I didn't mean to," he says apologetically. "How do you feel?"

This, I know, is him asking more than just how I slept. I turn toward him and, mindful that neither of us brushed our teeth last night, I give him a closed-mouth peck. "I have a crick in my neck," I admit. "Can we please aim for passing out in the bed tonight instead?"

Kit hesitates. "Are you sure? I don't have to stay if you'd rather—"

"I want you to," I say firmly. "You're warm, and if it were any colder in here, it'd be snowing."

He chuckles and holds me a bit tighter. "Very well. I'll be your personal Sandringham space heater, but only because you insist."

Once we untangle ourselves and Kit heads to his own room to get ready, I turn the shower on as hot as it'll go and stand under the scalding water long enough to boil a lobster. By the time I dry off and dress in my warmest sweater, I have some feeling in my fingers again, and I braid my damp hair and head out into the hallway, determined to find something hot for breakfast. Before I can take more than a couple of steps, however, a door across the corridor opens, and Ben appears.

Instantly our eyes meet. He's wearing contacts instead of his typical brown frames, making his stare even more penetrating than usual, and slowly I register the fact that his hunting outfit matches Maisie's.

"Evangeline," he says, and while his tone is as genial as ever, it still turns my blood to ice. "Are you not joining us today?"

"I'm not in the mood to kill things," I say coldly, and he chuckles.

"Pity. I rather think you'd be good at it." He smiles, but

there's no real warmth behind it—only a mimicry. "If you'll excuse me."

He starts to walk away, but with a surge of bravery—or, more likely, sheer recklessness and a generous lack of self-preservation—I follow, my footsteps matching his.

"I got your flowers," I say, and he slows. "I'd say thank you, but."

"Flowers?" he says innocently. There's a smirk tugging at the corner of his mouth, though, and I know he knows exactly what I'm talking about—the bouquet of blood-red gerbera daisies that accompanied the threatening note he sent to my first public appearance. "I'm afraid they must've been from someone else."

"Must've been," I agree in a tone that makes it clear I'm not the least bit fooled. "Why did you do it?"

"Send flowers?" says Ben. "I thought we just established—"

"Not that. All of it. Jasper, the video—everything that happened this summer. Why?"

Ben stills completely now, almost unnaturally so. "You've asked me that before."

"You didn't answer then, either," I say. "But I think I deserve to know. What is it that made you hate me so damn much that you tried to ruin my life?"

He tilts his head. "I didn't try to ruin your life, Evan. You did that on your own the moment you decided to join this family."

Before I can argue, a creak sounds behind me, and I glance over my shoulder. A member of the security team stands fifteen feet away, his gray suit a stark contrast to the rich velvets and dark woods that decorate the hallway. When I look back at Ben, his shoulders are squared and his posture is stiff as he takes in the sight of the officer.

"The family's expecting me," he says, his gaze once again meeting mine. We stand there for several eternal seconds until at last, with a mocking dip of his head that anyone else might assume is a bow, he turns and continues on his way down the corridor.

I watch him go, his footsteps muffled by the hunter-green carpet, and only once he's turned out of sight do I unclench and exhale. My legs feel like they're made of putty, and I lean against the wall, resting the back of my head on the edge of a gilded frame as I focus on my breathing.

Shit.

CHAPTER TEN

Aoife

it was grand seeing you yesterday, kitters. have you and evangeline got a spare hour today? or maybe after christmas?

Kit

We have a tight schedule today, I'm afraid, and we'll be leaving for Klosters on Boxing Day.

Aoife

damn

Aoife

I like her. she seems delightfully normal, or whatever passes for normal in that bloody family of yours.

Kit

It's a rather low bar, admittedly.

Aoife

some other time, then, yeah?

Kit

Some other time.

Aoife

you really never mentioned me or dylan?

Kit

You know why. She has enough to worry about.

Aoife

that's nothing, love. just a bit of fun. no reason to tie yourself into a twist over it.

Kit

I fear our definitions of fun are very different.

—*Text message exchange between Christopher Abbott-Montgomery, Earl of Clarence, and Aoife Marsh, 24 December 2023*

"EVAN?"

I'm still leaning against the gilded frame outside my bedroom, my heart racing from the encounter with Ben, when my name filters down the hallway.

My eyes fly open. The security guard is gone now, and in his place stands Kit. He's in a gray sweater with fitted jeans, and his hair is tied back in a half ponytail that he pulls off with astounding ease. But even as I take in the sight of him—which is usually more than enough to make me go all warm and fuzzy inside—I can't shake the coldness that's settled over me in Ben's wake.

"I'm fine," I say, seeing the worried crease in his brow as he makes his way toward me. "Just ran into Ben."

"Did he say anything?" says Kit, taking my arm, and I shake my head.

"Nothing menacing enough to hold up in a court of law," I mutter. "I love your hair like that."

"You do?" he says, mercifully letting the topic of Ben drop as he self-consciously touches his ends. "It's not quite long enough for a full ponytail, I'm afraid. And Aunt Helene will hate it."

Sure enough, as we enter the dining room a few minutes later, Helene's fork falls to her plate in a clatter.

"Kit, I am *begging* you—allow my assistant just a few minutes with that unruly mop of yours before church tomorrow. You can't be photographed like this."

"I think he looks exceptionally handsome," says Venetia, who sits across from Helene with her green eyes now fixed on Kit. "It's rather roguish, isn't it? If I were ten years younger . . ."

"You'd still be a decade too old," says Helene, now delicately spearing a strawberry.

Someone clears their throat behind me, and Kit and I both turn. My mother stands with a mug of coffee in one hand and a tote bag of painting supplies slung over her shoulder, and she smiles. "Longer hair suits you, Kit," she says, though unlike Ben's mother, there's nothing creepy about the way she says this.

"Thank you, Ms. Bright," says Kit politely, but there's a hint of amusement in his voice, too. "May I take your bag?"

Surprisingly, my mother hands it over, and while Kit sets it down in an unoccupied corner of the room, she drops a kiss on my forehead. "Good morning, Evie."

"Hi, Mom," I say quietly, and as I hug her, I have the sudden urge to lead her as far away from the dining room as we can get. "What are you—"

"Evangeline!" cuts in Venetia cheerfully, seemingly oblivious to our private conversation. "Now that you and your mum are both here, I've been meaning to ask—what time were you born, love?"

I blink. "What? Why?" We've barely said a word to each other, and this isn't exactly the kind of question you ask without a motive.

Helene must sense it, too, because she gives Venetia a look that could melt steel, but the duchess merely waves her off. "Oh, not like *that,* darling. I simply want to do her natal chart. It'll be similar to Maisie's, of course, considering they were born on the same day, but there must be all sorts of stories in the differences. Maisie's a Leo rising," she adds cheerfully. "You're so alike, the pair of you—I bet your ascendant is a fire sign, too."

"I don't know what that means," I say. "And I don't know when I was born. I was a little busy at the time."

Venetia laughs as if I've told the funniest joke in the world. "You certainly don't get your sense of humor from His Majesty, do you? Laura, surely you know her birth time."

I peer at my mother, whose expression has gone strangely fixed. She's still smiling, but it seems glued on now, and like it's taking a considerable amount of effort to keep it there.

"I'm afraid I have no idea, either," she says. "It was a difficult birth, and the doctors gave me the good stuff. I didn't know what day it was, let alone what time."

"You've never looked at her birth certificate?" says Venetia dubiously. And for a split second, I swear Helene and my mother exchange an unreadable look.

"Evan's early life was somewhat . . . turbulent for me," says my mom. "Alexander has all the official documentation now. You'll have to ask him about any specifics."

Venetia opens her mouth, then swiftly closes it, her overdone lips puckered like she's swallowed a lemon. And when Helene and my mother glance at each other again, I'm sure I'm not imagining things.

Despite this awkward interaction, Venetia shows no signs of being subdued throughout breakfast. Helene and my mother make sure most of the chatter is mercifully directed toward Kit, who seems happy to talk in bland generalities about his term at Oxford, but whenever the conversation drifts toward me, Venetia's questions go from polite to probing in seconds. Again and again, Kit intercepts, turning the conversation back on himself with masterful skill, until Venetia finally seems to grow bored and excuses herself, citing an urgent need to make a phone call.

As soon as she's gone, the four of us seem to exhale at once, and I shift to face my mom in the chair beside me. "Are you going somewhere to paint? Maybe Kit and I could come along and keep you company."

"I thought I'd stay here for a little while," she says, sipping the last of her coffee. "Helene and I have plenty to catch up on, and I'm not sure we'll have another chance before the boys return."

"What?" I say, so startled that for a moment, I forget we're all being polite. "But—"

"It has been a long time," agrees Helene. "And we do have quite a lot to discuss."

I look back and forth between them, baffled. Never in my life have I pictured the pair of them sitting at the same table, having a civil—let alone friendly—conversation, and the thought of all the cruel things Helene could say to my mother fills my ears with incessant buzzing and the pit of my stomach with dread. Helene was the trigger for my mother's psychotic break, and even though it's been fourteen years, those scars must still exist somewhere inside her. And I have no idea how delicate they might be.

"Evan," says Kit, his fingers lacing through mine underneath the table. "Why don't we go on that walk?"

"Walk?" I say, barely comprehending the word. "But—"

"That's a great idea," says my mother. "Do me a favor and look for a spot that captures your attention. I'd like to work on a new piece while we're here, and it should be something special."

I don't know how to say no to that, or how to say yes to Kit, but he stands and guides me to my feet. "We'll be back before lunch," he promises, but before he can lead me to the exit, I slip my hand out of his grip and fling my arms tightly around my mom.

"Are you sure?" I whisper, and she hugs me gently in return.

"Positive," she murmurs. "Helene and I both have what we want now, and that makes all the difference."

I'm not convinced, but my mother releases me, and Kit's there again, apparently every bit as sure as she is that this isn't a massive mistake. I glance over my shoulder as we leave the dining room, but rather than focusing on my mother, I meet Helene's eye instead. She nods once, slowly, and this is as much of a promise as I'm going to get.

The garden, as it turns out, isn't just a stretch of flowers, but a dozen paths that lead through meticulous hedges and shrubs, past stunning fountains and statues, and into the woods that are spread out across the estate. Kit's arm is wrapped around the waist of my black wool peacoat as we meander between tall trees, the branches bare in the winter morning light, but for once, his presence isn't enough to calm the hurricane of anxiety inside me.

"I hate that we don't know what they're talking about," I say, resisting the urge to look back at Sandringham House, or at least what little we can see of it from here. "If Helene says something that sets my mom off . . ."

"She won't," says Kit. "What would be the point? It would only upset you and Alexander, and she wouldn't gain anything. Besides, Aunt Helene may be many things, but she isn't malicious or sadistic."

"No, just spiteful and heartless," I mutter. "She told the entire world about my mom's illness."

"Because she thought it would protect Maisie. I'm not defending her," he adds gently as I start to protest. "I'm completely on your side. But I've known Aunt Helene my entire life, and if I thought for a moment that she might do something to shatter your mother's peace, I would've never walked out of that room. If anything, they're almost certainly talking about Alexander."

"What about him?" I say, silently desperate that he's right.

"Logistics, I'd expect, especially if he and your mother choose to carry on while he's still legally married to Helene."

I make a face. "I can't believe they're sharing a bedroom. Do you think—no, never mind, don't answer that."

He laughs and kisses my temple. "Are you all right with it? With them being together again, if they are. If they choose to be."

Something heavy settles over me, and I take a deep breath, considering the question. Unlike some kids with unmarried parents, I never fantasized about mine getting back together in a sweeping romance that fixed every problem in my life. If anything, the very thought makes me uneasy for reasons I'm not sure I can explain.

"I don't think I have any right to try to stop them," I admit at last. "But I don't like it. Not the idea of them—I think anyone who's ever seen them together knows how much they love each other, and they have a right to be happy. But I'm not sure that's possible. Alexander can love my mom more than anything in the world, but he's still King, and being with him will shine a spotlight on her that'll never go away. The press has already villainized her, and no amount of truth or damage control will change the fact that everyone—*everyone* knows about the darkest moments of her life."

"And because of that, they can't be together?"

I shake my head. "The media will never let it go, and the public will never forget what happened. No matter what comes next, she'll always be the—the *crazy mistress* who tried to drown her daughter in a bathtub. At least if she's out of the limelight, she'll have a chance to move on with her life. She'll have a chance to be *more*."

Kit is quiet as we head deeper into the trees. Overhead, a bird breaks into song, and I crane my neck to find it, but it's hidden in the endless bare branches.

"What if," he says slowly, "your mum doesn't want to be more?"

I frown. "Who wants to be defined by the worst thing that's ever happened to them?"

Kit purses his lips. "For years, she's been separated from the people she loves. She couldn't be with Alexander because—well, obvious reasons, and she was scared to be around you in case she hurt you again. But now that everything's out in the open, she's here—in England, with you and Alexander. There's nothing more the press can do to her. They have all her secrets, and you . . . you're healthy. Thriving, even. She's still careful with you—gentle, I mean," he adds when I shoot him a confused look. "I can't pretend to know what it must be like, surviving all she's gone through, but I would imagine she'll always be gentle with you. And the important thing is that she has you now, and you have her. And you both have Alexander. What would the point of all those terrible things be if she walked away? What could possibly be worth more than the love between the three of you?"

For a long moment, I say nothing, and I let myself picture it instead. My mom and Alexander, both of them happy—really, truly happy, despite the endless storm of bullshit the media would throw at them. "He'll never divorce Helene," I say. "And he'll never marry my mom, either—it'd make her queen, and he wouldn't do that to her. It would also be the biggest scandal in the history of the monarchy, besides maybe Henry VIII and his wives."

"No monarch has divorced since, I'll grant you," says Kit.

"But that's hardly the equivalent of beheading two queens and creating a new religion."

"Maybe not, but Helene's the most idolized woman in the world," I say. "There's no way Alexander can leave her without becoming public enemy number one."

"It would be . . . tricky," he agrees. "But perhaps—"

Crack.

A loud noise echoes through the woods, and I glance up, sure that a tree branch has broken. But before I can even comprehend what's happening, Kit's arms are around me, and he dives toward the base of the nearest tree as another crack rings out, and then another.

Kit and I hit the hard ground in a heap, his body pressed against mine, and I let out a yelp of pain as my left shoulder seems to bear the brunt of our fall. But Kit covers my mouth with his hand, stifling any sound, and I stare at him, my eyes wide.

What the hell is going on?

Another crack cuts through the still morning, and the tree trunk seems to explode a foot above our heads, showering us with wood chips.

Those cracks aren't breaking branches, I realize as cold horror spreads through me.

They're gunshots.

Kit catches my eye, and he must see my sudden surge of panic, because he presses his finger to his lips, and I manage a jerky nod. Only then does he remove his hand from my mouth, and he pulls out his phone to type a quick message, his body still covering mine.

My heart is pounding so hard that my chest hurts, and the edges of my vision slowly turn black from sheer terror. But as I lie perfectly still, my muscles taut while I wait for the next shot, I notice a dark red smear on the shoulder of Kit's tan coat. Maybe it's denial, or maybe just adrenaline, but for a split second, I can't wrap my head around what I'm looking at. When it hits me, however, all the air leaves my lungs, and the world seems to lurch sideways.

"Kit." His name is barely a breath, though it's enough to grab his attention. He follows my gaze, his brow furrowed, but his confusion turns to wild-eyed fear as he hastily shifts his weight off me. He's still hovering, barely an inch above me as his hair falls into my eyes, and he slides his hand between us to undo the buttons of my coat.

What are you— I mouth, but he's pushing my lapel away from my chest, and then I see it. A scarlet stain blooming in the cream of my sweater, just below my shoulder.

It's not his blood. It's mine.

CHAPTER ELEVEN

Sandringham Estate has gone into lockdown this morning after multiple ambulances and law enforcement vehicles were seen speeding onto the grounds. No further information is available at this time.

—Breaking news alert from the BBC,
9:41 a.m., 24 December 2023

I DON'T KNOW HOW LONG we lie there on the forest floor, Kit's body covering mine as he presses his hand to the wound in my chest, trying to stanch the blood that flows with horrific ease. Time doesn't seem to mean much anymore, and even though I'm aware of the pain spreading through me, deep and unyielding and unlike anything I've ever felt before, my mind is strangely blank.

Eventually, almost like an afterthought, it occurs to me that the gunshots have stopped. Kit's brown eyes are locked on mine, and his lips are moving, but even though I can hear the low murmur of his voice, my brain can't comprehend what he's saying. Maybe I'm panicking, or maybe I'm dying, or maybe it's something in between. Either way, I don't move, and neither does he.

The protection officer who escorted us into town is the first to reach us, and he radios his colleagues as he kneels beside us, the rush of air sending an agonizing tremor through me. Within seconds—or at least it feels like seconds—more officers appear, and when I blink, the forest is suddenly alive with red flashing lights. More people surround us now, but even as several paramedics try to usher Kit out of the way, he stays right where he is.

I blink again, and I'm suddenly in what I think is the back of an ambulance, but something is off. There's a wall of noise around me, and I catch sight of a cloud floating even with us through a small window. My thoughts are so muddled that I can't figure out what this means, but then Kit is there, his mouth moving even though I can't hear him, and I don't care about the cloud anymore.

This time, when I open my eyes, the oppressive sound is gone, replaced by a soft beeping. I'm in a dimly lit room with moss-green walls, and though a pair of curtains are covering the nearby window, a faint ray of gray light sneaks through a gap in the fabric. My body is heavy and numb, but my thoughts are clearer now, and when I notice the IV sticking out of my arm, I realize that this is a hospital room.

"Kit?" I manage, trying to sit up, but whatever medication is dripping through the plastic tube stops me from moving too much.

"Evie?"

Alexander's hoarse voice floats toward me, and he and my mother are beside the bed in an instant, both of them looking like they've aged a decade. My mother's eyes are red and swollen, and Alexander looks gaunt with worry. Which is ridiculous, because I'm fine.

"Where's Kit? Is he okay?" I say, and even though my mind

is scrambling to form a coherent picture from the fragments of my memories—the gunshots, the smear of blood on his coat, the whirling of what must have been helicopter blades—I sound *incredibly* drugged.

"Kit's in the hallway," says Alexander as my mother slides her hand into mine. "He's all right—grazed in the arm, but nothing a few stitches won't fix."

Grazed in the arm. By a bullet. The same kind of bullet that somehow hit me. Maybe even the same one. None of this feels real, and I shake my head, trying to . . . I don't know. Make it stick, maybe. Find something solid among all this haze.

"I'm so very sorry, Evie," continues Alexander, and he covers our hands with his. With a sharpness that's in stark contrast to the rest of this soft reality, I notice he isn't wearing a wedding ring, and I can't remember if he ever did. "Police and royal security are combing through the estate as we speak, but we've no idea how this happened."

"It was Ben," I mumble, and even though I haven't actually thought about who pulled the trigger, I'm absolutely sure it was him. "Where's your ring?"

"My—what?" says Alexander, taken aback.

"Your wedding ring. Don't you have one?" There's a signet ring on his pinky, but otherwise his left hand is bare. And it's only now, with the way both he and my mother are looking at me, that I realize how strange this question is, all things considered.

He clears his throat. "Er, yes, but I haven't worn it in private in years. Evan, it wasn't Benedict—he was with me and the rest of the hunting party, and we were miles from the house. There's simply no way it could've been him. But I swear to you, we *will* find whoever did this."

Alexander's voice catches, and my mother touches his arm with her free hand. He turns toward her, his face mostly hidden from me, and for the briefest of moments, she rests her forehead against his. Before it occurs to me that I probably shouldn't be staring, it's over, and Alexander steps back as my mother shifts closer to me.

"How do you feel, sweetheart?" she says, touching my cheek with her cool hand.

"I don't know. Weird." My body feels like it's made of cement, and the harder I try to get a handle on my drifting thoughts, the more they turn into smoke. With a faint and unsettling jolt, I realize that between the loss of control over my own limbs and the disjointed confusion, this feels like the night Jasper drugged me. Except this time, danger isn't hovering nearby, whispering in my ear as he tells me to relax. It's everywhere, and the part of me that trusts the world—that believes in my own survival—has cracked.

"The doctor said that will wear off soon," she says. "You lost a lot of blood, and you'll be sore for a while. But surgery went well. The—the bullet missed your heart and lung, and there's no major damage."

I nod slightly, flexing my fingers. These, at least, still work. "When can I go home?"

"If you're feeling up to it, we'll take you back in the morning," she promises, and belatedly I realize I should've been more specific. Sandringham isn't my home. Maybe Windsor is, or maybe in my stupor, I mean Virginia. But when I think about it, all I really want is her and Kit.

"You should talk to Ben," I say, my gaze sliding to Alexander again. "He'll know what happened. He was disappointed I wasn't going hunting this morning." At least I think it was this morning. But with the curtains blocking the window and my sense of time out of whack, I can't be sure. "I think I messed up his plan."

"Security told me the two of you had an . . . encounter," says Alexander thickly, and he hastily wipes his cheek. "I promise, Evie, I had my eye on him the entire time. He never slipped away."

"Doesn't mean anything," I mumble. "He has other people do his dirty work for him."

My parents exchange a look I don't understand. "We'll talk about it more when you're feeling better," says my mom, squeezing my hand again. "Why don't you rest?"

I know I should. My eyelids are growing heavy, and it won't be long before whatever the doctors are pumping through my system wins. But I take a deep breath, or at least as deep as I can manage right now, and I glance at the door. "Can I see Kit first?"

I have the vague sense that I could ask for the world right now, and my father would move heaven and earth to give it to me. Sure enough, almost as soon as Alexander steps out into the hall, Kit appears in the doorway. His sweater and coat are gone, and he wears a white T-shirt instead, with gauze wrapped around his right bicep. But even though he's clearly washed away the worst of the carnage, I can see a few smeared drops of blood on his neck, now dried to a sickening brown.

He says nothing as he crosses the room to my bedside, and my mother slips away as Kit carefully embraces me. His wet cheek presses against mine, and his shoulders shake as he cradles me, his breath coming in soft gasps.

I've never seen him really cry before, not like this. He's always so damn calm and stoic, taking everything life throws at us in stride, as if he can absorb any hit no matter how hard. But this is his breaking point, and I clumsily rub his back with my good hand, wishing I knew how to make any of this better.

"Are you okay?" I say, and he nods.

"How do you feel?" he says hoarsely. "Do you need anything?"

"Not anymore." The stubble on his jaw is scratchy against my skin, and I nuzzle his cheek. Kit's shoulders shake a little harder at that, and as I hold him, rage burns within me. Rage at the gunman for doing this to us, rage at the terror and pain Kit and my parents must have felt, but especially rage at myself, irrational as it may be, for letting this happen in the first place.

"I'm so sorry, Ev," he whispers at last, his voice thick with guilt and grief. "I should've—I should've done more. I should've protected you."

"My memory's a little fuzzy," I say, "but I'm pretty sure you stepped in front of a bullet for me." I touch the edge of the gauze. "Several bullets, possibly."

He clears his throat, and his fingertips brush against the pulse point of my neck like he's trying to reassure himself I'm really still here. "I don't know what I'd do without you."

"Live a long and happy life with Rosie," I say, and he lets out a choked laugh that sounds more like a sob.

"You have no idea how important you are to me, do you?" he says, burying his nose in my hair and breathing in my scent—

which can't be terribly attractive right now, all things considered. But he doesn't seem to care.

"Almost as important as you are to me?" I guess, and he manages another halting laugh. Finally he pulls away, just enough to gaze at me, and for a split second, I think he's going to say it. But as he brushes a stringy piece of hair from my eyes with aching tenderness, I decide he won't. Not because he wouldn't mean it, but because he doesn't have to for me to know.

"Stay with me?" I ask, and he nods.

As he settles on the very edge of my mattress, excruciatingly mindful of my injuries, I finally look past him and notice the table on the other side of my bed. It's flush against the wall and difficult to see from my vantage point, but someone has arranged several bouquets of flowers along the imitation wood.

Most feature a variety of roses and lilies and poinsettias—the kinds of flowers that are easy to find at the height of the Christmas season. But the plastic vase set closest to my bed is full of daisies. Not bright, cheerful daisies, with sunny yellow centers and crisp white petals—these daisies, like the ones Ben sent to Wimbledon, have black eyes that seem to sink into the darkness, and even in the faint gray light, I can make out the red petals, so deep and vivid that all I see when I stare at them is blood.

I reach for the small paper card among the gaping flowers, and though my fingers fumble at first, I manage to pluck it from its plastic holder. And there, in scarlet ink and Ben's spidery handwriting, are three innocent words that chill me to the bone.

Thinking of you.

CHAPTER TWELVE

HUNTING ACCIDENT AT SANDRINGHAM TRIGGERS MEDICAL EMERGENCY; EVANGELINE REPORTED VICTIM

Buckingham Palace has announced that a hunting accident is to blame for the frightening scene at Sandringham Estate on the morning of Christmas Eve, and a well-placed palace insider has confirmed that Evangeline Bright was the victim.

While no life-threatening injuries were reported, speculation about the seriousness of the incident was fuelled by the alleged evacuation of the royal family to Windsor Castle shortly after the shooting took place, leading many to fear that foul play was involved. A Twitter post from Venetia, Duchess of York, however, suggests that the move was made to be closer to the hospital where Evangeline was taken.

@duchessvofyork What a frightening day! An unexpected detour to Windsor Castle now . . . there's nothing more important than being with your family on Christmas. Hug your loved ones tight.

12:23 p.m. · 24 December 2023

Bright, who is not an official member of the royal family, was airlifted yesterday morning to an undisclosed hospital for emergency treatment. Though there have been no further updates on the alleged victim's condition or location, the royal standard has not been raised at Windsor Castle, Sandringham House, or any other royal residence, suggesting that His Majesty is spending

Christmas in hospital with his illegitimate daughter.

The identity of the shooter has not been released.

—*The Daily Sun,* 25 December 2023

THE NEXT MORNING, WHILE MOST families are opening presents and drinking hot cocoa, mine is escorted back to Windsor Castle by more than a half dozen police vehicles, complete with sirens, flashing lights, and a motorcycle leading the way.

Even with the gunman still on the loose, it's overkill, but I'm too exhausted to make any kind of snarky remark. I'm stretched out across the middle bench seat in a bulletproof SUV, my head in my mom's lap and a blanket covering the rest of me, while Kit and Alexander sit in the row behind us. The three of them speak in hushed voices, and even though I drift in and out of consciousness, I catch snatches of their conversation.

". . . didn't match the striations of any rifle in the Sandringham armory," says Alexander, and I can practically hear his frown.

"That's good, isn't it?" says my mother, her fingers gently combing through the tangles in my hair. "That no one on the estate was responsible, I mean."

"All it means is that they didn't use one of our hunting rifles," says Alexander grimly. "The police are doing their best, but the estate is twenty thousand acres, and much of it is open to the public. Even if they do find evidence . . ."

We hit a bump in the road, and though the doctors gave me a nerve block before our trip, rendering most of my upper-left side numb and useless, I still wince. But I only have myself to blame

109

for this whole setup, as I refused point-blank to get in an ambulance, and this was the only alternative Alexander would accept.

I must dip into sleep again, because the next thing I hear is Kit's voice. ". . . said you banned the family from attending the service at St. George's Chapel this morning?"

"I doubt she's terribly upset," says Alexander dryly. "But yes, with the service at Windsor open to the general public, it was too much of a security risk. Maisie knows that the safety of the family is paramount, and I'm sure God will forgive us, considering the . . ."

Alexander trails off, and Kit swears quietly under his breath. I open my mouth to ask what's wrong, but then I hear it.

Shouts—dozens of them all at once, a wall of voices that grow louder as the car creeps forward. I remember the protesters outside Sandringham, and a chill runs through my aching body, but the people with scarves covering their faces were silent. This crowd—

This crowd is calling my name.

"How do they know it was her?" says my mom, horrified.

"Who?" I say, my throat painfully dry. "What's going on?"

I try to sit up, but her hand is there, gently holding me down. "Photographers and journalists at the gate," she explains. "There must be nearly a hundred of them. Alex—"

"I don't know," he says in a strangled voice. "I told Doyle to release a statement calling it a hunting accident. Jenkins confirmed just an hour ago—"

"There's an article on the *Daily Sun*'s site," says Kit suddenly. "A 'well-placed palace insider' told them Evan was shot."

A few long seconds pass, and I assume Alexander's reading whatever post Kit has found. "Damn," mutters my father, followed by a few more colorful snarls. "That gold-digging, bloodsucking—"

"Venetia?" says Kit, and Alexander grunts in the affirmative.

"We knew she'd go to the press eventually," says my mother with a sigh. "I was hoping she would at least wait until Evan was out of the hospital, though."

The vehicle is moving at a snail's pace, and on the other side of the tinted windows, I can just make out several police officers guiding us through what must be a tightly packed crowd. My name is louder now, interspersed with what sound like questions, but I can't tell what any of them are saying. And I'm not sure I want to know.

At last, we must make it through the gate, because the shouting grows quieter as the SUV speeds up again, and I can feel my mother relax. She shouldn't be here—not at Windsor, not in the middle of everything. But I also know that nothing, not even Alexander, could send her away now. And I'm terrified.

"Security has locked down this part of the castle," says Alexander unprompted. "Though if you must go outside, do be certain to stick to the immediate grounds."

"I don't think any of us needs fresh air that badly," says Kit as the car pulls to a stop. Only then does my mother help me sit up, and I see the dozen staff members waiting for us at the door— including a man with a salt-and-pepper beard who wears a frown so deep that it's practically sliding off his face.

"Jenkins?" I gasp, wondering if I'm imagining things. But as a footman opens the door, he's there, his arms around me as he eases me gently onto the drive. And even though everyone's watching, I hug him in return and bury my face in his chest, finally letting myself feel the overwhelming grip of fear—of all that happened, of all that could've happened, and how close I came to losing everything.

"You're all right, Evan," he murmurs in a voice meant only for me. This kind of behavior would get any other member of the royal staff dismissed on the spot, but Jenkins has been the one constant in my life since my grandmother's death, and I refuse to let something as ridiculous as protocol steal that from us.

"You're here," I say, a little dizzy as I finally step back. "What about Louis? You shouldn't have to give up your Christmas."

"There's nowhere else I'd rather be," he says. "And I assure you, our nieces and nephews won't miss me, not when Louis's baking up a storm. Your Majesty," he adds, bowing his head as footsteps crunch against the gravel beside us.

"Jenkins," says Alexander. "Thank you for coming—and please, there's no need for formalities today. Has Dr. Gupta arrived?"

"He and his team have already set up their equipment in Evangeline's apartment, sir," says Jenkins, as proper as he always is, and he touches my good shoulder. "Let's get you inside, darling."

Somehow, miraculously, I manage the walk from the side entrance to my apartment, which feels like it's tripled in the two days we've been at Sandringham. The royal physician—Dr. Gupta—is waiting for me in my sitting room, and it's only after he checks my vitals and the small incision just below my shoulder that I'm finally allowed to pass out in my own bed.

Maybe it's the painkillers, or maybe the trauma of all that's happened is finally sinking in, but instead of sleeping soundly, I float from dream to dream, each more surreal than the last. Kit and I are back in the woods at Sandringham, but they're darker and full of blood-red daisies. I know what's coming—I can feel the gunman's eyes on me like heat from the sun—but when I turn, Venetia is there instead, asking me for the time I was born.

The trees morph into brick, and suddenly I'm standing in front of the gift shop Kit and I visited in Norfolk. Aoife chatters happily at me while I barely listen, too distracted by a garden of flowers made of jewel-like stones. When I look up, Dylan is there with us, staring at me with such intensity that I feel like I'm burning from the inside out. And as I cast around searching for Kit, I spot him lurking on the opposite side of the street—except as my vision focuses, I realize it's not him, but the faceless man with the teal scarf.

The buildings shift into the four posters of my bed in Windsor, almost exactly as they are, except the light pouring through the curtains is stained pink. Constance stands beside me with a silver-wrapped gift in her hand, and as our eyes meet, she doesn't look away. She opens her mouth to say something, but before she can utter a word, everything goes black. And then it's Ben standing there instead, his lips twisted into a half smirk in the indigo light.

My eyes fly open, and for a few horrible seconds, I forget where I am. My room is completely dark now, with the winter sun long set, and somewhere in the distance, I think I hear the sound of someone whispering my name again. Confused, I glance at the spot where Constance-then-Ben stood. There's no one there—of course there isn't, there never was—but I can't shake the feeling that I'm not alone.

"Evan?"

I suck in a breath, and the lamp on my desk switches on. But while the part of me that's still half-asleep expects Ben or Constance to be perched on my couch, it's my mom, her hair frizzy and the purple smudges beneath her eyes prominent. She looks like she's barely slept in days, and I feel a pang of guilt.

"Sorry," I say, clearing the thickness from my throat. My mouth is disgustingly dry, and I don't remember the last time I had any water. "Go back to sleep."

"I'm all right," she promises, climbing to her feet. "How do you feel?"

"I don't know," I say, slowly easing myself up into a sitting position. The nerve block has worn off, and there's a deep, constant ache in my shoulder that turns into a sharp stab every time I move. "Sore."

She heads to my bedside table, and as I gently probe the bandage covering my wound, she opens a pill bottle and pours a glass of water from a pitcher. "Here," she says, and I pop the painkillers into my mouth before downing the water in one go. "Are you hungry?"

As if on cue, my stomach growls. "I think that's a yes," I say, and she manages a breathy laugh.

"I'd say so, too." She offers me her hand. "Let's get you something to eat."

Once I've brushed my teeth, my mom helps me change into clean clothes—an oversized sweatshirt and ratty pajama bottoms that Tibby has been threatening to burn for months now—and eases my arm into a sling. I'm still unsteady on my feet, but the world isn't spinning anymore, and I feel more alert than I have since this all happened.

When she opens the door to my sitting room, however, I suddenly wonder if I'm still dreaming. Thousands of tiny colorful lights are strung up around the room, with longer strands crisscrossing overhead, giving everything a soft, ethereal glow. Garlands decorate the walls, and there are enough poinsettias crammed into corners that I could start my own flower shop. A wreath hangs on the inside of my door, and best of all, there's a large Christmas tree in front of the window, covered in the same colorful string lights with a glittering star on top.

"What—" I begin, baffled, but then I hear a knock on the door. It creaks open before either my mother or I can say anything, and Maisie pokes her head inside.

"Evan?" Her voice is hushed, like someone else is still sleeping in the other room. As soon as our eyes meet, however, the softness in her posture vanishes, and she strides into my apartment like she owns it. She's wearing an emerald-green ball gown and cherry-red lipstick, and when she reaches the spot where I'm rooted to the ground, she wraps her thin arms around me like I'm made of spun sugar, and one wrong move will make me collapse.

"Maisie?" I say, confused. "What's going on? Did you do this?"

She nods into my shoulder, but she doesn't say anything. And a moment later, I feel something warm drip down my neck and absorb into the collar of my shirt.

My sister is crying.

Ignoring the sharp ache in my chest, I carefully slip my good arm around her waist and hug her as tightly as I dare. "Everything's okay, Mais. I'm okay."

"Some—someone tried to kill you," she says thickly, and her shoulders shake. "You and Kit and—and we don't know who or—or why."

Privately I think I know exactly who did it, even if I don't know why. But before I can say anything, movement in the hallway catches my eye, and Alexander and Kit appear in the doorway. They're both wearing tuxedos every bit as formal as Maisie's gown, but my father's bow tie hangs loose, and Kit's sleeves are pushed up to his elbows, giving them both a strangely casual appearance.

"Why don't we let Evan sit down, darling?" says Alexander as he joins us. Reluctantly Maisie lets me go, though her fingers wrap briefly around my wrist, featherlight and delicate.

"I'm just—really, really glad you're all right," she says, eyes still brimming. As Alexander eases me down onto the nearest sofa, my mother wordlessly hands her a tissue, and she takes it, dabbing her eyes. She must be wearing waterproof mascara, because her makeup doesn't budge. "I—Kit and I, we didn't want you to miss your first Christmas with the family, so we thought we'd bring Christmas to you."

"Thank you," I say as I glance around the room again, taking in the lights and decorations. "Really. This is incredible."

"It was all Maisie's idea," says Kit, bending down over the arm of the sofa and giving me a peck on the cheek. "Happy Christmas, Evan. How do you feel?"

"Better, I think," I say, and he's still hovering close enough for me to steal a quick, but real, kiss, even though my parents are watching—and are probably the reason for his restraint. "I'm sorry for ruining Christmas."

"You didn't ruin a bloody thing," says Alexander as several footmen carry dome-covered platters into the room. "We've got a few hours left, so why don't we make the most of it?"

While he, Kit, and Maisie rally around the tree, decorating the branches with glittering ornaments that look like they're made of real crystal, my mother tucks a blanket around me and brushes my tangled hair. Christmas music plays softly in the background, and even though it's probably the blood loss, there's something magical about all of this—something that fills me with warm contentment and giddiness that only seems to expand, chasing away the last of the somber shadows. The royal family has always felt more *royal* than *family* to me, but in this moment, with the people I love most chatting and laughing together, I almost forget that my father is King, that my sister is the future queen, and that most of the country thinks my mom and I have no place here. Nothing outside my sitting room matters as we pass around plates full of food, and then presents, each more ridiculous than the last.

"Really?" says Alexander, holding up a bobblehead of himself, complete with a giant crown. When the head wobbles, a tinny voice declares, *"Gather 'round, ladies, to see the King's crown jewels!"*

My mouth drops open, and from the armchair, Maisie immediately pales. "I had no idea it did that," she insists, but she's mostly drowned out by Alexander's sharp guffaw.

"Of all the bloody things . . . ," he says, shaking the bobblehead again.

"King Philanderer II at your service, m'lady!"

He throws his head back, and any lingering hint of propriety dissolves into howls of laughter. My mother joins in, reaching for the toy to take a closer look, and even Kit chuckles as I manage a tired grin. Only Maisie, whose face is bright red, is unamused.

"I'm going to bloody *murder* Fitz," she mutters, and I immediately feel a stab of pity for her hapless private secretary.

"On the contrary," says our father, now wiping tears from his eyes, "I think I owe him a pay rise."

We pass around the bobblehead and listen to it repeat its assortment of sordid phrases until I wince from laughter, and my mother pointedly sets the toy aside. While most of the gifts are jokes—though none of the rest are nearly as funny—her gift to me is a framed photograph I've never seen before.

It's a picture of her and Alexander, both much younger, and a baby that can only be me. We're sitting beside a Christmas tree, the lights twinkling behind us, and they're focused on me as I seemingly do my best to rip the wrapping paper from a stuffed bear. They're smiling—the kind of secret, genuine smiles not meant for the camera—and I can just make out their joined hands.

"This was your first Christmas," says my mother softly. "I know you don't remember it, but your father and I do."

I touch the frame, not knowing what to say. I wish I could remember it. I wish I could remember every moment from those first few years, when my parents were still happy and together, even if Alexander was living a double life with Helene and Maisie. I wish I could remember a time when none of us had to make room for estrangements and arrests and the scandal of just existing.

"I love it," I say, setting my head on her shoulder. "Thank you."

"You're welcome, Evie," she murmurs as she kisses my hair. "I'm just relieved we have this Christmas, too."

Maisie leans over to peer at the photo. "Oh—that's the one that was on your desk for the Christmas speech, isn't it?" she says to Alexander, who nods.

"I hoped it might go a long way to silence the conspiracy theorists," he says, and I don't need to ask which ones he's talking about. My mother's been vilified and called all kinds of names in the press, which seems fixated on the lie that she trapped and extorted him with a pregnancy he didn't want. I didn't realize it bothered Alexander so much, but as he watches my mother, it's clear that it does.

"And that," says Maisie, pointing to the record player that's currently spitting out a Bing Crosby Christmas song, "is from me and Kit. Along with the record collection beneath it."

"Really?" I say, craning my neck as much as I dare. The cabinet the record player sits on is covered in Christmas decorations, but it's definitely new, and the shelves are crammed full of vinyl records. "You and Kit did that?"

He nods. "We had to guess at some of your favorites, but I think we found most of them. And," he teases, glancing at my sister, "only half or so are Taylor Swift albums."

Maisie lifts her chin defiantly. "She's universal. And they're signed," she adds, and I grin.

"One more reason for the entire world to hate me," I say. "I love it."

We're passing around something called Christmas pudding, which looks suspiciously like a steaming mountain of fruitcake, when another knock sounds on the door. Alexander calls for whoever it is to enter, but as soon as I see who's on the other side, I immediately wish he hadn't.

Venetia stands in the threshold, her blond hair pulled into a fancy updo that shows off the low bodice of her glittering scarlet gown. She wears a plastered-on smile that makes her Botox obvious, and a gift is tucked into her bare arms.

"I'm not interrupting, am I?" she says sweetly, curtsying to my father and Maisie. "I just wanted to see how Evangeline is feeling."

"I'm fine," I say, forcing a small smile. It quickly drops, however, when Venetia enters the room, and I spot a figure lurking in the corridor behind her.

Ben.

He, like Alexander and Kit, is also wearing a tuxedo, but his is still done up properly, and nothing about him is infused with Christmas cheer. To my dismay, he follows his mother inside my sitting room, and as his gaze slides to me, I instantly look away and suppress a shiver. Of all the brash and shameless things he's done in the past, showing his face tonight is a step too far, even for him.

"Oh, Evangeline," says Venetia, bending down to kiss my cheeks. "We're so *relieved* you're all right. I can't tell you how worried I was—my own niece, nearly killed on Christmas Eve!"

Hearing her call me her niece almost makes me choke, but

she shoves the gift into my hand and I busy myself with carefully undoing the sharply folded corners. I can tell it's a book at first touch, but when I finally get it open, I'm not prepared to see a younger Venetia staring up at me from the cover.

Royally Ever After: Tips and Tricks from the Duchess of York

"It's my third book," she says proudly. "I wrote it almost ten years ago, but the monarchy never changes, and it all still applies. It's about joining the royal family," she adds at what must be my blank stare. "It's meant for girls looking to marry into it, of course, but it's an excellent reference for you, too."

"Wow," I say, hoping this doesn't sound as hollow as I think it might. "This is . . . great. Thank you."

Venetia beams, and she takes my hands—including the one in the sling. "We're just so happy you're all right," she says again, this time with tears in her eyes. "We were so *worried,* darling."

Worried enough to cry on the shoulders of a *Daily Sun* journalist, but I don't say that. Instead, I let her kiss my cheeks again without complaint, but once she steps aside, Ben's there, and my expression drops.

Across the sitting room, Alexander tenses, and Kit shifts forward on the love seat, prepared to leap to his feet if need be. And while I'm grateful for both of them, I look straight at Ben now, refusing to offer him even a hint of goodwill.

"I'm relieved to see you up and about," he says with an amiable smile. "It seemed like it was touch and go there for a while."

"I'm not that easy to kill," I say in as neutral a voice as I can muster. There's still an edge of hatred to it, though, but Ben's smile doesn't falter.

"Lucky us," he says, and to my disgust, he leans in to brush his lips against my cheek. At his touch, I stay perfectly still, feeling like I've plunged into a tank of ice.

"You missed," I whisper in his ear.

"I never miss," he breathes, and when he straightens, there's a hint of a smirk tugging at the corner of his lips. "Here—I thought you'd like a reminder of how far you've come."

He offers me a shallow golden box tied with red ribbon, and when I refuse to take it, he sets it in my lap instead. We stare at each other for a painfully long moment, but at last Ben slips his arm into his mother's.

"We ought to get back to the party and let them enjoy the rest of their night," he says, and we finally agree on something.

"Of course," says Venetia as he leads her to the exit. "Happy Christmas, all!"

None of us says a word until Ben closes the door behind him, and only then do we all let out a collective exhale. "What did he give you?" says Maisie with an eager glint she can't hide as she kneels on the carpet beside the sofa.

"You can have it, whatever it is," I say, and my father clears his throat.

"Evan, I know you don't trust him, and I certainly don't blame you. But I truly believe he isn't responsible for this particular incident."

"It's hardly the first time someone's tried to have a go at one of us," says Maisie as she snatches up Ben's gift and starts to unwrap it. "Daddy, didn't a woman try to stab you on a walkabout once?"

"Mm, a few years after you and your sister were born," he says. "Your grandfather was shot at twice in the nineties."

"And Mummy was attacked when she was pregnant with me—broke her nose and everything," says Maisie, tossing the ribbon aside. "See? It happens."

"It won't happen again," says Alexander darkly. "I've already spoken to Victor Stephens, our head of security, and—"

"A photo album?"

We all look at Maisie now, who's staring into the box. She pulls out a red leather-bound book, and when she turns to the first page, I spot my face peering back.

It's one of the few photos the public has of me as a kid, from my third boarding school yearbook. I have uneven bangs, a zit on my chin, and I'm scowling at the camera, but Ben has blown it up so large that it takes up nearly the entire page. Confused, I reach forward to flip to another, and this time I'm looking at several pictures from a royal garden party held at Buckingham Palace this summer. But they aren't the official photos released on social media. These were taken by someone else, and I'm the focus of them all.

"Odd," says Maisie, seemingly bored of it already as she checks out one more page—which is full of more candid pictures of me at various appearances over the past month, including the one where Thaddeus Park is catching me in his arms. She eyes the photos for another beat before shutting the album with a satisfying snap, and she sets it on my lap again before turning back to her mulled wine. "The pictures aren't exactly flattering, are they? Ben may be a monster, but there's simply no excuse for immortalizing paparazzi dreck."

As she segues into a tirade about the terrible angles some of the Royal Rota have been using on her lately, I pick up the album, determined to hide it under the sofa until I can throw it in a dumpster myself. Something on the cover shimmers in the twinkling Christmas lights, however, and as I squint, I spot two lines of gold lettering embedded in the leather.

Evangeline Florence Phillipa Constance Bright
2005–

It's innocuous—my name and my birth year, that's all. But my heart starts to race, and as I lean forward, it takes me a moment to understand why.

The space after my birth year isn't blank. Instead, so faint that it might as well be my imagination, I can just make out the shape of four more digits that look like they've been removed.

2005–2025

CHAPTER THIRTEEN

"This past year, my family has been through a great many challenges that have tested our fortitude and courage. But it is our love for one another, and our love for our country and Commonwealth, that have allowed us to persevere in the face of trying circumstances. While the future may be—and always is— uncertain, we can count on this love, and our love for the people, to ensure that our faith and devotion to serve this great nation never waver."

—*Excerpt from His Majesty's Christmas Speech, 25 December 2023*

WHEN THE CLOCK STRIKES MIDNIGHT, Maisie has left, and both Kit and my mother are sleeping soundly on the red velvet sofas in my sitting room.

I should be resting, too, but my mind is buzzing even though my body feels like it's full of sand. The photo album Ben gave me is barely a foot beneath my mother's head now, seemingly forgotten among the other gifts scattered throughout the room, but I can feel its presence like a black hole, sucking me in whenever I so much as glance in that direction.

Alexander and I sit at the dining table now, the twinkling Christmas lights illuminating his tired face as we flip through my new record collection. I know I should say something—about the gold lettering on the cover that only I saw, about the death year that Ben didn't bother to properly remove, and about the very real possibility that his so-called gift was originally meant to be a memorial to me. But after Alexander's repeated assertions that Ben had nothing to do with the attack, I don't know how to tell him without sounding like a broken record that can't move on. Besides, I already know exactly what Ben will say—that the photo album was meant to only chronicle the first eighteen years of my life, but after the shooting, he thoughtfully removed the end date, realizing belatedly what it looked like. Or maybe he'll insist it was a simple printing error that arrived too late to correct. Either way, it'll be an uphill battle, and in the end, I still won't be able to prove a thing.

I'll tell Alexander soon, I decide. After the holidays, or if Ben refuses to crawl back underneath a rock and stay out of our lives. I can't make myself destroy the fragile contentment that's settled over my father, though, not after the few days we've all had. And so, for these last moments of my first Christmas with my family, I make myself focus on the selection of records Kit and Maisie chose for me instead. Most are predictable, from bands they know I love, but a few of them are curious choices, and I set them aside to listen to first.

"You and Kit have grown rather close lately, haven't you?" says Alexander in a low voice as he examines the back of a Fleetwood Mac album.

"Isn't that the whole point of dating?" I say, studying one

of the many Taylor Swift records Maisie included. She wasn't kidding—it really is signed specifically to me. The majority of the covers are, and it's daunting to see the evidence of just how many favors she can call in for a simple Christmas present.

"Does it feel like a long-term thing?" says Alexander, and my face grows hot as I set the album aside and select another. Ed Sheeran. Also signed.

"He jumped in front of a literal bullet for me," I point out. "I think I'm going to hold on to him for a while."

"And if none of that had happened?" says Alexander.

"Then he'd be stuck with me anyway. What about you and my mom?" I add, glancing at her sleeping form. My gaze automatically drifts to the space beneath the sofa, however, and I look back at my father. "What's the plan there?"

He clears his throat. "Your mother's the love of my life," he says. "I was a fool and walked away from her twice—once when my father died, and again when she needed me the most. I won't make that mistake a third time."

"What about Helene?" I say, picking up another album. Reignwolf. My favorite band, and definitely one of Kit's choices. "Are you planning on getting a divorce?"

A beat passes before Alexander answers. "I don't know," he admits. "That's a conversation she and I've been having for a very long time, and neither of us is eager to throw our family—your mother and Nicholas included—into that particular fire."

"So you want my mom to be your mistress again?" I say, and the words taste foul.

"Of course not. She never was my mistress," he says, and when I open my mouth to point out the obvious, he keeps going.

"She was always the real thing to me—the true center of my life. My marriage and the rest of it . . . that was the part I couldn't escape."

I pull another vinyl from the stack—a Spice Girls album bearing four signatures. Apparently even Maisie's power has limits. "You're going to hurt her again."

"I'd rather throw myself off a cliff," he says without affectation. "Regardless of what happens with the status of my marriage to Helene, I have every intention . . . no," he corrects himself. "I *will* spend the rest of my life making your mother happy and giving her every wonderful thing she deserves. I promise you, Evan, I will never hurt her again."

He says this with more conviction than I've ever heard from him before—maybe more than I've ever heard from anyone— but I still can't help the niggling doubt worming its way inside me. "What if Helene decides she does want a divorce? What happens then?"

"What do you mean?" says Alexander.

"I mean—will you marry my mom?"

This seems to bring him up short, even though this can't be the first time he's thought about it. "Why do you ask?" he says carefully.

"Because . . ." I hesitate. To me, it's obvious, but apparently not to him. "Because that would make her queen. And you said so yourself—she doesn't want that."

"No, she doesn't," he agrees quietly. "And I would never force her into a role she doesn't want."

"Then you wouldn't marry her?" I say. "She'd still be your mistress?"

"Partner," he corrects. "Exactly as she is now. Exactly as she has been since the day we met."

I consider that. It's not how I see them—maybe because of the power imbalance, or maybe because of all those years I thought my mom's relationship with him was a figment of her illness. But I remember how she silently comforted him in the hospital the day before, and how she can calm both his temper and his nerves with a touch, and something about the way I think of them both shifts. He's not a king when he's with her, and she's not a mistress or a home-wrecker or any of the other disgusting things the media calls her. They're just . . . together.

"You don't want her to leave, do you?" I say, and he purses his lips.

"We were going to wait to speak to you about it in the new year, but . . . no, I don't. And neither does she."

I shake my head, more out of instinct than conscious thought. "She can't stay. I want her here as much as you do, but the press is out for her blood, and the people will never give her a chance. She won't be able to set foot outside the castle without risking her life—"

"I can keep her safe," he insists, and I give him a look. "I mean it, Evie. What happened to you won't ever happen again."

"It's not just that," I say. "It's her routine. It's everything that's familiar. You know how important that all is for her mental health. Disruptions, big changes—they can confuse her, and she's already pushing herself too hard—"

"You're important for her mental health, too."

I shake my head again. "She went seven years without seeing me in person."

"Only because she thought it was the right thing to do," he says. "Those were the hardest years of her life, and I have no desire to watch her go through that again. As difficult as it might be for a little while, she'll be happier here, once she settles in. She'll be happier here with both of us."

"But—"

"Evie." He takes my good hand. His skin is warm and dry, and there's a comforting weight to his touch that I'm still not used to. "You've spent a very long time worrying about your mum, and I understand why. But she isn't delicate, and she won't shatter, not because of something like this. She's strong—stronger than you realize, I think—and she's had to deal with more than any of us can fully comprehend. This is what she wants—very badly—and even if you can't trust my judgment, you can trust hers."

I feel like I've swallowed my tongue, and tears prickle in my eyes as I try to sort my panicked thoughts into something tangible. "If anything happens to her . . ."

"It won't," he says, and he squeezes my hand. "Nothing will happen to either of you again, I swear it. I've spoken to the home secretary, and starting immediately, you'll be assigned your own around-the-clock protection officers."

"Me?" I say, stunned. "Or my mom, too?"

"You," he admits. "She isn't eligible, I'm afraid, though should she choose to venture out on her own, I will ensure she has a private security team with her at all times."

My heart's beating a little too fast now, and the lights around us start to blur together. "That won't protect her from Ben."

"Benedict won't hurt her, Evie," says Alexander with a frown.

"There's no denying he put you through hell last summer, and I will never forgive him for it. But he isn't responsible for the shooting. He may be arrogant and spoiled, but I've known him his entire life, and there are some things he simply isn't capable of."

Maybe Alexander means for this to be reassuring, but a hollow forms in the pit of my stomach, and I swallow, my throat dry. It won't matter if I tell him about the date on the photo album, I realize. He's already made up his mind about Ben, and nothing short of a smoking gun will change it.

"What if you're wrong?" I say. "What if he does try something? Or—what if he already has, and we just don't know it yet?"

"Then we'll cross that bridge if we come to it," he says quietly. "And in the meantime, you and your mother will be well-protected against all threats, both inside the castle and out. I promise."

He means it—it's obvious he means it with all his damn heart. But I still don't believe him.

"I want to learn how to defend myself," I blurt, and my father tilts his head like I've just suggested growing wings.

"Pardon?"

"Once I've recovered, I want someone to teach me how to fight," I say. "Not just with my hands, but with weapons, too. Something I can keep on me at all times in case security fails."

The thought of shoving a knife between Ben's ribs brings only a fraction of the comfort it should, but Alexander's nod helps considerably. "Very well. I will make the arrangements."

"Thanks," I mumble, picking up an album by a rock band

called Royal Blood. Either Kit chose this because of his impeccable analysis of my musical tastes, or it's Maisie's idea of a joke. "Why am I eligible for personal protection officers when my mom isn't?"

Alexander exhales. "Well—I was going to wait until you were older, but given the circumstances . . . I was hoping you'd agree to become a working royal."

I blink, positive I haven't heard him right. "What?"

"It's a bit unorthodox," he allows. "Considering you're not . . . well, *legitimate,* technically speaking."

"I'm not a royal, either," I point out, setting the record down.

"You're my daughter. That's good enough," he says firmly. "And should you want it, I could—I would—issue a letters patent to style you Her Royal Highness The Princess Evangeline."

For a split second, the room seems to tip sideways as the weight of his words settles over me. A princess. He wants to make me an actual princess, and when I suck in a stunned breath, I damn near choke.

"That," I wheeze, "is an excellent way to start an uprising and end the British monarchy for good."

He chuckles, even though absolutely none of this is funny. "Yes, well. You're worth it."

This is almost sweet of him, minus the threat of anarchy, and I take a sip of my cooling hot cocoa to ease the sudden block of ice in my stomach. "Are you only offering because I almost died?"

"Of course not," he says. "Though I suppose the whole incident did help . . . clarify a few things for me. And it certainly made me see that you deserve far better than what I've offered."

I shrug. "You've given me a family. I don't need titles or jewels or—or all the rest of it. Besides, it really would cause a riot, and Maisie would literally murder me if she never got to be queen."

"I'll take that as a no, then," says Alexander, who doesn't sound the least bit surprised.

"Absolutely, unequivocally, emphatically no," I say. "I'm not really into the whole princess thing anyway."

He laughs again, a quiet rumble that only carries between us. "And being a working royal? Is that something you'd be interested in? You'd receive a generous allowance, and you're already doing the majority of the work, with the appearances you've been making with Maisie and me. Your education would take top priority, of course, and you may step back whenever you'd like. But you could do a great deal of good for many people, and the country would be lucky to have you."

That last part is bullshit, but I study him for a moment. "What does my mom think?"

"Your mother is incredibly proud of you no matter what, and she wouldn't dream of taking away your choice in the matter," he says. "But I'm certain she would feel infinitely better if you had the protection that comes with the job. We both would."

"You could just hire private security for me, too," I say, even though the thought of being followed around all the time makes my skin crawl.

"I could," he says slowly, "and I will, if you decide this isn't for you. But if you'll excuse my candor . . . I'm sick of the media acting like you mean less to me because your mother and I aren't married. It's absurd. You're every bit as important to me as your sister, and if you won't accept a title, then this is what I have to offer instead. An official place in this business we call a family."

I toy with a loose thread on my sling. If I'm being honest with myself, I'm sick of it, too. I'm sick of my legitimacy—or lack thereof—being brought up in every article. I'm sick of being sneered at by royalists and media commentators who've never met me. And I am really, really sick of everyone treating me and my mother like something disgusting Alexander stepped in and now can't get rid of.

"Do I get paid time off?" I say at last. "And what are the benefits like? I can't agree unless I know what kind of pension and health-care plan you're offering."

This time he laughs loud enough for my mom to stir beneath her quilt, and we immediately fall silent again until she stills. "All excellent, I assure you," he teases in a whisper. "I've no doubt we can come to a satisfying arrangement."

"Then I suppose I could consider your offer," I say. "As long as Maisie isn't my boss."

"Not for a very long time." He leans forward to press a kiss to my forehead. "I have one more gift for you."

Alexander stands and fetches the jacket of his tuxedo, which he's long since discarded. He pulls a small package from the inner pocket, and as he sits back down, he offers it to me.

"What is it?" I say suspiciously, already tucking the slim box between my knees and untying the gold ribbon with my good hand.

"A necessity," he says. "One you can't turn down this time, I'm afraid."

As I rip away the rest of the wrapping and see the logo, I groan. "Seriously?"

"You need a mobile, Evie," says Alexander. "If Kit hadn't brought his yesterday, you would have bled to death. You don't need to use it, but you do need to have it on you—charged—at all times."

"But I'll already have protection officers," I say. "Isn't this overkill?"

"No," he says simply. "It's not."

Even though I've used plenty of smartphones before, I listen closely as he shows me how it works. This one has a few features I'm pretty sure don't come standard, including a tracking app that can't be turned off, and after my father has me repeat the sequence to trigger my panic button—two short presses of the volume keys, followed by a lengthier one—he seems to breathe a little easier.

"I love you, sweetheart," he says. "Our family leads a complicated life of service to this country, but it can be good, too. If you let it."

"It already is," I promise, briefly taking his hand. "Are you going to stay?"

He nods. "Just until your mother wakes. Why don't you get some rest?"

Even though I want nothing more than to curl up with Kit, I can barely get comfortable in my own bed right now, let alone on a stiff sofa made in the Victorian era. And so I allow Alexander to help me to my bedroom door, where he hugs me again, a little longer than usual.

"Happy Christmas, Evie," he murmurs, and when he lets me go, I smile up at him in the glow of the colorful lights.

"Merry Christmas, Dad," I whisper, and just as I turn toward my bedroom door, I swear I see his eyes glisten.

I'm so tired that I can barely brush my teeth, and I give up on braiding my hair almost as soon as the thought crosses my mind. I stumble to my bed and ease down onto the edge, warm and full and feeling more hopeful than I have in ages, despite the photo album under the sofa and the stitches below my shoulder and the ache that tells me I need to take another painkiller. But as I shift to turn off my bedside lamp, I notice something on the nightstand.

A gift wrapped in silver paper.

Instantly my dreams from earlier that day come flooding back to me, and I see Constance bathed in pink light from the window—the light of the setting sun, I realize. With my heart suddenly pounding, I gingerly tear open the present and reveal a black velvet box underneath.

Inside is a simple diamond pendant hanging from a white-gold necklace. It's beautiful, and as I touch the pendant, I can't help but wonder if it's a cubic zirconia, if only to drive home the metaphor of how I'll never be the real thing. But as much as Constance despises me, she's a queen, and I'm positive she'd never gift a fake diamond to anyone—even to me.

There's a folded piece of card stock tucked into the top of the box, and I open it. Her handwriting is cramped and almost archaically difficult to read, but her signature is clear.

Dear Evangeline,
　　Happy Christmas.

　　Sincerely,
　　Her Majesty Queen Constance

That's it. No explanation, no quippy insult—just a simple greeting, even less than I'd expect from a dentist or a site I ordered from three years ago trying to lure me back.

Exhausted and confused, I close the velvet box and set it aside. Maybe Alexander isn't the only one who found some clarity in the fact that I almost died, but even though I know it's uncharitable of me, I somehow doubt it.

As I finally rest my head on the pillow, however, another moment from that dream flashes through my mind. It wasn't just Constance standing over me. Ben was there, too, in the indigo of twilight.

My eyes fly open, and I look around the dark room, as if I'll find him lurking nearby, staring at me through the shadows. But he doesn't need to anymore. I have the pictures to prove he's always there, even when he isn't, and I pull the blanket tighter around my aching body.

No matter where he is in the world, he'll always be watching— and waiting for the right moment to make his next move.

CHAPTER FOURTEEN

"Henrietta, it's been ten days since Buckingham Palace confirmed a member of the royal family was seriously injured in a hunting accident on Sandringham Estate, yet we've had no further official updates."

"No, and I expect we won't, I'm afraid. Though with most of the royal family now enjoying the new year at the Klosters ski resort in Switzerland, simple process of elimination has all but confirmed the rumours that it was Evangeline who was injured."

"Process of elimination?"

"She, the King, and Christopher Abbott-Montgomery, Earl of Clarence, are the only three members of the royal family missing from the trip. While His Majesty has never been particularly fond of Klosters, Lord Clarence seemed to enjoy himself last year with Princess Mary and Prince Benedict, and one might expect him to be eager to ring in the new year with Evangeline, as the pair have been dating for quite a while now."

"Yet Buckingham Palace has refused to comment on any speculation regarding the incident."

"If it truly was an accident, then it's possible a devoted staff member or even a senior royal was also involved."

"Also involved? How?"

"Well, presumably someone must have pulled the trigger."

"And you believe it might have been another member of the royal family?"

"It would certainly be a twist, wouldn't it? And it would explain the palace's lack of communication regarding the matter. Royal courtiers would never allow such a thing to become public knowledge, even as a rumour."

"And if it wasn't an accident?"

"Well, that's pure conjecture, isn't it? But I will admit, there is some evidence that points to there being more to the story than we know. The police response to the incident was far stronger than one might expect from a simple hunting accident where all factors were known, and the subsequent investigation and search of the estate, as well as the royal family's hasty return to Windsor Castle, could possibly lead one to believe there may have been an active threat against the family."

"You're starting to sound rather like a conspiracy theorist, Henrietta."

[laughs] "Oh, dear me! That's hardly my intention, I assure you."

"It is all rather befuddling, though, isn't it? Particularly in light of the recent drama that has plagued the royal family."

"Yes, I rather think it is. And the fact remains—we have no idea who shot Evangeline. Or what the circumstances were that led to such a dangerous—and potentially fatal—mistake."

—ITV News's interview with royal expert Henrietta Smythe,
3 January 2024

FOR THE NEXT TWO WEEKS, while most of the family takes off to the Swiss Alps to enjoy a prolonged ski trip, I'm stuck haunting the halls of Windsor.

Kit and my parents stay behind with me, and while no one

says anything, I notice that my mother's wardrobe expands from a week's worth of nice sweaters and pants to paint-stained T-shirts and jeans with holes in the knees. They're not clothes she would have brought with her for a temporary holiday stay, and I'm sure Alexander's already had her things shipped over from Virginia.

Kit and I spend most of those weeks in my suite, watching Netflix, reading books, and listening to my new record collection. He's attentive to a fault, and even after my shoulder heals enough for me to use my arm again, he's constantly fetching things for me and acting like I'm incapable of anything more than light conversation. The only plus to the whole situation is that, without either of us really discussing it, he spends the night—every night—in my suite. Sometimes we fall asleep on the sofa, but other times, we're both awake enough to make it to bed. And while he always falls asleep with his arms around me or his hand in mine, he's annoyingly proper and respectful about it.

I wake up before him almost every morning—a switch from our usual routine, but I can't seem to sleep for longer than a few hours anymore. Maybe it's the lingering pain, or maybe it's the constant buzz of adrenaline that seems to course through me, always on alert for another crack, another bullet, another near miss that doesn't this time. Either way, I spend those predawn hours on my laptop, scrolling through everything I can find about Ben. Old articles about his birth and public appearances as a child, gossip posts about his seemingly endless supply of temporary girlfriends, pictures of him spilling out of nightclubs at four in the morning, sometimes with Jasper, sometimes with Maisie, and even sometimes with Kit—anything that might clue me in as to why he's doing this, or offer a single shred of proof that he's capable of sending a gunman after me in the middle of a royal estate.

But there's nothing. He is, as far as the internet knows, an astonishingly polite and intelligent young prince with a harmless taste for partying. There's no evidence of the malicious side of him that he's kept hidden from his own family, and the only hint I find of his ruthlessness is a glint in his eyes that I'm sure no one else sees—either because they refuse to acknowledge the monster underneath, or because I'm the only one who knows it's there in the first place.

Every morning, I close my tabs the instant I hear Kit stirring, and I never tell him about my research on Ben—not because I don't trust him, but because I'm sure he'll insist that it isn't my job to figure out what happened this time. That whoever shot us won't be bragging about it on social media, and right now, the only thing I need to worry about is healing, while the police do the hard work of tracking down the shooter and figuring out why they did it.

Kit wouldn't be wrong. But when no one else is willing to admit that Ben could still be a suspect even if he didn't pull the trigger, it would feel wrong for me to listen.

For now, I feel marginally better knowing exactly where Ben is—at Klosters, with Maisie, Helene, and the rest of the family. My phone remains mercifully silent for the first week of their trip, but a few days after New Year's, I wake up to sixteen text messages from Maisie, all screeching at me for not telling her about my new pocket-sized minder. She proceeds to send me pictures, videos, and voice notes informing me about every minute of her day in excruciating detail, and the only reason I don't complain is because of how many times I catch sight of Ben lurking in the background. I don't like the idea of him being anywhere near my sister, but as long as he's preoccupied, there's a chance he isn't plotting my death.

"Maisie seems happy," I say to Kit as we both ignore the romcom playing on my laptop. He's on his own mobile, texting with his brows knit, and I glance at him. "Everything okay?"

"What? Oh—yes," he says quickly, switching off his screen and offering me a smile. "Just my parents. What's this about Maisie?"

"She's in a good mood, that's all," I say. "I think she and Gia made up. Rosie really hasn't said anything?"

"I haven't heard from her since the photo she sent on New Year's Eve," he says, and I snort.

"I still can't believe she managed to include that much cleavage in a single selfie. It's a shame we know she was in Johannesburg for Christmas, otherwise I wouldn't put it past her to be the one who tried to off me."

Kit shakes his head. "She's far too good of a shot. She can fell a deer at a truly remarkable distance."

"Really?" I say, surprised. "She doesn't exactly seem like the hunting type."

"Maisie's the one who can't hit the broad side of a barn," he says. "Gia doesn't shoot, but Rosie has real talent."

"Either way, she wouldn't have risked hitting you," I say, glancing at his sleeve. The graze on his arm is well on its way to being healed, but every time I catch sight of it, dread fills the pit of my stomach as I imagine what could've happened. What almost did. And whenever Kit's eyes linger on me a little too long, I know he's thinking the same thing.

"Yes," he agrees quietly. "I think we can rule her out as a suspect."

His phone vibrates again, and he reaches for it before stopping himself, his mouth set in a thin line. As stoic as he is, he's terrible at hiding his emotions, and now it's my turn to frown.

"Are you sure everything's okay?"

"Positive," he says, and he sounds so genuine that I want to believe him. His brows are still furrowed, though, and as he pulls me into his arms so we can both settle in and watch the movie, he holds me a little tighter than usual.

Before I can decide if I want to press or not, my phone chimes, and I grumble as I grab it off the end table. "If this is another picture of Maisie's dinner . . ."

But it isn't. Instead, it's from an unknown American number, and with a jolt of familiarity, I notice the area code.

202. Washington, D.C.

Sure enough, when I open the message, there aren't any words—only a single emoji of a tiny hand making a heart with its pointer finger and thumb.

"I'm going to *murder* Maisie," I growl, tossing my phone aside. "She gave Thaddeus my number."

"Thaddeus? Park?" says Kit, and to my surprise, he chuckles. "Perhaps she thinks you need more friends."

"She should've asked me first," I mutter.

"You're not wrong, but this is also Maisie we're talking about," he says, drawing me to him again. "The concept of asking for permission is completely foreign to her."

I grumble a bit more. "I keep seeing Ben in the background of her pictures."

"Oh?" says Kit mildly. "She did mention wanting to keep an eye on him."

"Yes, but she doesn't have to actually hang out with him all day," I say. He doesn't disagree, at least, and after a moment I decide to test the waters. "I really think he had something to do with it, Kit. I know he was with Alexander and everyone else, I know they were watching him the whole time, but the gift he gave me at Christmas . . ."

"Gift?" says Kit, instantly more alert. "You mean that photo album? Is there something sinister inside?"

I shake my head, though I don't actually know, because I've refused to touch it. "It's the cover. Look—I think it's still under the couch."

Sure enough, when Kit bends down to grope beneath the sofa, he straightens a moment later with the album in his hand. His fingers brush against the gold lettering, and in the daylight, it's easier to see the slight indent of where the *2023* used to be. Without me saying a word, his eyebrows shoot up, and he leans in to get a better look.

"Is that . . . ?" he says, and I nod.

"My death year. Obviously he was wrong, but not for lack of trying."

Kit sucks in a breath. "Ev, you have to show someone. Even if Ben had nothing to do with the shooting, this is still a very real threat."

I frown. "He'll claim it was a mistake, or that he didn't mean for it to look like a memorial album."

"Maybe, but you still need to tell your father," he insists, and I sigh.

"I will, once Maisie's back and my mom's settled into her routine here. But it won't change anything, Kit—you know it won't. Alexander will make more excuses, and everyone will think I have an irrational vendetta against Ben, especially when he has a dozen witnesses who can truthfully say he was with them when we were attacked."

"It doesn't matter what anyone thinks," says Kit, setting the album aside and wrapping his arms around me again. "What matters is your safety."

"Alexander said he won't let him anywhere near me or my mom again," I say, resting against his chest. "I think that's the best I can hope for right now. I can't prove anything, not yet, but . . . there's just something about the way Ben looks at me. And his *smirk*—it's like he knows something bad is coming, and he's just waiting for the other shoe to drop."

Kit nuzzles the top of my head. "When—if—it does, we'll figure out how to beat him at his own game, Ev. I promise."

"What if we can't?" I say. "Or . . . what if it costs us something we don't want to lose?"

Our eyes meet, and the energy between us crackles with everything we haven't said. "Then we'll make him pay," says Kit quietly. And I know he means it.

THE NEXT MORNING, I WAKE to another round of faint whispers coming from somewhere nearby. It's still early, and when I glance at Kit, he's fast asleep, clearly unbothered by the eerie sound.

I head into my sitting room on the off chance someone really is out there, but of course it's empty, and the voices disappear as soon as I cross the threshold. Too rattled to remain in my apartment, I brush my teeth and head toward the family dining room instead. Alexander is already seated at the table with a newspaper in one hand and a piece of toast in the other, and he glances up when I enter.

"Good morning," he says, managing to conceal most of his surprise. To be fair, I'm usually not an early bird. "How did you sleep?"

"Fine," I lie, plopping down into the chair beside him. Telling him about the strange whispers feels dangerous, even though I can't figure out why. "My phone kept going off—Maisie went to some party, and she sent about a hundred pictures."

"Did I not show you how to silence your mobile?" he says before taking a bite of toast.

"I know how," I say, stealing a piece of bacon from his plate. "But I forgot, and it was on the other side of the room. Where's my mom?"

"She had a long night," he says, and at my glare, he shakes his head with faint amusement. "Painting, Evie. She had a long night painting. She hasn't been sleeping well since Christmas, and—well, we both know she needs her rest."

Yes, she does, and even though the shooting wasn't my fault, guilt slices through me anyway. A footman brings me a plate identical to my father's, and I thank him before stabbing the scrambled eggs with my fork. "How long before the press finds out she's still here, and that she didn't just fly over for Christmas?"

"A few months, if we're lucky," admits Alexander. "By then, I hope Helene will agree to announce our separation."

"And turn my mom into the bad guy all over again?" I say, and he sighs.

"I'm afraid that can't be helped at this point. But I promise you, I will do my very best to set the record—"

"Your Majesty."

Both of us turn. Jenkins stands in the doorway with a tablet in his hands, and while he's always been a master of worried looks and concerned frowns, he seems uncharacteristically apprehensive.

"Yes, Jenkins?" says my father in a voice that makes it clear he sees it, too.

"My sincerest apologies for interrupting, sir. But I've just received word that there's been an article published on the *Daily Sun*'s site, and . . ." He glances down at the screen. "I believe you may want to see the accompanying photographs."

I freeze, my heart pounding as Jenkins brings the tablet over to Alexander, who accepts it with the air of someone being handed a live snake.

"What is it this time?" I say, my mouth dry and my forkful of eggs forgotten. "Was someone taking pictures at the hospital? Were you and my mom photographed together? Did Maisie and Gia—" I stop and resist the urge to look guiltily at the footmen still in the room with us. Their relationship isn't a secret in the family anymore, but I'm not about to out my sister to the entire damn world.

Alexander swipes the screen methodically, his expression unreadable. The passing seconds are agony as a dozen possibilities flash through my mind, each worse than the last, but eventually his hand stills, and to my shock, he starts to chuckle.

"It isn't you or your mother or Maisie," he says. "It seems Helene and my wayward brother were caught together in a hot tub in Switzerland."

I gasp and scramble to his side, ignoring the protest from my healing shoulder. Sure enough, there are more than a dozen photos taken last night that show Helene and Nicholas in a private hot tub together, and there's no mistaking their steamy kisses and intimate touches for anything short of a hot and heavy affair.

"Holy shit," I whisper, and I look at Alexander, my eyes wide. "Holy *shit*."

He laughs again, a strangely dignified sound that carries two decades of relief with it, and he hands the tablet back to Jenkins. "Well, then," he says. "This will certainly be interesting."

CHAPTER FIFTEEN

In case you've been living under a rock for the past six hours, the *Daily Sun* has obtained pictures taken last night that show Queen Helene in a *very* compromising position with her brother-in-law, Prince Nicholas, the Duke of York.

While we can hardly fault the *Daily Sun* for posting the risqué series of exclusive photographs—we've been known to do so from time to time as well, after all—one must wonder if it might be considered high treason to do so of one's beloved Queen.

After all, who can blame Her Majesty for finding comfort in the nearest pair of exceptionally handsome arms, considering the decades of turbulence and humiliation she's suffered in her marriage to His Majesty? Not only has Queen Helene had to endure the knowledge that her husband was involved in an extramarital affair that produced a child he refused to denounce, but eighteen years later, she's been forced to accept his illegitimate issue into her home and treat her like family—*and* host the King's mistress during what should have been a private Christmas gathering.

Frankly, Her Majesty deserves a bit of fun, and we at the *Regal Record* congratulate Queen Helene and His Royal Highness on their affair. We very much hope this turns out better for both of them than their marriages.

For more *fascinating* royal relationships that might be more than they appear, click through our gallery below.

—*The Regal Record,* 4 January 2024

FOR ONCE, IT'S NOT MY name in the headlines, and even though I feel bad for Helene and Nicholas and the sudden white-hot scrutiny of their relationship, I can't pretend it isn't nice to get a break from all that attention.

What worries me, however, is the fact that the photographs were clearly taken by someone inside their private château. A member of the staff, maybe, but Alexander confirms that Helene and Nicholas brought their own personnel with them—all of whom have known about their affair for ages. Which means that if there is a mole, it's someone in the royal party. And while I can't pinpoint a motive, the part of my mind that's fixated on Ben tries to come up with a way that he could be responsible for leaking this, too.

I text Maisie twice that morning, but she doesn't respond. By the time noon rolls around, I'm on the verge of actually calling her when the protection officer now stationed outside my room—a no-nonsense woman in her thirties named Ingrid Straw—informs me that Her Royal Highness has returned to Windsor.

I pause just long enough to scribble a note for Kit, who's showering in his own suite, before I sprint down the long gallery. I'm at my sister's door fifteen seconds later, my shoulder aching and my lungs burning, and taking a deep breath, I knock with all the delicacy of someone defusing a bomb, not entirely sure what I'll find on the other side.

Silence. I scowl.

"Maisie, it's me," I call through the thick wood, glancing at the burly protection officer standing outside her room—a development I'm sure she's as thrilled with as I am. "I know you're in there. You can't text me nonstop and then decide to ignore me when—"

The door flies open, and a hand reaches through the crack, grabbing my good arm and yanking me through the tight space. As soon as I'm inside Maisie's apartment, which is easily twice the size of mine, the door slams shut behind me, and my sister faces me with a mixture of annoyance, fury, and very real fear mingling on her features.

"I can't believe Daddy's allowing someone to *stalk* me all bloody day," she says, and it takes me a moment to realize she's talking about the protection officer.

"Between the two of us, you're the logical choice," I point out.

"Hardly. *You're* the one who was nearly killed, not me."

"But you're the one inheriting the throne. I have a shadow now, too, if it makes you feel any better."

"It does not," she says with a sniff, and she whirls back around and marches to a cream-and-gold sofa, where she's strewn the contents of her purse. "I can't find my bloody mobile. I think I left it on the plane."

"You mean this mobile?" I say, picking up the phone that's lying face up on a side table, half-hidden by an enormous vase of hot-pink roses. "Who sent the flowers?"

Maisie snatches her phone out of my hand, checking it over like she expects it to be damaged. "No one," she mutters, but there's still a card nestled among the fragrant petals, and even though I don't mean to snoop, it's impossible to miss the blocky signature.

Thaddeus

I barely—*barely* manage to suppress a choked laugh. He's definitely barking up the wrong tree. "I'm sorry about the photos," I say. "How's your mom doing?"

"How do you think she's doing?" snaps Maisie as she scoops her things back into her purse. "About as well as you were after that bloody video of you and Jasper was posted, I'd expect."

That's not a fair comparison by any stretch of the imagination, considering Helene was fully conscious and consenting—to Nicholas, at least—but I bite my tongue. "It'll blow over. She and Alexander are already separated anyway, and—"

"I don't bloody *care* about the photos," my sister explodes, throwing her purse toward the white piano positioned in front of her floor-to-ceiling windows. The leather hits the keyboard in a discordant array of notes, and the contents go flying.

Right. Not just a run-of-the-mill bad mood, but a full-blown temper tantrum. I let her seethe for a few seconds before I say quietly, "What's really going on, Maisie? And don't tell me it's nothing. You've been blowing hot and cold for weeks."

She takes several deep breaths, each one with the kind of crescendo that makes me think she's going to hurl her phone at my head. But at last, after nearly half a minute of this, she sinks onto the sofa and buries her face in her hands.

"You already know what's going on," she mumbles, and I approach her slowly, still not convinced she won't lash out.

"Gia?" I guess, and she nods miserably.

"We tried to patch things up over the New Year, but I was awful to her this morning after we found out about Mummy's pictures, and . . ."

I ease down beside her. "Why were you awful to her?"

"Because—" The words seem to stick in her throat, and she swallows hard. "The *Regal Record* posted a bunch of photos."

"Of Nicholas and Helene?" I say, confused. "I thought that was—"

"Of me and Gia," she says, and she glances my way only long enough for me to see how red her eyes are. "As a bonus feature to their story about Mummy and Uncle Nicholas. 'Royal relationships that may be more than they seem,' or some other nonsense."

My hand twitches toward my phone, and Maisie must notice, because she sighs.

"Go ahead. It's the only way you'll understand."

With an apologetic look, I fish my phone out of my pocket and pull up the *Regal Record*. It's a simple blog with black text and a white background, free of the frills and ads of most other royal gossip sites, and that somehow makes it all the more unnerving—especially when they get things right.

It takes a few clicks to find the gallery she's talking about, and I swipe through it, studying each photo in turn. They're not all bad—most of them are paparazzi shots of Maisie and Gia leaving clubs or walking into exclusive parties together, and even with how close they're standing, their heads occasionally bent together, it could all easily be considered innocent. But two of the images stand out—both grainier than the others and clearly taken from a distance.

The first is a picture of Maisie, Gia, and Rosie inside the VIP area at a club I don't recognize—which isn't surprising, considering I've only joined them on their midnight excursions a handful of times. While Rosie is tugging on one of her blond curls and making eyes at a server holding a bottle of champagne, Maisie and Gia are leaning close together, and their heads are tilted in such a way to make them look like they're kissing. For all I know, they were.

That doesn't sound like my sister, though, who always at least pretends to be careful with her secrets. From an unbiased perspective, it's obvious the angle and lighting aren't doing them any favors, and I could easily argue that nothing is really happening. But when I find the second damning photo, I take a slow breath and release it, trying to keep the shock off my face.

It's impossible to positively identify Maisie and Gia in the shadows of the dimly lit room, which is full of people drinking and dancing. But the innocuous previous photo does the detective work for the viewer, plainly showing them arm in arm in the same distinct outfits they're wearing in the second picture. Maisie's hand—identifiable from the golden bangles she's wearing and the ring on her thumb—is resting dangerously high on Gia's deep brown thigh. Gia's fingers are tangled in Maisie's strawberry-blond waves, and while their faces are obscured, it's clear that they're taking advantage of the darkness and stealing a quick kiss. Or more.

"No one's supposed to take pictures at those parties," says Maisie miserably. "That's always been the deal. Anyone caught trying has been kicked out, but . . ."

"But someone got away with it," I say, flipping through the photos again. "Do you remember when this happened? Is there any chance you might be able to figure out who took it?"

"It's always the same people at those bloody parties," she says, pressing her palms into her eyes. "That was from October—

Rosie's birthday. I had a little too much to drink, and I wasn't thinking—"

"It's not your fault," I say. "Whoever sent this in—"

"Of course it's my bloody fault," she bursts, her temper flaring again. "I should've known someone would be watching. I should've never trusted any of them, I should've never taken the bloody risk—"

"You're allowed to kiss your girlfriend at a party," I say firmly.

"*You* might be, but I'm the future queen," she snaps. "If I'm outed, all hell will break loose. There are already whole social media accounts dedicated to Gia and me, watching our every move, reading far more into things than they should—"

"Are they, though?" I say, and she gives me a look that could set the ocean on fire. "Listen, I'm not trying to push you into something you're not ready for, but explain it to me—what's the worst that could happen if you and Gia go public?"

Maisie laughs suddenly, humorless and borderline hysterical. "That's easy. Benedict gets the crown."

"Well—yeah, obviously, if you two don't have kids. But—"

"You've no idea how the succession works, do you?" she says, and there are tears in her eyes now. "It's what you and your American sensibilities might refer to as *archaic*. I'll be the head of the Church of England as Queen, and while a portion of the world may have moved on from certain narrow-minded prejudices, I assure you that the archbishops have not."

"So this is a religious thing, not a royal thing?" I say slowly, and she scoffs.

"They're one and the same. Succession law very clearly dictates that my heirs—who I'd have to give birth to—would only be allowed to inherit the throne if I'm married to their biological father. Adoptees aren't eligible, and forget any sort of *donation*." She laughs again, raking her nails through her hair and grabbing fistfuls of it. "And the line of succession is set now, isn't it? Mummy and Daddy obviously aren't going to have any more children, and Nicholas is second in line after me. As soon as we all die, Benedict's going to win. No matter what I do, he's going to get exactly what he wants."

"Dunno," I say. "From what you've said, you might destroy the whole monarchy before he ever gets the chance to sit on the throne."

She buries her face in her hands, and her shoulders start to shake, but I don't know if she's laughing or crying. I set my hand on her back anyway, rubbing circles against her sweater, and my eyes fall on the hot-pink roses once more.

Oh.

"Does Thaddeus know about Gia?" I say delicately, and she sniffs.

"No."

"Are you going to tell him about Gia?"

"I don't know," she whimpers, and I wrap my arm around her shoulders in an awkward hug. She doesn't push me away, though, so that's progress.

"Is that what you're fighting about?" I say, but by now, I'm pretty sure I know the answer.

Maisie nods, wiping her wet eyes and smudging her mascara. Clearly she didn't think to wear the waterproof kind today. "I don't know what else to do. A few dates with Thaddeus would get the rumors off our backs, but Gia's furious."

"Thaddeus probably will be, too, if he finds out you're using him," I say. "Usually both halves of a fauxmance know they're in one."

"A what?" She turns her head to look at me properly, and I gently wipe the black smudges from her face with my thumbs.

"A fauxmance. A fake romance," I explain. "They're common in Hollywood, I think. There's always some rumor going around that two actors are together to publicize their new movie, or that they have a relationship contract—"

"A what?" she says again, and this time I see the spark of something I don't like in her eyes.

"I'm not here to give you ideas, Mais, and I don't know what to say to make any of this better. Just that . . . we'll figure it out, all right? I promise. And who knows—maybe Ben will do us all a favor and die young."

She focuses on the cream rug, and I notice her nails are short and ragged. I've never seen her with anything less than a perfect manicure before, and this more than anything tells me exactly how upset she really is.

"There are several monarchs whom historians suspect also . . . favored the same sex," she says softly. "They all married, though, and most of them had children. Queen Anne was pregnant at least seventeen times. *Seventeen.*" She looks at me again, her blue eyes almost pleading. "Maybe it wouldn't be so bad."

In that moment, my heart breaks for her. She has all the privilege and wealth and status anyone could ever ask for, but what's the point if it's really just a gilded cage?

"I can't tell you what to do," I say, taking her hand in mine. "But I will say that while those kings and queens didn't have much of a choice, you do. We don't live in the eighteenth century anymore, and the people love you—even the ones who are . . . less than open-minded. You have a right to be yourself. You have a right to be happy and to be with the person you love and to not give up such a huge part of who you are just so you don't make strangers uncomfortable. I mean—look where prioritizing the crown got our parents. They're all miserable. Or they were, at least, for longer than we've been alive."

Maisie shakes her head and, in what's possibly the most shocking thing I've ever seen her do, she wipes her nose on the sleeve of her cashmere sweater. "I really don't want to end up like them."

"Me neither," I admit. "Especially your mom. No offense."

"None taken." She sniffs again. "I don't think I've ever really seen her happy before, except when she's with Nicholas."

"And I don't think I've ever really seen you happy before, except when you're with Gia. Or ordering me around," I add as an afterthought.

Maisie sighs again, ignoring my quip. "I love her. I hate that we're fighting. I hate that this might be the end, all because of things we can't control. It isn't fair. Thaddeus is the perfect solution, and it wouldn't be forever."

"I'm not sure that would end well for anyone, though," I say.

"I know," she mumbles. "I don't want to lose her. I've tried talking to her about it a million times, but—"

Abrupt staccato footsteps sound in the hallway, growing louder as they approach Maisie's sitting room. No one knocks, however, and we both fall silent, listening as they fade—until the muffled but unmistakable sound of Helene's shrieks echoes down the corridor.

"Mummy's home," says Maisie grimly, and with one more pass at her face with her sleeve, she grabs my good arm and yanks me to my feet, dragging me to the door.

CHAPTER SIXTEEN

I am born for the happiness or misery of a great nation, and consequently must often act contrary to my passions.

—King George III (b. 1738, r. 1760–1820)

"MAISIE," I HISS AS WE creep toward the doorway that leads into Windsor's white drawing room. *"Maisie.* We shouldn't be doing this."

"Since when have you had a moral objection to eavesdropping?" she whispers, pulling me closer to the threshold. Though she and I are sneaking around like we're thieves in the night, our protection officers walk normally behind us, both looking vaguely bored by the whole thing as Helene's rising voice reverberates through the open door.

". . . all over," she cries. "Everything I've worked for, every terrible thing you've done that I've excused or ignored or endured—"

"This is hardly the end of the world," says Alexander's measured voice, far quieter than Helene's. "Does it truly matter if everyone knows you and Nicholas are a couple? You live together, after all, and that was hardly going to stay a secret forever—"

"No, of course not. How could it, with you parading *her* around?" snaps Helene, and it's only when I catch a glimpse of my mother's auburn hair through the doorway that I stop caring about being spotted. With Maisie still attached to my arm, I'm the one leading us inside the room now, over the threshold until the whole miserable scene is laid out before us.

My mother's seated with her back to the large bay window, facing an easel and a canvas I can't see, paintbrush poised in her hand even though it isn't moving. Nearby, Alexander sits unperturbed on one of the white-and-gold sofas beneath a massive portrait of some long-dead queen, and Helene paces frantically in front of him. Her thin frame is rigid and her silk skirt catches between her knees, and no amount of concealer can hide the dark hollows beneath her eyes—which, every time she turns toward the window, are glaring daggers at my mother.

"Oh, lovely," says Helene when she catches sight of me near the doorway. "Precisely who I was hoping to see at this very moment in my life. Shall we tell your secret family about all our private affairs, Alexander, and call it a day?"

"You're being unreasonable," he says, which even I could tell him is exactly the wrong thing to say. Sure enough, Helene sputters and whirls on him again, her face twisted into a caricature of its usual beauty.

"*I'm* being unreasonable? I didn't get a say in any of this, Alexander. I was twenty years old when I agreed to marry you—*twenty*. I didn't know what I was getting into, and *you* certainly didn't tell me you were in love with someone else."

"You knew it was an arranged marriage," says Alexander in a tired voice that makes it clear this is an argument they've had countless times before. "You knew you weren't the first woman I proposed to. And we both knew we didn't love each other—"

"So that made it all right for you to sneak around behind my back?" she snarls. "That made it all right for you to ruin my life barely a year into our marriage?"

Alexander is quiet for a moment. "Why is it," he says at last, "that whenever something goes wrong for you, you insist on laying it at my feet?"

"Because *everything* is your fault," she explodes. "You never tried to love me. Nicholas was the only one who ever paid me any attention, and—"

"When did your affair start, Helene?" says Alexander, now deadly quiet. She stops in her tracks, her face draining of color beneath her makeup.

"That has nothing to do with—"

"We both know that's not true," says Alexander. "If you want to have this argument here and now, then we will. But I don't think you do."

Helene swallows convulsively, and for a moment I think she might actually scream. "You didn't love me, Alexander," she says, so pitifully that I feel like an intruder. Which I am, but with my mom so close to the line of fire, I can't back away now.

"Yes, I did," he says. "Just not the way you wanted me to."

"Not the way you were supposed to," she counters. "Not the way you promised to."

"I loved you the only way I could," he says. "I'm sorry it wasn't enough. I mean it—I've always been sorry. And I'm especially sorry it's come to this."

"So am I," she says, and there's such an undercurrent of

bitterness beneath her words that I take half a step back, nearly running into Maisie. She shifts beside me, and we stand shoulder to shoulder in the doorway, watching our parents have the fight that's been brewing for twenty years.

"I'm sorry, too, Helene," says my mother softly. "What we did to you was inexcusable. You deserved better, and we will never be able to make it up to you."

"No," she says. "You won't. Neither of you can give me my life back, can you? And we're all stuck now. There's no wriggling out of any of this."

At last Alexander stands, his entire body heaving with a sigh. "I'll tell Doyle to draft a statement announcing our separation."

Helene's mouth drops open. "Alexander—*no*. You can't. The entire world will blame me—"

"I will make sure he is very clear on when, precisely, our separation took place," continues my father. "And that we are still deeply devoted to the country and to our family, despite this egregious intrusion into our private lives."

There are tears in Helene's eyes now, and she doesn't bother to wipe them away as they roll down her cheeks. "The details won't matter," she says. "Everyone will think it's my fault."

"I cannot erase those pictures, or go back in time and stop them from ever being printed," says Alexander. "But I will do everything I can to place the blame squarely at the feet of my affair, and to make it clear that the accusations of infidelity against you are baseless. I will also ask the courtiers to inform the press that I wholly and happily support your relationship with my brother." He glances at my mom. "In a few weeks' time, when we're ready, the four of us will make a joint appearance together, and we will all look happier than we ever have in our lives. Is that acceptable?"

"What?" I blurt before either my mother or Helene can say a thing. "You want to make a public appearance with my mom? *No—*"

"That's something for me and your father to discuss," says my mother, but I hear the apprehension in her voice, even if it doesn't show on her face.

"Mom, please—it's too dangerous," I insist. "The press will eat you alive—"

"I know," she says so quietly that I can barely hear her. "Evie, please, it's not the time—"

"Evangeline's right," says Helene suddenly, and I'm so taken aback that I fall silent. "The media will insist it's a cover-up, and they won't just go after Laura. They'll make up stories, call me horrible names, claim I'm some—some *villain* who went after your brother for revenge. They'll destroy me, Alexander. Everything I've worked for, everything I've ever wanted, everything I've had to put up with because of *you—*"

This time, she rounds on my mother, and I automatically move forward again, my pulse racing. Maisie's there beside me, though, her fingers curling around my elbow, and a hint of pain twinges below my shoulder.

"You should've left us alone," says Helene tearfully. "You should've never let him back into your life. You've ruined *everything,* all because you two had to have your way, consequences be damned. My family—my *life* is now a joke because of you, and—"

"And we will pick up the pieces as best we can," says Alexander, a few steps closer to my mother now, too. "Our marriage may have fallen apart, but we are still bound together, Helene, and I will not let you crash and burn."

"How can you possibly save me?" she says with astounding vitriol. "You can't even save yourself. Your reign is in tatters, Alexander, and history will hate you. Your people already do."

"That is entirely their prerogative," says Alexander, but I can tell this blow has landed.

Helene turns to me now, and the force of her animosity is so strong that only Maisie's grip keeps me in place. "None of this would've happened if you'd just stayed where you were," she hisses. "That was all you had to do, Evangeline. Live your life as far away from mine as possible. But you couldn't even manage that much, could you?"

"We all know I've never been very good at following directions," I say dryly, even though I feel like I'm staring down a rabid bear. "But all *you* had to do was learn to lock the door."

Maisie looks at me sharply, but it's Helene whose fingers twitch like she's itching to wrap them around my throat. "I was right the first time," she says thickly. "You *were* a mistake."

"That's enough—" snaps Alexander, but I'm already speaking over him.

"Maybe I was," I say. "But so were you."

Helene's face turns a sickly purple, and she pulls her shoulders back, drawing herself up to her full height. Slowly she turns to Alexander, her expression strangely unreadable.

"You're absolutely right, Your Majesty. It is enough. And if you can't protect me anymore, then I'll just have to protect myself."

She curtsies, a mocking gesture that oozes contempt and revulsion, and then storms straight toward me. Maisie finally lets me go, and I quickly step aside, knowing damn well that Helene will win this game of chicken if I play.

Sure enough, she breezes past me at speed, so close that I can smell her perfume, and only when she reaches the door does she pause. "Coming, Maisie?"

My sister, who hasn't said a word during this entire exchange, is staring at Helene like she's never seen her before. When she finally looks at me instead, I can see the apology in her eyes, but I don't try to stop her. Obviously she's always going to choose her mother.

And so, like Constance's dog trotting after its master, Maisie follows Helene out of the white drawing room and into the long corridor beyond, leaving Alexander, my mother, and me on our own. Or at least as *on our own* as we'll ever be in a place with footmen, courtiers, and protection officers lurking in every corner.

"That wasn't your fight, Evan," says my mom, finally setting her paintbrush down. "You shouldn't have gotten involved."

I shrug. "Helene's always going to make it my fight, too. I might as well get a few hits in while I can. Are you okay?"

I'm speaking to my mom, but I also watch Alexander. He's already sunk back onto the sofa, his hands clasped and his lips pressed together so hard that the skin around them is colorless. My mother nods, but he doesn't respond right away, instead taking a deep, shuddering breath that seems to burrow into his soul and expel something with it.

"More than all right," he says with a hint of forced cheer.

"Now none of us has anything to hide, and that's all we've wanted, isn't it?"

I manage a nod, but I'm not convinced. And as I glance at the empty doorway once more, dread nags at me, bringing with it a sense that somehow, this is about to get a whole lot worse before anyone finds their peace.

CHAPTER SEVENTEEN

@duchessvofyork My heart goes out to Her Majesty and His Royal Highness the Duke of York for this abhorrent invasion of their privacy. Happiness shouldn't have to be sacrificed in the name of crowns and thrones, and they have my deepest sympathy.

12:52 a.m. · 5 January 2024

@yorkiesfurever @duchessvofyork Does that mean it's really true? I'm so sad. I always thought you two made such a lovely couple and hoped you'd get back together.

12:55 a.m. · 5 January 2024

@dutchessdame172 @duchessvofyork did you know?? how long have they been together? and with her husband's BROTHER??? #ew #twotimingqueen #offwithherhead

12:59 a.m. · 5 January 2024

@mrshrhnickofyork @dutchessdame172 Can't you read? Those photos are revolting, and the Duchess is right. Even if they aren't photoshopped and the Queen and Duke are sneaking around behind His Majesty's back, maybe we should all be asking ourselves why.

1:05 a.m. · 5 January 2024

—Twitter exchange between Venetia, Duchess of York, and users @yorkiesfurever, @dutchessdame172, and @mrshrhnickofyork, 5 January 2024

#OFFWITHHERHEAD TRENDS FOR A FULL week after the pictures are released. I think it starts as a joke, but soon enough, a terrifying number of people are taking it much too seriously, and death threats—real, actual death threats against Helene and Nicholas—flood in. Each morning at breakfast, Jenkins briefs Alexander on the worst of them, and they grimly discuss the measures both the police and palace security are taking to ensure none of those threats turns into bloodshed.

In light of the scandal, Alexander cancels all royal appearances in hopes that the furor will die down, but it quickly becomes apparent that this isn't going away anytime soon. Helene and Nicholas retreat to Kensington Palace, where they remain for the week as a specialized crisis management team works overtime to quell the uproar, and Maisie joins her mother during the day to offer her support. I'm not surprised—if our positions were reversed, I wouldn't leave my mom's side. But I still check on my sister every night when she returns to Windsor Castle, if only to make sure she hasn't gone to pieces again.

By that Monday, four days after the photos are released, seemingly every royal correspondent in the UK has dived headfirst into the mess. Some insist it can't be true, while others write exposés about the whispers they've heard and the moments they've witnessed between the royal pair that gave them pause. Helene's die-hard fans spend countless hours online defending her, refusing to believe the pictures aren't photoshopped, but others gleefully jump to the conclusions those images offer, delighted to watch her downfall in real time. Every known photo of Helene and Nicholas is unearthed and dissected, and every glance they've ever exchanged in public suddenly becomes a conniving—or occasionally lovelorn—look between two people pulling a fast one on the entire world.

The promised press release from Buckingham Palace is simple and to the point, with no wordsmithery to manipulate the facts: Alexander and Helene have been separated since early July, and though my father deeply regrets the pain he's caused his wife of twenty years, he wishes her and Nicholas well in their new relationship. Most of the commenters and posters seem to take his statement at face value, but there's more than one corner of the internet that doesn't believe a word of it, and the rage against Helene only grows.

Amidst the chaos of the monarchy all but burning down around us, I start both physical therapy and, even though I'm nowhere near fully healed, self-defense lessons with Ingrid, my protection officer. She's careful with me, despite her gruff demeanor, and Kit is a ready and willing participant when she needs to demonstrate something she can't yet do on me.

"Oof," he grunts as he hits the mat that's been laid out in the green drawing room, his hair fanned out in a wild tangle. "That one hurt."

"That's the idea, Lord Clarence," says Ingrid without the faintest hint of apology, and she offers him a hand up.

"Just Kit, if you would," he says as he takes it, and she hauls him to his feet.

"I'm afraid that's against protocol, sir," she says, and he winces again.

"Considering you've been throwing me to the ground for the

past twenty minutes, perhaps we can consider ourselves above protocol. Just for the time being."

Ingrid makes a noncommittal sound in the back of her throat, and when she turns away, I see Kit's expression grow pained. His courtesy title, Earl of Clarence, is only his because his older brother died, and even though I never met Liam Abbott-Montgomery, I know without a doubt that Kit would give up every penny of his inheritance—titles and estates and future dukedom included—if it meant having him back.

"Call him Kit," I say suddenly. It's as close to an order as I've ever given, and he looks at me, surprised. "Or else I'll tell His Majesty that you call me Evangeline."

Ingrid raises an eyebrow, and I think I see a hint of amusement on her somber face. It's hard to tell, though, considering I'm pretty sure she hasn't smiled since she was in diapers. "If you insist, Miss Bright."

"I do," I say, amazed that this actually worked—and admittedly a little worried that Maisie is rubbing off on me. "Thank you."

The rest of our lesson goes off without a hitch, and though Ingrid slips up once or twice, she corrects herself immediately. She does seem to throw Kit a little harder than before, though, and by the time our session is over, I notice he's favoring his right side.

As soon as we return to my sitting room, I request an ice pack from the kitchens, and we spend the rest of the afternoon on my sofa together, lamenting Ingrid's unyielding toughness and fantasizing about the day I'm strong enough to throw her. Eventually Kit's phone buzzes, and as he checks it, his head resting in my lap and the warm ice pack discarded on the side table, I reach for my own. To my mild astonishment, I have no messages from Maisie, but there's a notification about a new post on the *Regal Record*. And as I read it, I swear under my breath.

"Everything all right?" says Kit, and I shake my head.

"The *Regal Record*'s reporting that Helene and Nicholas are living together at Kensington Palace," I say. "How do they know? How could they *possibly* know?"

"Someone trusted the wrong person," says Kit simply, and I grumble.

"Maybe Ben's still feeding the *Regal Record* information."

"It's possible," he allows. "Though as far as I know, Ben hasn't been anywhere near Kensington Palace in ages."

"He's in Florence with Venetia," I say, and Kit doesn't seem surprised I know this. "Nicholas probably told him."

"Son or not, you'd think he'd know better by now," says Kit, though his gaze is focused on his own screen again, and we lapse into silence.

As I scroll through the latest posts, a thought occurs to me. "I bet we could figure out who runs the site."

"The *Regal Record*?" says Kit, his thumbs typing furiously. "You know all about that computer stuff, don't you?"

"A little, but not enough to get around any privacy protection." I pause and glance at him. His frown is deeper now, but it's directed toward his phone, not me. "What about Aoife?"

Instantly he stills, and his brown eyes meet mine. "What about her?"

"She's studying computer science, isn't she? She might have some ideas."

Kit watches me for the space of several heartbeats, and I can practically see his mind turning this over. "You . . . want me to ask?" he says slowly, and I shrug.

"It's probably easier if you give me her number. If that's all right," I add, because based on his scowl, it isn't. But the moment I say this, he seems to realize his face is telling its own story, and it relaxes into a neutral expression.

"Er, yeah," he allows. "I'll text it to you. Just . . ." He hesitates. "She hasn't been vetted. By the palace, I mean. Whatever you say to her might end up in the papers, so be careful, all right?"

Now it's my turn to frown. "I thought she was your friend. Your *good* friend, according to her."

"More of an acquaintance," he mumbles. "We wouldn't know each other if it weren't for Dylan, and I'm not particularly chummy with him, either. We just go out to the pub together sometimes."

"Oh." This is at odds with the conversation they had in the gift shop near Sandringham, and I sift through the memory, trying to decide whether I'm imagining things. I don't think I am, but I also know the royal family and those connected to it are the evergreen targets of social climbers and sycophants. And Kit, who's a tabloid staple now because of me, is no exception.

"Just . . . promise me you won't trust her, yeah?" says Kit. "Not completely. That's all I mean."

"Okay," I say. "I'll be careful. I promise."

I watch as he types into his mobile, and a moment later, mine dings with her number. I add it to my contacts, but instead of messaging her, I set my phone aside and study him. He stares unseeingly at the ceiling now, and though he hasn't moved from my lap, I can sense a strange distance between us that wasn't there a minute ago.

"Are you okay?" I say at last. His gaze drifts to me, coming into focus as the faint furrow reappears between his eyebrows.

"Of course. I might be a bit sore in the morning, but it's nothing I can't handle."

"That's not what I mean," I say, running my fingers through his waves. "Something's been off for a while."

"We did both get shot," he points out, and I automatically glance at the pinkening scar on his bicep, visible now that he's wearing a T-shirt.

"You know it's more than that," I say quietly. "Something's going on, and I think it started before the attack. You don't have to talk about it if you don't want to," I add. "But if you do, I'm here to listen."

A moment passes, and then another, and part of me is sure he won't say anything. But then he lets out a weighty sigh, and his hand finds mine.

"I've been thinking about Liam a lot lately," he admits as he laces our fingers together. "When I went home over the summer to see my parents, my mother told me she'd kept a box of his things hidden from my father in the attic. I was looking through them, and . . ." He exhales again. "I don't know. I was hoping they'd offer answers. About why he did it, about . . . about who he was as a person toward the end. I didn't see him much in those last few years," he adds. "With him at Oxford and me at Eton. I just wanted some insight, I suppose. Some closure."

"Did you find it?" I say, and he hesitates.

"No. Not yet. But I've been doing more research about his time at university now that I'm there, too. His professors remember him. He was part of certain social groups and clubs, and . . . well, it's almost like following a ghost. Everywhere I go, a part of him is there."

I rest our joined hands on his chest, directly above his heart. It's racing, and I don't fully understand why. "I'm sorry."

"Don't be." He smiles, but it's weary. "Maybe there were never any answers to be found. But I do have to try."

"When I start in October, I'll help you," I offer. "If you're still looking, I mean."

He draws my hand to his lips and kisses it. "I'd like nothing more."

We fall asleep early that night, and it's a damn good thing, too, because there's a tap on my door well before the sun rises. Though the knock isn't loud, it sends a jolt through me, pulling me from my dreams so quickly that I'm dizzy, and I mumble a curse as Lady Tabitha Finch-Parker-Covington-Boyle strides into the room.

"Good morn—"

As light floods the room, she stops dead in her high-heeled tracks, her eyebrows climbing nearly to her hairline.

"Well, then," she says, and it takes me a beat to realize what's grabbed her attention.

"Get your mind out of the gutter, Tibby," I grumble as Kit shifts beside me, rubbing his eyes in the unexpected light. "What are you doing here?"

"What your father pays me to do," she says, and she resumes her stroll to my armoire, where she starts to rifle through a selection of designer dresses. "Doesn't your new term start in a few days, Kit?"

"I'll be there when it does," he says, his voice thick with sleep. "Does she always wake you up like this?"

"Every morning except Sundays," I mutter.

"I feel like I understand so much more about your relationship now," he says, and he gives me a quick peck. "I'll see you at breakfast."

Both Tibby and I watch as he rolls out of bed in his flannel pajamas, and once he's pulled on a robe and left my apartment, I turn the full force of my glare onto my smug private secretary.

"It's not a big deal," I say, and she hums in agreement.

"If anything, it's about bloody time. I expect the precautions I included in your luggage to Sandringham were put to good use, then?" she adds, and I flush.

"That's definitely none of your business."

"Everything you do is my business, Evan. It's my job to know the details, so I can help keep your private life private and prevent any sordid affairs from becoming public knowledge."

"Yeah? Then Helene probably needs you more than me right now."

"Mm. The staff at Kensington Palace *is* going through a rather brutal restructuring at the moment, but you're a far better long-term prospect. Speaking of," she adds as she pulls a burgundy coatdress from my closet, "His Majesty has decided to go ahead with your and Maisie's scheduled joint appearance today at the Royal London Children's Hospital."

"Really?" I say, still trying to digest the compliment I think is in there. "I thought everything was canceled."

"Yes, well, it seems the monarchy is currently in desperate need of good press, and Doyle believes that you and Maisie are the best bet. She's universally adored, and you provide . . . well, a distraction, shall we say?"

I narrow my eyes. "Is this about the *hunting accident?*"

"If you'd like to call it that. The public will no doubt be relieved to see you whole and well. You *are* whole and well, yes?" she says with something that sounds suspiciously like concern, and she studies me more intently now.

"I probably won't be able to wear strapless or low-cut dresses anymore," I say, pulling aside the collar of my shirt to show her the healing scar. "But that's Louis's problem."

As Tibby takes in the sight of the bullet wound, her throat contracts. "I see," she says quietly. "I was led to believe it was a shoulder injury, but that is . . . very close to . . ."

"Missed by a couple inches," I say, straightening my shirt. "The bullet nicked an artery, so there was a lot of blood, but it didn't hit anything else important. I keep asking if I can have it as a souvenir, but Jenkins ignores me every time I bring it up."

"I will see what I can do," says Tibby a bit shakily, and it might be the lack of sunlight, but her face has a slightly gray cast to it now. "In the meantime, it would be good for . . . for the people to see that you're all right."

"And you think the best way to do that is to send me to a hospital?" I say, and she sniffs.

"*I* didn't arrange it. Fitz did, ages ago, and I'll happily let him take the blame for any perceived blunder."

I finally climb out of bed and carefully start one of the

morning stretches my physical therapist recommended. "This isn't going to steal headlines away from Helene, you know."

"Darling," says Tibby in a dry tone that's much more her usual style, "you and Maisie could walk into the middle of Piccadilly Circus and stab someone, and it still wouldn't steal headlines from Helene right now. But Doyle's desperate."

"Clearly," I say. "And you never know—maybe he'll get lucky, and whoever shot me will try again. That would probably make a few front pages."

As Tibby goes ashen once more, my phone buzzes on the nightstand, and I glance at the screen. This early, I shouldn't have any messages, but there's a single text from an unknown number I don't recognize. And as I open up the conversation, my finger already hovering over the delete icon, I freeze, and every single cell in my body goes cold.

Good luck in London today. I'll be watching.

CHAPTER EIGHTEEN

You are a member of the British royal family.
We are never tired, and we all love hospitals.

—Mary of Teck (1867–1953)

THE CROWD WAITING FOR MAISIE and me in front of the Royal London Children's Hospital is enormous.

It's not just the usual group of fans and photographers. A clamoring mass of tabloid journalists is there, too, held back by a single line of police, and I can hear the questions they hurl at my sister and me as we greet well-wishers behind the metal barricade on the opposite side.

"Mary! Are your parents getting divorced?"

"How do you feel about your mother shagging your uncle?"

"Evangeline! Is it true the affair started after you arrived?"

"Is your mother sleeping with the King?"

"Mary! Do you have anything to say about your father's mistress?"

"Evangeline!"

"Mary!"

"Evangeline!"

"*Mary!*"

The fans aren't much better, with their worried looks and sympathetic words of support—some for Helene, some for us. A few want to know how I'm feeling, and more than one dares to ask Maisie directly about the Switzerland photos. But her dazzling smile never falters, and I follow her lead, not wanting to be the weak link.

At last a frazzled-looking Fitz and a steely Tibby usher us through the front doors, and we're greeted by an official photographer, members of the Royal Rota, and nearly two dozen hospital employees and board members. Doctors, nurses, administrative assistants, charity representatives—their names and positions all blur together, and my face starts to hurt from all the smiling. Maisie is a consummate professional, though, and she more than makes up for what I lack in grace and charm, asking questions, offering compliments, and laughing at every terrible joke. The photographer mercifully spends much more time focusing on her, and I take advantage of his inattention to find my footing.

I start to relax halfway down the line, and my interest is genuine as I ask about the hospital and the role each person plays. It's one of the things I've learned from Maisie over the past six months—my job here isn't to be the center of attention, but to make our hosts feel like the most important people in the world. My sister does it flawlessly, and while I'm still learning, it helps that I feel like I have to earn the welcome that's always given to her.

Finally we reach the end of the line, where the well-dressed head of the hospital charity greets Maisie like she's known her for years. They exchange kisses on the cheeks, and Maisie turns toward me with a flourish.

"And this is my sister, Evangeline," she says warmly. "Evangeline, this is my godmother, Lady Peggy Merrit, director of the Children's Trust."

Suddenly it makes sense that Alexander felt comfortable sending us here, and I take her offered hand. "It's really nice to meet you."

"And you, Evangeline," says Peggy—or Lady Merrit, I suppose, but I'm still stubbornly adverse to titles. "We've all been so very worried about you."

I smile graciously. "I feel great, and I'm honored to have the opportunity to learn more about the incredible things you do here," I say, which is the line Tibby's fed me in case anyone asks about the supposed hunting accident. It's not a lie, exactly, and it swiftly turns the conversation back to our visit.

"We've certainly been looking forward to it," says Peggy. "Come—we have a wonderful tour planned, and the children are so very excited to see you both."

Maisie takes the lead, as she always does, and I end up a step behind. But as we move through the lobby, I spot a collection of flower arrangements lining the front desk, and a chill runs down my spine.

Every single vase is full of blood-red daisies.

In an instant, the eerie text I received this morning makes sense, and a strange buzz hums in my ears, growing louder with each second. Of course it's Ben. Of course he's the one who's watching, who somehow knows exactly where I am and what I'm doing, even though he's hundreds of miles away.

Suddenly I'm acutely aware of the healing wound in my chest, and as my pace starts to slow, Tibby is by my side in an instant, every bit as calm and collected as she always is.

"Are you all right, Miss Bright?" she says, and I nod, even though I'm not really sure.

"The crowd was just . . . a lot," I say quietly as we fall a few steps behind. "And those flowers . . ."

"What about them?" says Tibby, glancing at the bouquets. But if she recognizes them from my appearance at Wimbledon, she says nothing.

"Ben sends them to me," I admit, my voice falling to a whisper. "And I got a weird text this morning that I think—"

"Miss Bright?"

I look up. Peggy has stopped at a pair of double doors, and both she and Maisie—and everyone else tagging along with us—are watching me, concerned.

"I'm sorry," I say with what I know isn't a convincing smile. "I was just admiring the flowers."

Peggy beams. "Oh, aren't they lovely? They arrived from the palace this morning. Just the touch of cheer we needed, wouldn't you say?"

I nod in polite agreement, ignoring the fact that Tibby is now in a hushed conversation with one of the protection officers nearby. "They're beautiful," I say, my mouth dry.

Peggy continues through the double doors, happily chatting away about the opening of the new wing we're touring, and Tibby presses something into my hand—a cold bottle of water.

"Small sips," she says under her breath. "And if you feel like you're about to faint, tell me so we can go somewhere private."

"I'm fine," I whisper, but I sip the water as instructed. The moment I'm done, Tibby steals the bottle back and hides it in her handbag, as if admitting that a member of the royal family can be thirsty is a cardinal sin.

The water helps, and I fall into step beside my sister as Peggy guides us through the wing, introducing us to more members of the staff and showing us the latest technological advances funded by the trust. Even among the bustle of saving lives, the atmosphere is warm and comforting, and everyone seems delighted to see us. It's such an about-face from the crowd outside that my overwrought nervous system finally begins to unclench, and by the time we reach a playroom full of waiting children, I'm sincerely happy to be there.

The kids are lined up to meet us—or at least the older ones are, while the younger ones are too busy with their toys to bother with two strangers in heels. There's a colorful banner stretched across the windows that reads WELCOME PRINCESSES, and it's so damn sweet that I almost feel like one.

Maisie and I read handmade cards, admire drawings, and listen to countless stories from the parents who hover nearby as they tell us all the hospital has done for their children. We split up at one point—Maisie sits at a low table to make paper flowers with a group of chatty kids, while I kneel on the floor in my coatdress to play blocks with a little girl named Elsie. Her mother looks on, a bit misty-eyed, and the official photographer spends an uncomfortable amount of time focused on the three of us. Maybe everything in the lobby was for show, but these moments feel personal.

At last, after more than ten minutes, I hug Elsie and thank her mother for her time. By now my feet are half-asleep, and

I stumble slightly as I stand, using the back of a nearby chair for support. But before I can even right myself, Tibby is there, her arm looped through mine and a fake smile plastered on her face.

"Miss Bright," says Tibby smoothly, "why don't we step out into the hallway for a moment?"

This is definitely not a suggestion, and before I can protest, she starts to lead me forward. I try to dig my heels in without making it obvious, but then Ingrid is there, and between the two of them, I don't stand a chance.

"Really, I'm okay," I insist once we've stepped into the hallway. "My foot fell asleep, that's all."

They both continue to ignore me as Tibby guides me into a nearby room, where a nurse is waiting, clearly on call for exactly this scenario. Ingrid stands guard outside, and I reluctantly sink into a chair, though only because my leg is tingling with pins and needles.

"This is totally unnecessary," I protest as the nurse takes my blood pressure. "Tibby, seriously, I'm fine—"

"Your color is off," says Tibby. "And you looked like you were seconds away from passing out in the lobby. While I expect that might do the trick of commandeering a few headlines from Her Majesty, that is *not* how your father wants it to happen."

"Her Royal Highness's pressure is low, and her skin's a bit clammy," says the nurse apologetically, like this is somehow her fault.

"I'm not a Royal Highness," I say with a sigh. "And I'm sweaty because the playroom was warm. Tibby, come on—I'm *fine,* and people are going to notice that I'm missing."

She sniffs. "If by some miracle Fitz is doing his job, Maisie ought to be handing out plastic tiaras and swords right about now, and I expect that will be enough to distract everyone for a while. *You* need to take a moment."

I grit my teeth, but no matter what I say, I know Tibby won't budge, not when she's convinced I'm one misstep away from collapsing in public. And so, when the nurse leaves us with another bottle of water and some cookies, I nibble on them grudgingly as Tibby checks her phone.

"Those flowers in the lobby," she says without preamble. "What did you mean, Ben sent them?"

"I'm sure it was him," I say, and in between bites, I explain everything—the bouquet and menacing note at Wimbledon, the flowers beside my hospital bed, and even the Christmas gift and Ben's insistence that he never misses.

"The photo album is unnerving, I'll grant you," says Tibby once I'm finished, her expression troubled. "But gerberas aren't exactly a rare flower."

"No, but they're the exact same shade, and it can't be a coincidence. He's trying to get under my skin."

"Clearly it's working." She raises an eyebrow. "And you believe he's doing this for what reason, precisely?"

"I don't know," I say, slumping in my chair. "A warning? A reminder that he's always watching? At Sandringham, he pretended everything was fine, but it isn't, Tibby. I'm the reason he was practically exiled last summer, and he wants revenge. But I don't even know why he did it all in the first place."

Tibby sighs. "Whatever his reasons were, you must remember that he's half a world away—"

"He arrived in Paris this morning," I say, before I can stop myself. Tibby gives me a strange look.

"Very well," she says slowly. "He's in Paris. Which means he isn't here, Evan. He could send an entire field of flowers, and it still wouldn't matter—they can't hurt you."

I shake my head, and my throat tightens as I resist the urge to press my palms to my tearing eyes. "He doesn't need to be here. He wasn't in the room when Jasper attacked me, either, and he was miles away when I was shot, but I'm sure he's behind that, too. Someone tried to kill me, and he just happened to show up the day before? But Alexander refuses to even acknowledge the possibility, and I can't talk to my mom about it, and Kit is supportive, but he isn't convinced, and—I just need someone to *listen* to me."

She takes a slow, steady breath and tucks her phone away. "I am listening, Evan," she says. "And I'm worried. Maybe Ben is behind it all, but it isn't your job to figure it out."

"Who else is going to do it?" I say. "No one believes me. No one's even looking for the person who tried to kill me and Kit—"

"On the contrary, your father has half the Home Office working round the clock to find the shooter," says Tibby.

"But no one's caught them yet. The shooter's wandering around free as a bird, and if they come after us again—"

"What happened at Sandringham was a fluke," says Tibby. "Someone was impossibly lucky, sneaking onto the grounds like they did, and you and Kit were undoubtedly victims of opportunity. Not intended targets. If it had been Maisie out there instead, or Helene . . ."

This has never once occurred to me over the last seventeen

days, and I open and shut my mouth, not sure what to say. "But . . . but what about the date on the photo album? I know there are other explanations, but—what if Ben *was* involved? What if it was all planned, and he tries again?"

Tibby says nothing for a long moment, and she eases down into the chair across from mine. "Where is this coming from, Evan? You were joking about the shooter this morning, and you certainly didn't seem worried then."

"I don't know. I don't *know*." I bury my face in my hands and take a shuddering breath. "Maybe it's the crowds, or—or being out in public again. I didn't think about that part. I didn't think about what it would feel like to be around hundreds of strangers when any one of them might want to kill me."

I feel Tibby's hand on my knee, but I can't make myself look at her. "You've no idea what kind of effort goes into your security, do you?" she says, but for once, there's no judgment in her voice. "You're safe, Evan—as safe as anyone in the world could possibly be. Your father wouldn't have sent you here otherwise. There are snipers on the roof as we speak, and an entire tactical team no more than fifty feet away, ready to set the world on fire to save you and your sister from every threat imaginable. Each room of this hospital has been searched, and everyone inside has been background-checked within an inch of their lives. Millions of pounds every year are spent protecting your family—"

"From other people," I say in a choked voice. "From crowds and overzealous fans who think they know us thanks to some twisted parasocial relationship. But who's supposed to protect us from each other?"

Tibby doesn't seem to have an answer to this, and she watches me with the intensity of someone trying to read between the lines—to see the three-dimensional shape that's hidden in the magic picture.

"I'll speak to Fitz," she says at last. "I think it's time for us to cut this visit short."

"What? *No*," I insist, rising to my feet and hastily wiping my cheeks. "Tibby, I'm fine. Really. And I'm obviously not going to mention any of this to the kids."

"They're not the ones I'm concerned about," she says, and I give her a withering look.

"I'm not bailing. And I know you don't want to be responsible for the rumors that'll inevitably crop up if I do," I say. "I just—I haven't been sleeping well lately, okay? I'm tired, I hate hospitals, the flowers rattled me, and I promise I'll rest when we get back. But we can't leave early—these kids deserve better, and Maisie will never forgive me. You know how she is when she's holding a grudge."

Tibby eyes me for a long moment. "Fair point," she allows reluctantly. "The Maisie bit, that is. And I'd rather not give the press another nasty headline, so you get one more chance, Evan. But if I so much as see you slouch, we're going back to Windsor."

"Deal," I say, and even though my eyes are still brimming with unshed tears, I plaster on my sunniest smile. "Let's go, then, before there aren't any swords and tiaras left to hand out."

After Tibby cleans up my smudged makeup, we spend another hour touring the rest of the facility and visiting patients in their rooms. Tibby watches me like a hawk the entire time, but I refuse to let my Evangeline mask slip, not wanting to give her a single reason to follow through with her threat. And at last, once we've hugged dozens of children, shaken what feels like hundreds of hands, and smiled for countless photos, Peggy escorts Maisie and me back down to the lobby.

As we say our goodbyes, I refuse to look at the flowers lining the front desk. But I can feel them there, like stares burning a hole in the back of my head, and it's a relief when our protection officers usher Maisie and me out the door and into the waiting crowd.

That relief doesn't last long, however. The teeming mass of onlookers is bigger than it was this morning, with so many rows of people packed against the creaking barriers that a wave of claustrophobia threatens to drown me. Even though all I want to do is climb into the Range Rover, Maisie heads straight for the fans eager to catch a glimpse of her, and I follow with an iron fist wrapped around my heart, knowing exactly how it'll look if I don't.

With a smile still glued onto my aching face, I shake hands and accept bouquets—none of which are daisies, thankfully, but there are plenty of deep-red roses. The roar of the crowd grows louder as Maisie and I make our way down the barriers, and anxiety spreads through me like a weed, choking what little composure I have left until I can barely speak. I want to leave—I *need* to leave, but when I glance at my sister, she's still chatting happily with her well-wishers, seemingly oblivious to the unrest around us.

"Miss Bright?" says Tibby, who lingers nearby with an armful of bouquets. I force another smile, afraid of what will happen if I open my mouth, and though she eyes me warily, she doesn't press. Maybe because there are a dozen cameras pointed our way, and a hundred more phones documenting our every move. Or maybe, unlikely as it is, I look more convincing than I think I do. Either way, for the first time that day, I desperately want her to take my arm and march me out of there, appearances be damned. But despite her many talents, even Tibby hasn't yet learned how to read my mind.

We're only ten feet from the SUV when I notice a flash of color in the crowd—a vivid teal. At first I think it must be someone's hat or sweater, but as I pose half-heartedly for a selfie I know Tibby will berate me for, I see it again. And this time, when I look up, he's there—the protester who stood outside the Sandringham gate.

I recognize him instantly. His face is once again covered in a teal scarf, and he has a beanie pulled down over his ears, leaving only his deep-set eyes exposed as he stares at me with the intensity of a predator who's found his prey. Though he's several rows back from the barrier, he elbows his way closer with each passing second, ignoring the protests of those he shoves out of his way.

Despite the frigid January weather, a drop of sweat trickles down my spine. The crowd is seething now, crushed against each other, fighting for enough space to breathe. Hands reach for me, touching my coat and gloves, but my heels are rooted to the pavement, and I can't take my eyes off the man with the scarf.

When he's less than three feet away—so close now that I can make out the ring of gold around his pupils—the sun breaks free of the heavy clouds. And as he pushes aside a woman filming me with her phone, I catch the glint of something metal in his hand, and unadulterated terror strikes me like lightning.

"*Gun!*" I cry as panic erases everything in my mind except the singular need to escape. A chorus of screams pierce the air as I spin away from the crowd, my vision blurred and my breath caught in my throat, but I don't look back.

The car—I have to get to the car.

As I stumble forward on my teetering stilettos, however, an earsplitting *crack* reverberates off the building, and I lose my footing completely. Cries of surprise and pain echo behind me, and I hit the ground hard, my injured shoulder taking the brunt of it.

Agony cuts through me, and for a split second, I think I've been shot again. I gasp, the edges of my vision going black, but when I glance down at the front of my coatdress, there's no sign of a bullet wound—only some slush from the sidewalk.

"*Evan!*"

My sister's scream rises above the commotion, and when I look up, the pathway between me and the hospital entrance has disappeared. Instead, the crowd surges past an overturned barrier, propelled by the crush of bodies behind them as they flood the empty space.

"Maisie!" I shout as I scramble to my feet, pain momentarily forgotten. I've lost sight of the man with the teal scarf, and the thought of him getting anywhere near my sister chills me to the bone. "*Maisie!*"

But before I can dive recklessly into the throng, a pair of arms wrap around me, and Ingrid drags me away from the tangle of human bodies. I fight to break free, but she's incredibly strong, and before I know what's happening, Ingrid shoves me unceremoniously into the back seat of the Range Rover.

I tumble over the soft leather, dazed and panicked and desperate to find Maisie. But by the time I right myself, ready to dash back into the melee, another protection officer bursts through the edge of the crowd—and he's holding my sister in his arms.

"Evan!" she sobs as he lifts her into the car. She's chillingly pale, and a button hangs loose from her lavender coat, but to my relief, she looks mostly unscathed. Ignoring my throbbing shoulder, I throw my good arm around her and hold her tight, and she clings to me like I'm the only thing in the world that can keep her from sinking into oblivion.

"They attacked me," she babbles, her voice too high and tight. "Evan—did you see? The crowd, they came out of nowhere, and—and they were everywhere—"

"I saw," I say, swallowing my own hot fear. Out of the corner of my eye, I notice Tibby and Fitz hastily climb into the vehicle behind ours. "Are you okay? I heard a gunshot, and—"

"Gunshot?" Her wide eyes brim with tears. "Someone had a gun?"

"In the crowd," I say shakily. "The man pushing his way up to me—he had a teal scarf—"

"He wasn't holding a gun, Miss Bright." Ingrid climbs into the passenger seat and pulls her door shut, cutting out the worst of the crowd. "It was a mobile with a metallic case."

"A—what?" I say, stunned. I glance out the window, part of me expecting to see him staring me down like he did outside Sandringham, but a line of police officers stand between us and the crowd now, blocking my view. "Are you sure?"

"Positive," she says, and despite her gruff demeanor, there's a hint of softness in her voice, too. "I had eyes on him the whole time, Miss Bright, I assure you."

"But—the gunshot—" I say as Maisie finally lets me go and digs a tissue out of her purse.

"The sound you heard was the barrier breaking from a surge in the crowd," says Ingrid. "You were never in any danger, Miss Bright."

As I stare at the back of her head, speechless and reeling, Maisie dabs her eyes. "But they attacked me," she insists. "They ran straight for me and knocked me down, and—and I understand them hating Evan, of course, but I'm their future queen. They love me. They *love* me."

Despite her barb, I take her trembling hand in mine as we pull away from the chaotic scene. And though my shoulder continues to protest every tiny move I make, I look out the window once more at the countless faces that watch us go. But I'm only searching for one.

Finally, just as we turn a corner, I see him—the man in the teal scarf. Despite the Range Rover's tinted windows, he's staring straight at us, and in that moment, I know beyond the shadow of a doubt that this won't be the last time we meet.

CHAPTER NINETEEN

Kit

Maisie, I've just seen the news—are you all right? Evan isn't answering my texts.

Maisie?

Maisie, please tell me you're both safe.

Gia

What news? What's happened?

Kit

A barrier broke during their walkabout, and the crowd rushed them.

Gia

What?? Are they safe? Do we know anything?

Kit

Their PPOs got them into the car, but that's all the footage shows. There had to be hundreds of people there.

Rosie

were they attacked??? xx

Kit

I don't know. I'm waiting on them at Windsor now.

Gia

Kit, tell the front gate to expect me. I'm on my way.

—*Text message exchange between Her Royal Highness The Princess Mary, Lady Georgiana Greyville, Lady Primrose Chesterfield-Bishop, and Christopher Abbott-Montgomery, Earl of Clarence, 10 January 2024*

WHILE MAISIE SPENDS OUR ENTIRE drive back to Windsor Castle in tears, babbling nonstop on a phone call to her mother, I don't say a word.

I replay the scene outside the hospital again and again in my mind, trying to figure out what happened, but once my heartbeat slows and the panic seeps from my body, it's obvious.

The surge was my fault. I'm the one who thought I saw a gun, after all—I'm the one who caused the crowd to panic, and I'm the reason the barrier broke. It doesn't matter that my fear was born out of trauma and the very real fact that I almost died seventeen days ago. No excuse will erase that terrifying moment for anyone, least of all myself, and I spend the rest of the ride staring unseeingly out the window, trying not to think about how many people must've been injured in the crush.

When we finally return to Windsor, Alexander is waiting for us with Jenkins at his side, and both look about as bleak as I feel. Maisie goes to our father as soon as her feet are planted on the gravel drive, and he embraces her while she sobs into his shoulder. I turn toward Jenkins, determined to give them some privacy, and he regards me gravely.

"That will never happen again," he says, and I shake my head.

"It was my fault," I say, my voice breaking. "I thought—I thought I saw someone in the crowd with a gun, and . . ."

As I take a shuddering breath, he opens his arms, and I go to him, pressing my cheek against his suit jacket. It wouldn't be the first of his that I've ruined, but even though I'm trembling now, my eyes are dry.

"The barrier broke, and the police were unprepared for the turnout," says Jenkins. "Neither of those things are your fault, darling, and I'm afraid you can't take the blame for this one."

Except I definitely can. "Where's my mom?" I say, hating how small I sound. But as Jenkins starts to reply, I hear hasty footsteps on the gravel.

"I'm right here, sweetheart," she says, and in an instant, she sweeps me into a comforting embrace, and Jenkins steps aside.

The smell of her shampoo floods my already-overwhelmed senses, and as my mom holds me close, I melt into her, inhaling that familiar scent. The maelstrom in my mind finally begins to calm, and I suddenly feel every bit as exhausted as I am.

"You're all right?" she says softly into my hair, and I nod.

"Just tired," I mumble.

"Nothing else for the rest of the day," she says firmly as she rubs my back. At first I relax at her touch, but when she gets a little too close to my shoulder, I wince.

"Are you injured?" says Jenkins, and the alarm in his voice must alert my mother, because she immediately lets me go. I shake my head.

"I fell, but I'm fine. I don't know why Tibby makes me wear

heels," I say, trying to play it off as a joke, but I can't dredge up any humor right now. "The crowd swarmed Maisie. I don't know if they hurt her."

"Dr. Gupta is already waiting," says Alexander, still holding my quaking sister. "Come—let's get you both inside."

My exam is mercifully quick, with the doctor prescribing me nothing more than rest and another round of anti-inflammatories. But Maisie's arms are red and already starting to bruise, and she seems startled when the nurse notices her left wrist is swollen.

"It doesn't hurt," she says, dazed, but when she tries to bend it, she whimpers.

"An X-ray, I think," says Dr. Gupta. And as Maisie dissolves into tears once again, guilt gnaws at me until I can't stand to be here anymore.

While everyone's busy tending to my sister, I slip out of the room and into the corridor, grateful for the cooler air. For a moment, I close my eyes and take a deep breath, trying to push the sounds of Maisie's sobs out of my head, but a familiar voice echoes down the hall.

"Ev?"

When I look up, Kit is hurrying toward me, and his arms are around me before I know what's happening. He's gentle with me—he's always gentle with me—but I still wince into his shirt as he accidentally jostles my shoulder.

"Are you all right?" he says thickly, and with a start, I realize he's been crying.

"I'm okay," I say. I can feel his pulse hammering through his sweater. "It was just—scary, that's all. One of the barriers broke, and I thought . . ."

I trail off. After everything Kit and I've been through together, I can't bring myself to tell him about the gun I thought I saw, or to admit that this was entirely my fault, no matter what Jenkins says. Kit's already terrified, and I can only imagine the scenarios that have been running through his mind since he heard. There's nothing he can do to fix this for me, and in turn, I don't want to make it any worse for him.

And so, even though I hate keeping secrets from him, I swallow my own jagged unease and hug him tighter. I'll tell him once we've both healed, I decide. Once this overwhelming fear doesn't matter anymore, and this is all just a footnote in our history that reminds us how far we've come.

To my relief, Kit doesn't push me for more, and instead he exhales into my hair, his breath warm against my skin. "You weren't answering my texts."

"Tibby has my phone, and she and Fitz were in the other car," I say apologetically. "I should've asked Maisie to let you know everything was okay. I'm sorry."

"Don't be," says Kit. "She wouldn't answer me, either. I was afraid . . ." His Adam's apple bobs.

"She's bruised, and her wrist might be sprained, but I think she's more shaken than anything." I brush my lips against his cheek. "We're both okay, Kit. I swear. Everything's okay."

It takes him a minute to release me, and once he does, I slip my hand into his and lead him back to my apartment. Ingrid trails us as we go, and for once, I'm grateful for her presence.

"Gia and Rosie are on their way here," says Kit as he rubs his swollen eyes. "I should let them know everything's okay."

"I need to change anyway," I say. "Do you want to track them down, and I'll meet you in Maisie's room?"

His frown makes it clear he doesn't want to go anywhere without me right now, but when we reach my door, I stand on my tiptoes and give him a lingering kiss.

"I'm fine, Kit. I promise," I say. "I'll join you in a few minutes, all right? Maybe you could order Maisie something from the kitchen. She was pretty shaken."

"Tea ought to steady her," he agrees, and he kisses me again. "Do you want anything?"

"A peanut butter and jelly—jam—sandwich," I request, even though my appetite is long gone. It gives him something productive to do, though, and I'll eat every sandwich in Windsor if it helps him feel a little less lost.

He sees me into my sitting room before heading off, and as soon as I'm alone, I head into my bedroom and sink down onto the edge of my mattress. For a moment, I stare at the cream carpet, my vision unfocused and my head swimming. But at last, without any conscious thought, I bury my face in my hands and finally let myself cry.

I don't know why the crowd scared me so damn much. I don't know why I'm suddenly afraid of everything outside the castle walls. But even though the broken barrier was an accident, even though the man in the scarf didn't have a gun and I was never in any real danger, every inch of me feels like I've escaped some horrible fate.

Was he the one who shot me and Kit? The thought is so

preposterous that I almost dismiss it immediately, but it's no less possible than the idea that Ben was somehow behind it. The man was at the protest in front of Sandringham, after all, and the fact that he was here today, too . . .

My head is spinning as the adrenaline finally leeches from me, leaving me with limbs that are too heavy and a body that doesn't feel quite right. I take one more deep breath before forcing myself to stand, and then, like I'm going through the motions, I wash the makeup off my face, change into a cozy sweater and leggings, and head back into the corridor.

Ingrid is waiting outside my apartment, and when I open the door, she greets me with a nod. "All right, Miss Bright?"

"Just tired," I mumble, echoing the same reply I gave Jenkins, and I hesitate. "I'm sorry about today. I really thought that man had a gun."

Ingrid regards me for a long moment, her light blue eyes studying me like she's not sure what she'll find. "Years ago, a sniper almost killed me in Afghanistan," she says, and I blink. "It took me a long time before I felt comfortable out in the open again, even after I came home. Our brain exists to try to keep us alive, and it'll take yours a while to realize there isn't a bullet with your name on it lurking around every corner. In the meantime, be kind to yourself. No one blames you for a thing."

I should say something—tell her I'm sorry she went through this, too, or thank her for putting herself in harm's way again just to protect me. But when I open my mouth, no words come out, and a lump forms in my throat.

She doesn't seem to expect a response, but as we make our way down the long gallery toward Maisie's apartment, Ingrid walks a little closer to me than usual, a comforting presence now rather than an unwanted shadow. And when we reach the turn near the dining room, I pause, still a couple doors down from Maisie's.

"Could you do me a favor?" I say, my throat still tight. "Will you ask the other protection officers to keep an eye out for that man in the scarf? He was at the protest outside Sandringham, too, and . . . I don't know. I just have a bad feeling."

"Of course, Miss Bright," she says, and even though I know this is part of her job, I'm absurdly grateful that someone else will be on the lookout for him, too.

As we approach Maisie's suite, I hear the sound of rising voices echoing from inside, and I pause, not entirely sure what to do. But as I'm reaching out to knock, the door opens, and to my surprise, Kit appears.

"There you are," he says softly, and he slides his arm around me. "Gia and Rosie are here, and—"

"—sent you *roses?*"

Gia's incredulous voice rises from somewhere inside the sitting room, and Kit grimaces. "We should—" he begins, but Maisie cuts him off.

"I didn't bloody ask for them. I didn't even know they were coming until they were already here, and what was I supposed to do? Reject them?"

"Are you texting him?" demands Gia.

"I—yes, a little, but only as friends—"

"Does he know about me? Did you tell him you have a girl-friend?"

Silence.

"We should go," Kit says to me, looking distinctly uncomfortable. "Your sandwich should be arriving from the kitchen soon, and I can ask them to deliver it to your room instead—"

"Is that Evan?"

Gia's voice is much closer now, and Kit steps aside to reveal her standing only a few feet inside the door. She's in a purple leotard and sweatpants, with her hair pulled into a tight bun, and it's obvious she came straight from ballet practice.

"Kit and I were just leaving," I say, but Gia steps toward me, her eyes blazing.

"Did you know about this?" she says, and over her shoulder, I see an anguished Maisie standing beside Rosie, who's picking nervously at the end of a single blond curl.

"About the flowers?" I say slowly. "Or the texts?"

"About how she's trying to replace me with a cocky American *boy*," she spits out, and Maisie immediately protests.

"I'm not *replacing* you! Gia, please, be reasonable—"

"I'm being perfectly reasonable," she snaps, though her furious gaze is still fixed on me. "You're accepting flowers—*roses*—from someone who's very clearly interested in you, and you haven't bothered to tell him you've been in a relationship for the past three years."

Rosie gasps. "You've been together that long?" she says in an injured tone, but both Maisie and Gia glare at her, and she falls silent.

"I really don't want to get in the middle of whatever's going on between you," I say, taking half a step back, but Gia closes the distance between us, grabbing my wrist and lowering her face so it's only inches from mine.

"Did you," she says, "or did you *not* know that she's planning on dating that American narcissist in front of the entire world because she's ashamed of me?"

"I'm not ashamed of you!" cries Maisie, her voice thick with tears. "I'm trying to protect you. Gia, please, that's all it is, I swear—"

"You're trying to protect me by pretending I don't exist?" says Gia, finally whirling around to face her again, though her grip on me doesn't loosen. "Even in your world, Maisie, that makes no sense."

"Yes, it does," she says, wiping her eyes as Rosie loops her arm around her. But Maisie slips away, walking toward Gia instead, and Rosie sinks dejectedly onto the sofa. "If they find out about you, they'll hunt you like you're prey. They'll stalk you. They'll dredge up every slightly scandalous thing about you and your family, and they'll turn it all into headlines—"

"Do you think I don't know that?" says Gia incredulously. "Do you think I've spent the past three years keeping my head down and my nose clean because I *like* being invisible? I've turned down modeling jobs, parties, friendships, business partnerships—Maisie, I don't even have a bloody Instagram account because I know what it could mean for you. Everything I *do* is to make sure that when we go public, when you finally pull your head out of your arse and stop feeling so bloody ashamed of something that isn't the least bit shameful at all, the press will have nothing on me. *Nothing.*"

Gia's in tears now, too, and the two of them stand only a few feet apart, but it might as well be a mile. Maisie's hugging herself even though her left wrist is wrapped in a bandage, and her pale face is splotchy, her lips parted in disbelief.

"It doesn't matter," she says brittlely. "They'll find something anyway, or they'll make it all up. Or—or they'll go after you because you're Black, or because your mother's Kenyan, or because you're stunningly beautiful and people will always be jealous of you—"

"I don't care," says Gia. "Don't you see? I don't care about any of that as long as I have you. I know the risks. I've seen what you and your family have to go through, I've seen how the press tortures you all, and I know what I'm getting into, Maisie. And it's worth it—every last bit of it—as long as it means getting to be by your side."

I try to ease my arm out of her grip, painfully aware that this should be a private conversation, but Gia's fingers tighten around me, and I still.

"I want you by my side more than anything," says my sister tearfully. "But I have a duty to my country and the crown—"

"Sod the bloody crown," spits Gia. "I didn't fall in love with a tiara. I fell in love with *you*. What's it all worth if you're not allowed to be happy?"

Maisie's lips are white, and she's shaking again. "You know I don't have a choice. I'm the only person who can stop Ben from inheriting the throne, and if the public turns on me—"

"There's no bloody reason you can't have both me and everything you've spent your life working toward," says Gia, and there's a hint of desperation in her voice now. "All you have to do is take a chance, Maisie. All you have to do is trust that it'll all work out, and it *will*. I'm not saying it'll be perfect, and I'm not saying that it'll be a fairy tale every step of the way, but whatever the world throws at us, we can face it together. Doesn't that sound better than a lifetime of lies and misery with Mr. America and those hideous roses?"

Maisie wipes her eyes with her uninjured hand. "I want that more than anything in the world," she manages. "But the press will destroy you—"

At last Gia drops my wrist, and she moves toward Maisie, towering over her even without her heels. "Let them try," she says in a dangerous voice. "It's worth it to me—every last risk, every last consequence. I know what I want, and it's you. But you're the one who needs to decide what *you* want."

"I want a life with you," she says in a tiny voice. "You know I do. But it's not that simple—it'll never be that simple."

"Of course it won't be," says Gia. "But that doesn't mean it isn't worth fighting for."

"I—of course, but—" begins Maisie, but Gia shakes her head and takes a step back, seeming to lose her last thread of patience.

"I don't care what you are or who you're going to be," she says, her tone ripe with heartbreak and disgust. "If you keep playing these games, one day, you'll finally look up, and you'll realize you've lost me for good."

Without another word, Gia slips past me and Kit and out the door, disappearing down the corridor as Maisie breaks down into gut-wrenching sobs.

CHAPTER TWENTY

We at the *Regal Record* can exclusively report that Princess Mary is under the care of the royal physician after a barrier broke outside Royal London Children's Hospital shortly after noon, causing a crowd surge that swarmed the heir to the throne.

The frightening incident was caught live by BBC World News, with footage showing Her Royal Highness and Evangeline Bright being ushered to safety after greeting fans outside the hospital, where they had spent the morning supporting the Children's Trust. Even though the event was thought to be cancelled, the crowd that gathered to meet the royal sisters was reported to be in the hundreds—not exactly surprising, considering the bombshell photos that were posted by the *Daily Sun* exposing the affair between Queen Helene and Prince Nicholas. One must wonder why His Majesty, in all his wisdom, sent his daughters out into the chaos like lambs to the slaughter, particularly when their security was clearly unprepared to handle the size and scope of the crowd.

While Evangeline is reportedly unharmed, Her Royal Highness was swept up in the surge, causing significant bruising and a sprained wrist. Royal insiders have revealed that Mary is resting comfortably at Windsor Castle, and we wish our brave little princess a speedy recovery.

—*The Regal Record,* 10 January 2024

MAISIE IS INCONSOLABLE.

I try for a while, but there's nothing I can say—nothing anyone except Gia can say—that will offer her any comfort. She sobs until she has no tears left, and Rosie, Kit, and I spend the rest of the day with her in her suite, alternating between listening to her rant, assuring her that she's not a terrible person, and discreetly picking up the trail of used tissues in her wake.

Rosie leaves after dinner, and Maisie ends up falling asleep with her head in my lap in the middle of some insipid vampire movie, but I don't have the heart to wake her. Instead, Kit drapes a pair of blankets over us, and even though I know I'll be sore tomorrow, I lean my head against the back of the sofa, close my eyes, and do my best to convince myself that no one will try to kill any of us in the morning.

I don't remember my dreams that night, but when I jolt awake shortly before sunrise, I have the vague sense of having just escaped something terrible. It takes me a moment to realize where I am, and I glance around the darkness as I try to calm my racing heart. Maisie has migrated from the sofa to the nest of pillows Kit's created in the middle of her sitting room, and they're lying with their feet inches from the other's face, in a way that feels so casually familiar that I'm sure this isn't the first family sleepover they—and likely Ben—have had.

Tap tap tap.

"Your Royal Highness?"

To my surprise, it isn't a member of the household staff or even Fitz who cracks open Maisie's door. Instead, as warm lamplight filters into the sitting room, I see Tibby standing in the doorway, hovering like she isn't sure whether she's allowed inside.

"Still asleep," I mumble, and Tibby breathes a sharp sigh of relief.

"*There* you are. I've been looking all over for you."

I sit up and run my fingers through my hair. It's sticking

up in every direction thanks to the hair spray my stylist used yesterday, and I make a face. "Maisie had a rough night. What time is it?"

"Nearly eight o'clock," she says softly. "His Majesty wishes to see you."

"Everything all right?" says Kit from his spot on the floor, and when I glance down, his eyes are open, though he hasn't moved. Maisie, mercifully, is still fast asleep.

"I couldn't say," says Tibby. "All Jenkins told me is that the King and Evan's mother have requested that she join them for breakfast."

"What about Maisie?" I say, slowly stretching my sore shoulder. It's better than it was last night, but the ache is still persistent.

"I believe it would be best to let Her Royal Highness sleep," says Tibby pointedly. And considering my sister's puffy face and the dark shadows beneath her eyes, I can't disagree.

After I leave a note for Maisie beside her phone, Kit and I extract ourselves from her sitting room, careful not to wake her. He ducks into his suite while I head into mine to shower and get dressed, and twenty minutes later, we're walking down the long gallery together, toward the private dining room.

"Any idea what this is about?" I say, and Kit shakes his head.

"Maybe just a family breakfast."

"Maybe," I echo, but considering everything that happened yesterday, I'm not convinced. And with each step we take, my anxiety grows, until I'm absolutely sure that whatever this is, it isn't good.

Alexander and my mother are waiting for us in the private

dining room, and immediately I notice that it's just us—there are no footmen lingering nearby, no kitchen staff bustling through the door with fresh dishes for the buffet, and I have to fight the urge to turn around and walk right back out.

"Good morning, Evie," says my mom, and she joins me and kisses my hair. "How do you feel?"

"Sore," I admit, gingerly flexing my shoulder. "We stayed the night with Maisie."

"How is she?" says Alexander from where he stands near the dining table. The smell of eggs and sausage and pancakes permeates the air, but my stomach only turns.

"Not great. Relationship stuff," I add as he frowns. "You should ask her."

Alexander nods grimly, but when I move to the buffet with my mom, I notice Kit is still lingering near the entrance.

"Should I . . . ?" he says, his hands behind his back and his body angled toward the door.

"If you wouldn't mind excusing us—" my father begins, but my mother cuts him off.

"Stay," she insists, beckoning for him. "There's plenty for everyone."

"Laura," says my father, but she gives him a look.

"He should be here for this," she insists, and though Alexander purses his lips, he doesn't argue. And while Kit looks about as nervous as I feel, he doesn't protest, either.

With my fear that this isn't a normal breakfast confirmed, my throat is tight, and all I get from the buffet is a cup of black coffee that's too bitter for me to enjoy. We stick to small talk until we're all seated at the table, with Kit beside me and my parents across from us, and as I study them both, I realize they look like they're bracing themselves for a fight. Terrific.

"What's going on?" I say, my stomach doing somersaults, and though my mother picks nervously at the dried paint on her nails, her gaze doesn't leave mine.

"We have something we'd like to speak to you about, Evie. Something important."

Instantly my exhaustion evaporates, and I glare at Alexander. "We talked about this."

He turns pink. "This isn't that, darling," he reassures me. "Nothing's changed between your mother and me. We simply . . ."

"We'd like to take you back to Virginia," says my mom. "For the time being, until everything settles down."

Despite all the possibilities running rampant through my mind, this one didn't even occur to me. "What?" I say. "Why?"

My mother glances at Alexander, but she doesn't wait for him to explain. "After everything that happened at Sandringham, and then yesterday, with the crowd surge . . . it isn't safe for you here," she says. "Not until we know who was behind the shooting."

"I already know who was behind the shooting," I protest. "Ben. Why isn't anyone looking into him?"

"Evie . . ." My mom presses her hands together, and I think I see her fingers twitch. "Tibby told us about your suspicions, and how they've been affecting you."

I grit my teeth. Of course she did. "That's no reason—"

"And if Ben is harassing you, then that's certainly something I can address with security," says my father, as if I haven't spoken.

"But your mother's right. It would be safer for you in the States for a little while."

"Safer how?" I argue. "Tibby made it clear that you're taking every precaution during our appearances, and the castle has armed guards surrounding it at all times. Unless you've significantly upped the security at my mom's house, I'll always be safer here."

My mom hesitates. "It isn't just about your physical safety, sweetheart. The incident outside the hospital—"

"That was an accident," I say. "The barrier broke, Mom. No one did it on purpose."

Alexander clears his throat. "Your protection officer mentioned that you thought you saw a man with a gun."

Beside me, Kit stiffens, and any warmth I feel toward Ingrid instantly evaporates. "I was wrong," I say. "Ingrid's positive he was only holding his phone."

"Yes, but . . ." My mom stares at a spot somewhere behind me, her gaze unfocused. "We're worried about you, Evie. What happened to you at Sandringham . . . it would rattle anyone. You need time to recover properly, and you won't have that here."

I open my mouth, but nothing comes out. They're not talking about physical recovery, I realize. They're talking about my mental health.

"I'm not going," I say flatly. "Maisie's falling apart, and she needs me."

"*You* need rest and recuperation—" begins Alexander, but I cut him off.

"Then I'll do that here," I say. "I'll even go to therapy if you insist. But I'm not leaving."

Kit takes my hand below the table, and I look at him, the edge of my anger melting away. He looks . . . hollow, I think. Deeply, utterly, bone-wearily wrung out, exhausted, and just— sad. It's so startling that I don't know what to say, or even what to think.

"They're right," he says, so quietly I can barely hear him. "The past seven months have been extraordinarily difficult, and you weren't given the proper time or space to come to terms with it. After what Jasper and Ben did to you, and after what happened at Sandringham . . ."

"I've spent almost three weeks up to my eyeballs in TV shows and movies and books and music with you," I say, my voice breaking slightly. "That's plenty of time. I'm fine, really—"

"I don't think you are," he says, sandwiching my hand between both of his now. "I'll go with you, if you'd like. You can show me where you grew up, and we'll go for walks in the park and order from your favorite restaurants, and we'll just . . . relax."

"But you have to go back to university," I say, and he shrugs.

"I can put it off. It won't be the end of the world. What will be the end of the world, though, is if something happens to you because of—all this." He gestures around the room, but he's not just talking about Windsor Castle. He's talking about everything. "Please, Evan. Consider it."

I swallow convulsively, my eyes growing hot with tears of frustration. "How long do you want to banish me?" I say acidly to my parents.

Alexander clasps his hands together so tightly that his knuckles are white. "We wouldn't be banishing you, sweetheart. You'd be welcome back anytime you'd like, and—"

"At least a few months," says my mother softly. "Maybe more."

I exhale sharply. Not days or weeks, but *months*. "Why can't I start therapy here? And if things get worse, maybe then—"

There's a knock on the door, and Alexander scowls. But before he can send whoever it is away, the door to the private dining room opens, and Jenkins steps inside. He's pale and his expression is drawn, and for one horrible moment, I'm sure something devastating has happened.

I'm not alone, and Alexander's anger seems to die in his throat. "Jenkins? What's going on?" he says, his hand finding my mother's.

"I beg your pardon for interrupting, Your Majesty," says Jenkins with a bow of his head. "But I fear this couldn't wait. I've just received word from Doyle—it seems Her Majesty recorded an interview with Katharine O'Donnell late last week, and as a courtesy, the BBC has let us know it will be airing tonight."

"An interview?" says Alexander, confusion muddling the worry on his face. "What sort?"

Jenkins hesitates. "While my source was not especially forthcoming, it seems Her Majesty has taken it upon herself to . . . disclose private information regarding her affair," he says. "And yours."

Instantly Alexander's expression darkens. "Of bloody course she did. Do we know how bad it is?"

"I fear it doesn't look good, sir," says Jenkins. "We're trying to negotiate a delay, especially in the aftermath of the incident with Miss Bright and Her Royal Highness yesterday, but I'm afraid the head of the BBC is refusing to reschedule. Or allow us access to the interview before it airs."

Jenkins crosses the room now, and he wordlessly offers my father a tablet. Alexander accepts it with some reluctance, and I stand, my fury at my parents' so-called intervention temporarily pushed aside as I lean over to get a better view.

Jenkins has already queued up a video, and when Alexander hits Play, Helene's face fills the screen, her makeup plain, her hair down, and her blue eyes brimming with tears.

". . . spent the best years of my life loving him," she says in her honeyed voice, soft and sweet and devastating. "But now that I know the real truth of it, I know it was all a lie."

Her face fades, and then, in big block letters, words appear.

HELENE—HER TRUTH, HER LOVE, AND HER GILDED CAGE

CHAPTER TWENTY-ONE

"Your Majesty, we have all watched with shock and awe over the past seven months as the private affairs of your family—of the royal family—have been exposed in a way that the country has never seen before."

"It's been devastating. Not just the emotional turmoil, but also that it's played out in such a terribly public way."

"It all started, didn't it, with the arrival of Evangeline Bright?"

"No. That marks the time when the public finally found out, but this particular storm has been brewing for longer than anyone knows."

"When would you say it all began?"

"During His Majesty's first year at Oxford, I suppose. That's when he met Laura Bright."

"They knew each other at university?"

"Oh, yes. My husband likes to call it love at first sight, and they were together quite a while—years, really. They were even engaged at one point, in the months before Alexander ascended the throne."

"Yet the public never knew?"

"It was easier in those days to keep secrets, before the invention of smartphones and social media. There were paparazzi, of course, but the intense focus on the family that exists now simply wasn't there in the nineties and early aughts."

"One might argue that that intensity exists because of you and your incomparable popularity after your marriage to His Majesty in 2003."

"Yes, so I've been told. But before Edward IX died so tragically and at such a young age, the royal gears turned rather like clockwork. The media didn't scrutinize the family's every move, and Alexander and Laura took advantage. She was even a guest at Sandringham the Christmas before Edward IX passed—as Alexander's fiancée."

"Yet the public was never told that the then-heir to the throne, the Prince of Wales, was set to be married?"

"No. I believe his intention was to quietly remove himself from the line of succession before the marriage took place."

[pause] "His Majesty wished to abdicate?"

"Laura had no desire to be queen—it's a job that comes with a great many responsibilities, after all, and they both anticipated pushback from an American assuming the role. Which I always thought was a rather silly excuse, considering Mary of Teck, who became queen in 1910, was the first royal consort to be born in England since Henry VIII's sixth wife, Catherine Parr."

"You don't believe that was the real reason His Majesty planned to give up his birthright?"

"It played a part, no doubt, but he never wanted the crown in the first place—it was only the tragedy of his father's death that made him set aside his own desires and accept the throne. He was never happy about it, though. He made that clear when we were discussing the possibility of becoming engaged. Alexander had a particular need to make sure I was willing to take on the duties that he so strongly resented—duties that, by then, had lost him the woman he called the love of his life."

"Did you know about Laura during your engagement?"

"In a sense. I knew he'd been in a relationship when his father died, and I knew that relationship had fallen apart because of it. He was forthcoming about that much, and I've known the royal family for my entire life—our mothers were close friends, after all, and I've been privy to a great many secrets over the years. I was aware he'd been away in America with a girlfriend, even though I didn't know the details."

"Would you have married him if you'd known he was still in love with her?"

[pause] "No. Looking back on it, I was very much hoodwinked, though I had no idea until more than a year into our marriage."

"When did you find out that they had rekindled their relationship?"

"The day I discovered I was pregnant. It was a tragedy, really, the way it played out—for all of us. I was over the moon about the baby, of course—Alexander and I had been trying for an heir since our wedding, and by then, I was starting to worry that perhaps something was wrong with me. He'd grown a bit distant, and I thought it was my fault. He had a great deal of pressure on him, after all, being King at such a young age, and my inability to give him an heir . . . well, I was convinced I was only making things worse."

"What happened that day?"

"I was pleased and relieved—and frightened, admittedly. We were still young, but I loved him so very much. All I wanted was to make him happy." [pause] "I took the test that morning, and it was that evening that he . . . he asked to speak with me alone. He'd been out all day—working, I thought—but . . . that was when he told me he was still in love with her. With Laura. And that they'd been seeing each other again for months by that point, and she . . ." [pause] "She was pregnant. And he wanted to abdicate to be with her and their child. It was the most devastating moment of my life."

"And that was when you told him about Princess Mary?"

[nods] "As I said, it was a tragedy for us all. He finally had a chance at the happiness he so desperately wanted with Laura, but when I told him I was

pregnant, too . . . well, that changed things, didn't it? He couldn't leave me then, not when it also meant leaving his heir. And I couldn't let him go. We'll both have to live with that moment for the rest of our lives, and I don't think either of us will ever fully recover."

"Did you love His Majesty when you married him?"

"Yes. I think so. As much as I could, given we didn't know each other very well."

"And did he love you?"

"He was fond of me, and I truly believe that he very much wanted to love me and had convinced himself that he would, in time. I was so certain that our love would grow, too, and it did—for me. I spent the best years of my life loving him. But now that I know the real truth of it, I know it was all a lie. Not just for me, though. Alexander also lied to himself, and we've both had to live with the consequences."

"And what were those consequences?"

"For him, a double life—a mirror life he could never truly have. A child—a daughter, Evangeline—he could only watch from a distance. They did meet a number of times when she was very young. Alexander and Laura spent some holidays together, playing family, but in the end, he always came home to me and Mary. And I could see it eating away at him, bit by bit, right before my eyes."

"And for you?"

"Well, that's rather obvious, isn't it? I had the love of the people, the love of my country, but never the love of my husband. And it's a very difficult thing, not being loved by the person who ought to love you most."

"Do you resent him?"

"No. How could I? Even to this day, I still love him—and in a way, he does love me, but it's not the kind of love I needed, then or now. It wasn't his fault, though. His father died, and everything rather snow-balled from there."

"Do you believe that your lives would've been different if Edward IX had lived longer?"

"Certainly. If he had, Nicholas would've been old enough to take the throne instead. That was what Alexander was waiting for—time to prepare his brother, the spare, for the role of the heir instead. Alexander has made many mistakes, but he's always put his family first. He would've never walked away without being certain that Nicholas was ready to lead the institution—the country and Commonwealth—without him."

"During the time after Princess Mary was born, when you knew Alexander was leading a double life . . . did that draw you and the Duke of York closer together?"

"No. By then, he had his own wife and son, and he was far too busy with his military career to bother with me. Don't get me wrong—he was considerate, of course. He checked in on me occasionally, as did all members of the family who knew about Laura and Evangeline. But we didn't grow closer until recently."

"When Evangeline joined the family?"

"Yes. By then, my marriage was over—had been over for years. Alexander and I are still friends. We'll always be friends, and we both take our duties to our country very seriously. But we decided many years ago that when our daughter turned eighteen, we would quietly separate. And we did."

"And is that when you and the Duke of York started seeing one another?"

"Yes. The stress of having Evangeline at Windsor Castle . . . well, it's no secret she struggled for several weeks after she arrived, between her identity being leaked and all that the Cunningham boy did to her. As a family, we were there for her, of course, but . . . it was difficult for us all, facing our new reality while the public sifted through the intimate details of our lives."

"How did your relationship with Prince Nicholas begin?"

"Innocently. Reluctantly. We both love Alexander, and neither of us wanted to hurt him. But he's known from the beginning, and he's been very supportive of us—very supportive of our happiness, as Nicholas and I've been supportive of his renewed relationship with Laura."

"The rumours are true, then?"

"Of Alexander and Laura being together again? Yes, I'd say so. She joined us at Sandringham for Christmas, and in truth, I've never seen Alexander happier. It's as if the weight of the past twenty years has gone."

"Do you resent her?"

[soft laughter] "Well . . . no, not really, though I've certainly had some difficult days. I think she made some poor choices, as did Alexander—choices that are ultimately inexcusable. But she's also faced a great deal of hardship in her life, and in the end, I'm truly happy to see her overcome it all. I'm truly happy for them both."

"Do you believe that one day, you and His Majesty will divorce?"

"No. As I've said, we've always taken our duties seriously, and in this family . . . in this institution, happiness always comes second to the crown. Sometimes third or fourth, and occasionally it isn't a consideration at all. We both know that, and we've both accepted it. And I expect—I hope, rather—that we've both found the relationships that will see us to our graves, but our friendship and partnership haven't diminished."

"What would you say to those who might feel . . . uncomfortable with knowing that the head of the Church of England is living such an . . . unconventional lifestyle?"

"I would say to them that we have both—that we have all made the best of what has been an unbearable and suffocating situation for the past two decades, and that I hope a loving and compassionate God would understand. And that the good people of the United Kingdom will, too. Our past mistakes, and what we do now in our private lives, will never affect our love and our devotion to this country."

"And Princess Mary? How do you believe this will affect her?"

"We've never lied to her about the situation, and I rather think she's relieved. While it may seem like we're setting a poor example for her in the present, I believe the poor example was set during those first eighteen years of her life. She's only now had the opportunity to see both her parents truly content, and that, I feel, will only make her a better queen when the time comes for her to take the throne."

"Do you have any regrets?"

[pause] "I regret it all. But time only goes one way, and no matter who we are or what lives we lead, the only thing we can really hope for is the chance to find our happiness any way we can."

—Excerpt from Katharine O'Donnell's interview with Her Majesty Queen Helene, 11 January 2024

AS THE HOUR-LONG INTERVIEW ENDS, the lights in the Windsor Castle conference room go up, and every single one of my father's advisers looks utterly shell-shocked.

None of it was new information to me, or at least nothing so significant that I'm speechless. But the fact that Helene has said it—openly, willingly, and in front of the entire world—is jaw-dropping. Alexander is completely still at the head of the table, while my mom, who sits to his right and my left, has tears in her eyes. Maisie's on his other side, so pale that she seems ill, and Kit's hand is on my good shoulder, gently massaging the tension from my neck.

"How did we not know about this?" says Alexander as the screen that descended from the ceiling slowly retracts with a faint whir. He's holding my mother's hand beneath the table, and Jenkins, who stands behind us, silently offers her a tissue.

Doyle, the royal press secretary, clears his throat. "It seems that part of Her Majesty's agreement with the BBC included keeping us in the dark until the day the interview aired," he admits. "Sir, if I may, we'll need to issue a statement—"

"More than a statement," says the dark-haired woman sitting beside him. Yara, whose title I still don't actually know, but she's the only person who ever challenges Doyle. "The claims Her Majesty has made could be extraordinarily damaging to the monarchy, and the sooner we refute them—"

"The problem is," says Alexander, "they're all true."

Silence. Several advisers glance between one another, clearly not knowing what to say, while Doyle sputters indignantly. But I shake my head.

"They're not, though," I say, looking at Alexander. "The timeline's wrong. Her affair with Nicholas started before—"

"A trivial detail," says Alexander quietly. "And if we go after her for it, it will come off as a personal attack when, arguably, Helene went out of her way to make it clear that no single one of us is at fault for what happened."

"Your Majesty," says Yara carefully, "if we're able to point out one inconsistency, then that would throw her entire interview into question—"

"And how do we prove that the timeline is wrong?" says Alexander. "More photographs? Personal testimony from the staff? Whispers from courtiers? I will not wage a war in the media against Her Majesty. Not when there's nothing to be gained from it, and so very much that we could lose."

"Sir, if we do nothing to contain the situation, we already stand to lose a great deal," argues Doyle. "The people expect the royal family to uphold the values of the Church, to offer consistency and stability when the country is in turmoil—"

"We certainly haven't been living up to our side of the bargain lately, have we?" says Alexander wearily. "But perhaps this is the moment we need to get back on track. Ripping off the plaster, so to speak."

"Sir," says Doyle, appalled. "You cannot possibly suggest that this could be *good* for the country."

"No," says Alexander, a hint of steel in his voice now. "I expect we're in for a rather bumpy ride. But the fact remains that Helene's spoken the truth—in far more detail than we would've liked, admittedly, but it *is* still the truth. She did not demonize me, she did not demonize Laura, and in the end, all she was trying to do was exonerate herself from the claims that the media has been making against her—and I certainly can't blame her for that."

The throng of advisers and senior staff members exchange yet another round of baffled glances, and for a long moment, no one seems to know what to say.

"What would Your Majesty prefer we do, then?" says Jenkins at last, as cool and levelheaded as always. "If you do not wish to speak out against Her Majesty or condemn the interview, then it will be accepted by the public as fact. Which will come with consequences we cannot predict."

"I am aware," says Alexander. "But they are consequences we must live with regardless."

"And the consequences that will be directed toward Ms.

Bright and Evangeline?" says Jenkins, and only now does Alexander's resolve seem to waver.

My mother sits up a little straighter, still holding his hand. "I've known the risks from the start," she says. "I knew it would be bad if we were caught, and we were—when Evangeline's identity was revealed. What Helene's interview gives us is context. It lets the world know that Alexander and I have been together for a very long time, and that Evangeline isn't . . ."

"The bastard product of a one-night stand?" I supply, and amidst the soft gasps from around the room, my mother's lips thin.

"Helene has cleared the air around a lot of things that Alexander and I were never going to be able to address on our own. Things I know have been bothering you," she adds as she looks at my father.

He nods, his throat working for a moment. "Yes," he finally manages. "Helene did not have to be kind or compassionate, but she was. And in the process, she offered us an opportunity—one I would very much like to take."

"And what opportunity is that, sir?" says Yara, unable—or maybe unwilling—to hide her skepticism.

"The opportunity for us all to have what we want," he says. "Myself, Helene, Laura—even my brother. We will continue to serve the country as we always have, without feeding into this situation or making it worse. I will speak with Her Majesty, and we will find a way to put forth a united front."

My fingers curl around the cuff of my sweater. I know what *a united front* means, and I don't like it. "It doesn't exactly sound like she's willing to play nice right now," I mutter.

"Perhaps when she knows there will be no retaliation, she may be more open to having that discussion," says Alexander, but even he doesn't sound convinced.

Doyle scowls. "Sir, with all due respect, burying our heads in the sand won't stop the media—and the people, for that matter—from turning this into a circus. We'll be lucky if it doesn't start a riot—"

"We will let it play out as it will," he says. "If it gets out of hand, then we'll reassess our strategy. But as it stands, there is nothing in the interview to refute, and Laura is right. It offers the people context that she and I would never have been able to publicly divulge. Perhaps this will, in the end, be a blessing to us all."

That doesn't seem likely, and as I glance around at the averted gazes and shuffling papers, it's clear no one else agrees with Alexander, either.

"We should, at the very least, cancel your upcoming appearances," says Yara, turning to what must be Alexander's schedule. "The Modern Music Museum opening tomorrow, the veterans' lunch next week—"

"No," says Alexander softly, though his voice still carries around the table. "Business as usual, Yara. I insist."

Her mouth opens and shuts several times. "Sir, we are on the precipice of a crisis—"

"We have been in crisis for months," he points out. "This is merely another chapter. Should there be security concerns, then I will certainly reconsider the matter. But unless there are any valid objections, I will continue my public duties."

Jenkins grimaces. "Sir, I understand the desire to maintain

status quo in the face of something that we are all still . . . processing. But without any official rebuttal, I must very strongly advise against it, at least until we have a better idea of what the fallout will be."

"And you know I value your opinion greatly, Jenkins," says my father. "But I will not hide from my people. Or my past."

"Can't we have it both ways?" I say before I even realize the thought's formed in my head. All eyes turn toward me, and I try to keep my expression neutral. "I mean—Alexander can stick to his duties, but we can also find a way to send a message to the public, too."

"What sort of message?" says Alexander, and I shrug.

"That we support you, I guess. That's what this is about, right? Who has more support? It wouldn't mean much coming from me, all things considered, but—"

"It would mean something coming from me," says Maisie. They're the first words she's spoken since the interview aired, and even though her hands are clasped together, I notice a slight tremor.

"It might mean something from me, too," says Kit quietly from behind me.

Faint amusement flickers across the deep shadows on Maisie's face. "Mummy may be your aunt, Kit, but we all know where *your* loyalties lie," she says, glancing suggestively at me.

"It's not a bad idea, Evangeline," says Jenkins as I narrow my eyes at my sister. "A display of unity, particularly from Her Royal Highness and Lord Clarence, might quell any rumors of a fracture within the family, and perhaps take the teeth out of the worst of Her Majesty's revelations."

"We could go with Alexander to the museum," I offer. "It sounds interesting anyway."

"No," says my father firmly. "You girls need your rest. It was a mistake sending you yesterday, and I won't compromise your safety."

"What happened at the hospital was an accident," I say, exasperated. "And this is important. If you won't issue a statement, then the best thing we can do for you—for the monarchy—is to show a united front."

"Evangeline is right, sir," grunts Doyle from his spot a few seats down, and I'm so surprised that I do a double take. "If she, Her Royal Highness, and Lord Clarence wish to support you publicly, then I can think of no better way for them to do so. It would certainly be the most efficient and effective way to signal the royal family's stability in the face of such . . . public uncertainty."

But even though Maisie nods in mute agreement, she pales and pulls her hands into her lap. I frown.

"Maybe Maisie shouldn't go," I say. "Not with her wrist wrapped up like that."

"I'm fine," she insists, but nothing about the way she looks or sounds supports this particular claim.

"You were nearly trampled yesterday, and you look like death warmed over," I say. Not to mention the emotional turmoil from her fight—and potential breakup—with Gia. "You really do need to rest."

"I agree," says Alexander before my sister can continue to argue. "It wouldn't do any good to bring you along, darling, not while you're injured. And without Mary, there's little point to Evangeline and Kit joining me—"

"Of course there's still a point," I protest. "I know I'm not Maisie, but I'm still your daughter, and I can support you. And Kit—"

"—is still an Abbott-Montgomery," says Doyle brusquely. "Despite his relationship with Evangeline, the press will expect him to side with Her Majesty. To show the three of you together, perhaps a few friendly moments between you and Lord Clarence . . ."

Alexander clenches his jaw, clearly unhappy about how this conversation is turning out. But he's the one who wants to carry on like nothing is happening.

"And we can all take a picture together tomorrow at breakfast, before the three of you head out," says Maisie, who sounds considerably more optimistic now that crowds aren't involved on her end. "I'll post it on Instagram with a suitably supportive caption—without mentioning Mummy's interview, of course—and everyone will see that you're wearing the same outfits from your appearance, so they'll all know it was taken that morning."

Our father shakes his head. "I'm afraid I must insist on going alone. The crowds tomorrow—"

"We'll skip the walkabout," I say. "But I *am* coming. If you don't want me there, then cancel the appearance, but those are your only options."

He scowls. "I am still your king—"

"You're also my dad," I snap. "And I'm not letting you go out there on your own tomorrow. If you do, you'll just be giving Helene and the media exactly what they want, and you know it."

Alexander and I stare at each other for a long moment—too long, probably, considering more than two dozen people are now gawking at us—and it's only when he straightens in his seat, clearly about to issue some kind of command, that I cut him off.

"I'll do it," I say quickly. "That—trip we talked about at breakfast. I'll do it, no argument, for a minimum of three months and a maximum of six. But only if you let me do this for you."

This seems to instantly take the wind out of his sails, and he glances at my mother, as if asking for her opinion. Or maybe her help.

"It's one appearance," she says quietly. "An hour or two at the most, and then Doyle will have his rebuttal, and you'll have your dignity and the public support of your family. And Evangeline . . ."

She trails off, but I know what she isn't saying. I'll have the break they think I so desperately need. I'll be out of this mess long enough to recover, and maybe, by the time my parents let me come home, this will all be sorted out. Or at least the rancor will have died down.

And maybe, just maybe, someone will finally believe me about Ben.

Alexander exhales. "Very well," he says at last. "One appearance as a family, and then we will carry on as we were before this abominable interview ever happened. Do we have a deal?"

"We have a deal," I say, and even though I'm the one now facing up to six months in purgatory, I still feel like I've won.

CHAPTER TWENTY-TWO

Nat4leele: Alexander's been seeing that American slag for TWENTY FIVE YEARS??? How did we never find out?? DIVORCE HIS ARSE.
gemino604: wait—so QH just put up with it all that time? girl. take that royal money and RUN.
MarciOSurley: The Queen is right, this is a tragedy. I hope they all find peace, happiness, and love.
guardenia93: I can't be the only person who thinks she and Nick make a super hot couple. Like, yeah, it's sad that she and the king didn't work out, but what an upgrade. Rooting for them. #royalwedding2025
AshPecla: What kind of person shags their husband's brother? Disgusting.
GRANdeVENtie3: yawn. rich people cheating on each other and being miserable. who cares.
yeetherish: Why are we deifying these inbred adulterers? Cancel the whole lot. They're nothing more than worthless grifters who've been living off the people for far too bloody long. Britain deserves better.
DutchessDame: time to bring back the guillotine. #offwithherhead

—The comments section of "Heartbroken Queen Regrets All," *The Daily Sun,* 12 January 2024

I BARELY SLEEP THAT NIGHT, and when I do, it's only to wake with a start, drenched in sweat, the last fragments of my nightmares already gone.

At first I can't figure out why. I was fine on Maisie's couch, after all, hours after the barrier broke in front of the hospital. But

I didn't know then that I'd be facing another crowd so soon—an angry crowd this time, with every right to hate me and Alexander for what we did to their beloved queen.

Our protection officers will be more cautious now, I tell myself, after what happened to Maisie and me. But this does nothing to soothe my anxiety—if anything, it only makes me fixate on what else they've overlooked, and what other small things with big consequences can go wrong. And how Alexander, Kit, and I will be the ones paying the price.

After I jerk awake for the second time, Kit rubs my back until his hand stills and his breathing evens out. Not wanting to disturb him again, I slip away and settle onto the sofa in my sitting room instead, taking my laptop with me.

I spend the next three hours distracting myself by reading the comments about Helene's interview on various gossip sites. Some call her a liar and insist she's trying to save face, while others support her wholeheartedly and drag my mother's name through the mud—and occasionally mine, calling us leeches and her a succubus and all kinds of things that would make Constance proud.

Most of all, though, the people blame Alexander. Not everyone, of course. Some empathize with him, or pity him, or focus on the real villain in all of this—an archaic system that imprisons everyone born into it, then drapes them in gold and jewels and privilege beyond compare so no one will ever believe their pain.

But too many push their anger onto him, assigning him motivations and emotions and sinister traits that turn him into the worst of humanity, ignoring that he was in an impossible situation and allowed to make mistakes. All they want is a demon to hate, and in Alexander, they've found one in spades.

The revelations from Helene's interview dominate the news cycle, with her face plastered on the front page of every single news site I visit. But when I type out the *Regal Record*'s address—more out of habit than any desire to see what they're saying—I'm instead faced with a paparazzi shot of Maisie and Gia exiting a club in what I think is Soho.

I recognize the outfit Maisie is wearing—a cute blue dress I helped her pick out sometime in September, before it grew too cold to need a jacket. Despite the packed pavement, there are several feet between her and Gia as they walk past a cluster of photographers, and unlike the shots featured in the roundup the *Regal Record* posted last week, they both look miserable.

PRINCESS MARY AND LADY GIA SUFFER FALLING-OUT AMIDST ROYAL ADULTERY SCANDAL

While the rest of the world is focused on the sensational surprise interview with Queen Helene that aired earlier tonight on the BBC—and we'll certainly get there, too—we at the Regal Record *have received word of yet another royal breakup: Princess Mary and Lady Georgiana Greyville, who have known each other since nappies, have reportedly suffered a dramatic falling-out.*

Lady Gia, as she's known to close friends and family, allegedly rushed to Windsor to check on her princess after a crowd barrier broke yesterday morning at the Royal London Children's Hospital, leaving Her Royal Highness with a sprained wrist and other minor injuries. Their reunion was short-lived, however, as Lady Gia stormed out of the heir to the throne's private apartment mere minutes later, leaving the princess utterly bereft. The catalyst behind their fight? A bouquet of roses from a very presidential American suitor.

While we wouldn't dare presume that these two besties have ever been anything more than the closest of friends, one must wonder why a sweet, but hardly personal, gift would lead to a shouting match heard throughout the halls of Windsor Castle.

To remember happier times between Her Royal Highness and Lady Gia, click the gallery below.

I read the article twice, too exhausted to be sure I'm not imagining things. But there they are, in neat black font on white background—details that no journalist or gossip blog should know about Maisie and Gia's fight. And as I scroll through the most recent entries, I realize it's more than the roses or their breakup. The *Regal Record* knew about Maisie's injuries, too. And the time stamp is less than an hour after we returned from London.

Someone in the castle—someone close to the royal family—is running directly to the *Regal Record* with insider information.

My mind races through the names and faces of everyone I saw at Windsor Castle that day, tripping over possibilities and half theories that don't make any sense, and I'm so distracted that I don't notice the whispers at first. They start out soft—so soft that they sound like a faint buzz, or maybe the rush of blood through my pounding heart. But as soon as I realize they have nothing to do with my too-fast pulse, they grow louder, and I slowly register the fact that the whispers are saying something— something I can't make out until I do. And this time, it isn't my name.

"You die today."

Terror cuts through me, so sharp and tangible that it might as well be a knife. I slam my laptop shut and leap to my feet, heading straight for the only weapon I can think of—a weighty silver candlestick on my mantel. Though it isn't much, I clutch it in both hands as the whispers surround me, repeating themselves again and again like some demonic nursery rhyme.

"You die today."

"You die today."

"You die today."

"Evan?"

I jump. Kit is standing in the doorway to my bedroom, his hair wild, his pajamas rumpled, and his eyes half-closed with sleep, and I'm so relieved to see him that I almost burst into tears.

"Can you hear that?" I say, not entirely sure I want to know the answer.

He cocks his head, listening for a long moment, and I can't tell if the faint whispers that echo in my mind are real, or if they're nothing more than figments of my imagination now.

"I'm sorry, Ev," he says at last. "I don't hear anything."

I close my eyes and take a deep breath, but the strange sounds have already disappeared. "I don't know what's wrong with me," I say, my voice tight and frantic and one wrong note away from snapping. "I keep hearing these whispers, ever since Sandringham. Mostly they say my name, but sometimes it's laughter or even music I've never heard before, and—and I can't tell where it's coming from, but today—just now—they said—they said—"

"Evan." Kit gently takes my shoulders and leans down so our

foreheads are pressed together. "Just breathe, all right? Just for a minute."

I stare into his liquid brown eyes as we both inhale and exhale at the same time. I'm dizzy again, but at least the whispers are gone, and when he touches my cheek, I don't know what to say.

"Did you sleep at all?" he murmurs, and I shake my head.

"Not really," I manage. "I was on my laptop."

He brushes his lips against mine. "You're exhausted. We have a few hours before you have to be at breakfast, so why don't we go back to bed? I'll chase Tibby off and wake you in time."

Breakfast. Maisie's Instagram picture. The museum opening. I can't do any of it like this—not when I feel like I'm about to jump out of my skin. "The whispers were saying I'm going to die today."

"You're not going to die today," he murmurs, tucking my tangled hair behind my ear. "You're not going to die for a very, very long time."

I blink hard. "What if my mom and Alexander are right?" I mumble. "What if I really am losing my mind?"

"We'll figure out what's going on when we get to Virginia, okay?" he says, but I shake my head.

"You need to go back to Oxford."

"What I need right now has nothing to do with university," he says. "But we'll talk about it later, all right? For now, let's get you tucked into bed."

He leaves a note for Tibby on the dining table, and once we're back in my bedroom, he chooses an ocean soundscape on

YouTube and plays it just loud enough to drown out any other noise—real or imagined. It reminds me of the nightmares I used to have when I was a kid, the ones where no matter what I did, I always ended up drowning. But this time, as he holds me and I slip into that same dream, he's on the shore with my mother and grandma, ready to show me the way back.

By the time he wakes me, a streak of sunlight sneaks in through a crack in the curtains, and it's nearly nine o'clock. Tibby is waiting in the sitting room, and though she's done an exceptional job of keeping to herself, as soon as she knows I'm up, she's back to ordering me around like I haven't been getting myself ready in the morning for practically my entire life.

I don't know what, if anything, Kit told her, and I don't ask as I brush my teeth and get dressed. A stylist is waiting for me in my sitting room, and thirty minutes later, my hair is dried and pulled into an artful half ponytail, my makeup is done, and Kit and I walk hand in hand to the breakfast room, where Alexander, Maisie, and my mother are all waiting for us.

I force a smile as Tibby takes picture after picture, some with all of us, some with just me and Maisie and our father. Even when we start to eat, I notice her sneaking a few shots when she thinks no one is looking. And although I'm calmer now, as I look around at my family gathered together, I can't shake the feeling that this is somehow a morning I'm always going to remember. Or that maybe those voices were right, and this is the last happy memory I'll ever have.

Our regular Range Rover is replaced with a Rolls-Royce bearing the royal standard, bulletproof windows, and an emergency airlock that, in case of a gas attack, will keep us safe. Security has more than doubled, with Ingrid accompanied by three other protection officers specifically there to keep an eye on me and Kit, and no fewer than six to protect Alexander.

Kit holds my hand the entire way, and he and my father chat about the museum we're about to visit—a newly renovated building along the Thames that's been nearly two years in the making. They pretend that nothing's wrong, that neither of them noticed there were no newspapers waiting for us at the breakfast table this morning, or that I've barely said a word. And none of us mentions the protesters lining the sidewalks as we approach the museum, or that the crowd waiting for us behind reinforced barriers is booing.

"Ready?" says Alexander, looking straight at me.

I try to take a steadying breath, but it hitches in my throat, and suddenly I want nothing more than to say no, to tell him we have to drive away and forget this photo op, forget this opening, forget that he has duties and responsibilities. The crowd is tense. The sky is an overbearing gray. And every cell in my body is screaming at me that we shouldn't be here.

But Alexander won't leave, even if I beg. And if I don't go into that museum, Kit will stay behind with me, and my father will be alone. The photographers will have their iconic picture of him walking up the steps surrounded by bodyguards, with no family or loved ones there to offer support, and I have to do this. I *have* to do this.

"Ready," I manage, trying to smile away the anxiety coursing through me, replacing my blood with ice and panic. It will be fine. It will be fine. It will be *fine*.

But as we step out of the car—Alexander first, then me, then

Kit—I nearly freeze on the spot. A wall of jeers hits us like an avalanche, and I notice a muscle tightening in Alexander's jaw as he smiles and waves to the hostile crowd. Our protection officers surround us, not letting us anywhere near the barriers, and I'm enormously grateful as Ingrid joins me on our walk to the front doors. Kit is on my other side, and I clutch his hand, afraid that if I let go, I'll never find it again.

Among the endless questions and accusations hurled at Alexander, none of which he acknowledges, the sound of my own name catches my attention. The voice is deep and clear, and out of habit—or maybe because I don't expect to be addressed today—I glance over into the sea of people watching us.

And there, right up against the barrier, is the man with the teal scarf.

He's not alone—there are three others with him, the lower half of their faces also covered by thick scarves, though I notice a single lock of red hair sticking out from beneath the smallest figure's hood. They're all staring at me, and I grip Kit's hand so tightly that he leans in until his lips are an inch from my ear.

"All right?" he says, barely audible. I shake my head.

"Ingrid," I manage. "To your right—the man with the teal scarf."

"I see him," says Ingrid quietly, and she hangs back for a moment to speak to the protection officers behind us. I feel strangely exposed without her there, and I practically glue myself to Kit's side as we finally ascend the steps.

The curator, who's willowy and blond and looks jarringly like Helene, greets us at the arched entrance with a curtsy. After introducing herself, she dives straight into a gushing speech about how grateful she is that we were able to make it, though she doesn't say a word about the interview or the antagonistic crowd. Alexander is polite and down-to-earth, without any indication that his estranged wife has just aired his dirty laundry to the entire world, and only when the doors close behind us do I release my death grip on Kit's hand.

"Sorry," I whisper as he flexes his fingers. "There's someone out there—he was at the hospital, too."

"The one you thought had a gun?" he says, and I nod grimly. But our conversation is quickly cut short as the curator introduces her team, and Kit and I both work our way down the line to greet everyone.

The lobby of the museum is an architectural wonder, with soaring arched ceilings and marble columns that seem to shimmer as we move. The curator tells us about the design of the museum—that everything was built with acoustics in mind, and that it could double as a concert hall if need be. Kit and I join Alexander, who looks thoroughly intrigued, and I almost manage to focus—until I see them.

Three vases of blood-red daisies, spaced perfectly apart on the welcome desk.

I take Kit's hand again and, without letting my own fake smile falter, I meet his questioning gaze and glance at the desk. He freezes in place for a moment, clearly seeing the flowers, too, and we fall out of step with the others.

"Is everything all right?" says the curator, and Alexander pauses.

"Evangeline?" he says, his worry obvious, but my mouth is dry, and I'm not sure what to say.

"We were just noticing the flowers," says Kit after a beat. "They're beautiful—and rather distinct, wouldn't you say?"

"Oh, yes," says the curator. "We were so pleased to receive them, Your Majesty. It was a lovely gesture from the Palace."

"We're very glad," says Alexander, so smoothly that for a moment, I think he doesn't understand. But he steps toward the welcome desk, the curator at his elbow, and I notice the slight tremble in his hand as he touches the card tucked in the middle bouquet. Finally, *finally*, he might actually believe—

Boom.

A noise unlike anything I've ever heard before seems to shatter the very air around us, rocking the marble beneath my feet. And before I can process what's happening, before I can wrap my head around the way the entire lobby is disintegrating before my eyes, Kit's hand is ripped from mine as something collides with me with the force of a concrete wall, and the world goes black.

CHAPTER TWENTY-THREE

An explosion has been reported at the Modern Music Museum in Central London, during an official visit from His Majesty the King, Evangeline Bright, and Lord Clarence. The area surrounding the museum has been evacuated, and there is no word yet on casualties.

—Breaking news alert from the BBC,
11:17 a.m., 12 January 2024

ALL I HEAR IS SILENCE.

I don't know where I am. I don't know what time it is, or what day it is, or why I can't see. Vaguely I'm aware that I hurt— that my body is aching in ways it shouldn't, that something has happened, something I should remember. But all I can feel is a strange tingling that seems to be holding the real pain at bay.

There's something warm beside me—warm and wet, I think, but I can't be sure. My senses aren't working properly, and I'm floating in the dark, yet at the same time held down by something foreboding and impenetrable. None of it makes sense, and I want to slip back into nothingness when a high-pitched sound pierces my eardrums, and the world around me seems to shift.

Suddenly it's daylight, bright and overpowering and filled with dust as it chases away the darkness. I squeeze my eyes shut, but not before I see the white arched ceiling of the museum high above me, partially collapsed where two of the shimmering columns should be.

"I've got Evangeline here!" The deep voice mingles with the whine in my ears, and I'm vaguely aware of someone touching the pulse point on my neck. That brush is enough to ignite the rest of my dormant nerves, and suddenly the pain hits me like a tidal wave, leaving me gasping for breath.

I open my eyes again, and there's a man in a firefighter uniform peering down at me as others clear the debris around us. It's mostly plaster, I think, but there are some heavier chunks of marble, too, and only then do I slowly start to understand what happened.

"What—" I manage, but it comes out as a gurgle. Another emergency worker lifts a piece of stone that landed inches from my head, and he inhales sharply.

"Found a body," he calls, and I notice the dark red stain on the bottom of the marble. Some small part of my mind is screaming at me, but I don't understand why—until I turn my head and see the mess of blood and bone beside me, so close that I can feel what's left of its heat.

"Keep still," orders one of the men working to excavate the rest of me. "I need a collar over here!"

I'm still staring at the body, mostly buried under marble that missed me by inches. That voice in my mind grows louder, clawing away at the fog until I finally hear what it's saying.

Kit. Kit. Kit.

Kit was next to me. Kit was exactly where this body is now, and—

The world goes dark once more, and when I come to again, I'm lying on a stretcher, surrounded by medics. There's an oxygen mask over my mouth, and a woman is doing something to one of my legs. When I glance up, I see the gray sky again, but this time there's no hole to look through. We're outside.

"Kit?" I whisper, but if anyone hears me, they don't react. Someone shouts nearby, and another team of medics rolls a second stretcher past mine, though I can't see who's on it. When it's gone, however, my blurred vision focuses on the top of the steps, where several long black bags are lined up side by side, one after another.

Body bags.

"Evangeline?" A woman with black hair and a nose stud shines a light in my eyes, and I blink, not sure if I'm crying or not. "Can you hear me, Evangeline?"

I nod—or at least I try to, but something is holding my neck in place. "Kit?" I repeat, louder this time.

"We're taking you to hospital now," she says like I haven't said anything at all. "We'll get you sorted there, all right?"

Time slips away from me again, even though I think I'm still awake. I hear the sirens, can feel every bump in the road as the ambulance rushes through traffic, and when we arrive at what must be the emergency room—*A&E in England,* says a dry voice in my mind that sounds an awful lot like Tibby—I'm surrounded yet again by a medical team.

"Kit?" I say desperately as a doctor removes my oxygen mask. "Is he okay?"

"Can you tell me where it hurts?" she replies, and if I wasn't crying before, I am now. I try to sit up, but hands hold me down as I babble Kit's name again and again, and all I can see is that crushed body in the rubble.

The doctor must sedate me, because the next time I open my eyes, I'm in a room that's eerily similar to the one I woke up in on Christmas Eve. The whining in my ears is fainter now, and in its place, I hear a steady *beep-beep-beep* that must be my pulse.

"Kit?" I say before I can even think of why. But then the memory of that morning hits me, and I suck in a breath. "Kit—"

"It's about bloody time," says a clipped voice from my bedside. "The doctors said you'd be awake an hour ago, but as always, they're utterly incompetent and haven't a clue what they're doing."

For a split second, I'm positive I'm dreaming. But sure enough, when I turn my head, I see my grandmother sitting straight-backed in a plastic hospital chair, her expression drawn, her eyes red and swollen, and her designer coatdress buttoned to her throat.

"Constance?" I manage. "What are you doing here?"

"You will address me as Your Majesty," says my grandmother sternly. "And I am here because I've long since done my duty to the crown, and no one cares what happens to me."

This doesn't make any sense, and I lift my head. The brace I wore on the stretcher is gone now, and even though every inch of my body aches, I can still move my fingers and toes. "Where's Kit?" I say as I struggle to sit up. "Is he—"

"Would you *please* lie still? For the love of . . ." Constance reaches forward, and a moment later, my bed begins to whir and guides me into a sitting position. "You're a very lucky girl, you know. You have a mild concussion and a nasty gash on your leg that needed stitches, but beyond that and a few bumps and bruises, you ought to be perfectly fine. *If you don't strain your-self over the next few days.*"

I shake my head. I don't feel lucky—I don't feel anything but creeping dread. "There was a body beside me," I whisper, my fingers digging into the thin mattress. "There was blood—so much blood—and before . . . before, Kit was there, and—"

"My understanding is that Lord Clarence is awake and being treated a few rooms down," says Constance so matter-of-factly that it knocks the wind out of me. "*He's* not the one who had the bloody ceiling fall in on him."

I look at her sharply, not sure I've heard her right. "Kit—he's alive?"

Constance sniffs. "Honestly, Evangeline, your life would be so much easier if you learned to listen."

Something hot and liquid seems to explode in my chest, and before I realize it, I'm sobbing. From relief, from shock, from delayed fear—I don't know what it is, but I'm crying harder than I ever have in my life.

Kit's alive. He's okay. It wasn't him. *It wasn't him.*

Constance stiffens, seemingly frozen in place by a show of actual emotion. But eventually I feel her tentative touch on my back, and a moment later, she snakes a thin arm around me with the kind of awkwardness usually reserved for middle schoolers at a dance.

I don't care that we've never said a nice word to each other. I don't care that she hates my guts and is only here because she has to be. I bury my face in her shoulder as every last emotion wrings itself from my body, leaving me quaking and boneless when my sobs finally start to subside.

"Who was it, then?" I say hoarsely as I let her go. "Who—"

But then another possibility occurs to me, and I study her face. Her swollen eyes. Her haggard expression. The way she suddenly looks every single one of her seventy-plus years, despite a lifetime of facials.

"Where's Alexander?" I say as cold horror sweeps through me, taking every ounce of my relief with it. "Constance, where—"

"Your Majesty," she corrects, but her voice hitches. "You will call me Your Majesty, Evangeline, or I—"

"Where is he?" The guttural sound that comes out of me is inhuman, and all I can think about is that broken body beside me, and how I know beyond a doubt that my father, king or not, would have done everything he could to protect me. Even if it meant taking the death that was supposed to be mine.

Constance swallows hard. "His Majesty was pulled from the rubble shortly after you were," she says slowly, like it's taking everything she has to keep her voice steady. "He sustained crush injuries to his legs and chest, and—"

"Is he alive?" I demand, sick with fear all over again. Her chin quivers now, and I reel, trying to brace myself for the reality I don't want to face.

"Yes," she whispers. "He's still alive. But he is critical, and the odds the doctors have given him . . ."

She closes her eyes, and twin tears escape down the sides of her nose. Before I can think better of it, I'm hugging her again, numb to the inconsequential aches and pains in my own body now. And when she slumps against me, all her carefully crafted royal veneer vanishing in a single shudder, I know that there's a very real chance I'll never see my father again.

CHAPTER TWENTY-FOUR

A total of eight deaths have been reported so far in the bombing of the Modern Music Museum in London during an official visit by His Majesty and members of the royal family. The identities of the victims have not yet been released, and Buckingham Palace has refused to comment on the status of the King.

—Breaking news alert from the BBC,
2:11 p.m., 12 January 2024

CONSTANCE REMAINS WITH ME THROUGHOUT the rest of the afternoon as we wait for an update on Alexander.

All details of his condition are kept from the media—a matter of national security at this point—and the hospital is crawling with police and personal protection officers, both for our safety and to hold the rabid journalists that surround the building at bay. No one is allowed to leave their room without a damn good reason, and while neither of us is thrilled about it, especially when I'm desperate to see Kit, Constance and I settle into something that resembles an uneasy truce.

After she dabs her eyes and resumes her prickly royal demeanor, I pepper her with questions, and she tersely explains that both Maisie and Helene have been told by the prime minister and home secretary to stay where they are, in case of another attack. This is what she meant when she said that no one cares what happens to her, I realize—she's not in the line of succession, and she's considered as expendable as I am. But Alexander is also her son, and as much as she and I don't like each other, I'm glad someone from the family is here.

Our shared fear and frustration with the lack of updates does a strange thing as we wait—it makes me feel like we actually have something in common. It's far from a familial bond, but by the time the sound of an argument filters in from the corridor outside my room, I'm almost starting to warm up to her. Almost.

"What on earth . . . ," mutters Constance as she stands and marches toward the door, but despite the high-pitched tone that still lingers in my ears, I immediately recognize one of the voices.

"That's Kit," I say urgently, climbing out of bed, but Constance flings open the door before my feet touch the ground.

"What is the meaning of this?" she demands. Kit stands a few steps away, physically blocked from the entrance by two protection officers with their holstered weapons now on full display.

"I just need to see—Evan!" says Kit, the relief in his voice palpable as he spots me over Constance's shoulder. "Are you all right? Would you bloody let me *go*?"

"Get your hands off him," says Constance sharply as I stumble across the freezing floor, my injured leg protesting as a dozen stitches tug against my skin. "Lord Clarence is family and well within his rights to be here."

The protection officers step aside, and Kit offers my grandmother a grateful bow of his head before hurrying past her and into the room. He catches me in his arms, lifting me off the ground as he holds me to him.

"Bloody hell, Ev," he mumbles into my hair, his voice choked with tears. "You have to stop doing this to me."

"Not my choice, trust me," I say, wrapping my arms around his neck. I can feel the edge of a bandage against my skin, and when I pull away enough to peer at him, I see several small cuts across his face, including one beneath his eye that required stitches. "You're okay?"

"Fine," he promises. "Climbing the bloody walls trying to find out how you are. MI5's here, and they wouldn't tell me anything—"

"No one is being told a thing," says Constance. "The press *must* be kept in the dark about the King's condition, is that understood?"

"He's alive?" says Kit, and I can tell by the catch in his voice that he wasn't expecting this. "At the museum, I thought . . . he was buried, and when they found him . . ."

His throat works hard, and I press my cheek to his. Dust still clings to his hair, turning parts of it ashy gray, and I realize he's dressed in hospital scrubs. "You saw what happened?"

"Only bits," he says. "One of the PPOs pinned me to the ground, but I could still see you. Ingrid threw herself at you, and then . . . then the column fell, and . . ."

My insides churn, and suddenly I think I'm going to be sick. "Ingrid?" I manage. "She was—she was with me?"

I see the body again, the blood and the bone and the parts I don't want to identify, and I press my lips together, as if that'll stop the contents of my stomach from coming up. But when Kit nods wordlessly, I let him go, and he sets me down just in time for me to grab the plastic bin next to my bed and be sick.

Someone calls for a nurse, and Kit crouches beside me, rubbing my back as I retch. He murmurs something, but the high pitch in my ears grows louder, drowning out his voice.

Ingrid was only there because of me—because I demanded that Alexander bring me. If I hadn't, if I'd listened to him and stayed behind, or if I'd trusted my gut and not gotten out of that car in the first place, she would still be alive. The other people in the body bags—maybe they'd still be alive, too. Alexander wouldn't have noticed the flowers, and he would've been in a different part of the lobby. And maybe, maybe—

I'm sick again, and a few seconds later, I feel the prick of a needle in my arm. I expect to black out—I expect them to sedate me like they did in A&E—but instead all that happens is that my nausea subsides as quickly as it came.

"There we go," says a nurse, offering me a tissue as I sit back up. Her voice is muffled by the ringing in my ears, but that, too, slowly eases until I can hear myself panting. Kit presses a glass of water into my hand, and I'm so dazed that I don't think twice before drinking it.

Ingrid's dead, and this time, it really is my fault.

Kit helps me back onto the bed as the nurse fetches some crackers, but I sit sideways, my legs dangling and my head in my hands. "I shouldn't have been there," I whisper. "Alexander didn't want me to go. If I'd listened to him, then Ingrid . . ."

"That's not fair," says Kit. "You didn't know this was going to happen, Ev."

"I think I did," I say, so softly I'm not even sure my voice carries. But he squeezes my knee, and I know he heard. "Those whispers in my sitting room . . ."

"That had nothing to do with this," says Kit. "Okay? You didn't know this would happen, and it isn't your fault. You had no control over any of it. Whoever did this—"

I look at him suddenly, my eyes bleary as I feel myself go pale. "The man in the teal scarf," I say. "The one in the crowd—"

"Who?" says an unfamiliar male voice in the doorway, and Kit and I both turn.

Constance has disappeared into the hallway, and in her place stands a tall man with thick black hair, dark skin, and a sharp charcoal suit. There's something overwhelmingly intimidating about him—even more so than the protection officers carrying loaded guns—and I look nervously at Kit.

Kit clears his throat. "Evangeline, this is Suraj Singh. He's from MI5."

"It's nice to meet you, Miss Bright," says Singh, stepping into the room and extending his hand toward me. "Though I wish it were under different circumstances."

I eye his hand like it might bite me. "MI5. Isn't that like the CIA?"

"More like your FBI," he says with the ease of someone who expects me to be difficult. "MI5 is the British security service, while MI6 deals in foreign intelligence. It's entirely possible they'll also be assisting with the investigation, but for now, you're stuck with me."

My experience with the police hasn't exactly endeared me to any kind of government authority, but his hand still hovers between us, and reluctantly I take it. His grip is firm, but brief, and as soon as he lets my hand go, I wedge both of mine between my knees.

"Lord Clarence was kind enough to tell me all he remembers about the incident at the Modern Music Museum this morning," he says smoothly. "And I was hoping you might feel up to the same, particularly if there's someone you've noticed or—"

"Who gave you permission to be in here?"

Before today, I never would've thought I'd be relieved to see Constance, but as she steps through the doorway, her face hard as stone, I could actually hug her.

Singh clears his throat. "Your Majesty," he says, bowing his head. "Forgive me. I'm Agent Suraj Singh, and I've been sent by the home secretary—"

"I don't care who sent you," says Constance, drawing herself up to her full height. "You've no right to be in this room, or to question a member of the royal family."

My mouth goes dry, though I'm not sure what part surprises me more—Constance being protective of me, or her referring to me as a member of the royal family.

"Ma'am," says Singh patiently, "we need Miss Bright's statement—"

"And you'll have it," says Constance. "Once Evangeline is out of a hospital gown and in the safety of a royal residence."

Singh purses his lips, and suddenly, in the face of Constance's ire, he doesn't seem nearly as intimidating. "My team is in the process of tracing the terrorists now, ma'am, and time is of the essence—"

"You know who did this?" I cut in, and Singh hesitates.

"We made several arrests at the scene," he admits. "And an anti-monarchist group that calls itself the Army of the British Republic has taken credit. But situations such as these can be chaotic and confusing, particularly in the initial hours and days, and the more information we have—"

"There is nothing Evangeline can tell you that other witnesses cannot," says Constance. But as Singh looks at me again, I can see he thinks otherwise.

"You said you saw a man in the crowd—one wearing a teal scarf," he says. "He seemed suspicious to you?"

I open my mouth, though I'm not entirely sure what's going to come out. Before I can make a sound, however, Constance steps between us, her arms crossed as she blocks his way.

"One more word, and I'll be having more than a few with the home secretary over your conduct in the hospital room of a traumatized eighteen-year-old girl," she says sharply. "Now go, before I have you physically thrown out in front of every single journalist camped outside."

Singh manages a tight smile. "Very well, ma'am," he says, and he pulls a card from his pocket, reaching past her to offer it to Kit. "When Miss Bright is ready to speak."

Kit takes the card, and Singh offers Constance another bow before exiting the room. As soon as he's gone, Constance shuts the door and begins to pace in her heels, clearly fuming.

"The nerve of that man," she mutters. "You must never answer any questions without legal representation present, is that understood? No matter how innocent you are, you mustn't say a word."

"I know," I say quietly. "I promise, I know."

Her frown deepens, but at least this seems to satisfy her for now. "I've just spoken to the doctors," she says, and Kit and I immediately sit up straighter.

"About Alexander?" I say. "Is he—"

"He's out of surgery," she says in a clipped voice. "Which was more than he was expected to survive. For now, he's in a medically induced coma, though the doctors can't say much more at this stage. If he . . ." Her voice catches again, and she takes a steadying breath. "If he survives the night, then we'll have a better idea of what the future might hold."

If. I swallow hard as Kit's fingers slip between mine. "Does my mom know how bad it is?" I say, and Constance shoots me a withering look.

"What have I been saying about how important it is that his condition not leak to the press?"

"My mom won't tell anyone," I insist. "Helene's the one who runs to the media every chance she—"

"I'm well aware," snaps Constance. "But she is still his wife, and she still has the right to make medical decisions for him. Which unfortunately means she is the only other person currently being updated on his condition."

Constance and I stare at each other, my mind racing as I try to put my thoughts into words. "So you're saying—you're saying my mom has no idea if he's even alive?"

She purses her lips. "No."

"What about me?" I say, my heart pounding. "Does she know I'm okay?"

Constance sets her jaw, and I slide off the bed, closing the distance between us.

"Go get her," I say in a low, dangerous voice. "Wherever she is—go get her, and bring her here."

Her eyes narrow. "Watch your tone with me, Evangeline. The hospital is on lockdown—"

"I don't care," I say. "And you shouldn't, either. I get why you don't trust her, but she loves him more than her own life, and we both know he feels the same. You can't keep her in the dark. Not now, not when . . ." I shake my head. "He'd want her here. You know he would."

Constance glances away, the lines in her forehead multiplying. I try to think of what to say next—of what combination of threats and pleas might make her relent—but just as I open my mouth again, she sighs.

"Very well," she says, so quietly that I almost don't hear her over the ringing in my ears. "I shall send for her."

Instantly the tension in my body deflates, and my limbs feel like rubber. "Thank you," I say, but it's all I can manage right now. She nods tersely, and as Kit helps me back onto the bed, she goes to the door to speak to one of the officers in the hall.

"Fetch Ms. Bright," she orders. "She's downstairs with one of your colleagues. Don't allow her to speak to anyone, and bring her directly to me."

"Yes, ma'am," says the officer, and when Constance reenters the room, I'm gaping at her.

"My mom's been here the whole time?"

"Of course she has," she says blisteringly, but there's no real bite in her voice now. "You're her daughter. Where else would she be?"

My mother arrives less than five minutes later, and I know instantly from the hollows beneath her eyes and the gray tint to her face that she's spent the entire afternoon desperately trying to convince herself that Alexander and I aren't dead. "I'm sorry," I say as she clings to me. "I thought someone would tell you. I didn't know—I'm so sorry—"

She shakes her head. "You're all right," she manages. "That's all that matters."

"Alexander's alive, too," I say, ignoring Constance's glare. "But . . . he's in really bad shape, Mom. They don't know if . . ."

My mom holds me tighter, and a dry sob escapes her. We stay like that, tangled together in the middle of the room, until my legs start to give out from the effort of supporting our combined weight. And once we've separated, me perched on the bed and my mom gripping my hand in both of hers, Constance looks between us, as if coming to some kind of decision.

"How far can you walk?" she says to me, and I glance at my leg. The cut is deep and jagged, and it's yet another scar to remind me of what's turning out to be the worst month of my life. But in the face of everything else, it's barely a blip.

"As far as I need to," I say, and she nods.

"Put on your dressing gown and follow me—both of you. Kit, stay here. I'll bring her back soon enough."

He doesn't argue, and I tie the sash of a hospital robe around my waist as my mom and I follow Constance into the corridor. The protection officers assigned to my room start to protest, but she silences them with a single look, and I tuck myself underneath my mom's arm as Constance leads us down the hall.

I don't know where we're going until we stop in front of a door guarded by two more protection officers. And as they exchange a grim look, I'm positive I know what's on the other side.

"You will let us all in," says Constance, "or you will lose your livelihoods."

There's a moment—just a moment—when I see both of them weighing her threat and wondering if she actually possesses the power to have them fired. But she's the former queen consort, mother of the current sovereign, and grandmother to the heir to the throne. If anyone has the power to do anything in this country, it's her.

And so they step aside and open the door, and with her head held high, Constance leads us into Alexander's hospital room.

The first thing I notice is the beeping. It isn't just a single steady *beep-beep-beep*, but several layers of tinny noise, all indicating that he's still alive—or, at the very least, that the machines are keeping him going for now. A nurse sits in the corner beside a computer that displays his vital signs, and another pair of protection officers stand near the door, eyeing us like we might be threats. I ignore them and, mustering up all the courage I have left, finally look at my father.

He lies in an oversized hospital bed, with so many bandages wrapped around his broken body that there's no real way to tell who he is. The only sign that it's him is the part of his swollen face not hidden under gauze, and even then, he's barely recognizable. I freeze, completely unprepared for the sight of him like this, and Constance stands stiffly beside me, also unmoving. But my mother doesn't hesitate as she walks toward his bedside and takes his bare hand, gently sandwiching it between hers.

"Oh, Alex," she says softly, her eyes raking over the damage. "My Alex. Look at you."

There's something so achingly tender about the way she says

his name that tears well in my eyes, but I blink hard, refusing to lose it right now. Not in front of my mom. Instead, I force myself forward and push a plastic chair beside the bed, giving her a place to sit.

"We should know more about His Majesty's condition in the morning," says the nurse in a gentle Scottish accent. "For now, the doctors have stabilized him, and we'll do all we can to help him make it through the night."

"He will," says my mother with quiet certainty. Her eyes linger on his face, and her thumb strokes the back of his hand. "I'd like to stay with him, if it's allowed."

The nurse looks at Constance, who still stands by the door, her cheeks bloodless and her eyes haunted. For all her arrogance and bad temper, right now she's nothing more than a mother faced with the possibility of losing her son, and her throat tightens before she nods.

"He would want you here," she says, and my mom offers her the tiniest of smiles before turning her gaze back to my father. And as she lays her head down beside their intertwined hands, I drag another chair over and join her.

CHAPTER TWENTY-FIVE

ARRESTS MADE IN MUSEUM BOMBING; KING'S CONDITION STILL UNKNOWN

The Home Office has announced that several arrests have been made related to the bombing of the Modern Music Museum in London yesterday, which has claimed the lives of eight people.

While the identities of the suspected terrorists have not yet been revealed, the Army of the British Republic, a previously unknown and self-declared anti-monarchist group, has reportedly taken credit for the bombing in a video posted anonymously to social media. Though the Home Office has yet to confirm their claim, several international leaders, including President Hope Park of the United States, have already condemned the organization for the attack.

While the King's condition remains unknown, a palace insider has revealed that Evangeline Bright, illegitimate daughter of the King, and Christopher Abbott-Montgomery, Earl of Clarence and nephew to the Queen, survived the attack. Both have been admitted to an undisclosed hospital for treatment, though the extent of their injuries remains unknown.

—*The Daily Sun,* 13 January 2024

IN THE EARLY HOURS OF the morning, long before the sun rises, Jenkins appears in the doorway of my hospital room.

Kit is asleep in the bed beside me, his body tense with

nightmares that aren't hard to guess, but I'm awake, staring at the ceiling as I try not to think about what's happening down the hall. Every time I hear someone hurry past my room, my adrenaline spikes, and I'm sure this is it—that Alexander's finally let go. But neither my mother nor Constance comes to break the news to me, and each time my anxiety drags me out of bed to check with the protection officers stationed outside my door, all they do is offer a reassuring nod. Somehow, against all odds, he's hanging on.

"Jenkins?" I whisper as he slips inside the room, closing the door softly behind him. He startles slightly, clearly not expecting me to be awake, and in the dim light, I see his apologetic grimace.

"Good morning, Evan," he says softly. "How do you feel?"

"Like a building fell on me," I deadpan, and to his credit, he tries to smile. "Is Alexander still . . . ?"

"His Majesty is a fighter," says Jenkins, and I breathe a sigh of relief. "Do you feel well enough to come home?"

"Already?" Technically Kit and I have both been discharged, but no one's argued about us staying in the room for a little while longer, considering Alexander's the only other patient on this floor.

"Her Royal Highness has asked that you be present for an emergency meeting this morning," he says. "In order to discuss the, er . . . plans for what will happen while His Majesty is incapacitated."

"Plans?" I say, confused. "What does that mean?"

"It means . . ." Jenkins clears his throat. "It means that though we all very much hope His Majesty will make a full recovery, we must decide how to carry on until he is ready to resume his duties. Her Royal Highness is the heir to the throne, of course, but until she is twenty-one, she is bound by the Regency Act of 2005, and that . . . complicates matters significantly."

I stare at him for a long moment. "Jenkins, I *just* learned the difference between MI5 and MI6. I have no idea what the Regency Act of 2005 is."

This finally gets a real—albeit faint—smile out of him. "It's an act that was put into place by Parliament shortly after your sister was born. It outlines what would happen—what will now happen—should something befall His Majesty before Her Royal Highness reaches the age of twenty-one."

"But he's not—he's not gone," I say. "He could wake up, right? Isn't a regency permanent?"

"The situation we're now in is . . . rather delicate, and we do not yet know if a true regency will be required. But it is possible."

I don't want to think about that, especially not now, in the early morning, with my ears still ringing from the bomb. "Why twenty-one?" I say. "I thought Queen Victoria was eighteen when she took the throne."

"She was," says Jenkins. "But while the Regency Act of 2005 was being drafted, your father asked to include a clause ensuring that so long as Her Royal Highness is under the age of twenty-one, she will be assisted by a council of senior royals, who are able to help make decisions and carry out the monarch's duties in his absence, whether temporary or permanent."

"So it won't all be on Maisie," I say, though I'm still confused.

"Precisely," he says. "And she wishes for you to be present during the discussion of the finer details."

I have no idea why, and spending hours listening to a dozen royal advisers arguing over political minutiae sounds like the worst way to spend any morning, let alone this one. But I nod, because the thought of what Maisie must be going through right now makes me shiver, and the idea of her facing it alone makes me ache with something I can't name. Protectiveness, maybe. Or maybe some kind of sibling connection I don't recognize. If Alexander takes a turn, or if he can't find his way back, my sister will be queen. And I don't think any of us are prepared, least of all her.

"Okay," I say. "But when it's over, I'm coming back to sit with my mom."

"I'll make sure no one stops you," says Jenkins. And after another beat, he wordlessly takes my hand, as if reassuring himself that I'm really there. "Sometimes I wish I'd never brought you to England in the first place," he admits so quietly that I barely hear him.

"But I'm glad you did," I say.

"Even after all this?"

"Especially after all this." I glance at Kit, who's still asleep. He looks calmer now, like his nightmare has passed. "I like having people in my life who are worth a few bombs and bullets."

"It's hardly our typical British welcome," he says, and I shrug.

"You're all worth it."

After I check in on my mom and Alexander, whose condition hasn't changed, Jenkins and several protection officers escort Kit and me into a parking garage beneath the hospital, and we emerge into the predawn London morning in a Range Rover with bulletproof windows and armored plating around its frame.

Even though our location is supposed to be a secret, half the journalists on the planet are waiting for us at the exit, and Kit and I watch wordlessly through the tinted windows as they try to swarm the vehicle. The police hold them back behind the barriers, though, and our security team sees us swiftly onto the dark city streets, where we speed away from the hospital toward the relative safety of Windsor Castle.

"How bad is it?" I say to Jenkins. "The press coverage, I mean."

"It's the top story in virtually every English-speaking country around the world, and the majority that aren't," he says. "The BBC has been running wall-to-wall coverage of the bombing, though with no official word on His Majesty's condition, it's all speculation. I'd imagine our exit is already being shown on a loop."

"Are they wearing black?" says Kit, and though I don't understand the reference, Jenkins shakes his head.

"Not yet. Though there are plenty of rumors that it's only a matter of time."

Kit grimaces. "Are there plans to release an official statement?"

"As soon as Her Majesty feels it will not be misleading."

Kit must notice my confusion, because he says quietly, "Aunt Helene is—or was—waiting to see if he makes it through the night."

"Oh." I don't know how I feel about the thought of Helene still being such an important part in all of this, not when she hung my parents out to dry less than two days ago. But her interview feels so inconsequential now that I can barely muster up any anger toward her. Just bone-deep exhaustion I'm not sure will ever go away.

We reach Windsor Castle as a hint of pink appears on the horizon, and even more journalists are waiting for us at the gates. This time, security has already cleared the road, and we speed through without so much as slowing down.

Tibby stands at the entrance nearest the private apartments, clutching her tablet as she watches us approach. I notice she's wearing low heels today, along with a gray dress that's so dark it's almost black, and somehow these are the details that make it all feel real to me—that make me realize this is going to impact the rest of our lives, and nothing will ever be the same.

She hugs me fiercely as soon as we're inside, and I let her fuss over me on our way to my apartment. She doesn't ask any questions about Alexander or the details of the bombing, and I don't know if it's out of respect or because there's a blanket ban on trying to wheedle information out of us. Either way, I'm grateful, though when she notices the bandage on my leg, I actually see her bite her tongue.

Kit and I separate long enough to wash the dust and blood away, and once I'm dressed, I head out into my sitting room, fully expecting Kit to be waiting for me alongside Tibby. But there's no sign of either of them, and instead I'm greeted by my frantically pacing sister.

"It's about bloody time." She pounces toward me with the speed and grace of a jungle cat, and I do my best not to grunt as she tackles me in a hug. I'm sorer now than I was in the immediate aftermath of the bombing, and my shoulder still aches, which doesn't exactly help. But I can tell from how tightly she holds me that she needs this, and I delicately hug her in return.

"Good call, staying home yesterday," I say in a pitiful attempt at a joke. But as soon as she pulls away and I see the tears brimming in her eyes, I immediately regret it.

"Have you seen him?" she says, her lower lip trembling. "No one will let me leave. Mummy told me it's touch and go, but beyond that, I don't know a thing, and I've been going mad trying to figure out a way to visit him—"

"I saw him right before we left," I say, trying to sound reassuring. "My mom and Constance have been with him all night. He's . . ."

I pause. I don't want to scare her more than she already is, but I don't want to give her false hope, either. My ears are ringing again, faintly now, and I suck in a breath.

"We'll find a way for you to see him after the meeting," I say at last. "Even if we have to sneak you out of here."

She wipes her eyes, and I can tell she understands everything I'm not saying. "I don't know if that'll be possible," she admits. "The prime minister himself told me to stay put. It's a matter of national security, apparently."

Privately I agree. I don't want to imagine the chaos if Maisie is somehow hurt in all this, too. "Then we'll VidChat my mom, all right? We'll figure it out. Now tell me about this meeting and why you decided to drag me out of bed so early."

I expect this to be a neutral topic, or at the very least easier to bear than the thought of Alexander's mangled body, but Maisie's lower lip quivers again, and I think she might actually burst into tears.

"The entire senior staff will be there," she manages, her voice not much more than a squeak. "I'm of age now, and—and they'll all be—looking to me for instruction, but—" She sniffs and dabs at her cheeks with the cuff of her midnight-blue sweater. "I don't know what to do, Evan. This wasn't supposed to happen for decades."

"It hasn't happened yet," I say, trying to sound reassuring, even though the idea still makes me reel. "Everyone coming to this meeting was hired by Alexander for a reason, and they know what they're doing. Listen to them. Listen to your mom and Nicholas, and remember they're all there to support you, not the other way arou—"

A sharp knock cuts me off, and even though this is my apartment, Maisie calls for whoever it is to enter. A beat later, Jenkins opens the door, his expression even more somber than it was when he left me in Tibby's hands.

My heart drops to my knees. "What's wrong? Is Alexander—"

"His Majesty's condition has not changed," he says hastily. "But I fear there is a . . . situation in the conference room that requires Her Royal Highness's immediate attention."

I glance at Maisie, and she smooths the fear from her face and draws herself up to her full height. In the space of a single heartbeat, she goes from my terrified half sister to heir to the throne—one who could become queen at any moment—and I bite my lip, silently wondering if this is the last time I'll see her like that. Raw and vulnerable and genuine, without the weight of the entire country and Commonwealth on her shoulders.

As the three of us head into the long gallery, we're joined by a nervous-looking Tibby and a silent but steady Kit, who gives me a questioning look. I shrug. Whatever's going on now, I suspect there are a lot of *situations* that are going to require Maisie's attention, and this kind of grave urgency is something we all need to get used to.

As we climb the staircase to the upper floors, I wince at the pain in my leg, and Kit wordlessly takes my elbow. I have no right to complain, not when Ingrid's dead and Alexander's fighting for his life, but I'm still embarrassingly slow, and by the time Kit and I catch up to the others, they're standing in front of the closed doorway to the conference room.

Fitz, Maisie's private secretary, is already waiting for her, his suit jacket wrinkled and his red hair sticking up like he hasn't brushed it in days. Tibby doesn't even try to hide her disdain, and as he briefs Maisie in a low voice, she joins Kit and me, her scowl deep and her jaw set.

"Utterly incompetent. Has he never heard of a bloody comb?" mutters Tibby before refocusing on me. "I expect you won't have to do or say much. Just listen, and remember that everyone inside that room is there to keep things running as smoothly as possible in His Majesty's absence. And if Maisie seems like she needs a break, it's completely within your rights to call for—"

"*What?*" My sister's voice cuts through Tibby's murmur, and Fitz flushes.

"I—I'm very sorry, Your Royal Highness, but there was nothing I could do—"

Maisie lets out a curse so vile that even Tibby looks taken aback, and Jenkins steps forward. "Security is on standby, Your

Royal Highness," he says. "Should you choose that particular route."

I have no idea what he's talking about, but my sister grits her teeth and pushes open the door with the force of a tornado. I glance at Kit, both alarmed and intrigued, and we follow her into the room just in time to see Maisie round on someone sitting near the empty seat at the head of the table.

"How *dare* you show your face now," she says, her voice shaking with fury. "You've no right to be here. *None.*"

"I think you'll find that I have every right to be here, especially now," says a mild voice that chases away every trace of exhaustion inside me, leaving nothing but adrenaline and anger behind.

Sitting beside his father, with his blond hair pushed back casually from his face and his lips twisted into the faintest hint of a smirk, is Ben.

CHAPTER TWENTY-SIX

A job well done.

That depends entirely on whether he's still breathing.

No updates yet. I'll let you know as soon as I hear.

How did you manage it, anyway?

What did I tell you about asking questions?

It's already done. There's no harm in telling me.

I lost loyal followers to this, and I've taken enough of a risk without giving you something else to hold over me.

What happened to mutually assured destruction?

Forgive me for thinking you'd ever pay the price.

Send me an update as soon as you hear. I need to plan our next move.

I've already moved forward with the photo. It should hit the news cycle any moment now. Was she one of them?

Yes. Not an easy loss.

It'll all be worth it. For both of us.

—Text message exchange between two prepaid mobile numbers, 13 January 2024

WHILE THERE ARE MORE THAN two dozen people crammed around the long conference table, no one says a word as Maisie takes a menacing step toward Ben, her fists clenched like she actually knows how to use them.

"Did you hit your head?" she says nastily. "Or have you conveniently forgotten what His Majesty told you before we left for Klosters?"

Ben leans back in his chair and surveys her with the arrogance of someone who thinks he's untouchable. "I believe the word 'banished' may have been batted around once or twice," he says. "By all means, if Uncle Alexander feels the need to remind me, he's more than welcome to do so."

"That is *enough*," says Constance sharply from the seat across from him, while Maisie looks like she's about to burst into flames. The Queen Mother sits beside an expressionless Helene, who, to her credit, seems like she's only barely managed to pull herself together for this meeting, with her hair limp, the cords of her neck strained, and the circles beneath her eyes so dark they're purple.

Ben's smirk is unmistakable now as he looks at us one by one, and while it may be my imagination, I swear his searing gaze lingers on me for a beat longer than the others. "I can't be the only one who's actually *read* the Regency Act of 2005," he says. "That is why we're all here, is it not?"

I barely have time to wonder how he knows that before Maisie speaks up again. "It has nothing to do with you, Benedict—"

"I think you'll find that it does," he says. "I don't have the exact wording in front of me, so forgive me if I'm paraphrasing, but I do believe it states that should the heir to the throne be eighteen at the time of ascension or regency, then the four most senior members of the royal family shall gather to advise her, and to rule by council until she turns twenty-one. Am I wrong?"

Maisie slowly turns a shade of red I've never actually seen on a human face before. "It doesn't mean *you*."

"As I said before, dear cousin, I think you'll find that it does," says Ben, and there's a hint of victory in his voice that makes me want to wring his neck.

My sister narrows her eyes. "Then I suppose we'll just have to remove you, won't we?" she says. "It should be a simple vote. Four to one, I think—"

"You aren't Queen yet, Your Royal Highness," says Ben. "And even if Uncle Alexander dies today, I believe you'll find that you won't have the power to get rid of me for another two and a half years. The act is ironclad. Uncle Alexander's rather clever that way, isn't he? Or . . . wasn't he?" He drums his fingers against the mahogany table. "I'm afraid I've been remiss in asking how our beloved King is doing. Or not doing, so to speak."

It's only Kit's tightening grip on my elbow that stops me from launching myself at Ben, and Maisie actually takes a step toward him. But whether it's the dozens of curious eyes on her, or the very real possibility that Ben does in fact know what he's talking about, she stops herself from getting too close and instead turns to Helene.

"Mummy," she demands, "he can't be here. He can't be part of this."

Helene exchanges a look with Nicholas, who's leaning slightly away from his son. "I'm afraid Benedict is correct," she says, her honeyed voice brittle. "Alexander was . . . very specific about the requirements in the event of his incapacitation, and unfortunately we're all bound to them. Any change would require an act of Parliament, which would surely take time, and it would, I fear, also require an explanation. A public explanation."

Ben pushes a lock of hair out of his eyes, practically basking in the glory of his win. "Would you like to be the one to explain to Parliament and the entire world why you don't want me here, Maisie? Or would you prefer I elaborate for you?"

For a split second, she tenses in a way that makes it seem like she really is about to knock him upside the head. But Jenkins clears his throat, and he pointedly positions himself between them, heading off the fight that Ben is so gleefully stoking.

"If I may, Your Royal Highness," he says to Maisie. She nods stiffly, still glaring at Ben with the heat of a thousand suns, and Jenkins turns toward him. "Your recollection of the Regency Act of 2005 is mostly correct, Your Royal Highness. But I fear there is one point in particular that you have misinterpreted."

Ben goes very still. "Is that so?" he says, an edge to his voice.

"Indeed," says Jenkins. "The act asks that the four *blood* relatives closest to His Majesty and the heir to the throne, including the Counsellors of State, step up to advise Her Royal Highness. It never specifies that they must be designated senior royals—or even royalty at all."

In an instant, all eyes are on me, and with sharp horror, I realize why I'm here. "Wait," I say suddenly. "*Wait—*"

"Is this a joke?" says Ben, leaning forward in his chair so quickly that he nearly leaps out of it. "Evangeline isn't any older than Maisie—"

"She meets the age requirement of eighteen," says Jenkins

mildly. "And forgive me, Your Royal Highness, but you yourself are only nineteen."

Ben sputters. "But—she's *American*. That alone invalidates her eligibility—"

A peal of laughter escapes from Maisie, so unexpected that even Ben looks taken aback. "Evan has a British passport," she manages. "And I'm fairly certain that as far as close relatives go, *daughter* trumps *estranged nephew* by a bloody mile."

I'm still reeling, trying to absorb what no one has actually said out loud, but Ben stands rigidly, fixing his glare on me. "A matter of interpretation," he says, like this is somehow my fault. "And I'm certain the palace lawyers will see it my way."

Jenkins clears his throat again. "I fear it is not a matter of interpretation," he says. "I helped His Majesty draft the clause in question, and he was exceptionally clear about his intention. He worded it in such a way to specifically ensure that Her Royal Highness would have the support of the three Counsellors of State—Her Majesty the Queen, Her Majesty the Queen Mother, and His Royal Highness the Duke of York—and her only sibling, Evangeline Bright, once they both turned eighteen. There was, in fact, no discussion regarding your involvement in any potential regency. Sir."

Jenkins says this last word with just a hint of bite, though his posture is straight and his expression unmoving. And I'm absolutely sure that even if Ben enlists half the lawyers in the UK to fight him on this, Jenkins will stand his ground until the bitter end.

Someone knocks on the doorjamb, and Kit and I turn to find two members of the palace security team standing directly behind us. They don't say a word, but they don't have to, and when I look at Ben again, he's turned an unhealthy shade of puce.

"I see," says Ben through his clenched jaw, and yet again, he eyes us one by one until his stare falls on me. There's a new layer to his hatred now—a malevolence so intense that it chills me to the bone. "Then I suppose that settles it. Though I wouldn't be terribly surprised if the public were . . . less than enthusiastic about Evangeline playing a role in this, all things considered."

He lets this hang in the air like it's an invitation, but I know better than to give him that kind of opening. And no one else, not even my viciously smug sister, takes it. After a beat, his smirk returns, and he smooths the front of his jacket.

"I'll see you all rather soon, I suspect," he says, as if he's the victor in this battle. And maybe, in his own mind, he is. "Father. Grandmother. Aunt Helene. Good luck."

He slides past Maisie without a second glance, but Jenkins, I notice, has to step aside to avoid being directly in his path. And when Ben reaches the door, he pauses as he peers down at me, and the air between us is so charged that a single spark could set it on fire.

"Rest assured, Evangeline, that this is only the beginning," he says with eerie calm. And just when I think he's about to keep going, he leans down so close that his lips brush against my ear. "It was meant to be you."

I suck in a breath, stunned. "What the hell is that supposed to mean?" I say raggedly, but as he tilts his head, the picture of innocence, I already know the answer.

I was the one who was supposed to die under a mountain of

rubble. Not Alexander, not Ingrid, not the seven other victims—that bomb was meant for me.

Kit steps forward, danger radiating from him. "I believe Her Royal Highness has made it clear that you are no longer welcome here," he says with inhuman calm, and Ben chuckles.

"My condolences on your most recent failure, Lord Clarence," he says. "Perhaps you'll finally get the job done next time."

And with an enormous wink at Kit, he finally passes through the doorway, waving aside the officers as he strides down the hall and out of sight.

The room is deadly silent. Rattled, I try to catch Kit's eye, but his gaze is focused on the empty doorway, and his lips are parted, almost like he's seen a ghost.

"What is he talking about?" I whisper, but Kit shakes his head and slides a protective arm around my shoulders.

"You should sit," he says, and before I can protest, he leads me around the table to the now-empty chair beside Nicholas. I hesitate, ready to insist that I'm perfectly fine standing, but once again, all eyes are on me. And so I ease down into the chair, my skin crawling when I discover the leather is still warm.

I don't want to be here. I don't want anything to do with Parliament or politics or a maybe-regency for my critically injured father, but even though no one's said it out loud, it's clear now that I'm the only thing standing between Ben and a position on this royal council. And while his whispered words and their terrible implication still slither through my mind, I can't discount the likelihood that they're designed to do exactly this—to shake me so badly that I race out of there and never come back, leaving his seat vacant once more.

And so, knowing I need to tell someone but also painfully aware that now is *not* the time, I shove my trembling hands between my knees and make myself as small as possible. Kit remains behind me, and I take all the comfort I can from his presence, though for once, it isn't enough.

"Well, then," says Maisie as she sits at the head of the table—Alexander's spot. "Shall we get on with it?"

"How is His Majesty?" says Yara immediately, her complexion bloodless. "Is his condition really so poor as to require . . . this?"

"The King's injuries are grave," admits Helene, her gaze fixed on the table in front of her. "And if he does survive, there is a . . . significant possibility they will have a permanent impact on his quality of life. And, potentially, his ability to rule."

This is new information to me, although considering I'm one of the only people in that room who's actually seen Alexander, it shouldn't be. Shock and devastation flicker across Maisie's face, and it's only thanks to what must be a supreme act of willpower that she pulls herself together before she falls to pieces.

"*When* my father recovers," she says, as if challenging not only her mother, but the entire universe to prove her wrong, "we will of course dissolve this council. But until then, we will do our solemn duty to protect and uphold His Majesty's rule."

I stay silent as Jenkins situates himself in the empty spot beside me and leads the meeting from topic to topic, starting with when to release a delicately worded statement about Alexander's condition, and then moving on to how to divide his duties between the members of the royal family—which, to my relief, doesn't seem to include me. Maisie and Helene take the lion's share, but when the topic of public appearances comes up, Nicholas stands.

"There will be no public appearances until we can be certain that all participants of the attack on His Majesty have been rounded up," he insists. "We will not put other members of the family at risk."

"MI5 has already made several arrests in the case, Your Royal Highness," says a man I recognize as the head of palace security—Victor Stephens. "We're working closely with the Home Office to ensure the royal family's safety."

Nicholas nods. "Good. And when we do start to venture out into the world again, I insist that Princess Mary be accompanied by another senior royal whenever she is in public."

Maisie stares at our uncle. "Pardon me?" she says, though there's no politeness in her voice. "With all due respect, our security is the best in the world. I don't need a minder."

"You're in an exceptionally vulnerable position," says Nicholas, "and you will need support from those of us with the experience to guide you."

"And I will have it, in private," says Maisie fiercely. "I suppose *you'd* prefer to escort me everywhere I go?"

"Yes," says Nicholas. "After what's happened to my brother, I very much would."

She gives him a contemptuous look. "You're not superhuman, Uncle Nicholas. You're not going to single-handedly stop a building from falling on me."

"Likely not," he agrees, "but my military background gives me insight into the security of public events that the other members of this family do not have."

"And you don't think our *actual* security team might have a problem with you stepping in to play bodyguard?" She shakes her head. "We need to give the people a sense of stability—a sense of continuity and safety and peace, and the last thing they need is a steady stream of images of their princess being followed around like a child who can't be trusted. I know I'm young, and I know I have a lot to learn, but I will *not* give the country a reason to doubt me, and I will *not* offer the media a single bloody excuse to claim I'm incapable of upholding my duties as the future—"

Suddenly the door flies open, and a sweaty Doyle bursts into the room, clutching a tablet. Despite the sea of people now staring at him, his wild eyes immediately find me.

"Pardon me, Your Majesties, Your Royal Highnesses," he says with a quick bow to the head of the table. "I'm afraid there's a matter that needs immediate attention."

"Is there something more important going on than the attempt on His Majesty's life?" says Jenkins calmly, and Doyle reddens.

"I—" He shakes his head, seeming to think better of it. "Jenkins, you need to see this."

Doyle maneuvers past an irritable Maisie, and Kit presses against my chair to give him enough space to reach Jenkins. Breathing heavily, Doyle hands the tablet over, and as Jenkins examines the screen, he grows very, very still.

"What am I looking at?" he says in a quiet voice that doesn't carry any farther than a few feet.

"That one right there . . ." Doyle reaches over to swipe to a separate page, still panting like he's run a marathon. "Her identity was just released. And as you can see, she's—"

"*Everyone out.*"

Jenkins's commanding voice echoes off the walls, louder than I've ever heard him before, and a shocked murmur ripples through the crowd. Confused, I glance up at Kit, but his eyes are fixed on the tablet, and his fingers dig so deeply into the leather of my chair that I can't even inch back enough to stand.

"You forget yourself, Jenkins," snaps Constance, while Helene looks like she's been slapped across the face.

"My apologies, Your Majesty," says Jenkins, his words unnervingly sharp as he pulls the tablet to his chest. "But I'm afraid we need to adjourn this meeting. I will be in touch with the Privy Council to make all the necessary arrangements, and in the meantime, it is my strongest recommendation that the royal family take a few hours to rest. The days ahead are bound to be difficult, and you will need your strength."

But Maisie climbs to her feet, her annoyance with Nicholas transferring seamlessly to Jenkins. "Nothing could possibly be more important than this meeting," she says hotly as she marches over. "We still have several matters to discuss, and—"

Jenkins bows his head as she approaches. "Forgive me, Your Royal Highness. Now that the royal council has been established, I fear this is currently a more pressing matter."

"What—" she says, but he shows her the tablet, swiping between what seems like two pages, and her perfectly plucked brows furrow. "Is that—"

"Yes, ma'am," he says.

"And that's one of the people who . . . ?"

"Yes, ma'am."

She goes white, and her eyes lock on mine for an unbearably long moment before she straightens. "You heard Jenkins," she says. "Everyone out. Not you," she adds, her gaze flickering toward me once more. "And *certainly* not you."

This is directed toward Kit, who visibly gulps. By now, I'm practically burning with both curiosity and dread, but Jenkins and Maisie don't offer a single hint as every senior adviser except Doyle shuffles out, all looking as baffled as I feel.

"I must insist that we stay," says Constance once the room is nearly empty. Helene and Nicholas stand together at the head of the table now, but the Queen Mother hasn't budged from her seat.

"And I'm afraid I must insist that you excuse us for the time being, Grandmama," says Maisie. "I'll see you all at breakfast as soon as we're done here."

Constance opens her mouth to argue, but Nicholas sets his hand on her shoulder. "Mother, let's go," he says quietly. "Whatever this is, the sooner it's resolved, the sooner we can return to the matter at hand."

She doesn't look convinced, but after several seconds, it becomes clear that Maisie isn't going to cave, and Constance narrows her eyes. "You're every bit as insolent as your father," she says as she stands. "Do try to remember that you aren't the sovereign yet, darling."

"A fact for which I am exceptionally grateful at the moment," says Maisie hotly, glaring at Kit once more.

As soon as they've left, royal protection officers in tow, I wiggle out from between my seat and the table and finally stand. "What's going on?" I demand, facing the four of them. "Kit?"

He shakes his head, his dark eyes focused on the carpet now. "I'm sorry, Evan," he says with a desperate note in his voice. "I didn't know. I thought . . ." He rakes his fingers through his hair and finally looks at me, and his face is full of such naked vulnerability and fear that my insides turn to lead. "I didn't *know.*"

"Out of all the things you two could've done," says Maisie, and to my shock, her voice catches like she's about to cry. "Are you both out of your bloody minds?"

"What are you talking about?" I say, alarmed. *"What is going on?"*

At last, with the reluctance of someone about to saw off their own limb, Jenkins shows me the tablet. I don't know what to expect, but the possibilities racing through my mind are too horrible to contemplate for long—and not at all like the innocuous picture on the screen.

The red brick buildings of the town near Sandringham fill the background, and in the corner of the image, I can just make out the sign from Noble Norfolk Novelties, the ice cream-slash-gift shop Kit and I visited. I'm standing on the sidewalk with the redheaded Aoife, who hugs me like we've known each other our whole lives. Kit lingers beside us, looking nervously over his shoulder, while Aoife's boyfriend—Dylan, I think—is facing away from the camera, his knit hat hiding any trace of his features.

Bewildered, I search the photo for some hidden image—some clue as to why they're all panicking. "Those are Kit's friends from school," I say. "We ran into them when we were picking up presents for my mom. That's right after Maisie texted Kit about Ben—we were heading back, and—"

"So you do know her?" says Maisie like this is somehow a massive betrayal.

"Aoife? No, not really. This is the only time we ever met. She hugged me before I could get away, that's all. Kit—" I say, turning to him for confirmation, but his entire body is hunched over the back of my chair now, and he looks like he's about to collapse.

"Evan," says Jenkins in a measured voice. "This woman's name is Aoife Marsh. You're *absolutely* certain this is the only time you two have met?"

"Positive," I say, my heart thumping so hard that I can hear my pulse. "Please, just tell me what's going on. You're scaring me."

For a split second, no one replies. But at last, with a heavy sigh, Jenkins swipes to another tab, and the BBC home page appears. A single headline dominates the screen:

TERRORISTS BEHIND BOMBING IDENTIFIED

"The Home Office has released the names of the suspects arrested yesterday in connection to the bombing," says Jenkins. "And Aoife Marsh—the girl you're hugging in this photo—is one of them."

CHAPTER TWENTY-SEVEN

We at the *Regal Record* can exclusively reveal that Evangeline Bright, illegitimate daughter of the King, is allegedly a close friend of one of the suspected terrorists in the bombing of the Modern Music Museum in London.

Evangeline and Aoife Marsh, 19, pictured together below, met last year through Christopher Abbott-Montgomery, Earl of Clarence, and the two have reportedly been in constant contact ever since. Marsh was one of three suspects arrested at the scene of the bombing yesterday morning, during an official visit from the King, whose condition remains unknown. Eight others were killed in the blast, including two royal protection officers thought to be guarding His Majesty.

Both Evangeline and Lord Clarence were present during the attack, though the couple, who began dating this past summer, were released from a London hospital in the early hours of this morning. Evangeline was infamously involved in the death of Jasper Cunningham this past June, but was not charged despite alluding to her guilt in a live interview that aired weeks later.

There has so far been no word from the Home Office on the connection between Evangeline, Lord Clarence, and Marsh, though we can only hope that with eight families mourning the loss of their loved ones today, no one, not even the daughter of the King, will be above the law this time.

—*The Regal Record,* 13 January 2024

AOIFE, KIT'S SWEET AND BUBBLY friend from university, tried to kill my father.

Aoife, whose beaming face is clearly visible over my shoulder in the image on Doyle's tablet, is responsible for the deaths of Ingrid and seven other innocent people.

Aoife, who's hugging me like we're best friends and have known each other our entire lives, is an actual terrorist.

And somehow the only picture of us together has surfaced barely twenty-four hours after the bombing.

My stomach twists so violently that I think I might be sick, and slowly, as if one wrong move will make me fall apart, I sink down onto the edge of the mahogany table, my head spinning.

I don't know what to say. There's nothing *to* say, not when the media will take this picture and wring every last drop of conjecture and bad-faith assumption out of it. Even if the palace tries to claim it's photoshopped, even if the royal press office manages to convince the BBC and CNN and every other major news outlet that Aoife and I've only met once, this single photo will inevitably make headlines around the world. And this time, it'll be my name trending with *#offwithherhead*.

"Do we know where it came from?" says Jenkins to Doyle, who grunts ambiguously.

"A gossip site called the *Regal Record* posted it fifteen minutes ago," he says, and Maisie sneers. "I already have my team trying to get them to take it down, but—"

"They won't," says Jenkins grimly, pinching the bridge of his nose. "Bloody hell. How do we get ahead of this?"

"I don't know that we do," admits Doyle. "We can release a statement making it clear that she and Evangeline have no connection, but it won't do any good, not if Lord Clarence knows her. The media will immediately frame it as a cover-up."

Maisie crosses her arms tightly over her chest, her lower

lip caught between her teeth before she speaks. "Talk to us, Kit. How do you know these people? *Why* do you know these people?"

Kit's eyes are still glued to the floor, and when he speaks, it seems to take him an enormous amount of effort. "I knew Dylan at Eton," he rasps like he hasn't had water in days. "We ended up on the same course at university. I . . . I didn't suspect anything was off until recently, but—"

"Until recently?" I blurt, stunned. "You knew they were . . . ?"

"No," he says firmly, and finally he looks at me. "I didn't know they were involved in this sort of thing, Evan, I swear. They—" He grimaces. "They're members of a group called Fox Rex."

"The dinner club?" says Doyle, seemingly flabbergasted. "I remember it from my Christ Church days. Wasn't it banned years ago?"

"Yes," says Kit, but his focus is still on me. "Though apparently it was resurrected as a secret society. Over the summer, I discovered that my brother was a member, and . . . they invited me to join at the start of term."

Secret societies aren't news to me—there were plenty of those at the boarding schools I attended, but as far as I know, none of them turned into terrorist organizations. "What does that have to do with the bombing?" I say.

"I'm getting there," he assures me, his Adam's apple bobbing. "I turned them down at first, and they started to push, particularly Dylan and Aoife. Dylan has always been . . . outspoken about his politics. He's a republican," he adds, and he must see the question on my face, because he clarifies, "In the

UK, it means he's an anti-monarchist. He doesn't support the royal family."

"Oh," I say. "Is that why you were nervous when we ran into them?"

"One of the reasons," he admits. "And . . . because it's relevant, if my aunt weren't who she is, I'd likely lean that way as well. Which I made the mistake of mentioning to Dylan while we were at Eton, before I ended up with a bloody courtesy title."

This is news, and I stare at him. "You're a . . . republican, too?"

He shakes his head, and I can see the pleading in his eyes. "Not in the way they are. *Never* in the way they are. The things Dylan would let slip when he was drinking . . ." A muscle in his jaw twitches. "He told me on Bonfire Night that among the more senior members of the club, it isn't Fox Rex. It's *Fawkes* Rex. As in Guy Fawkes."

"The fifth of November guy?" I say, and this earns a loud snort of derision from Maisie.

"Honestly, what *have* your tutors been teaching you?" she mutters. "Yes, the traitor who tried to blow up Westminster Palace in the Gunpowder Plot of 1605. He and his co-conspirators wanted to assassinate King James I. Though *they* intended to place a Catholic monarch on the throne in his stead," she adds. "Not abolish it entirely. That was far more of a Cromwellian thing."

"I don't know what that means—"

"And not one of us is surprised," she says, cutting me off. "Kit, will you *please* get to the bloody point?"

He flinches, and when he continues, he's looking at me again, as if I'm the only thing that matters about any of this. "The more Dylan let slip, the more I wondered if . . . perhaps it didn't have something to do with the reason why Liam . . ." He pauses, pain flickering in his deep brown eyes. "I was chasing ghosts, and Dylan could tell. He mentioned my brother a few times, hinted that I might find some answers, and finally I agreed to join. I didn't question *why* they wanted me so badly, but as soon as I became a member, it was clear my presence offered their more . . . extreme political leanings legitimacy."

"In what way?" says Jenkins. Kit exhales.

"I discovered that everyone invited was an anti-monarchist to some degree. And while I'm not—I'm *not*," he insists at Maisie's quirked eyebrow. "Even then, my courtesy title, my future dukedom, Aunt Helene . . . it was as if they could put me on a pedestal and claim they were surely on the right side of history, if even the nephew of the King and Queen wanted to be part of it. As soon as I realized what sort of mess I'd gotten myself into, I tried to disengage. We were nearing the end of term by then anyway, and it was easy to prioritize exams."

"Why didn't you tell me?" I say, my voice small and pathetic, but the words are out before I know they're coming.

"I'm sorry, Ev," says Kit, and his hand flexes like he wants to reach for me, but he doesn't close the distance between us. "I'm so bloody sorry. I wanted to tell you, but . . . I could never find the right words. And you've had enough on your plate lately, with everything that happened over the summer, and I didn't want you to worry."

Part of me isn't surprised, though that doesn't stop it all from hurting anyway. "You should have said something," I say. "I could have helped. Or—I would've at least listened."

"I know," he says, his voice barely audible now. "I'm sorry. It wasn't you—it was never you. I was . . . ashamed that I got taken in like that. That I didn't see them coming, and the last thing I wanted was for you to get tangled up in it as well."

"Too late now," I mutter, glaring at the tablet. "That picture . . . Kit, it makes it look like—like—"

"I know." His eyes are shining with tears now. "I had no idea. It must've been a setup—it was too much of a coincidence to run into them, and now the photo . . ."

"Do you have reason to believe there's a connection between this Fawkes Rex club and the Army of the British Republic?" says Jenkins. "They're the ones who've taken credit for the attack, though MI5 has yet to confirm their involvement."

Kit shakes his head, but at the same time, he gestures toward the screen. "Aoife's proof, isn't she? And the other names that were released . . . I recognize them, too."

Doyle mutters several curses under his breath, while Maisie's posture stiffens. "You're certain?" she says.

"That I recognize the names? Yes," says Kit. "That Fawkes Rex has any direct ties to this Army of the British Republic outside of Aoife and her cohorts? No. It could feed the other way— Aoife could have been involved with the bombers before she joined the club, or the other members could've roped her into it. I thought—I thought it was all theoretical," he adds, pinching the bridge of his nose. "If I'd known for a second that there was a plan, or any chance they might've taken action . . ."

He trails off, and my sister watches him, her expression unforgiving. "You need to speak to MI5 immediately," says Maisie. "The photo's already out there, and we've no hope of getting ahead of it now. But we can at least come up with a reasonable explanation that has a chance of mitigating the damage and proving your innocence. And Evan's," she adds, glancing at me. "But the fact that you two were there yesterday . . . it doesn't look good."

No, it doesn't, and as I stare at the picture again, I finally begin to understand just how bad this all is.

"Doyle," says Jenkins, "draft a statement for anyone who asks about the photograph. Make it clear that Evangeline's met thousands of people during her time in the UK, and find pictures of her hugging other fans to send to journalists who are friendly to us."

"I could spin it into a security issue," suggests Doyle. "Make it seem like we're deeply concerned that someone like Aoife Marsh was able to gain access to Evangeline and accost her in the street."

"Do whatever you have to do to steal the narrative," agrees Jenkins. "Lord Clarence, I'll have one of the palace lawyers join you before MI5 arrives. Follow their directions to the letter, is that understood?"

Kit nods mutely.

"Good. Your Royal Highness, as soon as everything is taken care of, I'll update you and the rest of the royal family."

"Please do," says Maisie with stiff bravado, but I can see the fear in her eyes.

"And Evan . . ." Jenkins takes my hand in his, and it's only then that I realize I'm trembling. "It's likely that you'll need to speak to MI5 as well, I'm afraid. Is that something you're willing to do?"

I try to nod, but it's taking everything I have not to cry. Jenkins watches me for a long moment before pulling me into a gentle hug, and I cling to him as a single sob finally escapes.

"We'll sort this out, darling," he murmurs into my ear. "I promise. None of this is your fault."

But as bad as it all is for me, that's not the reason I'm crying. Instead, I watch Kit over Jenkins's shoulder, both furious with him and terrified for him at the same time.

"I need to . . ." I try to say, but the words come out as a croak, and I clear my throat. "I need to talk to Kit. Alone. Please."

Doyle looks dubious at best, and even Maisie hesitates, but it's Jenkins who shakes his head. "I don't think that's a good idea, sweetheart."

I pull back. "What? Why not?"

"Because this way, the three of us can assure the Home Office that there's been no collusion between the two of you now that we know about Lord Clarence's connection to the suspects."

"Collusion?" I stumble over the word. "Jenkins, this isn't some spy movie—"

"He's right, Evan," says Kit thickly. "If this gets . . . sticky for me, the palace is going to focus on protecting you. And they can't do that if you're trying to protect me."

"I—" I look between them, stunned. "So what, you're going to separate us?"

Doyle dabs his forehead with a handkerchief. "For the time

being, it would be . . . wise for Lord Clarence to keep his distance from the royal family," he says. "Not only from a legal perspective, but the optics—"

"But he didn't do anything wrong," I protest. "If you kick him out, it'll look like we think he did. *Jenkins*—"

"I'm sorry, darling, but this is all rather serious, I'm afraid," he says, still holding my hand. "We'll know more once you and Lord Clarence speak to the Home Office."

I open and shut my mouth, momentarily speechless, and finally I look at my sister. "Maisie, please," I beg. "He's your cousin."

"So is Ben." Her eyes are red as she meets mine. "I'm sorry, Evan. You told me to listen to my advisers, and . . . I'm listening."

I push off the edge of the table with such force that my leg nearly buckles beneath me. "This isn't fair," I say jaggedly. "You know it's not fair. You can't just throw him to the wolves because it's easier—"

"We're not throwing anyone to the wolves," says Jenkins. "You're right, Evan. He didn't do anything wrong. But we need the opportunity to prove that. He'll have our best lawyers with him, and when it's all said and done, everything will be fine."

"How can you say that when—" I begin, but a tentative brush against my shoulder startles me, and as I whirl around, Kit snatches his hand back, every bit as fearful of touching me as he was during those first few weeks we knew each other. This, more than anything, is what breaks me, and when I finally close the distance between us and throw myself into his arms, it's a relief to feel him embrace me in return.

"It's all right," he murmurs into my hair—not a whisper, not a secret Jenkins and Doyle and Maisie can hold against us. "As soon as we talk to MI5, it'll all be settled. Dylan and Aoife have been texting me about the club for months, and I have everything I need to prove I had nothing to do with any of this. And that you didn't, either."

The ringing in my ears grows louder again as I hold him, refusing to let go. All I can picture are the terrible ways this could end—the worst-case scenarios that have Aoife and Dylan claiming Kit was part of this all along, that he offered them access and information and gave them everything they needed to pull this off. I can see the headlines. I can hear the jeers and the boos. I can imagine the talking heads and media figures tearing him down, mentioning his name in the same breath as Aoife Marsh and acting like they were in this together the entire time. And I'm terrified.

At last it's Kit who gently pushes me away, until I'm clutching the fabric of his jacket and staring up at his blurry face. "I'll see you soon, Ev," he promises, resting his forehead against mine. That small gesture is enough to remind me of what my parents have been through and how everything in their lives conspired against them, and I am desperate—*desperate* to not let that happen to us.

"I love you," I say, the words easy even if I have to force them past the lump in my throat. And despite the way everything is going so incredibly wrong, he manages a tiny, genuine smile.

"I love you, too," he says, pressing his lips to my temple. And then it's Jenkins's arm around me instead, leading me to the exit. I watch Kit over my shoulder until we reach the doorway, and the last image I see of him is of his hand pressed to his mouth, and the utter despair he must've been holding at bay finally creeping over him, stealing the last of his smile.

CHAPTER TWENTY-EIGHT

"Henrietta, with all that's happened in the past twenty-four hours, I scarcely know where to begin."

"It's all been rather shocking, hasn't it? But with the statement that was just released from Buckingham Palace regarding the King's condition, we're finally starting to see some answers."

"His Majesty is alive—that's certainly more than some were speculating."

"Alive, yes, but given the news that the royal family is invoking certain clauses of the Regency Act of 2005, it's clear that his injuries are extensive and potentially life-threatening."

"Can you tell us more about the Regency Act, Henrietta? And how it may affect us all in the days and weeks to come?"

"The first modern-day Regency Act was passed in 1936, after Edward VIII took the throne when his son, who later became Alexander I, was only seven years old. Parliament wanted to ensure that there was a clear path forward if Edward VIII died before his heir reached the age of eighteen, and that involved creating the position of Counsellors of State—members of the royal family over the age of twenty-one who may perform most of the sovereign's duties, should he be temporarily incapacitated or abroad. Traditionally these include the monarch's consort and the first four adults in the line of succession, though as the royal family began to slim down in recent generations, the number has fluctuated. Now the heir to the throne is included, should they be over the age of eighteen, as well as the consort of the former sovereign."

"The Queen Mother, you mean?"

"Indeed. Queen Florence, His Majesty's grandmother, was also a Counsellor of State until her retirement from public duties shortly before her death."

"And who are the Counsellors of State today?"

"Officially, the Queen, the Queen Mother, the Duke of York, and Princess Mary, now that she's eighteen, are the only four Counsellors of State. Prince Benedict, of course, is still under the age of twenty-one, and Prince Edgar, the fourth in line to the throne and second son of Alexander I, does not reside in Britain, nor do his descendants. After him come the descendants of Edward VIII's daughters, Princess Victoria and Princess Phillipa, none of whom have titles or are actively involved in royal life."

"So in this time of great need, we are short a Counsellor of State."

"Indeed. But there are several curiosities regarding the Regency Act of 2005, most important of which deals with precisely the situation we've found ourselves in now—what happens if His Majesty is incapacitated, either temporarily or permanently, before Princess Mary turns twenty-one."

"Presumably the monarchy would become a regency, yes?"

"It's possible, though a regency will only be established if His Majesty is permanently unable to perform his duties. In either case, after Princess Mary was born, the King worked with Parliament to outline a plan to ensure she would not be burdened with the full weight of the crown whilst still a teenager."

"And this is where this . . . royal council comes in, yes?"

"Precisely. His Majesty requested that should he be temporarily incapacitated, or should Her Royal

Highness be placed in a position of regent or monarch before the age of twenty-one, she be assisted by four individuals: the Counsellors of State, and should this equal less than four, then her closest blood relatives over the age of eighteen."

"Which, until now, we all assumed was included to allow for Prince Benedict's involvement, considering he was born the year before Princess Mary."

"Yes. But it seems His Majesty has, as they say, pulled a fast one on us all. At the time the clause was drafted, he was very much aware that he had a second daughter—Evangeline Bright. And the statement from Buckingham Palace announcing the arrangement has made it clear that *she* was always the intended final member of the council, *not* Prince Benedict."

"A rather unusual choice for His Majesty to make, considering Evangeline's existence was only revealed to the public last summer."

"'Unusual' doesn't even begin to cover it, I'm afraid. Parliament almost certainly wouldn't have accepted the wording as it stands had they known an illegitimate half sibling would be involved, and I'd imagine that this won't help calm the inevitable chaos in the palace at the moment."

"What should we expect from this royal council, moving forward?"

"It's difficult to say, as such a council has never been established before, let alone placed in a position of authority over the monarchy. But I have no doubt that everyone involved wishes to work together toward the best interests of this country and its people, and with the experience of two queen consorts at Princess Mary's disposal, we can only hope the transition—whether temporary or permanent—is as smooth as possible, given the tragic circumstances."

"And if His Majesty, God forbid, succumbs to his injuries?"

"Should the unthinkable happen, then with the royal council's continued guidance, Princess Mary will officially ascend the throne, and the United Kingdom will have our first queen regnant since the age of Victoria."

—ITV News's interview with royal expert Henrietta Smythe, 13 January 2024

I SPEND THE REST OF the morning in a much smaller conference room with Wiggs, the gray-haired palace lawyer who represented me during the investigation into Jasper Cunningham's death, as he takes me through every excruciating detail of my meeting with Aoife Marsh.

For the most part, he's sympathetic, but he has me repeat my story more than a dozen times, in different ways and from different angles, and I start to notice that his questions are designed to trip me up and catch me in a lie. And while I know that it's his job to make sure he has as much of the truth as I do before he squares off with MI5 for me, especially with the stakes so high, by the time Suraj Singh strides into the room with a laptop tucked under his arm, my nerves are frayed and my patience is dangerously close to zero.

"Miss Bright," he says politely, but instead of sitting down, he opens the laptop so I have a clear view of the blank screen. His suit is identical to the one he wore in the hospital the night before, and even though it looks clean and pressed, part of me wonders if he hasn't gone home.

"What's this about?" says Wiggs gruffly, eyeing the laptop. Singh taps a key, and the image of a human silhouette appears, its identifying features in shadow.

"This video was posted by the Army of the British Republic

less than twenty minutes ago," says Singh as he sets the computer down on the table, and before Wiggs can ask any more questions, he hits Play.

"—rocked the entire world with our message, and we're only getting started," says a pitched voice as the silhouette shifts. "We have shown our so-called rulers that they are not and will never be our betters, and that they sit on their thrones because we the people allow it. Because we the people *tolerate* their existence, not because they have any true power, and the time has come for us to refuse to stand by and endure the shame of their lechery and depravity in the name of our great country."

A chill runs through me at the sheer loathing in those words, but even though there's nothing really happening on-screen, I can't tear my eyes away.

"For now, we must live in the shadows, loyal soldiers dedicated to a single cause. We rejoice in our suffering because we know it will lead to a future where the people will no longer have to live with the corruption, the theft, the *evil* with which our kings and queens built their empires, and we know that we alone have the will to stop them.

"But not all of us have remained hidden," continues the voice, and the silhouette seems to lean closer to the camera. "We are proud of those who have risked their lives for our cause, and prouder still of those who have risked their legacies. To have their names among ours, to know that even those who live in the nest of snakes can see the cruelty and immorality of their existence—this is what sparks us all into action, for even those who benefit from the systems that have held the people hostage are able to see that justice must be served."

The silhouette fades, and to my horror, a video clip starts to play—one of me and Aoife on the street outside the gift shop, filmed from at least thirty feet away. We're chatting like old friends, and as we move toward the Range Rover, she throws her arms around me as she says goodbye—and in my attempt not to offend her, I look like I'm hugging back. It's everything that damn photograph is, but worse, because no one, not even the palace, will be able to claim it's fake now. Or that it was a simple meet and greet gone terribly, unthinkably wrong.

"Our undying thanks to Evangeline Bright for the important role she played," says the pitched voice again, and I clutch the table so hard that I break a nail. "Without her contribution, our cause would have been lost, but now we are stronger than—"

Singh taps the keys again, and the screen goes blank. I open and shut my mouth, my head spinning as I try to think of something—*anything*—to explain why the apparent leader of the Army of the British Republic thanked me personally.

"I—I didn't have anything to do with—" I begin shakily, but Wiggs covers my hand in a silent attempt to get me to shut up. I don't, though—I physically can't stop myself, and I pull away. "I don't know these people. I only met that girl once, I swear—"

"I believe you," says Singh, and the rest of my protest dies on my tongue.

"You—what?" I say as he glances at me, then at Wiggs, who must wear a similar expression of incredulity, because despite the fact that I'm staring down the barrel of treason, there's a faint smile tugging at the corners of Singh's mouth.

He finally sits in a chair at the head of the table, next to me rather than across. "Tell me, Miss Bright," he says. "If you were running an underground organization determined to destroy the monarchy, and you were lucky enough to convince a member of the royal family to help, would you turn around and thank them publicly after failing to assassinate the King?"

This time I know better than to answer the question, and Wiggs clears his throat instead. "Miss Bright had nothing to do with the attempt on His Majesty's life, and was herself a victim who very nearly died—"

"Yes," says Singh with compassion I don't expect. "I was sorry to hear about your personal protection officer, Evangeline. I've been to the site of the bombing, and there is no question that that could have been—perhaps was meant to be—you."

I dig my nails into my palms as I remember the words Ben whispered to me only a few hours earlier. "She died to protect me," I say roughly. "I would never—*never* help these people try to kill my family and friends."

"On the outside looking in, there seems to be no sense in it, I agree," he says. "Though just because I don't see the connection right away doesn't mean there isn't one. In this particular case, however," he adds, gesturing toward the laptop, "it is far too neat. It's so perfect that it's sloppy."

I don't know what to say to that, or if I should say anything at all, and so I let Wiggs do the talking yet again. "Miss Bright only met the alleged bomber once, during a brief outing in Norfolk—"

"A fact which Lord Clarence has confirmed—multiple times, each more insistent than the last," says Singh. "I *will* need to hear your version of events, Evangeline. But for now, I'm far more curious why the Army of the British Republic would name you, specifically, as their accomplice."

"Miss Bright had nothing to do with—"

"Yet again, Mr. Wiggs, I believe her." Singh eyes the pair of us. "Do you think it might be possible to work under the presumption that I am an ally, not an enemy? My goal is to find out what happened to His Majesty and the victims of the bombing, and to identify the members of this organization before they can do any more harm. It is quite curious to me that they would name Evangeline rather than the much more plausible Lord Clarence, and I'd like to hear her thoughts on why."

After a brief pause, Wiggs nods slightly toward me, and I gulp. "I don't know," I say at last. "None of it makes sense. That picture, the video—all of it had to be a setup, but I don't know *why.*"

My voice breaks on this last word, but I force myself to hold it together, and again I hear Ben's whisper.

It was meant to be you.

That wasn't the only thing he said before leaving the conference room, though. And with a sudden stark clarity, I look at Singh, my eyes wide.

"Ben," I blurt. "Prince Benedict, my cousin. He said something to me and Kit earlier—"

"Miss Bright," says Wiggs in a warning tone, but when I feel his touch again, I jerk away.

"I'd like to hear what His Royal Highness said," says Singh to Wiggs, but the words are already tumbling out of me.

"He told Kit—Christopher Abbott-Montgomery—he said

something like, 'my condolences for your most recent failure. Maybe you'll finally get the job done next time.' I didn't understand what he was talking about," I add quickly, before either Singh or Wiggs can interrupt. "But I didn't know about—about the group Kit joined, or that Aoife was working for the bombers, or any of it."

Singh pulls a small notepad out of his suit jacket and flips through a few pages. "I don't recall Lord Clarence mentioning this interaction."

"Ask him," I say. "He'll tell you. Ask everyone seated by the door in the conference room—they could hear it, too."

Singh scribbles a note. "So you believe that your cousin, His Royal Highness Prince Benedict, is also trying to frame you?"

"That's quite enough," blusters Wiggs. "It's one thing to question Miss Bright about her involvement when she has been named by the organization in question, but to drag His Royal Highness into this when he is not here to defend himself—"

"He told me it was meant to be me," I say, and my voice wavers as my face grows hot. "In the conference room, before he accused Kit of being involved in the bombing—he whispered in my ear and said it was meant to be me."

Singh leans forward before Wiggs can come up with a coherent response. "And you believe His Royal Highness was referring to . . . ?"

"Ingrid," I manage shakily. "Or maybe Alexander. I don't know. It was a threat. All he does is threaten me. Back in June, he told me he was going to destroy me, and now every time I see him, it's like he's trying to decide what to put on my gravestone.

He was there at Sandringham when someone tried to kill me and Kit, but even though he was with Alexander and the rest of the hunting party, I'm sure he had something to do with it, and—"

"I'm afraid Miss Bright has had a very difficult few days," says Wiggs suddenly. "Unless you have any further questions regarding her single brief meeting with Aoife Marsh, then I must insist that you allow her time to rest."

My eyes are blurry with tears of frustration now, but I can still see Singh watching me. I want to say more—I should say more—but Wiggs is right. I have no evidence. I have no proof that Ben is behind any of this, only a bone-deep certainty that every terrible thing that's happened somehow points back to him. But he has an alibi for all of it, and while Ben may be many things, he isn't the kind of reckless that would ever let him slip. At least not where anyone else could see it.

"Yes, I think it might be prudent to continue this conversation at another time," agrees Singh, his dark eyes still on me as he closes his notebook. "For now, I would suggest you remain in the comfort of the royal residences, Evangeline. We don't have a full picture of what the Army of the British Republic's intentions are, nor what other plans may already be in motion, and it's best not to give them any opportunities."

Opportunities. "You mean chances to try again," I mumble, and he nods.

"Yes, among other things."

I stare at the grain of the polished wooden table as all the fight and stubbornness drain out of me. If I stay at Windsor, then I won't be able to sit with my mom at Alexander's bedside. But the thought of making her a target, too, is enough to nauseate me all over again, and I take a deep breath and nod.

"Everyone's going to think Kit and I were behind this, aren't they?" I say in a small voice.

"It's likely, for the time being," says Singh plainly. "Should this all be a misunderstanding, however, no doubt the public will be relieved to hear it."

That's definitely not true. I'm still being blamed for Jasper's death in plenty of corners of the internet, and no matter what happens next, I know that those same people will latch onto these accusations like leeches until there's nothing left of the truth to believe. And by the time this is over, even if the prime minister himself declares on national television that I had absolutely nothing to do with this, it'll be too late.

Everyone in the world is going to think I tried to kill my father. And I have no way to prove I didn't.

CHAPTER TWENTY-NINE

BOMBERS CLAIM EVANGELINE BRIGHT AS ALLY

—BBC News, 13 January 2024

AMERICAN PRINCESS REPORTEDLY INVOLVED IN ROYAL BOMBING

—CNN, 13 January 2024

HEAD OF ARMY OF BRITISH REPUBLIC: THANK YOU, EVANGELINE

—*The Daily Sun,* 13 January 2024

ROYAL FAMILY ON LOCKDOWN—EVANGELINE REMAINS AT WINDSOR

—BBC News, 14 January 2024

PRESIDENT PARK WISHES KING ALEXANDER SPEEDY RECOVERY, CONDEMNS TERRORISTS RESPONSIBLE FOR MUSEUM BOMBING

—CNN, 14 January 2024

EVANGELINE NAMED OFFICIAL SUSPECT IN BOMBING BY HOME OFFICE

—*The Daily Sun,* 14 January 2024

EVANGELINE REMAINS AT WINDSOR WITH PRINCESS MARY DESPITE CONNECTION TO ROYAL BOMBING

—BBC News, 15 January 2024

PALACE INSIDER REPORTS EVANGELINE FROZEN OUT OF ROYAL FAMILY

—CNN, 15 January 2024

PRIME MINISTER ISSUES STATEMENT SUPPORTING KING, CALLING FOR FULL INVESTIGATION INTO EVANGELINE'S CONNECTION TO ABR

—*The Daily Sun,* 15 January 2024

OVER THE NEXT SEVERAL DAYS, I'm practically a ghost.

Singh confiscates my laptop and phone, leaving me with no way to see what the world is saying about me. Tibby, on the other hand, is glued to her screen, and while she refuses to spill any details about what's happening in the headlines and on social media, her favorite new pastime is declaring it all *utter bollocks.* And though part of me knows that remaining blissfully ignorant is undoubtedly for the best, the possibilities still eat away at me until I feel like I'm losing my mind.

My schedule isn't completely empty. Every morning, I sit in the conference room with Maisie, Helene, Constance, and Nicholas, along with a revolving door of senior advisers, as they all make plans and decisions I barely understand. While Jenkins attends the first few meetings and goes to significant lengths to make sure I'm included, he's conspicuously absent from the rest. And from then on, no one will look at me, and I never speak up. My only job is to fill a seat that would otherwise be Ben's, and that, I know, is the sole reason Helene hasn't thrown me out on my arse. Though she and Constance are both cold to the point of being unapproachable, neither seems to actually believe the ABR's claims about me, probably because it would also mean believing that Kit was involved. But the truth doesn't stop either of them from treating me like the whole wretched scandal is entirely my fault.

To make it all worse, Kit officially leaves Windsor for his family's townhouse in London. While he isn't far, we have no way of communicating—and even if we did, I'm sure he wouldn't risk it, not when it might give Singh a reason to reconsider my supposed innocence. But either way, the solid foundation Kit has offered me for the past seven months is gone, and I constantly feel like I'm walking on shaky ground, and one small push could send me spiraling into oblivion.

On the fifth day after the bombing, I wake up to another round of whispers. They're more frequent now that I'm on my own, and I lie in bed, my eyes squeezed shut as I try to ignore them.

"Evangeline."

"Evangeline."

"Evangeline."

At first my name is almost white noise in the quiet of the early morning. But as the seconds pass, the whispers seem to converge until they become a single voice pulsing in the air, and even when I roll over and bury my head underneath the pillow, I can still hear them. With a curse, I shove the blanket off me and sit up with dizzying force.

"Go *away!*"

The words ring through my bedroom, and silence rushes in as the whispers abruptly disappear. Startled, I look around in the darkness, but before I can figure out what just happened, my door swings open, and Tibby stands silhouetted in the lamplight from the sitting room.

"Evan?" she says. "Are you all right?"

"Fine," I mutter, though my heart is racing. I push a loose

lock of hair from my face, and I can hear the faint thud of Tibby's heels as she walks toward the windows. "What are you doing here so early?"

"Fitz is a wreck, so I stopped by to help him arrange Her Royal Highness's schedule for the rest of the week," she says as she opens the curtains, even though the sun hasn't come up yet. "Naturally the job took all of ten minutes. Did you have a nightmare?"

She says this in a strange, almost sympathetic tone that doesn't sound natural on her, and I shake my head. "It doesn't matter," I say, climbing to my feet. "I need to shower."

Tibby lets me trudge off to my bathroom without further comment, but I can feel her eyes on me as I go. And once I emerge half an hour later, she speaks to me like I'm a feral animal that's one wrong word away from biting her, and I know it's going to be a very long day.

I barely manage to choke down a croissant at breakfast, and I don't say a word during the meeting that follows. Vaguely I note the dark circles under Maisie's eyes—ones that are slowly beginning to rival Helene's—but she, like everyone else, does a remarkable job of acting like my seat is empty, and the moment the meeting is adjourned, I escape into the hall and make myself scarce.

This time, however, the thought of returning to my room and enduring Tibby's sympathy is too much to bear, and so rather than turning left when I reach the bottom of the staircase, I turn right, heading for the drawing rooms instead.

Even though seemingly every adviser is on call, the household staff has been reduced in the wake of the bombing, and the long gallery is empty. As I pass the series of doors that lead into the royal family's private apartments, I pause in front of one that's identical to the rest, but as far as I know, no one except cleaning personnel has been inside in months.

Ben's suite.

My fingers wrap around the handle before I know what I'm doing, and I give it an experimental twist. The knob doesn't give, and I take a deep breath, standing perfectly still. I shouldn't be here. I should keep walking and disappear into the maze that is the state apartments and not give this door another thought. But something compulsive—something irresistible—makes me slip my lockpicks out of the narrow pocket in the waistband of my leggings, and after a quick glance up and down the corridor to make sure no one is coming, I slide them into the keyhole.

Fifteen seconds later, I'm inside, my back pressed against the closed door as I look around the room. It's different from the last time I was in here—less lived-in, somehow, even though none of the blue-and-gold furniture has changed. But the floor-to-ceiling bookcases are full of generic leather-bound books and artfully arranged knickknacks, and when I peek inside the credenzas near the dining table, where Ben stashed the rest of his seemingly endless supply of paperback novels, they're empty.

That should be the end of it—solid evidence that any sign of Ben's time here has been vacuumed and dusted away. But something pulls me toward the door that leads into his former bedroom, and when the handle turns easily, I cross the threshold, feeling as if I'm entering a tomb.

It's nearly pitch-black inside, with heavy velvet curtains covering the windows and blocking out the sun, but I don't bother fumbling around for a switch. Instead, I let the light from the sitting room spill inside as I move straight toward the large wardrobe and open the doors. It's also empty, without even so much as a single stray sock or hanger left behind, but I'm not surprised. If his books are gone, then his clothes must be, too.

I crouch down and feel around the bottom of the wardrobe, until my fingers brush against a slight gap at the edge. With dread settling in the pit of my stomach, I lift the false bottom of Ben's favorite hiding spot and hold my breath.

At first, all I see is darkness. My body is blocking the light from the sitting room, and it isn't until I shift that I notice a shadow lurking inside. The last time I was here, the contents of the drawer were mostly organized, save for the pile of adult magazines that served as a decoy to keep anyone from searching too hard. But now, the Polaroids and media and manila envelopes are gone, and in their place sits something strange and irregular. Gathering my courage, I reach inside, and my fingers brush—

A flower.

I snatch my hand back, and it takes me several long seconds before I can make myself touch it again. The petals are velvety soft, and gingerly I pull it out of the hiding place, not at all surprised when the light reveals it's a blood-red gerbera daisy. Ben must have stashed it here before Maisie kicked him out of Windsor, but the daisy doesn't look like it's been lying at the bottom of a dark wardrobe for the past five days. It's healthy and thriving, as if it were plucked straight from a vase full of water. As if Ben placed it here minutes ago, knowing I was about to come looking.

Suddenly my skin prickles like something—or someone—is

watching me, and I scramble to my feet, the flower clutched in my hand. I don't bother to close the wardrobe as I hurry out of the bedroom. Ben will know I was here whether or not I cover my tracks, and I dash through the rest of his suite, my pulse racing and my vision blurring—with anger, with determination, with every answer I know I have, but can't prove. And maybe that's the point. Maybe, like a predator taunting its prey, Ben wants me to know I'm right—that his fingerprints are all over what's happened since the attack at Sandringham, and I'm the only one who knows he's playing the game.

I'm three long strides into the corridor when I run straight into something warm and solid, and it's a minor miracle I don't fall flat on my face. Instead, as I stumble, a hand reaches out to steady me, and I hear Jenkins's voice.

"Evan. *Evan.*"

I blink, and his face swims into focus. The line between his brows is deep with concern, and his blue eyes are so intensely fixed on me that it looks like he's trying to keep me upright through sheer willpower alone.

"Jenkins," I choke out, still clutching Ben's daisy. I didn't close the door to his room, I realize. And Jenkins isn't oblivious. "I—I was just—"

I trail off, the lump in my throat too big for me to finish, and to my horror, hot tears roll down my cheeks. Without a word, he pulls me to his chest, and we stand like that for a long moment, my face buried in his shoulder as he murmurs in my ear—murmurs that sound eerily like the whispers that I can still hear if I focus on the silence.

I don't know how to explain this. I *can't* explain this, not without telling him everything, but part of me—a very small, terrified part of me—wants to. Jenkins has spent half my life fixing my problems, but right now, with the monarchy on his shoulders, I refuse to add to a burden that must already be impossible to bear. And what can he do, anyway? Reassure me that Ben isn't allowed in Windsor anymore? Tell me everything will be all right, even though we both know it won't be?

"I'm worried about you, darling," he says at last. "You haven't been reading the papers, have you?"

"Tibby won't let me near them," I mumble. "Or social media. Or her phone."

"Good," he says, tucking my hair behind my ear as he studies me for a long moment. "Do you have any plans for the rest of the day?"

I wipe my eyes with the back of my hand. "I think Tibby has me down for a long, aimless walk around the castle from now until lunch, and then after that, I'll be busy staring at the walls and, if I can squeeze it in, having a minor breakdown before dinner. The major one comes after," I add, trying to smile, but my face won't cooperate. "And then, of course, there's the two to four hours of lying awake at night, worrying about everything. Sleep is optional."

"Mm, quite busy, then, I see," says Jenkins, and he plucks a handkerchief from his pocket and presses it into my hand. "Do you think, just for today, you might be able to make some room in your schedule for a hospital visit? Your mother's been asking after you, and I think it'd do you both some good to spend time together."

I open my mouth, but for a moment, nothing comes out. She

hasn't left Alexander's side since the bombing, and I miss her so much that just the thought of her makes me feel like I've swallowed acid. "MI5 told me to stay here."

"And since when do you do what you're told?" says Jenkins kindly. "Or is it only me you refuse to listen to?"

I shake my head. "Singh told me that if I go see her, I could make her a target."

"We'll be discreet," Jenkins assures me. "There's no safer place in England right now than your father's bedside. And, if you'll excuse my candor, given the state you're in, I think the real danger is what may happen if you stay away any longer."

I should say no. I should keep as much distance between my parents and me as possible until every member of the ABR is behind bars. But those damn tears start again, and my chin trembles as I nod.

"Okay," I say, barely audible, and he sets a comforting hand on my shoulder to guide me back down the corridor. My fingers tighten around the daisy stem, and I know that no matter how much space I put between me and that wardrobe, it—and Ben—will taunt me until I find a way to trap him in his own snare of lies.

CHAPTER THIRTY

LORD CLARENCE PICTURED COSYING UP TO BOMBER MONTHS BEFORE ATTACK

Christopher Abbott-Montgomery, Earl of Clarence, has been having a secret affair with close friend Aoife Marsh, one of three suspects arrested at the site of the Modern Music Museum bombing that claimed the lives of eight people and has left His Majesty the King in critical condition.

Photos of the pair cuddling at a local pub last November have surfaced, months after they met through mutual friends at Oxford University, and a member of the couple's inner circle has confirmed the relationship.

"Everyone knows Christopher and Aoife have been sneaking around, spending the night together and snogging in dark corners when they think no one is watching," says the source, who wished to remain anonymous. "He's tired of the constant drama surrounding Evangeline, and when he's had too much to drink, he always goes on about how she won't let him touch her after what that Jasper bloke did to her. I guess he finally got tired of waiting. I know I would."

Clarence, 19, is currently rumoured to be a suspect in the bombing, along with his girlfriend of seven months, Evangeline Bright, illegitimate daughter of the King, who was specifically thanked by the Army of the British Republic for her participation in the terrorist attack. Both the Home Office and the Palace have declined to comment on the duo's connection to the ongoing investigation.

—*The Daily Sun,* 17 January 2024

AN HOUR LATER, JENKINS AND I walk down the hallway of the hospital together as every single person—staff and guard alike—eyes me like I'm about to pull a grenade from my pocket and lob it into the nearest crowd.

It's jarring, to say the least, and it leaves me both queasy and questioning why I'm here in the first place. "Does my mom know?" I say softly as we pass through yet another checkpoint of the seemingly infinite layers of security that surround my father.

"She doesn't know anything about the investigation or the claims against you and Lord Clarence," says Jenkins at a volume that matches mine. "You may tell her if you'd like, and perhaps it would be good if you did. But I didn't want to do so without your permission."

The thought of telling my mother that the world thinks I helped plan the bombing is enough to make me wish I had a vomit bin. "Not yet," I mumble, and Jenkins nods, mercifully leaving it at that.

As we approach my father's hospital room, both protection officers at the door shift their stance as they scrutinize me. I try to pretend I don't see their hands twitch toward their hidden holsters, but they're not exactly subtle about it.

"Gentlemen," says Jenkins as we stop in front of the room. "Miss Bright is here to visit His Majesty."

The larger of the two steps toward me. "All visitors are required to be searched—"

"We've been searched three times already, as you very well know," says Jenkins. "Both the palace and Home Office have already determined that the claims against Miss Bright are base-less, and that she is not a threat. Do you know something we don't?"

The protection officers glance at each other, and one picks up a walkie-talkie to mumble something into it. A burst of static responds almost instantly, and he grimaces.

"Lovely," says Jenkins, as if this has all been settled, and with a grudging nod, the first guard opens the door for us. If the situation were any different, I'd be fascinated by this rare display of Jenkins's power. But as we enter the room, all I can do is stare at my father's prone and broken body, and my mother's hunched form on the small sofa that's situated a few feet from the edge of Alexander's bed. A new nurse sits at the computer, scribbling something down on a clipboard, and while she nods to us both in greeting, she returns to her work immediately.

"Whenever you're ready to leave, let the protection officers outside know, and someone will come to escort you," says Jenkins. "There's no rush, though, darling. Stay as long as you'd like."

I nod, but even though I want to be here, I'm not sure how much I can take. A heaviness surrounds this place, muffling any sense of the past or the future, and even though I knew exactly what to expect, it still feels like another world.

My mom looks up then, and her eyes are distant, like she's focused on something no one else could ever possibly see. The haziness clears up after a beat, however, and she manages a smile.

"There you are, Evie," she says, beckoning for me, and I notice a large open sketchbook resting on her lap. As I cross the room to join her, she clears a place for me among the pencils, brushes, and various other art supplies that always seem to follow her wherever she goes, and to my surprise, I notice the paint set Kit gave her for Christmas.

"You're really using that?" I say as I ease down beside her.

"This? Of course," she says, opening it to show me the half-empty tubes of paint. "It's incredibly useful. Your Kit has excellent taste, you know."

I try to smile, but I still can't manage it. Part of me knows I should tell her about the ABR's claims and about the picture with Aoife, but even if I wanted to, I don't know how. She'll find out eventually—there's no way to hide the accusations of murder and treason from her forever—but for now, her ignorance is a balm, and I need it more than I realized.

"Are you okay?" I say. "Do you have your medication with you? Is everyone treating you all right? Have you been eating?"

My mother pulls me closer and kisses my forehead. "I'm perfectly fine, sweetheart, don't worry. Jenkins is making sure I have everything I need."

Of course he is, and I make a mental note to thank him. "How is Alexander?" I say, glancing at the bed and the beeping machines presumably keeping him alive. She sighs.

"There hasn't been much improvement," she admits. "But he isn't getting any worse, either, and that's the important part. It can take a while for the swelling to go down, and until it does . . ."

She trails off, and instead of finishing, she rubs my back for a moment before focusing on her sketchbook. It's only because she isn't trying to hide it that I let myself look at the unfinished drawing, and when I do, I'm startled to see my own toddler face peering back at me.

I can't be older than two or three, and I'm laughing, all baby teeth and chubby cheeks as someone tickles me. The hands are large and nothing like my mother's, and as soon as I spot the rough sketch of a signet ring on the pinky, I realize they must be Alexander's.

"Wow," I say as my mother defines the knuckles, her pencil moving so quickly that it looks like she's revealing what's already there beneath the blank page. "Did that really happen?"

"Of course," she says, and she pauses long enough to flip back a page. There's another picture, this one of her and Alexander sitting in what I recognize as her backyard in Arlington, and she's filled in the garden with bursts of watercolor. They look young in the painting—just a few years older than I am—and it seems so real that it's almost like I'm staring into her memories.

"That's beautiful," I say softly, as if speaking too loudly will ruin it somehow.

"It's nothing," she says, but her cheeks grow pink as she turns to a third drawing. It's a detailed study of Alexander's sleeping face, whole and well, and his fingers peek through toward the bottom of the picture, laced with someone else's—my mother's, no doubt. He's young in this one, too, but as she moves to another page, there's a near-identical drawing, and this time, there are lines around his eyes, and his hairline isn't as thick as it was in his twenties.

One by one, she shows me each of the nearly two dozen drawings, all memories of their history together. By the time we reach the very first sketch, my vision is blurred, and I blink hard before taking in the details of a large building with remarkably detailed Gothic architecture. A girl—my mother—sits on the edge of a fountain in the foreground, sketch pad in hand, as a figure that can only be my father walks toward her. His face is hidden, but I'm struck by the look in her graphite eyes. Somehow, my mother's managed to convey an entire lifetime of love and joy with only a few pencil strokes, and I brush the tip of my finger against the page, far from any spot I might smudge.

"This is the day Alex and I met," she says, leaning her head against mine. "I used to think the idea of love at first sight was a fairy tale, but from the moment I laid eyes on him, I knew he was it for me."

"He told me the same thing about you," I say quietly as I gaze at those pencil figures, who have no idea what kind of heartbreak and tragedy are lying in wait for them. "Do you regret it at all? Going to Oxford, I mean. Meeting him. Maybe if you hadn't . . ."

"If I hadn't met him, I wouldn't have you," she says. "And even if Alexander and I hadn't worked out, even if he'd never spoken to me again after you were born, you're worth every moment of it, Evie. Good, bad, devastating—I'd do it all again a thousand times over if it meant bringing you into this world. You know that, right?"

My mom peers at me with such naked vulnerability that I nod, even though I don't know this. Even though I can't imagine that I really am worth the pain and suffering she's faced. She must see my uncertainty, because she sighs and sets the sketchbook aside.

"I hate that you only remember the worst parts," she says, clasping my hand between both of hers. "My mother—your grandmother thought it was best for me to keep my distance from you while I was still recovering. And she was right at first, especially . . . well, especially in the immediate aftermath. But it robbed you of seeing the good parts, too, even when they were messy and might've seemed like our darkest moments from the outside looking in."

"Like what?" I say, not entirely sure I want to know. Hearing her talk about Alexander makes me ache in a way I can't entirely face, but it's a good kind of pain, too, I think.

She hesitates. "For instance, when I was hospitalized after . . . well, after what I did to . . . what happened to you, I didn't see anyone for months. I refused, and I was . . ." Her throat tightens, and she glances at Alexander for a split second. "I was in a bad place. But your dad visited me every week. Every single week, he would take a red-eye from London, and he would sit in the visitors' lounge, waiting for me to come out."

"He did?" I say, but I'm not surprised. Nothing about how much they love each other surprises me anymore.

"He did. And eventually I started to look forward to it, even though I refused to see him. Just knowing he was there . . . during a time when I hated myself more than anyone else ever could, it gave me something to live for. And I think he knew that. I think he knew how much I needed him, even though I couldn't admit it. But when I did . . . when I finally worked up the courage to see him, he didn't blame me for hurting you. He didn't tell me what a terrible mother I was, even though I deserved it."

"You're not—" I begin, but she squeezes my hand.

"I thought I deserved it at the time," she amends. "But your dad made sure—still makes sure—that I know *he* didn't believe it. He made sure I knew that he understood what had happened, and all he wanted was to help me heal."

She looks at him again, and even though he's lying motionless on the bed, covered in bandages and bruises and stitches that will undoubtedly leave scars, there's no fear in her eyes. Just a depth of love I can't even begin to fathom.

"Now it's my turn to make sure that he knows I'm here for him," she continues, "and that I'm not going anywhere. And I won't pretend it's not one of the most difficult things I've ever done, seeing him like this, not knowing if he'll ever wake up or be the person he was before. But in a way, it gives me the chance to love him the way he loved me then, as painful as it is. And there's nothing more worthwhile than that. So no, I don't regret any of it," she says, turning back toward me. "How could I? You're the brightest stars in my sky, and without you, life wouldn't be worth living."

I don't know what to say to that, and so I just hold her hand as she shifts closer to me.

"All I want now," she says, "is for the three of us to have the chance to make new memories. Alexander's fighting to stay—I know he is, just like he's always fought for you and me. But even if he . . . even if he doesn't make it, even if these memories are all we'll ever have together, I'll always be here for you, Evie. I won't ever be able to make up for the time we lost, but I also won't ever leave you again. Okay?"

"Okay," I whisper, resting my head on her shoulder. Maybe it's the weariness, or maybe it's the number of times I've cried in the past five days, but suddenly all I want is to believe that she really is a permanent part of my life, in a way she's never been before. It seems like some distant dream—like a fantasy I'll never really have—but in that moment, leaning against her and listening to the soft sound of the beeps, I desperately want to believe it.

"*Evangeline.*"

My eyes fly open as the sound of my name seems to filter through the air, little more than a soft whoosh as a distant door closes. "Did you hear that?" I say, sitting up straight, and my mom frowns.

"Hear what?"

"Someone said my name," I say. "I heard it earlier, too, in—"

I cut myself off, but I can already feel the concern radiating from her. For a long moment, I listen, waiting to hear it again, and I'm so focused that when she touches my hair, I jerk away.

"Do you want to talk about it?" she says with gentleness I can't stomach, because I know what she's thinking. It's the same thing I've been afraid of ever since the voices began, and my mouth goes dry.

In the weeks and months that followed, Laura Bright was diagnosed with schizophrenia, a lifelong mental illness that often has a genetic component.

They're the words from the *Daily Sun* article that revealed my mother's history and diagnosis to the world. At the time, it was a not-so-subtle swipe at me, considering the paper is owned by Robert Cunningham, who was convinced I'd killed his son. But that sentence is seared into my brain, and finally I admit to myself that I'm terrified it might be right.

Auditory hallucinations. Paranoia. Confusion. The absolute certainty that I'm seeing something that no one else will admit is there. I feel like I'm standing at the edge of a cliff, painfully aware of my mother's worried gaze, and at last I bury my face in my hands.

"I've been . . . hearing things," I say softly into my palms. "Mostly whispers when I wake up and go to sleep at night. Sometimes they say things, like my name, or—or threats." I bite my lip, but now that I've admitted it, the words spill out of me like a waterfall. "And the flowers Ben's been sending me . . . he's behind this, Mom—I *know* he is, but whenever I try to tell someone, they make me feel like I'm—I'm—"

"Paranoid?" she offers quietly. "Imagining things? Connecting dots that aren't really there?"

I nod and finally work up the courage to look at her. "Nothing feels right anymore," I say thickly. "But I'm also so sure I'm not making any of it up that—I don't know what to think. I don't know what's *real*."

My mom sighs and gathers me in her arms, her auburn waves tickling my nose as I breathe in the scent of her. Even after nearly a week at Alexander's bedside, she still smells like home.

"You've been under an enormous amount of stress lately, Evie," she says. "It would take a toll on anyone. We'll find someone to help you sort through this, all right?"

I nod, though my heart feels like it's being squeezed in a vise. "But what if it's not just stress? What if . . . ?"

While I can't force the words out, my mom understands. "Then we'll make sure you have the care you need," she says. "It'll be okay, sweetheart, no matter what happens. I promise."

There's no fear or pity or disappointment in the way she says it. Instead, she's so calm about it, so matter-of-fact, that even though I'm all but clawing at the walls of my own mind, I let myself believe her. And for the first time since the bombing, I relax. Not entirely—not when I'm feet away from my father, whose chest rises and falls only because a machine is breathing for him—but enough that the crushing weight of anxiety inside me lessens to the point where, at least for the moment, it's bearable.

My mom nuzzles my hair. "Why don't I head back to Windsor with you tonight?" she says. "We can spend a little time together. Watch a movie, maybe, if you're up for it."

"Don't you want to stay with Alexander?" I say warily.

"I'll let Constance know so she can sit with him. He won't be alone."

And while I know I should say no—that every minute she's away from him, she'll only worry—I selfishly don't want to. Because even during all those years on my own at boarding school, even after everything Jasper did to me, even in the thick of the shooting and the bombing and every awful thing that's happened lately, I don't think I've ever needed her more than I do right now.

"Okay," I say. "But we'll be back tomorrow morning, all right? First thing."

"First thing," she agrees, and she kisses my hair again as we settle into silence, both of us lost in our thoughts as we listen to the steady beat of Alexander's heart.

CHAPTER THIRTY-ONE

Is it time to admit, once and for all, that teenagers are too young to rule?

Princess Mary might have been groomed from birth to be our future monarch, but at eighteen years, six months, and sixteen days old, she can barely be trusted to sign her name in the right place, and we as a United Kingdom and Commonwealth ought to be shaking in our boots at the very notion of her taking on the lifelong job of queen.

After all, what teen today isn't far more occupied with their follower counts and ever-evolving trends than with politics and diplomatic relations? The royal family has always been an exception to the plague of modernity, or so we're led to imagine. But while Princess Mary has been a shining star during her dozens of official appearances over the past six months, smiling for the cameras and shaking hands hardly qualifies her to lead on the global stage.

I know what many of you must be thinking—no doubt of the last great queen who ruled our nation, Victoria, who ascended the throne at the age of eighteen. But times were different nearly two hundred years ago, and children were far more prepared to take on the responsibilities that came with their station. Now one cannot make small talk with anyone under the age of twenty without being accused of a slip of the tongue that leads to theatrical claims of offense. And while we have watched Her Royal Highness as she has grown from fragile newborn to the sunny young woman she is today, the palace has only recently begun to present her as our future sovereign, and in a time of great turmoil, the British people deserve the stability and reassurance that comes with the known.

Though the Regency Act of 2005 makes it clear that Her Royal Highness would be assisted by a so-called royal council, with the third in line to the throne being deliberately passed over in favour of the King's illegitimate American daughter, it's time to pose the question we've all been thinking: Just how seriously are we meant to take this farce of temporary rule?

Should the worst come to pass and His Majesty fail to recover from his reportedly severe injuries after the 12 January bombing, would Britain not be better off in the hands of a prince who has decades of experience as a working royal? A proper regency would require that Prince Nicholas, the Duke of York, rule in Princess Mary's stead until her twenty-first birthday, allowing her more time to grow and mature into the monarch we all wish her to be. It would allow for fewer hiccups, no doubt, and certainly less wariness and scrutiny both within and beyond our borders.

With as much turmoil as the King and his wayward family have caused over the past seven months, is it too much to hope that perhaps the royals might finally prioritize the people and the stability of this country over their own privilege and entitlement? Or could we as a country finally find relief from this never-ending roller coaster of drama?

—Op-Ed in the *Daily Sun,* 17 January 2024

THE FIRST THING MY MOTHER does when we return to Windsor Castle is head straight for the shower.

"I'll meet you in your rooms in twenty minutes, all right?" she says, her fingers running through my hair. "I just need to wash the hospital smell off."

She says this with a slight shudder, and I'm too wrung out to tell if she's trying to keep things lighthearted, or if it really does bother her. Either way, I agree, and I drop her off at Alexander's apartment before sniffing my own hair. It also smells vaguely like antiseptic, and I wrinkle my nose.

"Evan?"

I whirl around. Rosie stands outside Maisie's door, only twenty feet or so from Alexander's. Her freckled face is pale and free of makeup, and she looks so startlingly lost that for a second, I'm sure something else has happened.

"Rosie?" I say. "What are you doing here? Is Maisie—"

"She's in her sitting room," says Rosie quickly, like she knows I can't take any more bad news right now. "Your mum's still in England? I thought . . ."

There's something strange about the way she says this, like she's putting the pieces of a puzzle together, and I can practically see the gears turning in her mind. "Yeah, she's still here," I say, glancing at Alexander's door. There's no point in lying, after all, not if Rosie's already seen her. "She's been staying at the hospital with Alexander."

"Oh." Rosie's lips thin. "I didn't know."

Even though I'm not exactly her favorite person, not when I'm the one dating Kit, I expect her to ask something else—why my mom's hanging around, maybe, or even how Alexander's doing. But instead she tugs nervously at one of her blond curls, and I swear I see her gulp.

"Is Gia here, too?" I venture, and she shakes her head, her green eyes growing round.

"Maisie texted me earlier. She's having a really bad day, and I thought maybe I could help, but all she's really done is throw things and scream. I don't . . . I don't know what to do anymore."

Her voice breaks, and I feel a sudden stab of pity for her. "I can try to talk to her, if you think she'll let me," I say, even though I know this is a terrible suggestion. Maisie's barely been able to look at me since the news of the photo broke, and there's

327

a very real chance I'll only make things worse. But Rosie nods eagerly, as if this is the greatest idea she's ever heard.

"Maybe she'll listen to you." But as she says it, the faint sound of shattering glass echoes from inside Maisie's apartment, and Rosie flinches. "Or at the very least, maybe she'll stop breaking things. Some of those are priceless, you know."

Taking a deep breath, I steel myself and approach Maisie's door. I can feel Rosie's nervous gaze on me as I knock, and I'm not at all surprised when Maisie's snarl cuts through the air like a knife.

"I told you to piss off, Rosie!"

"Off to a great start," I mutter before raising my voice. "It's me. Can I come in?"

Maisie lets out a string of curses so obscene that I nearly abandon the whole idea. But before I can talk myself out of this entirely, her door flies open, and I'm face to face with my seething sister.

"*What?*" she says, and over her shoulder, I notice several picture frames and chunks of glass scattered across her cream carpet. After almost seven years in boarding schools, I'm no stranger to tantrums, but the ones I've witnessed didn't involve artifacts older than most trees.

"My mom and I just got back from the hospital," I say with all the nonchalance I can muster. "I thought you'd like an update."

Maisie's jaw is clenched, and her entire body seems to vibrate with pent-up emotion as she inhales. "Rosie," she says after a beat. "Have someone bring us a pot of tea. Make sure it's hot."

The thought of Maisie being anywhere near boiling liquid

right now isn't exactly comforting, but Rosie nods and scurries off, and finally my sister stalks back into her apartment, leaving me room to step inside. I do so carefully, eyeing the floor for pieces of glass, not in the mood for another round of stitches.

"How is he?" she says waspishly, walking through the shards in her high heels with several loud crunches. I skirt the edges of the room as I head for her antique white telephone, which is set on an end table near her sofa.

"He's not getting worse," I say. "Which is about all anyone can ask for right now. My mom said the swelling takes time to go down, and when it does—"

"Daddy has to be okay," she says, cutting me off. "He has to be."

"I . . . No one really knows yet," I admit. "But my mom said—"

"I don't care what your bloody mother said," bursts Maisie, and I'm not sure which startles me more—her words or the fact that she's suddenly a teary mess. "I can't do this, Evan. I can't— I can't be queen, not yet. It's too bloody soon, and I'm supposed to have years—*decades* before I have to make these kinds of decisions, but suddenly everyone's looking to me like I have the answers, as if genetics alone is enough—"

"It's not all on you, not yet," I say, easing around the remains of what I think might've been a snow globe. "You have your mother and Constance and Nicholas—"

"The papers are calling for a regency," she says with such venom and heartbreak all at once that the words come out guttural. "If Daddy—if Daddy never wakes up, they want Nicholas to reign until I'm twenty-one."

I study her. "Is that a good thing, or . . . ?"

"Of *course* it's not a good thing!" she explodes, grabbing the nearest item—a lamp—and hurling it at the floor. As it shatters, a streak of red appears on her leg, though she doesn't seem to notice. "The people don't trust me. They don't think I'm up for the job, but of course *Nicholas,* perfect bloody Nicholas, is exactly what this country needs right now. Never mind that Victoria became queen when she was eighteen, or that Mary, Queen of Scots, was six days old. *Six days!* And obviously it's disputed, but Lady Jane Grey was fifteen when Edward VI, who was *nine* when he became king, died and named her his heir, and King Henry VIII was seventeen—"

"It's alarming that you know all this off the top of your head," I say.

"It's my bloody *job* to know this," she snaps, marching past her sofa toward her bookcase, where there's a hand-painted music box sitting beside a leather-bound set of Shakespeare plays. "My entire education has been to prepare me for becoming queen. I've studied history, politics, economics, constitutional law—all to be the best monarch I can be when the time comes. It didn't matter that I like maths and science. I learned some, of course, because I can't count on my bloody fingers in front of the world, can I? But who I am and who, in another life, I might've wanted to be—none of it matters, because I'm going to be queen. It's destiny. And now these people—*these bloody people*—are trying to take it from me like I'm not singularly qualified. Like I'm some—some *teenager* who can't control herself and who'll throw a tantrum if I don't get my—"

Maisie stops abruptly as her fingers close around the music

box, and without any prompting from me, she looks around at the utter destruction that is her sitting room. Picture frames torn off the walls. Trinkets and teacups and paperweights that are little more than dust now, and several antique books with freshly torn pages. Her hand falls to her side, and without warning, her face crumples as she dissolves into sobs.

Inwardly cursing the thin soles of my flats, I tiptoe as fast as I can through the wreckage until I reach her. She tries to push me away, but her attempts are half-hearted, and I capture her in a hug.

"From where I'm standing, you're doing an incredible job," I say. "Every single meeting, you take charge, and even when you don't know what the answer is, you listen, and you process, and you decide. Nicholas might have more experience, but you're a born leader, Maisie."

"I don't want to be," she whimpers, her arms snaking around me until she's the one holding me to her. "I want him back. I want more time. I shouldn't—I shouldn't have to *do* this yet."

"No, you shouldn't," I say quietly. "I'm sorry."

Maybe no one has actually said this to her, or maybe all she wants is for someone to understand, because this seems to trigger another flood of tears, and she clings to me like I'm a life raft. We stand there for a minute or two as she cries so hard that her entire body is wracked with sobs, until at last, with several wet sniffles, she lets me go.

"Sit down," I say, nodding toward a nearby love seat. "You're dripping all over the carpet."

"What?" she says, dazed, and only then does she notice the blood still trickling down her leg. With a curse, she limps over to the sofa, and I grab a cushion to keep her injury from ruining the white velvet.

As she's inspecting the cut, I pick up the corded handset of her telephone, and I'm instantly connected to an operator. "Yes, Your Royal Highness?" says a low female voice on the other end.

"This is Evangeline," I say. "I'm with Princess Mary. Everything's okay, but we need a maid and a doctor, please."

"Yes, Miss Bright," says the operator smoothly, as if this is hardly an unusual request. "I'll send for both right away."

"Thank you," I say, and I hang up the phone with a click. Almost as soon as I do, there's a knock on the door, and without waiting for a response, a protection officer steps inside.

"Your Royal Highness," he says, and I notice his hand is resting on his holster. "Is everything all right?"

As soon as he says it, he seems to notice the debris, and his gaze snaps straight to me. "Maisie had a rough afternoon," I say dryly, not at all appreciating the implication of his stare.

"I'm fine," she mumbles without glancing up from her leg. "I just need a bandage, that's all. And for you to go."

The protection officer heads for us anyway, the glass under his shoes crackling with each step he takes. He pulls a small first aid kit seemingly out of nowhere, and I watch as he snaps on a pair of latex gloves and removes several alcohol swabs, gauze, and medical tape from the pack.

"Thank you," says Maisie testily as he starts to mop up the blood for her. "That will be all."

"Ma'am—" he begins, but she cuts him off.

"I said *go*. I'm hardly going to bleed to death from a scratch."

The officer looks between us dubiously, but Maisie's glare doesn't waver, and at last he stands.

"I'll be outside if you need anything," he says, and this time, I notice that he takes the long route around the worst of the carnage before heading back out the door.

As soon as we're alone once more, Maisie lets out a muffled screech. "Do you see?" she says, tears flooding her eyes all over again. "This is my life now, and the people won't even let me have that. There are already rumors about what sort of queen I'll be, or that I'm impulsive and can't make decisions, and—have you read the *Regal Record* lately?"

"No," I say, offering her a tissue. She snatches it from me and dabs the cut with a distinct lack of gentleness. "My phone and laptop were taken by MI5, remember?"

"Probably for the best," she says with vague irritation, and though I want to know what she means, I don't push. "Yesterday, at the meeting, I asked Grandmama about how we might approach the weekly session with the prime minister today. If it ought to be all five of us, or if it should just be me and Mummy."

"I remember." Thankfully, Nicholas was the only one who voted for the entire royal council to attend.

"Well, less than three hours later, there was an article up on the *Regal Record* about it," she says with a sniff. "They went on and on about how I shouldn't be allowed to meet the prime minister without Nicholas, not when I'm not even regent yet, and since he's next in line after me, it'd only be prudent if . . . if . . ."

She wipes her eyes with the back of her wrist, and I offer her another tissue. "Can I tell you something?" I say uncertainly, and this immediately grabs her attention.

"You can tell me anything."

That's definitely not true, but I press on anyway. "I think there's a mole in the castle," I say. "One who's been leaking information to the *Regal Record*."

"Well, obviously," she mutters. "It was Ben, wasn't it? We figured that out ages ago."

"Yes, but—he hasn't been here," I point out. "He's in Belgium right now. But the *Regal Record* is still getting little scoops like that—information that no one outside of that meeting should have."

Her hand stills. "You think someone else is going to them now?"

I nod. "They knew about your injuries after the crowd surge, Maisie. And about your breakup with Gia. There are other things, too—little things they shouldn't know, but do, and it's *constant*. Someone close to you is selling secrets to the *Regal Record*."

Maisie looks up at me, the second tissue now pressed against her cut. "Who? And don't you dare hold back," she adds as I hesitate. "You wouldn't tell me this if you didn't have a theory."

"I . . ." I rip open an alcohol swab and hand it to her. "I don't know who. But it has to be someone close to you. Close to both of us. The breakup with Gia, for instance . . . who else knew about that except the five of us in the room?"

"I was upset," says Maisie defensively. "And with the way Gia stormed out of here, anyone could've guessed."

"Maybe," I say. "But they knew it was because of the roses

that Thaddeus sent you. Did you tell anyone else? Your mom, maybe? Or even Alexander?"

She grows quiet for a long moment. "No," she says at last. "I didn't tell anyone. Just you, Kit, Rosie, and Gia."

"Then one of us is the mole," I say. "Unless someone else found out, it's the only possibility."

"But—" Maisie stops. "It isn't me. *Obviously* it isn't me. And it can't be Gia or Rosie, either."

"Why not?" I say, and instantly I know I've waded into dangerous territory.

"Because," she says sharply, "they've been my best friends since we were in nursery together. They've never betrayed me—not once—and there's no reason in the world they might start now."

"No reason that you know of," I say, and her glare is so withering that I have to fight the urge to flinch.

"What about Kit?" she retorts. "He was there, too, *and* he's the one who's chummy with terrorists. Maybe he also tipped off the *Regal Record* and sent in that photo of you hugging the bomber. He's the only one of us who knew about it, after all, and with everything else the papers are saying—" She cuts herself off and shakes her head. "*He's* the most likely suspect."

I open my mouth to tell her in no uncertain terms that it couldn't be him—that he wouldn't do something so awful, that there's no way he would ever betray either of us—but it's the same knee-jerk reaction she had to my suggestion of Gia and Rosie. And instead, even though it takes every ounce of willpower I have, I press my lips together and consider it.

She's right. He *has* been there for all of it. He was the one to suggest the trip to the shop. He was the one to introduce me to Aoife. He also knew about Maisie's injuries, and the breakup, and the roses—everything that Gia and Rosie knew and more.

On paper, it makes sense. It more than makes sense—he really should be our prime suspect. But as I think about the things he's said, the things he's done to protect me, the changes he's been willing to make in his own life to keep me safe and unafraid . . . maybe I'm every bit as in denial as Maisie is, but it doesn't fit. It just doesn't.

"Did I ever tell you that I blamed him for leaking the story about my mom's illness to the press?" I say. "Back in June, the morning the news broke. He was the only one I ever told."

Maisie scowls. "What does that have to do with—"

"I was wrong. It wasn't Kit," I say. "Even though he let me believe it was, even though I almost lost him, it wasn't him. And I'm not going to put Kit through that again. Not unless we have irrefutable proof."

"And I'm not going to blame the only two friends I have because *you* can't see what's right in front of you," she snaps. "He was there for all of it."

"Yes, he was," I say. "And maybe that's the point. Maybe the real mole is trying to frame him, too, just like Ben tried to frame me last summer."

Maisie lets out a derisive snort and shakes her head. "You think this is still about Ben? The bombing, the attacks—" She shakes her head incredulously. "You're absolutely mad."

After the conversation I had with my mother that morning,

her words are a slap to the face. But I swallow the sting and press on, refusing to rise to her bait.

"Ben knew about the photo with Aoife before it was posted," I say with all the steadiness I can muster. "During that first meeting after the bombing—he said that he wouldn't be surprised if the public wasn't thrilled about me being part of the council."

"Yes, but that could've meant anything—"

"He offered Kit his condolences for his failure," I say, and this time it's my voice that rises. "Maisie, he meant the bombing. He knew Kit was in the picture, too—he knew Kit was part of that group. He knew it all. He even said—"

I stop suddenly, and Maisie pulls her leg from the pillow so she can face me properly.

"What, Evan?" she says, fury radiating from her. "What awful thing did Ben supposedly say that made you think he knew about the bombers?"

"He said . . ." I stare at her, positive she won't believe me. She didn't hear it, after all—no one else did. But I'm sure it was real. "He said it was supposed to be me. The people who died in the bombing—the ABR was after *me*, Maisie. Ben said—"

She laughs, a cold sound that seems to drop the temperature in the room a good twenty degrees. "You just have to make this all about you, don't you? Never mind that eight people died, and that Daddy's in hospital and might never wake up. Oh, no—this *must* all be about the great Evangeline Bright."

My mouth drops open, and for a long moment, I have no idea what to say. "Maisie, I'm not making this up—"

"And that's the worst part," she says. "That you actually

believe it. Fine, there might be a mole—I'll give you that. And yes, they're feeding secrets to the *Regal Record,* which Ben also manipulated for his own personal gain. But as awful as last summer was, there is an entire universe between blackmail and the murder of eight people."

"That doesn't—"

"I've known Ben my entire life, Evan. He's my cousin. I know how he thinks, what he's capable of—"

"You didn't seem to believe he was the one behind the video, either," I say, my voice breaking again.

"No, but this is *treason,* Evan. This is—it's unthinkable." She shakes her head, her face twisted with incredulity. "He loves this family. He loves the monarchy, and he would never do anything to destroy it. I *know* he wouldn't. You, on the other hand . . ."

Her words hit me like a semitruck, and as muffled voices sound in the corridor, I gawk at her, wondering if I've imagined this, too.

"What . . . ?" I say, but it's all I can manage to squeeze out of my rapidly tightening throat.

Something that might be a hint of regret flickers across Maisie's face, but it's gone before I'm sure it's real. "You're the only newcomer, Evangeline. Everyone else in my life has been there practically from the start, and they've proven time and time again that they're loyal. But if you want to talk about who might be feeding information to the *Regal Record,* let's look at you, shall we? Because *you* knew it all, too."

I open and shut my mouth so many times that I feel like a fish trying to breathe. "Maisie, it wasn't me—"

"And it wasn't me, it wasn't Gia, and it wasn't Rosie," she

snarls. "I know why you hate Ben. I hate him, too. But everything that's gone wrong in my life lately only happened after *you* showed up, and I'm beginning to think it isn't a bloody coincidence."

I try to speak—to defend myself, to swear it wasn't me—but the words don't come. And as the door opens once more, this time to a voice I recognize as Dr. Gupta's, I slowly step back from the couch.

"That's what I thought," says Maisie with such searing malice that it feels like she's ripped out some vital part of me and smashed it, too. "Leave, before I call security. And if you *ever* try to accuse my friends of treason again, I will make you regret the day you ever stepped foot in my country. Is that understood?"

My mouth is as dry as a desert, and I can't speak, but I can't nod, either. Because nodding feels like an admission somehow, and even though every bone in my body feels like it's turned into concrete, I can't give her that. Not when it isn't true. Not when she has it all so impossibly wrong that I don't know which way is up anymore.

Instead, as Gupta and his assistants file into the room, along with a small army of cleaners who immediately start picking up the glass, I turn around and slink toward the door. I wait for her to say something else—to get in a few last words, or maybe, impossibly, to take it all back. But she doesn't. And as I step over the threshold and into the cold corridor beyond, it feels like the delicate fabric that is our relationship has shredded into threads, and nothing will ever be able to weave it back together.

CHAPTER THIRTY-TWO

Is it done?

no, and I won't.

Why?

you lied to me.

About?

you know exactly what. I won't.

Then I'll just have to find someone else.

you can't! you'll hurt someone.

And if you don't do this, then I'll make sure you take the blame.
Do you think you're my only insider?

you can't. I didn't. I won't.

So you keep saying.

if you do this, i'll tell them the truth.

Will you?

[picture message attached]

you're a monster.

No, I'm simply following the rules. What will it be, love? It's entirely your decision.

—*Text message exchange between
two prepaid mobiles, 17 January 2024*

MY MOTHER DOESN'T LEAVE MY side all evening as I sob miserably into my pillow.

I don't tell her why I'm crying—I can't find the words, and even if I tried, I'd have to tell her about Aoife and the ABR, and I already feel like I'm at my breaking point. But once she realizes I don't want to talk about it, my mom doesn't push, and instead we curl up together underneath my blanket, and she tells me stories.

Most of them are fictional and only meant to distract me— the plots of books she's read, movies she half remembers, myths she's always liked—but inevitably they remind her of something that's happened in her life, and she veers into the truth. Stories about her childhood that I've never heard. About her friends growing up, and how they used to make jewelry to sell at craft fairs and how she designed the covers of all her high school yearbooks. She tells me about her time at Oxford, about the classes she took and the traditions I have to look forward to next year, and Alexander slides in and out of her anecdotes like his presence is as natural as breathing.

I don't remember falling asleep, but I must at some point, because I start to dream of her life like I'm her. Like my childhood was normal, or as normal as it could be when her own father died when she was three, and like the only thing eighteen-year-old me has to worry about is making it to my next class on time. But in the middle of this montage of memories that aren't mine, a shrill sound pierces the lecture hall I'm sitting in, spun entirely out of her words and my imagination, and my eyes fly open as my mom and I sit up in the darkness together.

"What is that?" she says, her voice low and sleepy, and I'm relieved she can hear it, too.

"I don't know," I say, already wriggling toward the edge of the bed. My limbs are heavy, and my head feels like it's full of sand, but the screech penetrates my brain like an ice pick. "It almost sounds like a—"

"Miss Bright!"

My bedroom door bursts open, and a protection officer holding a flashlight rushes inside, stopping only a few feet from the bed as he shines the light in our eyes. "Miss Bright—Ms. Bright—we need to go. *Now.*"

I shrink back, but his free hand is already reaching for my elbow, and he seizes it with the kind of force that makes it clear he'll drag me if he has to.

"What's going on?" says my mom, already on her feet.

"There's a fire in the private apartments," he says, pulling me upright. "The castle's being evacuated."

I stumble across the carpet, my mind fuzzy. My rooms are technically in the visitors' apartments, but the private ones—

"Maisie," I gasp, her name caught in my throat, and suddenly everything she said to me flies out of my mind like it was never there at all. "Is she—"

"Her Royal Highness is being seen to," he says, and this is so infuriatingly vague that I can't even begin to interpret what he's really saying. "I'm afraid we must go."

For a split second, I think he's going to pull me out the window. Instead, he leads me and my mother through the sitting room and into the corridor, which is already hazy with smoke.

"Maisie!" I shout down the long gallery. *"Maisie!"*

"This way, Miss Bright," says the protection officer, and he all but jerks me in the other direction. The exit and the safety that comes with it aren't far, but I can hear other panicked voices call to one another in the distance, and adrenaline spikes through me.

"Let me go," I say, trying to free my arm, but his grip is impossibly tight. "I said let me *go*—"

Out of instinct, maybe, or pure fear, I twist my wrist in the way Ingrid taught me, pushing against his thumb, and I finally break loose. Instantly I take off deeper into the gallery, toward the thickening smoke.

"Evie!" cries my mom as a crackle of radio static fills the air. "Evie, get back here!"

It's irrational—I know it's irrational. But after nearly losing Alexander, the thought of my sister, trapped and frightened and gasping for air, drives me forward as fast as my legs can carry me.

The shouts grow louder as I dash toward my sister's apartment. But I don't know where I am, exactly, not with the smoke so thick now that I can hardly see, and I'm coughing as I stumble directly into someone's arms.

"Found her!" calls a man whose voice I don't recognize, and before I know what's happening, he picks me up around the waist and carries me around the bend in the corridor.

"Maisie!" I yell, but her name dissolves into another coughing fit. Suddenly ruddy orange flames flicker through the haze, and I see the outline of a doorway—the entrance to Alexander's apartment.

"This way," booms another voice nearby, and just as I spot a second door—Maisie's, which is wide open as smoke pours from her sitting room—my so-called rescuer veers to the left and out into the freezing courtyard.

Almost instantly, the air clears, and I suck in a deep breath between coughs. Dimly I hear my mother calling my name nearby, and within moments, her arms are around me.

"Don't you *ever* do that again," she gasps, clutching me so tightly that I really can't breathe. "What were you *thinking?*"

"Maisie's still in there," I wheeze. Sirens sound nearby, and blue lights reflect off the walls of the courtyard as several fire trucks appear, along with multiple ambulances.

"And you were going to rescue her yourself?" says my mom, but she holds me even closer. "Come on—let's get you checked out."

I don't want to go anywhere without knowing my sister's all right, but another pair of protection officers usher us both toward the center of the courtyard, where an ambulance has parked. I crane my neck as we go, anxiously watching the doorway closest to Maisie's room, but no one comes or goes for nearly a minute.

"She probably went out through her window, sweetheart," says my mom as a technician presses a stethoscope to my chest, half an inch from my healing wound. "She'll be in the garden, no doubt."

"But it's a drop," I manage. "And if she jumped out the window—"

Suddenly the doors burst open, and a protection officer with an ash-streaked face barrels out of the castle, cradling a bundle with strawberry-blond curls.

My sister.

"Maisie!" I cry, even though my throat is raw from the smoke. This time, I dodge both my mother and the protection officer hovering nearby as I race across the courtyard toward a second ambulance near the doors. My lungs are on fire, but I don't care. All I can focus on is the fact that she isn't moving.

I reach the ambulance just as Maisie's rescuer sets her on a stretcher, and I skid to a stop a couple yards away. "Maisie?" I say as terror spreads through me, rooting my bare feet to the ground. *"Maisie."*

She's still—too still. The sleeve of her flannel pajamas is scorched, and her arm is red and angry, but the paramedics pay it no attention as they place an oxygen mask over her face. They move over her, listening to her heart and her lungs with calm urgency, but just as tears sting my already-watering eyes, hers fly open.

"Get—*off*—me!" she gasps, and my legs damn near give out from relief. But as soon as these three words escape her, she dissolves into a coughing fit so violent that I half expect her to expel a lung. She sits up, hunching over as her entire body contracts with each rattle, but even as the crowd around her gathers, she looks at me.

"Maisie," I choke out, only partially because of the smoke now. "Are you—"

She pushes aside a paramedic who has to be twice her size, and despite the way she's shaking, she slides off the stretcher and crosses the narrow distance between us, her hand pressing the oxygen mask to her face. I meet her halfway, and without a word, she hugs me fiercely, once again clinging to me like I'm the only thing keeping her standing—which, after a second or two, might actually be true.

"I'm sorry," she wheezes as she pulls her mask away. We're surrounded by protection officers and paramedics alike, but she shrugs off their touches as she holds on to me instead. "What I said—"

"It doesn't matter," I say. "Let them take care of you, okay? I'll be right here."

At last she allows the officers and medics to lift her back onto the stretcher, but as they tend to her, her gaze doesn't leave mine. And while the words she said and the accusations she slung hours earlier still hang between us, with the smoke rising from the castle and the flames flickering toward the night sky, they seem to fade until they, too, drift away on the wind.

CHAPTER THIRTY-THREE

A fire has broken out in the private royal apartments of Windsor Castle, the main residence of His Majesty, Princess Mary, and Evangeline Bright. The status of the royal family is currently unknown.

—Breaking news alert from the BBC,
5:14 a.m., 18 January 2024

RATHER THAN YET ANOTHER TRIP to the hospital, which our protection officers deem unsafe, Maisie, my mother, and I are escorted by half the city's police to Apartment 1A in Kensington Palace, a sprawling brick maze of a manor that borders a massive park in the heart of London.

"I'll come inside with you," says my mom, a hint of nervousness in her voice as we pass through the gate and into a dark courtyard. "But once you're both settled in, I think I'll head back to the hospital."

While the thought of her leaving sets my already-frayed nerves on edge, I don't argue. It's no secret why she doesn't want to be here—Apartment 1A is where Helene and Nicholas have been secretly living together since the summer, and after the interview Helene gave to the BBC, I can't blame my mom for not feeling welcome.

Both Helene and Nicholas are waiting for us beneath the inky predawn sky in front of their apartment, which is really a four-story, twenty-room wing of the palace that no one could ever seriously compare to the apartments in Windsor Castle—or any other actual apartment in London. One of the protection officers helps Maisie out of the car, her bandaged arm held tight against her chest, and Helene hurries toward her in a flood of tears.

"Oh, my darling," she cries. "Look at you. The doctors have already arrived, and we've arranged for you to be treated in one of the reception rooms."

"I'm perfectly all right, Mummy," says Maisie, but her voice is hoarse, the burn on her forearm is swathed in gauze, and there are still smudges of ash on her cheeks. "This is all completely unnecessary."

"I'll believe that once the doctors have said so themselves," says Helene, and she gently guides Maisie inside, leaving my mom and me behind without a hint of acknowledgment.

Nicholas lingers, however, and he clears his throat in the awkward silence. "Laura," he says with a nod. "Evangeline. We're relieved you're both all right. Have you been seen to?"

"I'm fine," says my mother before I can jump in. "But the paramedics were concerned about the amount of smoke Evan breathed in. She went after Maisie," she explains, giving me a hard look. "Straight toward the flames, like the entire building wasn't already looking for her."

My face grows warm. "I know, Mom. I'm sorry."

"We'll make sure she's examined, too," says Nicholas, ushering us both through the double doors. "That was brave of you, Evan. Reckless, but brave."

"Maisie would've done the same for me," I say, but that almost definitely isn't true. And judging by the quirk of Nicholas's left eyebrow, he's thinking the same thing.

As we walk across the marble floor of the foyer, warm light spills out from one of the reception rooms, and the crown molding over the arched doorways casts strange shadows on the walls, making this feel like some kind of fever dream. But my mom takes my hand, and I'm painfully aware that it's all very, very real.

She stays with me in the makeshift clinic until one of the doctors—a blond woman with a sleek bun—does a thorough exam, draws some blood, and declares that the worst I'll have to deal with is a temporary cough. Relieved, my mom kisses my forehead.

"If anything happens, let Jenkins know, and I'll come back immediately," she promises. "You're sure you're all right if I go?"

I nod. "I need to get some sleep anyway," I say, even though I want her to stay. But now that she knows I'm okay, I can tell she's desperate to check on Alexander. "I'll visit the hospital later today."

"Only if you're feeling up to it." She gives me one more lingering hug. "I love you, Evie."

"Love you, too, Mom," I say. And as I watch her with a heavy lump of unexplained dread in the pit of my stomach, she slips back into the foyer and the darkness beyond.

While my exam was relatively quick, Maisie is subjected to

a battery of tests on the other side of the room. My eyelids grow heavy as the adrenaline finally begins to wear off, and I can hear the low murmur of concerned voices while they examine her chest X-ray.

". . . need plenty of oxygen and rest," says Gupta. "We'll reevaluate her progress this afternoon, and should there be any concerning changes—"

"I'm *fine*," wheezes Maisie, who's once again holding an oxygen mask to her face. "Really. Please don't put me in hospital. Everyone already thinks I'm weak—"

"Darling, if you need further treatment, then we'll do whatever we must," says Helene. "But I'd rather she not be exposed to the public unless absolutely necessary."

"Agreed, ma'am," says the protection officer who brought us bandages the night before. "I'll have a team secure King Edward VII's Hospital just in case."

"Evan," says Nicholas quietly, and I jerk my head up so fast that I think I sprain something. My uncle stands beside the antique chaise I'm curled up on, his mouth pinched and his expression haggard. "Why don't I show you to one of the guest rooms?"

"Thanks," I say, "but I'd rather stay here."

Nicholas smiles faintly, like he was expecting this. "Then I'll have a pillow and blanket brought in for you. And some water," he adds, as on the other side of the room, Helene tries to coax a miserable Maisie to drink.

I don't know why he's being so nice to me, but I nod, too tired to really question it. Maybe it's guilt, or maybe with Alexander fighting for his life, Nicholas has decided it's his job to step up and make sure I don't suddenly keel over. Either way, I thank him again, and when the pillow and blanket and water arrive, I drain the glass and make myself comfortable, only intending to doze.

Instead, I wake up a disorienting amount of time later, to the sound of Helene's gasp. "You're certain? You're *absolutely* certain?"

"Yes, ma'am," says a deep voice I recognize, but can't place. "My team took pictures of the scene, if you'd like to see them."

I sit up groggily and rub my eyes. Gray winter light streams through the sheer curtains in the reception room, and as I glance around, I notice Maisie lying in a bed twenty feet away as a nurse checks her blood pressure. But even though Maisie should be asleep—we should both be asleep—her eyes are open, and she's watching me.

"Hey," I say softly. "How are you feel—"

Before I can finish, a series of curses echoes through the foyer, growing louder as the click of heels approach. "After all we did—after everything she's put us through—"

"Ma'am—" says the familiar voice, but suddenly Helene appears in the arched doorway, the fury on her face so consuming that for a split second, she looks like a completely different person.

"*You,*" she growls, rounding on me. "*You* did this."

"What?" I say, sitting up so fast that I'm light-headed.

"*You* set the fire," accuses Helene as she advances on me. "*You're* the one who nearly killed my daughter."

My mouth drops open. "I had nothing to do with—"

"Palace security found accelerant hidden in your sitting room," she says. "The same accelerant used to start the fire."

I stare at her, gaping, as a man I recognize from the morning council meetings appears with a tablet clutched in his hand. Stephens—the royal family's head of security.

"Turpentine," he clarifies, angling his screen to show me a picture of several bottles of paint thinner stored in a cabinet in my sitting room. "The brand matches the supply used by Ms. Bright in His Majesty's private apartment over the past few weeks."

"I—" For a moment, I forget how to breathe. "I don't know how those got in my room, I swear. I didn't put them there. I don't paint—"

"Then are you saying your mother is the one responsible for the fire?" says Helene viciously.

"Of course not," I protest. "Why would she do that? Why would *either* of us do that?"

"Why don't you tell me, Evangeline?" says Helene. "Every time something dreadful happens lately, it all seems to come back to you, doesn't it? Maisie's protection officer said you were in my daughter's room last night. You would've had ample opportunity to splash turpentine around her bedroom—"

"I wasn't anywhere near her bedroom," I argue. "I would never—"

"Actually, ma'am," says Stephens abruptly, we believe the fire started in His Majesty's bedroom and spread into Her Royal Highness's."

Helene lets out a humorless gasp of a laugh. "Lovely. Was it Laura after all? Have we been hosting an entire family of arsonists? No one's forgotten why you were expelled from your last boarding school," she adds, blue eyes narrowed at me. "You certainly have experience with this sort of thing, don't you? Perhaps your mother asked you for help, and you were all too eager to offer it."

I stand then, toe to toe with Helene, and even though I'm barefoot and more than half a foot shorter than her, I refuse to cower. "My mom and I didn't have anything to do with this. We were both in my apartment all night, and we didn't leave. Aren't there cameras all over Windsor? Can't you check the footage and—"

"There are none in the private apartments, at the request of Their Majesties," says Stephens, and his uncomfortable glance at Helene tells me exactly why. Because during her years of sneaking around with Nicholas, neither of them wanted to leave any evidence behind. And Alexander undoubtedly went along with it—probably out of guilt, or a misguided attempt to keep the peace.

And now I have no way of proving I didn't try to barbecue my own sister.

I let out a choking laugh, though while I mean for it to be sardonic, it comes out as more hysterical than anything. "Great. Terrific," I say, glaring at my stepmother. "I can't say anything to change your mind, can I? I could find whoever did this and have them confess in front of you, and somehow you'd *still* be convinced that it was me. But it wasn't. I would never hurt Maisie. She's my sister—"

"*Half* sister," corrects Helene sharply.

"She's my *family*," I say. "And that actually means something to me. I am not the source of all your problems, Helene. I'm sorry that my existence hurts you. I'm sorry my parents made some pretty awful choices, and you had to pay the price. But I didn't do this. My mother didn't do this. And the longer you insist that we did, the longer the real culprit is still out there, and the longer *you're* the one putting your entire family in danger by refusing to believe anything but the worst in me."

She stands there, cold as ice, for the better part of ten seconds. "Get out," she snarls.

"Mummy," says Maisie pleadingly. "Evan didn't do this. Someone must have planted the bottles, or maybe Laura stored them there ages ago, and—"

"Stay out of this, Maisie," orders Helene, her tone as hard as diamonds. To my dismay, Maisie falls silent, but I can see her staring a hole into the back of her mother's head. "*You,* Evangeline, will leave my home and stay away from my family. You've been nothing but a plague on us since the day you were born, and if you ever come near us again, I will go straight to the *Daily Sun* and tell them you were the one who started the fire."

I shouldn't be surprised—there's no low Helene won't stoop to, apparently, though I still stare at her in disbelief. "But I didn't," I insist. *"It wasn't me."*

"And yet all evidence points directly to you. What a terrible coincidence, if it truly wasn't." The honeyed venom in her voice is back, and a shiver runs through me like I've stepped outside into the winter chill. "You've already given the world plenty of reasons to hate you, Evangeline, but I am more than happy to offer them another. Now *go,* before I have you dragged out by your damn ear."

I swallow hard, and for a moment, I think I might cry, but I refuse to give Helene the satisfaction. Maisie looks furious, too, but she doesn't speak up again. And Stephens stares at his feet, still clutching his tablet and clearly uninterested in correcting his queen—or maybe he thinks I did it, too. Maybe they all do, and there's nothing I'll ever be able to say to get out of this one.

Fine. If Helene wants to burn it all down, then so be it.

"No matter how much the people hate me," I say through gritted teeth, "it'll never make them love you again. You will *always* be the heartless monster who left the King for his own brother—who lied to the people about your marriage for *decades,* and who hasn't visited her husband a single time since he was nearly blown to pieces. That's your legacy. That's what the world will remember about you. And there is nothing—*nothing* you can do to change it."

For a split second, Helene looks like I've slapped her, and part of me wishes I had. But as she opens her mouth—maybe to retort, maybe to tell Stephens to throw me into the courtyard by my hair—I slip past her and head toward the archway, refusing to look anyone in the eye. Even Maisie.

The entrance hall isn't empty, like I expect. Instead, Nicholas stands near the front door, along with another familiar man in an equally familiar suit. Suraj Singh.

Though I'm still in my pajamas, which carry more than a faint whiff of smoke, I hold my head high as I stride toward the exit, intent on ignoring them completely. But as I approach, Nicholas moves between me and the double doors.

"Evangeline," he says, barely audible over Helene's furious screeches echoing from the reception room, her words mercifully indecipherable. "Please accept my apologies for Her Majesty's behavior. We—she's had quite a scare this morning, and I'm afraid with everything else that's happened as of late, she isn't handling it well."

"I don't care," I say coldly. "She's your problem, not mine. I need to go."

"You're welcome to stay," he says, but we both know that's a lie. I give him a look, and he grimaces. "Well—at least let me escort you to Clarence House. Mother has plenty of room, and . . ."

He falters again at the expression on my face, and it takes all the effort I have left in me to be polite. "Thank you," I manage, "but I don't need your help. I'm going to the hospital to see my mom and Alexander."

"And after?" he says. "Perhaps I can ask the staff to ready Nottingham Cottage, or a room at Buckingham Palace, or any of the other properties nearby—"

"I'll figure something out," I say. "I just—I need to go."

Nicholas looks oddly crestfallen, but he nods. "There's a car waiting for you outside," he says. "It'll take you anywhere you want to go. And if there's anything you need . . ."

"Thanks," I say again, barely able to force myself to speak. But while he, at least, doesn't seem to believe I started the fire, there's no doubt in my mind that he'll follow Helene's lead, no matter where it might take him.

The cobblestones are icy against my bare feet as I step into the courtyard, and sure enough, there's a Range Rover idling several yards from the door. I'm halfway there when a sharp pebble digs into my heel, and I wince, pausing long enough to rub my foot against my other leg to dislodge the tiny rock.

In those few seconds, Singh appears in front of me, his hands in his pockets and his breath visible in the freezing morning air. I try to step around him, but he moves with me, blocking my way again.

"I don't want to hear it," I say sharply. "I didn't set the fire. I was in my room the entire night, and I had nothing to do with—"

"I never suspected you," says Singh in an infuriatingly neutral tone that doesn't give anything away, but it's enough to steal my indignation right out from under me.

"Do you know who did it, then?" I say warily.

"Haven't a clue," he admits, "but I am certain it wasn't you—or as certain as I can be, given the circumstances. Someone seems desperate to make everyone believe it was you, though, don't they? And that, to me, is exceptionally curious, especially considering everything else that's happened lately. Once again, this is all so very, very neat—and so very, very sloppy at the same time."

I frown. "You think the ABR might've been behind this, too?"

"They haven't taken credit, but the day is young," he says. "Though I sincerely hope they haven't breached the palace. If they have . . ."

I shiver again, and not because of the cold. "I just know it wasn't me or my mom."

"And as I said, Miss Bright, I believe you. In fact . . ." Singh reaches into the inner pocket of his suit jacket and produces a phone. "This belongs to you."

I take it gingerly, like this, too, might explode in my face. "You're giving me back my phone?"

"And your laptop, though I'm afraid I haven't got that in my pocket," he says with a hint of humor I'm too miserable to appreciate. "They were clean, as you undoubtedly know, other than a stray number under Aoife Marsh's name."

"It wasn't hers?" I say, confused.

"Not unless she's the owner of a Pizza Express in Derby," he says, and while this time I should be surprised, I'm not. Of course Kit didn't give me her real number, and I'm suddenly glad I never used it.

"What about Kit's phone?" I say as I press the power button. "Was it . . . ?"

"Lord Clarence's personal items have also been returned to him," he says. "Other than the emails and messages he exchanged with members of Fox Rex, all of which he shared willingly, we found nothing to connect either of you with the bombing."

It isn't until that moment that I realize part of me—a miniscule part, but one that still exists—worried that Kit was lying, and that something on his devices would incriminate him. Maybe both of us. But as I watch my phone boot up, my eyes sting with tears, and I nod mutely.

Kit's innocent. We're both innocent. And someone is still coming after us with everything they've—*he's*—got.

"I took the liberty of adding my direct number to your contacts," says Singh after it becomes clear I can't speak. "Not strictly aboveboard, but I thought it would be best if you had an easy way to keep in touch, should anything else pop up. I'm on your side, Evangeline," he adds. "I believe someone close to the royal family is framing you, with the assistance of the ABR. And whoever it is, I'm as keen to catch them as you are."

We both know exactly who it is, but all I can manage is another nod as I wipe my eyes with my sleeve. Even if I could form words right now, there's no use making my case again, not when I don't have proof. But Singh's support is an antidote to Helene's poison, and I almost—*almost*—believe him.

Singh opens the door to the Range Rover, and a blast of heat emanates from inside. "Keep in touch, Miss Bright," he says. "This is unlikely to be the end of it, I'm afraid, but if you and I are both lucky, perhaps we might find a way to help each other."

I have no idea what that means, but he doesn't elaborate as I climb into the SUV. Without another word, he closes the door behind me, and even though the windows are tinted, I can feel his gaze on me for a long moment before he heads back inside.

Closing my eyes, I try to take a deep breath to calm myself down. My irritated lungs aren't thrilled with the concept, however, and I end up in the middle of a coughing fit, painfully aware of the driver watching me through the rearview mirror.

"Good morning, Miss Bright," he says as soon as the coughs subside. "Where would you like to go?"

"The hospital," I say. "I want to visit my dad."

He nods, and as he radios in our location, I tug on the seat belt. It locks up before I can pull it all the way across my body, and I mutter to myself, vaguely wondering how this day could possibly get any worse—and that's when I hear it.

"Evangeline."

The sound of my name echoes off the brick and stone courtyard, and I clench my jaw. Not again. Not here—not now, not when everything else is falling apart.

"Evangeline."

As the Range Rover starts to roll down the concrete drive, my name grows louder, and I resist the urge to cover my ears. It won't help, not when it's in my head. But without any warning, the driver hits the brakes, and I have to catch myself on the seat in front of me.

"Evangeline!"

This time, when I hear my name, it's through the door, and I do a double take when I realize that Maisie's on the other side. She's breathing heavily, and Helene and Nicholas rush out of Apartment 1A after her, but there's a determined look in her eye that I know better than to challenge.

"Will you open the bloody door?" she says, exasperated, and I fumble with the handle until it pops open.

"Maisie? What are you—"

"Move," she orders, and I hastily shift to the other seat. Helene and Nicholas shout Maisie's name as they hurry across the courtyard, but she ignores them and slams the door shut. "Palace Gardens Terrace, Matthew," she says to the driver. "You know the number."

"Yes, Your Royal Highness," he says, and seconds before Helene and Nicholas reach the Range Rover, we take off, and neither Maisie nor I look back.

It's only as we pass through the gate and onto the main road that I realize Maisie is clutching a tablet—the same one Stephens was holding minutes earlier. "You should be resting," I say. "Not—whatever this is."

"You sound uncannily like Mummy," she mutters, waking the screen. "And I'm going with you. I would've thought that was obvious."

"Yes, but—why?" I say. Maybe it's a question I shouldn't be asking, but I can't help myself, not after our argument the night before.

"Because," she says simply, and she hands me the tablet. "You're right about Ben. And I've found proof."

CHAPTER THIRTY-FOUR

We at the *Regal Record* have exclusively learned that while His Majesty fights for his life, Laura Bright, his reported mistress, is treating the King's private apartment as her own—and even sleeping in his bed.

While one might argue that this is nothing short of expected for a woman who's spent more than two decades chipping away at the marriage between the King and Queen, to do so while His Majesty remains hospitalized in a critical state is perhaps Laura's most audacious move yet. Palace insiders claim that even after the revelation that her daughter, Evangeline, is working with the Army of the British Republic, Laura has insisted on spending much of her time ordering around the household staff, in anticipation of His Majesty's recovery.

"She's delusional," says an anonymous royal insider. "Maybe it's her illness, but she really is acting like she'll be queen someday."

As our country is thrown into chaos in the wake of the terrorist attack that claimed the lives of eight people, one would hope that Ms Bright might spare us all the reminder that a home-wrecker remains at Windsor Castle—and that the British people are paying for her royal accommodations.

—*The Regal Record,* 18 January 2024

YOU'RE RIGHT ABOUT BEN.

As Maisie hands me the tablet, her voice ricochets in my head like a bullet, and I examine the picture on the screen. Her supposed proof doesn't look like much—just a piece of metal no bigger than a dime taped to the inside of a hollowed-out book. Hardly irrefutable evidence that Ben enlisted someone inside the palace to leak secrets. Or potentially try to kill us.

"What's this?" I say, zooming in, but I still can't identify it.

Instead of answering, my sister swipes to another photograph, this time of the same kind of device concealed in the folds of a red velvet curtain. A third image shows one inside a lampshade, and then one more nestled in a wooden crevice that might be part of an armoire.

"I don't get it," I say as she swipes through several more. "What am I looking at?"

Maisie huffs. "I don't know how it's possible that your skull keeps getting thicker with age, but clearly you're a medical marvel."

She stops at a photograph of an entire room—my sitting room. It looks like a crime scene, with numbered markers seemingly everywhere, and from this angle, I can see the open cabinet where security found the paint thinner. The thought of anyone searching my apartment makes my skin crawl, but even amidst the feeling of utter violation, something else clicks.

"Are these . . . ?" I swipe back to look at the last picture. "Are these *bugs*?"

"If by 'bugs,' you mean covert transmitters and listening devices, then yes," says Maisie curtly. "They found no fewer than twenty in your apartment."

"Twen . . . ?" The word dies halfway off my tongue, and suddenly I feel like I'm falling through the air at a tremendous speed, as every single one of my internal organs finds a new place to settle. "Maisie—"

"Someone's been spying on you," she says. "And I'm positive that Ben had something to do with it."

"How?" I say in a choked voice, cycling through the pictures again. "How can you possibly connect this to Ben?"

"Because he used to do it to me," she says, and at my startled look, she waves off my concern. "Nothing untoward, of course. We were children. We saw these devices used in some film, I think, and we begged our parents for a set to play with. We used to hide them in the nursery—try to eavesdrop on our nannies, and even sometimes each other. It was fun," she added defensively. "We didn't have secrets then, of course."

My mouth is still dry, and it takes me a moment to speak. "And you think . . . you think he's behind this, too? You can prove it?"

"Well—I mean, no, I can't *prove* it," she says. "Not unless there are fingerprints on any of them. But he was here last week, wasn't he? He could've planted them then, or maybe he really does have someone in the palace working for him, and they did it ages ago. If he's been listening in, it would explain the leaks, wouldn't it?"

My mind is racing, and I shake my head, as if that'll somehow force things into neat little boxes so I can begin to make sense of it all. "I never talked to anyone about your injuries, though. Or about Thaddeus's roses, or any other secrets the *Regal Record* made public. I don't think Tibby ever brought them up, either. I don't even think she knows."

Maisie considers me for a long moment. "You're absolutely certain? There's no way you could've . . . I don't know, mentioned it to Kit, perhaps?"

"Maybe." I frown. "But I really don't think any of it came from . . ."

I pause as a horrifying thought swims to the forefront of my mind, as if it's been there all this time, waiting for me to notice.

"Maisie," I say slowly. "Are these just listening devices? Or are they speakers, too?"

Maisie takes the tablet and swipes to another picture. "Most are listening devices, but Stephens said that the ones that look like these are tiny speakers."

Every inch of me freezes into place, and I stare at the image until it's nothing but a blur of colors.

Speakers. I've had speakers in my apartment. Maybe for days, but possibly for weeks. Or longer.

My throat is tight, and I gasp for air, barely managing enough to speak. "Maisie—I've been hearing things—voices—"

"You're what?" she says, startled.

"For weeks, ever since Sandringham. I thought they were real. Or—that they were in my head, I mean," I say. "But I think—I think it was Ben. You're *sure* this is something he'd do?"

She nods, her eyebrows knit as she zooms in on the device again. "Positive. It's exactly his style."

I reach for one of the miniature bottles of water stored in the center console, my thoughts reeling. It was Ben. It was Ben this entire time, whispering my name, freaking me out, making me think I was having hallucinations—

"The day of the bombing, the voices told me I was going to die," I say, struggling to get the words out. "Kit was there— I don't think he heard them, but I told him, and—I was a mess."

"The day of the bombing?" she says, with a hint of skepticism. "You're sure?"

"That's not the kind of thing you forget," I mutter. "But I think . . . I think Ben was trying to scare me. To make me believe I was losing my mind, or—that maybe I was showing signs of schizophrenia."

Maisie scowls so deeply that she looks almost like a cartoon. "That's *ghastly*. Why on earth would he do that?"

"I don't know," I say, slumping against the seat as I twist off the plastic cap. "Why is he sending me flowers? Why did he give me that photo album? Why did he tell me it should've been me? Why is he trying to convince me I'm having auditory hallucinations? It doesn't make *sense*."

Maisie takes a water for herself, and she drinks half of it before slowly setting her bottle down. "Yes, it does. He's trying to discredit you. No one believes the mad girl, do they? That's why he felt he could say those things to you—because you've already been cracking, and don't deny it. I've known something was wrong for ages, but I thought it was—well, you know, getting shot. PTSD. That sort of thing."

"The voices started before then," I say, thinking back. "The morning you tried to get me and Kit to go hunting with you—the morning of the shooting. That's when they began."

Maisie sighs. "Well, it certainly fits the timeline, doesn't it? Of Ben lurking about and being . . . *Ben*."

"But why?" I press. "What's the point? No one cares what I think or do. Why bother with all this in the first place?"

It's the same question I've been asking myself for months. But even now, with so many new pieces of the puzzle snapping into place, I still can't see the bigger picture—I still don't understand why Ben is torturing me. And I'm beginning to wonder if I ever will.

"I don't know," says Maisie. "And neither do you, so let's focus on what we do know, shall we? We *do* know that yesterday, someone poured turpentine all throughout Daddy's apartment, including his bedroom, and set it on fire. But who was it?"

"Not me," I say automatically, and Maisie rolls her eyes again.

"Yes, *obviously*. I'm not accusing you. Honestly, Evangeline, you're too bloody sensitive sometimes."

"I'm not—" I pause and sip my water. It isn't worth the fight. "You really believe me?"

"Of course I do," she says with a faint wheeze. "The fire started in Daddy's apartment, and your mother's the only one staying there at the moment. You have no reason to hurt her. If anything, you go a bit feral whenever anyone so much as insinuates that she's not the single greatest human being on the planet—"

"You think whoever did this wanted to hurt my mom?" I say, stunned. But now that she's said it, it makes perfect sense, and a wave of nausea hits me.

"Well, yes," says Maisie. "I suppose they could've been coming after me, considering how close my rooms are to his, but it seems a rather roundabout way of assassinating someone, doesn't it?"

My mind is racing again, and I take another sip of water in hopes of calming my roiling stomach. "If they were going after my mom, why yesterday? Because she finally came back from the hospital? Was it their only opportunity? But it can't be, not when she's been staying at the castle for weeks. The whole staff knew. The family, everyone—"

I freeze, and Maisie leans in, her blue eyes bright. "What?" she says. "I know that look, Evan. What is it? *Tell me.*"

"I—" I swallow painfully. "You're not going to like it."

"I don't bloody care," she says, breathless again. "Spit it out already."

The last thing I want to do is reignite the fight we had yesterday, but I don't have a choice. Not really. Besides, it all makes sense, and I hate myself a little for not seeing it sooner.

"When my mom and I got back from the hospital yesterday . . ." I hesitate again. "I ran into Rosie, right by Alexander's apartment. My mom went inside, and . . . Rosie asked me about her."

"What did she say?" says Maisie, and I can hear the familiar defensiveness in her voice already.

"Something about how she had no idea that my mom was staying in Alexander's suite. That she'd thought she'd gone back to Virginia, and . . ." I take another sip of my water, but it does nothing to alleviate the dryness in my throat. "I don't know. The whole thing was weird. She almost seemed guilty, and she kept saying she had no idea, but . . ."

I trail off. Maisie isn't looking at me anymore, and there's a strange expression on her face as she types something into the tablet. A moment later, the *Regal Record* appears. The latest headline announces the fire, and as Maisie skims past the article that follows, I spot my name alongside *a history of arson.* And even though I should expect it—even though I know I've already been linked to the ABR, and no one in the country will give me the benefit of the doubt now—the reality of what's happening outside our isolated palace bubble hits me like a brick wall.

Everyone hates me. The *Daily Sun,* the *Regal Record,* every troll on social media—no doubt they're claiming that I'm the one who set the fire that could've killed my sister. Worse, I have no defense except my word. Because I *was* there that night. The turpentine *was* in my room. And even though I know it's all some twisted setup, most of the world already believes I was involved in the bombing, and I'm coldly certain that they won't think twice before accepting this as the truth, too.

It doesn't matter that I didn't do it. No amount of innocence will ever wipe the slate clean, and for as long as I live, these whispers will follow me around, one more black mark on an already scandalous list. *Treasonous* list, now, with the bombing and two attempted murders to add to my count.

At last Maisie turns the tablet toward me again, and I see the headline she was searching for, time-stamped shortly after midnight.

WHILE ALEXANDER FIGHTS FOR HIS LIFE, LAURA PLAYS WIFE

I blink once, twice, certain I'm reading it wrong, or at the very least making connections that aren't really there. But at the same time, I know I'm not—for exactly the same reason that, even though this article is made up of rumors and anonymous sources that add up to nothing but hot air, it happens to be right. That all the articles on the *Regal Record* happen to be right.

"Did you ever tell Rosie and Gia about my mom staying at

Windsor?" I say, choosing my words carefully despite my racing pulse.

"No," says Maisie, though she's already pulled out her phone and is scrolling through what looks like a group text. "No, I—no, I never talked to them about Laura. Even at Klosters, we all avoided the subject. No one wanted to upset Mummy."

"Did your mother mention it during the interview?" I press. "She didn't, right? I would've remembered that."

"I don't think she did, either," says Maisie, her voice slightly panicked now as she continues to scroll through her texts. "Evan . . . it can't . . . Rosie *wouldn't* . . ."

"Maybe not," I say, because as much as I dislike her, I can't imagine her trying to burn my mother alive. "But if there's even a chance that she knows who did . . ."

Maisie's eyes flutter shut, and her throat works convulsively, like she's trying not to cry. "It's just a coincidence," she says. "She would never."

I stay silent, partially because I really am afraid of starting another fight, but also because I can tell she doesn't need my help coming to the inevitable conclusion. And sure enough, when she opens her eyes again, they're red and watery, but there's a look of determination on her face, too.

"We need to talk to her," says Maisie, her wheeze back now. "Even if she has nothing to do with any of it, even if it's . . . it's nothing, maybe . . ."

"She could've seen someone else lurking around," I say. "Or maybe she heard something while we were in your room. Anything's possible."

"Anything's possible," she echoes, but there's no real feeling behind it. She plucks a tissue from the console and dabs at her eyes. "She'll deny it all, though. Even if she has vital information, she won't admit it, not if she thinks our friendship is on the line."

I shrug. "Then we'll just have to find another way to get her to talk."

The Range Rover begins to slow, and when I glance out the window, my heart skips a beat. We're on a residential street now, with a row of neat white townhouses on either side and expensive vehicles parked along the pavement. And just up ahead, standing by a wrought-iron gate, is a boy with a familiar head of wavy dark hair.

"How?" says Maisie miserably. "The more we push, the more scared she'll be."

Our driver stops in front of the gate, and even though it takes everything I have, I look back at Maisie and squeeze her hand.

"I think I have an idea," I say, and I flash her a reassuring smile before opening the door and leaping onto the sidewalk, where Kit is waiting for me with open arms.

CHAPTER THIRTY-FIVE

Kit:

Rosie, are you awake?

Rosie:

omg hi! yes, just taking snickers for a walk xx

Kit:

Did you hear about the fire?

Rosie:

fire?? what fire??? xx

Kit:

At Windsor this morning. Maisie's safe.
She's at KP with Aunt Helene.

Rosie:

omg

was she hurt??

was anyone hurt???

Kit:

Everyone's fine. Evan and Laura
are safe, too.

Rosie:

evan and her mum were there?

Kit:

Yes. And I think . . .

Rosie:

?????

kit???

is everything okay????

—*Text message exchange between Lady Primrose Chesterfield-Bishop and the mobile of Christopher Abbott-Montgomery, Earl of Clarence, 18 January 2024*

THE DOORBELL OF THE ABBOTT-MONTGOMERYS' townhouse rings at ten o'clock on the dot.

As Maisie and I watch through the nearest strategically placed security camera, Kit, wearing a gray sweater and black trousers that fit him a little too well, pads to the door and opens it, revealing a pink-faced and breathless Rosie.

"Kit!" she squeals, and even though Maisie and I are listening through headphones in the basement, we both wince at her high pitch. Without waiting for an invitation, Rosie leaps over the threshold and throws her arms around Kit, embracing him like they've been reunited after years apart.

"Rosie," he says, hugging her affectionately in return, though I don't miss the look he gives the camera. "It's lovely of you to pop by so quickly. I didn't interrupt anything, did I?"

"Of course not," she says as she finally releases him. "It sounded important. Is everything all right?"

"I . . ." Kit glances out toward the street in an impressive show of paranoia. "Let's go inside, shall we? I have a tea tray ready."

Rosie doesn't need persuading. She hugs his arm, and Kit leads her into a cozy sitting room as I switch the feed to a second camera. "What's this about?" she says as they sit side by side on the love seat, even though there are two armchairs and a separate sofa to choose from. "Are you sure Maisie's all right? Some people on social media are saying—"

"She's fine," he assures her. "The palace isn't releasing any information right now for security reasons, but no one was seriously injured."

Rosie nods, and while it might be the camera, she seems paler than usual. "Security reasons? Is something else going on?"

"I . . ." Kit hesitates. "I'm not supposed to say anything, but . . . Stephens and the protection officers think the fire was set on purpose."

Her mouth drops open a split second too late to be truly convincing. "*Really?* Do they know who . . . I mean, do they have a suspect, or . . . ?"

Kit stares at his knees, and his hair falls into his eyes, hiding his expression. "You have to swear you won't breathe a word of this to anyone," he says, so quietly now that the microphone barely registers his voice.

"Of course," she says immediately, and she takes his hand in hers. "Kit, you know I won't say anything. You can trust me."

Beside me, Maisie is slowly tearing a tissue to shreds. "Liar," she mutters, and even though I silently agree, I don't say a word as Kit launches into the story the three of us concocted. Which is, admittedly, less a work of fiction and more what everyone else will think by the time the sun sets.

"Palace security found accelerant in Evan's sitting room," he says in a hushed voice. "They think . . . they think she set the fire. And they think Maisie was the intended victim."

This time, the surprise on Rosie's face is real. Not, I suspect, because I've been framed, but because Rosie knows that Maisie was never supposed to be targeted.

"They . . . *what?*" she gasps, and there's an eagerness in the way she leans closer to Kit. "You really think it was Evan?"

Kit nods and rakes his hair out of his eyes, not quite looking at her. "I don't want to, but—what else am I supposed to believe? I just . . . I never thought she would ever . . ."

His voice breaks, and for a split second, I forget this isn't real. Rosie throws her arms around him, pressing her cheek to his. "Oh, Kit," she murmurs. "I'm so sorry. Of course you had no idea. None of us did. She seemed all right, didn't she? But she's had a troubled life, and all that nasty business with her mother . . . well, sometimes the apple doesn't fall far from the tree."

Kit's entire body tenses, but Rosie doesn't let go. "I just wish I understood why," he mumbles into her shoulder. "I thought she loved Maisie. They've fought a few times, but that's normal for sisters, and Maisie's always been a bit prickly—"

"I'll show you prickly," mutters Maisie, and I elbow her in the side.

"—but I never thought Evan would try to kill her," continues Kit. "It doesn't make *sense.*"

Rosie is quiet for several long seconds, her fingers now toying with the ends of Kit's hair. "Well . . . maybe it does," she says, and Maisie and I both go still.

"What do you mean?" says Kit, and he pulls away enough to look at her—but, I notice, he doesn't untangle himself completely.

"I . . ." Rosie pauses, and I can feel my heart pounding. For a few seconds, I don't breathe, terrified she might not finish. But then Kit takes her hand, and I can practically see Rosie melt.

"Go on," he says gently, lacing his fingers through hers. "I won't tell anyone. Not if you'd rather I didn't."

"It's important people know," she says, her voice wavering. "Motive is important. But . . . they can't know it came from me, all right?"

"They won't," he says, his eyes locked on hers now, and as she stares back, the tension seems to drain from her until she's curled against his chest.

"Do you know anything about the Legitimacy Act of 1959?" she says, and beside me, Maisie sucks in a breath.

"Er . . . I'm not acquainted with the particulars," says Kit, sounding as baffled as I am.

"Well," says Rosie, and there's a note of exhilaration in her voice now—either because she has a captive audience in Kit, or because she knows something the rest of us don't. "It's all a bit complicated, but it basically legitimizes children born of an adulterous affair—*if* their parents later marry."

The way she words this doesn't sound like her—it sounds like someone fed her this exact phrase, and she's relishing the chance to pass it on to Kit. But I'm so distracted by the way she says it that *what* she's saying doesn't start to sink in until I feel Maisie's nails digging into my forearm.

"Ow," I hiss. "What are you—"

"I know what's going on," she says, her eyes wide. "I know why Ben's doing this."

But before she can explain, Kit leaps to his feet, dislodging Rosie and forcing her to sit up. "Wait—*wait,*" he says, like he's also having trouble fully grasping the concept. "You think Evan tried to kill Maisie because . . . ?"

"Because if her parents marry, she'll be legitimate, and then she'll get to be queen," says Rosie, though she doesn't sound as sure of herself now. "That's what the law says, doesn't it?"

Kit shakes his head, and he begins to pace. "No—no, that's not true. Even if she's legitimized, she won't be placed in the line of succession. She can't be, not without an act of Parliament."

"But her heirs would be," says Rosie, yet again triumphant at knowing something he doesn't. "So if Maisie's dead, even if Evan can't be queen, her oldest child would still become the monarch."

Finally everything she's saying hits me, and something inside me—something I can't name—caves in on itself, suffocating me in the process. "Maisie, is that—"

She's already standing, though, and she flings her headphones aside as she hurries toward the stairs. Reeling, I race after her, and even though Maisie is wheezing so loudly that it's a miracle she can make it up the steps at all, she's still somehow faster than I am.

"Maisie—" I hiss, but it's too late. She marches straight through the kitchen and into the sitting room, stopping in the dead center of the archway.

"I didn't realize you were such a scholar when it came to succession law," says Maisie, her tone deceptively mild despite her heavy breathing, and Rosie's jaw practically drops to the floor.

"Maisie! Are you—" She scrambles off the love seat, but Kit loops his arm around hers.

"I think it'd be best if you stayed here with me for now," he says, and confusion flickers across Rosie's face—until she glances at the archway again and finally sees me lingering behind my sister.

I've never seen anyone lose their color so quickly, and for a split second, I'm positive she's about to faint. But somehow she manages to stay on her feet, and though she sways, Kit is there to steady her.

"Evan—you're here." She chokes out my name like it hurts, but I'm too stunned to feel any sense of satisfaction. "And—and Maisie—you're okay? Kit said—"

"How kind of you to be so concerned," says Maisie, her voice sweet venom now. "If Evan was the one to set the fire because she wanted the throne to herself, then explain to me why she started it in Daddy's bedroom, not mine."

"I—" Rosie gapes at her, but this time, she doesn't look the least bit surprised. "I don't know."

"And why would she be so careless as to keep evidence of

her crime hidden in her own sitting room?" says Maisie. "She may be American, but even she has the brains to think that one through."

"Really, Maisie?" I say, but there's no bite behind it. I don't have it in me. I don't have anything in me right now except bewildered disbelief and a healthy dose of panic.

"I—I don't know," says Rosie again. "Maybe . . . maybe the other doors were locked."

"Maybe the *hundreds* of other doors in Windsor Castle were locked," repeats Maisie, as if this is a legitimate possibility. "I see."

"I don't know. I don't *know*," cries Rosie. "Maisie, please—"

"You can't explain why you think Evan's the main suspect in a fire that could've—*should've*—killed her mother, yet you can paraphrase obscure and nearly obsolete legislation from sixty-five years ago," says Maisie calmly. "How curious."

Instantly Rosie shuts her mouth, and she yanks her elbow from Kit's grip. He lets her go, and she stumbles backward toward the mantel, her arms crossed tightly over her chest. "Maisie, I don't—whatever's going on—"

"That's precisely what I'm trying to discover," says Maisie. "Because you're one of my best friends, and because I know none of this could've possibly been your idea, I'll give you one chance to explain, Rosie. Tell me everything—and I do mean *everything*—and we won't involve the police."

Rosie stares at her, so pale now that her lips are bloodless. I expect her to object again, to insist this is all some kind of misunderstanding, but instead, her chin quivers, and she bursts into tears.

"It was him," she sobs. "All of it—it was all him. He wanted me to start the fire, and he told me how—he threatened me—but as soon as I saw Evan's mum there, I refused, and he threatened me again, but—"

She's crying so hard now that the rest of her words are lost on me, but neither Kit nor Maisie moves to comfort her. Instead, with her legs shaking like a newborn fawn's, Rosie teeters toward the nearest armchair and collapses.

"Who?" demands Maisie, but Rosie ignores the question as she weeps into her hands.

"I didn't hurt anyone. I didn't start the fire—I *didn't*, I swear. It was just supposed to be gossip. Tidbits. You know, things that—things that didn't matter. But then he kept asking for more, and more, and more, and—" She hiccups. "Then he wanted pictures and information and secrets, and I tried to refuse, but his threats got worse, and I couldn't tell him no, Maisie. I tried, but—"

"Who?" demands my sister.

"No one was supposed to get hurt," says Rosie. "He swore—he *swore*—"

"Rosie, if you don't say his name this instant, I will come over there and rip your curls out one by one," snarls Maisie, and Rosie gives her such a desperate look that for a moment, I almost feel sorry for her.

"You already know who," she whimpers.

Maisie advances across the threshold and into the sitting room. "Tell me."

"I can't."

"Say his bloody name, or so help me—"

"I *can't!*"

Rosie flies to her feet again, and Kit barely manages to dodge out of her way as she takes a few furious steps toward us. Then, almost as if she loses her nerve, she backtracks until her legs hit the edge of the armchair once more.

"I can't, Maisie," she whispers. "You don't understand. The things he has on me . . . the things he could do to me . . ."

"What about the things *I* could do to you?" growls my sister. "Because believe me, I am sorely tempted."

Rosie wipes her eyes. "He could do so, so, *so* much worse. He has pictures . . . and video . . . he could ruin my family . . . he could ruin *everything.*"

With nauseating clarity, I flash back to the night that the *Regal Record* posted the video of Jasper assaulting me. I remember how it felt, watching it all unfold, knowing that millions—*billions* of people could watch it, too, if they wanted. With a single click of a button, the worst thing that had ever happened to me was viewable to anyone with an internet connection and a questionable moral compass. And there isn't a doubt in my mind that if Ben had given me a chance, I would've done damn near anything to prevent it from going public.

"Do you swear on your life—on Snickers's life—that you had nothing to do with the fire?" I say, as Maisie struggles to sputter out a coherent response. Clearly Rosie has never told her no before, and the idea isn't landing well.

Rosie nods miserably. "I can show you the texts. He gave me a prepaid mobile—it's how he keeps in touch. He told me to spread the paint thinner and sneak the cans into Evan's room, and he said someone else would light it so it couldn't be traced back to me. I didn't want to, but maybe—maybe I would've—but as soon as I saw you and your mum there, I knew I couldn't. I swear," she says, crying again. "Evan, I *swear.*"

"Okay," I say quietly, my stomach churning with acidic fury that has nowhere to go. "Right now, until you give us a reason to change our minds, we're going to move forward like that's the truth."

"It *is*," wails Rosie, even as Maisie hisses my name, but I ignore them both.

"Now let's talk about the rest of this," I say, the steadiness of my voice an act of sheer willpower. "Is it true? That if my parents get married, I'll be legitimized?"

"Yes," says Maisie before Rosie can answer. "Though Kit's right—you wouldn't be in the line of succession, not without an act of Parliament that will never, ever happen."

"But my theoretical heirs would be," I say, and now it's Kit who nods.

"The line of succession would treat you as if . . . well, as if you weren't alive," he says. "But you're still the King's daughter, and if you were legitimized, your children would be placed after Maisie."

"And ahead of Ben," I say, and this time it isn't a question.

Silence settles between us as everything—*everything* finally falls into place. Why Ben's been after me since the moment I stepped foot in the UK. Why he's dragged my name through the mud again and again. Why he tried to make me question my own mental health. Why he convinced an actual terrorist group to claim me as one of their own and brand me a traitor who tried to kill my own father.

It's because he's afraid of me. And he's afraid of losing the crown that, since the moment he found out about Maisie and Gia, he thought was his for the taking.

I swear softly and lean against the archway, not sure I can hold my own weight anymore. Kit steps toward me, but I shake my head. He has to stay where he is, as close as Rosie will let him, in case she bolts.

"He's been doing this from the start," I say, a little light-headed as it all clicks. "He and Jasper—they drugged me and assaulted me and filmed it to try to chase me out of the country. To make sure I was too humiliated and broken to stay. And when that didn't work, when we figured out Ben was behind it and Alexander banished him, he stopped playing nice and tried to have me killed at Sandringham. And the bombing . . . he knew about it beforehand. What he said to me and Kit—he's connected to the ABR somehow. I know it. I *know* it. And the fire . . ." I grit my teeth. "Maisie's right. It should've killed my mom. He must have someone else in the castle, too—someone who really did light it, without realizing my mom was in my room instead."

Kit is already on his phone, texting someone—palace security, I assume, or maybe Helene—but Rosie looks back and forth between Maisie and me, terror written on her face.

"So—the whole point *was* to . . . to hurt your mum?" she manages.

"The whole point was to *murder* her mother," says Maisie flatly, but her eyes are wide now as she puts the pieces together, too. "Daddy, Laura, and Evan are the only ones standing in Ben's way now. If one of them dies, it's over—the line of succession stays as it is, and he's safe. That rotten bastard," she mutters. "That knob-headed, spiteful *maggot*—"

She goes on for several rounds, and I let her, mostly because I'm still stunned by how simple it is. How utterly transparent, now that I have all the facts. I'm not paranoid. I'm not imagining things. I'm not connecting dots that aren't there.

Ben really is behind every horrible thing that's happened, and we can almost—*almost* prove it.

"Rosie," I say, interrupting Maisie as she delves into what I'm fairly certain are curses in several different languages. "Has he ever mentioned the ABR to you?"

"The what?" she says faintly as she wipes her eyes again, creating a black smudge of mascara on her cheeks.

"The Army of the British Republic," I say. "The group behind the bombing."

"No. No, of course not," she says, a note of panic in her voice now. "I was just—I was only supposed to give him gossip, that's all. For the *Regal Record*. He and Jasper started it, and he runs it now, and sometimes he has me write bits, but I swear, it's all him—"

"It's *him*?" says Maisie, still sputtering. "All that rubbish—it's him?"

Rosie nods wretchedly. "I'm sorry, Maisie. I wanted to tell you, but—"

"It's not important," I say, and the three of them look at me like I've proclaimed marmite and ham to be the best sandwich combination on the planet. "Not right now, anyway. We need to prove that he's connected to the ABR. Rosie, you're *positive* he's never mentioned it? Even in passing?"

"Yes," she whispers, so faintly I can barely hear her. "I swear, I had no idea. I would've never . . . I would've *never.*"

"Yet you did," says Maisie bitterly. "And now you have to find a way to live with that."

Rosie stares at her for a long moment before dissolving into tears yet again. I sigh inwardly, but her emotional well-being is the least of our problems right now.

"Ben is being extraordinarily careful to ensure that none of this can be traced back to him," says Kit as he tucks away his mobile. "The burner phones, being out of the country during the attacks . . . and if he's using blackmail to get what he wants . . ."

"Then anyone could be caught in his web," says Maisie, still glaring at Rosie. "Even the people we trust most. And unless we catch them in the act, then it's highly unlikely anyone working for him will come forward of their own accord. Especially with treason on the line."

"Treason?" says Rosie, anguished, and she's crying so hard now that I think she might drown in her own tears.

"But the ABR is different—they have their own agenda," says Kit, ignoring her. "It's possible he's using them, and they're happy to be used, so long as they get what they want in the end."

"Which, if you'll recall, is the fall of the entire monarchy," says Maisie. "How Ben thinks *that* will help his cause—"

"Wait," I say suddenly. "I have an idea. Maisie—how far does your power extend?"

She squares her shoulders and raises her chin, as if just the thought of *not* getting her way is a challenge. "Significantly."

"Good," I say. "Because we're going to need it."

CHAPTER THIRTY-SIX

"Henrietta, with the news of a fire breaking out at Windsor Castle this morning, it's time to ask ourselves the obvious question—is our royal family under attack?"

"After the shooting at Sandringham, the bombing of the Modern Music Museum, and now reports of a fire intentionally set in the private apartments of Windsor, I'm afraid there's little room for doubt anymore. Our royal family—our monarchy—our *country* is under attack from the so-called Army of the British Republic."

"For our viewers who may have missed our breaking news bulletin just minutes ago, the ABR has released another video taking credit for the fire and yet again thanking Evangeline Bright for the role she played. What do you make of this? With so much suspicion now being cast on His Majesty's illegitimate daughter, why has she been allowed to remain on royal grounds?"

"Well, the answer's clear, isn't it? The palace doesn't believe the accusations have any merit."

"And yet the ABR insists she was the one who started the fire. Who are we supposed to believe?"

"There are those who will jump to the very worst conclusions without a second thought, of course, but I believe it is vital we all keep an open mind. Remember, Evangeline has only been in the country for seven months, and much of her time has been spent sheltered in Windsor Castle. How would she have made these connections? How would she have been radicalised so quickly?"

"We already know, of course. Lord Clarence, the nephew of Her Majesty the Queen and Evangeline's rumoured boyfriend, also has proven ties to the group through his friendship with terrorist Aoife Marsh."

"Perhaps, and perhaps I'm naive in thinking there's more to the story. But something about this doesn't add up for me. Evangeline was, after all, the alleged victim of the Christmas Eve hunting accident at Sandringham, which is now speculated to be the first of the ABR's attacks on the royal family."

"A hunting accident for which the ABR has never taken credit."

"A point well made. But let's put this all into perspective, shall we? What would the ABR gain by revealing such a well-placed member of their operation? And what would Evangeline gain by continuing to do their bidding after they revealed her supposed involvement in the bombing?"

"Perhaps she is being blackmailed."

"The royal family employs some of the most highly trained and decorated security experts in the world. If anyone tried to blackmail a member of the royal family . . . well, let's just say it wouldn't end well for them."

"Nor does it seem like this will end well for Evangeline. With calls for her arrest being made not only on social media, but by celebrities, international figures, and even members of Parliament, it is only a matter of time before the public loses their faith in the palace's judgment."

"We have no way of really knowing what's going on behind closed doors, particularly now that the royal family's inner circle has closed ranks. But should there be even a kernel of truth in the rumours of Evangeline's involvement, then we can only hope that for the sake of the country, the palace allows those investigating these attacks on the royal family to seek justice."

"And if she is found guilty?"

"Well—let's not get ahead of ourselves. The royal family is going through enough right now without us all playing judge, jury, and executioner for one of their own."

"But no one is above the law, are they?"

"No, of course not. Not even those of royal blood."

—ITV News's interview with royal expert
Henrietta Smythe, 18 January 2024

AS I STEP INTO THE interview room, which is little more than a featureless box only a few degrees above frosty, the heavy metal door clangs shut behind me, and the lock slides into place.

Suraj Singh is already inside, standing in a corner like a well-dressed sentry, and he acknowledges me with a single nod. His presence in the room is a condition of the deal Maisie and Jenkins managed to strike with the Home Office, but while I'm not thrilled about it, my attention immediately snaps to the girl sitting on the far side of the long metal table, her wrists and ankles bound in handcuffs and chained to the concrete floor.

Despite the red waves tumbling over her shoulders, Aoife Marsh seems colorless somehow, as gray as her oversized sweatshirt. Any hint of the bubbly girl I met in the gift shop near Sandringham is gone, replaced by hollow cheekbones, dark circles, and a hopelessness in her dull green eyes that feels excruciatingly familiar.

For a split second, when she sees me, there's a spark of something on her face—excitement, or possibly relief. Maybe even hope. But when she offers me a tentative smile and I refuse to return it, that spark vanishes so fast that it might as well have never existed at all.

"I can't believe you're really here," she says, and even though *here* is a Category A prison, surrounded by so many layers of security that I feel claustrophobic, her voice is as sweet as ever. "I've been begging to speak to you, and my lawyer promised he'd pass the message on, but of course they say those things, and I never thought—"

"No one asked me to come," I say flatly. "I'm here because I need answers."

"Oh." She parts her lips to say something else, but it takes her a moment to speak. "Did they tell you I'm innocent? It was all a setup, God's honest truth. I had no idea what they were planning—"

"Is Ben involved in the ABR?" I say. After listening to Rosie sob all morning, I have no interest in hearing more excuses. "Prince Benedict. Is he in any way connected to you?"

"Prince . . . ?" Her voice trails off, and she shakes her head. "Dylan talks about him sometimes, but I've never met him. Evangeline, I swear it on my grave, they were using me. I didn't know what was happening. I didn't know what Dylan and the others were planning. The club—Fox Rex, it was just supposed to be a laugh—something to do together at uni, an excuse to drink and meet other people who weren't so keen on the royals. I had no idea they were recruiting for a—a terrorist group, and if I had, I would've told someone, cross my heart—"

"What does Dylan say when he talks about Benedict?" I say, cutting her off. Aoife blinks.

"I—I don't know. He comes up sometimes, when Dylan

mentions Eton. I think they were mates, but I can't say for sure. I didn't know about the photo, Evangeline, I swear it. No one told me to hug you, and I didn't know they had a camera—I didn't know what they were planning—"

"So as far as you know, Benedict isn't involved in the ABR?" I say.

"I didn't even know there *was* an ABR," she insists, her voice cracking with desperation. "I was only at the museum because of your text."

"My text?" I say, startled. "What text?"

Aoife bites her lower lip. "You know, the one where you said you wanted me there. It's on my mobile. The police took it, but—"

"I didn't text you," I say, sharper than I should, given she looks like she's about to burst into tears.

"But—but it came from your number. It's the only reason I went to the opening. It's why I've been asking to see you— because you could prove that you invited me. Because you did, right? It had to be you. I'm sure it was."

Even though I know I shouldn't, I glance nervously over my shoulder. But Singh's already been through my phone—he knows every single message I've sent, and that none of them were to Aoife. Or the number Kit pretended was hers. "I never texted you, Aoife," I say. "Whoever gave you my number . . . it wasn't really mine."

"I . . ." Aoife falls short again, and this time she looks so crestfallen that I almost feel sorry for her. "It wasn't?" she whispers. "But . . . but Dylan said . . ."

A lump of frustration forms in my throat, and I force it down as I push my chair back with a hair-raising screech of metal against concrete. "I'm sorry if they really did trick you," I say in a measured voice, even though my patience is frayed to the last thread. "But if you don't know anything, then there's no point in me staying."

"Wait." Her voice catches as I stand. "Evangeline, please—you have to believe me. I didn't do this. I had no idea."

"You must've known something, Aoife," I say. "You can't tell me you spent months hanging out with terrorists and didn't overhear anything about Ben, or their leaders, or what they planned to do—"

"The leader's name is Guy," she blurts. "Except—I don't think that's his real name. But it's what everyone calls him."

"Guy? As in Guy Fawkes?" I say, and out of the corner of my eye, I see Singh shift his weight. This must be new information. "Who is he?"

Aoife's lips part, and she averts her gaze, staring at her ragged nails instead. Even from a distance, I can tell they've been bitten to the quick. "He's older than us. A graduate student, I think. He was with me at the museum opening. I didn't know he was there until—until he found me in the crowd, but he was."

I take my seat again, my mind racing. "Was he wearing a teal scarf?"

Her eyes dart back up to meet mine. "How did you . . . ?"

"I'm pretty sure he's been stalking me," I mutter. "Has he ever mentioned Ben?"

"Maybe. I don't know. He gives me the shivers, so I don't usually . . . I don't usually talk to him."

"Why does he give you the shivers?" I press, and Aoife lets out a single rueful laugh.

"Some people, you just know they're trouble, don't you? But everyone else loved him. Flocked to him when he bothered to show—which wasn't all that often, mind, but when he did, the rest of them thought it was grand. Like meeting a celebrity."

"Do you know the names of the other members of the club?" I say, but Aoife shakes her head.

"A few, maybe. But I was really only there for Dylan."

We're getting nowhere again, and my irritation must show, because she leans forward, her hands tugging at her chains.

"I know they have loads of contacts and donors—people who were part of the club when they were students, that sort. I couldn't say how many of them know about the ABR, or if they're in the dark, like me. But Guy likes to brag about it—how we're part of an illustrious group dating back decades, including members of Parliament, lawyers, doctors, journalists, barons, viscounts, and even people inside the palace—"

"People inside the palace?" I echo, alarmed. "Who? Did he ever give you names?"

"No, no one told me anything," insists Aoife. "I didn't know about the ABR, I didn't know about—about the bombing—but . . ."

She trails off, and I can see the wheels turning in her mind. "What?" I say, but it takes her another few seconds to respond.

"Outside of the museum opening," she says slowly—so slowly that I'm on tenterhooks now, "Guy seemed . . . happy. Like everything was going according to plan. I thought maybe he was pleased that Kit was there, since he was a new recruit to

Fox Rex, and maybe Guy was chuffed to have a member so close to the royal family. But . . ." She gulps. "I didn't think anything of it at the time, because Guy can be a bit . . . off, yeah? He said something about . . . about being glad the appearance hadn't been canceled. That it was the perfect location, exactly where he wanted it to be—"

Suddenly there's a buzz behind me, and I glance over at Singh again, only to see him punching a number into his phone. "If you'll excuse me," he says, and he hastily moves to the door and knocks. A beat later, it opens for him, and as he crosses the threshold, he starts to speak.

"Cooper. It's Singh. I need a list of staff at—"

The door shuts behind him, and for a moment, Aoife and I stare at each other, both of us confused into silence. I want to ask what this means—what clues Singh noticed that went over my head—but Aoife's eyes are overflowing again, and she tugs at her restraints like she wants to reach across the table for my hand.

"Evangeline, please," she begs, softer now. "You have to believe me. I'd never hurt anyone—I swear it. I'll admit, I'm not overly fond of the royals and all they stand for, but it's not personal. And I like you. I like Kit. I'm not a murderer. I'd never— I'd *never*—"

She's sobbing now, every bit as hard as Rosie was in Kit's sitting room. I should comfort her, maybe. Offer her words of assurance, promise to get to the bottom of it. But all I can see as I watch her are the bloody remains of Ingrid's body, and my father lying broken in a hospital bed, a single complication away from death.

"The ABR protested outside Sandringham the day we met,"

I say, and even to my ears, I sound hollow. "Were you part of that?"

"N-no," she hiccups, her watery eyes round, and even though I don't want to believe her, I think I do. "I arrived maybe an hour before Dylan suggested we go into town. And once we were there, he said there was an ice cream shop we had to try— that's why we went in. He suggested it. He suggested the whole thing."

She sniffs loudly, and her restraints rattle again as she tries to raise her hand. With a wince, she rubs her nose against her shoulder instead, leaving a streak of tears and mucus across her sweatshirt. I watch her, feeling strangely detached from her overt show of emotion, and at last I ask my final question.

"Do you know who shot me and Kit?"

Aoife's mouth opens again, and this time there's no mistaking her shock for anything but real. "I—it was both of you? I thought . . . the tabloids said it was only you."

"He threw himself in front of me," I say coldly. "And I want to know who almost killed him."

Aoife is silent for several seconds, but her hands are shaking now, and I know that finally, *finally* I've found a secret.

"I don't know," she whispers. "But . . . that morning, Dylan was texting someone, and he left early. Really early. Said he had a few more gifts to buy in town, but . . . but I peeked out the window to watch him go, and . . . he had . . . he had his rifle slung over his . . ."

Her face crumples as she chokes on the rest of her words, but she's already said enough. While this small bit of circumstantial evidence is just one more stone to add to the mountain that should—but doesn't—prove Ben's involvement, it's the piece of the puzzle that finally shows me the full picture.

Ben, who bugged my room at Sandringham, heard Kit telling Maisie where we'd be walking that morning. And there's no doubt in my mind that Ben sent Dylan to do his dirty work for him.

This time, when I stand, I'm careful not to drag the chair along the floor. I head toward the exit on silent feet, but once I reach it, I turn back to Aoife. "Dylan is a good shot, isn't he?" I say, and she manages a jerking nod.

"Y-yes," she gasps. "Please, Ev-Evangeline—*please,* you have to—to believe me—I didn't—*I didn't*—"

"Okay," I say, knocking on the door. "I believe you."

Her eyes widen, and she sits up straighter, her tear-streaked face full of astonishment. "You—you do?" she says, and the hope in her voice is a knife to my gut.

"I do," I say as the door opens. "But it won't make a difference, Aoife. You know that, right? Because the entire world thinks I'm guilty, too."

Her jaw goes slack, and she stares at me with dawning horror. But before she can say another word, I turn and walk away, and I don't—can't—look back.

Kit and Jenkins are waiting for me in a room down the hall, where three more agents from the Home Office are watching a weeping Aoife on a monitor and speaking quietly among themselves. Jenkins reaches me first, and he places his hands on my shoulders, his gaze searching mine.

"That was a brave thing you did, darling," he says, and I shake my head.

"Didn't really have a choice. She only wanted to talk to me," I say quietly, and as Jenkins lets me go, Kit takes his place, silently gathering me in his arms. But while I bury my face in the crook of his neck, I'm numb. Even though I finally have the answers I've been looking for, I still don't have the one thing I need—the one thing that ties this all together: irrefutable evidence that Ben is responsible for everything.

"What if we can never prove it?" I mumble. We can't speak freely, not in front of the agents, but Kit knows exactly what I'm talking about.

"We will," he murmurs as he rubs my back. "He'll slip up eventually."

I close my eyes as the soft sound of Aoife's wails echo through the room. "Maybe," I say. "But how many more people are we going to lose first?"

Someone clears their throat, and I look up to see Singh standing on the threshold, phone in hand. "Mr. Jenkins. I'm afraid that call is necessary," he says, and Jenkins stiffens.

"Very well," he says, and after offering me a small smile that isn't remotely convincing, he excuses himself to the other side of the room and pulls out his mobile.

"What's going on?" I say, but Singh gestures toward the hallway.

"If I could have a minute with both of you," he says, and it's the kind of request that isn't really a request at all.

Confused, I take Kit's hand and follow Singh into the wide corridor. It's empty, except for a few doors that remain firmly closed, and Singh glances over his shoulder before facing Kit and me head-on.

"Four of the doctors working at the hospital where His Majesty is staying studied at Oxford," he says in a low voice. "Three from colleges we know Fox Rex recruits from. We've pulled them from the floor, but that's only a temporary solution. As soon as it's safe to do so, I've recommended that His Majesty be moved to a more secure location, along with the rest of the royal family."

I frown. "But the hospital's crawling with security."

"I'm aware. Until we track down a full list of Fox Rex members, both past and present, however, we must assume that anyone who fits the profile could be working for the ABR," says Singh, and I stare at him, horrified.

"Wait—so anyone who went to Oxford—"

"Is to be treated as a danger to your family," he says. "Yes."

"But—that has to be thousands of people," I say. "Tens of thousands."

"Hundreds of thousands," he corrects. "Including several royal courtiers and senior advisers—such as Harry Jenkins."

I glance back through the open doorway and catch a glimpse of Jenkins pacing the length of the office, his spine ramrod straight as he speaks into his phone. "He's not a suspect," I say firmly. "He's family."

"So is Prince Benedict," says Singh, and I scowl.

"Don't you dare compare him to Jenkins—"

"It's not a comparison, Miss Bright," he says. "It's an example of how close the ABR could be. And as it stands, we have no way of knowing who might be an alumnus—or potentially still working for them."

"What if there is no list?" says Kit, taking my hand in what feels like a silent effort to calm me down.

"I guarantee you a record exists, if only to feed their leader's ego. We're already working on it, but it'll take time to get someone on the inside."

"What about Aoife?" I say. "If she's telling the truth about being used . . ."

Singh tilts his head. "Did you believe her story, then?"

I consider it. "Depends. Was she lying about the text I supposedly sent?"

"No," he says. "She wasn't lying. Someone was texting her as you under an unrelated number. And that someone asked her to come to the museum opening, exactly as she described."

My entire body goes cold. "So she really is innocent?"

"It's possible," he allows. "Or it could've all been set up in such a way to give her the benefit of the doubt, in hopes she might be released. Either way, she's not a viable asset to us. At best, the leaders of the operation will hold her at arm's length, *if* she's allowed back into the club at all. And if it turns out that she did in fact play a part in the bombing, then we'll be releasing a terrorist, and you and your family will have one more enemy out there gunning for your lives."

My fingers are now laced so tightly between Kit's that by all rights, he should pull away. But he doesn't. He strokes his thumb against the back of my hand instead, tracing invisible circles into my skin, and slowly I loosen my grip. I don't let go, though, and neither does he.

"Even if she's innocent, this will follow her for the rest of her life," I say.

"Yes," agrees Singh. "Some marks never rub off completely."

"And everyone thinks Kit and I . . . that we're part of it, too," I add, and he studies me for a long moment.

"Yes," he says again, slower this time. "They do."

I glance up at Kit, and he peers down at me, his warm brown eyes searching mine. We don't speak—there's no need, not really, not when we both know what the other is thinking. But there's a question there, too, that neither of us is ready to ask. Or answer.

"Why don't I walk you both out?" says Singh. "My colleagues will see to Jenkins once he's ready."

This time it's Kit's hand that tightens around mine. But he doesn't shake his head, and at last, with my heart in my throat, I tear my eyes away from his.

"Okay," I say. And as Kit and I follow Singh through the soulless corridor, the brick-and-concrete fortress weighs heavier over us with each step we take, threatening to bury the last dregs of everything familiar to us both.

CHAPTER THIRTY-SEVEN

Why has Evangeline Bright not been arrested? It's the question on everyone's mind, as the palace refuses to make a statement about her alleged ties to the terrorist organization known as the Army of the British Republic, which has claimed responsibility for the Modern Music Museum bombing that killed eight and grievously wounded His Majesty the King.

We certainly have the evidence. The pictures and video of Evangeline hugging friend Aoife Marsh, who was arrested at the scene of the attack and is a reported member of the ABR, have been confirmed as genuine. The leader of ABR himself has publicly thanked Evangeline for her help in the attempted assassination of her father, the King. And if that wasn't enough, with news breaking this morning of a fire at Windsor that reportedly targeted Princess Mary, palace insiders have revealed that accelerant was found in Evangeline's bedroom—and that the half sisters had fought the night before.

What more does MI5 need? The members of the royal family have long enjoyed a certain amount of privilege when it comes to bending the laws that the rest of us must follow, but we're not talking about a traffic ticket or a bit of light fraud. This is murder. This is terrorism. This is *treason.*

How many more people have to die before MI5 finally admits that the King's own daughter is responsible? How many more times must our beloved royal family fight for their lives before the senior courtiers stop using the palace's substantial power to protect a killer?

Evangeline Bright is a traitor—not only to her family, but to this country and its people. And we shudder to think of how many more tragedies we as a nation must face before she is finally brought to justice.

—The Regal Record, 18 January 2024

AS THE RANGE ROVER RACES down the expressway toward London, Jenkins stares at Kit and me, his silence louder than any rebuke.

He's in the passenger seat, his upper body twisted in what must be an uncomfortable position, but even when we hit a bump, he refuses to budge. The seconds tick by slowly, and though I expect him to speak, he doesn't have to—the look on his face says everything, and I toy with the cap on my water bottle as I hold his incredulous gaze.

"I know it's reckless," I say. "I know there are risks—"

"This is more than a risk, Evan," he says, his voice so rough that he doesn't sound like himself. "This is . . . it's unthinkable."

I shrug. "He gave me an opening, Jenkins. I have to take it."

"No, you don't," he says with gentle firmness. "As long as I've known you, Evan, your first instinct is to right wrongs with wrongs. You'll do whatever it takes to fight a perceived injustice, even when it means getting expelled, or setting your classroom on fire, or risking your future—or, it seems, your life."

"This isn't a *perceived injustice*," I insist. "He's trying to kill us. Not just me, but Kit, my mom, Alexander—"

"I know, sweetheart," says Jenkins. "And we have the best people in the world doing everything they can to protect you."

"But it isn't enough," I argue. "He knows the royal family's security protocols too well, and he also knows the loopholes and how to exploit them. He's grown up in this life—he knows exactly how to get to us, and I need to prove it's him before it's too late."

Jenkins sighs. "Even if you're right, darling, there's absolutely no reason it has to be you."

I look at Kit, who's tight-lipped and staring at his hands. "I think it does, though," I say. "I think I'm the only one who has a chance of making this work."

Before either Jenkins or Kit can respond, my phone buzzes in my lap, and I automatically check the screen.

"It's Maisie," I say as I accept the call and put the phone to my ear. "Hey, we just left the prison. Aoife Marsh didn't know anything about Ben, but—"

"Evan?" The connection crackles, and Maisie's voice sounds oddly distant as a swell of noise fills the background of the call. "What's going on? The prime minister's insisting we evacuate to Balmoral, which is positively *arctic* this time of year. And Daddy's coming by air ambulance even though he's still critical, but no one will tell me why—"

"It's the ABR," I say. "MI5 are worried they've infiltrated the hospital and the palace staff. Talk to Agent Singh—he'll give you the details. But they're right, Maisie. You need to get out of London, okay?"

Maisie mutters a few choice words under her breath, mostly about Scottish winters. "Yes, all right, fine. But I certainly won't enjoy it. How far away are you? The helicopter's already landed on the lawn at Kensington, and Mummy's insisting we leave as soon as possible."

"I—" I hesitate and look at Jenkins, whose stony expression offers me nothing in return. "My mom's going with them, right?"

"What? Who are you talking to?" says Maisie, confused, but I'm still watching Jenkins. At last the corners of his mouth tug downward, and he exhales in a heavy sigh.

"I'll make sure your mother remains with His Majesty," he promises, and I nod, grateful.

"My mom's going to join you at Balmoral, Maisie," I say. "Will you look after her for me? Make sure she takes care of herself?"

Maisie huffs. "I know you and Mummy had a bit of a spat, but Balmoral is my castle, not hers, and if I have to be there, then you most certainly do, too."

"I'll join you when I can," I promise. "But not yet, Mais. I'm sorry."

"What are you talking about?" she says, the indignation in her voice rising. But I hear a hint of fear, too. "You're coming with us, Evan. That's the whole bloody point, isn't it? He's after *you*."

"While I'm gone," I say as if she hasn't spoken, "let him take my spot on the council."

"*What?*" she sputters. "Evan—"

"You need to keep him close, all right? Close and busy. Let him think he's won. Let him think you believe I started the fire. Let him think you hate me, and that he's back in your good graces, or at least on his way. Pretend I'm not invited to Balmoral, that Kit and I are both being investigated—"

"Kit's part of this madness, too?" she says furiously. "Let me speak to him—"

"I need you to do this for me, Maisie, okay?" I say, talking over her once more. "It's important. *Keep him busy.*"

"I—" I can practically see Maisie opening and shutting her mouth. "Yes, all right, I'll keep him busy, but—"

"And don't let him anywhere near Dad," I say. "Not even for a moment, okay?"

"That we certainly agree on," she mutters. "Fine. I'll keep him busy, and I'll keep him away from Daddy—and your mother, naturally. But you *must* tell me what's going on."

My shoulders slump, and I lean forward, my seat belt cutting into my neck. "I'm going to fix this."

She scoffs. "That's alarmingly vague."

"I know. I'm sorry. Just—trust me, okay? Please. I love you."

"You—what?" says Maisie, and for a moment, her surprise overrides her fear. "Evan, what on earth—"

"I'll see you as soon as I can," I promise. "Stay safe. And don't trust anyone."

"Evan—*Evan!* Don't you *dare*—"

I hang up with her voice still ringing in my ears, and the silence in the vehicle is thick. Kit is watching me now, though his expression remains unreadable, and I desperately wish he'd say something. Even if it's not what I want to hear.

"I cannot condone this," says Jenkins, his words like steel as they cut through the quiet hum. "It's far too dangerous. If your father finds out—"

"Don't tell him," I say quickly. "Please. If—when he wakes up—"

"I cannot—I *will* not lie to my king," he says, and I hesitate, my mind a jumbled whirl.

"Then try to hold off on telling him for as long as possible," I say. "You don't have to lie, but just . . . buy me some time. Please."

Jenkins holds my pleading stare as the Range Rover veers toward an exit. He and I both know that this all might be a moot point—that Alexander might never wake up, and Jenkins will never have the chance to lie to him. Or tell him the truth.

But at last, his chin dips in the slightest of nods, and I reach forward, squeezing his fingers gratefully. "Thank you," I say, relieved. But Jenkins isn't looking at me anymore, and after a beat, he lets my hand go. Most people would hardly notice, but to me, it's a stab in the heart.

My throat tightens, and I force myself to push past the brief ache as I turn toward Kit. "You don't need to do this," I say. "I can figure it out on my own."

"I know you can," he says, his voice so low that he sounds hoarse. "But you won't have to."

My heart is thumping, and I don't know if it's from fear or nerves or excitement, or a potent combination of all three. "Are you sure?" I say, searching his face for any hint of reluctance or doubt.

But Kit takes my hand—the same one Jenkins dropped—and raises it to his lips, brushing them against my knuckles. "We're in this together," he says, his breath warm against my skin. "Let's finish it."

The cold rushes in as he lets me go, setting his palm on my knee instead, and I hold his gaze for several long seconds before picking up my phone once more. I dismiss another call from Maisie and open my contacts, where I have to scroll to find the right name. And as Jenkins speaks to the driver, grudgingly giving him our new destination, I type out my message.

We're in.

ACKNOWLEDGMENTS

This series wouldn't exist without the support and guidance from my agents, Rosemary Stimola and Allison Remcheck, Alli Hellegers, and everyone at the Stimola Literary Studio. I have no idea where I'd be without you all, but it'd probably be nowhere good.

The team at Delacorte Press continues to knock it out of the park in every possible way, especially my editor, Kelsey Horton, whose unending patience and wealth of creative knowledge have been equally invaluable to the process of creating this book. A huge thank-you to the rest of the team, including Beverly Horowitz, Shameiza Ally, Kenneth Crossland, Colleen Fellingham, Joey Ho, Shannon Pender, Tamar Schwartz, and Ray Shappell, and to Yordanka Poleganova for the incredible cover art.

Most of my friends are used to me sneaking chapters into their inboxes or snippets of new ideas into our texts, but it takes a special kind of dedication to commit to reading and offering feedback on sequels. My undying thanks to Sara Hodgkinson, Carli Segal, Caitlin Straw, and Andrea Hannah for reading this one and letting me pick their brains far beyond the point most people would tolerate.

Thank you to Veronica O'Neil, Malcolm Freberg, Kristin Lord, Becca Mix, Ashley Zajac, and Austin Webberly for the friendship and support, as always, and for listening to me spoil this entire trilogy. One day I'll learn to keep my mouth shut, but probably not anytime soon.

Several difficult situations cropped up in my life during the various writing and editing stages of this book, but especially toward the end, when we were up against a very strict deadline, and missing it would have meant moving the release date—something I am loath to do under any circumstances. But because of the understanding and grace of my publishing team and the support of the people in my life, this book was finished (mostly) on time. Thank you, thank you, thank you to Sadie Betro and Anthony Jacaruso, Ashley Oswald, Karla Olson-Bellfi, Ruth Rydstedt, and Jessica W. for being there when we needed you most.

Shout-out to my pets for the company during the writing process, and especially to Fred, my cat, who nearly died while I was editing this book but somehow came out of it even sweeter and more lovable than ever. I'm sure there's a lesson in there somewhere. A huge thank-you to the medical teams that kept her alive and made room in their schedules to see her literally dozens of times, which in turn helped me not be such an anxious mess—Dr. C., Kelsey, Courtney, Hayley, Dr. J., Sam, Lindsay, Terri, Rebekah, and Andrea.

And thank you to my dad, as always, who is the best person I know and my favorite human being. His love of writing has always inspired my own, and his support from the very first time I expressed interest in writing is the only reason any of my books exist. I love you most.

Catalyst QoS: Quality of Service in Campus Networks

nnagan, Richard Froom, Kevin Turek

t© 2003 Cisco Systems, Inc.

ess logo is a trademark of Cisco Systems, Inc.

d by:

ress

st 103rd Street

polis, IN 46290 USA

ed in the United States of America 1 2 3 4 5 6 7 8 9 0

ary of Congress Cataloging-in-Publication Number: 2002109166

N: 1-58705-120-6

arning and Disclaimer

Feedback Information

At Cisco Press, our goal is to create in-depth technical books of the highest quality and value. Each book is crafted
with care and precision, undergoing rigorous development that involves the unique expertise of members from the
professional technical community.

Readers' feedback is a natural continuation of this process. If you have any comments regarding how we could
improve the quality of this book, or otherwise alter it to better suit your needs, you can contact us through e-mail at
feedback@ciscopress.com. Please make sure to include the book title and ISBN in your message.

We greatly appreciate your assistance.

Trademark Acknowledgments

Cisco Catalyst QoS:
Quality of Service in Campus N

Mike Flannagan, CCIE No. 7651
Richard Froom, CCIE No. 5102
Kevin Turek, CCIE No. 7284

Cisco Press

201 West 103rd Street
Indianapolis, IN 46290 USA

Publisher	John Wait
Editor-In-Chief	John Kane
Cisco Representative	Anthony Wolfenden
Cisco Press Program Manager	Sonia Torres Chavez
Cisco Marketing Communications Manager	Scott Miller
Cisco Marketing Program Manager	Edie Quiroz
Executive Editor	Brett Bartow
Production Manager	Patrick Kanouse
Development Editor	Jennifer Foster
Copy Editor	Keith Cline
Technical Editors	Jason Cornett
	Lauren Dygowski
	Balaji Sivasubramanian
Team Coordinator	Tammi Ross
Book Designer	Gina Rexrode
Cover Designer	Louisa Adair
Compositor	Mark Shirar
Indexer	Tim Wright
Proofreader	Missy Pluta

CISCO SYSTEMS

Corporate Headquarters
Cisco Systems, Inc.
170 West Tasman Drive
San Jose, CA 95134-1706
USA
www.cisco.com
Tel: 408 526-4000
800 553-NETS (6387)
Fax: 408 526-4100

European Headquarters
Cisco Systems International BV
Haarlerbergpark
Haarlerbergweg 13-19
1101 CH Amsterdam
The Netherlands
www-europe.cisco.com
Tel: 31 0 20 357 1000
Fax: 31 0 20 357 1100

Americas Headquarters
Cisco Systems, Inc.
170 West Tasman Drive
San Jose, CA 95134-1706
USA
www.cisco.com
Tel: 408 526-7660
Fax: 408 527-0883

Asia Pacific Headquarters
Cisco Systems, Inc.
Capital Tower
168 Robinson Road
#22-01 to #29-01
Singapore 068912
www.cisco.com
Tel: +65 6317 7777
Fax: +65 6317 7799

Cisco Systems has more than 200 offices in the following countries and regions. Addresses, phone numbers, and fax numbers are listed on the
Cisco.com Web site at www.cisco.com/go/offices.

Argentina • Australia • Austria • Belgium • Brazil • Bulgaria • Canada • Chile • China PRC • Colombia • Costa Rica • Croatia • Czech Republic
Denmark • Dubai, UAE • Finland • France • Germany • Greece • Hong Kong SAR • Hungary • India • Indonesia • Ireland • Israel • Italy
Japan • Korea • Luxembourg • Malaysia • Mexico • The Netherlands • New Zealand • Norway • Peru • Philippines • Poland • Portugal
Puerto Rico • Romania • Russia • Saudi Arabia • Scotland • Singapore • Slovakia • Slovenia • South Africa • Spain • Sweden
Switzerland • Taiwan • Thailand • Turkey • Ukraine • United Kingdom • United States • Venezuela • Vietnam • Zimbabwe

About the Authors

Mike Flannagan, CCIE No. 7651, is a manager in the High Touch Technical Support (HTTS) group at Cisco Systems in Research Triangle Park, North Carolina. Mike joined Cisco in 2000 as a network consulting engineer in the Cisco Advanced Services group, where he led the creation and deployment of the QoS Virtual Team. As a member of the QoS Virtual Team, Mike was involved with the development of new QoS features for Cisco IOS and developed QoS strategies and implementation guidelines for some of the largest Cisco enterprise customers. Mike teaches QoS classes and leads design clinics for internal and external audiences and is the author of *Administering Cisco QoS for IP Networks*, published by Syngress.

Richard Froom, CCIE No. 5102, is a software and QA engineer for the Financial Test Lab at Cisco Systems in Research Triangle Park. Richard joined Cisco in 1998 as a customer support engineer in the Cisco Technical Assistance Organization. Richard, as a customer support engineer, served as a support engineer troubleshooting customers' networks and as a technical team lead. Being involved with Catalyst product field trials, Richard has been crucial in driving troubleshooting capabilities of Catalyst products and software. Currently, Richard is working with the Cisco storage networking products. Richard earned his bachelor of science degree in computer engineering at Clemson University.

Kevin Turek, CCIE No. 7284, is currently working as a network consulting engineer in the Cisco Federal Support Program in Research Triangle Park. He currently supports some of the Cisco Department of Defense customers. Kevin is also a member of the internal Cisco QoS virtual team, supporting both internal Cisco engineers and external Cisco customers with QoS deployment and promoting current industry best practices as they pertain to QoS. Kevin earned his bachelor of science degree in business administration at the State University of New York, Stony Brook.

About the Technical Reviewers

Jason Cornett is a customer support engineer at Cisco Systems, where he is a technical leader for the LAN Switching team in Research Triangle Park. Jason joined Cisco in 1999 and has a total of five years of networking experience. He holds a diploma in business technology information communications systems from St. Lawrence College. Previously Jason was a network support specialist with a network management company.

Lauren L. Dygowski, CCIE No. 7068, is a senior network engineer at a major financial institution and has more than eight years of networking experience. He holds a bachelor of science degree in computer science from Texas Tech University and a M.S.B.A. from Boston University. Previously, Lauren was a network manager with the United States Marine Corps and MCI. He resides with his wife and three sons in Charlotte, North Carolina.

Balaji Sivasubramanian is part of the Technical Assistance Center (TAC) based out of Research Triangle Park, where he acts as the worldwide subject matter expert in LAN technologies. He has been with Cisco TAC for more than three years. He has authored and reviewed many technical white papers on Cisco.com in the LAN technologies area. He has been a presenter/moderator of the Technical Virtual Chalk Talk Seminars for Partners. He has actively participated in early field trial testing of the Catalyst 4000/4500 platform series. Balaji holds a master of science degree in computer engineering from the University of Arizona and holds a bachelor of science degree in electrical engineering.

Dedications

Mike Flannagan:

I would like to dedicate this book to Anne. Thank you for your loving support and encouragement during the seemingly endless nights and weekends spent on this project.

Richard Froom:

I would like to dedicate this book to my wife Elizabeth for her support, understanding, and patience while I was authoring the book. I would also like to thank Elizabeth for her cooperation and assistance in reviewing my material.

Kevin Turek:

I would like to thank Tara for all of her encouragement and patience during my involvement in this project. I would not have been able to complete my portion of the book if not for your sacrifices and understanding. I would also like to thank the members of the Federal Support Program for their support. Finally, I would like to thank my family and friends for instilling in me the values and ethics that have allowed me to get to the point where I am today.

Acknowledgments

Richard would like to acknowledge his co-authors for asking him to work on this project and their efforts on their material. Furthermore, Richard would like to acknowledge Balaji Sivasubramanian for his aid and outstanding reviews of technical content pertaining to the Catalyst 4000 Family of switches.

Mike would like to acknowledge Dave Knuth and his other friends in Network Optimization Support for their support. Mike would especially like to thank Chris Camplejohn, Nimish Desai, and Zahoor Khan for asking the tough questions that always helped me learn. Thanks to the members of the AS QoS virtual team for their outstanding teamwork and technical expertise in support of our customers. Mike would especially like to recognize Richard Watts for his support of and contributions to the team. Finally, thanks to my new team in Cisco's HTTS group for an exciting new opportunity to learn.

Kevin would like to personally thank his co-authors for agreeing to do this book, and for their motivation, professionalism, and expertise, which ensured its timely completion without sacrificing quality. Thanks especially to Richard for his focus and acceptance of an additional load, despite his already busy schedule.

All the authors would like to thank Jeff Raymond for his time and recommendations that contributed to the technical accuracy and quality of the content pertaining to the Catalyst 6500 Family of switches.

A big thank you goes to the team at Cisco Press, especially Brett Bartow for his overall support of this project and Christopher Cleveland and Jennifer Foster for their suggestions and input. We would like to give special thanks to our review team of Jason, Lauren, and Balaji for their dedication to making this project successful.

Contents at a Glance

Contents

Icons Used in This Book

Throughout this book, you will see the following icons used for networking devices:

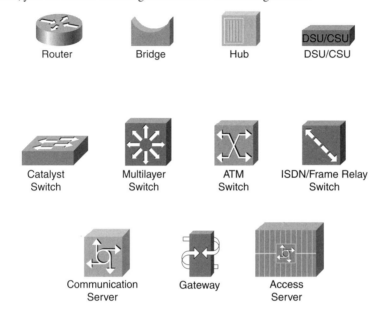

The following icons are used for peripherals and other devices:

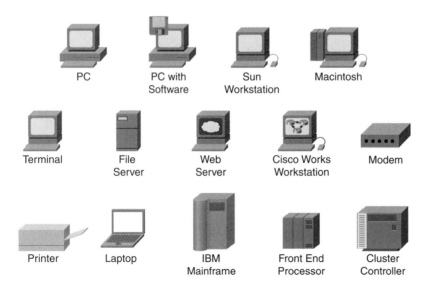

The following icons are used for networks and network connections:

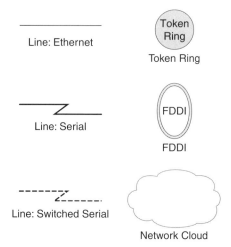

Command Syntax Conventions

The conventions used to present command syntax in this book are the same conventions used in the Cisco IOS Software Command Reference. The Command Reference describes these conventions as follows:

- Vertical bars (|) separate alternative, mutually exclusive elements.
- Square brackets [ ] indicate optional elements.
- Braces { } indicate a required choice.
- Braces within brackets [{ }] indicate a required choice within an optional element.
- **Boldface** indicates commands and keywords that are entered literally as shown. In actual configuration examples and output (not general command syntax), boldface indicates commands that are manually input by the user (such as a **show** command).
- *Italics* indicate arguments for which you supply actual values.

Introduction

This book is intended for all network engineers who deal with Catalyst switches and specifically for those looking for a deeper understanding of the QoS capabilities of those switches. In addition, any network engineer responsible for end-to-end QoS policies in a Cisco network will find, either now or in the near future, the need to thoroughly understand Catalyst QoS.

Besides the configuration syntax information provided in this book, the authors have made every attempt to discuss common practices and provide case studies. This treatment of the subject matter provides readers with more than just commands for configuring QoS on Catalyst switches; specifically, the authors wanted to make sure that readers understand the reasons for certain policy decisions, as those decisions would relate to a production environment.

Motivation for This Book

After countless hours spent trying to locate various pieces of information for our customers, the authors realized that there was not a good Catalyst QoS book anywhere to be found. Rather than continue to answer the same questions, we decided to publish our collection of the most commonly requested information plus some not-so-common information that would give readers a strong foundation in Catalyst QoS.

Goal of This Book

The purpose of this book is to provide readers who have a curiosity about Catalyst QoS, and end-to-end QoS involving Catalyst switches, with a well-rounded baseline of information about the RFCs involved in QoS, the configuration steps for enabling QoS, and the command syntax for fine-tuning the operation of QoS on Catalyst switches. In addition, the authors want to make sure that our readers walk away with more than command syntax; after completing this book, readers should actually be prepared to deploy Catalyst QoS in a production environment.

Prerequisites

Although anyone can read this book, the authors assume reader understanding of some fundamental networking concepts discussed in this book. If you do not have basic knowledge in the following areas, you might have trouble understanding certain examples and concepts presented in this text:

- Cisco IOS—Basic syntax
- Cisco Catalyst OS (CatOS)—Basic syntax
- Access-control list (ACL) configuration
- Virtual LANs (VLANs)
- IP addressing
- Routing protocols—Basic syntax and concepts
- TCP/UDP port assignments

How This Book Is Organized

Although this book could be read cover to cover, it is designed to be flexible and enable you to move easily between chapters and sections of chapters to cover just the material that you need more work with. Each chapter stands by itself; however, most chapters reference earlier chapter material. Overall, therefore, the order in the book is an excellent sequence to follow.

The material covered in this book is as follows:

- **Chapter 1, Quality of Service: An Overview**—This chapter defines quality of service (QoS), as it pertains to Cisco networks, provides a general overview of the necessity for QoS in multiservice networks, and discusses various QoS models. Several of the key RFCs pertaining to IP QoS are also explored in this chapter.

- **Chapter 2, End-to-End QoS: Quality of Service at Layer 3 and Layer 2**—This chapter explores QoS components such as congestion management, congestion avoidance, traffic conditioning, and link efficiency. This chapter also explores per-hop behaviors in the differentiated services architecture and includes an entry-level discussion of QoS on Catalyst platforms. The Catalyst platform discussion also cotains discussions of the Catalyst voice VLAN and trust concept.

- **Chapter 3, Overview of QoS Support on Catalyst Platforms and Exploring QoS on the Catalyst 2900XL, 3500XL, and Catalyst 4000 CatOS Family of Switches**—This chapter provides a basic overview of QoS support on each platform. In addition, a detailed explanation of QoS feature supported is provided for the Catalyst 2900XL, 3500XL, and Catalyst 4000 CatOS switches.

- **Chapter 4, QoS Support on the Catalyst 5000 Family of Switches**—This chapter discusses the limited hardware and software feature support for QoS on the Catalyst 5000 family of switches. In addition, concepts such as multilayer switches are explained in this chapter.

- **Chapter 5, Introduction to the Modular QoS Command-Line Interface**—This chapter discusses the need for the MQC and the steps required to configure QoS mechanisms using the MQC. In addition to providing an explanation of the commands necessary for configuration, this chapter also provides sample **show** command output for the various commands needed to verify the functionality of the configuration.

- **Chapter 6, QoS Features Available on the Catalyst 2950 and 3550 Family of Switches**—This chapter covers QoS feature support on both the Catalyst 2950 and 3550 family of switches. The QoS examples in this chapter present these switches as access layer switches. This chapter also includes an Auto-QoS discussion for those switches applicable to Voice over IP.

- **Chapter 7, QoS Features Available on the Catalyst 4000 IOS Family of Switches and the Catalyst G-L3 Family of Switches**—This chapter covers QoS feature support on the Catalyst 4000 IOS family of switches and the Catalyst G-L3 switches. The Catalyst G-L3 switches include the Catalyst 2948G-L3, 4908G-L3, and the WS-X4232-L3 Layer 3 services module for the Catalyst 4000 CatOS family of switches.

- **Chapter 8, QoS Support on the Catalyst 6500**—This chapter focuses on the QoS architecture for the Catalyst 6500 series platform. Specifically, it demonstrates how QoS on the Catalyst 6500 can support voice and other mission-critical applications in a converged environment. The chapter further demonstrates configuring QoS features using both CatOS and Cisco IOS.

- **Chapter 9, QoS Support on the Catalyst 6500 MSFC and FlexWAN**—This chapter discusses the QoS capabilities of the FlexWAN and MSFC in the Catalyst 6500. The chapter shows how the FlexWAN and MSFC extend the Catalyst 6500's QoS capabilities to the MAN and WAN. Examples demonstrate configuring QoS using the MQC available in Cisco IOS.

- **Chapter 10, End-to-End QoS Case Studies**—This chapter presents end-to-end QoS case studies using a typical campus network design. The network topology illustrates QoS end-to-end using the Catalyst 2950, 3550, 4500 IOS, 6500 switches.

Fundamental QoS Concepts

CHAPTER 1

Quality of Service: An Overview

The constantly changing needs of networks have created a demand for sensitive applications (such as *voice over IP* (VoIP) and video conferencing over IP), and networks are being asked to support increasingly mission-critical data traffic. Providing predictable service levels for all of these different types of traffic has become an important task for network administrators. Being able to provide predictable and differentiated service levels is key to ensuring that all application traffic receives the treatment that it requires to function properly.

This chapter covers several aspects of *quality of service* (QoS) and discusses how to provide QoS in Cisco networks. Specifically, this chapter covers the following topics:

- Understanding QoS
- Deploying QoS in the WAN/LAN: High-Level Overview
- Cisco AVVID (Architecture for Voice, Video, and Integrated Data)
- Overview of Integrated Services and Differentiated Services
- Differentiated Services: A Standards Approach

Understanding QoS

The following section defines QoS in terms of measurable characteristics. It is important, however, to recognize that fully understanding QoS requires more than a definition. To truly understand QoS, you must understand the concept of managed unfairness, the necessity for predictability, and the goals of QoS. In addition to a definition of QoS in measurable terms, the following section explains each of these things, to provide you with a well-rounded and practical definition of QoS.

Definition of QoS

QoS is defined in several ways, and the combination of all of these definitions is really the best definition of all. A technical definition is that *QoS* is a set of techniques to manage bandwidth, delay, jitter, and packets loss for flows in a network. The purpose of every QoS mechanism is to influence at least one of these four characteristics and, in some cases, all four of these

Bandwidth

Bandwidth itself is defined as the rated throughput capacity of a given network medium or protocol. In the case of QoS, bandwidth more specifically means the allocation of bandwidth, because QoS does not have the capability to influence the actual capacity of any given link. That is to say that no QoS mechanism actually creates additional bandwidth, rather QoS mechanisms enable the administrator to more efficiently utilize the existing bandwidth. Bandwidth is sometimes also referred to as *throughput*.

Delay

Delay has several possible meanings, but when discussing QoS, *processing delay* is the time between when a device receives a frame and when that frame is forwarded out of the destination port, *serialization delay* is the time that it take to actually transmit a packet or frame, and *end-to-end delay* is the total delay that a packet experiences from source to destination.

Jitter

Jitter is the difference between interpacket arrival and departure—that is, the variation in delay from one packet to another.

Packet Loss

Packet loss is just losing packets along the forwarding path. Packet loss results from many causes, such as buffer congestion, line errors, or even QoS mechanisms that intentionally drop packets.

Table 1-1 shows examples of the varying requirements of common applications for bandwidth, delay, jitter, and packet loss.

Table 1-1   *Traffic Requirements of Common Applications*

	Voice	**FTP**	**Telnet**
Bandwidth Required	Low to moderate	Moderate to High	Low
Drop Sensitive	Low	Low	Moderate
Delay Sensitive	High	Low	Moderate
Jitter	High	Low	Moderate

Managed Unfairness

Another, more pragmatic definition of QoS is *managed unfairness*. The best way to explain this definition is using an analogy to airline service. Sometimes airlines are unable to sell all of their seats in first class, but they rarely leave the gate with first class seats available, so there has to be some method by which they decide who gets those seats. The gate agent could swing open the door to the plane and tell everyone to rush onto the plane; whoever gets to the first class seats first gets them. Some would argue that would be the most *fair* way to handle the seating, but that would be very disorderly and probably not a very pleasant thing to watch. Anyone who flies regularly knows that frequent flier miles are valuable because you can earn free flights and so on. If you collect enough frequent flier miles from a specific airline in a single year, however, you will be moved into an *elite* frequent flier status and get some extra benefits. One of those benefits is typically some method by which the most frequent fliers are able to upgrade their coach seat to a first class seat, when available. Imagine paying full price for a coach ticket to Hawaii, and having no chance at all to upgrade, while the person beside you is able to upgrade just because he is a frequent flier. Some would argue that this is *unfair.* However, it is unfair in a very controlled way, because there is a specific policy in place that dictates who is eligible for this upgrade and who is not. This is managed unfairness.

In QoS, managed unfairness is important because sometimes it is necessary to allocate more bandwidth to one application than another. This doesn't specifically indicate that either application is more or less important than the other; rather it indicates a different level of service that will be provided to each application. That is, the applications may well have different bandwidth needs, and dividing available bandwidth equally between the two applications, although fair, might not produce the best results. A good example of such a scenario is the case of an FTP flow sharing a link with a VoIP flow. The FTP flow is characterized by a large bandwidth requirement but has a high tolerance for delay, jitter, and packet loss; the VoIP flow is characterized by a small bandwidth requirement and has a low tolerance to delay, jitter, and packet loss. In this case, the FTP flow needs a larger share of the bandwidth, and the voice flow needs bounded delay and jitter. It is possible to provide each flow with what it needs without significantly impacting the service provided to the other flow. In this case, the allocation of bandwidth is unfair, because the FTP flow will get more bandwidth, but it is unfair in a very controlled manner. Again, this is an example of the need for managed unfairness.

Predictability: The Goal of QoS

The successful management of bandwidth, delay, jitter, and packet loss allows for the differentiated treatment of packets as they move through the network. Unless an implementation error occurs, all implementations of the differentiated services architecture should provide the same treatment to each packet of the same type when those packets pass through a given interface. In Figure 1-1, multiple packets are sent from Bob to the web server, marked with IP precedence 2.

Figure 1-1   *Multiple Packets from Bob Are Sent to the Web Server Marked with IP Precedence 2*

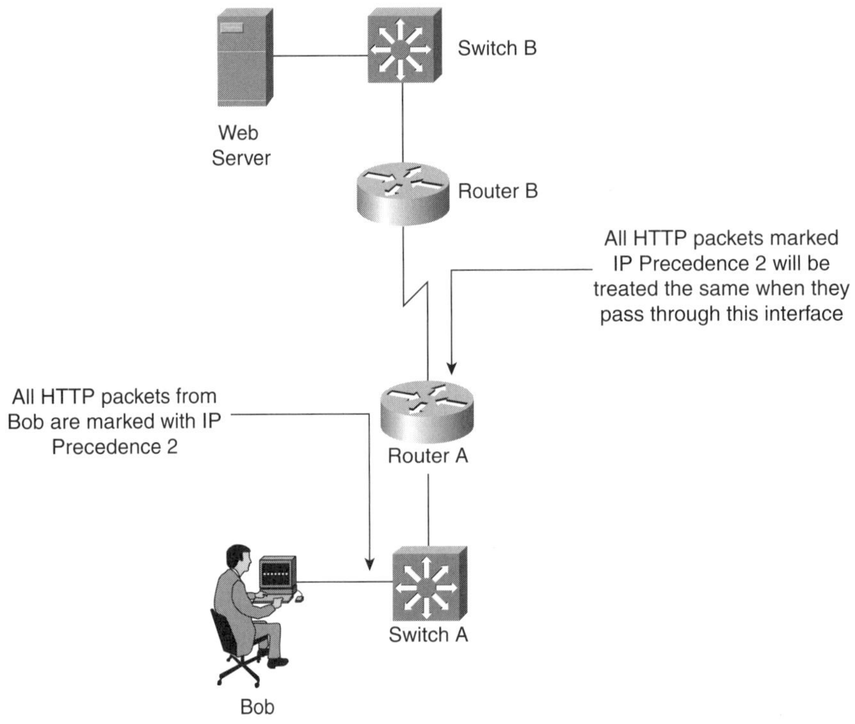

In this example, because all HTTP packets from Bob are marked with IP precedence 2, and the policy on router A's serial interface is to classify all HTTP packets with IP precedence 2 into the same class, you can assume that these packets will all receive the same treatment. Because all packets of the same type are going to be treated the same as they egress that interface, it's easy to predict the treatment that the next HTTP packet from Bob will receive. This is a simplified example of the overall goal of QoS: providing predictable service levels to packets as they move through a network.

It is very important to be able to predict the bandwidth, delay, jitter, and packet loss that can be expected as packets of a given flow traverse multiple hops in a network. Voice packets, for example, must not have a one-way delay greater than 150 ms and are very intolerant of jitter. Being able to say with confidence that voice packets will experience low latency and jitter at each hop along a given path is critical when provisioning IP telephony solutions.

Congestion Management

A variety of QoS mechanisms are available, but the most commonly used is congestion management. Congestion management provides the ability to reorder packets for transmission, which enables a network administrator to make some decisions about which packets are transmitted first and so on. The key to congestion management is that all congestion management QoS mechanisms only have an impact on traffic when congestion exists. The definition of congestion might differ from vendor to vendor and, in fact, is slightly different between Cisco platforms. However, one general statement can be made about the definition of congestion on Cisco platforms; *congestion* is defined as a full transmit queue. Figure 1-2 illustrates the decision model for congestion management.

Figure 1-2   *Congestion Management Decision Model*

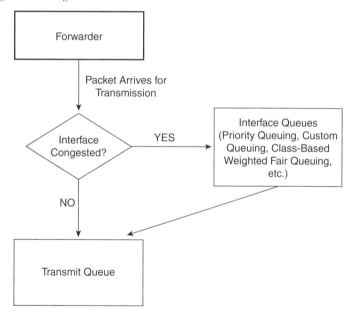

The need for interface queuing results because just a finite amount of buffer space exists in the transmit queue. This finite amount of buffer space is true across all platforms, so this logic applies to both switches and routers. If there were no interface queues, packets would just be dropped when the transmit queue was full.

Deploying QoS in the WAN/LAN: High-Level Overview

Different networks deploy QoS in the WAN and LAN for different reasons, but the overall intent is always to provide different treatment to different types of traffic. Sometimes the requirement is to provide better treatment to a select group of applications, such as VoIP or

Oracle. Other times, the requirement is to provide worse treatment to a select group of applications, such as peer-to-peer file sharing services such as Napster, KaZaa, and Morpheus.

Why QoS Is Necessary in the WAN

Originally, the queuing mechanism on all interfaces was *first-in, first-out* (FIFO), meaning that the first packet to arrive for transmission would be the first packet transmitted, the fifth packet arriving would be the fifth packets transmitted, and so on. This queuing mechanism works just fine if all of your traffic has no delay concerns (perhaps FTP or other batch transfer traffic). If you've ever worked with *data-link switching* (DLSw), however, you know how sensitive that traffic is to delay in the network.

For many networks, the first real need for QoS was to allow for priority treatment of DLSw traffic over low-speed WAN links. The need to provide basic prioritization of different types of data traffic was first seen in the WAN, because that is where bandwidth is most limited. In the case of Priority Queuing, the need was to prioritize a single traffic type (or a select few types of traffic) over all others. Custom Queuing addressed the need to provide basic bandwidth sharing, and Weighted Fair Queuing provided the ability to dynamically allocate more or less bandwidth to a given flow based on the IP precedence of the packets in that flow. *Class-Based Weighted Fair Queuing* (CBWFQ) and *Low Latency Queuing* (LLQ) are hybrid QoS mechanisms—that is, they provide a combination of the other functions to allow for greater flexibility.

As you can see, the Cisco congestion management mechanisms address a variety of needs in the WAN, and that only touches the surface of all the needs that can be addressed by QoS.

Why QoS Is Necessary in a Switched Environment

One of the most commonly asked questions is whether QoS is necessary in the Layer 2 environment. The basis for this question generally seems to be the belief that you can just "throw bandwidth at the problem"—that is, alleviate the problem of congestion by continuing to upgrade bandwidth.

Generally speaking, it's difficult to argue against the theory of providing *so* much bandwidth that congestion can be avoided. The truth is that if you install a 100-Mbps link between two switches that need only 10 Mbps, you're not going to have congestion. The cost of this theory starts getting ridiculous, however, when you approach congestion on higher-speed links.

The theory of continuing to upgrade bandwidth suffers from other problems: Primarily, the nature of TCP traffic is that it takes as much bandwidth as it can. For instance, you could upgrade your 100-Mbps link to a 200-Mbps Fast EtherChannel and still not have enough bandwidth to support good voice quality. In this case, perhaps FTP applications dominate the link. Whereas these applications were previously functioning well on the 100-Mbps link, due to TCP windowing, they are now taking far more bandwidth than before. In a case like this, it is difficult to get a true idea about how much bandwidth is required. You could upgrade to a 1-Gbps link, of course, but that confirms the fact that it's going to get expensive very quickly to follow that theory.

Still another problem helps make the case for QoS in the LAN. That problem is interactive traffic, such as voice and video conferencing. With most data traffic, there is no concern about jitter and little concern about delay, but that isn't the case with voice and video conferencing traffic. These real-time applications have special requirements with regard to delay and jitter that are just not addressed by adding more bandwidth. Even with abundant bandwidth, it is still possible that the packets of a voice flow could experience jitter and delay, which would cause call quality degradation. The only way to truly ensure the delay and jitter characteristics of these flows is through the use of QoS.

Cisco AVVID

As the incentives became greater and greater to migrate away from separate networks for data, voice, and video in favor of a single IP infrastructure, Cisco developed the Architecture for Voice, Video, and Integrated Data (AVVID), which provides an end-to-end enterprise architecture for deploying Cisco AVVID solutions. These solutions enable networks to migrate to a pure IP infrastructure; Cisco AVVID solutions include the following:

- IP telephony
- IP video conferencing
- MxU (that is, multi-tenant, hospitality, and so forth)
- Storage networking
- Virtual private networks
- Content networking
- Enterprise mobility
- IP contact center

The idea behind the AVVID architecture is that an enterprise environment can't possibly keep up with every emerging technology and adjust quickly to the individual changes in specific application deployments. With the AVVID architecture, Cisco provides a foundation of network engineering that allows an enterprise environment to quickly adapt to changes in all of these areas. In addition to the physical layer, the AVVID architecture also consists of the intelligent network services (such as QoS) that are necessary to transform a traditional data network into an advanced e-business infrastructure that provides customers with a competitive advantage.

AVVID is not a single mechanism or application; instead, it is an overall methodology that enables customers to build a converged network and adapt quickly to the ever-changing demands placed on that network. The requirements for IP-based voice and video, for example, may be different from the requirements for the next *x*-over-IP requirement.

QoS in the AVVID Environment

The foundation for the AVVID architecture is the assumption that all services (including VoIP) use a common infrastructure. The network requirements of VoIP traffic differ from those of a regular data flow (such as FTP). An FTP flow, for instance, requires a large amount of bandwidth, is very tolerant to delay and packet loss, and couldn't care less about jitter. Conversely, VoIP takes a relatively tiny amount of bandwidth, is very sensitive to packet loss, and requires low delay and jitter. By treating these two flows the same on your network, neither would be likely to get ideal service, and the FTP traffic could ultimately dominate the link, causing poor call quality for your VoIP.

For this reason, QoS is one of the cornerstones of the Cisco AVVID. Without QoS applied to the converged links in a network, all packets receive the same treatment and real-time applications suffer. Many QoS considerations exist in a Cisco AVVID environment, but the primary things that all QoS mechanisms are concerned with are constant: bandwidth, delay, jitter, and packet loss.

VoIP environments have multiple requirements. Assume that there is a T1 link between two branch offices, and you have determined that you can spare enough of that link for three concurrent VoIP calls. Figure 1-3 shows the minimum QoS mechanisms that you would configure.

Figure 1-3 *Minimum QoS Mechanisms for VoIP in a Specific AVVID Environment*

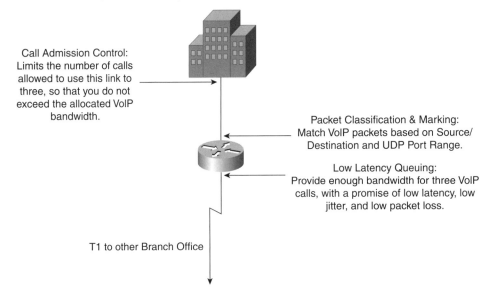

Call Admission Control: Limits the number of calls allowed to use this link to three, so that you do not exceed the allocated VoIP bandwidth.

Packet Classification & Marking: Match VoIP packets based on Source/ Destination and UDP Port Range.

Low Latency Queuing: Provide enough bandwidth for three VoIP calls, with a promise of low latency, low jitter, and low packet loss.

T1 to other Branch Office

If you modify that assumption, only slightly, the required mechanisms change. The changes are not dramatic, but call quality will certainly suffer if they are not made. Assume that the topology now is Frame Relay, rather than a point-to-point connection, with one end at full T1 speed and the other end at 384 kbps. Figure 1-4 shows the additional mechanisms that would be used.

Figure 1-4   *QoS Mechanisms for VoIP in a Mixed-Bandwidth Environment*

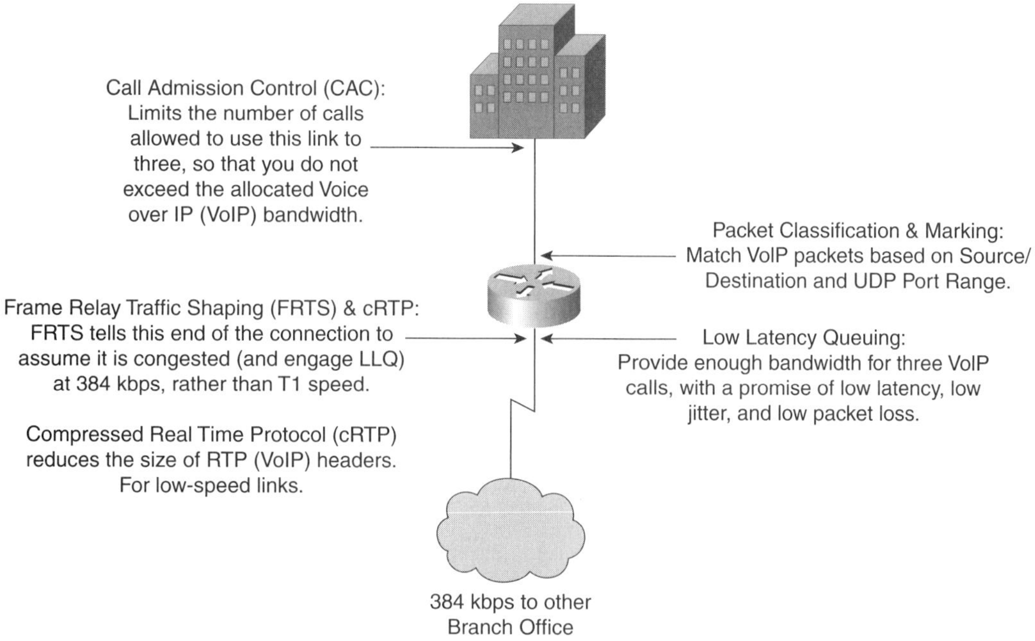

Call Admission Control (CAC):
Limits the number of calls
allowed to use this link to
three, so that you do not
exceed the allocated Voice
over IP (VoIP) bandwidth.

Packet Classification & Marking:
Match VoIP packets based on Source/
Destination and UDP Port Range.

Frame Relay Traffic Shaping (FRTS) & cRTP:
FRTS tells this end of the connection to
assume it is congested (and engage LLQ)
at 384 kbps, rather than T1 speed.

Low Latency Queuing:
Provide enough bandwidth for three VoIP
calls, with a promise of low latency, low
jitter, and low packet loss.

Compressed Real Time Protocol (cRTP)
reduces the size of RTP (VoIP) headers.
For low-speed links.

384 kbps to other
Branch Office

Overview of Integrated and Differentiated Services

QoS standards fit into three major classifications: integrated services, differentiated services, and best effort.

Integrated services and differentiated services are discussed individually, but *best effort* (BE) is not. BE is just the treatment that packets get when no predetermined treatment is specified for them. When there is no QoS at all, for example, all traffic is treated as BE. BE can also be used to refer to that traffic that is not given special (or defined) treatment with integrated services or differentiated services.

Integrated Services Versus Differentiated Services

Several models have been proposed to provide QoS for the Internet. Each has advantages and drawbacks, with regard to the Internet, but the model that has been more generally accepted recently is the differentiated services model. In an enterprise environment, however, both models can prove very useful. Note that you can also use these models in combination to achieve end-to-end QoS, taking advantage of the strengths of each model. At this time, only the differentiated services model is fully supported on the Catalyst 6500.

Definition of Integrated Services

Integrated services (IntServ) is the name given to QoS signaling. QoS signaling allows an end station (or network node, such as a router) to communicate with its neighbors to request specific treatment for a given traffic type. This type of QoS allows for end-to-end QoS in the sense that the original end station can make a request for special treatment of its packets through the network, and that request is propagated through every hop in the packet's path to the destination. True end-to-end QoS requires the participation of every networking device along the path (routers, switches, and so forth), and this can be accomplished with QoS signaling.

In 1994, RFC 1633 first defined the IntServ model. The following text, taken from RFC 1633, provides some insight as to the original intent of IntServ:

> We conclude that there is an inescapable requirement for routers to be able to reserve resources, in order to provide special QoS for specific user packet streams, or "flows". This in turn requires flow-specific state in the routers, which represents an important and fundamental change to the Internet model.

As it turns out, the requirement was not as inescapable as the engineers who authored RFC 1633 originally thought, as evidenced by the fact that the Internet still relies almost entirely on BE delivery for packets.

IntServ Operation

Resource Reservation Protocol (RSVP), defined by RFC 2205, is a resource reservation setup protocol for use in an IntServ environment. Specifics of operation are covered shortly, but the general idea behind RSVP is that Bob wants to talk to Steve, who is some number of network hops away, over an *IP video conferencing* (IPVC) system. For the IPVC conversation to be of acceptable quality, the conversation needs 384 kbps of bandwidth. Obviously, the IPVC end stations don't have any way of knowing whether that amount of bandwidth is available throughout the entire network, so they can either assume that bandwidth is available (and run the risk of poor quality if it isn't) or they can ask for the bandwidth and see whether the network is able to give it to them. RSVP is the mechanism that asks for the bandwidth.

The specific functionality is probably backward from what you would guess, in that the receiver is the one who actually asks for the reservation, not the sender. The sender sends a Path message to the receiver, which collects information about the QoS capabilities of the intermediate nodes. The receiver then processes the Path information and generates a *Reservation* (Resv) request, which is sent upstream to make the actual request to reserve resources. When the sender gets this Resv, the sender begins to send data. It is important to note that RSVP is a unidirectional process, so a bidirectional flow (such as an IPVC) requires this process to happen once for each sender. Figure 1-5 shows a very basic example of the resource reservation process (assuming a unidirectional flow from Bob to Steve).

Figure 1-5   *Path and Resv Messages for a Unidirectional Flow from Bob to Steve*

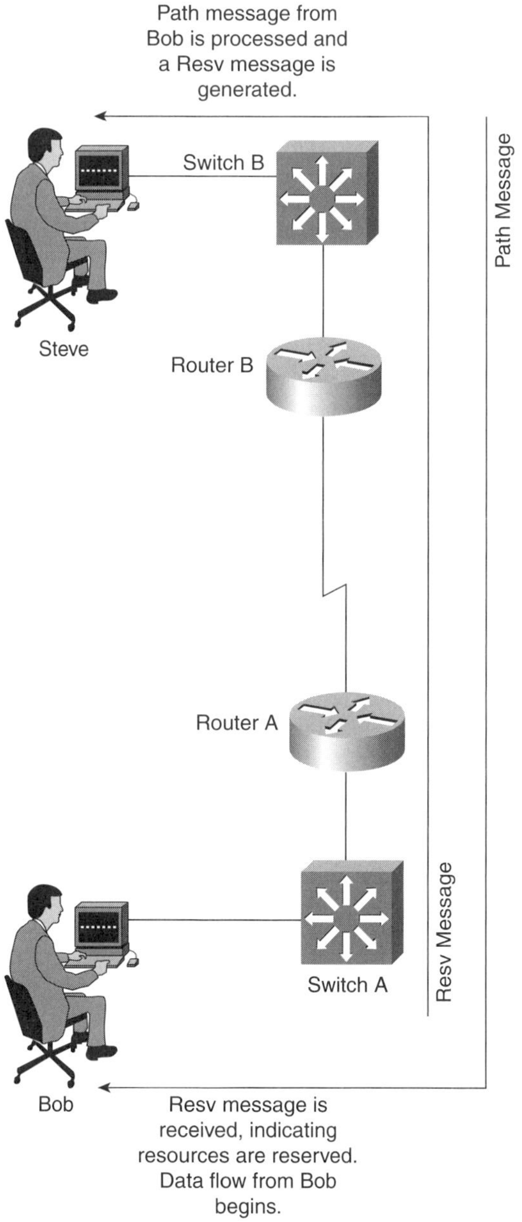

Path message from
Bob is processed and
a Resv message is
generated.

Switch B

Steve

Router B

Path Message

Router A

Switch A

Resv Message

Bob   Resv message is
received, indicating
resources are reserved.
Data flow from Bob
begins.

The other major point to note about RSVP is that RSVP doesn't actually manage the reservations of resources. Instead, RSVP works with existing mechanisms, such as Weighted Fair Queuing, to request that those existing mechanisms reserve the resources.

Although RSVP has some distinct advantages over BE and, in some cases, over differentiated services, RSVP implementations for end-to-end QoS today are predominantly limited to small implementations of video conferencing. That said, RSVP is making a strong comeback and some very interesting new things (beyond the scope of this book) are on the horizon for RSVP. If you're interested in a little light reading on the subject, have a look at RFCs 3175, 3209, and 3210.

Definition of DiffServ

To define *differentiated services* (DiffServ), we'll defer to the experts at the IETF. The following excerpt is from the "Abstract" section of RFC 2475:

This document defines architecture for implementing scalable service differentiation in the Internet. This architecture achieves scalability by aggregating traffic classification state which is conveyed by means of IP-layer packet marking using the DS field [DSFIELD]. Packets are classified and marked to receive a particular per-hop forwarding behavior on nodes along their path. Sophisticated classification, marking, policing, and shaping operations need only be implemented at network boundaries or hosts. Network resources are allocated to traffic streams by service provisioning policies which govern how traffic is marked and conditioned upon entry to a differentiated services-capable network, and how that traffic is forwarded within that network. A wide variety of services can be implemented on top of these building blocks.

To make that definition a little less verbose: The differentiated services architecture is designed to be a scalable model that provides different services to different traffic types in a scalable way. It must be possible to tell packets of one type from another type to provide the DiffServ, so techniques known as packet classification and marking are used. After packets of different types have been marked differently, it's possible to treat them differently based on that marking at each hop throughout the network, without having to perform additional complex classification and marking.

DiffServ Operation

DiffServ is a complicated architecture, with many components. Each of these components has a different purpose in the network and, therefore, each component operates differently. The major components of the DiffServ architecture perform the following tasks:

- Packet classification
- Packet marking
- Congestion management
- Congestion avoidance
- Traffic conditioning

These mechanisms can be implemented alone or in conjunction with each other. Figure 1-6 shows a possible implementation of these mechanisms in a production network.

Figure 1-6   *An Example of the Implementation of Various DiffServ Components*

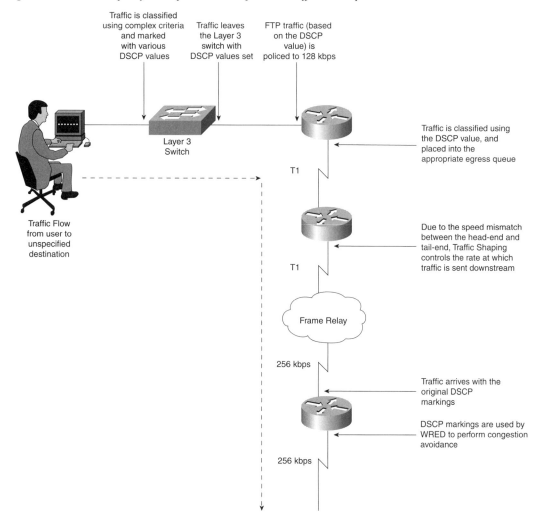

The sections that follow describe the five major components of the DiffServ architecture in greater detail.

Packet Classification

Packet classification can be simple classification, based on Layer 2 or Layer 3 information, and is, as the name implies, a set of mechanisms that can distinguish one type of packet from other. An example of a simple packet classification mechanism is matching against an access list that looks for packets with a specific source and destination IP address. This packet classification can also be far more complex, looking at things such as destination URL and MIME type. An example of a more complex packet classification mechanism available in Cisco routers is *network-based application recognition* (NBAR). NBAR is capable of matching on a variety of Layer 4 through Layer 7 characteristics, such as those listed previously. NBAR is also capable of stateful packet inspection, which dramatically increases the potential functionality. Whatever the actual classification capability of a specific mechanism, packet classification is typically performed as close as possible to the traffic source and is usually used in conjunction with packet marking. The words *typically* and *usually* were used intentionally here, because your particular setup may necessitate performing these functions at other places in your network.

Packet Marking

Packet marking is a function that allows a networking device to mark packets differently, based on their classification, so that they may be distinguished more easily at future network devices. Consider this analogy: Many states have smoking-prohibited sections in restaurants, but restaurants in North Carolina (where all of this book's authors live and work) still have smoking sections. Therefore, every time we walk into a restaurant, we have to state our personal preference about whether we want to sit in the smoking or non-smoking section. It seems like a lot of wasted time to ask and answer that question over and over again—wouldn't life be easier if I could just walk into a restaurant and they knew where to seat me? This is a loose analogy to the function of packet marking in the sense that a packet only requires complex classification (Do you prefer smoking or nonsmoking, sir?) to happen once. After the packet has been classified at the first router hop, a marking is applied so that all future network hops can just look at the marking and know what to do with that packet. Packet marking is, as previously mentioned, generally deployed in conjunction with packet classification as close to the source as possible. One of the reasons that the DiffServ model is so scalable is that the complex packet classification and packet marking are both recommended for deployment on only the first-hop Layer 3-capable device. In a typical enterprise network deployment, this means a branch office device (which serves a small subset of the total user community) performs the complex operations for that branch. Then that marking is carried with the packet throughout the network, limiting the burden on the core of the network to very simple classification of packets (based on the markings that were applied at the edge of the network) and the switching of those packets to the appropriate egress interface.

Congestion Management

Congestion management has many subcomponents (discussed in more detail later in this chapter, but the overall function of congestion management is to isolate various classes of traffic (based either on complex classification at the first hop or based on packet marking at nonedge devices), protect each class from other classes, and then prioritize the access of each class to various network resources. Typically, congestion management is primarily focus on re-ordering packets for transmission. This impacts the overall bandwidth given to each class, however, and also impacts the delay and jitter characteristics of each class. Because of limited queue lengths, the delay experienced by packets in a given class could impact the packet loss experienced by the traffic in that class. Stated another way, if a large amount of delay exists for a given traffic type and the queue fills, packets for that class will be tail dropped. Congestion management in Cisco routers is an egress function and includes mechanisms such as CBWFQ and LLQ. Congestion management is typically used at all network layers (access, distribution, and core) in a real-time environment, but no strict rules dictate where you must use congestion management in your network.

Congestion Avoidance

Congestion avoidance is specifically designed to discard packets to avoid congestion. The concept behind congestion avoidance is based on the operation of TCP. The details of TCP operation are beyond the scope of this text, but the basic concept is that when TCP traffic is sent, the receiver of the traffic is expected to acknowledge the receipt of said traffic by sending an *acknowledgment* (ACK) message to the sender. If the sender doesn't receive this ACK in a given amount of time, it assumes that the receiver didn't receive the transmission. In response to this assumption, the sender will reduce its TCP window size (which essentially reduces the rate of transmission) and retransmit the traffic for which it did not receive an ACK. Note that all of this happens without the sender ever actually being told by the receiver that packets weren't received. A good analogy is two people having a conversation; one person asks the other a question, but receives no answer. After some reasonable amount of time, the person probably assumes that the other person didn't hear the question and repeats the question. Congestion avoidance is implemented in Cisco routers as *Weighted Random Early Detection* (WRED) and is the process of monitoring the depth of a queue, and randomly dropping packets of various flows to prevent the queue from filling completely. This section covers the concept of congestion avoidance, however, not the WRED implementation specifics. Chapter 2, "End-to-End QoS: Quality of Service at Layer 3 and Layer 2," contains a more thorough discussion of WRED. By randomly discarding packets of various flows, two things are prevented. First, you prevent the queue from becoming completely full—if allowed to fill completely, "tail drop" would occur (that is, all incoming packets would be dropped). Tail drop is not good, because multiple packets from the same flows can be dropped, causing TCP to reduce its window size several times, thereby causing suboptimal link utilization. Second, it is possible to add intelligence to the decision-making process for which packets are "randomly" dropped; in the case of WRED, IP precedence or *DiffServ codepoint* (DSCP) markings can be used to influence which packets are dropped and how often.

Traffic Conditioning

Traffic conditioning contains two major components:

- **Policers**—Policers perform traffic policing, which means dropping packets that exceed a defined rate to control the rate at which traffic passes through the policer. Examples of policers implemented by Cisco are the *committed access rate* (CAR) policer and the class-based policer. The goal of policing is to rate limit traffic; an example of a practical application for a policer is to limit the amount of FTP traffic allowed to go out of a given interface to 1 Mbps. Traffic that exceeds this 1-Mbps rate limit is dropped. TCP retransmits dropped packets, UDP does not, which is a consideration when deciding whether a policer is right for a given situation.

- **Shapers**—Shapers perform traffic shaping, which, in Cisco equipment, takes many forms; *generic traffic shaping* (GTS), *Frame Relay Traffic shaping* (FRTS), class-based traffic shaping, and so on. The specific shaper that is used is not of consequence, because the concept is the same for all of them. The goal of the shaper is to limit the rate at which packets pass through the shaper by buffering packets that exceed a defined rate and sending those packets later. The goal is that, over time, the rate of transmission will be smoothed out to the defined rate. This is in contrast to the operation of a policer, where traffic is dropped if the defined rate is exceeded. Both policers and shapers have benefits and drawbacks, and each situation must be evaluated to determine which mechanism is best. For example, FTP traffic (which is TCP based and very tolerant of packet drops) can be policed without negatively impacting the usability of the application. Because FTP doesn't mind some delay in the transmission of its packets, in many cases FTP can also be shaped without any negative impact to the application. VoIP traffic, on the other hand, does not tolerate delay very well at all, so it is desirable to drop (police) a VoIP packet rather than delay (shape) it.

Differentiated Services: A Standards Approach

As you have just seen, many components comprise the DiffServ architecture, and those components can be used in many different ways. Of course, there are also different implementations of these mechanisms, which have been given different names by different vendors. The key to the DiffServ architecture's successful implementation in a multivendor environment, however, is that the entire architecture is standards-based. Regardless of what name each vendor uses to market a given feature, all the features that comprise the DiffServ architecture are standardized and should, therefore, interoperate between vendors with very predictable results. The idea of being able to provide predictable service to packets through the network is fundamental to being able to provide good QoS. This is especially critical when dealing with real-time interactive traffic, such as VoIP, but is also important for consistent data handling across multiple network nodes.

RFC 2475: Terminology and Concepts

The treatment given to a packet at each of these nodes, or hops, is called a *per-hop behavior* (PHB). PHBs are defined by RFC 2475 as "the externally observable forwarding behavior applied at a DS-compliant node to a DS behavior aggregate." For clarification, RFC 2475 also defines a DS behavior aggregate (or BA, which isn't nearly as complicated as it sounds) as, "a collection of packets with the same DS codepoint crossing a link in a particular direction." This concept was introduced earlier in this chapter, but RFC 2475 basically says that all packets with the same DSCP marking *must* be treated the same when passing through a given interface, in a given direction. It is possible to define a BA based on multiple criteria. Although not explicitly defined in the terminology of RFC 2475, the permissibility of such a BA definition can be inferred from the definition of the *multifield* (MF) classifier, "which selects packets based on the content of some arbitrary number of header fields; typically some combination of source address, destination address, DS field, protocol ID, source port and destination port." In other words, it is possible to group packets together, to receive a PHB, based on criteria other than the DSCP marking of those packets.

The question that naturally follows the definitions given by RFC 2475 is "what is a 'forwarding behavior?'" RFC 2475 states the following:

"Forwarding behavior" is a general concept in this context. For example, in the event that only one behavior aggregate occupies a link, the observable forwarding behavior (i.e., loss, delay, jitter) will often depend only on the relative loading of the link (i.e., in the event that the behavior assumes a work-conserving scheduling discipline). Useful behavioral distinctions are mainly observed when multiple behavior aggregates compete for buffer and bandwidth resources on a node. The PHB is the means by which a node allocates resources to behavior aggregates, and it is on top of this basic hop-by-hop resource allocation mechanism that useful differentiated services may be constructed.

Simply stated, it's something that you can distinctly measure (that is, bandwidth, delay, jitter, loss), and observing different forwarding behaviors is typically only possible when multiple traffic types compete for resources on a congested link. Further, this basic ability to provide different resource allocations to behavior aggregates on a hop-by-hop basis is the foundation for DiffServ.

RFC 2475 also gives a great example:

The most simple example of a PHB is one which guarantees a minimal bandwidth allocation of X% of a link (over some reasonable time interval) to a behavior aggregate. This PHB can be fairly easily measured under a variety of competing traffic conditions. A slightly more complex PHB would guarantee a minimal bandwidth allocation of X% of a link, with proportional fair sharing of any excess link capacity.

RFC 2474: Terminology and Concepts

As previously discussed, traffic can be grouped into behavior aggregates only by DSCP, or based on multiple fields (for example, DSCP *and* source IP address). As you read this section, keep in mind that the DiffServ RFCs focus mainly on the classification by DS behavior aggregate.

RFC 2475 states the following:

Nodes within the DS domain select the forwarding behavior for packets based on their DS codepoint, mapping that value to one of the supported PHBs using either the recommended codepoint → PHB mapping or a locally customized mapping [DSFIELD].

In more basic terms, a networking device decides which PHB to give a packet based on the DSCP value assigned to the packet. This value can either be one that is mapped to a PHB as defined by an RFC, or it can be a marking that is not standardized but has local signifi- cance. For example, DSCP value 26 (decimal) is mapped to a standardized PHB (called AF31, which is discussed later in this chapter), but DSCP value 27 (decimal) is not mapped to any standardized PHB. Therefore, when a network device receives packets marked with DSCP 26, certain assumptions can be made about the expected forwarding behavior. On the other hand, no assumptions can be made about the expected forwarding behavior for packets marked with DSCP 27, because that codepoint has no standardized PHB.

Because codepoint markings are very important in the DiffServ architecture, it seems prudent to discuss the origins of the DSCP values: RFC 2474. RFC 2474 obsoletes RFC 791, which defined the IPv4 *type of service* (ToS) octet, more commonly discussed as IP precedence. The Abstract section of RFC 2474 states the purpose of the document:

This document defines the IP header field, called the DS (for differentiated services) field. In IPv4, it defines the layout of the TOS octet; in IPv6, the Traffic Class octet. In addition, a base set of packet forwarding treatments, or per-hop behaviors, is defined.

Figure 1-7 shows the DS field format.

Figure 1-7   *DS Field Format*

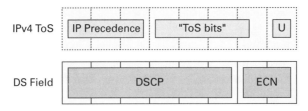

The addition of *explicit congestion notification* (ECN) to IP (RFC 2481) has since redefined bits 6 and 7 for use; however, a discussion of ECN is beyond the scope of this text.

RFC 2474 goes on to require that codepoint-to-PHB mappings must be configurable and that the default configuration should include recommended codepoint-to-PHB mappings. The exception to the requirement that codepoint-to-PHB mappings be configurable is for codepoints xxx000, because these codepoints, called class selector codepoints, are reserved for backward compatibility with IP precedence. The specifics of this backward compatibility are beyond the scope of this text, but the concept is that when bits 3, 4, and 5 of this byte are set to 0, and any of the first 3 bits of the byte (which were previously used for IP precedence) are not 0, the packet is handled as if it is marked with IP precedence. In other words, 001000 and 010000 are treated as if they are IP precedence 1 and IP precedence 2, respectively. No attempt is made in RFC 2474 to maintain any backward compatibility with bits 3 through 6 or 7 (previously used as the ToS bits and the *must be zero* [MBZ] bit, respectively).

Note as well that RFC 2474 documents the use of the codepoint 000000, which is the codepoint for BE treatment. BE is the treatment that packets get when no QoS is enabled in a network, and essentially means that the networking devices make every effort possible to get the packet to the destination, but ultimately there are absolutely no guarantees with regard to delay, jitter, packet loss, or bandwidth. In fact, there is no guarantee that the packet will even be transmitted. For example, a router might have three classes of traffic, each guaranteed 1/3 of the total link bandwidth. If all three classes are sending traffic equal to 1/3 of the total link bandwidth, the link is going to be totally congested. In a situation like this, BE traffic, which by definition is not classified into one of these three classes, has either very limited resources or none at all (depending on the implementation specifics). This situation could lead to significant delay and, ultimately, packet loss.

Assured Forwarding Versus Expedited Forwarding

Assured forwarding (AF, RFC 2597), and *expedited forwarding* (EF, RFC 2598) are PHBs that have recommended codepoints. EF has only 1 recommended codepoint, whereas AF has 12 recommended codepoints.

RFCs 2597 and 2598 both describe PHBs; beyond that, they are not specifically related, but the discussion of each has been combined in this section to contrast the two functions. The point of contrasting these two PHBs is to demonstrate how the DiffServ architecture allows for a great deal of flexibility in the PHBs that fall under the DiffServ umbrella. No relation or interdependency exists between AF and EF, but because the EF PHB is the easier of the two to understand, it is covered first.

RFC 2598, "An Expedited Forwarding PHB"

RFC 2598 defines "An Expedited Forwarding PHB" and states the following:

The EF PHB can be used to build a low loss, low latency, low jitter, assured bandwidth, end-to-end service through DS domains.

This means that when a network node receives a packet, it should be transmitted as soon as possible (adding as little delay as possible). This sounds a lot like voice service, right? Although RFC 2598 doesn't explicitly discuss the intended use of this PHB, it can probably be safely assumed that the primary intention for this PHB is real-time traffic, including voice and, in some cases, interactive video. That's not, of course, to say that this PHB isn't ever used for any other kind of traffic. I suppose that's one of the great things about the DiffServ architecture implementation in Cisco equipment; it is very flexible and entirely user configurable. When I teach QoS classes, my joke is that Cisco enables users to configure QoS any way they want to ... even if it's wrong. RFC 2598 is actually one of the few things in the DiffServ architecture that provides an opportunity to get into real trouble with misconfiguration.

Consider the fact that the EF PHB's main purpose is to provide a forwarding behavior that introduces as little delay and jitter as possible. If more traffic is received for transmission than an interface can transmit, a queue begins to form. When a device queues traffic, by definition it introduces delay. As such, it can be inferred that building a queue is undesirable when implementing the EF PHB.

Said another way, if a device queues traffic, it introduces delay; so to provide the EF PHB, a device should not queue (or queue very little) traffic. Because this requirement means that the EF traffic will be given strict priority for transmission (to minimize delay), there is a risk that the receipt of too much EF traffic could cause starvation for other traffic on the link. One might envision a situation in which there is a steady stream of EF traffic, received at the line rate of the egress interface, and a stream of other traffic, received at the line rate of the egress interface. In this situation, without a mechanism to prevent starvation, the strict priority of the EF traffic on that link means that all the EF traffic is transmitted and none of the other traffic is transmitted. That may very well be the intent of a particular user, but to prevent this situation from unintentionally occurring, RFC 2598 calls for a measure of protection.

The measure that is called for to prevent the starvation of other traffic, just because a device receives too much EF traffic, is the following provision:

The departure rate of the aggregate's packets from any DiffServ node must equal or exceed a configurable rate.

This behavior can be represented by stating that the rate of arrival must be less than or equal to the rate of departure, for packets receiving the EF PHB. To ensure that this is the case, the RFC suggests that a policer be used to rate limit the EF traffic, which is what is used in most Cisco devices. Specifically, if the configuration requires EF for all packets marked DSCP 46, and if 128 kbps is the configured egress rate for traffic receiving the EF PHB, and 129 kbps of traffic marked DSCP 46 is offered, 1k of traffic marked DSCP 46 is dropped to ensure that the rate of arrival into the EF queue does not exceed the rate of departure. This example, by the way, assumes link congestion is present. When no congestion exists, queuing does not become active and, therefore, the policing mechanism would also not become active. Stated another way, when there is no congestion, there is no policing of traffic that would, in the event of congestion, be placed in the priority queue for strict priority scheduling.

RFC 2597, "Assured Forwarding PHB Group"

In part, the Abstract of RFC 2597 states the following:

> The AF PHB group provides delivery of IP packets in four independently forwarded AF classes. Within each AF class, an IP packet can be assigned one of three different levels of drop precedence.

Until now, this text has only discussed single PHBs, so new terminology needs to be clarified before discussing AF in detail. The original RFC (2597) calls AF, as a whole, a PHB group. RFC 3260 later clarifies this definition and states that AF is actually a type of PHB group, which actually contains four separate PHB groups.

If you understand the implications of that correction, great! If you're scratching your head at the moment, don't despair. Before you finish reading this section, you'll understand the distinction and its importance.

RFC 2597 defines 12 DSCPs, which correspond to 4 AF classes, each class having 3 levels of "drop precedence." Visualize four totally separate buckets, each having three compartments, and you have the general idea. Each AF class (referred to as AF1x, AF2x, AF3x, and AF4x) is completely independent of the other classes. Within each class, however, there are three levels of drop precedence (for example, AF1x contains AF11, AF12, and AF13). These drop precedence levels, within each class, have relativity to the other drop precedence values in their class, but no relativity at all to the other classes. Note that the first number is always the AF class to which the packets belong, and the second number is always the packet's drop precedence value. For clarification, there is no such thing as AF10 or AF14; there are only three levels of drop precedence per AF class.

Stated more directly, each AF class is totally independent of the other three and no assumptions can be made regarding the treatment of packets belonging to one class when compared with the treatment of packets belonging to another class. Within a class, however, assumptions may be made regarding the treatment of packets with different drop precedence values.

All the classes and their drop precedence values are represented by the DSCP markings that are given to packets. Table 1-2 lists the 12 recommended codepoints defined by RFC.

Table 1-2   *Codepoints Recommended by RFC 2597*

Class	Low Drop Precedence	Medium Drop Precedence	High Drop Precedence
AF1	001010 (AF11)	001100 (AF12)	001110 (AF13)
AF2	010010 (AF21)	010100 (AF22)	010110 (AF23)
AF3	011010 (AF31)	011100 (AF32)	011110 (AF33)
AF4	100010 (AF41)	100100 (AF42)	100110 (AF43)

RFC 2597 dictates that packets with a low drop preference must be dropped with a probability less than or equal to the probability with which medium drop precedence packets would be dropped and that packets with a medium drop precedence must be dropped with a probability less than or equal to the probability with which high drop precedence packets would be dropped. The "or equal to" part allows for the equal treatment of all packets within an AF class but, assuming that the drop precedence is going to be used to treat packets differently, high drop precedence packets are going to be dropped first in an AF class. Again, there can be no assumptions made about the probability of a packet from AF1x being dropped, with respect to the probability of a packet from AF2x being dropped.

Recall, from the beginning of this section, the seemingly pointless clarification of the AF PHB standard as one that defines multiple PHB groups, rather than one large PHB group? The reason that distinction is so critical is that a PHB group has components that are somehow relative to each other. With the redefinition of the AF standard as one that defines four distinct PHB groups, the point is now very clear that AF1x is a PHB group by itself and is, therefore, *totally separate* from the other AF classes. This total separation makes sure that everyone implementing the AF standard knows that absolutely no relativity exists between the drop probabilities of packets in different AF classes.

RFC 2597 and RFC 2598: Practical Application in a Cisco Network

All the RFCs in the world don't do anyone any good until they are actually implemented in a network, so it seems prudent to look at the Cisco implementation of these two RFCs. Cisco routers provide EF or AF treatment to implement these RFCs. Later chapters detail the implementation specifics on the various Catalyst platforms, but it's important to first understand these RFCs as they are implemented on Cisco routers so that you can use the Catalyst information provided later to develop an end-to-end QoS strategy for your network.

EF Treatment

First, the EF PHB recommends DSCP 46 (101110) be used to mark packets that should received EF treatment. The mechanism for performing this marking is beyond the scope of RFC 2598, but many mechanisms can be used to perform this task, as the list that follows demonstrates:

- CAR
- Policy-based routing
- Dial peers
- Class-based marking
- Class-based policer

In almost every case, class-based marking and class-based policer are the recommended methods for performing packet marking in Cisco routers.

The mechanism in Cisco routers that actually provides the EF treatment to packets is called *Low Latency Queuing* (LLQ). A lengthy discussion of LLQ's operation is beyond the scope of this text, but the basic configuration defines a rate of departure for packets classified into the LLQ for EF treatment. This definition of the rate of departure activates a policer for the rate of arrival for packets into the LLQ. As such, a definition of 128 kbps of bandwidth with LLQ treatment means that, if 129 kbps of traffic is marked for EF, and offered to the LLQ, 1 kbps will be dropped. LLQ extends the CBWFQ model by introducing a single, strict priority queue.

AF Treatment

With regard to the same packet marking tools previously discussed, 12 codepoints are recommended for use with AF. These 12 codepoints, listed earlier in the chapter, are divided into 4 classes, each with 3 codepoints.

Figure 1-8 shows a possible implementation of AF.

Figure 1-8   *Possible Implementation of Assured Forwarding*

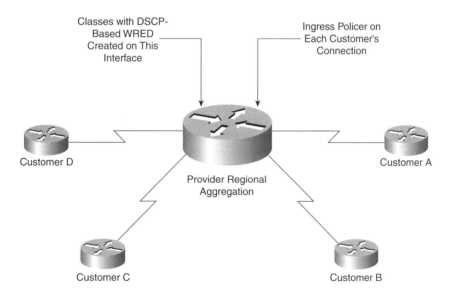

In this example

- A class called Customer-A will get AF11, AF12, and AF13 traffic.
- A class called Customer-B will get AF21, AF22, and AF23 traffic.
- A class called Customer-C will get AF31, AF32, and AF33 traffic.

- A class called Customer-D will get AF41, AF42, and AF43 traffic.

For each customer, an ingress policer marks the traffic based on the rate of the traffic. Up to 256 kbps is marked AFx1, above 256 kbps but below 768 kbps is marked AFx2, and above 768 kbps is marked AFx3. During periods of congestion, this traffic is placed into the classes described earlier as it egresses the aggregation router toward other regions. Because each class of traffic is independently forwarded, and each class is guaranteed a certain amount of bandwidth (using CBWFQ), the classes do not interfere with each other in any way.

Assume congestion and that Customers A, B, and C are all sending traffic at their CIR, but Customer D is sending traffic at 1.5 Mbps. It wouldn't be fair to punish the other customers because Customer D is not "behaving," so traffic is queued in the class called Customer-D and, when that queue begins to fill, WRED begins to discard packets. Per the RFC that defines AF, packets marked AF43 (those that were over 768 kbps) are discarded first, then packets marked AF42 (those that were between 256 kbps and 768 kbps), and packets marked AF41 are discarded only if no packets are marked AF43 or AF42.

It's not difficult to see how this could provide a service similar to Frame Relay where there is a CIR with burst and extended burst capabilities. However, no hard rule mandates the purpose for which AF must be used in your network.

Summary

This chapter defined QoS as the ability to create predictable service levels for various traffic types in the network, and also as "managed unfairness" (that is, the ability to provide different traffic types with unequal treatment while giving each type the treatment that it requires).

Integrated services and differentiated services have been discussed in detail, and you should now understand where you might find each of these useful in your network. The thorough discussion of some of the key DiffServ RFCs has provided the background information that you need in future chapters, which discuss Cisco's specific implementations of these standards. As these mechanisms are discussed, you should be able to relate their behavior to the standardized behaviors explained by the various RFCs that have been discussed in this chapter.

CHAPTER 2

End-to-End QoS: Quality of Service at Layer 3 and Layer 2

Chapter 1, "Quality of Service: An Overview," introduced several of the fundamental concepts of *quality of service* (QoS), various key RFCs, and explained various parts of the *differentiated services* (DiffServ) architecture. This chapter builds upon Chapter 1 by continuing to explore some DiffServ components and looking at mechanisms for traffic conditioning, link efficiency, and classification at Layer 3. This chapter also introduces the concept of Layer 2 packet marking for QoS and explains how Layer 2 markings relate to Layer 3 markings to facilitate end-to-end QoS. Although this chapter doesn't focus specifically on QoS for IP telephony applications, you will find examples of how Layer 2 QoS is used to allow voice traffic to traverse a switched infrastructure with limited delay and jitter. This chapter also looks at various traffic-conditioning components of QoS.

This chapter primarily focuses on QoS from a Cisco IOS router perspective. In addition, all the examples of this chapter were demonstrated on a Cisco IOS router. The last two sections of this chapter introduce QoS on the Catalyst platforms.

QoS Components

As discussed in Chapter 1, QoS is comprised of various components. This chapter discusses the following QoS components in detail:

- Congestion Management
- Congestion Avoidance
- Traffic Conditioning
- Link Efficiency

Each QoS component plays an important role in building an overall QoS strategy for your network, and each component offers unique characteristics that add value to your strategy.

In addition to discussing the various components, this chapter introduces you to some Cisco implementations of these components. After discussing the concepts in general terms, this chapter provides configuration examples and details how to verify your configurations using show commands.

Simply defined, *congestion* exists when an interface is offered more traffic for transmission than it is capable of transmitting. Congestion is usual in several common network design scenarios:

- **LAN-to-WAN connections**—When traffic is flowing from a LAN, where bandwidth is typically at least 10 Mbps, to a WAN, where bandwidth is typically less than 10 Mbps, the possibility of congestion is very real.

- **Aggregation**—When several links are aggregated and their traffic transmitted over a single link, the possibility exists that a situation may cause congestion. If ten 10-Mbps links were being aggregated into a Gigabit Ethernet connection, congestion would not be possible, because the single link's bandwidth would exceed that of the aggregated links. However, it is more common to see 24 or even 48 100-Mbps ports aggregated into a single Gigabit Ethernet uplink. In this situation, the sum of traffic from the aggregated links has the potential to exceed the capacity of the gigabit port.

- **Speed mismatch**—It is also possible to have congestion when traffic flows downstream, from higher-speed aggregation links to lower-speed access links. For example, traffic coming from the core of the network, through a Gigabit Ethernet link, to a PC that is connected by a 100-Mbps connection may experience congestion. In this example, the congestion point would occur at the 100-Mbps Ethernet port, as traffic tries to egress that port toward the PC.

Congestion Management

QoS involves many components and features, but the component that is most typically associated with the term QoS is congestion management. Congestion management is the key component for QoS on Catalyst switches. The congestion management component of QoS itself is made up of many different features in Cisco IOS and CatOS. All Catalyst switches that support QoS features support congestion management or congestion avoidance. The next section looks at these features in detail, but the purpose of this section is to define congestion management, in general.

As the name implies, congestion management enables you to manage the congestion that is experienced by packets at a given point in the network. Congestion management involves three main steps:

1 Queues are created at the interface where congestion is expected. Depending on the specific feature or mechanism being used to provide QoS and the platform on which the QoS is being configured, there could be only two queues or there could be several hundred (although there is currently no practical application for this many queues on any Catalyst platform).

2 Packets (this could also be frames, but for the sake of simplicity, the word *packets* is used) are then assigned to these queues, based on classification characteristics such as *DiffServ codepoint* (DSCP) value. The classification of packets by characteristics is typically user-defined, and packets are placed into queues by these predetermined characteristics. Some examples of packet characteristics that are typically used in classification are the values in the packet for IP precedence, DSCP, and Layer 2 *class of service* (CoS). It is also common to use extended access lists to match packets based on more complex criteria, such as port numbers.

3 Packets are then scheduled for transmission. Determining the scheduling of packets is specific to every congestion management mechanism, but it can generally be said that there will be a way to provide for the transmission of more packets out of some queues than some others. That is, you will be able to give some packets better treatment than others, with regard to the amount of bandwidth that those packets receive.

Congestion Management Mechanisms

As previously mentioned, several mechanisms in Cisco devices fall under the definition of congestion management. Although this chapter does not get deep into the specifics of these mechanisms, because there are several other books from Cisco Press that already cover these in detail, an overview of the various mechanisms will help explain the overall function of congestion management as part of an end-to-end QoS strategy.

The preceding section alluded to the need to queue packets, but did not explicitly discuss that need. When dealing with a situation where more traffic needs to be transmitted than an interface is capable of transmitting, some traffic must be queued while waiting for the resources necessary to transmit that packet. Cisco devices utilize four main types of queuing, as follows:

- First In, First Out
- Priority Queuing
- Custom Queuing
- Weighted Fair Queuing

First In, First Out

First In, First Out (FIFO) Queuing has no concept of priority for packets. FIFO is the most basic form of queuing, in that there is a default queue depth (64 packets in most cases) and that number of packets will be buffered, in the order that they were received, and transmitted in the order that they were received. A good analogy for FIFO is flying an airline where the first person to show up at the counter gets to board the plane first, and the last person to arrive boards last; there is no priority boarding for frequent flyers or other special treatment for certain passengers.

FIFO Queuing is the default behavior of most Catalyst switches where QoS is disabled and all Catalyst switches that do not support QoS.

Priority Queuing

Priority Queuing (PQ), on the other hand, is all about priority. With PQ, there are four queues to which packets are assigned. The queues are called High, Medium, Normal, and Low, and packets are serviced in that order, with all packets from the High queue being transmitted first. You can draw an analogy between PQ and the way that most airlines board their flights. All of the first-class passengers board first, then all of the elite frequent fliers, then the passengers in the rear of the main cabin, and then the passengers in the front of the main cabin. Unlike an airline, which eventually allows everyone with a ticket to board, PQ would continue to service "elite" packets to the point that other packets would not be able to get through. This condition is called *queue starvation*, because the applications with packets in lower-level queues can actually be starved of bandwidth by a high volume of traffic in higher-level queues.

Current Catalyst switches support PQ as an optional method for applying strict priority to *Voice over IP* (VoIP) traffic. Each platform that supports PQ varies slightly in implementation and architecture. Refer to the corresponding platform chapters for a discussion these variations.

Custom Queuing

Custom Queuing (CQ) does not have a strict priority scheduling mechanisms like PQ; instead, CQ tries to be fair by providing all classes with some ability to transmit packets in each interval of time. With CQ, there can be up to 16 queues and the packets in those queues are serviced in a round-robin fashion. That is, some packets from each queue are transmitted in each time interval. This method is similar to an airline deciding that in every 5-minute period, they will board 1 first-class passenger, 5 elite frequent fliers, 10 people seated in the rear of the main cabin, and 7 people seated in the front of the main cabin. If it seems like this method might become a little confusing at the airport, rest assured that it's fairly confusing to configure in a router, too.

Weighted Fair Queuing

Weighted Fair Queuing (WFQ) is a dynamic process that divides bandwidth among queues based on weights. The process is designed to be fair, such that WFQ ensures that all traffic is treated fairly, with regard to its weight.

There are several forms of WFQ, including *Class-based Weighted Fair Queuing* (CBWFQ) and *Low Latency Queuing* (LLQ).

CBWFQ is probably the form of WFQ that is most commonly being deployed these days. CBWFQ works quite a bit like CQ, but the algorithm is more efficient and the configuration is quite a bit easier to understand. With CBWFQ, classes are created and traffic is assigned to those classes, as explained earlier in this chapter. Bandwidth is then assigned to those classes, and the amount of bandwidth assigned to a given class determines the amount of scheduling that class receives. In other words, the bandwidth statement on a given class determines the minimum amount of bandwidth that packets belonging to that class receive in the event of congestion.

In the recent past, a PQ was added to the CBWFQ mechanism, specifically to handle VoIP traffic. This addition was necessary because, although CBWFQ did an excellent job of dividing up the available bandwidth, CBWFQ did not give any specific regard to the delay or jitter being introduced by queuing packets.

The LLQ mechanism is CBWFQ with a single PQ, which receives strict scheduling priority. To go back to airline analogies, this is the equivalent of preboarding courtesies that are often offered to persons with special needs or those traveling with small children. In spite of the fact that these people may not be in first class, or elite frequent fliers, they are moved directly to the front of the line and put on the plane first because they have special needs. In the case of VoIP traffic, it may not be the most important traffic on your network, but it has very specific requirements for delay and jitter and, therefore, must be moved to the front of the line for transmission.

Catalyst switches use classification to appropriate queuing frames for transmission. Although Catalyst switches only support the Cisco IOS features WFQ, CBWFQ, and LLQ on WAN interfaces, Ethernet interfaces use similar forms of queuing but vary in configuration and behavior.

Scheduling

Scheduling allows resource sharing, specifically bandwidth, among classes of traffic or queues; this scheduling becomes more important as congestion increases. On Cisco switching platforms, frames are scheduled in several ways. The most commonly discussed is *weighted round-robin* (WRR). Because the functionality and configuration of WRR on each specific platform is discussed in the chapter for that platform, this chapter does not attempt to explain the functionality of WRR. Instead, this section previews what is to come in future chapters. For additional information about WRR and its implementation on Catalyst switches, refer to Chapter 6, "QoS Features Available on the Catalyst 2950 and 3550 Family of Switches," Chapter 7, "QoS Features Available on the Catalyst 4000 IOS Family of Switches and the Catalyst G-L3 Family of Switches," and Chapter 8, "QoS Support on the Catalyst 6500."

Congestion Avoidance

In contrast to congestion management, which deals with congestion that already exists, congestion avoidance mechanisms are designed to prevent interfaces or queues from becoming congested in the first place. The actual methods used to avoid congestion are discussed shortly, but keep in mind that the entire concept of congestion avoidance is based on the presence of TCP traffic.

To understand why the benefits of congestion avoidance are only realized when the majority of network traffic is TCP, it is important to understand the fundamental behavior of TCP. This overview is intended to provide just such an understanding, and is not intended to be a comprehensive discussion of TCP's behavior.

Unlike UDP, which has no acknowledgment mechanism, with TCP, when a packet is received, the receiver acknowledges receipt of that packet by sending a message back to the sender. If no acknowledgment is received within a period of time, the sender first assumes that data is being sent too rapidly and reduces the TCP window size, and then the sender resends the unacknowledged packet(s). Gradually, the sender increases the rate at which packets are being sent by increasing the window size.

Without congestion avoidance, when a particular queue becomes completely full, something called *tail drop* occurs. Tail drop is the term used to describe what happens when the (n +1) packet arrives at a queue that is only capable of holding n packets. That packet is dropped and, consequently, no acknowledgment is sent to the sender of that packet. As previously mentioned, this causes a reduction in the window size and a retransmission.

Tail drop presents several problems, however. Most troublesome is the fact that tail drop does not use any intelligence to determine which packet(s) should be dropped; rather the ($n + 1$) packet is just dropped, regardless of what type of packet it is. This could mean that a packet of the most important traffic type in your network is dropped, whereas a packet from the least important traffic type is transmitted. Another problem associated with tail drop is global synchronization, which reduces the overall throughput of a link with many flows (but is beyond the scope of this discussion).

All Catalyst switches experience tail drop when transmit queues become full. However, several Catalyst switches support configuration of tail-drop thresholds among various queues to minimize full conditions with higher-priority traffic. Chapters 6 and 8 discuss tail-drop thresholds and configuration options available on the Catalyst 3550 Family and Catalyst 6500 Family of switches, respectively.

Random Early Detection (RED)

The problems of tail drop and global synchronization can both be addressed with congestion avoidance. Congestion avoidance is sometimes called *active queue management*, or *Random Early Detection* (RED). The Introduction section of RFC 2309 defines the need for active queue management as follows:

The traditional technique for managing router queue lengths is to set a maximum length (in terms of packets) for each queue, accept packets for the queue until the maximum length is reached, then reject (drop) subsequent incoming packets until the queue decreases because a packet from the queue has been transmitted. This technique is known as "tail drop", since the packet that arrived most recently (i.e., the one on the tail of the queue) is dropped when the queue is full. This method has served the Internet well for years, but it has two important drawbacks.

1. Lock-Out

In some situations tail drop allows a single connection or a few flows to monopolize queue space, preventing other connections from getting room in the queue. This "lock-out" phenomenon is often the result of synchronization or other timing effects.

2. Full Queues

The tail drop discipline allows queues to maintain a full (or, almost full) status for long periods of time, since tail drop signals congestion (via a packet drop) only when the queue has become full. It is important to reduce the steady-state queue size, and this is perhaps queue management's most important goal.

The naive assumption might be that there is a simple tradeoff between delay and throughput, and that the recommendation that queues be maintained in a "non-full" state essentially translates to a recommendation that low end-to-end delay is more important than high throughput. However, this does not take into account the critical role that packet bursts play in Internet performance. Even though TCP constrains a flow's window size, packets often arrive at routers in bursts [Leland94]. If the queue is full or almost full, an arriving burst will cause multiple packets to be dropped. This can result in a global synchronization of flows throttling back, followed by a sustained period of lowered link utilization, reducing overall throughput.

The point of buffering in the network is to absorb data bursts and to transmit them during the (hopefully) ensuing bursts of silence. This is essential to permit the transmission of bursty data. It should be clear why we would like to have normally-small queues in routers: we want to have queue capacity to absorb the bursts. The counter-intuitive result is that maintaining normally-small queues can result in higher throughput as well as lower end-to-end delay. In short, queue limits should not reflect the steady state queues we want maintained in the network; instead, they should reflect the size of bursts we need to absorb.

Cisco IOS Software devices implement RED as *Weighted RED* (WRED), which serves the same purpose as RED, but does so with preferential treatment given to packets based on their IP precedence or DSCP value. If it is not desirable in your network to give different treatment to packets of different IP precedence or DSCP values, it is possible to modify the configuration so that all packets are treated the same.

The basic configuration for WRED in a Cisco IOS router is fairly simple:

```
Router(config)#interface Serial 6/0
Router(config-if)#random-detect
```

With only that configuration, IP precedence-based WRED is enabled, and all the defaults are accepted. The configuration can be verified with the **show queueing interface** command as demonstrated in Example 2-1.

Example 2-1   *Verifying the WRED Configuration on a Cisco IOS Router Interface*

```
Router#show queueing interface serial 6/0
Interface Serial6/0 queueing strategy: random early detection (WRED)
    Exp-weight-constant: 9 (1/512)
    Mean queue depth: 0

class    Random drop      Tail drop       Minimum Maximum  Mark
         pkts/bytes       pkts/bytes      thresh  thresh   prob
0           0/0              0/0            20       40    1/10
1           0/0              0/0            22       40    1/10
2           0/0              0/0            24       40    1/10
3           0/0              0/0            26       40    1/10
4           0/0              0/0            28       40    1/10
5           0/0              0/0            31       40    1/10
6           0/0              0/0            33       40    1/10
7           0/0              0/0            35       40    1/10
rsvp        0/0              0/0            37       40    1/10
```

There are several values shown in the **show queueing** output that have not yet been explained.

- **Minimum threshold**—When the average queue depth exceeds the minimum threshold, packets start to be discarded. The rate at which packets are dropped increases linearly until the average queue depth hits the maximum threshold.

- **Maximum threshold**—When the average queue size exceeds the maximum threshold, all packets are dropped.

- **Mark probability denominator**—This number is a fraction and represents the fraction of packets that are dropped when the queue size is at the maximum threshold. In the preceding example, the mark probability denominator indicates that all IP precedence levels will have 1 of every 10 packets dropped when the average queue depth equals the maximum threshold.

In the **show queueing** output, notice that the minimum threshold is different for each IP precedence level. It was previously mentioned that it is possible to modify the configuration so that all IP precedence or DSCP values are treated the same. Example 2-2 shows one way to do this.

Example 2-2   *Configuring WRED Parameters on a Cisco IOS Router Interface*

```
Router(config)#interface s6/0
Router(config-if)#random-detect precedence 1 ?
  <1-4096>  minimum threshold (number of packets)

Router(config-if)#random-detect precedence 1 20 ?
  <1-4096>  maximum threshold (number of packets)

Router(config-if)#random-detect precedence 1 20 40 ?
  <1-65535>  mark probability denominator
  <cr>

Router(config-if)#random-detect precedence 1 20 40 10
Router(config-if)#random-detect precedence 2 20 40 10
Router(config-if)#random-detect precedence 3 20 40 10
Router(config-if)#random-detect precedence 4 20 40 10
Router(config-if)#random-detect precedence 5 20 40 10
Router(config-if)#random-detect precedence 6 20 40 10
Router(config-if)#random-detect precedence 7 20 40 10
Router(config-if)#exit
Router(config)#exit
Router#show queueing interface s6/0
Interface Serial6/0 queueing strategy: random early detection (WRED)
    Exp-weight-constant: 9 (1/512)
    Mean queue depth: 0

class   Random drop     Tail drop      Minimum Maximum  Mark
        pkts/bytes      pkts/bytes      thresh  thresh  prob
0          0/0             0/0            20      40    1/10
1          0/0             0/0            20      40    1/10
2          0/0             0/0            20      40    1/10
```

Example 2-2   *Configuring WRED Parameters on a Cisco IOS Router Interface (Continued)*

```
3               0/0            0/0          20    40  1/10
4               0/0            0/0          20    40  1/10
5               0/0            0/0          20    40  1/10
6               0/0            0/0          20    40  1/10
7               0/0            0/0          20    40  1/10
rsvp            0/0            0/0          37    40  1/10
```

As you can see from the **show queueing** output, the minimum threshold, maximum threshold, and mark probability denominator are now the same for all IP precedence values. This is not necessarily recommended; instead, it is shown to illustrate that the treatment of packets is entirely user configurable.

It is also possible to use DSCP-based WRED, and the configuration options for that differ slightly, as demonstrated in Example 2-3.

Example 2-3   *Configuring DSCP-based WRED on a Cisco IOS Router Interface*

```
Router(config)#interface s6/0
Router(config-if)#random-detect ?
  dscp-based  Enable dscp based WRED on an interface
prec-based  Enable prec based WRED on an interface
  <cr>
Router(config-if)#random-detect dscp-based
Router(config-if)#random-detect ?
  dscp                          parameters for each dscp value
  dscp-based                    Enable dscp based WRED on an interface
exponential-weighting-constant  weight for mean queue depth calculation
  flow                          enable flow based WRED
  prec-based                    Enable prec based WRED on an interface
  precedence                    parameters for each precedence value
  <cr>

Router(config-if)#random-detect dscp ?
  <0-63>   Differentiated services codepoint value
  af11     Match packets with AF11 dscp (001010)
  af12     Match packets with AF12 dscp (001100)
  af13     Match packets with AF13 dscp (001110)
  af21     Match packets with AF21 dscp (010010)
  af22     Match packets with AF22 dscp (010100)
  af23     Match packets with AF23 dscp (010110)
  af31     Match packets with AF31 dscp (011010)
  af32     Match packets with AF32 dscp (011100)
  af33     Match packets with AF33 dscp (011110)
  af41     Match packets with AF41 dscp (100010)
  af42     Match packets with AF42 dscp (100100)
  af43     Match packets with AF43 dscp (100110)
  cs1      Match packets with CS1(precedence 1) dscp (001000)
  cs2      Match packets with CS2(precedence 2) dscp (010000)
  cs3      Match packets with CS3(precedence 3) dscp (011000)
  cs4      Match packets with CS4(precedence 4) dscp (100000)
  cs5      Match packets with CS5(precedence 5) dscp (101000)
```

continues

Example 2-3 *Configuring DSCP-based WRED on a Cisco IOS Router Interface (Continued)*

```
  cs6      Match packets with CS6(precedence 6) dscp (110000)
  cs7      Match packets with CS7(precedence 7) dscp (111000)
  default  Match packets with default dscp (000000)
  ef       Match packets with EF dscp (101110)
  rsvp     rsvp traffic

Router(config-if)#random-detect dscp af11 ?
  <1-4096>  minimum threshold (number of packets)

Router(config-if)#random-detect dscp af11 20 ?
  <1-4096>  maximum threshold (number of packets)

Router(config-if)#random-detect dscp af11 20 40 ?
  <1-65535>  mark probability denominator
  <cr>

Router(config-if)#random-detect dscp af11 20 40 10 ?
  <cr>

Router(config-if)#random-detect dscp af11 20 40 10
Router(config-if)#exit
Router(config)#exit
Router#show queueing interface s6/0
Interface Serial6/0 queueing strategy: random early detection (WRED)
    Exp-weight-constant: 9 (1/512)
    Mean queue depth: 0

dscp      Random drop     Tail drop     Minimum Maximum  Mark
          pkts/bytes      pkts/bytes     thresh  thresh  prob
af11        0/0             0/0            20      40    1/10
af12        0/0             0/0            28      40    1/10
af13        0/0             0/0            24      40    1/10
af21        0/0             0/0            33      40    1/10
af22        0/0             0/0            28      40    1/10
af23        0/0             0/0            24      40    1/10
af31        0/0             0/0            33      40    1/10
af32        0/0             0/0            28      40    1/10
af33        0/0             0/0            24      40    1/10
af41        0/0             0/0            33      40    1/10
af42        0/0             0/0            28      40    1/10
af43        0/0             0/0            24      40    1/10
cs1         0/0             0/0            22      40    1/10
cs2         0/0             0/0            24      40    1/10
cs3         0/0             0/0            26      40    1/10
cs4         0/0             0/0            28      40    1/10
cs5         0/0             0/0            31      40    1/10
cs6         0/0             0/0            33      40    1/10
cs7         0/0             0/0            35      40    1/10
ef          0/0             0/0            37      40    1/10
rsvp        0/0             0/0            37      40    1/10
default     0/0             0/0            20      40    1/10
```

The **show queueing** output for af21, af31, and af41 indicates that the minimum threshold for af11 would have been 33 by default. As shown, the minimum threshold is 20, based on commands entered.

The af*xx* values shown in the **show queueing** output are related to the *assured forwarding per-hop behavior* (AF PHB) discussed in Chapter 1. From the **show queueing** output, you can see that afx3 packets will be dropped before afx2 packets, and afx2 packets will be dropped before afx1 packets. This behavior was explained in detail in Chapter 1.

Incidentally, the term *average queue depth* has been used several times during this discussion of WRED and, although a detailed explanation of this formula is beyond the scope of this chapter, the formula used to calculate average queue depth is as follows:

Average = (old_average * $(1 - 2^{-n})$) + (current_queue_size * 2^{-n}), where n is the exponential weight factor, which is user configurable.

CAUTION   If the value for n is set too high, WRED will not work properly and the net impact will be roughly the same as if WRED were not in use at all.

At time of publication, the Catalyst 3550 Family and Catalyst 6500 Family of switches support the WRED congestion management feature. Refer to the congestion management section in each product chapter for the Catalyst 3550 Family and Catalyst 6500 Family of switches for more details.

Token Bucket Mechanism

A *token bucket* is a formal definition of a rate of transfer. For this discussion, assume the token bucket starts full. This implies the maximum amount of tokens is available to sustain incoming traffic. Assume a bucket, which is being filled with tokens at a rate of *x* tokens per refresh interval. Each token represents 1 bit of data. To successfully transmit a packet, there must be a one-to-one match between bits and tokens. As a result, when a packet or frame arrives at the port or interface, and enough tokens exist in the bucket to accommodate the entire unit of data, the packet conforms to the contract, and therefore is forwarded. When the packet is successfully transmitted, the number of tokens equal to the size of the transmitted packet is removed from the bucket. Figure 2-1 illustrates the token bucket mechanism.

Figure 2-1 *Token Bucket Mechanism*

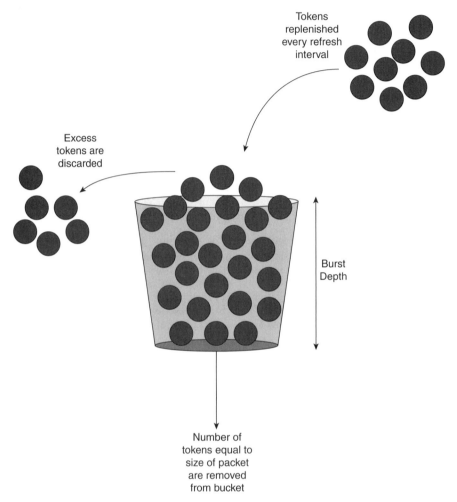

If the actual ingress traffic rate exceeds the configured rate, and there are insufficient tokens in the token bucket to accommodate the arriving traffic, the excess data is considered out-of-profile and can be dealt with in one of two ways:

- Re-assign QoS values to appropriate header
- Drop packet

If the decision is to mark down the nonconforming traffic, the DSCP value is derived from the mapping tables.

The token bucket mechanism has three components: a burst size, a mean rate, and a time interval (Tc). Although the mean rate is generally represented as bits per second, any two values may be derived from the third by the relation shown as follows:

Mean rate = burst size / time interval

Here are some definitions of these terms:

- **Mean rate**—Also called the *committed information rate* (CIR), it specifies how much data can be sent or forwarded per unit time on average.

- **Burst size**—Also called the *committed burst* (Bc) size, it specifies in bits (or bytes) per burst how much traffic can be sent within a given unit of time to not create scheduling concerns. (For a shaper, such as *generic traffic shaping* (GTS), it specifies bits per burst; for a policer, such as *committed access rate* (CAR), it specifies bytes per burst.)

- **Time interval**—Also called the *measurement interval*, it specifies the time quantum in seconds per burst.

By definition, over any integral multiple of the interval, the bit rate of the interface will not exceed the mean rate. The bit rate, however, may be arbitrarily fast within the interval.

A token bucket is used to manage a device that regulates the data in a flow. For example, the regulator might be a traffic policer, such as CAR, or a traffic shaper, such as *Frame Relay traffic shaping* (FRTS) or GTS. A token bucket itself has no discard or priority policy. Rather, a token bucket discards tokens and leaves to the flow the problem of managing its transmission queue if the flow overdrives the regulator. (Neither CAR nor FRTS and GTS implement either a true token bucket or true leaky bucket.)

In the token bucket metaphor, tokens are put into the bucket at a certain rate. The bucket itself has a specified capacity. If the bucket fills to capacity, newly arriving tokens are discarded. Each token is permission for the source to send a certain number of bits into the network. To send a packet, the regulator must remove from the bucket a number of tokens equal in representation to the packet size.

If not enough tokens are in the bucket to send a packet, the packet either waits until the bucket has enough tokens (in the case of GTS) or the packet is discarded or marked down (in the case of CAR). If the bucket is already full of tokens, incoming tokens overflow and are not available to future packets. Thus, at any time, the largest burst a source can send into the network is roughly proportional to the size of the bucket.

Note that the token bucket mechanism used for traffic shaping has both a token bucket and a data buffer, or queue; if it did not have a data buffer, it would be a policer. For traffic shaping, packets that arrive that cannot be sent immediately are delayed in the data buffer.

For traffic shaping, a token bucket permits burstiness but bounds it. It guarantees that the burstiness is bounded so that the flow never sends faster than the capacity of the token bucket plus the time interval multiplied by the established rate at which tokens are placed in the bucket. It also guarantees that the long-term transmission rate does not exceed the established rate at which tokens are placed in the bucket.

All Catalyst switches that support policing utilize the token bucket algorithm for bandwidth-limiting traffic flows. Chapters 6, 7, and 8 discuss the token bucket algorithm for the Catalyst 2950 and 3550, 4000 IOS, and 6500 Family of switches, respectively.

Traffic Shaping

Cisco devices utilize various types of traffic shaping, but this section is intended only to introduce the general concept of traffic shaping, not the specific implementations. For information about implementation on Cisco platforms, refer to Cisco.com.

The purpose of traffic shaping is to control the rate at which packets are sent out of an interface, while preventing packet loss. You might choose to use traffic shaping for any number of reasons, but the primary reasons are as follows:

- **Data rate mismatch**—In Frame Relay networks, it is common to have a main location with a large amount of bandwidth and remote locations with smaller amounts of bandwidth. Because the main location has no idea that the other end of the link has less bandwidth, traffic shaping must be used to control the rate at which traffic is sent to the remote locations.

- **Controlling access to bandwidth**—You might want to control access to bandwidth for various reasons, even when plenty of bandwidth is available. A good example is tiered-pricing or "burstable" Internet connections that have become popular in recent years. These connections deliver a circuit with a high possible speed (for example, a DS3) but charge based on average utilization of the circuit. So, if your company wants the flexibility to quickly move to a higher rate, but wants to control expenses, ordering this type of circuit and using traffic shaping to make sure that you do not exceed a certain subrate might be a good choice.

The key benefit of traffic shaping is that packet buffering, rather than packet drop, is used to achieve rate control. This is a crucial difference when dealing with drop-sensitive applications. There is also a potential downside to shaping, however, because shaping is accomplished through buffering, which introduces delay. Delay-sensitive traffic should not be shaped, unless the potential impact is fully understood and acceptable in your environment.

The decision of whether a packet should be sent immediately or buffered until the next time interval is based on the token bucket scheme that was introduced in the preceding section.

Policing

The purpose of the policer is to control the amount of bandwidth consumed by an individual microflow, or an aggregate of flows. Do not confuse policing with traffic shaping. Although traffic shaping limits flows to a specified rate, it buffers nonconforming traffic to ensure the flows remain within the confines of the configured contract. Policing, on the other hand, does not buffer nonconforming traffic. As a result, policing does not introduce additional jitter or delay, which could impact the timely delivery and performance of real-time voice or video applications.

In contrast to traffic shaping, policing accomplishes rate control by dropping packets. The two primary mechanisms for traffic policing in Cisco IOS are CAR and class-based policer. Cisco Catalyst platforms do not support CAR, but do support a policing function. Depending on the platform and supervisor engine, policing may be supported ingress only or both ingress and egress. In addition, policing may be aggregate or per-flow. On non-Catalyst platforms, policing is currently aggregate policing, although there are rumors that per-flow policing will be available sometime in the future.

It is important to understand that policing leads to packet loss, and to understand the impact of dropped packets on the application being policed. In the case of an application such as FTP, which is TCP-based and very tolerant of dropped packets, policing has very little impact other than the obvious impact of slowing the traffic rate. With an application such as IP-based video conferencing, however, dropped packets may cause poor picture and sound quality, so policing should be used with caution.

Networks use policing for dozens of reasons, but several of the most common reasons are as follows:

- **Subrate delivery**—Local Internet service providers may sell something less than a T1 connection (for example, 384 kbps), but are forced to deliver that over a full T1. Some providers choose to use a Frame Relay service that enables them to handle this problem another way, but it is often less expensive for the ISP to just use a point-to-point T1 and police the traffic coming into the provider's network. This also allows for an extremely simple bandwidth upgrade if the customer calls and requests more bandwidth.

- **Rate control of recreational traffic**—It is not uncommon these days for networks with no controls to be overrun with peer-to-peer file-sharing services such as Napster and Kazaa. Many networks have chosen to implement policing to limit the impact that these nonbusiness applications can have on their network.

- **Network security**—QoS mechanisms should never be viewed as an alternative to network security devices but, when used to compliment network security devices, QoS mechanisms can add to the overall security of the network. For example, policing ping traffic to a reasonable amount (what is considered reasonable depends on the network) will not stop someone from launching *Internet Control Message Protocol* (ICMP)-based attacks on your network, but will be able to drop a good portion of the attack traffic as it enters your network, thereby limiting the impact that the attack has on internal resources.

- **Safety mechanism**—If your network is implementing *connection admission control* (CAC) to make sure that only two concurrent video sessions can be established over a single link, there should not ever be more than two sessions in progress. As a safety mechanism, to prevent rogue video traffic from dominating the link in the event of a failure of your CAC device, a policer might be used to limit the total amount of video to equal the bandwidth required for two concurrent sessions. It is important to note that, if the CAC mechanism failed, policing would police the aggregate of the video traffic, which would likely impact video quality. Although poor video quality is not ideal, other network traffic would be protected.

As mentioned earlier, Cisco IOS has two main mechanisms for policing. CAR is a legacy mechanism and, although a lot of networks use CAR today, future development efforts will be put into class-based policer. Class-based policer was originally released to correspond to RFC 2697, which defines a single-rate three-color policer. The rate that is defined is the rate to which traffic should be policed. The three colors refer to the capability to use conform-action, exceed-action, and violate-action to specify different packet markings or actions (such as, drop) that can be configured when packets conform to, exceed, or violate the specified rate. If only the conform-action and exceed-action are specified, a single token bucket is used to perform the policing. If the violate-action is specified, a second token bucket is also used.

With the release of RFC 2698, which defines a two-rate, three-color policer, Cisco IOS version 12.2(4)T added to the functionality of the policing function. With the introduction of two-rate policing, it is now possible to specify both a CIR and a *peak information rate* (PIR).

CAR is not supported on Catalyst switches for shaping traffic between VLANs or Ethernet interfaces. CAR is supported for shaping of traffic across WAN interfaces. Instead, Catalyst switches use policers defined by policies to shape traffic across interfaces.

QoS Signaling

Resource Reservation Protocol (RSVP) is an IP service that enables hosts to make a request for reserved bandwidth along the path to the destination host. Allowing an explicit reservation of bandwidth end-to-end means that the traffic will have a guaranteed QoS.

It is important to understand that RSVP itself does not actually provide the bandwidth; it just signals the router that there is a request. In Cisco devices, RSVP works in conjunction with WFQ and WRED to provide the requested QoS.

Generally speaking, reserving bandwidth is not necessary for data flows other than real-time applications, such as VoIP or IP-based video conferencing. For these traffic types, latency and bandwidth are both critical to performance and it makes sense to have an explicit reservation for those characteristics along the network path.

RSVP works for unicast or multicast, and there are two types of reservations to be concerned with:

- **Distinct reservation**—This is a flow that originates from one and only one source. Distinct reservations are given a distinct reservation for each source on each link that the traffic crosses. Unicast traffic and "one-to-many" multicast would likely both use distinct reservations.

- **Shared reservation**—This is a flow that originates from one or more sources. A shared reservation is used by a "many-to-many" multicast application, and there is a single reservation, defined with a wildcard filter, such that any sender in the specified group has access to the reservation.

Subnet Bandwidth Manager (SBM), defined by RFC 2814, is a signaling protocol that deals with RSVP-based admission control on 802-based networks. Today, SBM is primarily used in switched Ethernet environments for LAN-based admission control for RSVP flows. Simply stated, SBM is responsible for handling admission control for resource reservations.

On each managed segment, an election process happens dynamically, and one device becomes the *Designated Subnet Bandwidth Manager* (DSBM). The DBSM is responsible for the admission control on that specific segment. There can be more than one SBM on a segment, but only one is elected as the DSBM.

The actual process of making a reservation, when a DBSM is present, includes the following steps:

1 When a DBSM sends an RSVP Path message out an interface that belongs to a managed segment, the message is sent to the DBSM. If the segment were not managed, this message would have gone directly to the RSVP session destination.

2 The DBSM builds a Path state for the message, and retains information about the node from which it received the message.

3 The DBSM forwards the message to the destination.

4 The DBSM then gets the RSVP Resv message and processes the message to determine what action to take next.

5 If there is bandwidth available for the reservation, the Resv message is sent to the previous hop. In this case, the local Path state is used for this session.

6 If bandwidth isn't available for the reservation, the DBSM returns a Resverr message to the requesting node.

On Cisco IOS routers, you can use the following command to configure SBM:

```
Router(config-if)# ip rsvp dsbm
candidate [priority]
```

The **show ip rsvp sbm detail** command can be used to verify the configuration of SBM.

Link Efficiency

Cisco IOS includes more and more features with every release. Some of the features in Cisco IOS are very specific, and may never need to be used in your network. However, link-efficiency mechanisms are likely to be of use in any network where there is a mixture of voice and data running over slower-speed links (T1 speed or less).

In general, link-efficiency mechanisms are designed to help maximize efficiency when voice is present on the network. Although quite a few mechanisms would be considered part of the group of link-efficiency features, only a few are discussed here; primarily, *Real Time Protocol Header Compression* (cRTP) and *Link Fragmentation and Interleaving* (LFI).

Link Fragmentation and Interleaving (LFI)

Before discussing the specifics of link-efficiency mechanisms, it seems wise to discuss the need for link efficiency in the first place. Primarily, when conversations take place about using VoIP, everyone jumps up and screams about the need for QoS or, more specifically, prioritization of traffic. Although prioritization is certainly necessary in a VoIP environment, lower-speed links (those under 768 kbps) create problems for VoIP that simple prioritization cannot solve. In these cases, link-efficiency mechanisms are necessary to ensure proper QoS for the VoIP traffic.

Serialization delay is the time that it takes to place bits on to the circuit. Table 2-1 shows the serialization delay for packets of various sizes, by link speed.

Table 2-1   *Serialization Delay of Various Packet Sizes on Links of Various Speeds*

Link Speed	Packet Size					
	64 bytes	128 bytes	256 bytes	512 bytes	1024 bytes	1500 bytes
56 kbps	9 ms	18 ms	36 ms	72 ms	144 ms	214 ms
64 kbps	8 ms	16 ms	32 ms	64 ms	128 ms	187 ms
128 kbps	4 ms	8 ms	16 ms	32 ms	64 ms	93 ms
256 kbps	2 ms	4 ms	8 ms	16 ms	32 ms	46 ms
512 kbps	1 ms	2 ms	4 ms	8 ms	16 ms	23 ms
768 kbps	0.640 ms	1.28 ms	2.56 ms	5.12 ms	10.24 ms	15 ms

As you can see from this table, the serialization delay for a 1500-byte packet on a link slower than 768 kbps is quite high. The "break point" for a 1500-byte packet happens at 768 kbps or higher speeds. When the link speed is 768 kbps, or greater, the serialization delay does not have a significant negative impact, so fragmentation is not necessary.

If the serialization delay would otherwise be greater than 15 ms, however, fragmentation is needed. Specifically, LFI is needed. All forms of LFI have the same function, but there are several types of LFI:

- **MLP Interleaving**—LFI on multilink PPP links
- **FRF.12**—LFI for Frame Relay data *permanent virtual circuits* (PVCs)
- **FRF.11 Annex C**—LFI for Frame Relay *Voice over Frame Relay* (VoFR) PVCs

The function of all of these types of LFI is to fragment large data packets and interleave the much smaller data packets. Figure 2-2 illustrates the basic concept.

Figure 2-2   *Link Fragmentation and Interleaving*

Configuring MLP Interleaving is as simple as using the following three commands:

```
Router(config-if)#encapsulation ppp
Router(config-if)#ppp multilink
Router(config-if)#ppp multilink interleave
```

Optionally, you can manually change the default fragmentation delay from 30 using the following command:

```
Router(config-if)#ppp multilink fragment-delay milliseconds
```

Table 2-2 shows the recommended settings for fragmentation

Table 2-2   *Recommended Settings for Fragmentation*

Link Speed	10 ms	20 ms	30 ms	40 ms	50 ms	100 ms	200 ms
56 kbps	70 bytes	140 bytes	210 bytes	280 bytes	350 bytes	700 bytes	1400 bytes
64 kbps	80 bytes	160 bytes	240 bytes	320 bytes	400 bytes	800 bytes	1600 bytes
128 kbps	160 bytes	320 bytes	480 bytes	640 bytes	800 bytes	1600 bytes	3200 bytes
256 kbps	320 bytes	640 bytes	960 bytes	1280 bytes	1600 bytes	3200 bytes	6400 bytes
512 kbps	640 bytes	1280 bytes	1920 bytes	2560 bytes	3200 bytes	6400 bytes	12800 bytes
768 kbps	1000 bytes	2000 bytes	3000 bytes	4000 bytes	5000 bytes	10000 bytes	20000 bytes
1536 kbps	2000 bytes	4000 bytes	6000 bytes	8000 bytes	10000 bytes	20000 bytes	40000 bytes

Shaded values indicate that fragmentation is not needed.

Configuring *Frame Relay Fragmentation* (FRF.12 or FRF.11 Annex C) requires only one command; note that the following command is entered within a Frame Relay map class, not under the interface directly:

```
Router(config-map-class)#frame-relay fragment fragment_size
```

You can verify the configuration of LFI for Frame Relay with the **show frame-relay fragment** command. These commands are, at present, only applicable to the FlexWAN module for the Catalyst 6500 Family of switches.

Real Time Protocol Header Compression (cRTP)

Real Time Protocol (RTP) is the standard protocol for the transport of real-time data, and is defined in RFC 1889. As defined, an RTP packet includes the payload plus an RTP/UDP/ IP header. The total header is 40 bytes and breaks down as follows: The RTP header is 12 bytes, the UDP header is 8 bytes, and the IP header is 20 bytes. Depending on the application, the payload is typically between 20 bytes and 160 bytes. That means that it's possible that the header would be twice the size of the payload! Clearly, that is not efficient, so the folks at the IETF came up with a way to take advantage of similarities between successive packets and reduce the 40-byte header to somewhere between 2 and 5 bytes. For VoIP, this header compression can yield an overall reduction in packet size on the order of 200 percent or more.

Although the idea of using cRTP everywhere sounds good at first glance, the trade-off, in terms of performance, on link speeds higher than T1 are not desirable. Therefore, use of cRTP should be limited to links with speeds of T1 or less. Speaking of performance, prior to Cisco IOS 12.0(7)T, cRTP happened in the process switching path, which often slowed the processing of packets to the point that it was not desirable to use cRTP. As of 12.0(7)T, however, cRTP will use the *Cisco Express Forwarding* (CEF) switching path, or fast switching path (if CEF is not enabled). Only if both CEF and fast switching are disabled will cRTP packets be process switched.

The configuration of cRTP on a serial interface is simple, as shown in the following example:

```
Router(config-if)#ip rtp header-compression [passive]
```

The **passive** keyword tells the routers to compress outgoing RTP packets only if the incoming RTP packets on that interface are compressed.

For Frame Relay PVCs, the configuration of cRTP is as follows:

```
router(config-if)#frame-relay map ip ip-address dlci [broadcast] rtp header-
compression [active | passive]
```

To verify the configuration and operation of cRTP, use the following commands for Frame Relay and non-Frame Relay interfaces, respectively:

```
Router#show frame-relay ip rtp header-compression [interface type number]
```

```
Router#show ip rtp header-compression [type number] [detail]
```

Classification and Marking at Layer 3

RFC 791 first defined Layer 3 packet marking in terms of IP precedence and *type of service* (ToS), whereas RFC 795 expanded on the service mappings of the TOS bits. The discussion of these RFCs provided here is for historical purposes, and it should be noted that both of these RFCs are obsolete, due to various RFCs that are part of the DiffServ architecture. Refer to Chapter 1 for a discussion of current RFCs that are part of the DiffServ architecture.

IP Precedence and the Type of Service Byte

RFC 791 defines the three most significant bits of the ToS byte as the IP precedence bits, and the next 3 bits as delay, throughput, and reliability. Table 2-3 shows the original definition of the ToS byte.

Table 2-3　*Definition of ToS Byte*

Bits	Precedence
Bits 0–2	Precedence
Bit 3	0 = normal delay, 1 = low delay
Bit 4	0 = normal throughput, 1 = high throughput
Bit 5	0 = normal reliability, 1 = high reliability
Bits 6–7	Reserved for future use

Keep in mind that the bits are numbered left to right, with the left bits (0–2) being the most significant. Table 2-4 shows the values assigned to the 3 bits used for IP precedence.

Table 2-4　*IP Precedence Bits and Their Definitions*

Bits	IP Precedence
111	Network control (precedence 7)
110	Internetwork control (precedence 6)
101	CRITIC/ECP (precedence 5)
100	Flash override (precedence 4)
011	Flash (precedence 3)
010	Immediate (precedence 2)
001	Priority (precedence 1)
000	Routine (precedence 0)

The concept of IP precedence became wildly popular and is in use in many networks today. The use of the next three most significant bits (defined for delay, throughput, and reliability) was not as well received for a variety of reasons. For the most part, these bits were not used due to confusion over the proper implementation to deliver the service levels specified. RFC 1349 redefined these 3 bytes and made use of 1 additional bit (bit 6). Table 2-5 shows how RFC 1349 defined what were now the four types of service bits.

Table 2-5 *Definition of ToS Bits in RFC 1349*

Bits	Precedence
1000	Minimize delay
0100	Maximize throughput
0010	Maximize reliability
0001	Minimize monetary cost
0000	Normal service

Unfortunately, this new definition was not implemented much more than the previous definition of these bits. Because these bits are not commonly used, and have been made obsolete due to later RFCs, they are not discussed here. You can find more information about the service mappings in RFCs 795 and 1349.

The Differentiated Services Field (DS Field)

As stated in RFC 2474, DiffServ enhancements to IP are designed to allow service differentiation on the Internet in a scalable manner, primarily because per-flow classification will not be necessary at each hop. There is a great deal more explained in RFC 2474 than is covered here. The purpose of this section is only to discuss packet marking, using the DS field.

The idea behind DiffServ is that packets will be marked (much like with IP precedence) at the edge of a network and those markings will then be read by each router (hop) that a packet passes through. Based on the specific rules that have been defined within that hop, the packet is assigned to a traffic class and that traffic class will have been given some amount of access to scheduling and other resources.

With IP precedence, only the 3 left-most bits were used for IP precedence, and the next 3 bits were rarely used. So RFC 2474 redefines the ToS byte to make use of the 6 left-most bits (bits 0–5) for packet marking. Doing so increases the number of possible packet markings from 8 to 64 and eliminates "wasted" bits (those that were rarely used). The 2 least significant bits of the ToS byte are not defined by RFC 2474, but have since been defined by RFC 2481. RFC 2481 is beyond the scope of this discussion, but is an interesting concept called *explicit congestion notification* (ECN). You can view RFC 2481 (and all other RFCs) at www.ietf.org, under the RFC Pages section.

Figure 2-3 illustrates the ToS byte with IP precedence and the redefined ToS byte with DiffServ:

Figure 2-3   *ToS Byte: With IP Precedence and Differentiated Services*

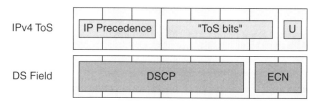

Per-Hop Behaviors

With the introduction of the DSCP markings, there were significantly more possible markings for packets (0–63 are the possible markings for packets). Because there were so many more possible markings, the IETF decided to standardize what some of the codepoints meant. In part, this is to provide backward compatibility to IP precedence and, in part, this is to facilitate certain types of behaviors that were seen as fundamental to the DiffServ architecture.

The following definition of a per-hop behavior is taken from Section 2.4 of RFC 2475:

A per-hop behavior (PHB) is a description of the externally observable forwarding behavior of a DS node applied to a particular DS behavior aggregate … In general, the observable behavior of a PHB may depend on certain constraints on the traffic characteristics of the associated behavior aggregate, or the characteristics of other behavior aggregates.

For a definition of forwarding behavior, refer to Chapter 1.

For the purpose of backward compatibility, it is important to note that a router that understands IP precedence, but is not DiffServ-aware, looks only at the 3 most significant bits (left-most bits) in the ToS field, whereas a DiffServ-capable router looks at the 6 most significant bits. Therefore, the marking 000000 is defined in RFC 2474 as Best Effort. This means that a router that only understands IP precedence would read that field as 000, which is the definition of Best Effort in an IP precedence environment. Similarly, all markings in the format *xxx*000 are reserved by RFC 2474 to provide backward compatibility with IP precedence values, as shown in Table 2-6.

Table 2-6   *Backward Compatibility with IP Precedence Values*

Bits	Precedence
001000	Class selector 1; read as 001 by a non-DiffServ node and treated like IP precedence 1.
010000	Class selector 2; read as 010 by a non-DiffServ node and treated like IP precedence 2.
011000	Class selector 3; read as 011 by a non-DiffServ node and treated like IP precedence 3.
100000	Class selector 4; read as 100 by a non-DiffServ node and treated like IP precedence 4.

continues

Table 2-6   *Backward Compatibility with IP Precedence Values (Continued)*

Bits	Precedence
101000	Class selector 5; read as 101 by a non-DiffServ node and treated like IP precedence 5.
110000	Class selector 6; read as 110 by a non-DiffServ node and treated like IP precedence 6.
111000	Class selector 1; read as 111 by a non-DiffServ node and treated like IP precedence 7.

These backward-compatible markings were necessary to not break networks while the conversion from IP precedence to DiffServ was taking place.

RFC 2597: The Assured Forwarding PHB

Other than those defined in RFC 2474, there are two main PHBs, RFC 2597 defines the first of these. It is called the *assured forwarding* (AF) PHB, and the concept behind the PHB is to provide a level of assurance as to a given packet's probability of being forwarded during congestion.

RFC 2597 defines four classes, and each class is completely independent of the other classes. In addition, each class has three level of "drop precedence" to which packets of that class can be assigned.

From a high level, the concept is that you can have four different classes of traffic and, within those classes, you can have three different levels of probability that a packet will be dropped if that class becomes congested. Table 2-7 shows the code point markings for the AF PHB and the decimal values associated with each.

Table 2-7   *Codepoint Markings for the AF PHB*

Drop Precedence	Class 1	Class 2	Class 3	Class 4
Low	AF11	AF21	AF31	AF41
	(001010)	(010010)	(011010)	(100010)
	10	18	26	34
Medium	AF12	AF22	AF32	AF42
	(001100)	(010100)	(011100)	(100100)
	12	20	28	36
High	AF13	AF23	AF33	AF43
	(001110)	(010110)	(011110)	(100110)
	14	22	30	38

To understand a possible use for the AF PHB, assume that you have four branch offices aggregating into a single router. Each branch has been told that they should not send more than 256 kbps of FTP traffic, but sometimes they do anyway. In fact, sometimes they send more than 1 Mbps of FTP traffic. The problem is that when one branch sends a lot of FTP traffic, it sometimes interferes with another branch's FTP traffic, even if they are sending at or below the 256-kbps limit. A possible solution for this problem can be found by using the AF PHB, as illustrated in Figure 2-4.

Figure 2-4 *An Example of the AF PHB*

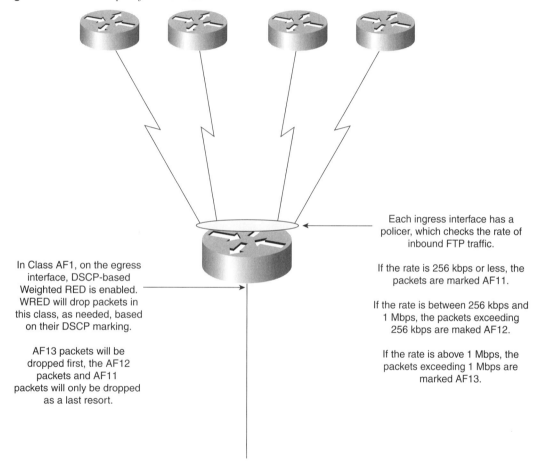

In Class AF1, on the egress interface, DSCP-based Weighted RED is enabled. WRED will drop packets in this class, as needed, based on their DSCP marking.

AF13 packets will be dropped first, the AF12 packets and AF11 packets will only be dropped as a last resort.

Each ingress interface has a policer, which checks the rate of inbound FTP traffic.

If the rate is 256 kbps or less, the packets are marked AF11.

If the rate is between 256 kbps and 1 Mbps, the packets exceeding 256 kbps are maked AF12.

If the rate is above 1 Mbps, the packets exceeding 1 Mbps are marked AF13.

In Cisco devices, this PHB is implemented on egress interfaces using a combination of CBWFQ and DSCP-based class-based WRED. Each site has contracted for 256 kbps of FTP traffic, so the bandwidth statement reflects a minimum reservation of 1024 kbps. The entire configuration of the egress interface seen in Figure 2-4 would be entered as shown in Example 2-4.

Example 2-4 *Configuring CBWFQ and Class-based WRED*

```
Router(config)#class-map match-any FTP
Router(config-cmap)#match ip dscp af11
Router(config-cmap)#match ip dscp af12
Router(config-cmap)#match ip dscp af13
Router(config-cmap)#exit
Router(config)#policy-map AF-PHB
Router(config-pmap)#class FTP
Router(config-pmap-c)#bandwidth 1024
Router(config-pmap-c)#random-detect dscp-based
Router(config-pmap-c)#exit
Router(config-pmap)#exit
Router(config)#exit
Router#
```

The running-config for this would then appear as in Example 2-5.

Example 2-5 *Verifying the Configuration of CBWFQ and Class-based WRED*

```
!
class-map match-any FTP
  match ip dscp af11
  match ip dscp af12
  match ip dscp af13
!
!
policy-map AF-PHB
  class FTP
    bandwidth 1024
    random-detect dscp-based
```

When attached to an interface, the functionality of this policy can be verified with the **show policy-map interface** command.

RFC 2598: The Expedited Forwarding PHB

The *expedited forwarding* (EF) PHB is designed to build a low-loss, low-latency, and low-jitter, assured bandwidth class. If all of those characteristics sound a bit like how you would want to treat VoIP traffic, you are already well on your way to understanding the purpose of this PHB.

Although RFC 2598 does not specifically say that this PHB should be used only for voice, this is the likely service for which this PHB would be used. Other types of interactive traffic could no doubt benefit from this type of treatment, however.

The idea behind the EF PHB is that traffic of this class should be forwarded with strict priority, as soon as that traffic is received. Note that the EF PHB should not normally be used for TCP traffic, due to the bursty nature of TCP. The reason behind this recommendation is that the EF PHB, in order not to starve other traffic classes of bandwidth, implements a policing function. This policing function ensure that the EF class receives all the bandwidth to which it is entitled, but is limited in the total amount of bandwidth that it can consume.

The EF PHB is implemented in Cisco devices as LLQ. Note that prior to Cisco IOS version 12.2, the policing function was implemented differently for different media types and, in some cases, the policing function happened regardless of congestion. In newer versions of Cisco IOS, however, this inconsistency has been resolved and the policing function of the LLQ only happens in the event of congestion on the interface.

If added to the configuration already shown for the AF PHB, the configuration for the EF PHB would be as shown in Example 2-6.

Example 2-6 *Configuring LLQ (EF PHB)*

```
Router(config)#class-map VOICE
Router(config-cmap)#match ip dscp ef
Router(config-cmap)#exit
Router(config)#policy-map AF-PHB
Router(config-pmap)#class VOICE
Router(config-pmap-c)#priority 56
Router(config-pmap-c)#exit
Router(config-pmap)#exit
Router(config)#exit
Router#
```

Notice that, in this example, the policy map is still named AF-PHB. Because this name was already being used for the interface, the EF configuration was just added to this policy. Of course, the name of the policy doesn't really matter.

The running-config for the entire policy would now appear as shown in Example 2-7.

Example 2-7 *Verifying the Configuration of LLQ and WRED*

```
class-map match-any FTP
  match ip dscp af11
  match ip dscp af12
  match ip dscp af13
class-map match-all VOICE
  match ip dscp ef
!
!
policy-map AF-PHB
  class FTP
   bandwidth 1024
   random-detect dscp-based
  class VOICE
    priority 56
```

This example reserves 56 kbps of bandwidth for the LLQ, which means that, under congestion, there will also be a policer that limits the VOICE class to 56 kbps. Again, when applied to an interface, this policy can be verified with the **show policy-map interface** command. The use of this command is currently limited to the FlexWAN module.

Classification and Marking at Layer 2

Before the days of VoIP and IP-based video conferencing, Layer 3 packet marking was the only packet marking that was ever discussed. Seemingly, Layer 3 markings were all that would ever be needed; the reasoning behind that line of thought was that the links in the switched environment were so fast that there would never be a need to prioritize access to bandwidth. Of course, VoIP and other real-time traffic also have very low tolerance for delay or jitter. Therefore, a clear need exists to place bounds on the amount of delay and jitter that a given packet will experience in the switched network.

A method of marking frames at Layer 2 was developed to allow differentiation of frames in terms of the characteristics that those frames would receive as they traverse the switched infrastructure. However, the only way to mark frames at Layer 2 is in the ISL or 802.1Q header. The location of bits used for this purpose is different for ISL and 802.1Q, as illustrated in Figure 2-5.

Figure 2-5   *The Layer 2 Class of Service Bits*

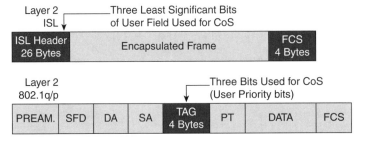

Mapping Layer 2 to Layer 3 Values

As frames/packets move from the Layer 2 environment to a Layer 3 environment, the ISL or 802.1Q header is lost. To preserve end-to-end QoS, this loss creates a need for the ability to map Layer 2 CoS values to Layer 3 ToS values (either IP precedence or DSCP). As frames/packets move back from the routed network to the switched network, ISL or 802.1Q headers will again be able to carry Layer 2 QoS markings. This is especially important when Layer 2 devices that have no Layer 3 capabilities are involved, because they may understand CoS markings, but not ToS markings. Again, to preserve end-to-end QoS, it would be necessary to use the Layer 3 marking to mark a Layer 2 CoS value on these downstream packets.

The commands for handling these mappings differs between platforms, but the command for setting a CoS-to-DSCP map on the Catalyst 6500 Family of switches is as follows:

```
set qos cos-dscp-map {dscp1, dscp2, dscp3, dscp4, dscp5, dscp6, dscp7, dscp8}
```

The variables *dscp1* through *dscp8* represent the DSCP values that you would enter. The seven positions shown correspond to the seven nonzero CoS values.

Because there are only eight CoS values, it is easy to map CoS to DSCP, but slightly more complicated when you map DSCP to CoS, because it's not possible to map all 64 DSCP values to an individual CoS value. As such, groups of DSCP values must be mapped to a single CoS value. On the Catalyst 6500 Family of switches, that configuration is as follows:

```
set qos dscp-cos-map 20-25:7 33-38:3
```

This example maps DSCP values 20 to 25 to CoS value 7 and DSCP values 33 to 38 to CoS value 3. It is a little confusing at first, but makes more sense as you become familiar with the syntax.

There are also default mappings in most switching platforms, but you should consult the chapters in this book that deal directly with the platforms that you are working with to determine what those defaults are and whether they are suitable for your network.

A General View of QoS on the Catalyst Platforms

This chapter mostly focuses on very detailed descriptions of the exact functionality of QoS on specific platforms. This section, however, provides a general overview of QoS concepts and a glimpse into the material covered in the later chapters. This section purposely avoids details about the operation of specific mechanisms on Cisco Catalyst switches. Instead, this section introduces some ideas that you will learn about in more detail in later chapters. The later chapters discuss the following QoS concepts for each Catalyst switching platform in more detail than they are introduced here:

- Classification
- Marking
- Policing
- Congestion Management
- Congestion Avoidance

Not all of Catalyst switching families support all the listed features, and those features are omitted from discussion on nonapplicable switch families. The following sections briefly discuss these features and their relation to Catalyst switches.

Catalyst QoS Classification

Classification determines how a switch or router marks, processes, and schedules frames. Currently shipping Catalyst switches utilize an internal DSCP value to correctly schedule and mark frames for egress transmission. Chapter 6 first introduces the concept of internal DSCP.

Moreover, Catalyst switches classify frames based on a variety of ingress frame parameters such as CoS, DSCP, IP precedence, trust, ingress interface, or IP address. Trust, based either on platform-specific default or user configuration, is an indication of whether the network administrator trusts the QoS markings of ingress frames on a per-interface basis. Generally, network administrators do not trust user ports because operating systems enable users to set the CoS value on egress packets. This situation may yield a negative impact on the network because users determine the priority of their traffic. Conversely, network designs typically trust infrastructure connections such as switch-to-switch, switch-to-router, or switch-to-IP Phone connections. The assumption in this case is that the other switches are already configured properly for trusting, classification, and marking.

Trusted interfaces do not alter the QoS marking of ingress frames. Untrusted interfaces alter the QoS markings to a configurable value CoS or DSCP. This value is typically zero (Best Effort) for untrusted interfaces. The command-line configuration and restrictions associated with trusted or untrusted interfaces are per platform. Later chapters discuss these configurations and restrictions, when the focus is on platform-specific properties. This trust concept is discussed in more detail in the section "Cisco Catalyst QoS Trust Concept" later in this chapter.

Catalyst QoS Marking

Marking is the act of a switch or router rewriting the CoS, DSCP, or IP precedence fields of frames based on classification. Marking modifies the intended ingress frame behavior as set by the originating device. Catalyst switches use interface configurations or policers to define marking parameters.

Catalyst QoS Policing

Catalyst switches define policers for applying bandwidth limits to ingress and egress traffic. In addition, Catalyst switches use policers to mark traffic. For example, it is possible to configure a policing policy such that all traffic of a certain type below 1 Mbps is marked with a DSCP value of af31 and all traffic above 1 Mbps is marked with a DSCP value of af32.

As with several with Catalyst QoS features, the configuration syntax and actual behavior for policing on Catalyst platforms is platform-specific and is discussed in later chapters. However, common to all platforms is the use of a token bucket concept for the policing bandwidth function.

Catalyst QoS Congestion Management

Catalyst switches use scheduling and transmit queues to achieve congestion management. All the currently shipping switches in the Catalyst product line support a form of scheduling that is more advanced than FIFO. The specific mechanisms differ on a platform basis.

With regard to output scheduling, the QoS marking determines the scheduling and output queue. In the case of the Catalyst 6500 Family of switches, for example, there are different queue types and drop thresholds per line module. Other platforms, such as the Catalyst 3500 Family and the Catalyst 4000 IOS Family of switches, use a single queue type for all line modules and product families.

Congestion Avoidance

At time of publication, only the Catalyst 3550 Family and the Catalyst 6500 Family of switches support congestion avoidance. In brief, congestion avoidance attempts to prevent congestion by applying specific queuing parameters. The Catalyst 3550 Family and the Catalyst 6500 Family of switches utilize WRED and several other queuing configurations to support congestion avoidance. This book discusses the Catalyst 3500 Family and Catalyst 6500 Family of switches in Chapters 6 and 8, respectively.

Cisco Catalyst QoS Trust Concept

The trust concept is a classification configuration option supported on all Catalyst switches that support QoS classification. The trust state of a switch port or interface defines how ingress packets are classified, marked, and subsequently scheduled. For a Cisco Catalyst switch that bases QoS only on CoS values, a port that is configured as untrusted reclassifies any CoS values to zero or to a statically configured CoS value. The CoS values of packets arriving on an untrusted port are assumed not verifiable and deemed unnecessary by the system administrator of the switch. Depending on the platform, untrusted ports may be configured to reclassify or mark IP precedence, DSCP, or CoS values on any ingress frame based on an 802.1q tag or access list.

Figure 2-8 illustrates the QoS trust concept. A workstation attached to a Catalyst 6500 switch is sending 802.1q tagged frames to the Catalyst 6500 switch with a CoS value of 5. If the port is configured as untrusted, the switch sets an internal DSCP value associated with the frame to 0. The switch does not actually alter the CoS value of the frame until transmission. All untrusted ports set the internal DSCP to 0 by default. However, the overriding internal DSCP value is configurable on various platforms. If the switch port is configured for *Trust-CoS*, the CoS value is not altered on ingress. Figure 2-6 applies to trusting IP precedence and DSCP values as well.

Figure 2-6   *Catalyst QoS Trust Concept*

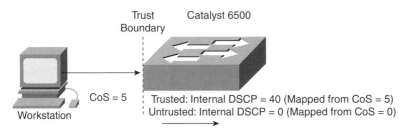

Switches that support classification of frames based on DSCP values derive an internal DSCP value for internal priority as the packet transits the switch. Several options exist to derive this internal DSCP value depending on platform. In brief, the general possible configurations for mapping an internal DSCP value are as follows:

- **Trust-IPPrec**—Internal DSCP is derived from the received IP precedence.

- **Trust-DSCP**—Internal DSCP is derived from the received DSCP.

- **Trust-CoS**—Internal DSCP is derived from the received CoS.

- **Untrusted**—Internal DSCP is derived from port configuration.

Additional configuration parameters are involved in determining an internal DSCP value, and caveats apply to this process. These caveats and configuration parameters are discussed on a per-platform basis throughout the book.

In summary, trusted ports are assumed to have ingress packets marked with IP precedence, DSCP, or CoS values that are valid. Untrusted ports are considered to have ingress frames marked with IP precedence, DSCP, or CoS values that are not deemed valid or desired by the system administrator of the switch.

The Cisco IP Phone

The Cisco IP Phone plays an important role in Cisco Catalyst QoS. A large majority of customers implement Cisco Catalyst QoS for the sole purpose of VoIP using Cisco IP Phones. Although a variety of IP Phone models exist, each phone uses a similar architecture. All current Cisco IP Phones include an internal three-port Layer 2 switch. As shown in Figure 2-7, the internal three-port switch enables customers to connect workstations through the IP Phone, which is in turn connected to a Catalyst switch using a single cable. Most customers actually use this daisy-chaining feature for both the phone and workstation to reduce the cable plant size and cost.

Network administrators generally accept a Cisco IP Phone as a trusted device. Most QoS campus network designs suggest using the trust feature with Cisco IP Phones.

Figure 2-7   *Cisco IP Phone Physical Network Example*

Workstation   IP Phone   Catalyst
                                        Switch

The internal switch ports of the Cisco IP Phone are referred to as P0, P1, and P2. P0 internally connects to the internal IP Phone appliance, P1 is an external 10/100-Mbps Fast
Ethernet port that connects PCs and workstations, and P2 is an external 10/100-Mbps Fast
Ethernet port that connects to the Catalyst switch. Figure 2-8 illustrates the integrated
switch architecture in the Cisco IP Phone.

Figure 2-8   *Cisco IP Phone Integrated Switch Architecture*

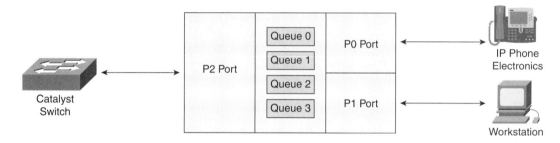

Each Cisco IP Phone port has four queues comprised of a single threshold statically
configured at 100 percent, 4q1t. Queue 0 functions as a high-priority queue for traffic with
a CoS value of 5. Spanning-tree *bridge protocol data units* (BPDUs) also use this queue.
Voice traffic from the internal IP Phone appliance has a CoS value of 5 by default. All
queues are serviced in a round-robin fashion. However, a timer maintains queue priority by
limiting service to the low-priority queues when there is traffic in the high-priority queue.
Subsequently, the Cisco IP Phone itself manages input and output scheduling for traffic
traversing the integrated switch ports.

Voice VLANs and Extended Trust

Through the use of dot1q trunks, voice traffic from an IP Phone connected to an access port
can reside on a separate VLAN and subnet. The workstation attached to the IP Phone might
still reside on the access, or native, VLAN. This additional VLAN on an access port for
voice traffic is referred to as a *voice VLAN* in Cisco IOS Software and *auxiliary VLAN* in
CatOS. Subsequently, with the use of voice VLANs, all voice traffic is tagged to and from
the Cisco IP Phone and Catalyst switch. The Catalyst switches use *Cisco Discovery
Protocol* (CDP) to inform the IP Phone of the voice VLAN ID. By default, Cisco IP Phone

voice traffic has a CoS value of 5. Figure 2-9 provides an example logical depiction of a voice VLAN. A common network design is to deploy both voice VLANs with trusting configurations for Cisco IP telephony applications (such as Cisco IP Phones).

Figure 2-9   *Example Logical Depiction of Voice VLAN*

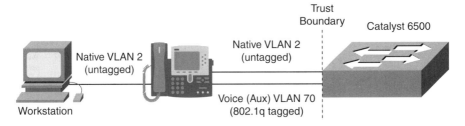

Another QoS option for IP Phones is extended trust. The switch can inform the IP Phone via CDP whether to trust ingress frames on its P1 port. The IP Phone may also be informed to overwrite the CoS value of the ingress frames on the P1 port with a specific CoS value. By default, the IP Phone does not trust frames arriving on the P1 port and rewrites the CoS value to 0 of any tagged frames. Untagged frames do not have CoS value.

Extended trust is a feature available to any device that can interpret the CDP fields describing the voice VLAN information. At the time of publication, Cisco IP Phones and other Cisco appliances are the only devices to use this feature.

Figure 2-10   *Catalyst Extended Trust Concept*

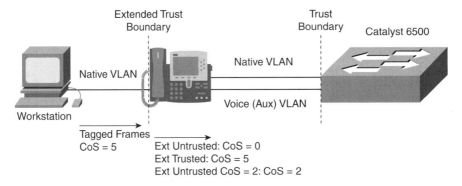

Summary

This chapter has given you a broad view of the QoS theories and mechanisms at Layer 2 and Layer 3, but hopefully left you hungry for more details. Those details are coming in each of the remaining chapters of this book. Now that you are familiar with the RFCs and overall concepts that drive the development of QoS mechanisms on Cisco devices, you will read about the very specific and often intricate details of these mechanisms on Cisco Catalyst platforms. You may find, as you read through some of the more detailed chapters, that you want to refer back to this chapter to see where a specific implementation detail fits into the end-to-end QoS strategy.

The next chapter includes a broad overview of QoS feature support on all Catalyst switches, and then focuses on QoS specifics on the Catalyst 2900XL, 3500XL, and 4000 CatOS Family of switches.

As you read the implementation specifics in the following chapters, keep an eye on the big picture of end-to-end QoS. From the Catalyst 3550 Family of switches to the Catalyst 4000 IOS Family of switches to the Catalyst 6500 Family of switches, think about how the configuration of each platform can be customized to fit the exact needs of your network. After all, you want to build a custom QoS policy that allows for the use of all the platforms in a single network, with a single end-to-end policy.

Overview of QoS Support on Catalyst Platforms and Exploring QoS on the Catalyst 2900XL, 3500XL, and Catalyst 4000 CatOS Family of Switches

Previous chapters described the necessity for QoS in campus networks and the fundamentals behind QoS operation. This chapter explains the various platform QoS features available across the Cisco Catalyst product family. A group of concise tables in the beginning of this chapter provides a quick reference for QoS features available for each Catalyst platform. In addition, this chapter, along with subsequent chapters, begins the product tour of the access layer Catalyst switches with the fewest QoS features and continues with the high-end core Catalyst switches with industry-leading QoS features. Although the access layer switches support only a few QoS features, these switches provide an excellent foundation for exploring QoS fundamentals in the campus network.

Specifically, this chapter covers the following topics:

- Brief Per–Catalyst Platform QoS Features Table
- QoS Features Overview
- QoS Features on the Catalyst 2900XL and 3500XL Switches
- QoS Features on the Catalyst 4000 CatOS Switches

The Cisco Catalyst 2900XL, 3500XL, and 4000 Family of switches share Layer 2 QoS features needed on access layer switches. These features include the following:

- Classification
- Marking
- Congestion Management

This chapter covers these topics on the respective platforms with command references, examples, and case studies. Upon completion of this chapter, you will understand each Catalyst platform's supported QoS features and be able to configure the Catalyst 2900XL, 500XL, and 4000 CatOS Family of switches for packet classification, marking, and congestion management.

From a platform perspective, the Catalyst 4000 CatOS Family of switches must be distinguished from the Catalyst 4000 Cisco IOS Family of switches due to individual differences in QoS features and configuration. The supervisor engine model determines whether a Catalyst 4000 switch operates on CatOS or Cisco IOS. In addition, the Catalyst 4000 Layer 3 services module also has exclusive Layer 3 QoS features (discussed in Chapter 7, "Advanced QoS Features Available on the Catalyst 4000 IOS Family of Switches and the Catalyst G-L3 Family of Switches"). This chapter is only applicable to the Catalyst 4000 CatOS switches. Table 3-8 shows which Catalyst 4000 switches are applicable to this chapter.

Catalyst Feature Overview

Cisco Catalyst switches support a wide range of QoS features. Generally, the high-end platforms support more QoS features especially platforms that support Layer 3 IP routing. Tables 3-1 through 3-5 provide a quick reference for QoS features for each platform. All platforms may have limitations and caveats per feature, and each QoS feature is discussed in the appropriate chapter of this book in additional detail.

Furthermore, QoS features are also dependent on whether the platform supports IP routing. The Catalyst 3550, Catalyst 4000 Cisco IOS Software family, Catalyst 5500 with *Route Switch Module* (RSM) or *Router Switch Feature Card* (RSFC), and the Catalyst 6000/6500 with Multilayer Switch Module (MSM) or *Multilayer Switch Feature Card* (MSFC) I/II support IP routing. Other platforms may support Layer 3 QoS features, such as classification based on *differentiated services codepoint* (DSCP) and marking of IP precedence; however, these platforms do not actually support routing of IP frames. As a result, network designs do not require platforms that support IP routing to classify, mark, police, or schedule traffic based on DSCP or IP precedence values. Therefore, network designers may choose lower-cost switches that do not support IP routing to enable Layer 3 QoS features.

The next sections provide quick reference tables for supported QoS features per platform. The tables only provide a glimpse into QoS feature support of each platform and do not indicate the benefits or restrictions of each feature. Refer to the appropriate chapters later in this book for thorough discussions of QoS feature support on each platform.

Specifically, the next sections highlight the following QoS features supported on each platform:

- Input Scheduling
- Policing
- Classification and Marking
- Output Scheduling

Table 3-1 indicates at a simplistic level, QoS feature support on a per-platform basis for most of the currently shipping Catalyst switches. The table only indicates at the fundamental level where a feature is supported and does not indicate the restrictions or caveats.

Table 3-1   QoS Feature Overview on Current Catalyst Switches

Product Family	Classification	Marking	Policing	Congestion Management	Congestion Avoidance
2950	Yes	Yes	Yes	Yes	No
3550	Yes	Yes	Yes	Yes	Yes
4000 IOS Family	Yes	Yes	Yes	Yes	No
6500 Family	Yes	Yes	Yes	Yes	Yes

Input Scheduling

Input scheduling is currently available only on the Catalyst 6000/6500. Input scheduling priorities and schedules packets out of ingress packet queues based on several QoS values including CoS and DSCP. However, most of Catalyst switches can deliver packets to the switching fabric at line rate or a specified rate. This specific rate defines the maximum throughput of the switch. If the input rate is not exceeded, input scheduling is not crucial in implementing QoS architecture. Furthermore, ingress policing is an option on many Catalyst switches that aids in preventing oversubscription of the switch fabric by limiting ingress traffic. Table 3-2 summarizes Catalyst platform support for input scheduling. The Comments column also denotes any switch capable of ingress policing.

Table 3-2   *Catalyst Platform QoS Input Scheduling Support*

Catalyst Switch	Input Scheduling	Ingress Policing	Comments
Catalyst 2900XL	No	No	Switching fabric is capable of 1.6 Gbps ingress.
Catalyst 2948G-L3/ 4912G-L3/4232-L3	No	Yes	
Catalyst 2950	No	Yes	
Catalyst 3500XL	No	No	Switching fabric is capable of 5.0 Gbps ingress.
Catalyst 3550	No	Yes	
Catalyst 4000 CatOS Family	No	No	Nonblocking line cards can deliver ingress traffic at line rate to switching fabric

continues

Table 3-2   *Catalyst Platform QoS Input Scheduling Support (Continued)*

Catalyst Switch	Input Scheduling	Ingress Policing	Comments
Catalyst 4000 Cisco IOS Family (Supervisor III and IV)	No	Yes	Non-blocking linecards can deliver ingress traffic at line rate to switching fabric.
Catalyst 5500	No	No	
Catalyst 5500 w/NFFC* II	No	No	
Catalyst 6000/6500	Yes	Yes	Based on Layer 2 CoS**; option for ingress Priority Queue.

*NFFC = NetFlow Feature Card

**CoS = class of service

Classification and Marking

Classification and marking support and features vary per switch. Table 3-3 indicates which platforms support specific classification and marking features. All switches that support QoS also support classification based on CoS values. Current generation switches that support IP routing also support classification and marking using IP precedence or DSCP values in addition to classification and marking of CoS values.

Table 3-3   *Catalyst Platform QoS Classification and Marking Support*

Catalyst Switch	Classification Marking of Untagged Frames	Marking CoS on Tagged Frames	Marking DSCP on Tagged Frames	Classification Based on DSCP of Ingress Frames
Catalyst 2900XL	Yes	No	No	No
Catalyst 2948G-L3/ 4912G-L3/4232-L3	No	No	No	No, IP precedence only
Catalyst 2950	No, IP precedence only	Yes	Yes	Yes
Catalyst 3500XL	Yes	Yes, on specific models	No	No
Catalyst 3550	Yes	Yes	Yes	Yes
Catalyst 4000 CatOS Family	Yes	Yes	No	No
Catalyst 4000 Cisco IOS Family (Supervisor III and IV)	Yes	Yes	Yes	Yes

Table 3-3   *Catalyst Platform QoS Classification and Marking Support (Continued)*

Catalyst Switch	Classification Marking of Untagged Frames	Marking CoS on Tagged Frames	Marking DSCP on Tagged Frames	Classification Based on DSCP of Ingress Frames
Catalyst 5500	Yes, requires NFFC II	Yes, requires NFFC II	Yes, requires NFFC II	Yes, requires NFFC II
Catalyst 6500	Yes	Yes	Yes	Yes

Policing

Table 3-4 indicates which Catalyst platforms support policing. Feature support and platform implementation of policing varies between each Catalyst switch. Three types of policing exist for Catalyst platforms:

- Individual policing
- Aggregate policing
- Microflow policing

Individual policing applies the bandwidth limit of a policer per interface. For example, an individual policer configured to constrain ingress traffic to 32 kbps limits each applicable interface to 32 kbps on ingress. An aggregate policer configured for the same bandwidth constraint limits the bandwidth collectively among all interfaces. Microflow policing is available on the Catalyst 6500, and it applies bandwidth limits to each *access-control entry* (ACE) of a defined policer. Chapter 8, "QoS Support on the Catalyst 6500," discusses ACEs and microflow policing in more detail.

Each platform has unique support, restrictions, and requirements surrounding policing. Refer to each product chapter for specifics.

Table 3-4   *Catalyst Platform QoS Policing Support*

Cisco Catalyst Platform	Ingress Policing	Egress Policing	Individual Policing	Aggregate Policing	Microflow Policing
Catalyst 2900XL	No	No	No	No	No
Catalyst 2948G-L3/ 4912G-L3/4232-L3	Yes, per-port rate-limiting	Yes, per port rate-limiting and traffic shaping	No	No	No
Catalyst 2950	Yes	No	Yes	No	No
Catalyst 3500XL	No	No	No	No	No
Catalyst 3550	Yes	Yes	Yes	Yes	No
Catalyst 4000 CatOS Family	No	No	No	No	No

continues

Table 3-4   *Catalyst Platform QoS Policing Support (Continued)*

Cisco Catalyst Platform	Ingress Policing	Egress Policing	Individual Policing	Aggregate Policing	Microflow Policing
Catalyst 4000 Cisco IOS Family (Supervisor III and IV)	Yes	Yes	Yes	Yes	No
Catalyst 5500 w/NFFC II	No	No	No	No	No
Catalyst 6500	Yes	No	No	Yes	Yes

Congestion Management

Congestion management is supported on all Catalyst switches that support QoS features. Congestion avoidance and management is achieved via the use of output scheduling using the tail-drop and *Weighted Random Early Detection* (WRED) queuing mechanisms. Chapter 2, "End-to-End QoS: Quality of Service at Layer 3 and Layer 2," explains the difference between congestion management and congestion avoidance, and later chapters explain the tail-drop and WRED queuing mechanisms in the congestion avoidance section of each chapter where applicable. Moreover, only the Catalyst 3550, Catalyst 4000 IOS Family of switches, and the Catalyst 6500 support congestion avoidance.

The nomenclature for output scheduling queues is a follows:

XpYqZt

- *X* indicates the number of strict-priority queues.

- *Y* indicates the number of queues other than strict-priority queues.

- *Z* indicates the configurable thresholds per queue.

For example, 1p3q2t indicates that a switch has an egress output queue with one strict-priority queue and three normal-priority queues each with two configurable thresholds per queue.

Table 3-5 indicates the available output queues per platform.

Table 3-5   *Catalyst Platform Congestion Management Support*

Cisco Catalyst Platform	Output Scheduling	Scheduling Queues
Catalyst 2900XL	Yes	Global 2q1t
Catalyst 2948G-L3/4912G-L3/4232-L3	Yes	4q
Catalyst 2950	Yes	4q
Catalyst 3500XL	Yes	Global 2q1t
Catalyst 3550	Yes	1p3q2t, 4q4t

Table 3-5   *Catalyst Platform Congestion Management Support (Continued)*

Cisco Catalyst Platform	Output Scheduling	Scheduling Queues
Catalyst 4000 CatOS Family	Yes	2q1t
Catalyst 4000 Cisco IOS Family (Supervisor III and IV)	Yes	1p3q1t, 4q1t
Catalyst 5500 w/NFFC II	Yes	1q4t
Catalyst 6500	Yes	Ingress: 1q4t, 1p1q4t, 1p1q, 1p2q1t Egress: 2q2t, 1p2q2t, 1p3q1t, 1p2q1t, 1p1q8t, and 1p1q0t

Material Presentation for Catalyst Switching Platforms

Figure 3-1 shows the general QoS packet-flow architecture for Cisco Catalyst switches. The architecture presents only the standard model for QoS features on each Catalyst platform. However, support for each feature of the architecture is platform dependent and varies significantly for each Catalyst switch.

For each Catalyst platform, this book discusses QoS features using the following flowchart:

- QoS Architecture Overview
- Input Scheduling
- Classification and Marking
- Policing
- Congestion Management and Avoidance
- Sample Configurations and Case Studies
- Summary

As indicated in the Tables 3-1 through 3-5, not every Cisco Catalyst platform supports all the QoS components and features. For those platforms, the QoS component is omitted or discussed as an unsupported feature. Chapter 10, "End-to-End QoS Case Studies," concludes with comprehensive case studies using several Cisco Catalyst switches and QoS features.

Figure 3-1   *General Catalyst QoS Packet-Flow Architecture*

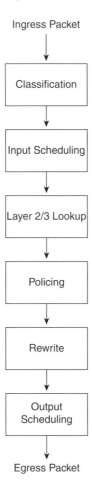

General Catalyst Switch CoS Architecture

Ingress Packet

Classification

Input Scheduling

Layer 2/3 Lookup

Policing

Rewrite

Output
Scheduling

Egress Packet

QoS Support on the Catalyst 2900XL and 3500XL

Specific models of the Catalyst 2900XL and 3500XL support QoS classification and congestion management. Ingress packet CoS values and configured port priorities exclusively determine classification of ingress frames for placement into either a low-priority or high-priority global transmit queue. The two global transmit queues with priority scheduling create the congestion management mechanism. The following sections discuss these QoS features with detailed overviews, configuration guidelines, and examples.

Catalyst 2900XL Product Family Delineation

QoS support on the Catalyst 2900XL and 3500XL platforms is software and model dependent. For the 2900XL, the original-edition models do not support QoS features, including the uplink modules for the Catalyst 2916M. All standard- and enterprise-edition models do support QoS features. Table 3-6 indicates which 2900XL models support QoS features. All models of the 3500XL support QoS features. In addition, the Catalyst 3524XL-PWR-XL and the 3548XL support CoS reclassification. This QoS feature is not available on other 3500XL platforms.

Table 3-6   *QoS Support by Model of 2900XL*

Catalyst 2900XL/ 3500XL Model	Description	QoS Support
WS-C2908-XL	8-port 10/100BASE-TX switch	No
WS-C2912-XL-A/EN	12-port 10/100BASE-TX switch	Yes
WS-C2912MF-XL	12-port 100BASE-FX switch	Yes
WS-C2916M-XL	16-port 10/100BASE-TX switch + 2 uplink slots	No
WS-C2924-XL	24-port 10/100BASE-TX switch	No
WS-C2924C-XL	22-port 10/100BASE-TX + 2-port 100BASE-FX switch	No
WS-C2924-XL-A/EN	24-port 10/100BASE-TX switch	Yes
WS-C2924C-XL-A/EN	22-port 10/100BASE-TX switch + 2-port 100BASE-FX switch	Yes
WS-C2924M-XL-A/EN	24-port 10/100BASE-TX switch + 2 uplink slots	Yes
WS-C2924M-XL-EN-DC	24-port 10/100BASE-TX switch + 2 uplink slots (DC power)	Yes

Catalyst 2900XL and 3500XL QoS Architectural Overview

The Catalyst 2900XL and 3500XL switches are limited to QoS features that suit access layer switches. These features include classification, marking, and congestion management via the use of output scheduling. Because of these features, the 2900XL and 3500XL fit well into an end-to-end QoS design with core switches. Figure 3-2 shows a sample network deploying access layer QoS features with comprehensive QoS features in the core.

Figure 3-2   *Network Topology Using Catalyst 3524XLs*

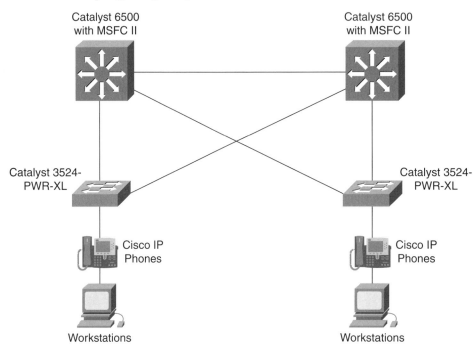

Figure 3-3 shows the basic QoS architecture model for the Catalyst 2900XL and 3500XL discussed in the following sections.

Software Requirements

For QoS feature support, the 2900XL and 3500XL require Cisco IOS Software Release 12.0(5)XP or higher. The 3524-PWR-XL and the 3548XL require 12.0(5)XU or higher for the reclassification of class of CoS values in frames.

Input Scheduling

The Catalyst 2900XL and 3500XL do not perform input scheduling as ingress packets are immediately copied to a global, shared memory buffer. As long as the packet-forwarding rate of the switch is not exceeded, input congestion is not critical to implementing QoS. The packet-forwarding rates of the Catalyst 2900XL and the Catalyst 3500XL are 1.6 Gbps and 5.0 Gbps, respectively.

Figure 3-3   *Basic QoS Architecture for the Catalyst 2900XLs and 3500XLs Switches*

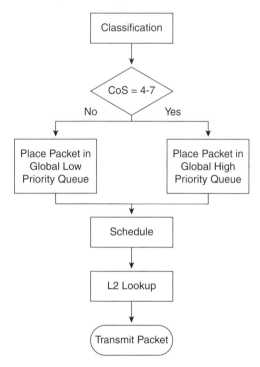

Classification/Reclassification

The Catalyst 2900XL and 3500XL switches both support classification of untagged frames. Two models of the Catalyst 3500XL switch, the Catalyst 3524-PWR-XL and the Catalyst 3548XL switches, support marking of ingress tagged frames. Classification and marking is configurable only on a per-port basis, and each port may be configured with a unique CoS value to be classified.

To configure a Catalyst 2900XL and 3500XL for classification or marking of frames, use the following interface command:

```
switchport priority {default default-priority-id | extend {cos value | none |
trust} | override}
```

- The *default-priority-id* parameter is the CoS value to be assigned to untagged ingress frames.

- The **extend** option is to configure the 802.1p trust configuration of the connected appliance on the P1 port of the IP Phone. For example, a Cisco IP Phone can be configured to trust or reclassify frames received on its P1 port.

- The **override** option is used to mark tagged frames with the *default-priority-id*. Only the Catalyst 3524-PWR-XL and the Catalyst 3548XL switches support this marking feature.

Example 3-1 shows a Catalyst 3548XL switch port configured to classify untagged frames with a CoS value of 2.

Example 3-1   *Catalyst 3548XL Switch Port Configured to Classify Untagged Frames*

```
Switch#show running-config
Building configuration...

Current configuration:
(text deleted)
!
interface FastEthernet0/48
 switchport priority default 2
 spanning-tree portfast
 (text deleted)
end
```

Example 3-2 shows a Catalyst 3524-PWR-XL switch port configured for a voice VLAN. In Cisco IOS Software Release 12.0.x, voice VLAN ports must be configured as trunk ports.

Example 3-2   *Catalyst 3548XL Switch Port for Voice VLANs*

```
Switch#show running-config
Building configuration...

Current configuration:
(text deleted)
!
interface FastEthernet0/24
 switchport trunk encapsulation dot1q
 switchport trunk native vlan 2
 switchport mode trunk
 switchport voice vlan 70
 spanning-tree portfast
 (text deleted)
end
```

NOTE   The Catalyst 2900XL and 3500XL software configuration for voice VLANs differs from the Catalyst switches that run Cisco IOS Software Release 12.1, such as the Catalyst 4000 Supervisor III and IV. Cisco IOS Software Release 12.1 does not require voice VLAN ports to be configured as trunks.

Congestion Management

The 2900XL and 3500XL switches use a shared memory buffer system because each individual port does not have its own output queue. This shared memory buffer is divided into two global transmit queues. Each ingress packet is placed into one of two global transmit queues based on CoS value for tagged frames and CoS classification for untagged frames. One of the transmit queues is designated for packets with a CoS value of 0 to 3, and the other transmit queue is reserved for packets with a CoS value of 4 to 7. The queues use a 100-percent threshold value. These queues are not configurable for different CoS values or thresholds. This queue scheme creates a logical high-priority and low-priority queuing mechanism. Priority scheduling is applied such that the high-priority queue is consistently serviced before the low-priority queue. The use of two global transmit queues based on CoS value is default behavior and cannot be altered. As a result, no global configuration is required to enable QoS output scheduling.

NOTE	Untagged packets that are classified with a CoS value transmitted on trunk ports are appropriately tagged with an 802.1q header with the respective CoS. For packets transmitted on nontrunk ports, the untagged classification only determines which queue the frame is placed in for egress transmission.

Case Study: Classification and Output Scheduling on Cisco Catalyst 3500XL Switches

To demonstrate classification and output scheduling on the Catalyst 3500XL series, a Catalyst 3524-PWR-XL was set up with two Cisco 7960 IP Phones, a Call Manager, and a traffic generator connected to three Fast Ethernet ports and a Gigabit Ethernet port, respectively. Figure 3-4 shows this topology. Two trials were conducted taking voice quality statistical measurements from each IP Phone based on a 1-minute, G7.11 voice call between IP Phone 1 and 2. To create traffic congestion, the traffic generator attached to Gigabit Ethernet port was sending multicast at line rate with a CoS value of 0. The multicast traffic was flooded to all ports, including the Fast Ethernet IP Phones, causing output congestion.

Figure 3-4 *Catalyst 3500XL Case Study Network Diagram*

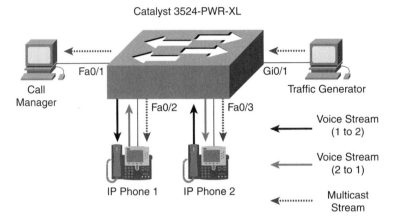

The Catalyst 3524XL switch was running software version 12.0(5)WC5 for the trial. The configuration only included voice VLANs on the Cisco IP Phone ports. The remaining port configuration of the switch was default. Example 3-3 shows the relevant configuration.

Example 3-3 *Catalyst 3548XL Switch Port Configuration for Case Study*

```
Switch#show running-config
Building configuration...

Current configuration:
(text deleted)

interface FastEthernet0/1
  switchport access vlan 70
!
interface FastEthernet0/2
 switchport trunk encapsulation dot1q
 switchport trunk native vlan 2
 switchport mode trunk
 switchport voice vlan 70
 spanning-tree portfast
!
interface FastEthernet0/3
 switchport trunk encapsulation dot1q
 switchport trunk native vlan 2
 switchport mode trunk
 switchport voice vlan 70
 spanning-tree portfast
!
(text deleted)

interface GigabitEthernet0/1
  switchport access vlan 70
(text deleted)
end
```

The variant in the two trials was the CoS value placed on the telephony frames between the IP Phones. With a CoS value of 0, the telephony stream was treated with a low priority (the same priority as the multicast traffic). With a CoS value of 5, the telephony stream was treated with a high priority. Table 3-7 summarizes the number of frames transmitted and lost as well as jitter from each trial.

Table 3-7   *QoS Trial Results on Catalyst 3524-PWR-XL*

Trial	Total Frames Transmitted (Phone 1/2)	No. of Receive Lost Frames (Phone 1/2)	Maximum Recorded Jitter (Phone1/2)
CoS = 0 on voice stream	3100/3110	1551/1549	51/49 ms
CoS = 5 on voice stream	3104/3106	0/0	51/49 ms

As indicated in Table 3-7, the Catalyst 3524XL did not drop a single frame due to output congestion on the IP Phone ports for packets with a CoS value of 5. Similar results are achievable with multiple Cisco IP Phones in a campus network using the Catalyst 2900XL and 3500XL. The jitter did not vary between the trials because all Catalyst switches drop frames under congestion and only buffer a few frames. The maximum recorded jitter is around 50 ms, which is above the recommended 30 ms for *Voice over IP* (VoIP). Only the first few frames of the IP flow recorded jitter near 50 ms.

Summary

The Catalyst 2900XL and 3500XL suit basic QoS needs for an access layer switch. If additional features such as policing and classification based on DSCP are required, network designers should consider the Catalyst 2950 and 3550 switches for use as an access layer switch. You can summarize QoS feature support on the Catalyst 2900XL and 3500XL switches as follows:

- No support for input scheduling.
- Classification based on CoS only; no support for classification based on IP precedence or DSCP.
- Two global queues for high-priority and low-priority traffic.
- No configurable CoS mapping to queues or queue threshold.
- Ports are trusted by default.
- Untagged frames are mapped to high-priority or low-priority queues based on configured classification CoS value.
- The Catalyst 3548XL and 3524-PWR-XL support reclassification of tagged frames.

QoS Support on the Catalyst 4000 CatOS Family of Switches

Catalyst 4000 CatOS switches provide for QoS classification and congestion management solely based on CoS values. The Catalyst 4000 IOS switches, discussed in Chapter 7, support a wider range of QoS. For the Catalyst 4000 CatOS switches, a high- and low-priority transmit port queue with round-robin scheduling accomplish congestion management. The Catalyst 4000 CatOS switches do not support policing or input scheduling. The following sections discuss the Catalyst 4000 CatOS QoS features with detailed overviews, configuration guidelines, and examples.

Catalyst 4000 Product Family Delineation

This section covers the Catalyst 4000 CatOS Family of switches. As discussed in the introduction to this chapter, the Catalyst 4000 Cisco IOS switches, the Catalyst 4000 CatOS switches, and the Layer 3 services module each have unique QoS feature support. The Catalyst 4000 Cisco IOS switches and the Layer 3 services module are covered in Chapter 7. Table 3-8 summarizes the Catalyst 4000 switches into the CatOS or IOS category. This chapter applies to the Catalyst 4000 switches that run CatOS Software.

Table 3-8 *Catalyst 4000 CatOS Versus Cisco IOS Software Platform Support*

Catalyst 4000 Model	Family	Description	Software
Catalyst 2948G	Catalyst 4000	48-port 10/100BASE-TX switch ports + 2 1000BASE-X GBIC* switch ports	CatOS
Catalyst 2980G	Catalyst 4000	80-port 10/100BASE-TX switch ports + 2 1000BASE-X GBIC switch ports	CatOS
Catalyst 2980G-A	Catalyst 4000	80-port 10/100BASE-TX switch ports + 2 1000BASE-X GBIC switch ports	CatOS
Catalyst 2948G-L3	Catalyst G-L3	48-port 10/100BASE-TX + 2 1000BASE-X GBIC Layer 3 switch	IOS
Catalyst 4003 + WS-X4012 Supervisor I Engine	Catalyst 4000	3-slot modular chassis + 2 1000BASE-X GBIC ports on Layer 2 supervisor	CatOS
Catalyst 4006 + WS-X4013 Supervisor II Engine	Catalyst 4000	6-slot modular chassis + 2 1000BASE-X GBIC ports on Layer 2 supervisor	CatOS
Catalyst 4006 + WS-X4014 Supervisor III Engine	Catalyst 4000	6-slot modular chassis + 2 1000BASE-X GBIC ports on Layer 2/3 supervisor	IOS
Catalyst 4006 + WS-X4515 Supervisor IV Engine	Catalyst 4000	6-slot modular chassis + 2 1000BASE-X GBIC ports on Layer 2/3 supervisor	IOS
Catalyst WS-X4232-L3 Layer 3 Services Module	Catalyst G-L3	Layer 3 router module for Catalyst 4003 and 4006 chassis with Supervisor I or II Engine	IOS

Table 3-8   *Catalyst 4000 CatOS Versus Cisco IOS Software Platform Support (Continued)*

Catalyst 4000 Model	Family	Description	Software
Catalyst 4503 + WS-X4013 Supervisor II Engine	Catalyst 4000	3-slot modular chassis + 2 1000BASE-X GBIC ports on Layer 2 supervisor	CatOS
Catalyst 4503 + WS-X4014 Supervisor III Engine	Catalyst 4000	3-slot modular chassis + 2 1000BASE-X GBIC ports on Layer 2/3 supervisor	IOS
Catalyst 4503 + WS-X4515 Supervisor IV Engine	Catalyst 4000	3-slot modular chassis + 2 1000BASE-X GBIC ports on Layer 2/3 supervisor	IOS
Catalyst 4506 + WS-X4013 Supervisor III Engine	Catalyst 4000	6-slot modular chassis + 2 1000BASE-X GBIC ports on Layer 2 supervisor	CatOS
Catalyst 4506 + WS-X4014 Supervisor III Engine	Catalyst 4000	6-slot modular chassis + 2 1000BASE-X GBIC ports on Layer 2/3 supervisor	IOS
Catalyst 4506 + WS-X4515 Supervisor IV Engine	Catalyst 4000	6-slot modular chassis + 2 1000BASE-X GBIC ports on Layer 2/3 supervisor	IOS
Catalyst 4507R + WS-X4515 Supervisor IV Engine	Catalyst 4000	7-slot modular chassis + 2 1000BASE-X GBIC ports on Layer 2/3 supervisor	IOS
Catalyst 4840G	Catalyst G-L3	40-port 10/100BASE-TX + 1000BASE-X GBIC Layer 3 server load-balancing switch	IOS
Catalyst 4908G-L3	Catalyst 4000	8 1000BASE-X GBIC Layer 3 switch	CatOS
Catalyst 4912G-L3	Catalyst G-L3	8 1000BASE-X GBIC switch ports	IOS

*GBIC Gigabit Interface Converter

Catalyst 4000 CatOS Family of Switches QoS Architectural Overview

The Catalyst 4000 CatOS switches support only QoS classification, marking, and congestion management. Classification and marking is based on the CoS value of 802.1q frames and port trust. Using two transmit queues for output scheduling achieves congestion management of egress traffic. Input scheduling is limited to *first-in, first-out* (FIFO) ingress queuing only. Figure 3-5 shows the basic QoS model for the Catalyst CatOS switches.

Software Requirements

The Catalyst 4000 CatOS switches require CatOS Software version 5.2(1) or higher for QoS feature support.

Enabling QoS Features on Catalyst 4000 CatOS Switches

QoS must be globally enabled on CatOS switches before classification, marking, and output scheduling configurations are applied. To enable QoS on the Catalyst 4000 CatOS switches, enter the following command:

```
set qos {enable | disable}
```

Figure 3-5   *Basic QoS Architecture for the Catalyst Cat4000 CatOS Switches*

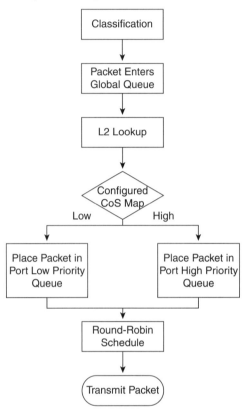

Example 3-4 shows a user enabling QoS on a CatOS switch.

Example 3-4   *Enabling QoS Features on a Catalyst 4000 CatOS Switch*

```
Console> (enable) set qos enable
QoS is enabled.
Console> (enable)
```

Input Scheduling

Similar to other access layer switches, the Catalyst 4000 CatOS switches performs only FIFO Queuing of ingress packets. For line-module ports that are nonblocking, FIFO Queuing does not pose an issue because nonblocking line-module ports can deliver traffic to the switching fabric at line rate. Ports that are oversubscribed to the switching fabric are also referred to as *blocking ports*. Oversubscribed ports share bandwidth and data transmit contention in groups of two to eight ports depending on line module. Campus network design must consider oversubscribed ports very carefully on the Catalyst 4000 because of the lack of input scheduling. Furthermore, when using the nonblocking modules, consider aligning the front panels to minimize oversubscription. For example, avoid placing workstations utilizing real-time voice and video applications on the same group of ports that share oversubscribed bandwidth with high-traffic servers and network appliances. The product release notes contain detailed information on which ports share bandwidth. Moreover, all line-module ports support 802.1x flow control for constraining host traffic. 802.1x flow control is useful in limiting traffic for hosts connected to oversubscribed ports.

Table 3-9 lists the available line modules at the time of publication and denotes whether the ports are blocking or nonblocking. Several line modules are both nonblocking and blocking depending on the front-panel port. The table also describes how the ports are subscribed to the switching fabric.

Table 3-9   *Catalyst 4000 Line Modules Architecture*

Module	Ethernet Ports (Media Type)	Architecture to Switch Fabric
WS-U4504-FX-MT	4 100BASE-FX (MTRJ)	Nonblocking.
WS-X4012	2 1000BASE-X (GBIC)	Nonblocking.
WS-X4013	2 1000BASE-X (GBIC)	Nonblocking.
WS-X4014	2 1000BASE-X (GBIC)	Nonblocking.
WS-X4515	2 1000BASE-X (GBIC)	Nonblocking.
WS-X4124-FX-MT	24 100BASE-FX (MTRJ)	Nonblocking.
WS-X4148-FX-MT	48 100BASE-FX (MTRJ)	Nonblocking.
WS-X4148-RJ21	48-port 10/100BASE-TX (RJ21)	Nonblocking.
WS-X4148-RJ45	48-port 10/100BASE-TX (RJ45)	Nonblocking.
WS-X4148-RJ45V	48-port 10/100BASE-TX with Inline Power (RJ45)	Nonblocking.
WS-X4306-GB	6 1000BASE-X (GBIC)	Nonblocking.
WS-X4232-GB-RJ	32-port 10/100BASE-TX (RJ45) + 2 1000BASE-X (GBIC)	Nonblocking.
WS-X4232-L3	32, L2 10/100BASE-TX L2 (RJ45) + 2 L3 1000BASE-X (GBIC)	32 10/100BASE-TX ports are nonblocking.
WS-X4412-2GB-T	12-port 1000BASE-T (RJ45) + 2 1000BASE-X (GBIC)	The 2 1000BASE-X ports are nonblocking. The 1000BASE-T ports are group 3 front-panel ports to a 1-gigabit switch fabric connection.
WS-X4418-2GB	18 1000BASE-X (GBIC)	Front-panel ports 1 and 2 are nonblocking. Ports 3 through 18 are grouped 4 front-panel 1000BASE-X ports to a 1-gigabit switch fabric connection.
WS-X4424-GB-RJ45	24-port 10/100/1000BASE-T (RJ45)	Each consecutive group of 4 ports is connected to a 1-gigabit switch fabric connection.

continues

Table 3-9   *Catalyst 4000 Line Modules Architecture (Continued)*

Module	Ethernet Ports (Media Type)	Architecture to Switch Fabric
WS-X4448-GB-LX	48-port 1000BASE-LX (SFP)	Each consecutive group of 8 ports is connected to a 1-gigabit switch fabric connection.
WS-X4448-GB-RJ45	48-port 10/100/1000BASE-T (RJ45)	Each consecutive group of 8 ports is connected to a 1-gigabit switch fabric connection.

Classification, Marking, and Trusting

The Catalyst 4000 CatOS switches are unable to differentiate between trusted and untrusted ports. As a result, the Catalyst 4000 CatOS switches consider all ports trusted, and the switch does not alter the CoS value for any Ethernet 802.1q tagged frames. System administrators need to be aware of servers, network appliances, or workstations that may be inappropriately marking CoS values in transmitted 802.1q tagged frames because the incorrectly marked frames could effect high-priority traffic such as voice or video.

Classifying Untagged Frames

The Catalyst 4000 CatOS switch may mark untagged frames with a default CoS value. The default CoS value is a global parameter applied to all ports for untagged frames received by the switch. This default CoS value marking technique cannot be applied to selective ports or selective frames. Marking is strictly a global parameter for untagged frames. To configure the default CoS value for untagged frames, enter the following command:

    set qos defaultcos default-cos-value

default-cos-value indicates the CoS value to be marked on untagged frames.

Example 3-5 shows a user configuring a global default CoS value.

Example 3-5   *Defining Default CoS Value on Catalyst 4000 CatOS Switch*

```
Console> (enable) set qos defaultcos 5
qos defaultcos set to 5
```

NOTE   Extended trust configuration is not supported on the Catalyst 4000 CatOS switches.

The Catalyst 4000 CatOS switches support only 802.1q trunking; *Inter-Switch Link* (ISL) trunking is not supported. The Catalyst 4000 Supervisor III and IV Engine both support ISL on existing linecards with a few exceptions.

Congestion Management

Congestion management is handled through the use of output scheduling. The Catalyst 4000 CatOS Software manages output scheduling by the use of a per-port, two-queues, one-threshold (2q1t) system. Packets are mapped to a logical high- or low- priority output queue depending on the switch QoS configuration and CoS value in the frame. There is only one threshold setting, 100 percent; therefore, the only threshold configuration is to tail drop packets when a queue is full. Packets are removed from the queues round-robin with each queue getting serviced 1:1. Because packet flows with higher CoS values of less bandwidth are generally mapped to one specific queue, those packets are less likely to be dropped due to output congestion with the lower-priority, high-bandwidth packet flows.

To configure the CoS values to map to specific queues and verify the configuration, enter the following commands:

```
set qos map port_type q# threshold# cos cos_list
show qos info [runtime | config]
```

For the Catalyst 4000 CatOS switches, the *port_type* is always 2q1t with a *threshold#* of 1. *q#* identifies the queue to map the CoS value to, and the *cos_list* identifies what queue frames of specific CoS values are mapped. The *cos_list* must be configured in pairs: 0-1, 2-3, 4-5, and 6-7. Because QoS configurations are saved to the *nonvolatile random-access memory* (NVRAM) configuration at run time, the **runtime** and **config** options have no significance and both display the current and saved configuration. Not mapping CoS values after enabling QoS may result in unexpected performance because all CoS values map to the same transmit queue by default when QoS is enabled. Example 3-6 shows a user configuring and verifying the CoS mapping.

Example 3-6   *Configuring Catalyst 4000 QoS CoS Mapping*

```
Console> (enable) set qos map 2q1t 2 1 cos 4-7
Qos tx priority queue and threshold mapped to cos successfully.

Console> (enable) show qos info runtime
Run time setting of QoS:
QoS is enabled
All ports have 2 transmit queues with 1 drop thresholds (2q1t).
Default CoS = 0
Queue and Threshold Mapping:
Queue Threshold CoS
----- --------- ---------------
1      1         0 1 2 3
2      1         4 5 6 7
```

The Catalyst 4000 CatOS switch records the number of frames tail dropped as a result of the transmit port queue being full. The counters record the tail-drop frames as txQueueNotAvailable in the **show counters** *mod/port*. In addition, both the *out-lost* counter from the **show mac** [*mod*[/*port*]] command and the *Xmit-Err* counter from the **show port** [*mod*[/*port*]] command include the txQueueNotAvailable counter. Note that the *out-lost* and *Xmit-Err* are not inclusively counters for txQueueNotAvailable and increment for other packet counters as well. Example 3-7 shows some extrapolated output from the **show counters** [*mod*[/*port*]], **show port** [*mod*[/*port*]]**,** and **show mac** [*mod*[/*port*]] commands from the QoS case study later in the chapter .

Example 3-7   **show counters**, **show port**, *and* **show mac** *Command Output Excerpts*

```
Console> (enable) show counters 5/1
(text deleted)
23 txQueueNotAvailable      = 19422994
(text deleted)
Console> (enable) show mac 5/1
(text deleted)
MAC     Dely-Exced MTU-Exced  In-Discard Lrn-Discrd In-Lost    Out-Lost
------- ---------- ---------- ---------- ---------- ---------- ----------
 5/1             0          0          0          0          0   19422994
(text deleted)
Console> (enable) show port 5/1
(text deleted)
Port  Align-Err  FCS-Err    Xmit-Err   Rcv-Err    UnderSize
----- ---------- ---------- ---------- ---------- ----------
 5/1          -          0   19422994          0          0
(text deleted)
```

Auxiliary VLANs

For VoIP appliances, such as the Cisco IP Phone, the 2q1t system works well. IP Phones should be configured in conjunction with auxiliary VLANs. Through the use of *Cisco Discovery Protocol* (CDP) packets, the IP Phone is informed of the auxiliary VLAN ID to use in sending tagged frames.

To configure a port for an auxiliary VLAN for tagged traffic, use the following command:

```
set port auxiliaryvlan mod [/ports] {vlan | untagged | none}
```

The **vlan** option specifies the VLAN ID of the auxiliary VLAN. The **untagged** option tells the port to use untagged frames for the auxiliary VLAN, and **none** disables the auxiliary VLAN configuration on the port.

A LAN IP Phone conversation based on *pulse code modulation* (PCM) (G.711) compression uses only 83 kbps, far below the output rate of an Ethernet port operating at 10 Mbps. Cisco IP Phones connect at 100 Mbps full-duplex by default. Mapping only VoIP frames exclusively to a single queue based on CoS value allows voice traffic to flow egress from the output queue without packet loss even under output port loads above line rate.

Case Study: Output Scheduling on the Catalyst 4000 Series Switches

To illustrate the output scheduling behavior on the Catalyst 4000 Family, a Catalyst 4006 with a Supervisor II Engine running CatOS Software version 6.3.7 is connected to two Cisco 7960 IP Phones, a Cisco Call Manager server, and a traffic generator connected to three Fast Ethernet ports and a Gigabit Ethernet port as shown in Figure 3-6.

Figure 3-6   *Catalyst 4000 Case Study Network Diagram*

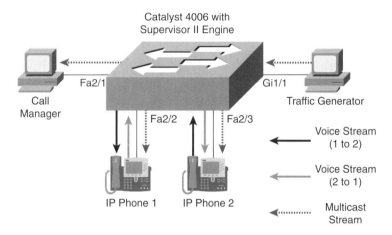

Two trials were conducted taking voice quality statistical measurements from each IP Phone based on a 1-minute, G7.11 voice call between IP Phone 1 and 2. To create traffic congestion, the traffic generator attached to the Gigabit Ethernet port was sending multicast at line rate with a CoS value of 0. The multicast traffic was flooded to all ports, including the Fast Ethernet ports connected to the IP Phones. This flooding of traffic led to output congestion.

The switch port configuration only included auxiliary VLANs on the Cisco IP Phone ports. The remaining port configuration of the switch was default. Example 3-8 outlines the relevant configuration.

Example 3-8   *Catalyst 4000 CatOS Switch Configuration for Case Study*

```
begin
(text deleted)

#qos
set qos enable

(text deleted)
#module 1 : 2-port 1000BaseX Supervisor
set vlan 70   1/1
set trunk 1/1  off dot1q 1-1005
set spantree portfast    1/1 enable
```

continues

Example 3-8 *Catalyst 4000 CatOS Switch Configuration for Case Study (Continued)*

```
set port channel 1/1 mode off
(text deleted)
#module 2 : 48-port Inline Power Module
set vlan 70    2/1
set port auxiliaryvlan 2/2 70
set port auxiliaryvlan 2/3 70
set trunk 2/1  off dot1q 1-1005
set trunk 2/2  off dot1q 1-1005
set trunk 2/3  off dot1q 1-1005
set spantree portfast    2/1-3 enable
set port channel 2/1-3 mode off
(text deleted)
```

QoS was enabled for both trials. In the first trial, however, QoS was enabled but the CoS mapping was left as default. As a result, frames of CoS values 0 through 7 mapped to the same output queue. In the second trial, frames with a CoS value of 4 to 7 were mapped to queue 1, and the remaining frames were mapped to queue 0. Example 3-9 shows the QoS configuration for each trial.

Example 3-9 *Catalyst 4000 QoS CoS Mapping Configuration for Each Trial of Case Study*

```
! Trial 1:

Console> (enable) show qos info runtime
Run time setting of QoS:
QoS is enabled
All ports have 2 transmit queues with 1 drop thresholds (2q1t).
Default CoS = 0
Queue and Threshold Mapping:
Queue Threshold CoS
----- --------- ---------------
1     1         0 1 2 3 4 5 6 7
2     1
! Trial 2:
Console> (enable) show qos info runtime
Run time setting of QoS:
QoS is enabled
All ports have 2 transmit queues with 1 drop thresholds (2q1t).
Default CoS = 0
Queue and Threshold Mapping:
Queue Threshold CoS
----- --------- ---------------
1     1         0 1 2 3
2     1         4 5 6 7
```

As Table 3-10 indicates, the voice stream statistical measurements clearly showed significant frame loss and poor voice quality when all frames shared the same output queue. When the frames were output scheduled appropriately, no loss of frames occurred and voice quality was excellent. The maximum jitter was well within the recommended boundary of less than 30 ms.

Table 3-10 *QoS Trial Results on Catalyst 4006 with Supervisor II Engine*

Trial	Total Frames Transmitted (Phone 1/2)	No. of Receive Lost Frames (Phone 1/2)	Maximum Recorded Jitter (Phone1/2)
1 queue	3245/3300	2536/2459	20/22
2 queues	3130/3240	0/0	15/9

Summary

The Catalyst 4000 CatOS Family of switches suits basic QoS needs for an access layer switch. If additional features such as policing and classification based on DSCP are required, network designers need to consider the Catalyst 4000/4500 Cisco IOS Family of switches using the Supervisor Engine III or IV. The Catalyst 4000/4500 Cisco IOS Family switches support classification based on DSCP or CoS, ingress and egress policing, and output scheduling based on a 1p3q1t or 4q1t port queuing system. You can summarize the QoS feature support on the Catalyst 4000 CatOS Family of switches as follows:

- No support for input scheduling.
- Classification based on CoS only; no support for classification based on IP precedence or DSCP.
- Extended trust options are not supported.
- Output ports have two queues with one threshold (2q1t).
- Frames are tail dropped when queue is full.
- Tail dropped frames are recorded as txQueueNotAvailable in the **show counters** *mod/port*.
- CoS mapping to queues are configurable in pairs: 0-1, 2-3, 4-5, and 6-7.
- Ports are trusted by default irrespective of the QoS global configuration.
- The queue threshold is not configurable.
- Untagged frames can be mapped to the queue based on configured CoS value.
- Tagged frames cannot have CoS values rewritten.
- Layer 3 services module can be added to Catalyst 4000 CatOS switch for policing of IP routed traffic between VLANs. However, the Layer 3 services module rewrites ingress CoS to zero.

In summary, the Catalyst 2900XL, 3500XL, and Catalyst 4000 CatOS Family of switches only support a subset of QoS features compared to the Catalyst 2950, 3550, 4000 IOS, and 6500 Family of switches.

The available QoS features depend on the platform; they also depend on whether the platform supports IP routing. The Catalyst 3550, Catalyst 4000 Cisco IOS Software Family, Catalyst 5500 with RSM or RSFC, and the Catalyst 6000/6500 with MSM or MSFC I/II support IP routing. Other platforms may support Layer 3 QoS features, such as classification based on DSCP and marking of IP precedence; however these platforms do not actually support routing of IP frames.

For a list of the QoS features supported by each platform, see Tables 3-1 through 3-5.

CHAPTER 4

QoS Support on the Catalyst 5000 Family of Switches

This chapter discusses QoS feature support on the Catalyst 5000 Family of switches. The Catalyst 5000 Family of switches supports only a small subset of QoS features. Furthermore, QoS feature support on these switches has important hardware and configuration restrictions. This chapter discusses all the restrictions and configuration requirements for implementing QoS on the Catalyst 5000 Family of switches and provides command references, examples, and a case study. Specifically, this chapter covers the following topics:

- QoS Architectural Overview
- Enabling Qos Features
- Input Scheduling
- Classification
- Marking
- Congestion Avoidance
- Case Study

Upon completion of this chapter, you will understand the restrictions surrounding QoS feature support on the Catalyst 5000 Family of switches and be able to configure the switches for packet classification, marking, and congestion avoidance.

Catalyst 5000 Family of Switches QoS Architectural Overview

The Catalyst 5000 Family of switches forwards frames strictly based on MAC address and VLAN ID. To route frames with a Catalyst 5000, the switch requires a router module, either a *Route Switch Module* (RSM) or a *Router Switch Feature Card* (RSFC). Catalyst 5000 switches with a *NetFlow Feature Card* or *NetFlow Feature Card II* (NFFC or NFFC II, respectively), router module, and specific line modules can perform *multilayer switching* (MLS). MLS enables the RSM or RSFC to offload the Layer 2 rewrite functionality of routers to hardware components on the supervisor engine and line cards. In relation to QoS functionality, MLS-enabled switches handle QoS packet rewrites slightly different than do switches without MLS enabled. Because of the system architecture deployed on the

Catalyst 5000 Family of switches, these switches support the following QoS features in specific hardware configurations:

- Classification of untagged frames

- Trusting of tagged frames

- *Class of service* (CoS) rewrite based on destination MAC and VLAN ID or ingress port

- CoS and *type of service* (ToS) rewrite based on *access-control entries* (ACEs)

- Output scheduling using one queue with four thresholds

For supporting QoS in network designs, especially networks delivering *Voice over IP* (VoIP) or using *DiffServ codepoint* (DSCP) for differentiated service, the preferred switches are the Catalyst 6500 Family of switches, the Catalyst 4000 IOS Family of switches, the Catalyst 3550, or the Catalyst 2950. By today's standards, the Catalyst 5000 Family of switches is a legacy product and does not support the features necessary for end-to-end QoS implementations. Furthermore, Cisco Systems, Inc., no longer sells the Catalyst 5000 Family of switches. Nonetheless, a large number of networks still use the Catalyst 5000 Family of switches; therefore, network designs need to exploit the QoS features available on these switches. Figure 4-1 illustrates a sample network design using a Catalyst 5500 switch in the core layer. The Catalyst 5500 switches include a router module for Layer 3 routing and the RSMs utilize HSRP for router redundancy. The Catalyst 5500 switches connect Layer 2 to the Catalyst 4000 CatOS switches used as access layer switches. Generally, legacy networks deploying Catalyst 5500's only utilize Layer 3 routing in the core. As a result, these networks only connect Layer 2 to access layer switches and perform no routing of traffic on the access layer switches. Although not shown on the diagram, several VLANs are deployed in this topology to minimize broadcast domains.

Figure 4-1   *Sample Network Topology Using Catalyst 5000 Switches*

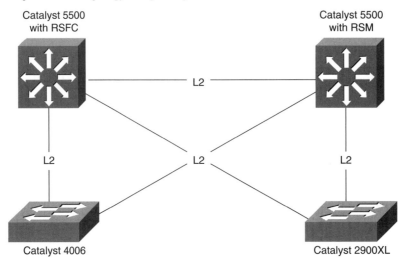

Catalyst 5500 with RSFC

Catalyst 5500 with RSM

L2

L2   L2   L2

Catalyst 4006

Catalyst 2900XL

Software Requirements

The Catalyst 5000 Family of switches requires CatOS software version 5.1(1) or higher for QoS feature support. The Catalyst 5000 Family of switches runs CatOS software up to CatOS software version 6.4. The Catalyst 5000 Family of switches does not support Native IOS software or the CatOS software version 7 train.

MLS changes the behavior of QoS on the Catalyst 5000 Family of switches. MLS support on the Catalyst 5000 Family of switches requires a NFFC and a Cisco router running Cisco IOS Software version 11.3 WA, 12.0, or higher. The recommended routers for deploying MLS are the RSMs or RSFCs. The RSM is a line module for the Catalyst 5000 Family, and the RSFC is a daughter card for the Catalyst 5000 Supervisor IIG and IIIG engines. External routers including the Cisco 3600, 7200, and 7500 support MLS as well and are alternatives to using the RSM or RSFC for MLS.

Hardware Requirements

Only a limited subset of the Catalyst 5000 Family of switches supports QoS features. To enable these QoS features, an NFFC II must be present on the supervisor engine. EARL 3 and NFFC II are the same hardware component, and the names are used interchangeably. EARL is an acronym for the Layer 2 forwarding logic on the supervisor engine and exists in several versions across all the Catalyst supervisor engines of the Catalyst 5000 Family.

The NFFC II enables QoS support for classification, marking, and congestion avoidance. The Supervisor IIIG and IIG include an NFFC II, whereas specific models of the Supervisor Engine III include the NFFC II. Table 4-1 illustrates which supervisor engines include an NFFC II. The Supervisor Engine IIIs without an NFFC II are upgradeable to include an NFFC II.

Table 4-1   *NetFlow Feature Card II to Supervisor Engine Matrix*

Model Number	Supervisor Engine	NetFlow Feature Card	EARL Version	EARL Subtype Model	QoS Feature Support
WS-X5550	Supervisor IIIG	NFFC II	EARL 3	WS-F5531	Yes
WS-X5540	Supervisor IIG	NFFC II	EARL 3	WS-F5531	Yes
WS-X5534	Supervisor IIIF	n/a	EARL 1++	WS-F5520	No
WS-X5530-E3	Supervisor III (NFFC II)	NFFC II	EARL 3	WS-F5531	Yes
WS-X5530-E3A	Supervisor III (NFFC II-A)	NFFC II-A	EARL 3	WS-F5531A	Yes
WS-X5530-E2	Supervisor III (NFFC)	NFFC	EARL 2	WS-F5521	No
WS-X5530-E2A	Supervisor III (NFFC A)	NFFC	EARL 2	WS-F5521A	No
WS-X5530-E1	Supervisor III	n/a	EARL 1++	WS-F5520	No

continues

Table 4-1 *NetFlow Feature Card II to Supervisor Engine Matrix (Continued)*

Model Number	Supervisor Engine	NetFlow Feature Card	EARL Version	EARL Subtype Model	QoS Feature Support
WS-X5509	Supervisor II	n/a	EARL 1+	WS-F5511	No
WS-X5506	Supervisor II	n/a	EARL 1+	WS-F5511	No
WS-X5505	Supervisor II	n/a	EARL 1+	WS-F5511	No
WS-X5009	Supervisor I	n/a	EARL 1	WS-F5510	No
WS-X5006	Supervisor I	n/a	EARL 1	WS-F5510	No
WS-X5005	Supervisor I	n/a	EARL 1	WS-F5510	No
WS-C2926G	Supervisor II	n/a	EARL 1+	WS-F5511	No
WS-C2926T	Supervisor II	n/a	EARL 1+	WS-F5511	No
WS-C2926GS	Supervisor III	NFFC II	EARL 3	WS-F5531	Yes
WS-C2926GL	Supervisor III	NFFC II	EARL 3	WS-F5531	Yes
WS-C2902	Supervisor I	n/a	EARL 1	WS-F5520	No
WS-C2901	Supervisor I	n/a	EARL 1	WS-F5520	No

Example 4-1 demonstrates use of the **show module** command to determine the supervisor engine model number, the EARL version subtype model, and NFFC type for a Catalyst 5000 Family of switches.

Example 4-1 shows sample output from a Supervisor Engine III with an NFFC II.

Example 4-1 *Sample Output from the* **show module** *Command*

```
Console> (enable) show module
Mod Slot Ports Module-Type              Model              Sub Status
--- ---- ----- ------------------------ ------------------ --- --------
1   1    2     100BaseFX MMF Supervisor  WS-X5530           yes ok
(text deleted)

Mod Module-Name       Serial-Num
(text deleted)

Mod MAC-Address(es)                          Hw     Fw          Sw
--- ---------------------------------------- ------ ----------- ----------------
(text deleted)

Mod Sub-Type Sub-Model Sub-Serial Sub-Hw
--- -------- --------- ---------- ------
1   NFFC II  WS-F5531  0012152468 1.0
1   uplink   WS-U5533  0010450920 1.0
```

The output from the **show module** command indicates not only supervisor engine type, NFFC, and EARL versions, but also includes software version, MAC addresses, hardware and firmware revisions, and serial numbers of all line modules in the chassis. For supervisor engines without an NFFC or NFFC II, the subtype indicates EARL version.

Moreover, QoS feature support requires traffic ingress and egress from specific Catalyst 5000 line modules. Table 4-2 summarizes the modules required for front-panel support of QoS features.

Table 4-2   *Required Line Modules for QoS Support*

Model No.	Description
WS-U5537-FETX	4-port 10/100BASE-TX uplink module
WS-U5538-FEFX-MMF	4-port 10/100BASE-FX uplink module
WS-X5234-RJ45	24-port 10/100BASE-TX RJ-45
WS-X5236-FX-MT	24-port 100BASE-FX MT-RJ
WS-X5239-RJ21	36-port 10/100BASE-TX Telco

To obtain supported features per line module from the *command-line interface* (CLI), use the following command:

```
show port capabilities mod/ports
```

Example 4-2 shows sample output from the **show port capabilities** command for the WS-X5224 and WS-X5234 line modules, respectively. The output from the commands indicate that the WS-X5224 does not support QoS features, whereas the WS-X5234 supports CoS and ToS rewrite as well as output scheduling.

Example 4-2   *Sample Output from the **show port capabilities** Command*

```
Console> (enable) show port capabilities 2/1
Model                   WS-X5224
Port                    2/1
Type                    10/100BaseTX
Speed                   auto,10,100
Duplex                  half,full
Trunk encap type        no
Trunk mode              no
Channel                 no
Broadcast suppression   pps(0-150000),percentage(0-100)
Flow control            no
Security                yes
Dot1x                   yes
Membership              static,dynamic
Fast start              yes
QOS scheduling          rx-(none),tx-(none)
CoS rewrite             no
ToS rewrite             no
Rewrite                 no
```

continues

Example 4-2 *Sample Output from the* **show port capabilities** *Command (Continued)*

```
UDLD                    yes
AuxiliaryVlan           no
SPAN                    source,destination

Console> (enable) show port capabilities 3/1
Model                   WS-X5234
Port                    3/1
Type                    10/100BaseTX
Speed                   auto,10,100
Duplex                  half,full
Trunk encap type        802.1Q,ISL
Trunk mode              on,off,desirable,auto,nonegotiate
Channel                 3/1-2,3/1-4
Broadcast suppression   percentage(0-100)
Flow control            receive-(off,on),send-(off,on)
Security                yes
Dot1x                   yes
Membership              static,dynamic
Fast start              yes
QOS scheduling          rx-(none),tx-(1q4t)
CoS rewrite             yes
ToS rewrite             IP-Precedence
Rewrite                 yes
UDLD                    yes
AuxiliaryVlan           1..1000,untagged,dot1p,none
SPAN                    source,destination
```

Enabling QoS Features on the Catalyst 5000 Family of Switches

QoS must be globally enabled on the Catalyst 5000 Family of switches before the switch enacts on classification, marking, and output scheduling configurations. To enable QoS on the Catalyst 5000 Family of switches, enter the following command:

set qos {enable | disable}

Example 4-3 illustrates a user enabling QoS on a Catalyst 5000 Switch.

Example 4-3 *Enabling QoS Features on a Catalyst 5000 Switch*

```
Console> (enable) set qos enable
QoS is enabled.
```

Input Scheduling

Similar to other access layer switches, the Catalyst 5000 Family of switches performs only FIFO queuing of ingress packets. Input scheduling is not supported, but this does not pose a significant issue if traffic does not exceed the backplane bandwidth. Backplane bandwidth depends on the chassis model and supervisor engine. All Supervisor I and II Engines utilize a single 1.2-Gbps system bus for the backplane architecture. The Supervisor III Engines utilize three 1.2-Gbps system buses for total of 3.6-Gbps bandwidth in a three-system bus chassis for the backplane architecture. The three-system bus chassis encompass the 5505, 5500, and 5509 models.

The three system buses on the 5505, 5500, and 5509 chassis aggregate at the supervisor engine. The supervisor engine is responsible for moving traffic between the three buses. All Ethernet line cards except the three-port, WS-X5403, and nine-port Gigabit Ethernet modules utilize a single bus connector. With the exception of the WS-X5403 and WS-X5410, all line cards attach to the first bus connector in a slot. The WS-X5403 attaches a single front-panel Gigabit Ethernet port to each bus connector on the backplane, whereas the WS-X5410 distributes traffic from all nine front-panel Gigabit ports to the three bus connectors on the backplane. The switch references the three buses as bus A, B, and C, respectively.

To distribute traffic across the buses for single bus connecting line cards, each chassis employs a different bus connector layout per slot. In this manner, the switch distributes traffic on a line card basis by placing the three backplane bus connectors in a different order depending on a chassis slot. In a Catalyst 5505 chassis, for instance, the first bus connector in slot 3 is A, whereas slots 4 and 5 utilize B and C, respectively, as the first bus connector. Placing three single bus line cards in slots 3 to 5 results in traffic from each line card occupying a different 1.2-Gbps system bus. Tables 4-3 to 4-6 illustrate the bus layout for each of the Catalyst 5000 Family of switches chassis.

Table 4-3   *Catalyst 5000 Chassis Bus Layout*

Slot	Backplane Connector
1	A
2	A
3	A
4	A
5	A

Table 4-4   *Catalyst 5505 Chassis Bus Layout*

Slot	Backplane Connector
1	A B C
2	A B C
3	A B C
4	B A C
5	C B A

Table 4-5   *Catalyst 5509 Chassis Bus Layout*

Slot	Backplane Connector
1	A B C
2	A B C
3	A B C
4	A B C
5	B A C
6	B A C
7	B A C
8	C B A
9	C B A

Table 4-6   *Catalyst 5500 (13-Slot) Chassis Bus Layout*

Slot	Backplane Connector
1	A B C
2	A B C
3	A B C
4	A B C
5	B A C
6	B
7	B
8	B
9	B or ATM
10	C or ATM
11	C or ATM
12	C or ATM
13	Reserved for ATM switch processor

The Catalyst 5500 chassis utilizes slots 9 through 12 for ATM or Ethernet line modules. This chassis only supports an ATM switch process in slot 13 and does not accept an Ethernet line module in this slot.

In addition to referencing the system architecture, use the **whichbus** {*mod/port*} command to determine which bus a line module utilizes.

Example 4-4 illustrates a user enabling the **whichbus** {*mod/port*} command.

Example 4-4   *Example of Using the **whichbus** Command*

```
Console> (enable) whichbus 4/1
B
```

Because the Catalyst 5000 Family of switches does not support input scheduling, maintaining backplane utilization within the 1.2 Gbps per system bus is important when implementing a QoS architecture. When oversubscribing the system bus, the switch tail drops frames from front-panel ports. Therefore, to avoid the arbitrary tail dropping of frames, do not oversubscribe the bus. Use the **show traffic** command to view the current and peak loads on each system bus as demonstrated in Example 4-5.

Example 4-5   *Sample Output of the **show traffic** Command*

```
Console> (enable) show traffic
Threshold: 100%


Switching-Bus Traffic Peak Peak-Time
------------- ------- ---- ------------------------
A             3%      10% Sun Mar 30 2002, 09:52:14
B             5%      11% Sun Mar 30 2002, 09:52:14
C             17%     63% Sun Mar 30 2002, 09:52:14
```

Use the **show system** command to view the collective utilization of all three buses. Example 4-6 displays sample output of the **show system** command.

Example 4-6   *Sample Output of the **show system** Command*

```
Console> (enable) show system
(text deleted)

Modem   Baud  Traffic Peak Peak-Time
------- ----- ------- ---- ------------------------
disable 9600  7%       13% Sun Mar 30 2002, 09:52:14
(text deleted)
```

As a generally accepted practice when using the Catalyst 5000 Family of switches, avoid utilizing more than 50 percent of a system bus's bandwidth. For networks requiring more bandwidth, use the Catalyst 3550 Family of switches, the Catalyst 4000 IOS Family of switches, or the Catalyst 6500 Family of switches.

For more information regarding the system architecture of the Catalyst 5000 Family of switches, refer to the following technical documents at Cisco.com:

- "Hardware Troubleshooting for Catalyst 5500/5000/2926G/2926 Series Switches" Document ID: 18810

- "Preparing to Troubleshoot Hardware for Catalyst 5500/5000/2926G/2926 Series Switches" Document ID: 18826

Classification and Marking

The Catalyst 5000 Family of switches bases classification solely on Layer 2 CoS values. Although the switch can rewrite Layer 3 IP precedence values in specific configurations, the switch does not use ToS values, including IP precedence values or DSCP values to make any QoS classification, marking, or congestion avoidance decisions. With regard to classification, the Catalyst 5000 Family of switches is similar to the Catalyst 4000 CatOS Family of switches and the Catalyst 2900XL and 3500XL switches.

Classification and Marking of Untagged Frames Based on Ingress Port

The Catalyst 5000 switch does not support any port-level rewriting of DSCP or ToS values, the switch only rewrites the ingress frames' CoS value and does not alter the DSCP or ToS bits even on untrusted ports. In this respect, the Catalyst 5000 Family of switches, by default, does not trust CoS values but always trusts DSCP or ToS values. Nevertheless, the Catalyst 5000 Family of switches can reclassify and mark untagged frames with a specific CoS value similar to the Catalyst 2900XL and 3500XL switches on line modules that support QoS features as indicated in Table 4-2. The switch must transmit the frame with a dot1q tag or *Inter-Switch Link* (ISL) header for the respective CoS value to be present on egress. Use the following command to configure a port to classify untagged ingress frames with a specific CoS value:

    set port qos mod/ports cos cos_value

cos_value represents the overriding CoS value. To clear the configuration, use the **clear port qos** {*mod/ports*} **cos** command. Example 4-7 illustrates a user configuring a switch port to classify untagged ingress frames with a specific CoS value and then clearing the configuration.

Example 4-7 *User Configuring Port to Classify Untagged Frames with Specific CoS Value*

```
Console> (enable) set port qos 3/1 cos 5
Port  3/1 qos cos set to 5

Console> (enable) clear port qos 3/1 cos
Port  3/1 qos cos setting cleared.
```

No options exist on the Catalyst 5000 Family of switches for trusting CoS, trusting DSCP, or trusting IP precedence.

Classification of Tagged Frames Based on Ingress Port

The Catalyst 5000 Family of switches trusts ISL- or dot1q-tagged frames' CoS value by default and does not support reclassification or marking of tagged frames based on port configuration.

Classification and Marking Based on Destination VLAN and MAC

The Catalyst 5000 Family of switches supports rewriting the CoS value of selected destination MAC address on a VLAN basis. For a CoS value to be present on the egress frame, the switch must transmit the frame with a dot1q tag or ISL header on a port configured for trunking. Figure 4-2 illustrates an example of using classification and marking based on destination VLAN and MAC. In this example, a Workstation 1 is sending traffic to Workstations 2 and 3 with a CoS value of 0. The configuration applied to the switch marks traffic destined for MAC address 0001.4200.0005 with a CoS value of 5. The marking subsequently also effects output scheduling for the frames.

Figure 4-2   *Topology Illustrating Classification and Marking Based on Destination MAC Address and VLAN*

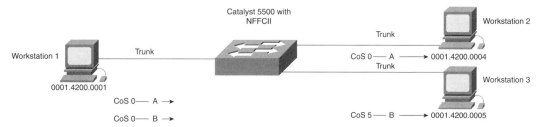

Use the following command to configure marking based on a destination MAC address on a VLAN basis:

set qos mac-cos *dest_MAC_addr VLAN cos_value*

The parameters for this command are defined as follows:

- *dest_MAC_addr* represents the destination MAC address.
- *VLAN* represents the VLAN ID where the destination MAC address resides.
- *cos_value* symbolizes the CoS value to write on the frame.

Example 4-8 illustrates a user configuring classification and marking based on the destination MAC address using the topology in Figure 4-2.

Example 4-8   *User Configuring Classification and Marking Based on the Destination MAC Address and VLAN*

```
Console> (enable) set qos mac-cos 00-01-42-00-00-05 5 4
CoS 4 is assigned to 00-01-42-00-00-05 vlan 5.
```

Classification and marking based on destination MAC address and VLAN does not scale in large topologies and requires knowledge and continuous updates to MAC addresses. The preferable methods of classification and marking are to utilize ingress port configuration or ACEs. The next section discusses classification and marking based on ACEs.

Classification and Marking Based on ACE

Classification and marking based on ACE provides a method of classifying and marking IP version 4 traffic for traffic crossing a routed boundary. Traffic crossing a routed boundary always passes through a router or switch capable of routing in hardware. The Catalyst 5000 Family of switches may use an RSFC or RSM for this functionality; however, any IP router supporting MLS is sufficient. Classification and marking based on ACEs supports the following ACE options:

- IP source address(es)
- IP destination address(es)
- UDP, TCP, or both protocols
- TCP/UDP source port(s)
- TCP/UDP destination port(s)

When ACE-based classification occurs, the switch marks the IP precedence bits in the IP header to match the CoS value. This behavior differs completely from newer platforms, such as the Catalyst 4000 IOS Family of switches. Later chapters discuss the differences in classification and marking behavior of the newer platforms. In addition, ACE-based marking rewrites CoS values written by the ingress port configuration or the destination and VLAN-based classification and marking configuration. CoS-to-IP precedence mapping or any other mapping table is not configurable.

Furthermore, classification and marking based on ACE behaves differently depending on the MLS configuration. In brief, without MLS enabled, the switch carries out ACE-based classification on all traffic. With MLS enabled, the switch executes ACE-based classification only on MLS-switched traffic. The following sections provide more details on this subject.

MLS Fundamentals

As discussed in the "Catalyst 5000 Family of Switches QoS Architectural Overview" section of this chapter, enabling MLS allows the supervisor engine to perform Layer 2 rewrites of routed packets. Layer 2 rewrites include rewriting the source and destination MAC addresses and writing a recalculated *cyclic redundancy check* (CRC). Because the source and destination MAC address changes during Layer 3 rewrites, the switch must recalculate the CRC for these new MAC addresses. The switch learns Layer 2 rewrite information from the MLS router via an MLS protocol. Figure 4-3 illustrates the fundamentals behind MLS.

Figure 4-3   *Logical Representation of Creating MLS Flow*

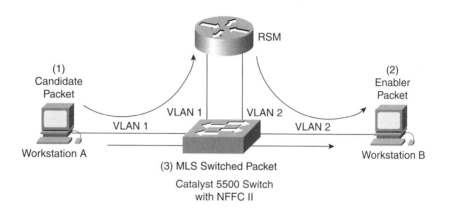

In Figure 4-3, when Workstation A sends a packet to Workstation B, Workstation A sends the packet to its default gateway. In Figure 4-3, the default gateway is the RSM. The switch (MLS-SE) recognizes this packet as an MLS candidate packet because the destination MAC address matches the MAC address of the MLS router (MLS-RP). As a result, the switch creates a candidate entry for this flow. Next, the router accepts the packets from Workstation A, rewrites the Layer 2 destination MAC address and CRC, and forwards the packet to Workstation B. The switch refers to the routed packet from the RSM as the enabler packet. The switch, upon seeing both the candidate and enabler packets, creates an MLS entry in hardware so that the switch rewrites and forwards all future packets matching this flow. The MLS Switched Packet arrow in Figure 4-3 indicates this flow. For more details and examples on the MLS architecture, consult the following technical document at Cisco.com:

"Troubleshooting IP MultiLayer Switching" Document ID: 10554

When using the MLS feature on the Catalyst 5000 Family of switches in conjunction with QoS classification and marking based on ACEs, classification and marking only occurs on MLS-switched packets. This limitation presents the following important caveats.

- MLS-RP must see both the candidate and enabler packets to create a flow.

- Candidate and enabler packets are not subject to classification or marking based on ACEs.

- The switch removes MLS entries when the MAC Aging-time expires; therefore, flows must be symmetrical.

- Packets with a destination network via a WAN port adapter on an RSM module are not subject to classification and marking based on ACEs.

- MLS ages entries based on an absolute timer; when flows age, the switch must relearn the entries via the candidate and enabler packets.

- IP routing table changes cause all MLS entries to purge.

As a result of these limitations, a QoS implementation with ACE-based marking and MLS enabled commonly yields packets without the ACE-based classification and marking. For networks requiring strict application of ACE-based classification and marking, disable MLS. Disabling MLS may have side effects, such as a higher CPU utilization on the MLS-RP. As a result, disabling MLS needs careful consideration and planning.

Configuring ACE-Based Classification and Marking

The switch determines which packets are destined for a router by the destination MAC address. As a result, the switch requires knowledge of the destination MAC of the router before any ACE-based classification and marking occurs. Use the following commands to configure and verify the destination router MAC for ACE-based classification and marking, respectively:

```
set qos router-mac MAC_addr vlan
show qos router-mac [MAC_addr | vlan]
```

Configure multiple router MAC addresses for ACE-based classification and marking on multiple VLANs or routers. Example 4-9 illustrates a user configuring and verifying a Catalyst 5000 switch for the router MAC address on multiple VLANs.

Example 4-9   *User Configuring and Verifying Router MAC Address for MLS*

```
Console> (enable) set qos router-mac 00-30-f2-c8-8e-dc 4
Router MAC/Vlan is set for QoS.
Console> (enable) set qos router-mac 00-30-f2-c8-8e-dc 5
Router MAC/Vlan is set for QoS.

Console> (enable) show qos router-mac
Number  MAC address       Vlan #
---------------------------------
     1  00-30-f2-c8-8e-dc  4
     2  00-30-f2-c8-8e-dc  5
```

ACEs used for classification and marking utilize several options. Use the following configuration command to configure an ACE based solely on source and destination IP address and mask:

```
set qos ip-filter cos src_IP_addr_spec dest_IP_addr_spec
```

cos represents the CoS value that the switch writes to frames matching the ACE. *src_IP_addr_spec* represents the source IP address(es) and mask of the ACE, whereas *dest_IP_addr_spec* represents the destination IP address(es) and mask. The keyword **any** is optional for specifying all IP addresses, and the keyword **host** represents an IP address for a single entry, (that is, 255.255.255.255 mask). Enter the **host** keyword before entering the IP address. Example 4-10 illustrates two example ACE entries using the **host** and **any** keywords, respectively.

Example 4-10 *ACE Example Using* **host** *and* **any** *Keywords*

```
Console> (enable) set qos ip-filter 5 any host 10.10.10.10
qos ip-filter is set successfully.

Console> (enable) set qos ip-filter 5 192.168.1.0 255.255.255.0 any
qos ip-filter is set successfully.
```

Use the following command structure for specific TCP and UDP ports for an ACE:

set qos ip-filter *cos* {**tcp** | **udp** | **any**} *src_IP_addr_spec src_port dest_IP_addr_spec*
    dest_port src_IP_addr_spec/dest_IP_addr

The **any** keyword proceeding the CoS value is available to specify the ACE for both TCP and UDP protocols. Example 4-11 illustrates several examples of using ACEs with TCP and UDP port number references.

Example 4-11 *ACE Example Using TCP and UDP Ports*

```
Console> (enable) set qos ip-filter 5 UDP any 30000 any 30000
Warning: This command will only apply to Unicast addresses.
qos ip-filter is set successfully.

Console> (enable) set qos ip-filter 4 TCP 192.168.100.0 255.255.255.0 16000
192.168.101.0 255.255.255.0 16000
qos ip-filter is set successfully.

Console> (enable) set qos ip-filter 6 any host 10.1.1.1 50000 host 10.1.1.2 50000
qos ip-filter is set successfully.
```

Use the following command to view the current configured ACEs on the switch:

show qos ip

Example 4-12 illustrates an example of using the **show qos ip** command.

Example 4-12 *Example Output from the* **show qos ip** *Command*

```
Console> (enable) show qos ip
There are 3 IP filter(s).
ACE# Src IP and Mask                 Dest IP and Mask
---- ------------------------------  -------------------------------
  1 any                              host 10.10.10.10
    Protocol Src Port Dst Port CoS
    -------- -------- -------- ---
    any      0        0        5


  2 192.168.1.0 255.255.255.0        any
    Protocol Src Port Dst Port CoS
    -------- -------- -------- ---
```

continues

Example 4-12 *Example Output from the* **show qos ip** *Command (Continued)*

```
         any        0         0         5


      3 any                            any
        Protocol Src Port Dst Port CoS
        -------- -------- -------- ---
        udp      30000    30000     5


      4 192.168.100.0 255.255.255.0    192.168.101.0 255.255.255.0
        Protocol Src Port Dst Port CoS
        -------- -------- -------- ---
        tcp      16000    16000     4


      5 host 10.1.1.1                  host 10.1.1.2
        Protocol Src Port Dst Port CoS
        -------- -------- -------- ---
        any      50000    50000     6
```

The switch executes ACE entries in order, the same as access-control lists in Cisco IOS Software. As a result, it may be necessary to rearrange the order of the ACE entries. Use the following suffixes to the **set qos ip-filter** command to place ACE entries in the configuration in a specific order:

[**before** *ACE#* | **modify** *ACE#*]

Example 4-13 illustrates a user determining the existing ACE order, placing an ACE entry in a specific order, and verifying the configuration.

Example 4-13 *Placing ACE Entries in Specific Order*

```
Console> (enable) show qos ip
There are 3 IP filter(s).
ACE# Src IP and Mask                   Dest IP and Mask
---- --------------------------------- --------------------------------
   1 any                               host 10.10.10.10
     Protocol Src Port Dst Port CoS
     -------- -------- -------- ---
     any      0        0         5


   2 192.168.1.0 255.255.255.0         any
     Protocol Src Port Dst Port CoS
     -------- -------- -------- ---
     any      0        0         5
```

Example 4-13 *Placing ACE Entries in Specific Order (Continued)*

```
  3 any                         any
    Protocol Src Port Dst Port CoS
    -------- -------- -------- ---
    udp      30000    30000    5



  4 192.168.100.0 255.255.255.0   192.168.101.0 255.255.255.0
    Protocol Src Port Dst Port CoS
    -------- -------- -------- ---
    tcp      16000    16000    4



  5 host 10.1.1.1              host 10.1.1.2
    Protocol Src Port Dst Port CoS
    -------- -------- -------- ---
    any      50000    50000    6


Console> (enable) set qos ip-filter 3 192.168.20.0 0.0.0.255 192.168.21.0 0.0.0.255
before 3

Console> (enable) show qos ip
There are 5 IP filter(s).
ACE# Src IP and Mask              Dest IP and Mask
---- ------------------------------ ------------------------------
  1 any                         host 10.10.10.10
    Protocol Src Port Dst Port CoS
    -------- -------- -------- ---
    any      0        0        5



  2 192.168.1.0 255.255.255.0     any
    Protocol Src Port Dst Port CoS
    -------- -------- -------- ---
    any      0        0        5



  3 192.168.20.0 0.0.0.255       192.168.21.0 0.0.0.255
    Protocol Src Port Dst Port CoS
    -------- -------- -------- ---
    any      0        0        3



  4 any                         any
    Protocol Src Port Dst Port CoS
```

continues

Example 4-13 *Placing ACE Entries in Specific Order (Continued)*

```
   --------  --------  --------  ---
   udp       30000     30000     5




 5 192.168.100.0 255.255.255.0      192.168.101.0 255.255.255.0
   Protocol Src Port Dst Port CoS
   --------  --------  --------  ---
   tcp       16000     16000     4



 6 host 10.1.1.1                     host 10.1.1.2
   Protocol Src Port Dst Port CoS
   --------  --------  --------  ---
   any       50000     50000     6
```

Use the following commands to clear ACE entries:

```
clear qos ip-filter ace_num
clear qos ip-filter all
```

Extended Trust Option

The Catalyst 5000 Family of switches supports instructing an attached appliance of extended trust options via the *Cisco Discovery Protocol* (CDP). CDP is a Layer 2 protocol used to inform Cisco devices of each presence and parameters such as IP address, system name, Native VLAN, and egress port. Chapter 2, "End-to-End QoS: Quality of Service at Layer 3 and Layer 2," in the "Voice VLANs and Extended Trust" section discusses the concept of extended trust. The following commands configure the extended trust options for a Catalyst 5000 switch:

```
set port qos mod/ports cos-ext cos_value
set port qos mod/ports trust-ext [trust-cos | untrusted]
```

cos_value represents the requested reclassification CoS value sent to the attached appliance via CDP. The **trust-cos** option requests the attached appliance to trust ingress CoS values on frames, whereas **untrusted** signifies the appliance to not trust the CoS value in ingress frames and rewrite any ingress CoS values to zero. The most common appliance is the Cisco IP Phone.

Although the Catalyst 5000 Family of switches supports extended trust parameters in CDP messages to attached appliances and auxiliary (voice) VLANs, it does not support the ability to provide power over the cabling infrastructure to power Cisco IP Phones or other appliances. For example, if you are using the Catalyst 5000 Family of switches to apply extended trust parameters in CDP messages to a Cisco IP Phone, you need a power outlet for the phone rather than relying on inline power.

Congestion Avoidance

The Catalyst 5000 Family of switches achieves congestion avoidance through the use of queue management on certain line modules based on CoS values. No support for output scheduling or queuing based on DSCP or IP precedence values exists for the Catalyst 5000 Family of switches. The two uplink modules and three line modules described in Table 4-2 represent the only line modules to support output scheduling. All other line modules only utilize a single transmit queue, and the transmit queue tail drops all frames when exhausting buffer queue space.

The uplink modules and line modules in Table 4-2 utilize a single transmit queue with four configurable transmit queue drop thresholds, 1q4t, to achieve congestion avoidance. The switch drops packets with specific CoS values when the transmit buffer reaches specific thresholds. The CoS values assigned to each threshold are configurable. This method of congestion avoidance delivers *Weighted Random Early Detection* (WRED) for a single queue. Chapter 1, "Quality of Service: An Overview," discussed WRED in more detail.

For example, Table 4-7 describes the default behavior of congestion management on the Catalyst 5000 Family of switches.

Table 4-7   *Default Output Scheduling Behavior of Ports Supporting 1q4t Transmit Queue*

Threshold No.	Threshold of Transmit Queue Buffer	CoS Values
1	30% Full	0 and 1
2	50% Full	2 and 3
3	80% Full	4 and 5
4	100% Full	6 and 7

Use the following command to configure the CoS values that map to a specific threshold number:

```
set qos map port_type q# threshold# cos cos_list
```

port_type is always **1q4t** and *q#* is always **1** on the Catalyst 5000 Family of switches. The *threshold#* represents one of four thresholds used for CoS value mapping. After making configuration changes to the transmit queue, use the following commands to verify the configuration changes:

```
show qos info <runtime | config> <mod/port>
show qos info config port_type tx
```

Example 4-14 illustrates a user configuring and verifying the QoS threshold number to CoS mapping. Only module 3 of this chassis supports QoS features; and therefore, the switch warns that QoS is not supported on modules 1, 2, 4, and 15.

Example 4-14 *User Configuring and Verifying QoS Threshold to CoS Mapping*

```
Console> (enable) set qos map 1q4t 1 1 cos 0-2
QoS is not supported on module 1.
QoS is not supported on module 2.
QoS is not supported on module 4.
QoS is not supported on module 15.
Qos tx priority queue and threshold mapped to cos successfully.

Console> (enable) set qos map 1q4t 1 2 cos 4
QoS is not supported on module 1.
QoS is not supported on module 2.
QoS is not supported on module 4.
QoS is not supported on module 15.
Qos tx priority queue and threshold mapped to cos successfully.

Console> (enable) show qos info config 1q4t tx
QoS setting in NVRAM for 1q4t transmit:
QoS is enabled
Queue and Threshold Mapping:
Queue Threshold CoS
----- --------- ---------------
1     1          0 1 2
1     2          3 4
1     3          5
1     4          6 7
Queue #  Thresholds - percentage
-------  ------------------------------------------
1        20% 40% 50% 100%
```

The threshold's values are also configurable on a global basis. Use the following command to configure the threshold percentage drop values:

set qos wred-threshold *port_type* **tx queue** *q# threshold_percentage_values*

As with all Catalyst 5000 QoS commands, *port_type* is always **1q4t** and *q#* is always **1**. *threshold_percentage_values* represents the four threshold drop values. Example 4-15 illustrates a user configuring the threshold drop values.

Example 4-15 *User Configuring Drop Thresholds for Transmit Queues*

```
Console> (enable) set qos wred-threshold 1q4t tx queue 1 20 30 40 95
WRED thresholds for queue 1 set to 20 and 30 and 40 and 95  on all WRED-capable 1q4t
   ports.
```

To view the number of packets dropped per threshold number, use the following command:

show qos statistics *mod_num/port_num*

Example 4-16 illustrates the use of the **show qos statistics** command.

Example 4-16 *User Displaying the Number of Dropped Packet per Threshold Number*

```
Console> (enable) show qos statistics 3/24
On Transmit: Port 3/24 has 1 Queue(s) 4 Threshold(s)
Q #  Threshold #:Packets dropped
---  --------------------------------------------
1    1:59378 pkts, 2:14 pkts, 3:7 pkts, 4:8 pkts
```

For IP telephony networks, a CoS value of 5 generally represents VoIP traffic. As a result, the desired behavior is to never drop VoIP traffic unless the output buffer queue is full. As a result, use the following best practice configuration for switch ports connected to IP telephony devices, such as Cisco IP Phones:

Example 4-17 *Best Practice Output Scheduling Configuration for IP Telephony Networks*

```
!
Console> (enable) show config
This command shows non-default configurations only.
Use 'show config all' to show both default and non-default configurations.
(text deleted)
!
#qos
set qos enable
set qos map 1q4t 1 1 cos 2
set qos map 1q4t 1 2 cos 4
set qos wred-threshold 1q4t tx queue 1 20 30 100 100
!
(text deleted)
end

Console> (enable) show qos info config 1q4t tx
QoS setting in NVRAM for 1q4t transmit:
QoS is enabled
Queue and Threshold Mapping:
Queue Threshold CoS
-----  ---------  ---------------
1      1          0 1 2
1      2          3 4
1      3          5
1      4          6 7
Queue #  Thresholds - percentage
-------  -------------------------------------------
1        20% 30% 100% 100%
```

The configuration in Example 4-17 assigns traffic with CoS values of 5 to threshold #3. In this manner, the switch drops traffic for CoS values 5, 6, and 7 only when the output buffer is full. In addition, the switch aggressively drops low-priority traffic for CoS values 0 to 4 when the queue is 20 percent to 30 percent full to avoid output buffer full conditions from ever occurring.

Case Study

Figure 4-4 illustrates a network that consists of two Catalyst 5000 switches implementing several QoS features to differentiate service in network.

Figure 4-4 *Case Study Topology*

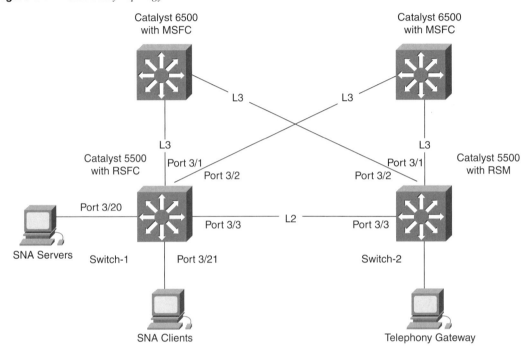

A time-sensitive application using the *Systems Network Architecture* (SNA) protocols exists in the network depicted in Figure 4-4. In this topology, the application handles banking transactions. The client and servers send only untagged frames. To classify frames accordingly, the Switch-1 configuration consists of classification based on ingress port. This configuration is illustrated by the **set port qos** command in Example 4-17.

Furthermore, a telephony gateway exists in the network. The telephony gateway sends keepalive packets to other telephony devices across VLAN boundaries to the core of the network. The telephony gateway transmits all keepalives with UDP source and destination ports of 25000. The telephony gateway does not tag the frames, and as a result does not apply a CoS value to transmitted frames. To classify the frames appropriately, both Catalyst 5500 switches use ACL-based classification and marking to set the CoS value of frames matching the signature of the telephony keepalives. As a result, these switches only classify the keepalive frames and not regular traffic. Example 4-17 illustrates this ACL-based classification configuration for Switch-1.

For appropriate congestion management of frames, the switch-to-switch connections and the ports connecting the SNA servers and the telephony gateway all utilize WRED scheduling. The WRED scheduling is nondefault to apply heavier weighted scheduling to packets with a CoS value of 5. Example 4-18 shows this configuration for Switch-1.

Example 4-18 *Case Study Configuration for Switch-1*

```
Switch> (enable) show config
This command shows non-default configurations only.
Use 'show config all' to show both default and non-default configurations.
(text deleted)
begin
!
# ***** NON-DEFAULT CONFIGURATION *****
!
(text deleted)
!
#qos
set qos enable
set qos ip-filter 5 udp any 25000 any 25000
set qos map 1q4t 1 1 cos 2
set qos map 1q4t 1 2 cos 4
set qos wred-threshold 1q4t tx queue 1 20 30 100 100
!
# default port status is enable
!
!
#module 1 : 2-port 1000BaseX Supervisor IIIG
set vlan 5    1/1-2
set trunk 1/1  off negotiate 1-1005
set trunk 1/2  off negotiate 1-1005
!
#module 3 : 24-port 10/100BaseTX Ethernet
set vlan 1    3/1
set vlan 2    3/2
set vlan 4    3/20-24
set vlan 5    3/3-19
set port qos 3/20-21 cos 5
!
(text deleted)!
#module 15 : 1-port Route Switch Feature Card
!
#module 16 empty
!
(text deleted)
!
#qos router-mac
set qos router-mac 00-30-f2-c8-8e-dc 5
set qos router-mac 00-30-f2-c8-8e-dc 4
end
```

Summary

The Catalyst 5000 Family of switches supports QoS with only specific Supervisors and line modules. These switches support QoS features limited to classification of untagged frames, marking based on ACEs, and output scheduling. These features classify frames solely on CoS values. For most applications, DSCP classification is desirable. As a result, network designs should not introduce the Catalyst 5000 Family of switches into a QoS end-to-end architecture; instead, utilize the Catalyst 5000 Family of switches only in existing deployments. In summary, the QoS feature support on the Catalyst 5000 Family of switches is as follows:

- QoS support requires one of the following Supervisors: Supervisor III with NFFC II, Supervisor IIG, or Supervisor IIIG.

- QoS support requires traffic ingress and egress using the following line modules or uplink modules: WS-X5234-RJ45, WS-X5236-FX-MT, WS-X5239-RJ21, WS-U5537-FETX, or WS-U5538-FEFX-MMF.

- No support for input scheduling exists.

- Classification based on CoS only; no support for classification based on IP precedence or DSCP.

- Marking of CoS and ToS supported with limitations with regard to MLS.

- CoS value determines ToS value for ACE-based marking.

- Congestion avoidance achieved via WRED using a 1q4t mechanism.

- Global mapping of CoS values to thresholds is configurable.

- Thresholds are configurable on a global basis.

Advanced QoS Concepts

Introduction to the Modular QoS Command-Line Interface

Not long ago, a unique *command-line interface* (CLI) existed for every QoS mechanism. This meant that if a user wanted to configure traffic shaping and congestion management, that user had to learn two totally different CLI structures. This made being proficient in the configuration of all available QoS mechanisms quite a challenge. Fortunately, Cisco IOS now has a better method for configuring the components of QoS. This new method is called the *Modular QoS CLI* (MQC).

This chapter covers the following aspects of MQC:

- MQC features and concepts
- Class maps
- Policy maps
- Servic policies

MQC Background, Terms, and Concepts

The MQC was originally introduced to support the configuration of *Class-Based Weighted Fair Queuing* (CBWFQ), but has now been expanded to include support for the configuration of nearly every QoS component. Although this list is not comprehensive, some of the QoS components that can be configured via the MQC include the following:

- Traffic classification
- Traffic marking
- Congestion management
- Congestion avoidance
- Traffic conditioning
- Header compression

The fact that so many different components of QoS can be configured via the MQC, and the fact that each of the components previously listed has several possible mechanisms, makes the MQC one of the most versatile parts of Cisco IOS. When discussing technology, versatility usually means complexity, which is one of the amazing things about the MQC. The MQC was specifically designed to *reduce* configuration complexity *and* provide versatility.

The simplicity of configuration is made possible through the use of a common configuration structure for all QoS components within the MQC. That is, the basic configuration steps for configuring all QoS mechanisms is the same, with only small variations in the configuration that are specific to the actual mechanism. You can configure all the mechanisms through a three-step process:

Step 1 Class map configuration

Step 2 Policy map configuration

Step 3 Service policy application

This chapter describes each step in the configuration process, as well as the configuration options, and also provides examples of MQC commands.

Step 1: The Class Map

The first step for configuring any QoS mechanism in the MQC is the configuration of a class-map. Simply stated, the *class map* defines which traffic you want the router to match. This is the fundamental step that allows the router to differentiate one traffic type from another. This is traffic classification, and without classification there can be no QoS.

To differentiate traffic, it is possible to match on one traffic characteristic or multiple characteristics. If you need to differentiate between traffic from 10.1.1.1 and traffic from 10.1.1.2, for example, the source IP address is the only characteristic that you need to configure. If you have multiple traffic streams from 10.1.1.1 and need to differentiate between those, however, as well as differentiate between multiple streams from 10.1.1.2, you probably need to classify traffic based on multiple criteria, such as TCP or UDP port.

A possible scenario in which this would come into play might be server 10.1.1.1 that serves production HTTP and FTP to the Accounting department, and server 10.1.1.2 that serves nonproduction HTTP and FTP to the IT group that develops applications for the Accounting department. Understanding that production traffic is the top priority, the development group needs their traffic to have a minimum bandwidth guarantee to enable that group to properly test a new HTTP application before delivering it to the Accounting department for production use. This means that there will be QoS requirements for *all* traffic from 10.1.1.1 and *some* traffic from 10.1.1.2. As such, just matching by IP address does not suffice. In this case, there is a requirement to match on multiple characteristics.

Configuring the Class Map

When matching on multiple characteristics, two options exist for creating the class map: **match-any** and **match-all**, as demonstrated in Example 5-1.

Example 5-1 *Class Map Options*

```
R1(config)# class-map ?
  WORD      class-map name
  match-all  Logical-AND all matching statements under this classmap
  match-any  Logical-OR all matching statements under this classmap
```

The **match-any option** is a logical OR operation, in which only one of the match conditions must be met for a packet to belong to a specific class. The **match-all option** is a logical OR operation, in which all match criteria must be met for a packet to belong to a specific class. You must choose one of these options before you configure the remaining class map parameters.

This section discusses the various configuration parameters for the class map, followed by a configuration example. The distinction between **match-any** and **match-all** is discussed as part of the configuration example later in this chapter.

In the examples that follow, the **match-all** parameter is used.

```
R1(config)#class-map match-all ?
   WORD  class-map name
```

Next it is necessary to provide a name for the class map. For this example, the class map is named HTTP.

```
R1(config)#class-map match-all HTTP
R1(config-cmap)#
```

Notice that this router is now in **config-cmap**, which is class map configuration mode. The class map has now been created, but it does not have any information about which traffic it should pay attention to. There are, however, a few options within the class map other than which traffic to match, as the output in Example 5-2 demonstrates.

Example 5-2 *Additional Class Map Options*

```
R1(config-cmap)# ?
QoS class-map configuration commands:
  description  Class-Map description
  exit         Exit from QoS class-map configuration mode
  match        classification criteria
  no           Negate or set default values of a command
  rename       Rename this class-map
```

It is possible, and highly recommended, to enter a description of the class map, using the **description** command. Use this in the same way that you would use the **description** command on an interface, and with the understanding that it has no actual impact on traffic. It is also possible to rename this class map, without losing the configuration of the class map. For example, if you decide that just calling the class HTTP is ambiguous, and decide that you want the class to be called ACCOUNTING-HTTP, you can change the name without destroying the configuration. This command was not always available, and it is a very convenient addition to the MQC.

```
R1(config-cmap)#rename ?
   WORD  new class-map name
```

The major function of the class map, however, is to match traffic. As such, the **match** argument has quite a few options. As with any software package, new features are constantly being added to Cisco IOS Software, so the list is constantly expanded. Example 5-3 shows a sample of the commands available.

Example 5-3   *Options for the* **match** *Command*

```
R1(config-cmap)# match ?
  access-group        Access group
  any                 Any packets
  class-map           Class map
  cos                 IEEE 802.1Q/ISL class of service/user priority values
  destination-address Destination address
  fr-de               Match on Frame-relay DE bit
  input-interface     Select an input interface to match
  ip                  IP specific values
  mpls                Multi Protocol Label Switching specific values
  not                 Negate this match result
  protocol            Protocol
  qos-group           Qos-group
  source-address      Source address
```

Within some of these match possibilities are additional match options. An example of that is the **match ip** option shown in Example 5-4.

Example 5-4   *Class Map* **match** *Option*

```
R1(config-cmap)# match ip ?
  dscp        Match IP DSCP (DiffServ CodePoints)
  precedence  Match IP precedence
  rtp         Match RTP port nos
```

You can view a list of the available options by using the interactive help menu.

Class Map Options: A Closer Look

The values on which the class map can be configured to match are explained in the previous output, but this list provides more detailed explanations of some of these options:

- **access-group**—Allows the configuration of an *access-control list* (ACL) and the matching of the criteria defined within that ACL.

- **any**—Allows for the matching of all packets. This option is typically used in a last-resort class, where the intention is to have all traffic not classified elsewhere put into a given class. This can also be used effectively with the **not** keyword, which is explained later in this list.

- **class-map**—This is the only way to combine the functions of the **match-any** and **match-all** class maps into a single match. Suppose, for instance, that you want traffic that is from either 10.1.1.1 or 10.1.1.2 *and* the destination IP address is 10.2.2.1 to match this class. You could accomplish this by having a **match-any** class with an access-group statement to match the source IP address of 10.1.1.1 (defined by an ACL) and an **access-group** statement to match the source IP address of 10.1.1.2 (defined by another ACL). Then, a **match-all** class would be configured with one condition being that it matches the first class map and another condition being that it matches an ACL that defines the destination IP address of 10.2.2.1. Example 5-5 shows the needed configuration.

Example 5-5   *Combining* **match-any** *and* **match-all** *Options*

```
Router(config)# class-map match-any SOURCES
Router(config-cmap)# match access-group 103
Router(config-cmap)# match access-group 104
Router(config-cmap)# exit
Router(config)# class-map match-all DESTINATION
Router(config-cmap)# match class-map SOURCES
Router(config-cmap)# match access-group 105
Router(config-cmap)# exit
R1(config)# access-list 103 permit ip host 10.1.1.1 any
R1(config)# access-list 104 permit ip host 10.1.1.2 any
R1(config)# access-list 105 permit ip any host 10.2.2.1
```

- **cos**—Allows for the matching of the Layer 2 *class of service* (CoS) value in either the 802.1Q or *Inter-Switch Link* (ISL) header.

- **destination-address**—Don't be fooled, this is not for matching the destination IP address. This allows matching of the destination MAC address.

- **fr-de**—Allows for matching of packets that have the Frame Relay *discard eligible* (DE) bit set.

- **input-interface**—Allows for the matching of packets based on the interface through which they entered the router. This is useful in an environment in which multiple remote sites are connected via Frame Relay to a head-end router. In that environment, provided that point-to-point Frame Relay with subinterfaces is configured, all traffic from a given remote site can be matched based on the subinterface on which that traffic arrived.

- **ip**—Allows for matching based on the IP-specific values previously listed (IP precedence, *DiffServ codepoint* [DSCP], RTP port numbers).

- **mpls**—Currently, this allows only for the matching of packets based on the *multiprotocol label switching* (MPLS) experimental bits. The command has multiple levels to provide flexibility for future matching of other MPLS-specific values.

- **not**—This is a very useful option, which can be used with the **match-any** option in a **match-all** class map to match all packets *except* those listed in the not criteria. For example, you could match all packets (using **match-any**) and then configure a **match not** statement for access group 101, which would match all packets *not* belonging to access group 101.

- **protocol**—Allows for the matching of certain predefined protocols. *Network-based application recognition* (NBAR) is a new classification engine that can recognize a large number of applications based on both static and dynamically assigned port numbers. On routers that support NBAR, the list of protocols is extensive, as shown in Example 5-6.

Example 5-6 **match protocol** *Possibilities Where NBAR Is Supported*

```
R1(config-cmap)# match protocol ?
  aarp               AppleTalk ARP
  apollo             Apollo Domain
  appletalk          AppleTalk
  arp                IP ARP
  bgp                Border Gateway Protocol
  bridge             Bridging
  bstun              Block Serial Tunnel
  cdp                Cisco Discovery Protocol
  citrix             Citrix Traffic
  clns               ISO CLNS
  clns_es            ISO CLNS End System
  clns_is            ISO CLNS Intermediate System
  cmns               ISO CMNS
  compressedtcp      Compressed TCP
  cuseeme            CU-SeeMe desktop video conference
  custom-01          Custom protocol custom-01
  custom-02          Custom protocol custom-02
  custom-03          Custom protocol custom-03
  custom-04          Custom protocol custom-04
  custom-05          Custom protocol custom-05
  custom-06          Custom protocol custom-06
  custom-07          Custom protocol custom-07
  custom-08          Custom protocol custom-08
  custom-09          Custom protocol custom-09
  custom-10          Custom protocol custom-10
  decnet             DECnet
  decnet_node        DECnet Node
  decnet_router-l1   DECnet Router L1
  decnet_router-l2   DECnet Router L2
  dhcp               Dynamic Host Configuration
  dlsw               Data Link Switching
  dns                Domain Name Server lookup
  egp                Exterior Gateway Protocol
  eigrp              Enhanced Interior Gateway Routing Protocol
  exchange           MS-RPC for Exchange
  fasttrack          FastTrack Traffic - KaZaA, Morpheus, Grokster...
  finger             Finger
  ftp                File Transfer Protocol
  gnutella           Gnutella Traffic - BearShare,LimeWire, Gnutella...
  gopher             Gopher
  gre                Generic Routing Encapsulation
  http               World Wide Web traffic
  icmp               Internet Control Message
  imap               Internet Message Access Protocol
  ip                 IP
  ipinip             IP in IP (encapsulation)
```

Example 5-6 **match protocol** *Possibilities Where NBAR Is Supported (Continued)*

```
ipsec         IP Security Protocol (ESP/AH)
ipx           Novell IPX
irc           Internet Relay Chat
kerberos      Kerberos
l2tp          L2F/L2TP tunnel
ldap          Lightweight Directory Access Protocol
llc2          llc2
napster       Napster Traffic
netbios       NetBIOS
netshow       Microsoft Netshow
nfs           Network File System
nntp          Network News Transfer Protocol
notes         Lotus Notes(R)
novadigm      Novadigm EDM
ntp           Network Time Protocol
pad           PAD links
pcanywhere    Symantec pcANYWHERE
pop3          Post Office Protocol
pppoe         PPP over Ethernet
pptp          Point-to-Point Tunneling Protocol
printer       print spooler/lpd
qllc          qllc protocol
rcmd          BSD r-commands (rsh, rlogin, rexec)
realaudio     Real Audio streaming protocol
rip           Routing Information Protocol
rsrb          Remote Source-Route Bridging
rsvp          Resource Reservation Protocol
secure-ftp    FTP over TLS/SSL
secure-http   Secured HTTP
secure-imap   Internet Message Access Protocol over TLS/SSL
secure-irc    Internet Relay Chat over TLS/SSL
secure-ldap   Lightweight Directory Access Protocol over TLS/SSL
secure-nntp   Network News Transfer Protocol over TLS/SSL
secure-pop3   Post Office Protocol over TLS/SSL
secure-telnet Telnet over TLS/SSL
smtp          Simple Mail Transfer Protocol
snapshot      Snapshot routing support
snmp          Simple Network Management Protocol
socks         SOCKS
sqlnet        SQL*NET for Oracle
sqlserver     MS SQL Server
ssh           Secured Shell
streamwork    Xing Technology StreamWorks player
stun          Serial Tunnel
sunrpc        Sun RPC
syslog        System Logging Utility
telnet        Telnet
tftp          Trivial File Transfer Protocol
vdolive       VDOLive streaming video
vines         Banyan VINES
vofr          voice over Frame Relay packets
xns           Xerox Network Services
xwindows      X-Windows remote access
```

On routers that do not support NBAR, the list is quite a bit smaller, as shown in Example 5-7.

Example 5-7   **match protocol** *Possibilities Where NBAR Is Not Supported*

```
R1(config-cmap)# match protocol ?
  aarp              AppleTalk ARP
  apollo            Apollo Domain
  appletalk         AppleTalk
  arp               IP ARP
  bridge            Bridging
  bstun             Block Serial Tunnel
  cdp               Cisco Discovery Protocol
  clns              ISO CLNS
  clns_es           ISO CLNS End System
  clns_is           ISO CLNS Intermediate System
  cmns              ISO CMNS
  compressedtcp     Compressed TCP
  decnet            DECnet
  decnet_node       DECnet Node
  decnet_router-l1  DECnet Router L1
  decnet_router-l2  DECnet Router L2
  dlsw              Data Link Switching
  ip                IP
  ipv6              IPV6
  ipx               Novell IPX
  llc2              llc2
  pad               PAD links
  qllc              qllc protocol
  rsrb              Remote Source-Route Bridging
  snapshot          Snapshot routing support
  stun              Serial Tunnel
  vines             Banyan VINES
  vofr              voice over Frame Relay packets
  xns               Xerox Network Services
```

- **qos-group**—Allows for the matching of a packet based on its **qos-group** marking. QoS groups are locally significant to a given router and are not carried with the packet once it leaves the router. Further, QoS groups are not mathematically significant. That is, a packet belonging to QoS Group 1 is no more, or less, important than a packet belonging to QoS Group 2. Assigning a packet to a QoS group is fairly simple as Example 5-8 demonstrates.

Example 5-8   *Assigning a Packet to a QoS Group*

```
route-map set-qos-group permit 10
match community 3
set ip qos-group 30
```

- **source-address**—Again, don't be fooled by the name of this option. This is for matching the source MAC address, not the source IP address.

Class Map Configuration Example

The most commonly used method is to match an ACL through the **access-group** option. Do not be fooled by the options for matching source and destination address. Those options refer to the MAC address; so if you want to match source or destination IP address, you will have to use an ACL. In the Accounting department example given earlier in the chapter, both the source address and a port number (either for HTTP or FTP) need to be matched. Because the class map configuration does not provide the capability to do that directly, ACLs are required for each. Example 5-9 shows traffic matching using ACLs.

Example 5-9   *Using ACLs to Match Traffic*

```
R1(config)# access-list 101 permit tcp any any eq www
R1(config)# access-list 102 permit tcp any any eq ftp
R1(config)# access-list 103 permit ip host 10.1.1.1 any
R1(config)# access-list 104 permit ip host 10.1.1.2 any
```

ACL 101 matches all HTTP traffic; ACL 102 matches all FTP traffic (on port 20 only), ACL 103 matches all traffic from 10.1.1.1, and ACL 104 matches all traffic from 10.1.1.2. The trick now is to combine the ACLs and class map configuration commands correctly, to achieve the desired result. Example 5-10 shows the class map configuration for matching HTTP traffic from 10.1.1.1.

Example 5-10   *Class Map Configuration for Matching HTTP Traffic from a Specific Network*

```
R1(config)# class-map match-all HTTP
R1(config-cmap)# match access-group 101
R1(config-cmap)# match access-group 103
```

This is where the difference between **match-any** and **match-all** comes into play. As highlighted earlier in the chapter, **match-any** is a logical OR operation, meaning if access group 101 *or* access group 103 are a match, the traffic belongs to this class. In this case, that would not be the desired behavior, because the intent is to match only traffic that matches *both* ACLs. That behavior is accomplished through the use of a **class-map match-all**, which is a logical AND operation. That means that access group 101 *and* access group 103 must be match for the traffic to belong to this class.

You can verify the configured class map with the **show class-map** command, as demonstrated in Example 5-11.

Example 5-11   *Verifying the Class Map*

```
R1# show class-map
 Class Map match-all HTTP (id 2)
   Match access-group  101
   Match access-group  103

 Class Map match-any class-default (id 0)
   Match any
```

The output from **show class-map** displays all the configured classes (in this case, there is only one), whether classes are a **match-any** or a **match-all** class, what the name of each class is, and which traffic belongs in those classes. Overall, this is a very useful command.

Also notice the **class-default**, which is automatically created whenever any other class is created. The purpose of **class-default** is to give all traffic that does not belong to any other class a place to go.

The ID numbers that are given in parentheses next to each class cannot be changed and have no meaning, other than to assist Cisco IOS Software in keeping the classes organized.

Going back to the Accounting department example, a total of four classes are needed: one to match HTTP traffic from 10.1.1.1, one to match FTP traffic from 10.1.1.1, one to match HTTP traffic from 10.1.1.2, and one to match FTP traffic from 10.1.1.2. Example 5-12 shows the complete configuration of the classes. Notice that the classes have been renamed for clarity.

Example 5-12 *Displaying the Class Configuration*

```
R1# show class-map
 Class Map match-any class-default (id 0)
   Match any

 Class Map match-all ACCOUNTING-HTTP (id 2)
   Match access-group   101
   Match access-group   103

 Class Map match-all DEVELOPMENT-FTP (id 5)
   Match access-group   102
   Match access-group   104

 Class Map match-all DEVELOPMENT-HTTP (id 4)
   Match access-group   101
   Match access-group   104

 Class Map match-all ACCOUNTING-FTP (id 3)
   Match access-group   102
   Match access-group   103
```

Now all four of the traffic source/type pairs that were presented earlier in the chapter have been classified, allowing for differentiated treatment to be given to each.

Step 2: The Policy Map

The function of the class map is only to identify traffic, based on the characteristics given within the class map; the actual treatment of that traffic is specified in a policy map. As discussed earlier in the chapter, many different QoS mechanisms can be configured via the MQC, so the policy map has quite a few options. Note that, on switching platforms, not all of these options are supported in hardware. Switching platforms, such as the Catalyst 6500, may support some options in software. For performance reasons, you should not configure policies that are not supported in hardware unless absolutely necessary, because there could be a severe performance penalty for doing so. Cisco constantly adds new hardware support for features and the hardware support is different for different hardware (such as, PFC1 versus PFC2). As such, you should always check the hardware support for these actions before configuring them. NBAR was discussed earlier in this chapter and is a good example of something that was not supported in hardware on the 6500 at the time of this writing.

Configuring the Policy Map

Like the class map, the policy map is configured from the global configuration mode in Cisco IOS Software and requires a name.

```
R1(config)#policy-map ?
  WORD  policy-map name

R1(config)#policy-map ACCOUNTING-POLICY
R1(config-pmap)#
```

The policy map ACCOUNTING-POLICY is now configured, and the router automatically moves into policy map configuration mode, as indicated by the config-pmap in the router's prompt. This configuration mode allows for the configuration of the specific policy map that was created and has several options, as demonstrated in Example 5-13.

Example 5-13 *Policy Map Options*

```
R1(config-pmap)# ?
QoS policy-map configuration commands:
  class       policy criteria
  description Policy-Map description
  exit        Exit from QoS policy-map configuration mode
  no          Negate or set default values of a command
  rename      Rename this policy-map
```

As with the class map configuration, it is recommended that a description be configured for all policy maps, but this is not required. Again there is a rename option, which is just a convenient way of renaming the policy map without losing the configuration. Before the rename option was available, the only way to change the name of a policy map was to delete the policy map and then re-add the same configuration under the new name. For anyone who works with QoS on a daily basis, this was a great addition. The main purpose of the policy map is, however, to create the policy or policies that will be applied to traffic of a given class. As such, the option for selecting a class is of the most interest. For more complicated QoS configurations, using meaningful names for classes and policies along with the description feature is of great operational value.

The only option listed under the **class** command is for you to enter the name of the class for which you want to configure a policy. A list of available classes is not given, but the supported classes include those that have been configured manually plus **class-default**.

Example 5-14 shows the options available under **class-default**.

Example 5-14   *Policy Map Options Available Under* **class-default**

```
R1(config)# policy-map ACCOUNTING-POLICY
R1(config-pmap)# class class-default
R1config-pmap-c)# ?
QoS policy-map class configuration commands:
  bandwidth       Bandwidth
  exit            Exit from QoS class action configuration mode
  fair-queue      Enable Flow-based Fair Queuing in this Class
  no              Negate or set default values of a command
  police          Police
  priority        Strict Scheduling Priority for this Class
  queue-limit     Queue Max Threshold for Tail Drop
  random-detect   Enable Random Early Detection as drop policy
  service-policy  Configure QoS Service Policy
  shape           Traffic Shaping
  set             Set QoS values
```

Notice that a new prompt appears, after a class has been selected, to indicate that you have entered the class configuration submode within the policy map configuration. The options shown, other than the **fair-queue** option, are the same for all classes. The **fair-queue** option is available on some classes, but not all. A discussion of the details of this behavior is beyond the scope of this text but can be found at Cisco.com.

Policy Map Options: A Closer Look

Because the policy map is the portion of the configuration that dictates the actual treatment of traffic by the router, a more detailed explanation of the behavior of each option is provided here. **exit** and **no** are not covered because their behavior is the same as elsewhere in Cisco IOS Software.

- **bandwidth**—Allows for the configuration of CBWFQ. The specifics of CBWFQ operation are beyond the scope of this explanation, but this command provides a minimum bandwidth guarantee to this class of traffic.

- **fair-queue**—Not available in all classes. This command enables Flow-based Weighted Fair Queuing within this class.

- **police**—Allows for the configuration of a policer, also known as *rate limiting*. The **police** command, when used within a class, is called class-based policing.

- **priority**—Designates that this class is a *Low Latency Queuing* (LLQ) class, which should receive strict scheduling priority to minimize delay, jitter and packet loss. Also specifies the amount of bandwidth for this class.

- **queue-limit**—Designates the maximum number of packets that can be in this queue.

- **random-detect**—Enables Weighted Random Early Detection (WRED) for congestion avoidance. By default, IP precedence is used for weight determination, but additional options within this command allow for the WRED algorithm to look at the DSCP. This command also provides an option for enabling *explicit congestion notification* (ECN) on this class.

- **service-policy**—Allows for the configuration of hierarchical policies (policy within a policy), which may be used to achieve functionality not possible in a single policy. For example, a T1 can be shaped to 512 kbps via a top-level policy, and then that 512 kbps can be divided (using CBWFQ/LLQ) within a second-level policy. Top-level policies are sometimes called *parent policies*, and second-level policies are sometimes called *child policies*.

- **shape**—Allows for the configuration of class-based shaping, which is generic traffic shaping performed on a per-class basis. In this case, only the traffic in this class would be shaped. This is in contract to interface-based shaping, in which all traffic on the entire interface is shaped.

- **set**—Allows for the marking of packets. Several fields can be marked through the use of the **set** command, including IP precedence, IP DSCP, MPLS experimental bits, Layer 2 CoS, the ATM *cell loss priority* (CLP) bit, and the QoS group.

Back to the Accounting department example again, because it is time to configure the actual policies for the classes that have been defined. In this example, the only parameter that is used is bandwidth. This is not necessarily the policy that you would use in your production environment and is intended only as a sample of the configuration parameters.

Policy Map Configuration Example

Assuming that the link speed is 1.544 Mbps, and the intent is to give 128 kbps to each of the production classes, 64 kbps to the DEVELOPMENT-HTTP class, and 32 kbps to the DEVELOPMENT-FTP class, the configuration would look like Example 5-15.

Example 5-15 *Configuring a Policy Map with Class Maps*

```
R1(config-pmap)# policy-map ACCOUNTING-POLICY
R1(config-pmap)# class ACCOUNTING-HTTP
R1(config-pmap-c)# bandwidth 128
R1(config-pmap-c)# exit
R1(config-pmap)# class ACCOUNTING-FTP
R1(config-pmap-c)# bandwidth 128
R1(config-pmap-c)# exit
R1(config-pmap)# class DEVELOPMENT-HTTP
R1(config-pmap-c)# bandwidth 64
R1(config-pmap-c)# class DEVELOPMENT-FTP
R1(config-pmap-c)# bandwidth 32
```

Notice that between the bandwidth statement for DEVELOPMENT-HTTP and the class name for DEVELOPMENT-FTP that there is no **exit** command. It is acceptable to exit from each class after configuring it, but not necessary. When you type a new class name, the MQC automatically moves to the configuration mode for that class.

You can confirm the configuration that has been entered through the use of the **show policy-map** command, as shown in Example 5-16.

Example 5-16   *Verifying the Policy Map*

```
R1# show policy-map
  Policy Map ACCOUNTING-POLICY
    Class ACCOUNTING-HTTP
          Bandwidth 128 (kbps) Max Threshold 64 (packets)
    Class ACCOUNTING-FTP
          Bandwidth 128 (kbps) Max Threshold 64 (packets)
    Class DEVELOPMENT-HTTP
          Bandwidth 64 (kbps) Max Threshold 64 (packets)
    Class DEVELOPMENT-FTP
          Bandwidth 32 (kbps) Max Threshold 64 (packets)
    Class class-default
```

As indicated by the output, the queue limit for each of these classes is set to 64 packets (the default). This output also shows the policy map's name, the names of all the class maps within the policy, and the policy that has actually been configured for each class. Notice that this command does *not* show any information about the traffic that will belong to each class or whether each class is a **match-any** or a **match-all**.

As discussed previously, one of the greatest benefits to the MQC structure is the lack of a learning curve for configuring new options. Suppose, for instance, that you now need to add traffic shaping to the ACCOUNTING-FTP class, to prevent the class from using more than 256 kbps under any conditions. If you were not using the MQC, it would be necessary to learn an entirely new command structure. Because the MQC uses the same structure to configure many QoS components, however, the configuration requires only one additional line of configuration.

Example 5-17 is the same example configuration as Example 5-15, but with the addition of traffic shaping.

Example 5-17   *Traffic Shaping Within a Class Map*

```
R1(config-pmap)# policy-map ACCOUNTING-POLICY
R1(config-pmap)# class ACCOUNTING-HTTP
R1(config-pmap-c)# bandwidth 128
R1(config-pmap-c)# exit
R1(config-pmap)# class ACCOUNTING-FTP
R1(config-pmap-c)# bandwidth 128
R1(config-pmap-c)# shape average 256000
R1(config-pmap-c)# exit
R1(config-pmap)# class DEVELOPMENT-HTTP
R1(config-pmap-c)# bandwidth 64
R1(config-pmap-c)# class DEVELOPMENT-FTP
R1(config-pmap-c)# bandwidth 32
```

The only additional command is the command to add traffic shaping, which makes the learning curve much shorter for learning how to configure a new QoS mechanism.

Further, the verification of the new configuration doesn't require anything new. As shown in Example 5-18, to verify both the CBWFQ configuration and the newly added traffic shaping configuration you can use the same command that was previously used to verify the CBWFQ configuration.

Example 5-18 *Verifying the Policy Map Configuration*

```
R1# show policy-map
  Policy Map ACCOUNTING-POLICY
    Class ACCOUNTING-HTTP
          Bandwidth 128 (kbps) Max Threshold 64 (packets)
    Class ACCOUNTING-FTP
          Bandwidth 128 (kbps) Max Threshold 64 (packets)
      Traffic Shaping
        Average Rate Traffic Shaping
              CIR 256000 (bps) Max. Buffers Limit 1000 (Packets)
    Class DEVELOPMENT-HTTP
          Bandwidth 64 (kbps) Max Threshold 64 (packets)
    Class DEVELOPMENT-FTP
          Bandwidth 32 (kbps) Max Threshold 64 (packets)
    Class class-default
```

After configuring both the class map, which defines the traffic that the router should pay attention to, and the policy map, which defines the action(s) that the router should apply to each class of traffic, the only thing that is left is to define the interface(s) to which the policy map should be applied.

Step 3: Attaching the Service Policy

All the configuration options and steps outlined so far in this chapter mean nothing until the resulting policy map is applied to an interface. This is much the same as configuring an ACL; the configuration means nothing until the ACL is applied to an interface.

For the service policy, only two options affect functionality: **input** and **output**. There is also a **history** option, not covered here in detail because it is for information only and does enable you to configure any functionality. Example 5-19 shows the two functional options.

Example 5-19 *Service Policy Options*

```
R1(config-if)# service-policy ?
  history  Keep history of QoS metrics
  input    Assign policy-map to the input of an interface
  output   Assign policy-map to the output of an interface
```

The **input** option means that the policy map is applied to traffic that enters the router through this interface, and the **output** option means that the policy map is applied to traffic that leaves the router through this interface. The ability to apply a policy map input or output on a specific interface depends on which QoS mechanisms are used in the policy map. Some actions are only allowed in output policies.

If the policy map called ACCOUNTING-POLICY is going to be applied to traffic leaving the router through Serial1/0, the commands in Example 5-20 are used.

Example 5-20 *Applying the Service Policy*

```
R1# conf t
Enter configuration commands, one per line.  End with CNTL/Z.
R1(config)# interface serial 6/0
R1(config-if)# service-policy output ACCOUNTING-POLICY
```

If you need to apply another policy in the input direction, you could do so easily, as follows:

```
R1(config-if)#service-policy input ANOTHER-POLICY
```

If you forget that you already have a service policy applied in the input direction and attempt to apply another policy, however, the router issues a friendly reminder that you are not allowed to apply more than one policy to an interface:

```
R1(config-if)#service-policy input THIRD-POLICY
 Policy map ANOTHER-POLICY is already attached
```

You now have the option of detaching the policy that was previously applied, which would then enable you to apply the THIRD-POLICY to this interface, or you can just do nothing and the original policy will remain attached.

Because the policy named ANOTHER-POLICY was only used to illustrate the ability to attach multiple policies (one input and one output), it is not included in the following **show** command outputs.

There is no service policy–specific command, but there is a command to show the interface-specific policy map information, and you should use that command to view the details of the policy map after it has been applied to an interface. Example 5-21 demonstrates output from the **show policy-map interface ?** command.

Example 5-21 *Options for Verifying Policy Map Configuration*

```
R1# show policy-map interface ?
  Async          Async interface
  BVI            Bridge-Group Virtual Interface
  CTunnel        CTunnel interface
  Dialer         Dialer interface
  Ethernet       IEEE 802.3
  Group-Async    Async Group interface
  Lex            Lex interface
  Loopback       Loopback interface
  MFR            Multilink Frame Relay bundle interface
  Multilink      Multilink-group interface
```

Example 5-21 *Options for Verifying Policy Map Configuration (Continued)*

```
Null                Null interface
Serial              Serial
Tunnel              Tunnel interface
Vif                 PGM Multicast Host interface
Virtual-Template    Virtual Template interface
Virtual-TokenRing   Virtual TokenRing
input               Input policy
output              Output policy
|                   Output modifiers
```

The interface types speak for themselves, but the **input** and **output** options are interesting because they can be used to show you all the policies that are applied in either the input or output direction (depending on which command you choose). More commonly, however, you will probably use the more specific command in Example 5-22.

Example 5-22 *Verifying Policy Map Configuration for a Specific Interface*

```
R1# show policy-map interface serial 1/0
 Serial1/0

  Service-policy output: ACCOUNTING-POLICY

    Class-map: ACCOUNTING-HTTP (match-all)
      0 packets, 0 bytes
      5 minute offered rate 0 bps, drop rate 0 bps
      Match: access-group 101
      Match: access-group 103
      Queueing
Output Queue: Conversation 265
        Bandwidth 128 (kbps) Max Threshold 64 (packets)
        (pkts matched/bytes matched) 0/0
        (depth/total drops/no-buffer drops) 0/0/0

    Class-map: ACCOUNTING-FTP (match-all)
      0 packets, 0 bytes
      5 minute offered rate 0 bps, drop rate 0 bps
      Match: access-group 102
      Match: access-group 103
      Queueing
        Output Queue: Conversation 266
        Bandwidth 128 (kbps) Max Threshold 64 (packets)
        (pkts matched/bytes matched) 0/0
        (depth/total drops/no-buffer drops) 0/0/0
      Traffic Shaping
           Target/Average   Byte    Sustain   Excess    Interval  Increment
             Rate           Limit   bits/int  bits/int  (ms)      (bytes)
           256000/256000    1984    7936      7936      31        992

        Adapt  Queue   Packets   Bytes   Packets  Bytes    Shaping
        Active Depth                     Delayed  Delayed  Active
        -      0       0         0       0        0        no
```

continues

Example 5-22 *Verifying Policy Map Configuration for a Specific Interface (Continued)*

```
         Class-map: DEVELOPMENT-HTTP (match-all)
           0 packets, 0 bytes
           5 minute offered rate 0 bps, drop rate 0 bps
           Match: access-group 101
           Match: access-group 104
    Queueing
             Output Queue: Conversation 267
             Bandwidth 64 (kbps) Max Threshold 64 (packets)
             (pkts matched/bytes matched) 0/0
             (depth/total drops/no-buffer drops) 0/0/0

         Class-map: DEVELOPMENT-FTP (match-all)
           0 packets, 0 bytes
           5 minute offered rate 0 bps, drop rate 0 bps
           Match: access-group 102
           Match: access-group 104
           Queueing
             Output Queue: Conversation 268
             Bandwidth 32 (kbps) Max Threshold 64 (packets)
             (pkts matched/bytes matched) 0/0
             (depth/total drops/no-buffer drops) 0/0/0

         Class-map: class-default (match-any)
           0 packets, 0 bytes
           5 minute offered rate 0 bps, drop rate 0 bps
           Match: any
```

As you can see, the output is far more detailed than the output from the previous command. In fact, this command probably provides one of the most detailed outputs of any command in Cisco IOS. Certainly, this is the most comprehensive output of any MQC command.

Summary

This chapter examined the three-step process for configuring all the QoS mechanisms supported by the MQC. These steps are as follows:

Step 1   Class map configuration

Step 2   Policy map configuration

Step 3   Service policy application

Class maps come in two types:

- **match-any**—A logical OR operation, which means that only one of the match conditions must be met for a packet to belong to this class

- **match-all**—A logical AND operation, which means that all match criteria must be matched for a packet to belong to this class

match-all is the default, if no option is specified. Class maps are capable of matching certain criteria, but the majority of matches come via the matching of an access group. As detailed earlier in the chapter, you can combine **match-all** and **match-any** class maps with access group matching to accomplish fairly complex matching criteria.

Policy maps define many different actions that you can apply to a given class. Some actions may only be applied in a single direction, not both. Not all of these actions can be applied to packets entering an interface; instead, they are only allowed as an output policy (for packets leaving an interface). Traffic shaping is a good example of a policy map action that cannot currently be applied to inbound packets. Further, not all actions that are specified are supported in hardware on Catalyst products, which could mean a severe performance impact for certain features. Always check your Cisco IOS version and specific hardware type to determine hardware support for software features.

The next chapter introduces the platform-specific configuration options and specific hardware available for the Catalyst 2950 and 3550 products. The following chapter includes examples, using the MQC explained in this chapter, that show you how to configure QoS features on these products.

CHAPTER 6

QoS Features Available on the Catalyst 2950 and 3550 Family of Switches

This chapter continues the discussion of QoS feature support on Catalyst switches with the Catalyst 2950 Family and 3550 Family of switches. From an architectural perspective, the Catalyst 2950 Family of switches supports only Layer 2 MAC address forwarding and does not support Layer 3 routing. However, the Catalyst 2950 Family of switches supports a multitude of Layer 3 features such as classification based on CoS or DSCP, security and QoS *access-control list* (ACL) support, policing, and *Internet Group Management Protocol* (IGMP) snooping. Because the Catalyst 2950 Family of switches does not support IP routing, the typical network installations find the Catalyst 2950 Family of switches acting as access layer switches. Moreover, the Catalyst 3550 Family of switches supports IP routing and is applicable as an access layer or distribution layer switch. The Catalyst 3550 Family of switches may act as a core switch in small networks aggregating Catalyst 3550 switches and other access layer switches, such as the Catalyst 2950, 2900XL, and 3500XL Family of switches.

Both the Catalyst 2950 and 3550 Family of switches supports a wide range of QoS features that rival higher-end switches, including the Catalyst 4000 IOS Family of switches and the Catalyst 6500 Family of switches. Because the Catalyst 2950 and Catalyst 3550 switches use the same Cisco IOS code base, both support a base set of QoS features while the Catalyst 3550 Family of switches supports a few additional QoS features. Table 6-1, in the "Software Requirements" section of this chapter, outlines the QoS features supported by both the Catalyst 2950 and 3550 Family of switches along with those features only supported on the Catalyst 3550 Family of switches.

Specifically, this chapter discusses QoS support on the Catalyst 2950 and 3550 Family of switches, and includes the following topics:

- Architectural Overview
- Input Scheduling
- Classification and Marking
- Policing
- Congestion Management and Avoidance
- Auto-QoS
- Case Study
- Summary

This chapter discusses both the Catalyst 2950 and Catalyst 3550 Family of switches concurrently because of the feature overlap of these switches. This chapter also indicates those features supported only on the Catalyst 3550 Family of switches on a per-feature basis.

Catalyst 2950 and Catalyst 3550 Family of Switches QoS Architectural Overview

The Catalyst 2950 and 3550 switches follow a standard model for QoS features. At the time of publication, all models of the Catalyst 2950 and 3550 Family of switches utilize the same QoS architecture. Specifically, the Catalyst 2950 and 3550 switches base QoS architecture on the following model.

Figure 6-1   *Catalyst 2950 and 3550 QoS Architecture Model*

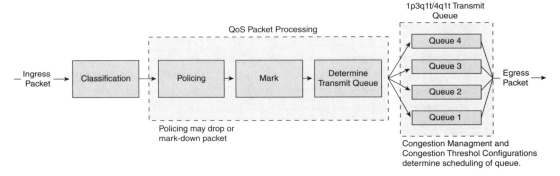

These switches do not modify the packet on ingress for classification and marking; instead, these switches assign an internal *differentiated services codepoint* (DSCP) value to the packet. These switches use the internal DSCP to make policing, queuing, and scheduling decisions. Furthermore, the internal DSCP determines the egress DSCP and *class of service* (CoS) values. The switches use the internal DSCP method of classification whether or not a packet contains an IP header. Policing may mark down the internal DSCP value for packets out-of-profile of a respective policer. As with the internal DSCP value, the switch carries the markdown DSCP value but does not modify the packet during rate policing.

Both switches utilize *ternary content addressable memory* (TCAM) to carry out QoS features such as classification based on ACLs and policing. TCAM provides a high-rate packet-matching algorithm for determining result actions. Security ACLs and IP routing decisions also use TCAM for pattern matching. The use of TCAM is the method of choice for packet processing among current Catalyst switches.

In brief, switches populate TCAM with masks, values, and results. Values may represent IP addresses, protocol ports, DSCP values, or any other packet-matching field. Masks represent wildcard bits. Results represent packet actions such as Permit or Deny packets, as in the case of a security ACLs, or a pointer to more complex action such as marking the packet in the case of a classification ACL. The switch generates lookup keys for ingress packets in order to search TCAM tables for results. The switch compares lookup keys against masks and values. The first match provides a result. Catalyst switches utilize TCAM on packet ingress, during packet progressing, and on egress to gather results for actions such as Layer 3 forwarding and packet rewriting, QoS classification, policing, and security ACLs processing.

Figure 6-2 shows a logical example of a security ACL. The figure does not indicate exact hardware implementation of TCAM, but rather a logical representation for understanding the use of TCAM. Actual hardware implementation of TCAM varies on each Catalyst Family of switch.

Figure 6-2   *Logical Representation of TCAM*

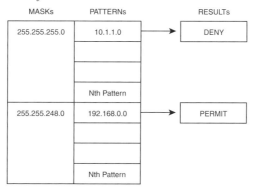

For additional technical information on the architectural use of TCAM, refer to the following technical document at Cisco.com:

> "Understanding ACL Merge Algorithms and ACL Hardware Resources on Cisco Catalyst 6500 Switches"

Exact implementations of TCAM vary significantly between Catalyst switching platforms. In addition, TCAM is a limited resource. The amount of ACLs that fit into TCAM are limited by the number of entries, range of ports specified, range of IP addresses, masks, and various other platform-specific constraints. These limitations are found in the configuration guides for each platform.

From a network design perspective, the QoS features supported on the Catalyst 2950 and 3550 Family of switches fit these switches into any end-to-end QoS design. Because the Catalyst 3550 Family of switches also supports IP routing features, the switch also fits well as a small distribution or core switch. Networks requiring more internal redundancy and additional port density should instead utilize the Catalyst 4500 or Catalyst 6500 Family of switches. Figure 6-3 shows a sample network design using Catalyst 2950 and Catalyst 3550 Family of switches in a small end-to-end design. Figure 6-4 illustrates the Catalyst 2950 and 3550 Family of switches in a campus network utilizing Catalyst 6500 switches in the core. The section, "Cisco IOS Software Feature Sets," discusses the EI and EMI acronyms found in Figures 6-3 and 6-4.

Figure 6-3 *Sample Network Topology Using Catalyst 2950 and Catalyst 3550 Family of Switches*

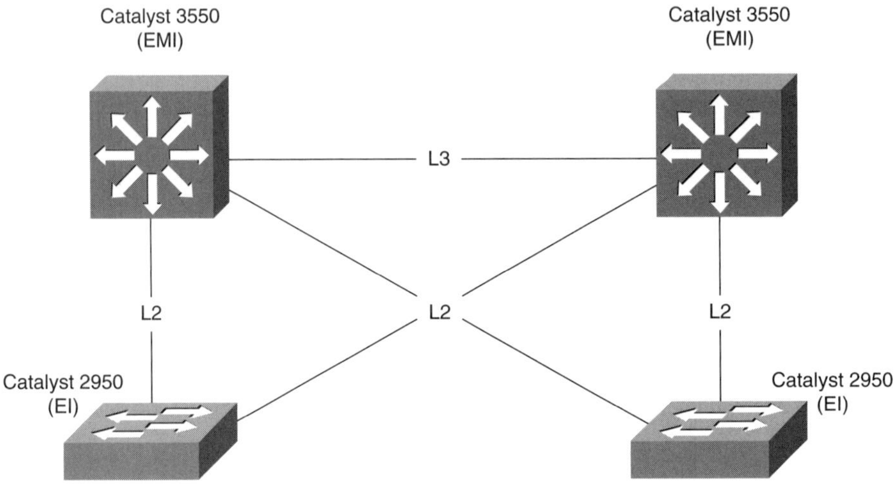

Figure 6-4 *Sample Campus Network Topology Using Catalyst 2950 and Catalyst 3550 Family of Switches*

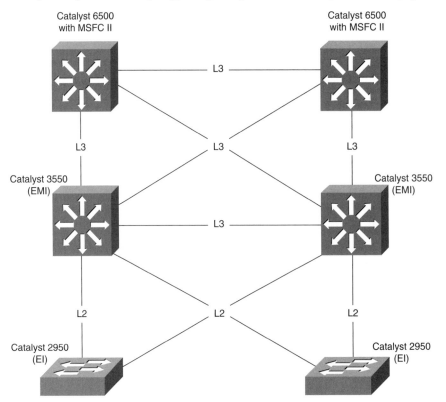

Software Requirements

Both the Catalyst 2950 and Catalyst 3550 Family of switches utilize Cisco IOS Software. At the time of publication, these switches run the Cisco IOS 12.1 EA Software train.

These switches support many campus QoS features including policing, classification, marking, and scheduling of packets or frames. The Catalyst 2950 and 3550 switches share many common QoS features. Most of the common QoS features impart the same configuration and operational characteristics. One noteworthy difference in QoS support between the platforms is output scheduling. The Catalyst 2950 Family of switches supports only congestion management, whereas the Catalyst 3550 Family of switches supports both congestion management and congestion avoidance. The Catalyst 3550 Family of switches supports congestion management and avoidance using *weighted round-robin* (WRR) with configurable tail drop or *Weighted Random Early Detection* (WRED) thresholds. Both switches support strict-priority queuing. Furthermore, the Catalyst 3550 Family of switches supports several additional QoS features, including egress policing and several QoS mapping table configurations not supported on the Catalyst 2950 Family of switches. Table 6-1 outlines the supported QoS features of the Catalyst 2950 and 3550 Family of switches.

Table 6-1 *Feature Parity Between the Catalyst 2950 and Catalyst 3550 Family of Switches in Cisco IOS 12.1(11)EA1*

Feature	Platform Support
Classification	**2950 (EI) 3550**
Classification based on port trust state	2950 (EI) 3550
Classification based on ACLs	2950 (EI) 3550
Classification based on policy maps	2950 (EI) 3550
Classification based on trusting CoS	2950 (EI) 3550
Classification based on port CoS configuration	2950 (EI) 3550
Classification based on trusting DSCP	2950 (EI) 3550
Classification based on IP precedence	3550
Classification based on CDP from Cisco IP Phone	2950 3550
Marking	**2950 (EI) 3550**
Policing	**2950 (EI) 3550**
Ingress policing	2950 (EI) 3550
Egress policing	3550
Configuration of Mapping Tables	**2950 (EI) 3550**
CoS-to-DSCP	2950 (EI) 3550
IP precedence-to-DSCP	3550

continues

Table 6-1　*Feature Parity Between the Catalyst 2950 and Catalyst 3550 Family of Switches in Cisco IOS 12.1(11)EA1 (Continued)*

Feature	Platform Support
DSCP-to-CoS	2950 (EI) 3550
Policed DSCP mapping table	3550
IP precedence-to-DSCP mapping table configuration	3550
DSCP-to-DSCP mapping	3550
DSCP-to-CoS	2950 (EI)
Output Queuing and Scheduling	**2950 3550**
Strict-priority scheduling	2950 3550
WRR scheduling	2950 3550
WRED congestion avoidance	3550
Tail-drop congestion avoidance	3550
Transmit queue size manipulation	3550

CDP = Cisco Discovery Protocol

Cisco IOS Software Feature Sets

The Catalyst 2950 Family of switches runs two feature sets of Cisco IOS, a *standard image* (SI) and an *enhanced image* (EI). Several feature differences exist between the SI and EI versions. The SI version only supports 64 VLANs, for instance, whereas the EI version supports 256 VLANs with ACL support on physical interfaces. The SI only supports the output scheduling QoS features, whereas the EI adds support for classification, marking, and policing. Table 6-1 illustrates which QoS features are available in the SI and EI versions by noting EI for features that require the EI software version. Those switches that employ SI versions are upgradable to EI with specific restrictions. Refer to the product release notes for details.

The Catalyst 3550 Family of switches also runs two different feature sets of IOS, a *standard multilayer image* (SMI) and an *enhanced multilayer image* (EMI). With regard to IP routing, the SMI version only supports IP routing and a few routing features such as static routing and *Routing Information Protocol* (RIP). The EMI version supports other routing protocols and IP routing features including inter-VLAN routing, *Open Shortest Path First* (OSPF), *Interior Gateway Routing Protocol* (IGRP), *Extended Interior Gateway Routing Protocol* (EIGRP), *Border Gateway Protocol* (BGP), and the *Hot Standby Routing Protocol* (HSRP). Furthermore, the EMI version supports router ACLs and a higher number of multicast groups and MAC addresses per switch. Nevertheless, the QoS features are identical between the SMI and EMI versions. As a result, this chapter does not differentiate between the two versions. The Catalyst 3550 Family of switches is upgradable to the EMI version. Refer to the product release notes for details.

NOTE   In Cisco IOS 12.1(9)EA1, several software changes occurred that optimized the use of the TCAM space for QoS and security ACLs. As a result, both the Catalyst 2950 and 3550 Family of switches possibly support more ACL entries in Cisco IOS 12.1(9)EA than previous versions.

Global and Default Configuration

The Catalyst 2950 Family of switches does not require global configuration to enact on QoS configuration. The default trust behavior of the Catalyst 2950 is untrusted. The Catalyst 2950 Family of switches uses the default port CoS value of zero by default for the internal DSCP value. See the "Internal DSCP and Mapping Tables" section later in this chapter for more detailed information about internal DSCP.

The Catalyst 3550 Family of switches does support a global QoS configuration. By default, the QoS is disabled on the Catalyst 3550 Family of switches and, as a result, does not modify any CoS or DSCP value of a packet on ingress or egress. In addition, the switch does not carry out any congestion management or avoidance mechanisms. Use the following configuration command to globally enable QoS on a Catalyst 3550 switch:

    [no] mls qos

Example 6-1 illustrates a user globally enabling QoS and verifying the configuration on a Catalyst 3550 switch.

Example 6-1   *Enabling and Viewing QoS Global Configuration on a Catalyst 3550 Switch*

```
Switch#config terminal
Switch(config)#mls qos
Switch(config)#end
Switch#show mls qos
QoS is enabled globally
```

The default trust behavior of the Catalyst 3550 Family of switches is untrusted when QoS is enabled. Furthermore, the switch carries out WRR scheduling with each queue receiving 25 percent of transmit bandwidth by default. The "Congestion Management" section of this chapter discusses WRR in more detail.

Input Scheduling

As with the other Catalyst platforms, neither the Catalyst 2950 nor the 3550 Family of switches support input scheduling, and they perform only *First-In, First-Out* (FIFO)

Queuing of ingress packets. Not supporting input scheduling on any switch is not an issue when maintaining the supported packet-forwarding rate of the switch. Consult the Cisco product documentation for more information regarding the packet-forwarding rate of the Catalyst 2950 Family and Catalyst 3550 Family of switches.

Classification and Marking

Classification establishes an internal DSCP value, which the switches use to differentiate packets during packet processing, policing, and output scheduling and queuing. The Catalyst 2950 Family of switches supports the following classification options:

- Ingress port CoS configuration
- Trust CoS
- Trust DSCP
- Extended trust on voice and VLANs
- ACL-based classification
- Classified model based on internal DSCP
- CoS and DSCP mapping tables

The Catalyst 3550 Family of switches supports the following classification options:

- Ingress port CoS configuration
- Trust CoS
- Trust DSCP
- Trust IP precedence
- Extended trust on voice and VLANs
- Trust Cisco IP Phone
- ACL-based classification
- Classification model based on internal DSCP
- CoS and DSCP mapping tables

Both the trust CoS and trust DSCP options allow for DSCP and CoS passthrough, respectively. In addition, the trust DSCP option on the Catalyst 3550 Family of switches supports DSCP mutation.

Internal DSCP and Mapping Tables

As mentioned in the architecture overview section, the Catalyst 2950 Family and 3550 Family of switches utilize an internal DSCP value to represent classification and marking of frames as the frames traverse the switch. Because the switches use internal DSCP values, the switch maps ingress DSCP, CoS, and IP precedence to the internal DSCP values when dictated by the classification configuration. When trusting DSCP, the switch maps ingress packets' DSCP directly to an internal DSCP value. The only exception is in configuring DSCP mutation. Figure 6-5 illustrates the logical depiction of internal DSCP as a packet traverses a Catalyst 2950 or 3550 switch.

Figure 6-5   *Logical Depiction of Internal DSCP*

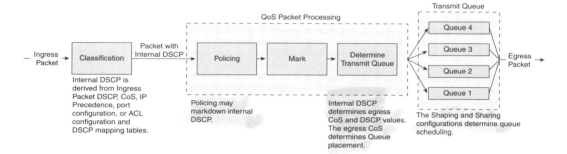

For CoS and IP precedence mapping to an internal DSCP, the switches use a CoS-to-DSCP and an IP precedence-to-DSCP mapping table, respectively. Tables 6-2 and 6-3 indicate the default mappings for the CoS-to-DSCP and IP precedence-to-DSCP mappings, respectively.

Table 6-2   *Default CoS-to-DSCP Mapping Table*

CoS	0	1	2	3	4	5	6	7
DSCP	0	8	16	24	32	40	48	56

Table 6-3   *Default IP Precedence-to-DSCP Mapping Table*

IP Precedence	0	1	2	3	4	5	6	7
DSCP	0	8	16	24	32	40	48	56

The IP precedence-to-DSCP mapping table is configurable on the Catalyst 3550 Family of switches, whereas both the Catalyst 2950 Family and the Catalyst 3550 Family of switches support custom configuration of the CoS-to-DSCP mapping tables. To configure the CoS-to-DSCP and IP precedence-to-DSCP mapping tables, use the following commands, respectively:

```
mls qos map cos-dscp DSCP-list
mls qos map IP-prec-dscp DSCP-list
```

DSCP-list represents the eight DSCP mapping values for each IP precedence value 0 to 7. For example, a *DSCP-list* of 0 10 16 25 36 46 48 50 for a CoS-DSCP mapping configuration results in the CoS value of 0 mapping to a DSCP value 0, CoS value of 1 mapping to a DSCP value of 10, and so forth. Examples 6-2 and 6-3 illustrate a user configuring and verifying configuration of a CoS-to-DSCP mapping table and a IP precedence-to-DSCP mapping table, respectively.

Example 6-2 *User Configuring and Verifying CoS-to-DSCP Mapping Table*

```
Switch#config terminal
Enter configuration commands, one per line. End with CNTL/Z.
Switch(config)#mls qos map cos-dscp 0 8 16 30 30 46 50 50
Switch(config)#end
Switch#show mls qos map cos-dscp
   Cos-dscp map:
        cos:  0  1  2  3  4  5  6  7
        -------------------------------
       dscp:  0  8 16 30 30 46 50 50
```

Example 6-3 *User Configuring and Verifying IP Precedence-to-DSCP Mapping Table*

```
3550#config terminal
Enter configuration commands, one per line. End with CNTL/Z.
3550(config)#mls qos map ip-prec-dscp 0 8 16 28 30 46 50 55
3550(config)#end
3550#show mls qos map ip-prec-dscp
   IpPrecedence-dscp map:
      ipprec:  0  1  2  3  4  5  6  7
      -------------------------------
        dscp:  0  8 16 28 30 46 50 55
```

Ingress Port CoS Configuration

The Catalyst 2950 Family and 3550 Family of switches allow for static configuration of ingress CoS values used for DSCP mapping. The switches use ingress port CoS configurations to classify untagged frames and override CoS values on tagged frames.

To configure a switch interface to represent a CoS value for an untagged frame, use the following interface commands:

```
mls qos trust cos
mls qos cos cos_value
```

cos_value represents the CoS value to assign to untagged frames. The switch requires both configuration commands for assigning CoS values to untagged frames.

Example 6-4 illustrates an example of an interface configured for trusting CoS for tagged frames and the default configuration of assigning a CoS value of 0 to untagged frames.

Example 6-4 *Example Interface Configuration of Trusting CoS Values of Tagged Frames and Assigning Default CoS Value 0 to Untagged Frames*

```
Switch# show running-config
Building configuration…
!
(text deleted)
interface FastEthernet0/1
```

Example 6-4   *Example Interface Configuration of Trusting CoS Values of Tagged Frames and Assigning Default CoS Value 0 to Untagged Frames (Continued)*

```
 switchport access vlan 53
 switchport voice vlan 701
 no ip address
 mls qos trust cos
 spanning-tree portfast
(text deleted)
end
```

Example 6-5 illustrates an interface configured for trusting CoS for tagged frames and assigning a CoS value of 5 to untagged frames.

Example 6-5   *Sample Interface Configuration of Trusting CoS Values of Tagged Frames and Assigning a Port CoS Value 5 to Untagged Frames*

```
Switch# show running-config
Building configuration…
 !
(text deleted)
interface FastEthernet0/1
 switchport access vlan 53
 switchport voice vlan 700
 no ip address
 mls qos cos 5
 mls qos trust cos
 spanning-tree portfast
(text deleted)
end
```

To configure an overriding CoS value on untagged and tagged frames on a switch interface, use the following commands:

```
mls qos trust cos
mls qos cos cos_value
mls qos cos override
```

The **mls qos cos override** signifies to override tags frames with the CoS value specified in the **mls qos cos** *cos_value* command. Example 6-6 shows an interface configuration using the override feature.

Example 6-6   *Sample Interface Configuration of Trusting and Assigning a Port CoS Value 5 to Untagged and Tagged Frames*

```
Switch# show running-config
Building configuration…
 !
(text deleted)
interface FastEthernet0/1
 switchport access vlan 53
 switchport voice vlan 700
 no ip address
```

continues

Example 6-6   *Sample Interface Configuration of Trusting and Assigning a Port CoS Value 5 to Untagged and Tagged Frames (Continued)*

```
 mls qos cos 5
 mls qos trust cos
 mls qos cos override
 spanning-tree portfast
 (text deleted)
 end
```

Assigning a port CoS value to an ingress frame does not necessarily result in the switch transmitting the frame with that CoS value. The port CoS value only determines the internal DSCP value of the ingress frame, and the switch may mark the frame, mark down the frame during policing, or use a nondefault DSCP-to-CoS mapping table before egress transmission of the frame.

To verify any classification configuration of an interface, use the following command:

show mls qos interface *[interface-name]*

Example 6-7 illustrates sample output from this command on a Catalyst 3550 switch.

Example 6-7   *Sample Output from the* **show mls qos interface** *Command*

```
Switch#show mls qos interface GigabitEthernet 0/1
GigabitEthernet0/1
trust state: trust dscp
trust mode: trust dscp
COS override: dis
default COS: 0
DSCP Mutation Map: Default DSCP Mutation Map
trust device: none
```

Trust DSCP

The trust DSCP configuration maps an ingress packet's DSCP value directly to the internal DSCP value. Trust DSCP is the recommended trust configuration for directly attached switches that perform classification and marking on ingress. Because classification and marking occurs on ingress for interconnected switch ports, just trusting DSCP allows the current switch to maintain the original ingress classification and marking of the connected switch. Trusting DSCP is also a choice configuration for interfaces connected to Cisco IP Phones. Cisco IP Phones mark frames with DSCP and CoS values, and just trusting DSCP on frames from the Cisco IP Phone is a common practice.

Figure 6-6 illustrates an example of this behavior. Switch-2 trusts DSCP on the attached Cisco IP Phone. Switch-1 preserves the classification of Switch-2 by just trusting DSCP on the interface connecting the two switches. As a result, Switch-1 preserves the classification done by Switch-2.

Figure 6-6   *Trust DSCP Example*

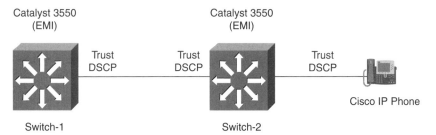

To configure a switch interface to trust DSCP, use the following interface command:

`mls qos trust dscp`

Example 6-8 illustrates an interface configured for trusting DSCP on ingress packets.

Example 6-8   *Sample Interface Configuration of Classifying Frames Based on DSCP Values*

```
Switch# show running-config
Building configuration. . .
!
(text deleted)
interface FastEthernet0/1
 switchport access vlan 53
 switchport voice vlan 700
 no ip address
 mls qos trust dscp
 spanning-tree portfast
(text deleted)
end
```

Trust IP Precedence

The trust IP precedence configuration mirrors trusting CoS. Trusting IP precedence is a feature only available on the Catalyst 3550 Family of switches. Trusting IP precedence uses the IP precedence mapping table to map an ingress packet's IP precedence value to an internal DSCP value. Because some applications only mark IP precedence, trusting IP precedence rather than DSCP allows for ease of understanding and configuration. Table 6-3, in the "Internal DSCP and Mapping Tables" section, shows the default mapping table for mapping IP precedence to internal DSCP. Example 6-3, in the same section, illustrates a user modifying the IP precedence to internal DSCP mapping table.

To configure a switch interface to assign a trust DSCP, use the following interface command:

`mls qos trust ip-precedence`

Example 6-9 shows a sample configuration of a switch interface configured for trusting IP precedence.

Example 6-9   *Sample Interface Configuration of Classifying Frames Based on IP Precedence Values*

```
Switch# show running-config
Building configuration…
!
(text deleted)
interface FastEthernet0/1
 switchport access vlan 53
 switchport voice vlan 700
 no ip address
 mls qos trust ip-precedence
 spanning-tree portfast
(text deleted)
end
```

Voice VLANs and Extended Trust

Both the Catalyst 2950 Family and 3550 Family of switches support voice VLANs and extended trust options. The "Voice VLANs and Extended Trust" section of Chapter 2, "End-to-End QoS: Quality of Service at Layer 3 and Layer 2," discusses the concept and configurations of voice VLANs and extended trust.

Trust Cisco IP Phone Device

The trust CoS configuration trusts the CoS values of all ingress frames on tagged frames. The trust DSCP configuration trusts the DSCP values of all ingress frames. In the case of an attached Cisco IP Phone, the desired configuration is to trust CoS or trust DSCP depending on desired configuration.

In most configurations, workstations attach directly to Cisco IP Phones, which, in turn, are attached to switches as shown in Figure 6-7.

Figure 6-7   *Cisco IP Phone Physical Network Diagram*

Catalyst   IP Phone   Workstation
Switch

Because the trust CoS or trust DSCP configuration does not validate the ingress frames, it is possible to send frames with specific DSCP values for malicious use on interfaces configured for trusting CoS or DSCP. As a result, the Catalyst 2950 Family and 3550 Family of switches support trusting CoS only when the switch connects to a Cisco IP Phone. In addition, the Catalyst 3550 Family of switches also supports trusting DSCP only when the switch connects to a Cisco IP Phone. These switches achieve this level of security by using the CDP. Because all Cisco IP Phones send CDP periodically and on linkup by default, the switch learns of connected Cisco IP Phones dynamically. When using this configuration option with trusting enabled, these switches only trust ingress frames when a Cisco IP Phone is attached. If the switch does not detect CDP packets from a Cisco IP Phone using this configuration, the switches use the port CoS configuration for determining CoS values associated with ingress frames. Because CDP is a proprietary protocol, only Cisco IP Phones support CDP.

To configure a switch interface to trust CoS only when a Cisco IP Phone is attached, use the following interface commands:

```
mls qos trust cos
mls qos trust device cisco-phone
```

To configure a switch interface to trust DSCP only when a Cisco IP Phone is attached, use the following interface commands:

```
mls qos trust dscp
mls qos trust device cisco-phone
```

Example 6-10 illustrates a sample configuration of an interface on a Catalyst 3550 configured for trusting DSCP when a Cisco IP Phone is connected to interface FastEthernet 0/1.

Example 6-10 *Sample Interface Configuration of Classifying Frames Based on DSCP and Whether an IP Phone Is Connected to an Interface*

```
Switch# show running-config
Current configuration : 157 bytes
!
(text deleted)
interface FastEthernet0/1
 switchport access vlan 53
 switchport voice vlan 700
 no ip address
 mls qos trust device cisco-phone
 mls qos trust dscp
 spanning-tree portfast
(text deleted)
end
```

Classifying Traffic by Using ACLs

The Catalyst 2950 Family and 3550 Family of switches support standard and extended IP ACLs and MAC ACLs for security and QoS purposes. For QoS purposes, these switches utilize ACLs in class maps for classifying packets. Using ACLs for classification allow for granularity when classifying packets. By using ACLs for classification, for example, the switch can classify packets that match only specific IP addresses or Layer 4 ports.

These switches use class maps to organize and group multiple ACLs for application to policy maps. Policy maps group class maps and class actions such as trusting, marking, and policing.

Chapter 5, "Introduction to the Modular QoS Command-Line Interface," expands on how to create and implement class maps and policy maps and includes examples. Consult Chapter 5 before reading the configuration examples and guidelines in the "Class Maps and Policy Maps" section later in this chapter.

To apply a policy map to an interface for ingress-supported classification, marking, or rate policing, use the following command:

```
service-policy input policy-map-name
```

policy-map-name refers to the name you configure for the policy map.

To apply a policy map to an interface for egress-supported classification, marking, or rate policing, use the following command:

```
service-policy output policy-map-name
```

policy-map-name refers to the name you configure for the policy map.

Example 6-11 illustrates a policy map, class map, and interface configuration for classifying traffic based on an ACL.

Example 6-11   *Sample Configuration for Classifying Traffic Based on an ACL*

```
Switch#show running-config
Building configuration…
!
mls qos
!
class-map match-all MATCH_ACL_100
  match access-group 100
!
!
policy-map Classify_ACL
  class MATCH_ACL_100
    trust dscp
!
!
(text deleted)
!
interface FastEthernet0/1
 switchport access vlan 2
 switchport voice vlan 700
 no ip address
 duplex full
 speed 100
 service-policy input Classify_ACL
 spanning-tree portfast
!
(text deleted)
!
access-list 100 permit ip 10.1.1.0 0.0.0.255 10.2.1.0 0.0.0.255
!
(text deleted)
end
```

Classification Passthrough Option

The classification passthrough option forces the switch to treat CoS and DSCP independently. The default behavior, and the lone behavior for all software versions prior to Cisco IOS versions 12.1.11(EA)1, of the switch is to modify the CoS or DSCP value depending on internal trust DSCP and any mapping tables. This is the behavior described in the previous sections of this chapter.

To recap earlier chapters, an interface configured for trusting DSCP modifies the CoS value on the frame on egress based on the internal DSCP and DSCP-to-CoS mapping table. Conversely, an interface configured for trusting CoS modifies the internal DSCP value on ingress according to the CoS-to-DSCP mapping table. The internal DSCP values determine the egress DSCP value.

To force the switch to treat CoS and DSCP independently, use the classification passthrough option. For trusting CoS configurations, the classification DSCP passthrough option uses the ingress CoS value of a frame for policing and scheduling without modifying the DSCP value of the frame on egress. Both the Catalyst 2950 Family and 3550 Family of switches support the trust CoS passthrough DSCP option.

The Catalyst 3550 Family of switches also supports the opposite behavior, trust DSCP passthrough CoS. Trust DSCP passthrough CoS enables the interface to classify, mark, police, and schedule packets without modifying the egress CoS value.

In practice, network administrators occasionally use these features to preserve CoS and DSCP values of frames when packets cross multivendor and multiplatform networks or ISP networks.

To configure an interface to trust CoS and passthrough DSCP, use the following interface command:

```
mls qos trust cos pass-through dscp
```

To configure an interface on a Catalyst 3550 Family of switches to trust DSCP and passthrough CoS, use the following interface command:

```
mls qos trust dscp pass-through cos
```

Example 6-12 illustrates a sample interface configuration of trusting CoS while passing through DSCP values.

Example 6-12 *Sample Interface Configuration of Trusting CoS and Passthrough DSCP*

```
Switch#show running-config
Building configuration…
!
mls qos
!
(text deleted)
!
interface FastEthernet0/1
 switchport access vlan 2
```

continues

Example 6-12 *Sample Interface Configuration of Trusting CoS and Passthrough DSCP (Continued)*

```
switchport voice vlan 700
no ip address
duplex full
speed 100
mls qos trust cos pass-through dscp
spanning-tree portfast
!
(text deleted)
!
end
```

Ingress DSCP Mutation

Classification using ingress DSCP mutation enables the switch to map ingress DSCP values to alternate configured DSCP values. In essence, DSCP mutation is the logical equivalent to a DSCP-to-DSCP mapping. Ingress DSCP mutation is commonly used when connecting multiple autonomous QoS domains, as illustrated in Figure 6-8. This feature is only available on the Catalyst 3550 Family of switches.

Figure 6-8 *DSCP Mutation*

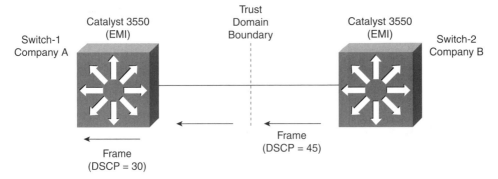

In this example, Switch 1 remaps packets with ingress DSCP values of 45 to 30 by way of the internal DSCP value. Example 6-13 provides a sample configuration of ingress DSCP mutation illustrating this behavior.

With regard to the DSCP mutation configuration, each Gigabit Ethernet interface supports a single DSCP mutation map. However, each group of 12 Fast Ethernet interfaces supports a single DSCP mutation map.

To configure the DSCP mutation map, use the following configuration command:

```
mls qos map dscp-mutation dscp-mutation-name in-dscp to out-dscp
```

dscp-mutation-name indicates the name assigned to the globally configured DSCP mutation map. *in-dscp* represents up to eight ingress DSCP vales for mapping to the single *out-dscp* value.

To configure and assign an interface for ingress DSCP mutation, use the following interface commands:

```
mls qos trust dscp
mls qos dscp-mutation dscp-mutation-name
```

dscp-mutation-name is the DSCP mutation global map name. The switch requires the trust DSCP configuration to enact on the DSCP mutation configuration.

Example 6-13 illustrates a sample configuration of ingress DSCP mutation for Figure 6-8.

Example 6-13 *Sample Configuration for Ingress DSCP Mutation Applied to Figure 6-8*

```
Switch#show running-config
Building configuration…
!
mls qos map dscp-mutation 40-45_reduce_30 40 41 42 43 44 45 to 30
mls qos
!
(text deleted)
!
interface FastEthernet0/1
 switchport access vlan 2
 switchport voice vlan 700
 no ip address
 duplex full
 speed 100
 mls qos trust dscp
 mls qos dscp-mutation 40-45_reduce_30
 spanning-tree portfast
!
(text deleted)
!
end
```

To verify the DSCP mutation map configurations, use the following command:

```
show mls qos maps dscp-mutation
```

Example 6-14 illustrates sample output for the preceding command for Example 6-13.

Example 6-14 *Displaying QoS DSCP Mutation Mappings*

```
Switch#show mls qos maps dscp-mutation
   Dscp-dscp mutation map:
   40-45_reduce_30:
     d1 :  d2 0  1  2  3  4  5  6  7  8  9
     ---------------------------------------
      0 :     00 01 02 03 04 05 06 07 08 09
      1 :     10 11 12 13 14 15 16 17 18 19
      2 :     20 21 22 23 24 25 26 27 28 29
```

continues

Example 6-14 *Displaying QoS DSCP Mutation Mappings (Continued)*

```
        3 :   30 31 32 33 34 35 36 37 38 39
        4 :   30 30 30 30 30 30 46 47 48 49
        5 :   50 51 52 53 54 55 56 57 58 59
        6 :   60 61 62 63
    Dscp-dscp mutation map:
    Default DSCP Mutation Map:
        d1 :  d2 0  1  2  3  4  5  6  7  8  9
        ----------------------------------------
        0 :   00 01 02 03 04 05 06 07 08 09
        1 :   10 11 12 13 14 15 16 17 18 19
        2 :   20 21 22 23 24 25 26 27 28 29
        3 :   30 31 32 33 34 35 36 37 38 39
        4 :   40 41 42 43 44 45 46 47 48 49
        5 :   50 51 52 53 54 55 56 57 58 59
        6 :   60 61 62 63
```

Policing

Both The Catalyst 2950 Family and 3550 Family of switches support policing with trusting, marking, and DSCP markdown actions. Both switches use the modular *command-line interface* (CLI) as discussed in Chapter 5 for configuring class maps and policy maps used for policing.

The Catalyst 2950 Family of switches supports only ingress policing on a per-port basis, whereas the Catalyst 3550 Family of switches supports per-port and aggregate policing in both ingress and egress configurations. Table 6-4 summarizes the policing options available to each switch. This section discusses each of the following policing topics as it relates to the Catalyst 2950 and Catalyst 3550 Family of switches:

- Policing Resources and Guidelines
- Class Maps and Policy Maps
- Ingress and Egress Policing
- Individual and Aggregate Policing
- Port-Based, VLAN-Based, and Per-Port Per-VLAN-Based Policing
- Policing Actions

Table 6-4 *QoS Policing Feature Available Per Platform*

QoS Policing Feature	Catalyst 2950 EI	Catalyst 3550
Port-based policing	Supported on all interfaces	Supported on all physical interfaces
Aggregate port-based policing	Not supported	Supported on all physical interfaces
Per-port VLAN-based policing	Not supported	Supported on ingress only

Table 6-4   *QoS Policing Feature Available Per Platform (Continued)*

QoS Policing Feature	Catalyst 2950 EI	Catalyst 3550
Policing rate parameters	Rate and burst only	Rate and burst only
No. of ingress policers per Gigabit Ethernet interfaces	60	128
No. of ingress policers per Fast Ethernet interfaces	6	8
No. of egress policers per Gigabit Ethernet interfaces	Not supported	8
No. of egress policers per Fast Ethernet interfaces	Not supported	8
Egress policers	Not supported	Supported

Policing Resources and Guidelines

Table 6-4 summarizes the QoS policing resource restrictions and guidelines for software version 12.1(11)EA1. As indicated in Table 6-4, the Catalyst 3550 Family of switches provides for additional QoS features over the Catalyst 2950 Family of switches. These features include per-port VLAN-based policing and egress policing. Furthermore, the Catalyst 3550 Family of switches supports additional policing resources that provide for a larger number of policers.

Class Maps and Policy Maps

As with mainline Cisco IOS Software, class maps group ACLs and match statements for application on policy maps. The class maps in effect define the classification criteria for policy maps that define actions. Example 6-15 illustrates a sample configuration of a policy map.

Example 6-15 *Sample Class Map and Policy Map Configuration*

```
Switch#show running-config
Building configuration…
!
(text deleted)
mls qos
!
class-map match-any MATCH_LIST
  match access-group 100
  match ip precedence 5
  match ip dscp 35
!
!
policy-map RATE_MARK
  class MATCH_LIST
```

continues

Example 6-15 *Sample Class Map and Policy Map Configuration (Continued)*

```
     police 1000000 8000 exceed-action drop
     set ip dscp 55
 !
(text deleted)
interface GigabitEthernet0/1
 switchport trunk encapsulation dot1q
 switchport mode trunk
 no ip address
 service-policy input RATE_MARK
(text deleted)
access-list 100 permit ip 10.1.1.0 0.0.0.255 10.2.1.0 0.0.0.255
(text deleted)
 !
end
```

The class map **MATCH_LIST** defines a class map with several classification matching rules. Because the class map uses the **match-any** option, matching any of the three match statements results in policy map executing the class actions. The other matching option, **match-all**, configures the switch to subject the packet to all the match statements in order to enact on the policy map class actions.

Furthermore, the class map defines three matching rules. For the switch to execute the class actions in the policy map, a packet must match ACL 100, have an IP precedence value of 5, or have an IP DSCP value of 35. Otherwise, the switch does not execute the class actions for the packet. Because the switch applies the policy map on ingress, the switch performs the matching operation on all ingress frames on GigabitEthernet0/1.

For packets that match the classification rules in the class map, the switch executes the class actions defined in the policy map. In Example 6-15, the switch rate limits this traffic by dropping frames above the defined rate of 1.0 Mbps and sets the internal DSCP value to 55. Chapter 5 provides additional configuration information on class maps and policy maps. The "Traffic-Rate Policing" section later in this chapter discusses the rate policer in Example 6-15.

Ingress and Egress Policing

Ingress policing logically refers to applying a set of class actions such as trusting, marking, or rate policing to specific packets as the switch receives packets inbound. Ingress policing logically occurs when a switch receives a packet, but actually occurs later in packet processing on Catalyst switches. Nevertheless, the logical concept of ingress policing is applying class actions to received packets. Egress policing applies a set of class actions on transmit; however, this feature is not found on all Catalyst switches. At the time of publication, only the Catalyst 3550 Family and 4000 IOS Family of switches support egress policing and the Catalyst 3550 Family of switches supports only traffic-rate policers for egress policing.

Applying a policy on ingress versus egress may result in significant behavioral differences in packet flow. In Figure 6-9, for example, an ingress policer is rate limiting the traffic to 100 Mbps ingress on interfaces GigabitEthernet0/1. As shown in the diagram, ingress traffic from Switch-1 is at 1.0 Gbps. Based on the rate limiting, the switch restricts ingress traffic collectively to 100 Mbps. Assuming all ingress traffic into Switch-2 is unicast, only 100 Mbps of total traffic is sent out interfaces GigabitEthernet0/2 and 0/3. In Figure 6-10, the switch applies the same policer outbound, and the switch only limits the traffic transmitted out interfaces Gigabit Ethernet0/2 and 0/3 to 100 Mbps individually. Traffic from interface GigabitEthernet0/4 to other interfaces flows without any restriction on rate.

Figure 6-9   *Ingress Policing*

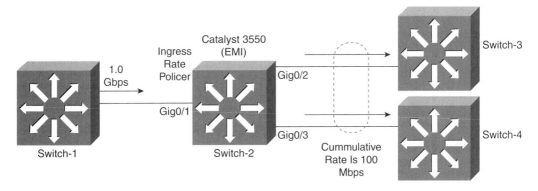

Figure 6-10   *Egress Policing*

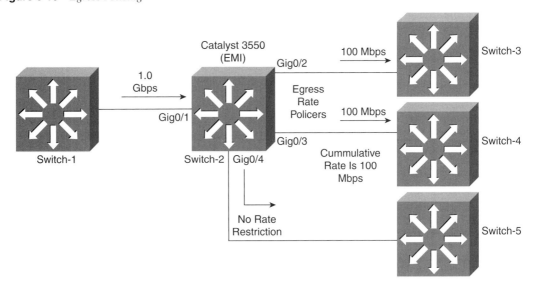

Individual and Aggregate Policing

Individual policers apply bandwidth limits discretely to each interface for defined policy maps. The Catalyst 2950 Family of switches supports only individual policers; however, the Catalyst 3550 Family of switches supports aggregate policers.

Class maps define traffic classes within a policy map. Use the following policy map class clause configuration command to configure individual policers:

police *rate burst* [**exceed-action** {**transmit** | **drop** | **policed-DSCP-transmit**}]

Example 6-16 illustrates a sample configuration for individual policing. The policy map in Example 6-16 drops packets exceeding the 100-Mbps rate defined in the policer for all packets ingress on interface GigabitEthernet0/1.

Example 6-16 *Sample Configuration of Individual Policer*

```
Switch#show running-config
Building configuration…
!
(text deleted)
mls qos
!
class-map match-all MATCH_ALL_PCKTS
  match any
!
!
policy-map RATE_RESTRICT
  class MATCH_ALL_PCKTS
    police 100000000 16000 exceed-action drop
!
(text deleted)
!
interface GigabitEthernet0/1
 switchport trunk encapsulation dot1q
 switchport mode trunk
 no ip address
 service-policy input RATE_MARK
!
```

Aggregate policers apply rate-limiting constraints collectively among multiple class maps within the same policy map. This behavior is unique compared to other switch platforms such as the Catalyst 4000 IOS Family and Catalyst 6000 Family of switches. These switches use aggregate policers to apply rate-limiting constraints among multiple ports or VLANs.

Use the following global configuration command to configure an aggregate policer:

mls qos aggregate-police *aggregate-policer-name rate-bps burst-byte* **exceed-action** {**drop** | **policed-dscp-transmit**}

aggregate_policer_name defines the name to represent the aggregate policer. Aggregate policers support dropping or marking down packets that exceed the define rate. Later sections in this chapter cover rate and burst parameters in more detail. To attach the aggregate policer, use the following policy map class clause configuration command:

police aggregate *policer_name*

Aggregate policers cannot be used across different policy maps or interfaces. Define multiple aggregate policers to work around this limitation. Example 6-17 illustrates an aggregate policer.

Example 6-17 *Sample Configuration of an Aggregate Policer*

```
Switch#show running-config
Building configuration…
!
(text deleted)
mls qos aggregate-policer RATE_500MBPS 500000000 64000 exceed-action drop
mls qos
!
class-map match-all MATCH_ACL_100
  match access-group 100
class-map match-all MATCH_ACL_101
  match access-group 101
!
policy-map AGGR_TRAFFIC_LIMITING
  class MATCH_ACL_100
    set ip precedence 0
    police aggregate RATE_500MBPS
  class MATCH_ACL_101
    set ip precedence 5
    police aggregate RATE_500MBPS
!
(text deleted)
!
interface GigabitEthernet0/1
 switchport trunk encapsulation dot1q
 switchport mode trunk
 no ip address
 service-policy input AGGR_TRAFFIC_LIMITING
!
access-list 101 permit ip any any
access-list 101 permit ip 10.1.1.0 0.0.0.255 10.2.1.0 0.0.0.255
!
end
```

In Example 6-17, the switch subjects all traffic ingress from interface GigabitEthernet0/1 to the aggregate rate limiting policer of 500 Mbps. However, the switch rewrites the IP precedence value differently based on class maps while maintaining the aggregate policer of 500 Mbps to traffic that matches either policer.

Use the following command to display the policy maps-to-policer configuration:

show mls qos aggregate-policer [*aggregate-policer-name*]

Example 6-18 illustrates the use of the **show mls qos aggregate-policer** command.

Example 6-18 *Displaying Policy Map–to–Aggregate Policers Mapping*

```
Switch#show mls qos aggregate-policer
aggregate-policer RATE_500MBPS 500000000 64000 exceed-action drop
Used by policy map AGGR_TRAFFIC_LIMITING
```

Port-Based, VLAN-Based, and Per-Port Per-VLAN-Based Policing

Port-based policing entails binding policy maps to individual ports. VLAN-based policing involves attaching a policy map to a VLAN interface. The Catalyst 2950 Family of switches supports only port-based policing. The Catalyst 3550 Family of switches supports port-based policing and a variant of VLAN-based policing referred to as per-port per-VLAN policing. The Catalyst 3550 Family of switches does not support applying policers to VLAN interfaces. Per-port per-VLAN policing consists of the typical class map clauses nested in a second-class map with a VLAN-class match clause. The switch is only able to bind per-port per-VLAN to trunk ports and VLAN access ports. Example 6-19 illustrates a sample configuration of per-port per-VLAN-based policing.

Example 6-19 *Sample Configuration of Per-Port Per-VLAN Policing*

```
Switch#show running-config
Building configuration. . .
(text deleted)
!
mls qos
!
class-map match-any MATCH_LIST
  match access-group 100
  match ip precedence 5
  match ip dscp 35
class-map match-all MATCH_VLAN_LIST
  match vlan  2 100-105
  match class-map MATCH_LIST
!
!
policy-map RATE_LIMIT_VLAN_2_100-105
  class MATCH_VLAN_LIST
  set ip dscp 22

!
(text deleted)
!
interface GigabitEthernet0/1
 switchport trunk encapsulation dot1q
 switchport mode trunk
 no ip address
 service-policy input RATE_MARK
!
(text deleted)
!
```

Example 6-19 *Sample Configuration of Per-Port Per-VLAN Policing (Continued)*

```
access-list 100 permit ip 10.1.1.0 0.0.0.255 10.2.1.0 0.0.0.255
!
(text deleted)
!
end
```

The only difference between Example 6-19 and Example 6-17 is Example 6-19 applies the policy map only to packets ingress from VLANs 2 and 100 through 105. This per-port per-VLAN configuration requires the nested class map configuration to operate correctly. Furthermore, a per-port per-VLAN configuration requires that the class map that nests the match VLAN classification rule with the regular class map must use the **match-all** configuration option. Also, a per-port per-VLAN class map requires the match VLAN class map clause before the match class map clause.

Policing Actions

The Catalyst 2950 Family and 3550 Family of switches support the following class actions:

- Trusting
- Marking
- Traffic-rate policing

Policing is similar to Cisco IOS rate limiting. Policing limits traffic flow the same as rate limiting. However, policing uses the leaky token bucket algorithm, discussed in Chapter 2, to apply a burst parameter to rate limiting. Both the Catalyst 2950 Family and 3550 Family of switches support dropping or marking down traffic exceeding the rate.

Trusting Action

The use of trusting as a policing action is identical to trusting based on an ACL. The Catalyst 3550 Family of switches supports trusting as a policing action. The supported trusting options include trusting CoS or DSCP.

Policy maps organize the trusting actions using the following policy map class clause command:

```
trust [DSCP | CoS]
```

Example 6-20 illustrates a Catalyst 3550 configured to trust DSCP for packets that match ACL 100.

Example 6-20 *Sample Configuration of Trusting as a Policing Action*

```
Switch#show running-config
Building configuration…
(text deleted)
!
mls qos
!
class-map match-all MATCH_ACL_100
  match access-group 100
!
!
policy-map Classify_ACL
  class MATCH_ACL_100
    trust dscp
!
!
(text deleted)
!
interface FastEthernet0/1
 switchport access vlan 2
 switchport voice vlan 700
 no ip address
 duplex full
 speed 100
 service-policy input Classify_ACL
 spanning-tree portfast
!
(text deleted)
!
access-list 100 permit ip 10.1.1.0 0.0.0.255 10.2.1.0 0.0.0.255
!
(text deleted)
end
```

For configurations using trusting in class map clauses, there is no need for a trusting configuration on the interface. You must carefully consider whether to configure an interface for trusting and whether to configure a policing action of trusting because the policing action takes precedence over the port configuration.

Marking Action

Both the Catalyst 2950 Family and 3550 Family of switches support marking as a policing action. Both switches supports marking of DSCP using the following policy map class action command:

set ip dscp *new-dscp*

new-dscp indicates the DSCP value used to mark the frame in the policing action. The marking occurs on the internal DSCP value and the internal DSCP determines the DSCP value in the frame on egress. The Catalyst 3550 Family of switches also supports marking of IP precedence. To configure marking of IP precedence in a policing action, use the following policy map class action command:

set ip precedence *new-precedence*

new-precedence indicates the IP precedence value used to mark the frame. The marking actually occurs on the internal DSCP value by marking the 3 MSBs of the DSCP. Example 6-21 illustrates a Catalyst 3550 switch configured to mark frames as a policing action.

Example 6-21 *Sample Configuration of Marking as a Policing Action*

```
Switch#show running-config
mls qos
!
class-map match-all MATCH_ACL_100
  match access-group 100
!
!
policy-map Mark_Frames
  class MATCH_ACL_100
    set ip dscp 45
!
(text deleted)
!
interface FastEthernet0/1
 switchport access vlan 2
 switchport voice vlan 700
 no ip address
 duplex full
 speed 100
 service-policy input Mark_Frames
 spanning-tree portfast
!
(text deleted)
!
access-list 100 permit ip 10.1.1.0 0.0.0.255 10.2.1.0 0.0.0.255
!
(text deleted)
end
```

Traffic-Rate Policing

The Catalyst 2950 Family and 3550 Family of switches use the leaky token bucket algorithm to determine whether a packet is conforming or exceeding a specified policer rate. The leaky token bucket algorithm is transparent to the policing behavior of the switch. An understanding of the leaky token bucket is only necessary when refining the burst size parameter of a policer. For more information about the leaky token bucket algorithm, see Chapter 2.

Use the following command to configure the Catalyst 2950 Family of switches traffic-rate and burst parameters of a class map policer:

police *rate-bps burst-byte* [**exceed-action** {**drop** | **dscp** *dscp-value*}]

Use the following commands to configure the rate and burst of a class map policer and an aggregate policer on a Catalyst 3550 switch, respectively:

```
police rate burst [exceed-action {drop | policed-DSCP-transmit}]]
mls qos aggregate-policer policer_name rate burst [exceed-action {transmit | drop |
policed-DSCP-transmit}]
```

rate defines the actually policing rate. For the Catalyst 2950 Family of switches, the supported rates are 1 Mbps to 100 Mbps in 1-Mbps increments for Fast Ethernet interfaces and 8 Mbps to 1 Gbps for Gigabit-capable interfaces. For the Catalyst 3550 Family of switches, the supported rates are 8 kbps to 2 Gbps in 1-bps increments for all interfaces. The switch may adjust the configured rate to a hardware supported rate.

burst defines the burst size in bytes. The burst size needs to be at least the maximum packet size of frames touched by the policer for accurate policing. The following sections discuss determining the applicable burst size. For the Catalyst 2950 Family of switches, the supported burst sizes are 4096, 8192, 16384, 32768, and 65536 bytes for Fast Ethernet ports and 4096, 8192, 16348, 32768, 65536, 131072, and 262144 bytes for Gigabit Ethernet-capable interfaces. For the Catalyst 3550 Family of switches, the switches support configuring the burst size in the range of 8 MB to 2 GB. Example 6-22 illustrates a Catalyst 3550 configured for policing traffic at 100 Mbps with a burst size 16000 bytes.

Example 6-22 *Sample Configuration of Rate Policing as a Policing Action*

```
Switch#show running-config
mls qos
!
class-map match-all MATCH_ACL_100
  match access-group 100
!
!
policy-map RATE_RESTRICT
  class MATCH_ALL_PCKTS
    police 100000000 16000 exceed-action drop
!
(text deleted)
!
interface FastEthernet0/1
 switchport access vlan 2
 switchport voice vlan 700
 no ip address
 duplex full
 speed 100
 service-policy input Mark_Frames
 spanning-tree portfast
!
(text deleted)
!
access-list 100 permit ip 10.1.1.0 0.0.0.255 10.2.1.0 0.0.0.255
!
(text deleted)
end
```

The traffic-rate policer supports two actions for traffic exceeding the configured rate. These actions are to drop the packet or mark down the DSCP value of the frame. Marking down the frame actually occurs on an internal DSCP value.

For the Catalyst 2950 Family of switches, use the follow command to configure the exceed-action of a traffic-rate policer:

```
police rate-bps burst-byte [exceed-action {drop | dscp dscp-value}]
```

dscp-value indicates the DSCP value used to mark down the frame. Example 6-23 illustrates a sample configuration of marking down the DSCP value for traffic exceeding the rate specified in the policer.

Example 6-23 *Sample Configuration of Marking Down for the Exceeding Action of a Rate Policing*

```
Switch#show running-config
Building configuration...
mls qos
!
class-map match-all MATCH_ACL_100
  match access-group 100
!
!
policy-map RATE_RESTRICT
  class MATCH_ALL_PCKTS
    police 100000000 16000 exceed-action dscp 35
!
(text deleted)
!
interface FastEthernet0/1
 switchport access vlan 2
 switchport voice vlan 700
 no ip address
 duplex full
 speed 100
 service-policy input Mark_Frames
 spanning-tree portfast
!
(text deleted)
!
access-list 100 permit ip 10.1.1.0 0.0.0.255 10.2.1.0 0.0.0.255
!
(text deleted)
end
```

For the Catalyst 3550 Family of switches, the switch uses a DSCP-policed transmit mapping table to determine the DSCP value used for marking down the packet. By default, the policed DSCP mapping table maps packet DSCP values directly to the marked-down DSCP. As a result, the default behavior for the DSCP-policed transmit table is to not mark down the DSCP value associated with the packet. Use the following command to configure the policed DSCP mapping table:

```
mls qos map policed-dscp dscp-list to mark-down-dscp
```

dscp-list represents up to eight DSCP values. The switch marks down frames with these DSCPS to the DSCP value specified by the *mark-down-dscp* value when exceeding the configured rate. To configure the exceed-action of the traffic-rate policer, use the following command:

police *rate-bps burst-byte* [**exceed-action** {**drop** | **policed-dscp-transmit**}]

Example 6-24 illustrates a user configuring and verifying the policed DSCP mapping table.

Example 6-24 *User Configuring and Verifying the Policed DSCP Mapping Table*

```
Switch#configure terminal
Switch(config)#mls qos map policed-dscp 30 31 32 33 34 35 to 20
Switch(config)#end
Switch#show mls qos map policed-dscp
   Policed-dscp map:
     d1 :  d2 0  1  2  3  4  5  6  7  8  9
     ---------------------------------------
      0 :    00 01 02 03 04 05 06 07 08 09
      1 :    10 11 12 13 14 15 16 17 18 19
      2 :    20 21 22 23 24 25 26 27 28 29
      3 :    20 20 20 20 20 20 36 37 38 39
      4 :    40 41 42 43 44 45 46 47 48 49
      5 :    50 51 52 53 54 55 56 57 58 59
      6 :    60 61 62 63
```

Burst Size

Because of the behavior of TCP/IP and UDP applications, packet drops due to policing may significantly impact traffic throughput and may result in a packet-per-second throughput far below the configured policer rate. The burst parameter of policing attempts to handle this behavior by allowing periodic surges of traffic into the bucket.

Configuration of the burst size follows several other Catalyst platform recommendations. For TCP applications, use the following formula to calculate the burst size parameter used for policing:

<Burst> = 2 * <RTT> * <Rate>

RTT defines the approximate round-trip time for a TCP session. If RTT is unknown, use a RTT value of 1 ms to 1 second depending on estimated latency. The burst calculation for a rate of 64 kbps and an RTT of 100 ms is as follows

<Burst> = 2 * <.100 sec> * <64000 bits/sec>
<Burst> = 12800 bits = 1600 bytes

Nevertheless, from an application standpoint, rate policing always results in actual rates less than the configured rate regardless of the burst size. UDP applications react closer to the configured rate in bits per second; nevertheless, some UDP applications retransmit heavily upon packet loss resulting in performance far less than the configured rate. In brief, carefully consider burst rate and its effects on application before applying policers.

Congestion Management and Avoidance

After the switch classifies, marks, and polices a packet against QoS rules, the switch queues the packet into a transmit queue for output scheduling. Placing the packet into one of multiple queues allows for the switch to differentiate service by transmitting packets from the queue with specific order and priority. The Catalyst 3550 Family of switches utilizes WRED and tail-drop queuing mechanisms for congestion avoidance; the Catalyst 2950 Family of switches does not support congestion avoidance. Both the Catalyst 2950 Family and 3550 Family of switches support four transmit queues. Although both switches support output scheduling utilizing WRR, the Catalyst 3550 Family of switches supports additional output scheduling and queuing configurations.

In brief, the Catalyst 2950 Family of switches supports the following output scheduling mechanism:

- Strict-priority scheduling
- WRR scheduling

Strict-priority scheduling services packets placed into higher-priority queues before servicing packets in lower-priority queues. Although this mechanism works well for high-priority traffic such as *Voice over IP* (VoIP), this mechanism may starve transmission of traffic in lower-priority queues. As a result, the second option of using WRR scheduling exists. WRR transmits traffic based on a weight value. In this manner, each queue receives an assigned weight of the total bandwidth. Therefore, during any period of time, the switch sends traffic out of every queue based on its weighted value. Subsequent sections discuss these mechanisms in more detail with configuration examples.

In brief, the Catalyst 3550 Family of switches supports the following queuing and output scheduling mechanisms:

- Expedite (strict-priority) queue
- WRR scheduling
- Configurable drop thresholds per output queue
- WRED congestion avoidance algorithm

The Catalyst 3550 Family of switches uses WRR scheduling for output scheduling in a manner similar to the Catalyst 2950 Family of switches. However, the Catalyst 3550 Family of switches allows for designation of an expedite queue and configuration of congestion avoidance mechanisms using tail-drop thresholds or WRED. The designation of the expedite queue forces strict priority of transmission on the respective egress queue. The congestion avoidance algorithms attempt to subside congestion by dropping packets with lower priority before higher-priority packets in the same transmit queue. Later sections of this chapter discuss these features in more detail.

Congestion Management with the Catalyst 2950 and 3550 Family of Switches

As noted in the preceding section, both the Catalyst 2950 Family and Catalyst 3550 Family of switches perform output scheduling via strict-priority queuing and WRR, although each family of switches exploits different default configurations. In summary, both the Catalyst 2950 Family and Catalyst 3550 Family of switches support the following congestion management configuration options:

- DSCP-to-CoS Mapping
- CoS-to-Transmit Queue Mapping
- Strict-Priority Queuing
- Configurable Weights for WRR

DSCP-to-CoS Mapping

The Catalyst 2950 Family and 3500 Family of switches use an internal DSCP value to differentiate service as a packet traverses the switch. Because marking may occur on a packet during the marking and policing of packet process, the CoS value of the packet needs to be updated on transmit. As a result, the switch employs the use of a DSCP-to-CoS mapping table for mapping the internal DSCP value to CoS value on packets before the switch schedules the packet into a transmit queue. Table 6-5 indicates the default DSCP-to-CoS mapping table.

Table 6-5   *Default DSCP-to-CoS Mapping Table*

DSCP Value	0–7	8–15	16–23	24–31	32–39	40–47	48–55	56–63
CoS Value	0	1	2	3	4	5	6	7

The DSCP-to-CoS mapping table is configurable on a global basis. Use the following global configuration command to configure the DSCP-to-CoS mapping values:

```
mls qos map dscp-cos dscp-list to cos
```

dscp-list represents up to eight DSCP values separated by a space. CoS corresponds to the transmitted CoS value on the egress frame. Example 6-25 illustrates a user configuring and verifying the QoS DSCP-to-CoS mapping.

Example 6-25   *Verifying and Configuring the DSCP-to-CoS Mapping*

```
Switch#configure terminal
Switch(config)#mls qos map dscp-cos 37 38 39 to 5
Switch(config)#mls qos map dscp-cos 32 to 3
Switch(config)#end
Switch#show mls qos map dscp-cos
  Dscp-cos map:
     d1 :  d2 0  1  2  3  4  5  6  7  8  9
```

Example 6-25   *Verifying and Configuring the DSCP-to-CoS Mapping (Continued)*

```
------------------------------------
   0 :    00 00 00 00 00 00 00 00 01 01
   1 :    01 01 01 01 01 01 02 02 02 02
   2 :    02 02 02 02 03 03 03 03 03 03
   3 :    03 03 03 04 04 04 04 05 05 05
   4 :    05 05 05 05 05 05 05 05 06 06
   5 :    06 06 06 06 06 06 07 07 07 07
   6 :    07 07 07 07
```

CoS-to-Transmit Queue Mapping

With the Catalyst 2950 and 3550 Family of switches, output scheduling uses the strict-priority queuing or WRR algorithm with four transmit queues. The switch queues traffic into the four transmit queues based solely on the CoS value associated with the frame. By default, the switch places frames with higher CoS values into the higher-number queues. The internal DSCP value actually determines the CoS value and subsequently the transmit queue. Before the switches places packets into the transmit queues, the switch determines the egress CoS value of the frame using the internal DSCP value and the DSCP-to-CoS mapping table.

In retracing the path of the packet, refer to the following outline and Figure 6-5 to understand the role of internal DSCP in CoS-to-transmit queue mapping.

- Switch receives packet.

- Switch classifies packets with an internal DSCP value based on configuration.

- Switch polices, marks, or marks down the internal DSCP value.

- Switch determines egress CoS value based on internal DSCP value and DSCP-to-CoS mapping table.

- Switch queues the packet into one of four transmit queues based on egress CoS value, CoS-to-transmit queue mapping table, and any configured congestion avoidance configurations.

- Switch schedules packet out of the transmit queue based on strict-priority queuing or WRR.

Table 6-6 illustrates the default CoS-to-transmit queue mapping.

Table 6-6   *Default CoS-to-Transmit Queue Mapping Table*

CoS Value	Transmit Queue
0, 1	1
2, 3	2
4, 5	3
6, 7	4

Use the following command to display the CoS-to-transmit queue mapping:

```
show wrr-queue cos-map
```

The Catalyst 2950 Family of switches allows for custom configuration of the CoS-to-transmit queue mapping on a global basis. The Catalyst 3550 Family of switches supports CoS-to-transmit queue mapping on a per-interface basis. Use the following global and interface configuration command to configure the CoS-to-transmit queue mapping:

```
wrr-queue cos-map qid cos1..cosn
```

q_id represents one of the four transmit queues. *cos1..cosn* represents configuration for up to eight CoS values to map to a transmit queue.

Example 6-26 illustrates a user custom configuring the CoS-to-transmit queue mapping table and verifying the DSCP-TxQueue mapping table configuration.

Example 6-26 *User Configuring and Verifying the DSCP-to-Transmit Queue Mapping Table*

```
Switch#configure terminal
Switch(config)#wrr-queue cos-map 1 0 1 2
Switch(config)#wrr-queue cos-map 2 3 4
Switch(config)#wrr-queue cos-map 3 5
Switch(config)#end
Switch#show wrr-queue cos-map
CoS Value      :  0  1  2  3  4  5  6  7
Priority Queue :  1  1  1  2  2  3  4  4
```

Strict-Priority Queuing

By default, the Catalyst 2950 Family of switches schedules packets from transmit queues using the strict-priority algorithm. Using this algorithm, the switch transmits all packets out of the higher-priority queues before servicing lower-priority queues.

The Catalyst 3550 Family of switches utilizes the strict-priority queue configuration with WRR for scheduling all the packets out of transmit queue four before servicing any other queue. The switch still utilizes WRR for scheduling packets out of the remaining queues. The behavior of this configuration is slightly different from the behavior on the Catalyst 2950 Family of switches. Priority Queuing on the Catalyst 2950 Family of switches services higher-priority queues before lower-priority queues in order and does not support the concept of a single expedite queue.

To configure the Catalyst 3550 Family of switches for the strict-priority scheduling of transmit queue four, use the following interface command:

```
priority-queue out
```

As a result of the strict-priority scheduling algorithm on both the Catalyst 2950 and 3550 Family of switches, the switches may never transmit traffic out of lower-priority queues when line-rate traffic exists in higher-priority queues. Although this behavior is warranted for high-priority traffic such as VoIP, many applications of strict-priority queuing may starve lower-priority traffic. To remedy this situation, consider configuring the switch for WRR bandwidth and WRED as discussed in the next section.

Configurable Weights for WRR

By default, the Catalyst 3550 Family of switches utilizes WRR for congestion management. The Catalyst 2950 Family of switches supports WRR as an optional configuration. Both the Catalyst 2950 Family and 3550 Family of switches support adjusting the scheduling weight for each transmit queue. For the Catalyst 2950 Family of switches, WRR configuration is a global configuration. On the Catalyst 3550 Family of switches, WRR configuration is per interface. The scheduling weight effectively determines the egress bandwidth per queue. Use the following egress bandwidth formula to determine WRR weight:

$$(W/S) * B = n$$

W represents the WRR weight of the queue, and S represents the sum of all weights of the active queues. B is the available bandwidth of the outgoing interface(s), and n represents the egress bandwidth.

For example, each queue, 1 through 4, is assigned the following WRR weights on a Gigabit Ethernet interface, respectively:

50 50 100 200

The S of the weights is 400. As a result of this configuration, each transmit queue receives the following egress bandwidth:

Queue 1: 125 Mbps
Queue 2: 125 Mbps
Queue 3: 250 Mbps
Queue 4: 500 Mbps

To configure the scheduling weight of total bandwidth per queue, use the following global configuration command for the Catalyst 2950 Family of switches and interface configuration command for the Catalyst 3550 Family of switches:

```
wrr-queue bandwidth weight1...weight4
```

weight1...weight4 represent four weighted values assigned to transmit queues 1, 2, 3, 4 respectively. Use the following command to display the configured WRR bandwidth per queue:

```
show wrr-queue bandwidth
```

Example 6-27 illustrates a user configuring the WRR bandwidth per queue for heavier weights on higher-priority queues and verifying the WRR bandwidth configuration on a Catalyst 2950 switch. In this example, queue 1 receives 10 percent of the bandwidth, queue 2 receives 20 percent of the bandwidth, queue 3 receives 30 percent of the bandwidth, and queue 4 receives 40 percent of the bandwidth on egress.

Example 6-27   *User Configuring and Verifying a WRR Bandwidth Configuration*

```
Switch#configure terminal
Switch(config)#wrr-queue bandwidth 10 20 30 40
Switch(config)#end
Switch#show wrr-queue bandwidth
WRR Queue  :   1   2   3   4
Bandwidth  :  10  20  30  40
```

To demonstrate and measure the scheduling behavior of strict-priority queuing and WRR on transmit queues, three packet-generator ports were connected to the switch as shown in Figure 6-11 using the switch configuration shown in Example 6-28. The first traffic-generator port connected to interface GigabitEthernet0/1 was sending 1 Gbps of traffic with a CoS value of 0, whereas the traffic-generator port connected to interface GigabitEthernet0/2 was sending 100 Mbps of traffic with a CoS value of 5. A third traffic generator connects to interface FastEthernet0/1 to measure the received rate of each packet type. Table 6-7 shows the result of a strict-priority queue versus several configurations using WRR with default CoS-to-transmit queue mappings.

Figure 6-11 *Network Topology for Demonstrating Strict-Priority Queuing Versus WRR*

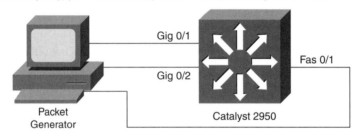

Example 6-28 *Interface Configuration for Demonstrating Strict-Priority Queuing*

```
Switch#show running-config
Building configuration...
(text deleted)
!
interface FastEthernet0/1
 switchport access vlan 2
 switchport mode access
 mls qos trust cos
 spanning-tree portfast
!
(text deleted)
!
interface GigabitEthernet0/1
switchport access vlan 2
 switchport mode access
 mls qos trust cos
 spanning-tree portfast
!
!
interface GigabitEthernet0/2
switchport access vlan 2
 switchport mode access
 mls qos trust cos
 spanning-tree portfast
!
end
```

Table 6-7 *Demonstrating Strict-Priority Queuing Versus WRR on Transmit Queues on the Catalyst 2950*

Trial Description	No. of Packets with CoS = 0 Received	No. of Packets with CoS = 5 Received
Default configuration (strict-priority queuing)	0	148,805
WRR queue bandwidth 25 25 25 25	74,400	74,400
WRR queue bandwidth 10 20 30 40	35,705	113,100
WRR queue bandwidth 10 20 100 100	13,000	135,805

Congestion Avoidance with the 3550 Family of Switches

The Catalyst 3550 Family of switches supports the following congestion avoidance mechanisms on Gigabit Ethernet-capable interfaces:

- Tail-drop thresholds
- WRED drop thresholds
- Transmit queue size manipulation

Furthermore, the Catalyst 3550 Family of switches supports only configuration of minimum reserve levels for congestion avoidance on Fast Ethernet interfaces.

Tail Drop

The Catalyst 3550 Family of switches utilizes two thresholds for congestion avoidance. By default, the switch maps all packets to a single threshold per queue. As a result, when a transmit queue becomes full, the switch drops any further packets needing placement into the respective transmit queue. This behavior is the default when any queue becomes congested and is subsequently unable to hold additional packets.

The Catalyst 3550 Family of switches allows for two tail-drop thresholds, whereas the switch tail drops packets with a lower priority over packets with a higher priority. The switch CLI refers to these thresholds as thresholds-1 and thresholds-2, respectively. The Catalyst 3550 Family of switches employs priorities for thresholds strictly on internal DSCP. The ingress interface determines the egress tail-drop threshold mapping and this configuration is only applicable to Gigabit Ethernet-capable interfaces. As a result, the switch treats all ingress packets from Fast Ethernet interfaces with the threshold-2 configuration.

In practice, tail-drop thresholds are useful in mitigating congestion. Consider, for example, a large network consisting of high-priority data and voice applications. The high-priority data application is built on TCP/IP and provides for file sharing between network users. The application adapts well to TCP/IP back-pressure and packet loss. The network uses voice applications for IP telephony. Because both applications are critical, the network administrators assign a DSCP value of 40 to the file-sharing application while using the default

DSCP value associated with Cisco IP Phones, 46. Packets from both applications occupy transmit queue 3. The switch is using WRR to service queue 3 with half the available bandwidth on egress interfaces. Before implementing tail-drop thresholds, the network administrators noticed that the file-sharing application was filing the transmit queue 3 causing excessive drops for voice applications. To remedy this situation, the network administrators implemented tail-drop thresholds. The network administrators configured the switch to tail drop packets from the file-sharing application when the queue becomes 30 percent full while only dropping voice application traffic when the queue is 100 percent full. This configuration yields ample transmit queue space for the voice applications, while the file-sharing program maintained high-priority service in transmit queue 3 but was unable to monopolize the buffer space.

To configure an interface for tail-drop congestion avoidance, use the following interface command.

`wrr-queue threshold` `queue-id threshold-percentage1 threshold-percentage2`

queue-id refers to the respective transmit queue, 1 through 4. *threshold-percentage1* and *threshold-percentage2* refer to the tail-drop percentage thresholds respectively. Valid percentages are in the range 1 to 100.

To configure the ingress interface for threshold mapping, use the following interface configuration command:

`wrr-queue dscp-map` `threshold-id dscp1 ... dscp8`

threshold-id represents a number 1 or 2 for *threshold-precentage1* or *2*, respectively. *dscp1 ... dscp8* represents up to eight DSCP values for threshold mapping.

NOTE   As mentioned previously, the DSCP-to-threshold mapping resides on the ingress interface of traffic. As a result, for packets to adhere to specific thresholds on the egress interfaces, the switch requires the mapping configuration on the ingress interfaces. In addition, only Gigabit Ethernet-capable interfaces support DSCP-to-threshold mapping.

Example 6-29 illustrates sample interface configurations for DSCP mapping to tail-drop thresholds. GigabitEthernet0/1 is the ingress interface, whereas GigabitEthernet0/2 is the egress interface of the packet flow. Ingress packets with DSCP values 40 and 46 on GigabitEthernet0/1 map to threshold 2. The threshold percentages are 50 percent and 100 percent, respectively.

Example 6-29 *Sample Interface Configuration for Congestion Avoidance Using Tail-Drop Thresholds*

```
Current configuration : 198 bytes
!
interface GigabitEthernet0/1
 switchport trunk encapsulation dot1q
```

Example 6-29 *Sample Interface Configuration for Congestion Avoidance Using Tail-Drop Thresholds (Continued)*

```
 switchport mode trunk
 no ip address
 wrr-queue dscp-map 2 40 46
 !
interface GigabitEthernet0/2
 switchport trunk encapsulation dot1q
 switchport mode trunk
 no ip address
 mls qos trust dscp
 wrr-queue threshold 1 50 100

 !
```

WRED Drop

With the tail-drop congestion avoidance mechanism, the Catalyst 3550 Family of switches drops packets when queues reach a certain percentage threshold or become full. The use of tail drop may result in an undesirable behavior of applications that specifically use TCP/IP. When a queue becomes full or reaches a certain percentage for packets matching a specific threshold, the tail drop instantaneously drops packets until the respective queue is no longer full. When these packet drops occur, TCP/IP applications reduce bandwidth accordingly. When the queue is no longer full and able to accept more packets, however, TCP/IP applications begin to increase throughput, which results in another full transmit queue condition. To utilize the transmit queue more effectively and prevent TCP/IP from increasing and decreasing throughput at relatively the same time, the condition also known as *global synchronization of TCP*, the Catalyst 3550 Family of switches supports WRED. Chapter 2, in the "Congestion Avoidance" section, discusses global synchronization of TCP in more detail.

The Catalyst 3550 Family of switches uses the WRED algorithm to randomly drop packets in a transmit queue before thresholds and queue full conditions. In this manner, multiple TCP/IP applications randomly reduce bandwidth instead of simultaneously reducing the transmit rate. Tail-drop conditions may still occur when using the WRED algorithm under periods of considerable congestion, low-percentage threshold values, or with applications that do not decrease throughput accordingly. A practical example is using WRED to handle congestion on an interface to a core switch that carries multiple file transfers and voice application traffic. To prevent congestion of higher-priority traffic and prevent all the file transfers from throttling bandwidth at the same time, WRED provides the best solution over tail dropping.

Configuration and implementation of WRED mirrors tail drop. The Catalyst 3550 Family of switches utilizes two configurable thresholds that signify percentages to randomly discard packets. In this manner, the switch is configurable to allow for random drop of packets with a lower priority over packets with a higher priority. The switch CLI refers to these thresholds as thresholds-1 and thresholds-2, respectively. The Catalyst 3550 Family of switches employs assignment to thresholds strictly based on internal DSCP. The ingress interface determines the egress tail-drop threshold mapping and this configuration is only applicable to Gigabit Ethernet-capable interfaces. As a result, the switch treats all ingress packets from Fast Ethernet interfaces with the threshold-2 configuration.

To configure the egress interface for WRED, use the following command:

```
wrr-queue random-detect max-threshold queue-id threshold-percentage1 threshold-percentage2
```

queue-id refers to the respective transmit queue, 1 through 4. *threshold-percentage1* and *threshold-percentage2* refer to the tail-drop percentage thresholds, respectively. Valid percentages are in the range 1 to 100.

To configure the ingress interface for threshold mapping, use the following interface configuration command:

```
wrr-queue dscp-map threshold-id dscp1 ... dscp8
```

threshold-id represents a number 1 or 2 for *threshold-precentage1* or *2*, respectively. *dscp1 ... dscp8* represents up to eight DSCP values for threshold mapping.

Example 6-30 shows a sample interface configuration for DSCP mapping to WRED thresholds. GigabitEthernet0/1 is the ingress interface, whereas GigabitEthernet0/2 is the egress interface of the packet flow. Ingress packets with DSCP values 40 and 46 on GigabitEthernet0/1 map to threshold 2. The threshold percentages are 50 percent and 100 percent, respectively.

Example 6-30 *Sample Interface Configuration for Congestion Avoidance Using WRED Thresholds*

```
Current configuration : 198 bytes
!
interface GigabitEthernet0/1
 switchport trunk encapsulation dot1q
 switchport mode trunk
 no ip address
 wrr-queue dscp-map 2 40 46


!
interface GigabitEthernet0/2
 switchport trunk encapsulation dot1q
 switchport mode trunk
 no ip address
 mls qos trust dscp
 wrr-queue random-detect max-threshold 1 20 90
 wrr-queue random-detect max-threshold 2 25 100
 wrr-queue random-detect max-threshold 3 50 100
 !
```

Use the following command to gather statistics about queue drops per threshold:

```
show mls qos interface [interface_name] statistics
```

Example 6-31 illustrates sample output from the **show mls qos interface statistics** command for WRED statistics.

Example 6-31 *Sample Output from the* **show mls qos interface statistics** *Command for WRED Statistics*

```
Switch#show mls qos int gig0/1 statistics
GigabitEthernet0/1
Ingress
  dscp: incoming   no_change  classified policed    dropped (in bytes)
Others: 0          0          0          0          0
Egress
  dscp: incoming   no_change  classified policed    dropped (in bytes)
Others: 547610028    n/a        n/a      0          0
WRED drop counts:
  qid  thresh1    thresh2    FreeQ
  1 : 385873    7637384    511
  2 : 0         0          1024
  3 : 0         0          1024
  4 : 0         0          1024
```

Transmit Queue Size

The Catalyst 3550 Family of switches allows for transmit queue size manipulation on a per-queue basis on Gigabit Ethernet-capable interfaces. By default, each queue receives 25 percent of the transmit queue. At the time of publication, the Catalyst 3550 Family of switches supports 4096 packet queues per Gigabit Ethernet interface; subsequently, each queue receives 1024 packet queues per Gigabit Ethernet interface. Queue size manipulation is useful when wanting to increase or decrease queue sizes based on protocol application. For example, queuing large amounts of voice and live video is not necessary. By the time the voice or video arrives at the destination, the application will most likely discard the packets. Hearing delayed audio or seeing delayed video for live sources such as IP telephony is undesirable. Nevertheless, data transfers are less sensitive to delay. As a result, storing a fair amount of data packets in a queue may not affect the performance of the data-centric applications.

A practical example is to minimize the queue size for delay-sensitive applications such as voice and video while utilizing larger queue sizes for data transfers. To configure the percentage of transit queues size for each queue, use the following interface command:

wrr-queue queue-limit *weight1 weight2 weight3 weight4*

Use the following formula to determine the queue size for a Gigabit Ethernet interface:

$$(W/S) * Q = n$$

W represents the WRR weight of the queue, and *S* represents the sum of all weights of the active queues. *Q* is the total queue size of the outgoing interface. Gigabit Ethernet interfaces on the Catalyst 3550 Family of switches utilize 4096 packet buffers. *n* represents the queue size per queue.

For example, each queue, 1 through 4, is assigned the following queue size weights on a Gigabit Ethernet interface, respectively:

10 20 30 40

The S of the weights is 100. As a result of this configuration, each interface configures for the following queue sizes:

Queue 1: 410
Queue 2: 820
Queue 3: 1228
Queue 4: 1638

Because of hardware implementation, the Catalyst 3550 Family of switches rounds the queue size to the closest configurable queue size. Use the **show mls qos interface** *interface* **statistics** command while the port is in the shutdown state to view the exact queue size provided by the hardware.

Minimum Buffer Size for Fast Ethernet Interfaces

The Catalyst 3550 Family of switches supports configuration of minimum buffer size for Fast Ethernet interfaces. The buffer size manipulation allows for adjusting the buffer queue size for different types of traffic. Generally, time-sensitive data such as VoIP traffic requires smaller queue sizes to avoid jitter, whereas large data transfer of images and files benefits from larger queue size.

The Catalyst 3550 Family of switches uses globally configured, minimum buffer levels for application to Fast Ethernet interfaces. These switches support up to 8 distinct buffer levels, and each buffer level denotes the packet buffer size in a range of 10 to 170 packets. Use the following global command to configure the minimum buffer levels:

[**no**] **mls qos min-reserve** *min-reserve-level min-reserve-buffersize*

min-reserve-level represents of the eight global configurable buffer levels, and *min-reserve-buffersize* represents the buffer size in number of packets.

To attach the *mim-reserve-level* to an interface queue, use the following command:

[**no**] **wrr-queue min-reserve** *queue-id min-reserve-level*

queue-id represents the interface transmit queue; *min-reserve-level* refers to the global minimum buffer level to attach to the transmit queue.

Use the following command to verify the minimum buffer level configuration:

show mls qos interface [*interface_name*] **buffers**

Example 6-32 illustrates a user displaying a sample interface configuration using minimum buffer levels and verifying the configuration. In this example, the switch uses small packet buffers for higher-priority traffic and larger packet buffers for low-priority traffic:

Example 6-32 *User Verifying Configuration of Minimum Buffer Levels*

```
Switch#show running-config
Building configuration...
!
(text deleted)
!
mls qos min-reserve 1 170
mls qos min-reserve 7 20
mls qos min-reserve 8 10
mls qos
!
!
interface FastEthernet0/4
 no ip address
 mls qos trust dscp
 wrr-queue bandwidth 10 20 30 40
 wrr-queue min-reserve 2 5
 wrr-queue min-reserve 3 7
 wrr-queue min-reserve 4 8
!
(text deleted)
!
end
Switch#show mls qos interface buffers
FastEthernet0/1
Minimum reserve buffer size:
 170 100 100 100 100 100 20 10
Minimum reserve buffer level select:
 1 2 3 4
```

Auto-QoS

Auto-QoS eases the deployment of QoS on Catalyst switches by applying recommended QoS configuration for typical networks, especially those deploying VoIP. For the Catalyst 2950 Family and Catalyst 3550 Family of switches, the Auto-QoS feature, as supported in 12.1.12c(EA1), aids in configuration of QoS for classification, egress scheduling, and congestion management of VoIP traffic for Cisco IP telephony. Upcoming software versions will offer additional Auto-QoS features.

Auto-QoS Classification

The Catalyst 2950 Family and 3550 Family of switches support two methods of classification when Auto-QoS is enabled. The first method classifies traffic strictly based on ingress CoS. Moreover, this configuration option just adds the trust CoS command to the interface for classification purposes. This method is useful for classifying traffic for interfaces connecting other switches.

The second method uses the trust Cisco IP Phone classification method as discussed in the "Trust Cisco IP Phone Device" section of this chapter. In brief, this method trusts ingress CoS only when a Cisco IP Phone is connected to an interface. This configuration option just adds the **mls qos trust device cisco-phone** and **mls qos trust cos** commands to the interface for classification.

To configure an interface for Auto-QoS of classification based on trust, use the following interface command:

```
auto qos voip trust
```

To configure an interface for Auto-QoS of classification based on trust and whether a Cisco IP phone is discovered on the interface, use the following interface command:

```
auto qos voip cisco-phone
```

Both of these classification options for Auto-QoS trust CoS for ingress frames. With these configuration, the switch classifies all untagged frames with a CoS value of zero regardless of the DSCP value. As a result, Auto-QoS is not the method of choice for applying classification based on DSCP or IP precedence.

Auto-QoS Congestion Management

Both the configuration options discussed in the preceding section also configure the Catalyst 2950 Family and Catalyst 3550 Family of switches for congestion management.

Foremost, the Auto-QoS feature modifies the CoS-to-DSCP mapping resulting in the nondefault internal DSCP values for classified frames. On the Catalyst 2950 Family of switches, the CoS-to-DSCP mapping is a global configuration. On the Catalyst 3550 Family of switches, the CoS-to-DSCP mapping is an interface configuration. The nondefault CoS-to-DSCP mapping is a follows for CoS values 0 through 7, respectively: 0 8 16 26 32 46 48 56. In addition, Auto-QoS configures both switches for mapping CoS 5 to queue 4.

In addition, the Auto-QoS feature modifies egress scheduling such that the switch only uses three egress transmission queues. The Auto-QoS feature achieves this configuration by assigning CoS value 5 to queue 4; CoS values 3, 6, and 7 to queue 3; and CoS values 0, 1, and 2 to queue 1. The Auto-QoS feature assigns the CoS value of 5 to queue 4, the expedite queue, because Cisco IP Phones mark voice traffic with CoS value 5. The Auto-QoS assigns CoS value 3 along with the CoS value 6 and 7, which are used by routing protocols and spanning-tree *bridge protocol data units* (BPDUs), because Cisco IP Phones mark control traffic with a CoS value of 3.

Auto-QoS also assigns different weights for WRR to each queue. For the Catalyst 2950, queuing is based on strict priority for queue 4. Therefore, queue 4 does not receive a weighted value. Similarly, for the Catalyst 3550 Family of switches, Auto-QoS configures queue 4 as the expedite queue. On both switches, queue 3 and queue 1 receive weights of 80 percent and 20 percent, respectively.

Finally, on the Catalyst 3550, Auto-QoS adjusts the buffer size of the Gigabit Ethernet and Fast Ethernet interface queues. The higher-priority queues receive a smaller queue size, whereas the lower-priority queues receive a larger queue size. This algorithm is used because high-priority traffic is affected by jitter and queuing packets increases jitter. Furthermore, data traffic occupying lower-priority queues is less affected by jitter; therefore, storing more packets prevents excessive drops while maintaining low-priority service.

In summary, the Auto-QoS provides a macro for configuring classification and congestion management based on trusting CoS for all ingress frames or only on interfaces connected to Cisco IP Phones.

Auto-QoS on the Catalyst 2950 Family and Catalyst 3550 Family of switches adds the following configuration commands as illustrated in Tables 6-8 to 6-12 in software version 12.1.12c(EA1):

Table 6-8   *Catalyst 2950 Auto-QoS-Added Global Configuration Commands*

wrr-queue bandwidth 20 1 80 0
wrr-queue bandwidth 20 1 80 0
wrr-queue cos-map 1 0 1 2 4
wrr-queue cos-map 3 3 6 7
wrr-queue cos-map 4 5
mls qos map cos-dscp 0 8 16 26 32 46 48 56

Table 6-9   *Catalyst 2950 Auto-QoS-Added Interface Configuration Commands*

mls qos trust cos
mls qos trust device cisco-phone

The **mls qos trust device cisco-phone** command is only added by Auto-QoS when the interface is configured for the **cisco-phone** option.

Table 6-10   *Catalyst 3550 Auto-QoS-Added Global Configuration Commands*

mls qos map cos-dscp 0 8 16 26 32 46 48 56
mls qos min-reserve 5 170
mls qos min-reserve 6 10
mls qos min-reserve 7 65
mls qos min-reserve 8 26
mls qos

Table 6-11 *Catalyst 3550 Auto-QoS-Added Gigabit Interface Configuration Commands*

mls qos trust cos
mls qos trust device cisco-phone
wrr-queue bandwidth 20 1 80 0
wrr-queue queue-limit 80 1 20 1
wrr-queue cos-map 1 0 1 2 4
wrr-queue cos-map 3 3 6 7
wrr-queue cos-map 4 5
priority-queue out

Table 6-12 *Catalyst 3550 Auto-QoS-Added Fast Ethernet Interface Configuration Commands*

mls qos trust cos
mls qos trust device cisco-phone
wrr-queue bandwidth 20 1 80 0
wrr-queue min-reserve 1 5
wrr-queue min-reserve 2 6
wrr-queue min-reserve 3 7
wrr-queue min-reserve 4 8
wrr-queue cos-map 1 0 1 2 4
wrr-queue cos-map 3 3 6 7
wrr-queue cos-map 4 5
priority-queue out

Auto-QoS supports a debug output that displays all commands applied globally and to each interface upon configuration of Auto-QoS on an interface. Use the following debug command to display this output:

```
debug autoqos
```

In addition, use the following command to display all configuration commands previously added by Auto-QoS:

```
show auto qos
```

Case Study

Figure 6-12 shows several QoS features in a campus network topology. To illustrate several QoS features in a single case study, this case study exaggerates the practicality of the use of QoS in this topology.

Figure 6-12   *Case Study Topology*

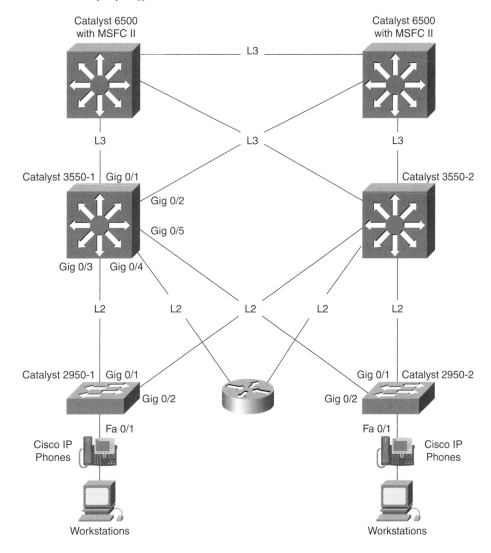

Example 6-33 illustrates the configuration for the Catalyst 2950s in Figure 6-12. A review of the configuration follows the example.

Example 6-33 *Catalyst 2950 Case Study Configuration*

```
Switch#show running-config
Building configuration...
!
(text deleted)
!
wrr-queue bandwidth 10 20 30 40
wrr-queue cos-map 1 0 1
wrr-queue cos-map 2 2 3
wrr-queue cos-map 3 4
wrr-queue cos-map 4 5 6 7
!
!
class-map match-all MATCH_FILE_SHARING
  match access-group 100
!
!
policy-map RATE_LIMIT_FILE_SHARING
  class MATCH_FILE_SHARING
    police 8000000 8192 exceed-action drop
!
(text deleted)
!
interface FastEthernet0/1
 switchport access vlan 2
 switchport voice vlan 701
 no ip address
 service-policy input RATE_LIMIT_FILE_SHARING
 mls qos trust device cisco-phone
 mls qos trust dscp
 spanning-tree portfast
!
(text deleted)
!
interface GigabitEthernet0/1
 switchport mode trunk
 no ip address
 mls qos trust dscp
!
(text deleted)
!
access-list 100 permit tcp any any eq 29999
!
(text deleted)
!
end
```

The Catalyst 2950s in Figure 6-12 act as access layer switches and configure identically. These switches aggregate access ports for Cisco IP Phones and workstations. In this topology, the workstations connect directly to the Cisco IP Phones. Because the Cisco IP Phones assign a DSCP value of 46 to all egress voice frames, an ideal configuration is to trust DSCP of ingress frames on the switch interface when a Cisco IP Phone is attached. As a result, the sample configuration uses the **trust dscp** command based on an attached Cisco IP Phone. The commands **mls qos trust device cisco-phone** and **mls qos trust dscp** achieve this configuration.

Furthermore, to isolate the VoIP traffic into a separate VLAN, the configuration applies voice VLANs; the example uses VLAN 701 for voice traffic and VLAN 2 for all workstation traffic. The **spanning-tree portfast** configuration command tells the switch to immediately forward frames on linkup instead of waiting on spanning-tree convergence.

The design uses a policer to limit the amount of file-sharing traffic received on each port. The policer classifies the file-sharing traffic on TCP port 29999 and limits the traffic to 8 Mbps ingress on each interface.

For output scheduling, the design uses WRR for all interfaces with each queue 1 through 4 getting 10 percent, 20 percent, 30 percent, and 40 percent of the egress bandwidth, respectively. In addition, all frames with a CoS value of 5 are designated to the highest queue 4. Because all VoIP traffic uses CoS 5 by default, CoS 5 frames were chosen for queue 4.

Example 6-34 illustrates the configuration for the Catalyst 3550s in Figure 6-12. A review of the configuration follows the example.

Example 6-34 *Catalyst 3550 Case Study Configuration*

```
Switch#show running-config
Building configuration...
!
(text deleted)
!
mls qos map dscp-mutation 40_down_32 40 to 32
mls qos map policed-dscp  1 2 3 4 5 6 7 8 to 0
mls qos map policed-dscp  9 10 11 12 13 14 15 16 to 0
mls qos map policed-dscp  17 18 19 20 21 22 23 24 to 0
mls qos map policed-dscp  25 26 27 28 29 30 31 32 to 0
mls qos map policed-dscp  33 34 35 36 37 38 39 to 0
mls qos map policed-dscp  40 41 42 43 44 45 46 47 to 1
mls qos map policed-dscp  48 49 50 51 52 53 54 55 to 1
mls qos map policed-dscp  56 57 58 59 60 to 1
mls qos map policed-dscp  61 62 63 to 2
!
!
class-map match-all RESTRICT_INTERNET_ONLY
  match access-group 151
!
!
policy-map RESTRICT_INTERNET
  class RESTRICT_INTERNET_ONLY
```

continues

Example 6-34 *Catalyst 3550 Case Study Configuration (Continued)*

```
      police 10000000 16000 exceed-action policed-dscp-transmit
 !
interface GigabitEthernet0/1
 ip address 10.1.1.0 255.255.255.248
 mls qos trust dscp
 service-policy input RESTRICT_INTERNET
 wrr-queue random-detect max-threshold 1 20 100
 wrr-queue random-detect max-threshold 2 40 100
 wrr-queue cos-map 4 5
 priority-queue out
 !
 !
interface GigabitEthernet0/2
 ip address 10.1.2.0 255.255.255.248
 mls qos trust dscp
 service-policy input RESTRICT_INTERNET
 wrr-queue random-detect max-threshold 1 20 100
 wrr-queue random-detect max-threshold 2 40 100
 wrr-queue cos-map 4 5
 priority-queue out
 !
 !
interface GigabitEthernet0/3
 ip address 10.10.1.2 255.255.255.0
 mls qos trust dscp
 service-policy input RESTRICT_INTERNET
 wrr-queue random-detect max-threshold 1 20 100
 wrr-queue random-detect max-threshold 2 40 100
 wrr-queue cos-map 4 5
 priority-queue out
 standby 101 ip 10.10.1.1
 !
 !
interface GigabitEthernet0/4
 switchport trunk encapsulation dot1q
 switchport mode trunk
 ip address 10.10.2.2 255.255.255.0
 mls qos trust dscp
 service-policy input RESTRICT_INTERNET
 wrr-queue random-detect max-threshold 1 20 100
 wrr-queue random-detect max-threshold 2 40 100
 wrr-queue cos-map 4 5
 priority-queue out
 standby 102 ip 10.10.2.1
 !
interface GigabitEthernet0/5
 switch access vlan 5
 switchport mode access
 ip address 10.11.1.1 255.255.255.252
 mls qos trust dscp
 mls qos dscp-mutation 40_down_32
 service-policy input RESTRICT_INTERNET
```

Example 6-34 *Catalyst 3550 Case Study Configuration (Continued)*

```
 wrr-queue random-detect max-threshold 1 20 100
 wrr-queue random-detect max-threshold 2 40 100
 wrr-queue cos-map 4 5
 priority-queue out
 !
 (text deleted)
 !
access-list 151 permit ip any 10.0.0.0 0.0.0.255
access-list 151 permit ip 10.0.0.0 0.0.0.255 any
access-list 151 permit ip any 172.16.0.0 0.0.255.255
access-list 151 permit ip 172.16.0.0 0.0.255.255 any
 !
(text deleted)
 !
end
```

The Catalyst 3550s in Figure 6-12 act as distribution layer switches, and both Catalyst 3550s configure identically except for IP addresses. These switches aggregate access layer switches for distribution into the core. As a result, the design utilizes the Catalyst 3550s as IP routers; hence, the IP addresses on the Gigabit Ethernet interfaces.

Because these Catalyst 3550s act as distribution switches on interfaces GigabitEthernet0/1 through 0/4, there is no need to reclassify traffic. As a result, these switches accept the classification and marking done by the access layer Catalyst 2950 switches and the core Catalyst 6500 switches.

The switch mutates DSCP from the router connected to interface GigabitEthernet0/5. The DSCP mutations mark down frames with DSCP values of 40 to 32. In effect, this configuration is marking down IP precedence values of 5 to 4. The goal of this configuration is to reduce the priority of traffic originating from networks connected off the router.

With regard to policing, the distribution switches are responsible for limiting traffic destined strictly for the Internet. The campus network uses the private network addresses, 10.0.0.0/8 and 172.16.0.0/16, for all intranet traffic. As a result, the Catalyst 3550 switches rate limits the Internet traffic to 100 Mbps per link to each core switch. The design uses the Catalyst 3550 rather than the Catalyst 2950 for limiting intranet traffic due to the larger number of ACLs and ACL options supported on the Catalyst 3550 Family of switches.

For congestion management, the design uses WRR for each interface with bandwidth configurations of 100 Mbps, 200 Mbps, and 300 Mbps for each transmit queue 1 through 3. The switch transmits traffic occupying queue 4 before the switch services any other queue because it is configured as a priority queue. As a result, the WRR bandwidth associated with this queue has no meaning. For queues 1 through 3, using WRR with the configured bandwidth parameters allows for higher-priority traffic to consume more bandwidth per interface. Furthermore, each interface employs the use of congestion avoidance through WRED. Only the low-priority queues drop traffic at specific thresholds.

This configuration assists in avoiding congestion on a per-queue basis. Finally, the **wrr-queue cos-map 4 5** configuration informs the switch to map CoS 5 traffic to transmit queue 4. Because CoS 5 traffic usually represents VoIP traffic, the ideal situation is to transmit the traffic with strict priority.

Summary

The Catalyst 2950 Family of switches provides for a wide range of QoS features suited specifically for access layer implementation. You can summarize QoS feature support on the Catalyst 2950 Family of switches as follows:

- Classification, marking, and policing require the EI software.
- Support exists for classification based on port CoS configuration, trusting configuration, and ACLs.
- Per-port ingress policing is supported.
- DSCP-to-CoS mapping table is configurable on a global basis.
- Output scheduling uses strict-priority queuing by default.
- WRR scheduling is configurable as an alternative to strict-priority queuing.

The Catalyst 3550 Family of switches provides for a wide range of QoS features suited specifically for access layer and distribution layer implementation. You can summarize QoS feature support on the Catalyst 3550 Family of switches as follows:

- No QoS feature differences exist between SMI and EMI software versions.
- Support exists for classification based on port CoS configuration, trusting configuration, and ACLs.
- Ingress and egress policing is supported on individual interfaces.
- A variant of VLAN-based policing exists as per-port VLAN-based policing.
- The DSCP-to-CoS mapping table is configured on a per-interface basis.
- Congestion management uses WRR with a strict-priority queuing option.
- Congestion avoidance utilizes the tail-drop and WRED techniques.

QoS Features Available on the Catalyst 4000 IOS Family of Switches and the Catalyst G-L3 Family of Switches

This chapter continues the tour of QoS feature support on Catalyst switches. This chapter covers two distinct product lines, the Catalyst 4000 IOS Family of switches and the Catalyst G-L3 Family of switches. The Catalyst 4000 IOS Family of switches encompasses any Catalyst 4000 chassis with a Supervisor III or IV Engine. The Catalyst G-L3 switches includes the Catalyst 2948G-L3, 4908G-L3, and the Catalyst WS-X4323-L3 (the Layer 3 services module for a Catalyst 4000 switch). Table 7-1 describes the various Catalyst 4000 platforms. Table 7-1 is identical to Table 3-7 in Chapter 3, "Overview of QoS Support on Catalyst Platforms and Exploring QoS on the Catalyst 2900XL, 3500XL, and Catalyst 4000 CatOS Family of Switches," and is included here for quick reference.

Table 7-1 *Catalyst 4000 CatOS Versus Cisco IOS Software Platform Matrix*

Catalyst 4000 Model	Reference Family	Description
Catalyst 2948G	Catalyst 4000 CatOS	48-port 10/100BASE-TX switch ports + 2 1000BASE-X GBIC* switch ports
Catalyst 2980G	Catalyst 4000 CatOS	80-port 10/100BASE-TX switch ports + 2 1000BASE-X GBIC switch ports
Catalyst 2980G-A	Catalyst 4000 CatOS	80-port 10/100BASE-TX switch ports + 2 1000BASE-X GBIC switch ports
Catalyst 2948G-L3	Catalyst G-L3 Switch	48-port 10/100BASE-TX + 2 1000BASE-X GBIC Layer 3 switche ports
Catalyst 4003 + WS-X4012 Supervisor I Engine	Catalyst 4000 CatOS	3-slot modular chassis + 2 1000BASE-X GBIC ports on Layer 2 supervisor
Catalyst 4006 + WS-X4013 Supervisor II Engine	Catalyst 4000 CatOS	6-slot modular chassis + 2 1000BASE-X GBIC ports on Layer 2 supervisor
Catalyst 4006 + WS-X4014 Supervisor III Engine	Catalyst 4000 IOS	6-slot modular chassis + 2 1000BASE-X GBIC ports on Layer 2/3 supervisor
Catalyst 4006 + WS-X4515 Supervisor IV Engine	Catalyst 4000 IOS	6-slot modular chassis + 2 1000BASE-X GBIC ports on Layer 2/3 supervisor
Catalyst WS-X4232-L3 Layer 3 Services Module	Catalyst G-L3 Switch	Layer 3 router module for Catalyst 4003 and 4006 chassis with Supervisor I or II Engine

continues

Table 7-1   *Catalyst 4000 CatOS Versus Cisco IOS Software Platform Matrix (Continued)*

Catalyst 4000 Model	Reference Family	Description
Catalyst 4503 + WS-X4013 Supervisor III Engine	Catalyst 4000 CatOS	3-slot modular chassis + 2 1000BASE-X GBIC ports on Layer 2 supervisor
Catalyst 4503 + WS-X4014 Supervisor III Engine	Catalyst 4000 IOS	3-slot modular chassis + 2 1000BASE-X GBIC ports on Layer 2/3 supervisor
Catalyst 4503 + WS-X4515 Supervisor IV Engine	Catalyst 4000 IOS	3-slot modular chassis + 2 1000BASE-X GBIC ports on Layer 2/3 supervisor
Catalyst 4506 + WS-X4014 Supervisor III Engine	Catalyst 4000 IOS	6-slot modular chassis + 2 1000BASE-X GBIC ports on Layer 2/3 supervisor
Catalyst 4506 + WS-X4515 Supervisor IV Engine	Catalyst 4000 IOS	6-slot modular chassis + 2 1000BASE-X GBIC ports on Layer 2/3 supervisor
Catalyst 4507R + WS-X4515 Supervisor IV Engine	Catalyst 4000 IOS	7-slot modular chassis + 2 1000BASE-X GBIC ports on Layer 2/3 supervisor
Catalyst 4840G	Catalyst Layer 3 server load-balancing switch	40-port 10/100BASE-TX + 1000BASE-X GBIC Layer 3 server load-balancing switch
Catalyst 4908G-L3	Catalyst G-L3 Switch	12-port 1000BASE-X GBIC Layer 3 switch
Catalyst 4912G	Catalyst 4000 CatOS	12-port 1000BASE-X GBIC Layer 3 switch

*GBIC = Gigabit interface converter

This chapter provides information about architecture, supported QoS features, configuration examples, and case studies for both the Catalyst 4000 IOS Family of switches and the Catalyst G-L3 Family of switches.

QoS Support on the Catalyst 4000 IOS Family of Switches

QoS feature support on the Catalyst 4000 IOS Family of switches surpasses those features supported in the Catalyst 4000 CatOS Family of switches. Tables 3-1 through 3-5 in Chapter 3 summarize the general QoS feature support on the Catalyst 4000 IOS Family of switches.

Specifically, the first section of this chapter covers the following topics and QoS features supported on the Catalyst 4000 IOS Family of switches:

- Architecture Overview
- Software Requirements
- Global Configuration
- Input Scheduling
- Internal DSCP
- Classification and Marking

- ACL-based Classification
- Policing
- Congestion Management
- Auto-QoS
- Case Study

Catalyst 4000 IOS Family of Switches QoS Architectural Overview

The Catalyst 4000 IOS Family of switches bases packet-processing performance solely on the use of *ternary content addressable memory* (TCAM). Packet processing includes application of QoS rules utilizing TCAM. These switches also use TCAM for Layer 2 lookups, Layer 3 lookups, Layer 3 rewrite information, and *access-control list* (ACL) processing. The use of TCAM in this manner allows the Catalyst 4000 IOS Family of switches to achieve line-rate performance at 64 Gbps.

The use of TCAM and the unique architecture of the Catalyst 4000 IOS Family of switches allows for application of QoS rules while maintaining line-rate performance for nonblocking ports. Table 3-9 in Chapter 3 discusses which front-panel ports are nonblocking per line card. The switches' architecture processes every packet against all QoS rules regardless of whether any configured QoS rules exist. A default QoS rule of null exists for application to every packet processed. As a result, when the switch subjects packets to QoS rules and processing, no change occurs in system performance. This behavior holds for ACL processing as well.

The industry term *hardware switching* refers to the discussed use of the TCAM component for packet processing. If the switch is unable to hardware switch a packet, the CPU must process the packet instead. The term *software switched* describes the packet processing orchestrated by an onboard CPU. An onboard CPU employs Cisco IOS Software for instruction on how to process and forward packets. Packets handled by the CPU experience lower packet-processing performance compared to hardware-switched packets because of the limited speed of the onboard CPU. In relation to QoS on the Catalyst 4000 IOS Family of switches, packet processing needs to occur in hardware, because of the limited software-switching performance of the CPU. A trade-off of utilizing TCAM for the line-rate performance is that hardware switching does not support all the Cisco IOS QoS features available in the latest Cisco IOS Software versions. Hardware switching only supports a subset of Cisco IOS QoS features for packet processing. The content of this chapter focuses only on QoS features that support hardware switching. In addition, TCAM is a limited resource varying per platform. The resource limitations affect the size and number of ACLs entries and policy maps allowed. ACLs that do not fit into TCAM are not executed on the Catalyst 4000 IOS Family of switches. Chapter 6, "QoS Features Available on the Catalyst 2950 and 3550 Family of Switches," presents the first platform to utilize TCAM for QoS features. This chapter includes more detailed information on the TCAM architecture. Figure 7-1 depicts the logical model of QoS packet flow in a Catalyst 4000 IOS switch. Later sections refer to this figure.

Figure 7-1 *Logical QoS Architecture for the Catalyst 4000 IOS Family of Switches*

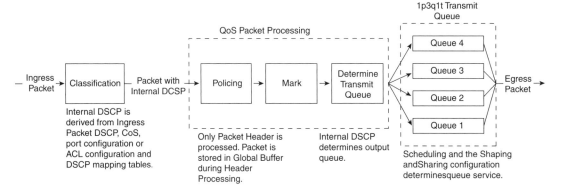

Because of the QoS features supported on the Catalyst 4000 IOS Family of switches, these switches fit well into an end-to-end QoS design as core, distribution, or access layer switches. Networks that require more than 64 Gbps or 48 Mpps in the core need to use the Catalyst 6500 platform instead. Figure 7-2 illustrates a sample network design using a Catalyst 4000 IOS switch in the distribution layer.

Software Requirements

All versions of the Catalyst 4000 IOS Software support QoS features. Several QoS attributes differ between the existing software versions. The initial releases of the Cisco IOS Catalyst 4000 software are Cisco IOS versions 12.1(8a)EW and 12.1(8a)EW1. A notable software change applicable to QoS occurs in Cisco IOS Software version 12.1(11b)EW1. In the original software versions, the switch counts packet drops that result from transmit queue overflow as output errors. In 12.1(11b)EW1 and later software versions, the switch counts output queue buffer drops as output drops rather than output errors. Example 7-1 compares how the switch counts output queue drops in 12.1(8a)EW and 12.1(8a)EW1 versus 12.1(11b)EW1 and later software versions.

Figure 7-2   *Sample Network Topology Using Catalyst 4000 IOS Switches*

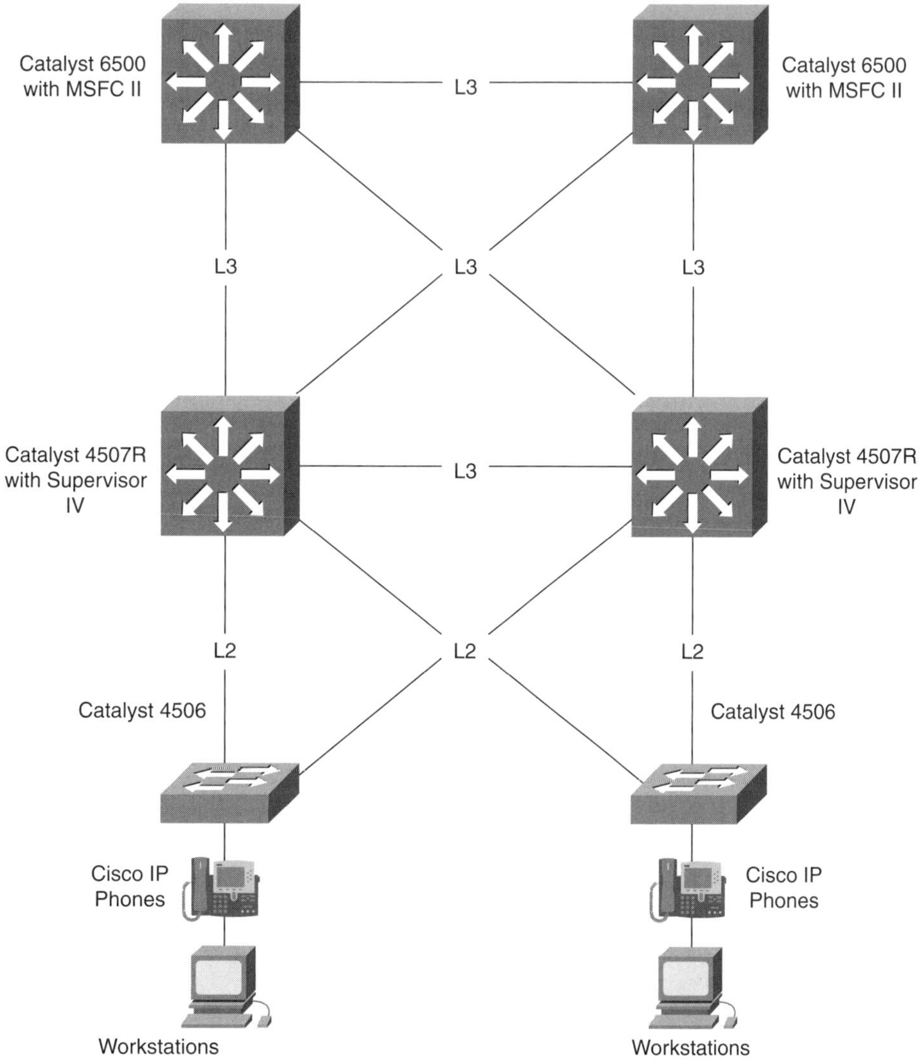

Example 7-1 *Transmit Buffer Overflow Counter Differences Between Software Versions 12.1(8a)EW and 12.1(8a)EW1 and Later Versions*

```
! 12.1(8a)EW:
Switch#show interface FastEthernet 6/1
FastEthernet6/1 is up, line protocol is up
  Hardware is Fast Ethernet Port, address is 0007.508b.84e0 (bia 0007.508b.84e0)
  MTU 1500 bytes, BW 100000 Kbit, DLY 100 usec,
     reliability 255/255, txload 1/255, rxload 1/255
  Encapsulation ARPA, loopback not set
  Keepalive set (10 sec)
  Full-duplex, 100Mb/s
  input flow-control is off, output flow-control is off
  ARP type: ARPA, ARP Timeout 04:00:00
  Last input never, output never, output hang never
  Last clearing of "show interface" counters never
  Input queue: 0/2000/0/0 (size/max/drops/flushes); Total output drops: 0
  Queueing strategy: fifo
  Output queue: 0/40 (size/max)
  5 minute input rate 0 bits/sec, 0 packets/sec
  5 minute output rate 0 bits/sec, 0 packets/sec
     373781138 packets input, 2447156352 bytes, 0 no buffer
     Received 11 broadcasts, 0 runts, 0 giants, 0 throttles
     4 input errors, 1 CRC, 0 frame, 0 overrun, 0 ignored
     0 input packets with dribble condition detected
     926574 packets output, 76097292 bytes, 0 underruns
     3120970731 output errors, 0 collisions, 0 interface resets
     0 babbles, 0 late collision, 0 deferred
     1 lost carrier, 0 no carrier
     0 output buffer failures, 0 output buffers swapped out
! 12.1(11b)EW1 and Later:
Switch#show interface FastEthernet 6/1
FastEthernet6/1 is up, line protocol is up
  Hardware is Fast Ethernet Port, address is 0007.508b.84e0 (bia 0007.508b.84e0)
  MTU 1500 bytes, BW 100000 Kbit, DLY 100 usec,
     reliability 255/255, txload 1/255, rxload 1/255
  Encapsulation ARPA, loopback not set
  Keepalive set (10 sec)
  Full-duplex, 100Mb/s
  input flow-control is off, output flow-control is off
  ARP type: ARPA, ARP Timeout 04:00:00
  Last input never, output never, output hang never
  Last clearing of "show interface" counters never
  Input queue: 0/2000/0/0 (size/max/drops/flushes); Total output drops: 250355824
  Queueing strategy: fifo
  Output queue: 0/40 (size/max)
  5 minute input rate 0 bits/sec, 0 packets/sec
  5 minute output rate 0 bits/sec, 0 packets/sec
     373781138 packets input, 2447156352 bytes, 0 no buffer
     Received 11 broadcasts, 0 runts, 0 giants, 0 throttles
     0 input errors, 0 CRC, 0 frame, 0 overrun, 0 ignored
     0 input packets with dribble condition detected
     926574 packets output, 76097292 bytes, 0 underruns
     0 output errors, 0 collisions, 0 interface resets
     0 babbles, 0 late collision, 0 deferred
     1 lost carrier, 0 no carrier
     0 output buffer failures, 0 output buffers swapped out
```

Moreover, Cisco IOS Software version 12.1(11b)EW adds support for voice VLANs and inline power, whereas Cisco IOS Software version 12.1(12c)EW adds the ability to disable the IP header *differentiated services* (DiffServ) *codepoint* (DSCP) rewrite functionality. The switch rewrites the IP header DSCP by default. Disabling the rewrite feature prevents all untrusted ports from rewriting DSCP to zero. In addition, the switch ignores any port DSCP configuration or marking, because the policing with the IP header DSCP rewrite functionality is disabled.

Use the following command to enable and disable the QoS IP header DSCP rewrite functionality:

```
[no] qos rewrite ip dscp
```

Global Configuration

The Catalyst 4000 IOS Family of switches requires QoS to be enabled globally for the switch to execute any QoS configurations. To enable QoS globally on the Catalyst 4000 IOS Family of switches, enter the following command in the global configuration mode:

```
[no] qos
```

Example 7-2 illustrates a user globally enabling QoS and verifying the configuration on a Catalyst 4000 IOS switch.

Example 7-2   *Enabling and Viewing QoS Feature Support on a Catalyst 4000 IOS Switch*

```
Switch#config terminal
Switch(config)#qos
Switch(config)#end
Switch#show qos
QoS is enabled globally
IP header DSCP rewrite is enabled
```

The global QoS configuration applies to all interfaces by default. However, the Catalyst 4000 IOS Family of switches supports disabling of QoS on a per-interface basis. The same command, **no qos** disables QoS on a per-interface basis. Example 7-3 shows a user disabling QoS feature support on interface FastEthernet 1/1.

Example 7-3   *Disabling QoS Feature Configuration on a Per-Interface Basis*

```
Switch#config terminal
Switch(config)#interface FastEthernet 1/1
Switch(config)#no qos
Switch(config)#end
```

Input Scheduling

As with the Catalyst 4000 CatOS switches, the Catalyst 4000 IOS Family of switches does not support input scheduling and performs only FIFO queuing of ingress packets. For line-module ports that are nonblocking, FIFO queuing does not pose a significant issue. Nonblocking line-module ports can deliver traffic to the switching fabric at line rate. Oversubscribed ports share bandwidth and data transmit contention in groups of two to eight ports, depending on line module. Chapter 3 in the "Input Scheduling" section discusses input scheduling as it relates to the Catalyst 4000 platform in general. Chapter 3 also includes Table 3-9, "Catalyst 4000 Line Modules Architecture," which discusses whether line modules are nonblocking and the oversubscription architecture.

Internal DSCP

The Catalyst 4000 IOS Family of switches represents all frames with an internal DSCP value. This internal DSCP value characterizes packet priority as the frame traverses the switch. Internal DSCP values range from 0 to 63, which is the same as the DiffServ specification for DSCP discussed in RFC 2474 and 2475. Packet processing involves policing, marking, and congestion management of packets using internal DSCP values for differentiating services.

By default, Cisco IP Phones mark RTP packets with a DSCP value of 46. On trusted ports, the switch derives the internal DSCP value from the ingress DSCP. Placing these Cisco IP Phones' *Voice over IP* (VoIP) packets into a strict priority queue illustrates an example of differentiating service using internal DSCP.

The switch must determine internal DSCP values for all ingress packets. Many parameters exist for determining internal DSCP values. These parameters include ingress packet's DSCP or *class of service* (CoS) value, trusting configuration, static port DSCP or CoS configuration, and ACL-based configurations.

The following section discusses the available parameters for determining internal DSCP and their relationship to the QoS mapping tables.

Classification and Marking

Classification determines the internal DSCP value, which distinguishes packets as they traverse the switch. The switch uses internal DSCP values to make policing, marking, and output scheduling decisions. Refer to Figure 7-1 for a logical diagram of QoS packet flow.

Classification is the primary focus of this section. For IP and non-IP traffic, several options exist for classifying frames to a specific DSCP value. The following sections discuss these options.

Trusting DSCP

This section explains trusting DSCP on the Catalyst 4000 IOS Family of switches. For a detailed explanation of the Cisco Catalyst trust concept, consult the Chapter 2, "End-to-End

QoS: Quality of Service at Layer 3 and Layer 2," section "Cisco Catalyst QoS Trust Concept."

The concept of trusting DSCP denotes that the switch uses an ingress frame's IP DSCP value to derive the internal DSCP value. For example, frames received on a trusted interface with a DSCP value of 50 directly denote the internal DSCP value of 50.

Use the following interface command to configure an interface to trust DSCP on ingress packets:

`qos trust dscp`

Example 7-4 illustrates a sample configuration of a Catalyst 4000 IOS switch interface configured to trust DSCP values on ingress packets.

Example 7-4 *Sample Configuration of an Interface Configured for Trusting DSCP*

```
Switch#show running-config
Building configuration...
(text deleted)
!
qos
!
(text deleted)
!
interface FastEthernet6/1
 switchport access vlan 2
 qos trust dscp
 no snmp trap link-status
 spanning-tree portfast
!
(text deleted)
!
end
```

For interfaces configured for trusting DSCP, the switch does not rewrite an ingress packet's CoS value; however, the egress CoS value of the final transmitted frame depends on the DSCP-to-CoS mapping tables. This chapter covers DSCP-to-CoS mapping tables for the Catalyst 4000 IOS Family of switches in the section titled "Mapping Internal DSCP to CoS."

NOTE   Because the DSCP value includes the IP precedence bits, all configurations use DSCP values rather than IP precedence values. A trust IP precedence configuration option does not exist on the Catalyst 4000 IOS Family of switches.

Trusting CoS

For the Catalyst 4000 IOS switch, the notion for trusting CoS signifies that the switch derives the internal DSCP value from the CoS value of an ingress frame. The CoS-to-DSCP mapping determines exactly how a CoS value maps to an internal DSCP value. For example, when trusting CoS, an ingress CoS value of 5 maps to an internal DSCP value of 40 with the default CoS-to-DSCP mapping table.

In addition, the switch does not rewrite the DSCP value of the packet on ingress when configured for trusting CoS. The packet's DSCP is not rewritten by the switch on ingress since the internal DSCP value serves as the classification parameter during packet-processing. Consequently, the egress DSCP value of the final transmitted frame depends solely on the internal DSCP. A multitude of factors determine the internal DSCP, including classification, marking, policing, and mapping tables. For example, a switch configured for trusting CoS that receives frames on an interface with a DSCP value of 26 and a CoS value of 5, uses only the CoS value of 5 to derive the internal DSCP. Assuming default CoS to DSCP mapping, the switches calculate the internal DSCP as a value of 40. Without any marking occurring and assuming default DSCP to CoS mapping, the DSCP value and CoS value of the egress frame will be 40 and 5, respectively.

Use the following interface command to configure an interface to trust CoS on ingress packets:

```
qos trust cos
```

Example 7-5 illustrates a Catalyst 4000 IOS interface configured to trust CoS values for internal DSCP mapping on ingress packets.

Example 7-5   *Sample Configuration of an Interface Configured for Trusting CoS*

```
Switch#show running-config
Building configuration...
(text deleted)
!
qos
!
(text deleted)
!
interface FastEthernet6/1
 switchport access vlan 2
 qos trust cos
 no snmp trap link-status
 spanning-tree portfast
!
(text deleted)
!
end
```

Table 7-2 indicates the default CoS-to-DSCP mapping that occurs on ingress frames on an interface configured for trusting CoS.

Table 7-2   *Default CoS-to-Internal DSCP Mapping Table*

CoS Value	0	1	2	3	4	5	6	7
DSCP Value	0	8	16	24	32	40	48	56

The CoS-to-DSCP mapping table is configurable such that any ingress packet's CoS value may map to any internal DSCP value. Use the following command to configure the CoS-to-DSCP mapping table:

qos map cos *cos-list* **to dscp**

cos-list represents the CoS values to map to the configured DSCP value. The command accepts the *cos-list* entries separated by a space.

For displaying the current configured CoS-to-DSCP mapping, use the following command:

show qos maps cos dscp

Example 7-6 illustrates an example of a user displaying, configuring, and verifying the CoS-to-DSCP mapping table.

Example 7-6   *Displaying, Configuring, and Verifying the CoS-to-DSCP Mapping Table*

```
Switch#show qos maps cos dscp
CoS-DSCP Mapping Table
   CoS:   0  1  2  3  4  5  6  7
  --------------------------------
  DSCP:   0  8 16 24 32 40 48 56
Switch#configure terminal
Switch(config)#qos map cos 1 2 3 to dscp 35
Switch(config)#qos map cos 4 5 6 to dscp 45
Switch(config)#end
Switch#show qos maps cos dscp
CoS-DSCP Mapping Table
   CoS:   0  1  2  3  4  5  6  7
  --------------------------------
  DSCP:   0 35 35 35 45 45 45 56
```

To restore the CoS-to-DSCP mapping table back to the default configuration, use the following global configuration command:

no qos map cos to dscp

Untrusted Interfaces

The term *untrusted port* refers to an interface that does not utilize the DSCP or CoS value of an ingress frame for determining the internal DSCP value. Unlike the default behavior of the Catalyst 4000 CatOS switches where all ports are trusted, the default behavior for all interfaces of a Catalyst 4000 IOS switch is to not trust DSCP or CoS (that is, untrusted). As a result, the switch classifies the frame with an internal DSCP value of zero by default. The terms *port DSCP configuration* and *port CoS configuration* identify untrusted ports as well. Unless the switch changes the DSCP value of the frames by policing or marking, the egress value is also zero.

Use the following commands to configure a switch to override an untrusted interface with specific DSCP and CoS values:

```
qos dscp dscp_value
qos cos cos_value
```

dscp_value and *cos_value* symbolize the DSCP or CoS value used in determining the internal DSCP value.

Example 7-7 illustrates a sample configuration of an interface configured for reclassifying the DSCP value to 40.

Example 7-7   *Sample configuration of an Interface Configured for Reclassifying DSCP*

```
Switch#show running-config
Building configuration...
(text deleted)
!
interface FastEthernet6/1
 switchport access vlan 2
 qos dscp 40
 no snmp trap link-status
 spanning-tree portfast
!
(text deleted)
!
end
```

Non-IP Frames

IP frames contain bits for IP precedence and DSCP; non-IP frames do not include an IP header or bits for IP precedence or DSCP. The Catalyst 4000 IOS switch prioritizes packets based only on DSCP or CoS. As a result, the switch classifies non-IP frames exclusively based on ingress CoS values or port CoS configuration. Trusting CoS is a valid configuration for non-IP frames. Port CoS configuration treats a port as untrusted and rewrites CoS values to a specified value. By default, the switch reclassifies the CoS value to zero. Because the internal DSCP value does not require an IP header, the switch subsequently maps the configured or trusted CoS value to an internal DSCP value using the configurable CoS-to-DSCP mapping table. The preceding classification sections—"Trusting CoS" and "Untrusted Interfaces"—include examples for displaying, configuring, and verifying trusting CoS configurations and untrusted configurations.

Displaying Port Trust Configuration

To verify an interface trust configuration, use the following command:

```
show qos interface {{FastEthernet interface-number} | {GigabitEthernet interface-
number} | {VLAN vlan_id} | {Port-channel number}}
```

Example 7-8 displays a sample output of the **show qos interface** *interface_name* command. This example illustrates an interface configured for trusting DSCP. The output displays both the global and interface QoS configuration. In addition, the command displays the trust port state as either DSCP, CoS, or untrusted with the respective reclassification values for the untrusted configuration.

Example 7-8 *Sample Output of the* **show qos interface** *Command*

```
Switch#show qos interface GigabitEthernet 1/1
QoS is enabled globally
Port QoS is enabled
Port Trust State: 'DSCP'
Default DSCP: 0 Default CoS: 0
Appliance trust: none
Tx-Queue    Bandwidth    ShapeRate    Priority    QueueSize
            (bps)        (bps)                     (packets)
   1        250000000    disabled     N/A         1920
   2        250000000    disabled     N/A         1920
   3        250000000    disabled     normal      1920
   4        250000000    disabled     N/A         1920
```

The appliance trust field indicates the 802.1p trust configuration to communicate via *Cisco Discovery Protocol* (CDP) to a neighbor appliance. *Appliance trust* is the IOS term for extended trust, as discussed in Chapter 2. The "Output Scheduling" section of this chapter discusses the transmit queues, bandwidth, and shape rate output.

ACL-Based Classification

Because the ultimate goal of classification is to determine the marking and scheduling of the frame, multiple methods of classification exist. The Catalyst 4000 IOS Family of switches allows for classification of ingress packets based on standard, extended, and named IP ACLs in addition to the port trust configuration. In addition, the switches support classification occurring strictly on IP precedence values or DSCP values without the use of an ACL. ACL-based classification often inherits properties of the untrusted configuration because the switch does not use the packet's DSCP or CoS values for determining packet classification.

Chapter 5, "Introduction to the Modular QoS Command-Line Interface," elaborates on how to create and implement class maps and policy maps and includes examples that show you how to do so. Consult Chapter 5 before reading the following "Class Map" and "Policy Map" sections. The following sections discuss class maps and policy maps, with a focus on options supported by hardware switching.

Class Maps

As with mainline Cisco IOS Software, class maps label ACLs for application on policy maps. A limited subset of available Cisco IOS class map **match** commands is available for hardware switching on the Catalyst 4000 IOS Family of switches. The following class map criteria are available for hardware switching:

- Standard, extended, or named IP or MAC ACLs
- IP precedence values
- DSCP values
- All packets MAC-address based ACL is also supported

To create class map clauses for ACL-based classification, use the following class map configuration command:

```
match access-group {acl_index | name acl_name}
```

acl_index represents the ACL number and *acl_name* refers to a named ACL. Up to eight class clauses are configurable per class map. Example 7-9 illustrates a user configuring a class map for matching packets against either of two ACLs.

Example 7-9   *User Configuring a Class Map Matching One of Two Configured ACLs*

```
Switch#configure terminal
Enter configuration commands, one per line.  End with CNTL/Z.
Switch(config)#access-list 110 permit udp any host 10.1.1.2 eq 12000
Switch(config)#access-list 111 permit tcp any host 192.168.100.1 eq 50000
Switch(config)#class-map match-any TEST
Switch(config-cmap)#match access-group 110
Switch(config-cmap)#match access-group 111
Switch(config-cmap)#end
```

To configure IP precedence and DSCP value matching criteria, use the following class map commands, respectively:

```
match ip precedence ipp_value1 [ipp_value2 [ipp_valueN]]
match ip dscp dscp_value1 [dscp_value2 [dscp_valueN]]
```

To match against IP precedence or DSCP, you must use the **qos trust dscp** configuration on the interface. Otherwise, the switch uses the default or port DSCP configuration value.

The **match-any** class map configuration command configures the class map to match packets on any ACL. Moreover, the **match-all** class map configuration command option configures the class map to match packets against all ACLs.

Example 7-10 shows a class map configured to match packets against several DSCP values.

Example 7-10   *Class Map Configured to Match Against DSCP Values*

```
Switch#configure terminal
Enter configuration commands, one per line.  End with CNTL/Z.
Switch(config)#class-map match-all MATCH_DSCP_VALUES_4-7
Switch(config)#match ip dscp 50 51 52 53 54 55
Switch(config-cmap)#end
```

For additional information about creating and applying class maps, see Chapter 5.

Policy Maps

Class maps define classification criteria; policy maps organize the class map classification criteria with policing and marking actions. Policing and marking configuration derive the class actions. Do not confuse policing with policy maps. Whereas policy maps may include an action based on rates, they also include support for other QoS actions such as marking.

On the Catalyst 4000 IOS Family of switches, policy maps tie up to eight class map actions together. A class map action may consist of a traffic-limiting policer. Each interface on the Catalyst 4000 IOS Family of switches supports a single policy for ingress traffic and a single policy for egress traffic.

Example 7-11 illustrates a sample policy map configuration for marking packets based on UDP port. The class action shown, **set ip precedence 5**, rewrites all ingress packets received on interface FastEthernet2/1 matching the ACL 101 criteria.

Example 7-11 *Sample Policy Map and Class Map Configuration*

```
Switch#show running-config
Building configuration...
(text deleted)
!
qos
!
(text deleted)
!
class-map match-all UDP_PORT_50000_59000
  description MATCH PACKETS ON UDP PORTS 50000 TO 59000
  match access-group 101
!
policy-map TEST
 description MARK FRAMES ON UDP PORT 50000 TO 59000 WITH IP PRECEDENCE 5
   class UDP_PORT_50000_59000
     set ip precedence 5

!
interface FastEthernet2/1
 service-policy input TEST
 no snmp trap link-status
 spanning-tree portfast
(text deleted)
!

(text deleted)
!
access-list 101 permit udp any any range 50000 59000
!
(text deleted)
!
end
```

To view ingress packet matching against the class map clauses of a policy map, use the following command:

```
show policy-map interface [{FastEthernet interface-number} | {GigabitEthernet
    interface-number} | {Port-channel number} | {VLAN vlan_id}] [input | output]
```

Example 7-12 shows the sample output of the **show policy-map interface** command for the policy map sample configuration in Example 7-11.

Example 7-12 *Viewing Class Map Matches of a Policy Map*

```
Switch#show policy-map interface FastEthernet6/1
 FastEthernet6/1
  service-policy input: TEST
    class-map: UDP_PORT_50000_59000 (match-all)
      9628 packets
      match: access-group 101
      set:
        ip precedence 5
    class-map: class-default (match-any)
      3948 packets
      match: any
        3948 packets
```

Policing

The Catalyst 4000 IOS Family of switches supports individual and aggregate policing in both ingress and egress configurations. In brief, aggregate policing limits a shared rate and burst parameter among all associated ports or VLANs. With individual policing, each port or VLAN uses its own exclusive rate and burst parameters. This section discusses the following policing topics:

- Policing Resources
- Port-based and VLAN-based Policing
- Individual and Aggregate Policing
- Policing Actions
- Traffic-Rate Policing
- Leaky Token Bucket Algorithm
- Burst Size Parameter
- Guaranteed Rate of Policer
- Policing Accuracy
- DSCP Policed Action
- Marking Action
- Trusting Action

Policing Resources

The architecture of the Catalyst 4000 IOS Family of switches limits the number of input policers and output policers to 1024. The architecture processes all packets for policing regardless of configuration. As a result, the Cisco Catalyst 4000 IOS reserves two input and two output policers for null processing. Subsequently, 1022 policers for input policing and 1022 policers for output policing are available.

Port-Based and VLAN-Based Policing

Port-based policing entails binding policy maps to individual ports. VLAN-based policing involves attaching a policy map to a VLAN interface.

For a configuration in which a VLAN-based policy exists but a port-based policy does not exist, the switch subjects ingress packets to the VLAN-based policer. This behavior occurs regardless of the port's policing configuration for VLAN-based or port-based policing. To work around this behavior, create and attach a null policy map to the interface. A null policy map consists of a defined police map with a class map clause to match all packets and no configured actions. The use of this null policer to work around VLAN-based policing behavior applies to both ingress and egress policers.

To configure an interface to use VLAN-based policies and to fall back on port-based policies if no VLAN-based policies exist, use the following interface command:

```
qos vlan-based
```

Example 7-13 shows and interface configured for VLAN-based QoS.

Example 7-13 *An Interface Configured for VLAN-Based Policing*

```
Switch# configure terminal
Enter configuration commands, one per line.  End with CNTL/Z.
Switch(config)# interface fastethernet 2/1
Switch(config-if)# qos vlan-based
Switch(config-if)# end
```

Individual and Aggregate Policing

Individual policers apply bandwidth limits discretely to each interface for defined policy maps. Class maps define traffic classes within a policy map. Use the following policy map class clause configuration command to configure individual policers:

```
police rate burst [[conform-action {transmit | drop}]  [exceed-action {transmit |
   drop | policed-dscp-transmit}]]
```

Example 7-14 shows a sample configuration of an individual policer. In this example, the policer limits ingress traffic from both FastEthernet 6/1 and 6/2 separately to the 1.54 Mbps specified in the individual policer.

Subsequent sections cover configuring the policer rate, burst, and actions parameters shown in Examples 7-14 and 7-15.

Example 7-14 *Sample Configuration of an Individual Policer*

```
Current configuration : 327064 bytes
!
(text deleted)
qos
(text deleted)
!
(text deleted)
!
class-map match-any UDP_PORT_1200
  description MATCH PACKETS ON UDP PORT 1200
  match access-group 102
!
policy-map TEST_INDIVIDUAL
  class UDP_PORT_1200
    police 1.54 mbps 16000 byte conform-action transmit exceed-action drop
!
(text deleted)
!
interface FastEthernet6/1
 switchport access vlan 2
 service-policy input TEST_INDIVIDUAL
 no snmp trap link-status
!
interface FastEthernet6/2
 switchport access vlan 2
 service-policy input TEST_INDIVIDUAL
 no snmp trap link-status
!
access-list 102 permit udp any any eq 1200
!
(text deleted)
!
end
```

Aggregate policers cumulatively restrict bandwidth among all ports and VLANs per class map clauses of the policy map. Use the following global configuration command to configure aggregate policers:

```
qos aggregate-policer policer_name rate burst [[conform-action {transmit | drop}]
    [exceed-action {transmit | drop | policed-dscp-transmit}]]
```

policer_name defines the name to represent the aggregate policer. To attach the aggregate policer, use the following policy-map class clause configuration command:

```
police aggregate policer_name
```

Example 7-15 provides a sample configuration of an aggregate policer. In this example, the policer limits ingress traffic from both FastEthernet 6/1 and 6/2 cumulatively to the specified 1.54-Mbps rate specified in the aggregate policer.

Example 7-15 *Sample Configuration of an Aggregate Policer*

```
Current configuration : 327064 bytes
!
(text deleted)
!
qos aggregate-policer 1_MBPS_RATE_EXCEED_DROP 1540000 bps 8000 byte conform-action
transmit exceed-action drop
qos
(text deleted)
!
interface FastEthernet6/1
 switchport access vlan 2
 service-policy input TEST_AGGREGATE
 no snmp trap link-status
!
interface FastEthernet6/2
 switchport access vlan 2
 service-policy input TEST_AGGREGATE
 no snmp trap link-status
!
(text deleted)
!
class-map match-any UDP_PORT_1200
  description MATCH PACKETS ON UDP PORT 1200
  match access-group 102
!
policy-map TEST_AGGREGATE
  class UDP_PORT_1200
    police aggregate 1_MBPS_RATE_EXCEED_DROP
!
(text deleted)
!
access-list 102 permit udp any any eq 1200
!
(text deleted)
!
end
```

To demonstrate and measure this behavior, two packet generator ports were connected to the switch on ports FastEthernet 6/1 and 6/2 as shown in Figure 7-3. The packet generator ports sent traffic at 100 Mbps unicast to a destination connected off interface FastEthernet 6/3. A packet generator port connected off FastEthernet 6/3 measured the traffic rate for this flow.

Figure 7-3   *Topology for Demonstrating Individual and Aggregate Policing*

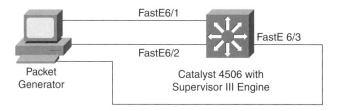

Three trials were conducted. For each trial, the packet count and traffic rate were measured. The trials included measuring traffic against a configuration without a policy, using the individual policer shown in Example 7-14, and using the aggregate policer shown in Example 7-15. Table 7-3 displays the results.

Table 7-3   *Demonstration of Individual Versus Aggregate Policer*

Trial	No Policers	Individual Policer Shown in Example 7-15	Aggregate Policer Shown in Example 7-16
Rate Received on FastEthernet 6/3	100 Mbps	3.08 Mbps	1.5 Mbps

The trial results clearly indicate that the individual policers apply traffic rates respective to each port, whereas aggregate policers apply traffic rates as the sum of all applicable ports.

Policing Actions

The Catalyst 4000 IOS Family of switches supports the following policing actions:

- Traffic-rate policing
- Marking IP DSCP
- Marking IP precedence
- Trusting DSCP
- Trusting CoS

The Catalyst 4000 IOS Family of switches supports transmitting or dropping the packet for both the conforming and exceeding actions of a traffic-rate policer. In addition, the exceeding action is configurable for marking down the DSCP on the respective packet. With regard to the Catalyst 4000 IOS Family of switches, a **policed-dscp-transmit** action refers to the marking down of a packet.

Traffic-Rate Policing

The packet-processing step of the QoS model from Figure 7-1 is responsible for determining whether each processed packet is conforming to or exceeding a specified rate of a policer. The Catalyst 4000 IOS Family of switches uses the leaky token bucket algorithm to determine whether a packet is conforming to or exceeding a specified policer rate.

The following commands configure the *rate* and *burst* of a class map policer and an aggregate policer, respectively:

```
police rate burst [[conform-action {transmit | drop}] [exceed-action {transmit | drop |
  policed-dscp-transmit}]]
qos aggregate-policer policer_name rate burst [[conform-action {transmit | drop}]
  [exceed-action {transmit | drop | policed-dscp-transmit}]]
```

rate defines the actual policing rate. The supported rates for the Catalyst 4000 IOS Family of switches range from 32 kbps to 32 Gbps in 1-bps increments. When entering the value for rate, the prefixes kilo, mega, and giga are optional using the **k**, **m**, and **g** command, respectively.

burst defines the burst size in bytes. The burst size needs to be at least the maximum packet size of frames touched by the policer for accurate policing. The burst size parameter also supports the following optional prefixes: kilo, mega, and giga. The following sections discuss determining the applicable burst size.

Leaky Token Bucket Algorithm

The switch applies the rate and burst parameters defined in the policer to all packets processed. The leaky token bucket algorithm takes snapshots of packet flow to determine whether a packet is conforming or exceeding the specified rate. The configured policer rate defines the number of tokens removed at each interval. The leaky token bucket algorithm does not actually store, process, or buffer any packet. Rather, the switch architecture relies on the leaky token bucket algorithm to distinguish a packet in a flow as conforming or exceeding the configured policer rate. The switch architecture uses the algorithm for both ingress and egress policing.

The number of tokens entering the bucket correlates to the ingress packet size of a frame. A specific number of tokens leak from the bucket every 16 nanoseconds for the Catalyst 4000 IOS Family of switches. The number of tokens leaking from the bucket relates to the configured policer rate. The burst size defines the maximum number of bytes in the bucket at any interval.

When the token bucket cannot accommodate any new tokens, the algorithm determines that the packets corresponding to these tokens are exceeding the policer rate and the packet processing engine executes the exceed action of the policer.

In brief, the token bucket algorithm provides a logical, visual portrait of how policing limits traffic. The portrait defined becomes useful when considering the burst size and the effect of the token bucket algorithm on TCP and UDP protocols.

NOTE Buffering does not occur on the packets in the bucket. The Leaky Token Bucket Algorithm only snapshots traffic to determine whether a packet is conforming or exceeding the configured police rate.

Burst Size Parameter

Because of the flow-control nature of TCP/IP and UDP application behavior, packet drops significantly impact traffic behavior and may result in a packet-per-second performance far below the configured policer rate. The burst parameter of policing attempts to handle the torrent nature of TCP/IP and web traffic by allowing period surges of traffic into the bucket.

Configuration of the burst size follows several other Catalyst platform recommendations. For TCP applications, use the following formula for calculating the burst size parameter used for policing:

<burst> = 2 * <RTT> * <rate>

RTT defines the approximate *round-trip time* for a TCP session. If RTT is unknown, use a RTT value of 1 millisecond or 1 second depending on estimated latency. Example 7-16 illustrates the burst calculation for a rate of 64 kbps and an unknown RTT.

Example 7-16 *Sample Burst Calculation*

```
<burst> = 2 * <1 sec> * <64000 bits/sec>
<burst> = 128000 bits = 16000 bytes
```

Nevertheless, from an application perspective, TCP/IP traffic-rate policing always results in actual rates less than the configured rate regardless of the burst size. UDP applications police closer to the configured rate in pure bits per second; however, some UDP applications retransmit heavily upon packet loss. As a result, the rate for applications that use UDP may also fall well below the configured rate. In summary, system administrators must carefully plan and consider application behavior and resiliency to rate policing before applying policers.

Guaranteed Rate of Policer

During any time interval, the leaky token bucket algorithm implementation on the Catalyst 4000 IOS Family of switches guarantees the following conforming policing rate:

Conforming rate <= (<configured_rate bits/sec> * <1 byte/8 bits> * <period>) + <burst_size> + 1 packet

Consider Example 7-14, for example, where the aggregate policer defines a rate of 1.54 Mbps and a burst size of 8000 bytes. Using the preceding formula, the guaranteed conforming traffic rate for a 1-second interval calculates as follows:

Conforming rate <= (1540000 bits/sec * 1 byte/8 bits * 1 sec) + 8000 bytes + 1 packet = 200500 bytes

In bits per second, the conforming rate is 2.006 Mbps, assuming an average 100-byte packet size.

Because of the nature of applications that use the TCP/IP and UDP/IP protocols, use careful planning when configuring the burst size.

Policing Accuracy

Moreover, the architecture of the Catalyst 4000 IOS Family of switches bestows policing at a finite set of rates distributed between 32 kbps and 32 Gbps in 1-bps increments. Because of the hardware architecture, specified rates adjust up or down to the nearest hardware-capable rate. The adjusted policy rate is always within 1.5 percent of the configured rate. Subsequently, two distinct policy rates must differ by at least 3 percent.

DSCP-Policed Action

The Catalyst 4000 IOS Family of switches uses the DSCP-policed concept to mark down packets. For DSCP-policed traffic, the switch marks the frame with a DSCP value derived from the QoS DSCP-policed mapping table. The default mapping table maps 1:1 with the internal DSCP values; therefore, the default mark down action results in no change to the DSCP value. The QoS DSCP-policed mapping table requires a nondefault configuration to actually mark down packets that exceed the rate specified in the policing action.

Use the following command to configure the QoS DSCP-policed mapping tables:

```
qos map dscp policed dscp-list to dscp mark-down-dscp
```

dscp-list represents up to eight DSCP values that configure to represent the DSCP *mark-down-DSCP* value. Example 7-17 displays the default QoS DSCP-policed mapping table, configures the DSCP-policed mapping table for marking down DSCP values 50 to 59 to 0, and verifies the configuration.

Example 7-17 *Displaying, Configuring, and Verifying the QoS DSCP-Policed Mapping Table*

```
Switch#show qos map dscp policed
Policed DSCP Mapping Table (DSCP = d1d2)
d1 : d2  0  1  2  3  4  5  6  7  8  9
---------------------------------------
  0 :    00 01 02 03 04 05 06 07 08 09
  1 :    10 11 12 13 14 15 16 17 18 19
  2 :    20 21 22 23 24 25 26 27 28 29
  3 :    30 31 32 33 34 35 36 37 38 39
  4 :    40 41 42 43 44 45 46 47 48 49
  5 :    50 51 52 53 54 55 56 57 58 59
  6 :    60 61 62 63
Switch(config)#qos map dscp policed 50 51 52 53 54 55 56 57 to dscp 0
Switch(config)#qos map dscp policed 58 59 to dscp 0
Switch#show qos map dscp policed
Policed DSCP Mapping Table (DSCP = d1d2)
```

continues

Example 7-17 *Displaying, Configuring, and Verifying the QoS DSCP-Policed Mapping Table (Continued)*

```
d1 : d2  0  1  2  3  4  5  6  7  8  9
-------------------------------------
  0 :    00 01 02 03 04 05 06 07 08 09
  1 :    10 11 12 13 14 15 16 17 18 19
  2 :    20 21 22 23 24 25 26 27 28 29
  3 :    30 31 32 33 34 35 36 37 38 39
  4 :    40 41 42 43 44 45 46 47 48 49
  5 :    00 00 00 00 00 00 00 00 00 00
  6 :    60 61 62 63
```

To configure the traffic-rate policer for marking down the DSCP value for the exceed action, use the **policed-dscp-transmit** keyword for the **exceed-action** parameter for the following individual policy map and aggregate global policer configuration commands:

```
police rate burst [[conform-action {transmit | drop}] [exceed-action {transmit | drop |
   policed-dscp-transmit}]]
qos aggregate-policer policer_name rate burst [[conform-action {transmit | drop}]
   [exceed-action {transmit | drop | policed-dscp-transmit}]]
```

Example 7-18 *Sample Configuration for* **policed-dscp-transmit** *Exceed Action of an Individual Policer*

```
Current configuration : 327064 bytes
!
(text deleted)
!
qos map dscp policed 50 51 52 53 54 55 56 57 to dscp 7
qos map dscp policed 58 59 to dscp 7
qos
(text deleted)
class-map match-all UDP_PORT_10000
  description MATCH PACKETS ON DESTINATION UDP PORT 10000
  match access-group 105
!
policy-map MARK_BASED_ON_RATE
  class UDP_PORT_10000
    police 32000 bps 16000 byte conform-action transmit exceed-action policed-dscp-
transmit
!
interface FastEthernet6/1
 switchport mode access
 service-policy input MARK_BASED_ON_RATE
 spanning-tree portfast
!
(text deleted)
!
access-list 105 permit udp any any eq 10000
!
end
```

Marking Action

Policy maps allow for marking of packets using ACL-based classification. Class maps frame ACLs for policy maps. Review the "ACL-Based Classification" section earlier in this chapter for discussion of class maps and ACL options.

Policy maps organize the marking action using the following policy map class clause command:

```
set ip [dscp | precedence] [value]
```

value represents the actual value to mark on the packet for DSCP or IP precedence. Example 7-19 illustrates marking based on ACL-based classification.

Example 7-19 *Sample Configuration of Marking Based on ACL Classification*

```
Current configuration : 327064 bytes
!
(text deleted)
!
qos
!
(text deleted)
!
class-map match-all UDP_PORT_10000
  description MATCH PACKETS ON DESTINATION UDP PORT 10000
  match access-group 105
!
!
policy-map ACL_MARK
  class UDP_PORT_10000
    set ip dscp 40
!
!
interface FastEthernet6/1
 switchport mode access
 service-policy input ACL_MARK
 spanning-tree portfast
!
(text deleted)
access-list 105 permit udp any any eq 10000
(text deleted)
!
end
```

Trusting Action

Trusting DSCP or CoS using a policing action is another way to refer to trusting DSCP or CoS based on an ACL. Packets that match the configured class clause have the internal DSCP determined based on ingress packets' DSCP or CoS value. The switch does not alter the internal DSCP of frames that do match the class clause ACLs. For configurations using trusting in class map clauses, there is no need for a trusting configuration on the interface.

Configuring an interface for trusting and configuring a policing action of trusting needs careful consideration because a trusting configuration on an interface classifies ingress frames before a policy.

Policy maps organize the trusting actions using the following policy map class clause command:

```
trust [dscp | cos]
```

Example 7-20 illustrates a policy map configured to trust DSCP for a specific class map.

Example 7-20 *Sample Configuration for a Policy Map Configured to Trust DSCP*

```
Current configuration : 327064 bytes
!
(text deleted)
!
qos
!
(text deleted)
!
interface FastEthernet3/1
 switchport access vlan 2
 switchport voice vlan 700
 service-policy input TRUST_UDP_GT_10000
 no snmp trap link-status
 tx-queue 3
   priority high
 spanning-tree portfast
!
(text deleted)
!
class-map match-all UDP_PORT_GT_10000
  match access-group 150
!
!
policy-map TRUST_UDP_GT_10000
  class UDP_PORT_GT_10000
    trust dscp
!
(text deleted)
access-list 150 permit udp any any gt 10000
(text deleted)
end
```

Congestion Management

After the switch classifies and processes packets against QoS policies, the switch places the packet in transmit queues for output scheduling. Refer to Figure 7-1 for a logical diagram of this behavior.

The Catalyst 4000 IOS Family of switches supports congestion management through the use these queuing and scheduling mechanisms that occur after packet processing. Classification distinguishes packets into multiple egress queues, whereas scheduling differentiates service by transmitting packets out of these queues in a specific order.

Queuing and scheduling use the following QoS-specific features for building the congestion management model:

- Port Transmit Queues
- Mapping Internal DSCP to Transmit Queues
- Strict-Priority Queuing
- Sharing
- Shaping
- Mapping Internal DSCP to CoS

Port Transmit Queues

The Catalyst 4000 IOS Family of switches uses a shared memory architecture. The shared memory architecture handles all output queuing and scheduling on the supervisor engine versus other Catalyst platforms that depend on line-module architecture for output queuing and scheduling. As a result, all ports utilize four transmit egress queues labeled 1 to 4. Gigabit Ethernet interfaces employ a queue size of 1920 packets, whereas Fast Ethernet and nonblocking Gigabit Ethernet interfaces utilize a queue size of 240 packets. Table 3-9 in Chapter 3 discusses which line-module interfaces are nonblocking. Software versions available at the time of publication do not allow for configuration of the queue size.

Mapping Internal DSCP to Transmit Queues

After packet processing occurs, the switch places the packet into a transmit queue for scheduling. By default, the switch places packets with higher DSCP values into higher-numbered transmit queues. Nevertheless, the switch services all transmit queues round-robin by default. The strict-priority queue, shaping, and sharing configurations allow for differentiating service based on the transmit queue. Table 7-4 lists the default internal DSCP to transmit queue mapping.

Table 7-4   *Default Internal DSCP-to-Transmit Queue Mapping Table*

DSCP Values	Transmit Queue
0–15	0
16–31	1
32–47	2
48–63	3

Use the following command to display the internal DSCP–to–transmit queue mapping:

```
show qos maps dscp tx-queue
```

Use the following global configuration command to configure the internal DSCP to the transmit queue:

```
[no] qos map dscp dscp_values to tx-queue queue-id
```

dscp_values represents configuration for up to eight DSCP values to map to a transmit queue. *queue_id* represents one of the four transmit queues. For configuring mapping of more than eight DSCP values, use multiple commands.

Example 7-21 displays the default DSCP-TxQueue mapping table, configures the DSCP-TxQueue mapping table for assigning DSCP values 40 to 49 to queue 1, and verifies the DSCP-TxQueue mapping table configuration.

Example 7-21 *Displaying, Configuring, and Verifying the DSCP-to-Transmit Queue Mapping Table*

```
Switch#show qos maps dscp tx-queue
DSCP-TxQueue Mapping Table (DSCP = d1d2)
d1 : d2  0  1  2  3  4  5  6  7  8  9
-------------------------------------
 0 :     01 01 01 01 01 01 01 01 01 01
 1 :     01 01 01 01 01 01 02 02 02 02
 2 :     02 02 02 02 02 02 02 02 02 02
 3 :     02 02 03 03 03 03 03 03 03 03
 4 :     03 03 03 03 03 03 03 03 04 04
 5 :     04 04 04 04 04 04 04 04 04 04
 6 :     04 04 04 04
Switch#configure terminal
Enter configuration commands, one per line.  End with CNTL/Z.
Switch(config)#qos map dscp 40 41 42 43 44 45 46 47 to tx-queue 1
Switch(config)#qos map dscp 48 49  to tx-queue 1
Switch(config)#end
Switch#show qos maps dscp tx-queue
DSCP-TxQueue Mapping Table (DSCP = d1d2)
d1 : d2  0  1  2  3  4  5  6  7  8  9
-------------------------------------
 0 :     01 01 01 01 01 01 01 01 01 01
 1 :     01 01 01 01 01 01 02 02 02 02
 2 :     02 02 02 02 02 02 02 02 02 02
 3 :     02 02 03 03 03 03 03 03 03 03
 4 :     01 01 01 01 01 01 01 01 01 01
 5 :     04 04 04 04 04 04 04 04 04 04
 6 :     04 04 04 04
```

Strict-Priority Queuing

The Catalyst 4000 IOS Family of switches offers strict-priority, Low-Latency Queuing by designating transmit queue 3 as a high-priority transmit queue. By assigning transmit queue 3 as a high-priority transmit queue, the switch transmits packets out of transmit queue 3 before any other queue until the queue reaches its share rate. The next section, "Sharing," discusses share rate.

The recommended use of the high-priority queue is for time-sensitive packet flows, such as VoIP flows, stock tickers, and, in some cases, video conferencing. Because of the aggressive scheduling nature of the higher priority, strict-priority queues may starve lower-priority queues when the high-priority queue consistently contains packets to transmit.

Use the following interface transmit queue command to configure transmit queue 3 as a high-priority queue:

```
priority high
```

Example 7-22 shows a sample configuration of an interface configured with a strict-priority queue.

Example 7-22 *Sample Configuration of Interface Configured for Strict-Priority Queuing*

```
Current configuration : 327064 bytes
!
(text deleted)
qos
!
(text deleted)
!
interface FastEthernet3/1
 switchport access vlan 2
 switchport voice vlan 700
 no snmp trap link-status
 tx-queue 3
   priority high
 spanning-tree portfast
!
(text deleted)
!
end
```

Sharing

The Catalyst 4000 IOS Family of switches supports QoS bandwidth sharing per transmit queue on nonblocking Gigabit Ethernet interfaces. Table 3-9 in Chapter 3 discusses which Gigabit Ethernet line modules and ports are nonblocking.

Because different DSCP and CoS values map to different queues, sharing differentiates services by guaranteeing queue bandwidth. Bandwidth sharing forces minimum bandwidth per transmit queue. A practical example of using sharing is with high-bandwidth applications such a *Network File System* (NFS). Generally, applications using NFS require high bandwidth with minimal packet loss. Configuring sharing at 500 Mbps for transmit queue 2 and mapping NFS packets to transmit queue 2 forces the switch to provide 500 Mbps of egress traffic to the adjacent switch for NFS packets. In this configuration, the system administrator must adjust other transmit queues' bandwidth rates to compensate for the 500 Mbps of traffic for transmit queue 2 given that the total bandwidth of the egress interface is limited to 1 Gbps. Example 7-23 provides a sample configuration for the described application of sharing.

Example 7-23 *Sample Configuration of Shaping*

```
Building configuration...
Current configuration : 225 bytes
!
qos
!
(text deleted)
!
interface GigabitEthernet1/1
 switchport trunk encapsulation dot1q
 switchport mode trunk
 no snmp trap link-status
 tx-queue 1
   bandwidth 125 mbps
 tx-queue 2
   bandwidth 500 mbps
 tx-queue 3
   bandwidth 125 mbps
!
(text deleted)
!
end
```

The switch maintains sharing rates by treating all queues as high-priority queues during periods when a transmit queue's egress traffic rate is below the configured share values. Initially, the switch round-robins packets until a queue reaches its share. At this instance, the switch services round-robin all other queues under the defined share. The switch still handles a configured strict-priority queue as defined in the "Strict-Priority Queuing" section. The switch services the strict-priority queue before all other queues until it reaches its configured share value. When all queues reach their share rate, the switch services the queues round-robin. The default bandwidth parameter applied to each transmit queue is 250 Mbps. Misconfiguring bandwidth parameters may result in transmit queue starvation, where the switch does not service a queue with a low-bandwidth parameter sufficiently.

To configure guaranteed minimum bandwidth per output queue, use the following interface transmit queue command:

bandwidth *bandwidth*

bandwidth specifies the guaranteed minimum bandwidth in bps using the optional prefixes kilo, mega, and giga, using the **k**, **m**, and **g** command options, respectively.

Example 7-24 illustrates configuration of 17.1 Mbps as the minimum bandwidth on transmit queue 3.

Example 7-24 *Configuring Interface with Bandwidth Parameter*

```
Switch#config terminal
Switch(config)#interface GigabitEthernet 1/1
Switch(config-if)#tx-queue 4
Switch(config-if-tx-queue)#bandwidth 17.1m
Switch(config-if-tx-queue)#end
```

To demonstrate and measure the behavior of sharing on transmit queues, two packet-generator ports were connected to the switch as shown in Figure 7-4. The packet-generator port connected to Gigabit Ethernet 1/1 was sending traffic with a DSCP value of zero at 1.0 Gbps. The packet-generator port connected to Gigabit Ethernet 1/2 was sending traffic with a DSCP value of 40 at 1.0 Gbps. The traffic sent by both interfaces was intended for another traffic port connected to interface Gigabit Ethernet 5/1. Connected to interface Gigabit Ethernet 5/1 was a traffic-generator port measuring the traffic rate for each DSCP flow. Three trials were conducted. The first trial involved the default configuration of bandwidth, whereas the remaining trials applied the bandwidth parameter at 200 Mbps, 750 Mbps, and 900 Mbps, respectively. Table 7-5 summarizes the results of the trial. Example 7-25 displays the basic configuration used for the trial.

Figure 7-4 *Network Diagram that Demonstrates Sharing*

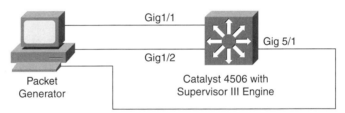

Table 7-5 *Sharing on Transmit Queues*

Received Rate	Default Configuration	Configured Bandwidth (200 Mbps)	Configured Bandwidth (750 Mbps)	Configured Bandwidth (900/100)
Rate received on Gigabit Ethernet 3/1 for traffic with DSCP value of 40	500 Mbps	480 Mbps	750 Mbps	900pps
Rate received on Gigabit Ethernet 3/1 for traffic with DSCP value of 0	500 Mbps	520 Mbps	250 Mbps	100Mbps

For the default configuration, the switch just load balances the egress traffic between the two egress queues containing packets for this test, queue 3 and queue 1. When the minimum bandwidth is configured for 200 Mbps for queue 3, the switch guarantees 200 Mbps to that queue. The switch must still guarantee 250 Mbps to the remaining queues and schedule traffic out of all queues using round-robin for traffic in excess of the configured bandwidth. As a result, a slight disparity in equality occurs when using a configured bandwidth of 200 Mbps on queue 3 and 250 Mbps for queue 1.

The second-to-last column in Table 7-5 illustrates results for configuring queue 3 for 750 Mbps and queue 1 for 250 Mbps. While the last column illustrates results for configuring queue 3 for 900 Mbps and queue 1 for 100 Mbps.

Example 7-25 *A Sample Sharing Configuration*

```
Current configuration : 102 bytes
!
interface GigabitEthernet1/1
 no switchport
 ip address 10.0.1.1 255.255.255.0
 qos trust dscp
end
Switch#show run interface GigabitEthernet 1/2
Building configuration...
Current configuration : 102 bytes
!
interface GigabitEthernet1/2
 no switchport
 ip address 10.0.2.1 255.255.255.0
 qos trust dscp
end
Switch#show run interface gigabitEthernet3/1
Building configuration...
Current configuration : 136 bytes
!
interface GigabitEthernet3/1
 no switchport
 ip address 10.0.3.1 255.255.255.0
 qos trust dscp
 tx-queue 3
   bandwidth 200 mbps
end
```

Shaping

The Catalyst 4000 IOS Family of switches supports traffic shaping in addition to policing. Traffic shaping has different characteristics than policing has. Chapter 2, "End-to-End QoS: Quality of Service at Layer 3 and Layer 2," discusses the differences between policing and traffic shaping.

Traffic shaping configures per transmit queue to a specified rate. The switch schedules packets out of the queue over time to maintain the configured rate. Packet drops occur only when a switch is unable to place a packet into a full transmit queue.

All Fast Ethernet and Gigabit Ethernet support shaping. Shaping is configurable between 16 kbps and the maximum rate of the interface in 1-bps increments. Use the following interface transmit queue command to configure shaping:

shape *rate*

rate defines the traffic shaping maximum rate associated with a transmit queue.

Example 7-26 illustrates configuration of traffic shaping at 1.54 Mbps on transmit queue 1.

Example 7-26 *Configuring the Bandwidth Parameter for a Transmit Queue*

```
Switch#config terminal
Switch(config)#interface GigabitEthernet 1/1
Switch(config-if)#tx-queue 1
Switch(config-if-tx-queue)#shape 1.54m
Switch(config-if-tx-queue)#end
```

To demonstrate the behavior of traffic shaping against traffic-rate policing using a policer, two TCP/IP throughput tests were conducted against a traffic policer and a traffic shaper. Two workstations running an application called TTCP were used to measure TCP/IP throughput against a policer and a traffic-shaping configuration. TTCP was configured with an initial window size of only 4096.

Three trials were conducted. The first trial did not consist of any traffic policer or traffic-shaping configurations. Therefore, the two workstations were able to achieve maximum throughput. The second trial consisted of an individual policer similar to the one shown in Example 7-15 (except that the burst size was lowered to 4000 bytes). The third trial consisted of the traffic-shaping configuration shown in Example 7-27. Figure 7-5 illustrates the simple topology used for this trial. Table 7-6 displays the results from the trial.

Figure 7-5   *Topology Used to Demonstrate Traffic Shaping Versus Traffic Policer*

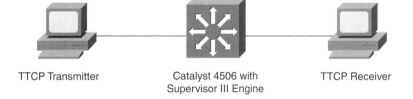

TTCP Transmitter   Catalyst 4506 with   TTCP Receiver
                             Supervisor III Engine

Table 7-6 *Shaping on Transmit Queues*

Trial	Maximum TTCP Throughput	Individual Policer at 1.54 Mbps	Traffic Shaping at 1.54 Mbps as Illustrated in Example 7-27
Measured TTCP rate	5.34 Mbps	224 bps	832 bps

As evident from the trial, the behavior of TCP/IP traffic against traffic policers and traffic shaping varies. Although both yield TCP/IP throughput below the configured rate, the individual policer generates a significantly smaller throughput rate. Because the policers were not buffering traffic and the individual policers were configured with a small burst size, the TCP/IP throughput measured significantly less than the traffic-shaping throughput. Because all network applications perform differently with different operating systems, apply these concepts carefully on a case-by-case basis.

Mapping Internal DSCP to CoS

As discussed throughout this chapter, the Catalyst 4000 IOS Family of switches uses the internal DSCP to differentiate service among packets. Because marking may occur on a packet as it traverses the switch, the CoS value of the packet needs to be updated on transmit. As a result, the switch employs the use of a DSCP-to-CoS mapping table for egress packets. The internal DSCP value determines the CoS value of the egress frame. Table 7-7 indicates the default DSCP-to-CoS mapping that occurs on egress frames.

Table 7-7 *Default DSCP-to-CoS Mapping Table*

DSCP Value	0–7	8–15	16–23	24–31	32–39	40–47	48–55	56–63
CoS Value	0	1	2	3	4	5	6	7

To display the current configured DSCP-to-CoS mapping, use the following command:

```
show qos maps dscp cos
```

The DSCP-to-CoS mapping table is configurable such that any internal DSCP value may map to any CoS value. Use the following command to configure the DSCP-to-CoS mapping table:

```
qos map dscp dscp-list to cos cos
```

dscp-list represents up to eight DSCP values separated by a space. *cos* corresponds to the transmitted CoS value on the egress frame. Example 7-27 displays, configures, and verifies QoS DSCP-to-CoS mapping.

Example 7-27 *Displaying, Configuring, and Verifying the QoS DSCP-to-CoS Mapping Table*

```
Switch#show qos map dscp cos
DSCP-CoS Mapping Table (DSCP = d1d2)
d1 : d2  0  1  2  3  4  5  6  7  8  9
-------------------------------------
 0 :     00 00 00 00 00 00 00 00 01 01
 1 :     01 01 01 01 01 01 02 02 02 02
 2 :     02 02 02 02 03 03 03 03 03 03
 3 :     03 03 04 04 04 04 04 04 04 04
 4 :     05 05 05 05 05 05 05 05 06 06
 5 :     06 06 06 06 06 06 07 07 07 07
 6 :     07 07 07 07
Switch#configure terminal
Switch(config)#qos map dscp 30 31 32 33 34 35 36 37 to cos 0
Switch(config)#qos map dscp 38 39 to cos 0
Switch(config)#end
Switch#show qos map dscpcos
DSCP-CoS Mapping Table (DSCP = d1d2)
d1 : d2  0  1  2  3  4  5  6  7  8  9
-------------------------------------
 0 :     00 00 00 00 00 00 00 00 01 01
 1 :     01 01 01 01 01 01 02 02 02 02
 2 :     02 02 02 02 03 03 03 03 03 03
 3 :     00 00 00 00 00 00 00 00 00 00
 4 :     05 05 05 05 05 05 05 05 06 06
 5 :     06 06 06 06 06 06 07 07 07 07
 6 :     07 07 07 07
```

Auto-QoS

The Catalyst 4000 IOS Family of switches will support Auto-QoS in the second half of 2003. The goal of Auto-QoS is to provide for autoconfiguration of QoS configurations for IP Phone ports and interface QoS configurations of access-distribution ports.

Case Study

Generally, system administrators do not configure more than a few QoS features simultaneously on a single switch. The topology displayed in Figure 7-6 illustrates a network that requires several QoS features. The topology maximizes the use of QoS to illustrate several QoS features simultaneously. Nevertheless, these features are commonly used in a variety of networks, especially those that require bandwidth restrictions (such as university campuses). For example, the case study illustrates restricting file-sharing traffic because file-sharing profiles are becoming increasingly important in applying QoS features to campus networks.

Figure 7-6 *Case Study Topology*

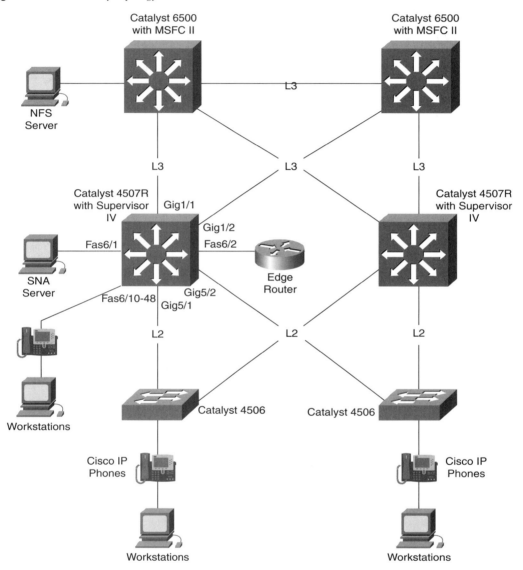

Example 7-28 illustrates several QoS features applied to the topology in Figure 7-6.

Example 7-28 *Case Study Configuration*

```
Switch#show running-config
Building configuration...
(text deleted)
!
qos aggregate-policer LIMIT_32KBPS 32 kbps 4000 byte conform-action transmit exceed-
action drop
qos
```

Example 7-28 *Case Study Configuration (Continued)*

```
vtp domain qos_TEST
vtp mode transparent
ip subnet-zero
!
!
class-map match-all MATCH_FILE_SHARING_FRAMES
  match access-group 100
!
!
policy-map LIMIT_FILE_SHARING
  class MATCH_FILE_SHARING_FRAMES
    police aggregate LIMIT_32KBPS
!
!
!
vlan 501-506,700
!
interface GigabitEthernet1/1
 description Uplink to Core
 no switchport
 ip address 10.1.1.2 255.255.255.0
 qos trust dscp
 tx-queue 1
   bandwidth 100 mbps
 tx-queue 2
   bandwidth 500 mbps
 tx-queue 3
   bandwidth 100 mbps
   priority high
 tx-queue 4
   bandwidth 50 mbps
!
interface GigabitEthernet1/2
 description Uplink to Core
 no switchport
 ip address 10.1.2.2 255.255.255.0
 qos trust dscp
 tx-queue 1
   bandwidth 50 mbps
 tx-queue 2
   bandwidth 500 mbps
 tx-queue 3
   bandwidth 100 mbps
   priority high
 tx-queue 4
   bandwidth 100 mbps
!
interface GigabitEthernet5/1
 description Link to Access Switch 501
 switchport trunk encapsulation dot1q
 switchport trunk allowed vlan 501,700
 qos trust dscp
```

continues

Example 7-28 *Case Study Configuration (Continued)*

```
 tx-queue 1
   bandwidth 100 mbps
 tx-queue 2
   bandwidth 500 mbps
 tx-queue 3
   bandwidth 100 mbps
   priority high
 tx-queue 4
   bandwidth 50 mbps
 !
(text deleted)
interface FastEthernet6/1
 description SNA Server
 switchport mode access
 qos cos 2
 spanning-tree portfast
 !
interface FastEthernet6/2
 description Edge_Router
 ip address 192.168.1.2 255.255.255.0
 tx-queue 1
   shape 1.0 mbps
 tx-queue 2
   shape 1.0 mbps
 tx-queue 3
   shape 500 kbps
 tx-queue 4
   shape 500 kbps
 !
(text deleted)
 !
interface FastEthernet6/10
 switchport mode access
 switchport voice vlan 700
 qos trust dscp
 tx-queue 3
   priority high
 spanning-tree portfast
 !
(text deleted)
 !
interface Vlan501
 description Data VLAN
 ip address 10.1.51.2 255.255.255.0
 no ip redirects
 service-policy input LIMIT_FILE_SHARING
 service-policy output LIMIT_FILE_SHARING
 standby 51 ip 10.1.51.1
 !
(text deleted)
 !
interface Vlan700
```

Example 7-28 *Case Study Configuration (Continued)*

```
 description Voice VLAN
 ip address 10.70.1.2 255.255.255.0
 no ip redirects
 standby 70 ip 10.70.1.1
 standby 70 preempt
!
(text deleted)
!
access-list 100 permit tcp any any eq 30000
!
(text deleted)
!
end
Switch#
```

In Example 7-28, interfaces Gigabit Ethernet 1/1 and 1/2 connect directly to the core as Layer 3 interfaces; therefore, trusting DSCP on ingress frames is desirable. The **qos trust dscp** configuration on each interface achieves this desired configuration. Although not illustrated in the configuration, interfaces Gigabit Ethernet 5/1 through 5/6 connect directly to access layer Catalyst 4506 switches. In this example, the access layer switches are responsible for determining the legitimacy of DSCP values on ingress frames. As a result, trusting DSCP on these connections is advantageous. In addition, the Cisco IP Phones connected to interfaces Fast Ethernet 6/10 through 6/48 require trusting of DSCP to differentiate the VoIP frames.

An SNA server connected off Fast Ethernet 6/1 is sending non-IP frames. These packets control a critical application and need classification and scheduling as appropriate. The frames have no IP header, and the server transmits the frames with a CoS value of zero. As a result, configuring the interface for **qos cos 2** applies an internal DSCP from the CoS-to-DSCP mapping table sufficient for prioritizing these frames. In this example, the SNA frames map to transmit queue 2.

The application of the policy map in the configuration intends to limit the amount of file-sharing traffic crossing VLAN boundaries. As a result, the switch applies the LIMIT_FILE_SHARING policy map to the access VLANs, ingress and egress. The policy map uses an aggregate policer to limit traffic to only 32 kbps for file-sharing applications that match the class map clause defined in ACL 100.

For more accurate output scheduling, the interfaces connected to other switches use a nondefault sharing configuration. Transmit queues 1 to 4 share traffic at rates of 50 Mbps, 500 Mbps, 100 Mbps, and 100 Mbps, respectively. NFS applications are marking their traffic with a DSCP value of 20 by default. To provide adequate sharing of traffic up to 500 Mbps, transmit queue 2 receives 500 Mbps as a share rate. Transmit queue 3 is strictly for VoIP traffic. The topology consists only of 100 Cisco IP Phones and restricting the transmit queue 3 to 100 Mbps is more than adequate for the amount of voice traffic passing between the switches. Because VoIP traffic maps to transmit queue 3 by default, configuring transmit queue as a high-priority queue forces the switch to service packets in transmit queue 3 first, and thus reduces the chance of latency or jitter for VoIP traffic. All interfaces that connect to other switches and Cisco IP Phone ports use transmit queue 3 as a high-priority queue.

Finally, the configuration consists of traffic shaping of transmit queues connected to an edge router. The edge router only routes data traffic and therefore traffic-shaping works well in this example. The edge router connects to an ATM cloud, which can service only about 3.0 Mbps of data. As a result, the traffic-shaping configuration limits traffic to specific rates per queue.

QoS Support on the Catalyst 2948G-L3, 4908G-L3, and Catalyst 4000 Layer 3 Services Module

The following sections discuss the Catalyst 2948G-L3 and 4908G-L3 switches, and the Catalyst 4000 Layer 3 services module. These switches resemble IOS-based routers from a configuration perspective and are generally referred to as G-L3 switches. However, these switches support only a few QoS features. The supported QoS features include rate limiting, IOS-based traffic shaping, and output scheduling. These switches base classification just on IP precedence values and have no support for marking.

These features use hardware TCAM to achieve 6 million packets-per-second performance. As with other Catalyst platforms, the term *hardware switching* represents using high-speed hardware components such as TCAM for packet processing.

These Layer 3 switches provide for classification based on IP precedence only. These switches do not support classification based on DSCP or classification based on the Layer 2 CoS field of a packet. Furthermore, these Layer 3 switches do not support classification based on ACLs, reclassification, or marking. As a result, these Layer 3 switches function solely as a QoS packet-forwarding switch. In other words, the intended QoS function of these Layer 3 switches is to route and schedule packets. In an end-to-end design, these switches rely on the adjoining switches and edge routers for classification and marking.

This part this chapter covers the following topics and QoS features for the G-L3 switches:

- Architecture Overview
- Software Requirements
- Global Configuration
- Classification
- Output Scheduling
- Per-Port Traffic Shaping
- Rate Limiting
- Case Study

Catalyst 2948G-L3, 4908G-L3, and 4232-L3 Services Module QoS Architectural Overview

The 2948G-L3 and 4908G-L3 Layer 3 switches and the WS-X4232-L3 Layer 3 services module share the same architecture with different port densities. The architecture of these switches uses TCAM memory for packet processing and forwarding of IP, IPX, and Layer 2 frames. As with the Catalyst 4000 IOS Family of switches, packet processing and forwarding needs to occur via hardware switching rather than software switching. Hardware switching allows for high-rate traffic flows with several QoS features. The QoS features supported on these switches include *weighted round-robin* (WRR) scheduling, traffic policing, and traffic shaping for IP packets. QoS features do not exist for IPX and bridged traffic, and these QoS features cannot coexist with IPX configurations.

The WS-X4232-L3 Services Module Architecture

The Catalyst 4000 Layer 3 services module, WS-X4232-L3, employs a unique architecture for integration into the Catalyst 4000 CatOS switch. At the time of publication, the Catalyst 4000 IOS Family of switches does not support the Catalyst 4000 Layer 3 services module.

The WS-X4232-L3 module consists of 4 Gigabit Ethernet ports and 32 10/100-Mbps ports. Two of the four Gigabit Ethernet ports connected directly to the supervisor interconnect on the Catalyst 4000 or 4500 chassis backplane. The other two Gigabit Ethernet ports are available as front-panel ports. The architecture of WS-X4232-L3 modules intends for the two front-panel ports to function as Layer 3 ports only. All four Gibabit Ethernet ports support port channeling (Gigabit EtherChannel). However, port-channel interfaces do not support QoS features. Furthermore, the WS-X4232-L3 does not support *integrated routing and bridging* (IRB). The 32 10/100-Mbps front panels are Layer 2-only ports. These 32 10/100-Mbps front panels are configurable only from the CatOS *command-line interface* (CLI) and not from the WS-X4232-L3 services module. Figure 7-7 provides a logical depiction of the WS-X4232-L3 module architecture when configured in a Catalyst 4000 CatOS switch.

The configuration of the G-L3 switches is rather unique, with many restrictions because the switch configures just like an IOS router. For instance, VLAN interfaces do not exist in the configuration. Because of the unique configuration of these Layer 3 switches, consult the following technical documents at Cisco.com for more details regarding configurations, limitations, and caveats:

- "Configuration and Overview of the Router Module for the Catalyst 4000 Family (WS-X4232-L3)" Document ID: 6198

- "Catalyst 4908G-L3 VLAN Routing and Bridging Example Configuration" Document ID: 14972

- "Catalyst 2948G-L3 Sample Configurations - Single VLAN, Multi-VLAN, and Multi-VLAN Distribution Layer Connecting to Network Core" Document ID: 12020

Figure 7-7 *WS-X4232-L3 in a Catalyst 4000 Switch Architecture Depiction*

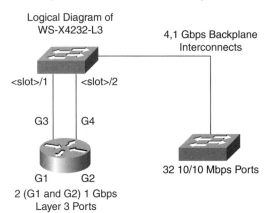

Software Requirements

All software versions for the Catalyst 2948G-L3 and 4908G-L3 Layer 3 switches and the WS-X4232-L3 Layer 3 services support output scheduling using WRR. Cisco IOS Software versions 12.0(10)W5(18e) and later add feature support for per-port traffic shaping and rate limiting.

Catalyst 4000 CatOS switches require Cisco CatOS Software version 5.5 or higher for use of the WS-X4232-L3 module.

Global Configuration

The Catalyst 2948G-L3 and 4908G-L3 Layer 3 switches and the WS-X4232-L3 module schedule packets based on IP precedence by default. Use the following command to disable QoS on these switches:

```
[no] qos switching
```

The **show qos switching** command displays the state of global QoS configuration. The **show qos mapping** outputs the global QoS WRR mapping configuration. The **show qos mapping** [**destination** *egress-interface*] command displays the QoS WRR mapping configuration for an egress interface.

Example 7-29 shows samples of the **show qos switching** and **show qos mapping** commands, respectively.

Example 7-29   *Sample Use of* **show qos switching** *and* **show qos mapping** *Commands*

```
Router#show qos switching
qos Based IP Switching enabled
Router#show qos mapping destination GigabitEthernet 1
Precedence WRR-Weight
      0        1
      1        2
      2        3
      3        4
```

Classification

The Catalyst 2948G-L3 and 4908G-L3 Layer 3 switches and the WS-X4232-L3 module output schedule packets using a four-queue class model. Classification differentiates packets into one of four queue classes for output scheduling.

The Catalyst 2948G-L3 and 4908G-L3 Layer 3 switches and the WS-X4232-L3 module derive classification solely based on IP precedence information. Furthermore, these switches classify frames based on the two *most-significant bits* (MSBs) of the IP precedence field. Table 7-8 illustrates how IP precedence bits map to the queue classes.

Table 7-8   *Default IP Precedence–to–Queue Class Mapping*

IP Precedence (Binary)	Queue Class
0 (000)	Queue 0
1 (001)	Queue 0
2 (010)	Queue 1
3 (011)	Queue 1
4 (100)	Queue 2
5 (101)	Queue 2
6 (110)	Queue 3
7 (111)	Queue 3

Output Scheduling

The Catalyst 2948G-L3 and 4908G-L3 Layer 3 switches and the WS-X4232-L3 module support output scheduling using WRR scheduling, rate limiting, and traffic-shaping features. These switches support traffic shaping only on egress traffic flows. Rate-limiting support is applicable to either ingress or egress traffic flows. The following sections discuss WRR scheduling, rate limiting, and traffic shaping applicable to the Catalyst 2948G-L3 and 4908G-L3 Layer 3 switches and the WS-X4232-L3 module.

WRR Scheduling

WRR scheduling imparts higher bandwidth to higher-priority queues while still providing service to lower-priority queues. Maintaining service to lower-priority queues avoids queue starvation.

The premise for WRR on the Catalyst 2948G-L3 and 4908G-L3 Layer 3 switches and the WS-X4232-L3 module is to apply effective bandwidths to each of the four queues. Use the following effective bandwidth formula to determine WRR weight:

$$(W/S) \times B = n$$

W represents the WRR weight of the queue, and S represents the sum of all weights of the active queues. B is the available bandwidth of the outgoing interface(s), and n represents the effective bandwidth. Table 7-9 displays the default effective bandwidth per queue.

Table 7-9   *Default WRR Weights Assigned to Queue Class*

Queue Class	Two MSB of IP Precedence	Weight	Effective Bandwidth	Percent of Total Bandwidth
Queue 0	0	1	100 Mbps	10%
Queue 1	1	2	200 Mbps	20%
Queue 2	2	3	300 Mbps	30%
Queue 3	3	4	400 Mbps	40%

Chapter 2 discusses the behavior of WRR in more detail.

The queue mapping of the two MSBs of IP precedence to the WRR weighted value configures globally and per interface. Interface configuration overrides the global configuration. Use the following command to globally adjust the IP precedence to the WRR weighted value:

```
qos mapping precedence value wrr-weight weight
```

To adjust the mapping of IP precedence to the WRR weighted value, use the following global configuration command:

```
qos mapping [destination egress-interface] precedence value wrr-weight weight
```

For both commands, *value* defines the two MSBs of IP precedence, and *weight* represents the WRR weight. *egress-interface* defines the egress interface to apply the command configuration.

Example 7-30   *Sample Configuration of Mapping IP Precedence to WRR Weights Globally and Per Interface*

```
Router#show running-config
Building configuration...
(text deleted)
qos mapping precedence 1 wrr-weight 1
qos mapping destination GigabitEthernet1 precedence 2 wrr-weight 1
(text deleted)
!
end
```

To demonstrate WRR behavior, several trials were performed using the topology in Figure 7-8. In each trial, a traffic generator transmitted traffic to the switch at 1 Gbps on both supervisor ports 1/1 and 1/2. The ingress traffic on port 1/1 had an IP precedence value of 0, and ingress traffic on port 1/2 had an IP precedence value of 7. The traffic was routed from interfaces 1/1 and 1/2 out to interface Gigabit Ethernet 1 on the WS-X4232-L3 module. The traffic generated was also connected to this port to measure the egress traffic rate for both streams.

In the first trial, the default QoS mapping configuration was used. In the second trial, the QoS mapping configuration was changed such that traffic from both streams mapped to the same WRR weight. Table 7-10 summarizes the results of the trial.

Table 7-10   *WRR on the Catalyst WS-X4232-L3 Module*

Trial	Default WRR Mapping	All IP Precedence Map to the Same WRR Weight
Measured rate of traffic for frames with IP precedence (0)	200 Mbps	500 Mbps
Measured rate of traffic for frames with IP precedence (7)	800 Mbps	500 Mbps

Based on the WRR bandwidth formula, both trials yielded expected results. For the default WRR mapping trial, the router used only two queues. As a result, the sum of all weighted values was 5 (because Q1 has a weight of 1 and Q4 has a weight of 4). Therefore, the derived formula for the effective bandwidth for the IP precedence traffic of 7 was computed as follows:

(W/S) x B = n
$(4/5)$ x 1.0 Gbps = 800 Mbps for IP precedence 7 traffic

For the second trial, mapping all the IP precedence values to the same WRR weight yields an even distribution of egress traffic for both streams.

Per-Port Traffic Shaping

Traffic shaping uses the leaky token bucket algorithm. The leaky token bucket algorithm discussed earlier in this chapter for the Catalyst 4000 IOS Family also applies to the Catalyst 2948G-L3 and 4908G-L3 Layer 3 switches and the WS-X4232-L3. Although the hardware architecture and leaky token bucket algorithm implementations differ significantly between the two types of switches, the algorithm still applies for understanding the rate and burst parameters for the Catalyst 2948G-L3 and 4908G-L3 Layer 3 switches and the WS-X4232-L3 Layer 3 services switches. Note that unlike rate-limiting policers, traffic shaping actually buffers packets that exceed the specified rate.

Use the following command to configure traffic shaping in the interface configuration mode:

```
traffic-shape rate burst
```

rate represents the traffic-shaping rate in bps. The Catalyst 2948G-L3 and 4908G-L3 Layer 3 switches and the WS-X4232-L3 module support configuration of 32 kbps to the maximum interface speed in 1-bps increments for egress shaping. *burst* defines the burst size in bits. Example 7-31 illustrates a sample configuration of traffic shaping.

Example 7-31 *Traffic Shaping Sample Configuration*

```
Router#show running-config
Building configuration...
(text deleted):
!
interface GigabitEthernet1
 ip address 192.168.1.1 255.255.255.0
 no ip directed-broadcast
 traffic-shape rate 1540000 20000
(text deleted)
!
end
```

Rate Limiting

Applications that are sensitive to delay and jitter, such as VoIP, interactive video, and stock tickers, do not tolerate the buffering that occurs when traffic shaping is active. Therefore, caution is necessary when configuring and applying traffic shaping to VoIP networks.

Rate limiting does not buffer packets. Instead, the switch drops packets over the specified rate and above burst. The Catalyst 2948G-L3 and 4908G-L3 Layer 3 switches and the WS-X4232-L3 switches do not support any other action for out-of-profile packets other than drop. These switches do support configuration of ingress and egress rate limiting in both ingress and egress applications.

Use the following interface command to configure rate limiting:

> **rate-limit** [**input** | **output**] *rate burst*

rate defines the target rate on a per-interface basis in bps. The Catalyst 2948G-L3 and 4908G-L3 Layer 3 switches and the WS-X4232-L3 support rates from 32000 bps to the maximum link speed in 1-bps increments. *burst* represents the burst size in bits configured in 1-byte increments between 0 and 64000 bytes. Example 7-32 shows a sample interface configuration for rate limiting.

Example 7-32 *Sample Configuration of Rate Limiting Applied Ingress*

```
Router#show running-config
Building configuration...
(text deleted):
!
interface GigabitEthernet2
 ip address 192.168.2.1 255.255.255.0
 no ip directed-broadcast
 rate-limit input 5000000 64000
(text deleted)
!
end
```

Case Study

Example 7-33 illustrates a typical configuration of a WS-X4232-L3 in slot 2 of a Catalyst 4000 chassis as illustrated in Figure 7-8.

Figure 7-8   *Case Study Topology*

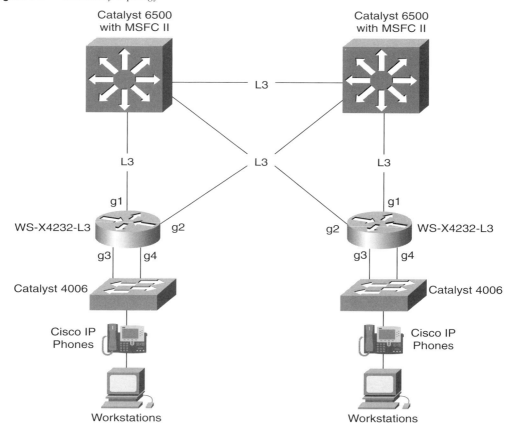

Example 7-33   *Case Study Configuration for Figure 7-8*

```
Router#show running-config
Building configuration...
(text deleted)
!
qos mapping destination GigabitEthernet1 precedence 0 wrr-weight 1
qos mapping destination GigabitEthernet1 precedence 1 wrr-weight 1
qos mapping destination GigabitEthernet1 precedence 2 wrr-weight 4
qos mapping destination GigabitEthernet1 precedence 3 wrr-weight 2
qos mapping destination GigabitEthernet3 precedence 0 wrr-weight 1
qos mapping destination GigabitEthernet3 precedence 1 wrr-weight 1
qos mapping destination GigabitEthernet3 precedence 2 wrr-weight 4
qos mapping destination GigabitEthernet3 precedence 3 wrr-weight 2
qos mapping destination GigabitEthernet4 precedence 0 wrr-weight 1
```

continues

Example 7-33 *Case Study Configuration for Figure 7-8 (Continued)*

```
qos mapping destination GigabitEthernet4 precedence 1 wrr-weight 1
qos mapping destination GigabitEthernet4 precedence 2 wrr-weight 4
qos mapping destination GigabitEthernet4 precedence 3 wrr-weight 2
(text deleted)
!
interface GigabitEthernet1
 ip address 10.0.1.2 255.255.255.0
 no ip directed-broadcast
 rate-limit output 100000 64000
!
interface GigabitEthernet2
 ip address 10.0.2.2 255.255.255.0
 no ip directed-broadcast
 !
interface GigabitEthernet3
 no ip address
 no ip directed-broadcast
 no negotiation auto
!
interface GigabitEthernet3.1
 encapsulation dot1Q 1
 ip address 10.1.1.2 255.255.255.0
 no ip redirects
 no ip directed-broadcast
 standby 1 ip 10.1.1.1
 !
interface GigabitEthernet3.3
 encapsulation dot1Q 3 native
 ip address 10.1.3.2 255.255.255.0
 no ip redirects
 no ip directed-broadcast
 standby 3 ip 10.1.3.1
 !
interface GigabitEthernet4
 no ip address
 no ip directed-broadcast
 no negotiation auto
 !
interface GigabitEthernet4.2
 encapsulation dot1Q 2
 ip address 10.1.2.2 255.255.255.0
 no ip redirects
 no ip directed-broadcast
 standby 2 ip 10.1.2.1
 !
interface GigabitEthernet4.4
 encapsulation dot1Q 4
 ip address 10.1.4.2 255.255.255.0
 no ip redirects
 no ip directed-broadcast
 standby 4 ip 10.1.4.1
 !
(text deleted)
!
end
```

The configuration applies dot1q subinterfaces to each Gigabit Ethernet interface separately to achieve load balancing without using port channeling.

The QoS mapping configuration consists of prioritizing IP precedence values 4 and 5 with 50 percent of the effective bandwidth of interfaces Gigabit Ethernet 1, 3, and 4. By default, Cisco IP Phones assign an IP precedence value of 5, which maps to queue class 2, to voice traffic (thus the reasoning for using a higher WRR weight for this queue class).

Furthermore, interface Gigabit Ethernet 1 connected to the core switch applies a rate-limiting configuration. The rate limiting limits all egress traffic flowing to the core to 100 Mbps.

Summary

The Catalyst 4000 IOS Family of switches provides for a wide range of QoS features. The switch bases classification, marking, policing, and output scheduling on not only DSCP values but also CoS values. The fine granularity of QoS features and configuration options allow for these switches to reside in either the core, distribution, or access layer of the campus network topology. You can summarize QoS feature support on the Catalyst 4000 IOS Family of switches discussed in the first part of the chapter as follows:

- At the time of publication, the Catalyst 4000 IOS Family of switches includes the Catalyst Supervisor Engines III and IV in a Catalyst 4000 or 4500 series chassis.
- Support exists for classification, reclassification, marking, and output scheduling.
- QoS packet processing occurs in hardware to achieve line-rate performance.
- 1022 ingress and 1022 egress policers applied as aggregate or individual policers are supported.
- Each interfaces uses four transmit queues for output scheduling.
- Sharing and traffic shaping are configurable per transmit queue.

The Catalyst 2948G-L3 and 4908G-L3 and the Catalyst 4000 Layer 3 services module, WS-X4232-L3, act only as QoS forwarding switches. For QoS features such as trusting and marking, these switches rely solely on externally connected switches or routers. You can summarize the QoS feature support on these switches discussed in the second part of this chapter as follows:

- Support exists for classification and output scheduling.
- Classification is determined by IP precedence only.
- Output scheduling uses WRR to differentiate service.
- Rate limiting is configurable per interface on ingress or egress.
- Traffic shaping is configurable per interface on egress only.
- Port-channel interfaces do not support any QoS features.

CHAPTER 8

QoS Support on the Catalyst 6500

The Cisco Catalyst 6500 series incorporates the industry's leading platforms, with regard to QoS features and functionality. The Catalyst 6500 Family of switches offers a broad catalogue of mechanisms to help ensure the timely end-to-end delivery of mission-critical and delay-sensitive applications. The Catalyst 6500 series is also capable of performing these mechanisms in hardware, with no impact to the overall operation of the switch.

Because of the Catalyst 6500's versatility, you can deploy it in all aspects of the campus environment. By integrating additional hardware components, the Catalyst 6500 is capable of transporting converged data, voice and real-time video across a LAN, MAN, or even WAN environment. Features such as inline power for phone support, trust, and per-port queuing and scheduling allow the Catalyst 6500 to be a viable solution for access layer deployment. Dual-rate policing, *Weighted Random Early Detection* (WRED), and marking extend the Catalyst 6500's reach to the distribution and core layers, as well as the WAN edge. Figure 8-1 shows how the Catalyst 6500 can be positioned in a small campus network.

Figure 8-1 *Positioning the Catalyst 6500 Series in the Campus*

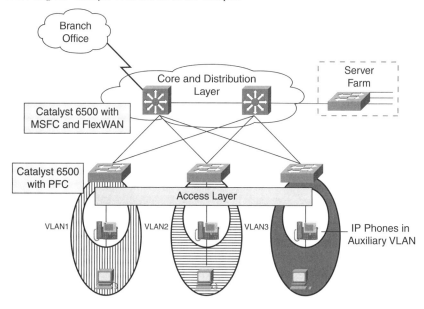

Chapter 2 "End-to-End QoS: Quality of Service at Layer 3 and Layer 2," introduces many of the QoS features and capabilities found on the Catalyst 6500. This current chapter expounds on these concepts and discusses how these features specifically relate to the Catalyst 6500. The chapter opens with an architectural overview of the Catalyst 6500, and then discusses the hardware and software requirements necessary to support QoS. The QoS discussion ensues with a quick demonstration of enabling QoS on the platform, immediately followed by the features outlined in the following list:

- Input Scheduling
- Classification and Marking
- Mapping
- Policing
- Congestion Management and Congestion Avoidance
- Automatic QoS

This chapter focuses on the campus LAN aspect of QoS for the Catalyst 6500 and addresses how the various QoS mechanisms function on this Catalyst switch without focusing on the role of the *Multilayer Switch Feature Card* (MSFC) or FlexWAN. Numerous configuration examples are provided, reinforcing the concepts discussed. CatOS versions 6.3, 6.4, and 7.5 and Cisco IOS version 12.1(13)E were used to configure the examples. The command references demonstrate how to configure the various QoS capabilities using both CatOS (Hybrid mode) and Cisco IOS (Native mode).

The Catalyst 6500 Family consists of both the Catalyst 6000 and Catalyst 6500. Despite some architectural differences, the Catalyst 6500 encompasses all features available on the Catalyst 6000. The following section lists the critical hardware components essential to QoS operation on the Catalyst 6500.

NOTE   The Catalyst 6000 chassis is "end-of-sale." However, the QoS mechanisms described in this chapter apply to both the Catalyst 6000 and the 6500 chassis. QoS capabilities depend on the installed modules.

Catalyst 6500 Architectural Overview

This section introduces the various components relevant to QoS operation on the Catalyst 6500. The section covers hardware resources and terms presented throughout the chapter.

Figure 8-2 shows the QoS architecture of the Catalyst 6500. The ingress and egress ports depict the queuing architecture found on more recent Gigabit Ethernet ports. The figure demonstrates the order in which the QoS functions occur and also denotes which switch components are responsible for the different mechanisms.

Incorporating an MSFC and a FlexWAN line module further enhances the platform's QoS support. With these modules, additional QoS features include traffic shaping, Low Latency Queuing, Class-Based Weighted Fair-Queuing, and complex traffic classification based on Layer 4 through Layer 7 application recognition. For information about QoS in conjunction with the MSFC and the FlexWAN module, see Chapter 9, "QoS Support on the Catalyst 6500 MSFC and FlexWAN."

Figure 8-2   *Overview of QoS on the Catalyst 6500 Family Architecture*

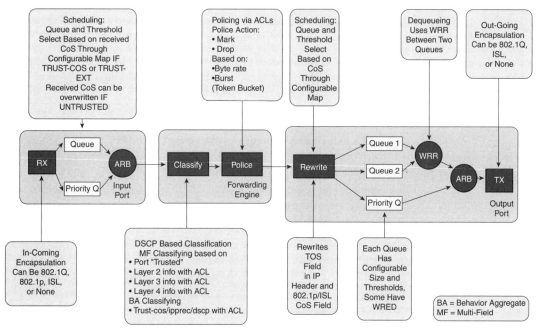

Both the Catalyst 6000 and the Catalyst 6500 chassis utilize a 32-Gbps bus for communication with non-fabric-enabled modules. Non-fabric-enabled linecards denote modules only capable of accessing the 32-Gbps bus architecture available on the Catalyst 6000 and Catalyst 6500. The 32-Gbps bus is referred to as the *data bus* or *D-bus*. The D-bus transports all frames between the various linecards. All information traversing the D-bus is viewed by all modules, including the supervisor engine. In addition to the D-bus, the Catalyst 6500 utilizes two additional buses, the *results bus* (R-bus) and the control bus or *Ethernet out-of-band channel* (EOBC). The R-bus forwards the appropriate rewrite information from the supervisor engine to the individual port *application-specific integrated circuits* (ASICs). The rewrite data includes the destination MAC and egress port information, and any QoS classification or policing policies applied to the frame. The CoS values derived from these QoS mechanisms may differ from the original *class of service* (CoS) value present when the frame entered the switch. The EOBC provides a conduit for the supervisor engine to perform system management functions with the various linecards.

Again, the bus architecture facilitates communication between traditional non-fabric-enabled modules, as well as between non-fabric-to-fabric-enabled modules.

The Catalyst 6500, unlike the Catalyst 6000, offers additional connectivity to a 256-Gbps crossbar switching fabric, accessible by incorporating a *switch fabric module* (SFM) and fabric-enabled linecards. *Fabric-enabled cards* are modules with the capability to connect to the crossbar fabric. The crossbar fabric provides high-speed communication between fabric-capable linecards only. Accessibility to the fabric is the fundamental difference between the Catalyst 6000 and the Catalyst 6500 from an architectural perspective. Incorporating a switch fabric module significantly increases the packet-forwarding rate relative to the traditional bus architecture. Table 8-2 lists the various modules and their connectivity to the backplane.

The MSFC and the *Policy Feature Card* (PFC) daughter cards of the Catalyst 6500 supervisor engines are responsible for the Layer 3 routing of packets through the switch. The MSFC and PFC have specialized functions. Not only does the PFC switch Layer 2 frames, it also routes Layer 3 packets based on Layer 3 information provided by the MSFC. Consequently, the MSFC's function is to build the Layer 3 routing and *Address Resolution Protocol* (ARP) tables, which may subsequently be passed to the PFC, in addition to handling any Layer 3 routing functionality the PFC cannot perform. Because the Layer 3 forwarding performance for the MSFC is substantially less than the PFC, the intent is not to forward all the packets using the MSFC. The goal of the Catalyst 6500 architecture is to Layer 3 route all packets via the PFC.

For CEF-based systems, the MSFC passes Layer 3 forwarding information through the EOBC to the appropriate ASICs on the PFC2. *Mulilayer switching* (MLS)-based systems do not use the EOBC to forward Layer 3 information. Instead, when a switched path is completed by the MSFC, a flow is created and cached and the PFC1 forwards all subsequent packets for that flow. *Cisco Express Forwarding* (CEF) and MLS allow the PFC to switch packets in hardware.

Layer 3 forwarding depends on the supervisor engine. For Supervisor I Engines, the forwarding information is based on MLS flows, whereas the PFC2 on Supervisor II Engines utilizes hardware-based CEF. MLS operation is covered in Chapter 4, "QoS Support on the Catalyst 5000 Family of Switches," in the section titled "MLS Fundamentals." Regardless of the Layer 3 switching method, QoS features are applied to the packet prior to it being Layer 3 switched.

NOTE   For additional information on MLS-based switching on the Supervisor I Engine, refer to the following technical document at Cisco.com:

"Configuring IP Unicast Layer 3 Switching on Supervisor Engine 1"

For additional information on CEF-based switching on the Supervisor II Engine, refer to the following technical document at Cisco.com:

"Configuring CEF for PFC2"

In addition to the PFC, which is centrally located on the supervisor engine, fabric-enabled linecards may incorporate a *Distributed Forwarding Card* (DFC). At the time of writing, the WS-X6816 linecard is the only module that comes equipped with a DFC by default. However, other fabric-enabled linecards can be upgraded to accept a DFC. The DFC is a daughter card that sits on a fabric-enabled linecard. The DFC's architecture and operation is exactly the same as the PFC2. As a result, the DFC is capable of performing distributed Layer 3 CEF-based forwarding, Layer 2 bridging, *access-control lists* (ACLs), and QoS. Therefore, by adding a DFC, forwarding decisions are localized to the linecard. Again, similar to the PFC2, the MSFC is responsible for building the CEF information that is distributed out to the DFC.

Finally, the *ternary content addressable memory* (TCAM) is a finite portion of memory resident on the PFC1 and PFC2. The TCAM is essentially a table that stores ACL entries and masks used to apply defined QoS policies. The TCAM allows multiple *access-control entries* (ACEs) to share a single mask. Storing the ACL information in memory on the PFC ensures high-speed lookups are performed, and thus maximizes the throughput and minimizes the latency for processing packets and applying QoS policies. Because QoS ACL lookups are performed in hardware, applying the policies results in no impact to system switching performance. TCAM is discussed in more detail in Chapter 6, "QoS Features Available on the Catalyst 2950 and 3550 Family of Switches," as well as later in this chapter.

For more detailed information regarding the architecture of the Catalyst 6500, consult the following technical document at Cisco.com:

> "Catalyst 6000 and 6500 Series Architecture"

Software and Hardware Requirements

QoS feature support for the Catalyst 6500 began with software version 5.1. Initially, with the Supervisor I Engine, the platform was limited in QoS functionality and only capable of performing Layer 2 functions. Specifically, it was only capable of supporting port-based CoS, as well as assigning a CoS based on destination MAC address. With the introduction of the PFC1 in CatOS Software version 5.3, QoS support on the Catalyst 6500 broadened to include policing, marking, and classification based on QoS ACLs for IP, IPX, and MAC layer traffic. QoS is also fully supported in Cisco IOS (Native mode). Initially, QoS support only included IP traffic in the first Cisco IOS Software version release 12.0(7)XE. Marking, policing, classification and congestion avoidance were the features included for IP traffic. Cisco IOS release 12.1(1)E expanded QoS support for Native mode to include IPX and MAC layer traffic. Table 8-1 depicts the different QoS processes covered in this chapter.

The table specifies the hardware responsible for the different operations and the software capable of supporting the various features.

Table 8-1 *Hardware Support for QoS*

QoS Operation	Hardware Responsible for QoS Operation	Supported Software
Input queue scheduling*	Linecards (port ASIC)—PFC not required	CatOS/Cisco IOS
Classification	Supervisor—Responsible for Layer 2 (CoS)	CatOS/Cisco IOS
	PFC—Responsible for Layer 2 and 3 (CoS/IP precedence/DSCP)	
Policing	Layer 3 switching engine in PFC	CatOS/Cisco IOS
Marking/rewrite	Linecards (port ASIC)—Based on classification/policing performed by supervisor or PFC	CatOS/Cisco IOS
Output queue scheduling	Linecards (port ASIC)—Based on priorities established during classification/policing	CatOS/Cisco IOS

*Input queue scheduling is contingent on the trust state of the inbound port. If the inbound trust policy is set for untrusted, traffic is sent to the default queue and is serviced FIFO.

As demonstrated in Table 8-1, the port ASICs on the linecards play a significant role in the end-to-end QoS implementation within the Catalyst 6500. Table 8-2 shows the different modules available for the platform and the default queuing architecture for both receive and transmit ports.

Table 8-2 *Overview of Modules Supporting QoS*

Module	Linecard Composition	Receive Ports	Transmit Ports	Priority Queue	Architecture to Backplane
WS-X6K-Sup1	2 X 1000	1q4t	2q2t	No	Bus
WS-X6K-Sup1A	2 X 1000	1p1q4t	1p2q2t	RX/TX	Bus
WS-X6K-Sup2	2 X 1000	1p1q4t	1p2q2t	RX/TX	Bus/Fabric
WS-X6024	24 X 10	1q4t	2q2t	No	Bus
WS-X6148	48 X 10/100	1q4t	2q2t	No	Bus
WS-X6224	24 X 100	1q4t	2q2t	No	Bus
WS-X6248	48 X 10/100	1q4t	2q2t	No	Bus
WS-X6316	16 X 1000	1p1q4t	1p2q2t	RX/TX	Bus
WS-X6324	24 X 100	1q4t	2q2t	No	Bus
WS-X6348	48 X 10/100	1q4t	2q2t	No	Bus
WS-X6408	8 X 1000	1q4t	2q2t	No	Bus
WS-X6408A	8 X 1000	1p1q4t	1p2q2t	RX/TX	Bus
WS-X6416	16 X 1000	1p1q4t	1p2q2t	RX/TX	Bus

Table 8-2   *Overview of Modules Supporting QoS (Continued)*

Module	Linecard Composition	Receive Ports	Transmit Ports	Priority Queue	Architecture to Backplane
WS-X6501	1 X 10GE	1p1q8t	1p2q1t	RX/TX	Bus/fabric
WS-X6502	1 X 10GE	1p1q8t	1p2q1t	RX/TX	Bus/fabric
WS-X6516	16 X 10/100/1000	1p1q4t	1p2q2t	RX/TX	Bus/fabric
WS-X6524	24 X 100	1p1q0t	1p3q1t	RX/TX	Bus/fabric
WS-X6548	48 X 10/100	1p1q0t	1p3q1t	RX/TX	Bus/fabric
WS-X6816*	16 X 1000	1p1q4t	1p2q2t	RX/TX	Fabric only

*Modules are only supported with Supervisor II.

As mentioned earlier, the Catalyst 6500 is capable of supporting QoS utilizing multiple modes of software. One software option is to support both the supervisor engine and MSFC with two separate images; this configuration is known as *Hybrid mode*. The alternative is to load one single image to support the entire platform. This software option is referred to as *Cisco IOS* (*Native mode*).

When running in Hybrid mode, the administrator must load one version of code for the supervisor module, referred to as the *Catalyst Operating System* (CatOS). If an MSFC exists on the supervisor, a separate version of IOS supporting the MSFC also needs to be loaded. The IOS on the MSFC is also responsible for supporting any FlexWAN modules and installed port adapters.

Native mode allows for the seamless integration of both the supervisor and MSFC, offering the administrator one command line to configure both components. This chapter provides numerous examples of the support for QoS in both Hybrid and Cisco IOS. These examples demonstrate QoS configurations utilizing both modes of operation.

Identifying the Catalyst Software

After the desired operational mode has been determined, it is necessary to download the appropriate software version. When running Hybrid, as already noted, the administrator must download separate images for the supervisor and MSFC components. For the supervisor engine, two software versions are available. One version supports the Supervisor I module, the other supports the Supervisor II module.

The fundamental difference between the two images is based on the numeric value prefaced by "cat6000-sup", which indicates the software is a supervisor image. If the string cat6000-sup is not immediately followed by a number, the software supports Supervisor I and IA engines. If the string is followed by a 2, however, the software supports all Supervisor II Engines. The same naming convention applies to images available for the MSFC. For 6500s utilizing an MSFC 1, the image name is preceded by "c6msfc". For switches equipped with an MSFC 2, the "c6msfc" string is immediately followed by the numeral 2.

The supervisor engine naming convention for Hybrid images is as follows:

- "cat6000-sup" indicates image supports Supervisor I/IA Engines.
- "cat6000-sup2" indicates image supports Supervisor II Engines.

The MSFC naming convention for Hybrid images is as follows:

- "c6msfc" indicates image supports MSFC 1.
- "c6msfc2" indicates image supports MSFC 2.

When running in Native mode, the image is bundled, incorporating the software essential for operating both the supervisor and the MSFC. In this instance, the string used to identify the version of code as a Cisco IOS image is "c6sup". Again, the numeric values immediately following the string specify the supervisor and MSFC versions supported by the image, respectively.

The naming convention for bundled Cisco IOS images is as follows:

- "c6sup11" indicates the image supports Supervisor I/IA engines and MSFC 1.
- "c6sup12" indicates the image supports Supervisor I/IA engines and MSFC 2.
- "c6sup22" indicates the image supports Supervisor II engine and MSFC 2.

NOTE   "c6sup" was the original designation used to identify the initial release of Cisco IOS for the Catalyst 6500. Images with this naming convention supported platforms with a Supervisor I Engine and MSFC 1.

Table 8-3 summarizes some of the fundamental differences applicable to operating in Hybrid and Native modes on the Catalyst 6500. For additional comparative information about CatOS and Cisco IOS, consult the following technical document at Cisco.com:

> "White Paper: Comparison of the Cisco Catalyst and Cisco IOS Operating Systems for the Cisco Catalyst 6500 Series Switch"
> www.cisco.com/warp/public/cc/pd/si/casi/ca6000/tech/catos_wp.pdf

Table 8-3   *Default Differences Between Hybrid and Cisco IOS*

Feature	Hybrid	Cisco IOS
Required software images	2 software images: Supervisor and MSFC.	1 software image: bundled Supervisor and MSFC.
Required configuration files	2 configuration files: Supervisor and MSFC.	1 configuration file: combined Supervisor and MSFC.
Default interface/port state	All ports default to Layer 2 switch ports.	All interfaces default to Layer 3 routed interfaces.
Default interface/port status	All ports default to enabled.	All interfaces default to administratively shut down.

Enabling QoS on the Switch

QoS first needs to be enabled globally on the switch, before this discussion turns to an explanation of the different QoS features. Example 8-1 shows how to initialize QoS on the Catalyst 6500 and shows the commands to verify the configuration.

Example 8-1   *Enabling QoS on the Switch*

```
(Hybrid)
hybrid(enable)> set qos enable
Command Verification:
hybrid(enable)> show qos status
   QoS is enabled on this switch.
(Native)
native(config)# mls qos
Command Verification:
native# show mls qos
   QoS is enabled globally
!
(text omitted)
```

After QoS has been enabled on the switch, the features can be configured. This chapter now focuses on the individual QoS mechanisms available on the Catalyst 6500. The first topic is input scheduling.

Input Scheduling

As shown in Table 8-1, the Catalyst 6500, through the use of individual port ASICs, can support input queue scheduling. This feature is beneficial if contention for the bus or switching fabric exists. At the time of writing, for instance, fabric-enabled cards have an 8-Gbps full-duplex connection to the switching fabric. Voice and real-time application performance may be severely impacted if the receiving module is a WS-X6516, with all 16 ports receiving traffic at close to line rate. To ensure that voice traffic and other real-time applications maintain required service levels, you can use input scheduling to assign traffic to the appropriate queues and thresholds. The recommendation is to assign voice traffic to the priority queue to minimize the end-to-end delay and jitter. To take advantage of this feature, however, the inbound port must be configured to trust the arriving CoS. To view the scheduling capabilities of a particular port, use one of the following commands:

Example 8-2   *Viewing Input Scheduling Capabilities*

```
(Hybrid)
Show port capabilities [mod[/port]]
hybrid (enable) show port capabilities 4/1
Model                    WS-X6408A-GBIC
(text omitted)
QOS scheduling           rx-(1p1q4t),tx-(1p2q2t)
(text omitted)
              or
```

Example 8-2 *Viewing Input Scheduling Capabilities (Continued)*

```
(Native)
show interface {type num} capabilities
native# show interface gigabitEthernet 2/1 capabilities
  Model:                 WS-X6516-GBIC
(text omitted)
QOS scheduling:         rx-(1p1q4t), tx-(1p2q2t)
(text omitted)
            or
show queueing interface {type num} [| include Receive]
native# show queueing interface fastEthernet 6/1 | include Receive
  Receive queues [type = 1q4t]:
```

NOTE   The following section on classification covers the concept of trust and how it operates on the Catalyst 6500.

All other settings result in the arriving frames being placed in a default queue and forwarded directly to the switching engine based on FIFO. Figure 8-3 represents the decision path for an arriving frame.

Figure 8-3   *Decision Path for an Ingress Frame*

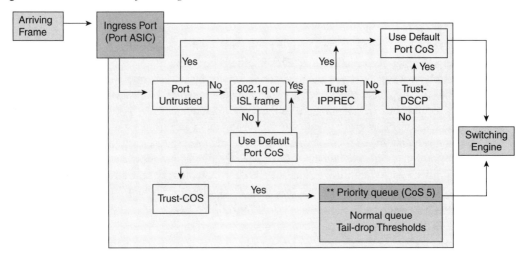

** Priority queue only available on ports
with 1p1qXt architecture.

Because input scheduling is only applicable when the port is set to trust an ingress frame's CoS value, assume the appropriate configuration has been made. If the arriving frame has an 802.1q or *Inter-Switch Link* (ISL) header, the port logic maintains the CoS value specified in the user priority field or the user field for the respective frames. For all other frames, the port ASIC uses the default CoS setting specified by the administrator for the given port.

NOTE   802.1q headers have a user priority field, and ISL headers contain a user field; these fields enable the network administrator to specify that a certain stream of traffic should be handled more expeditiously. However, frames not tagged with a trunk header lack any additional fields that accommodate a CoS setting. As a result, all untagged frames utilize the default CoS value specified on the ingress port. By acquiring the default port CoS value, the derived value determines how the frame is processed through the switch. This setting may also impact how the frame is handled on an end-to-end basis across the network.

After the CoS value of an inbound frame has been determined, the frame is placed into the appropriate queue. For most 10/100 ports, there is one queue with four configurable tail-drop thresholds, designated as 1q4t. For additional information on queue nomenclature, refer to the section "Catalyst Feature Overview" in Chapter 3, "Overview of QoS Support on Catalyst Platforms and Exploring QoS on the Catalyst 2900XL, 3500XL, and Catalyst 4000 CatOS Family of Switches." Each CoS is mapped to one of these four thresholds. Table 8-4 shows the exact CoS-to-threshold assignment for 1q4t port types. The exception to this is the fabric-enabled 10/100 modules, whose ports offer an additional strict-priority queue for frames marked with CoS 5. These port types are designated as 1p1q0t. This module is covered later in the section "Input Scheduling and Congestion Avoidance for 1p1q0t and 1p1q8t."

Similar to the non-fabric-enabled 10/100 ports, earlier Gigabit Ethernet ports could only provide a single queue with congestion avoidance handled by the four configurable tail-drop thresholds. (Refer back to Table 8-2 to view the queue architecture for the various modules.) However, recent Gigabit linecards offer the additional use of a strict-priority queue, noted as 1p1q4t. The priority queue is responsible for transmitting delay-sensitive and critical network traffic, namely voice. Because the priority queue can starve remaining traffic, it is recommended that only low-bandwidth traffic be placed in the strict-priority queue. By default, frames marked with CoS 5 are mapped to the strict-priority queue. This ensures the expeditious handling of voice traffic, because Cisco IP Phones mark voice frames with CoS 5. To minimize the delay and jitter, which impact voice quality, the strict-priority queue is provided immediate access to the switch backplane. If traffic exists in the strict-priority queue, it is serviced prior to any other queues. Contrary to the normal queue, however, the priority queue does not possess a configurable threshold. When the strict-priority queue reaches 100-percent capacity, frames are discarded due to buffer exhaustion.

Figure 8-4 shows input scheduling on 10/100 ports from an architectural perspective.

Figure 8-4 *Ingress QoS on the Coil ASIC*

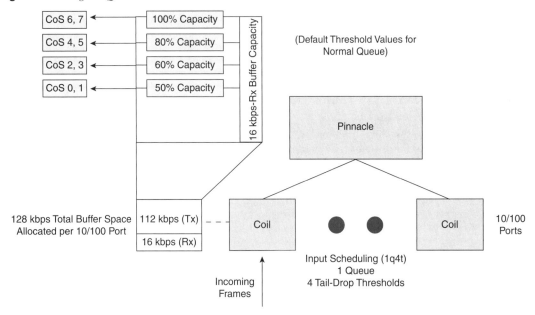

Figure 8-4 does not reflect the architecture of the fabric- enabled 10/100 modules. They use different ASICs and utilize a centralized buffer accessible to each port on the linecard. Although the architecture is centralized, the net result is a finite buffer being statically allocated to each port.

As depicted in Figure 8-4, input queue scheduling and congestion management on the 10/100 modules are accomplished by using the Coil ASIC.

The Pinnacle serves as the connection to the switching bus, and branches out to four Coil ASICs. Each Coil ASIC is responsible for servicing twelve 10/100 ports on a single linecard. The Coil is also responsible for allocating a finite amount of buffer space to each port. As shown in the figure, each individual port receives 128 KB of buffer space. The figure depicts the architecture for both the WS-X6348 and WS-X6148. Each block of memory is further subdivided, leaving 112 KB for the transmit buffer and 16 KB for the receive buffer. Within the 16 KB of space allocated for the receive queue, four tail-drop thresholds are specified. The different CoS values are mapped to these threshold levels.

Figure 8-5   *Ingress QoS on the Pinnacle ASIC*

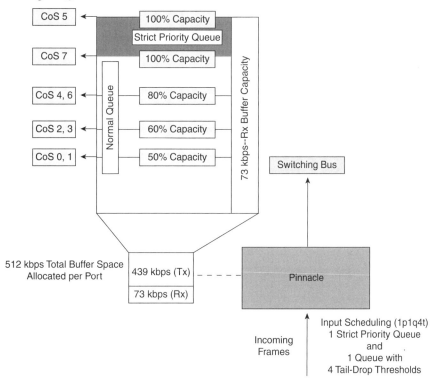

Figure 8-5 shows the ASIC responsible for Gigabit Ethernet ports. In this case, the Pinnacle ASIC controls four Gigabit ports. Each port receives 512 KB of buffer space, which is subdivided into 439 KB for the transmit side and 73 KB for the receive side. For earlier Gigabit linecards that do not have a strict-priority queue, the buffer architecture differs slightly and the default threshold settings and CoS mappings match the default settings for the 10/100 ports, shown in Table 8-4. For ports with a strict-priority queue, the default differs slightly. Instead of being mapped to the third tail-drop threshold setting of 80 percent, all frames arriving with CoS 5 are mapped to the priority queue by default. It is up to the network administrator to ensure that CoS 5 is, in fact, the critical traffic. The strict-priority queue then ensures that all arriving critical traffic is forwarded prior to traffic in the normal queue. When the priority queue is depleted, the normal queue is serviced. Again, the priority queue is only intended to accommodate low-bandwidth, low-latency traffic, such as voice. Continuous traffic present in the priority queue can potentially starve out lower queues. The priority queue does not have a configurable threshold. Therefore as soon as the queue is full, it tail drops any excess frames. Figure 8-5 depicts the priority queue, the default thresholds, and the CoS mappings. Now that input queue scheduling has been introduced, the focus turns to assigning receive queue drop thresholds and how to map CoS values to the thresholds and queues.

Configuring Receive Queue Tail-Drop Thresholds

To configure the different receive queue tail-drop thresholds and verify the configuration, use the following commands. Table 8-4 provides the default threshold drop values and the CoS values mapped to the thresholds.

```
(Hybrid)
set qos drop-threshold {port-type} rx queue {queue#} {thr1} {thr2} {thr3} {thr4}
show qos info {runtime {mod/port}} | {config {mod/port} | {{port-type} rx}}
(Native)
rcv-queue threshold 1 {thr1} {thr2} {thr3} {thr4}
show queueing interface {type num} [| begin Receive]
```

Table 8-4   *Default Receive Queue Threshold Configuration*

Standard Receive Queue Thresholds	Default Mapped CoS Values	Buffer Capacity Filled (Percent)
Threshold 1	0,1	50
Threshold 2	2,3	60
Threshold 3	4,5*	80
Threshold 4	6*,7	100

*CoS 5, by default, is mapped to the strict-priority queue if present.

CoS 6 is mapped to threshold 3 if a strict-priority queue is present. All other threshold mappings remain unchanged.

When configuring the receive queue thresholds in Hybrid, *port-type* is either 1q4t or 1p1q4t. Regardless of the presence of a priority queue, the *queue#* is always 1, which indicates the normal queue. The tail-drop threshold for the strict-priority queue, which is represented by *queue#* 2, is set for 100 percent, which is not configurable. In both cases, *thr1* represents the first drop percentage, which by default is 50 percent and corresponds to CoS values 0 and 1. *thr2* by default is set to 60 percent and maps to CoS 2 and 3. *thr3* defaults to 80 percent and corresponds to CoS 4 and 5, unless the port has a priority queue, in which case the CoS values are 4 and 6. Finally, *thr4* defaults to 100 percent and maps to CoS 6 and 7; in the presence of a priority queue, however, by default CoS 7 is the only value mapped to the final tail-drop threshold. **rcv-queue threshold**, which is configured under interface configuration mode, is the equivalent command in Cisco IOS. Verifying the configuration in Hybrid using the **config** *{port-type}* **rx** option enables the administrator to more accurately display the desired results. Examples 8-3 and 8-4 demonstrate how to configure the drop thresholds and verify the configurations.

Example 8-3   *Configuring Receive Queue Tail-Drop Thresholds in Hybrid Mode*

```
hybrid (enable) set qos drop-threshold 1p1q4t rx queue 1 65 75 85 100
Receive drop thresholds for queue 1 set at 65% 75% 85% 100%
hybrid (enable) show qos info config 1p1q4t rx
QoS setting in NVRAM for 1p1q4t receive:
QoS is enabled
Queue and Threshold Mapping for 1p1q4t (rx):
Queue Threshold CoS
```

Example 8-3   *Configuring Receive Queue Tail-Drop Thresholds in Hybrid Mode (Continued)*

```
.....  .........  ...............
1    1         0 1
1    2         2 3
1    3         4 6
1    4         7
2    -         5
Rx drop thresholds:
Queue #  Thresholds - percentage
-------  ------------------------------------
1        65% 75% 85% 100%
(text omitted)
```

Example 8-4   *Configuring Receive Queue Tail-Drop Thresholds in Native Mode*

```
native(config)# interface gigabitEthernet 1/1
native(config-if)# rcv-queue threshold 1 65 75 85 100
  threshold configured on:  Gi1/1 Gi1/2
native# show queueing interface gigabitEthernet 1/1 | begin Receive
  Receive queues [type = 1p1q4t]:
    Queue Id    Scheduling   Num of thresholds
    -----------------------------------------
        1         Standard          4
        2         Priority          1

    queue tail-drop-thresholds
    --------------------------
     1     65[1] 75[2] 85[3] 100[4]
(text omitted)
```

At the time of writing, only Gigabit Ethernet interfaces support configuring the receive queue thresholds while running Native mode. Fast Ethernet interfaces default to 100 percent for all thresholds in the receive queue. All Gigabit ports on the linecard must be configured to **mls qos trust** [**cos**], prior to altering the default threshold settings. After the thresholds have been adjusted, all ports inherit the configuration. For 16-port Gigabit cards, ports 1 through 8 receive the same threshold and map configuration, whereas 9 through 16 receive the same settings. For switches running Hybrid, it is necessary to use **set port qos** [*mod/port*] **trust** [**trust-cos**] to activate and use the receive queue thresholds.

Mapping CoS to Queues and Drop Thresholds

After the different queue thresholds have been configured, you can map the various CoS values to the desired tail-drop threshold. To map a CoS to a particular threshold and verify the configuration, use the following commands:

```
(Hybrid)
set qos map {port-type} rx {queue#} {thr #} cos {cos-list}
show qos info {runtime {mod/port}} | {config {mod/port} | {{port-type} rx}}
(Native)
```

```
wrr-queue cos-map {queue-id} {thr #} {cos1 [cos2] [cos3] [cos4] [cos5] [cos6] [cos7]
[cos8]}
rcv-queue cos-map {queue-id} {thr #} {cos1 [cos2] [cos3] [cos4] [cos5] [cos6] [cos7]
[cos8]}
show queueing interface {type num} [ | begin Receive]
(Mapping CoS to the priority queue)
priority-queue cos-map 1 {cos1 [cos2] [cos3] [cos4] [cos5] [cos6] [cos7] [cos8]}
```

After all the ports have been configured to trust the ingress CoS, the default threshold mappings take affect, as described in the preceding section. When mapping to receive thresholds in Hybrid mode, *port-type* refers to 2q2t, 1p1q4t, 1p1q0t, or 1p1q8t. (1p1q0t and 1p1q8t are addressed in the next section). The 2q2t port type keyword is used to configure the CoS mappings for both 1q4t receive and 2q2t transmit queues. In this case, queue 1 and thresholds 1 and 2 represent queue 1 and thresholds 1 and 2 for 1q4t port types. However, queue 2 and thresholds 1 and 2 represent queue 1 and thresholds 3 and 4. This behavior is discussed later in the chapter in the section titled "Mapping CoS Values to Transmit Queues and Thresholds" and demonstrated in Example 8-35.

The equivalent command in Cisco IOS for configuring 1q4t port types is **wrr-queue cos-map**. Again, the same 2q2t configuration principle applies. With the exception of the 2q2t port types, *queue#* or *queue-id* indicates the CoS is to be mapped to either the standard normal queue, specified as 1, or the priority queue, specified as 2. *thr #* designates the threshold within the applicable queue the CoS is mapped to. Because there is only one threshold for the priority queue, the appropriate parameter is 1. Finally, the *cos-list* enables the administrator to specify a specific CoS or range. When using the **priority-queue cos-map** command, the administrator does not specify the keywords **receive** or **transmit**. Therefore, all CoS values mapped to the priority queue apply in both directions. Example 8-5 demonstrates mapping a CoS to the normal queue and threshold and the priority queue and also verifies the configuration in Hybrid. Example 8-6 shows the same configuration with Native mode.

Example 8-5 *Mapping a CoS to a Queue and Threshold in Hybrid Mode*

```
hybrid (enable) set qos map 1p1q4t rx 1 4 cos 6
QoS tx priority queue and threshold mapped to cos successfully.
hybrid (enable) set qos map 1p1q4t rx 2 1 cos 7
QoS tx priority queue and threshold mapped to cos successfully.
hybrid (enable) show qos info config 1p1q4t rx
QoS setting in NVRAM for 1p1q4t receive:
QoS is enabled
Queue and Threshold Mapping for 1p1q4t (rx):
Queue Threshold CoS
----- --------- ---------------
1     1         0 1
1     2         2 3
1     3         4
1     4         6
2     -         5 7
(text omitted)
```

In Example 8-5, CoS 6 is changed from its default mapping in the normal queue, previously threshold 3, and mapped to threshold 4. CoS 7 is mapped to the priority queue. The following example demonstrates the same parameters in Native mode.

Example 8-6   *Mapping a CoS to a Queue and Threshold in Native Mode*

```
native(config-if)# rcv-queue cos-map 1 4 6
  cos-map configured on:  Gi2/1 Gi2/2 Gi2/3 Gi2/4 Gi2/5 Gi2/6 Gi2/7 Gi2/8
native(config-if)# priority-queue cos-map 1 7
  cos-map configured on:  Gi2/1 Gi2/2 Gi2/3 Gi2/4 Gi2/5 Gi2/6 Gi2/7 Gi2/8
native# show queueing interface gigabitEthernet 2/1 | begin Receive
  Receive queues [type = 1p1q4t]:
    Queue Id    Scheduling  Num of thresholds
    ----------------------------------------
        1          Standard          4
        2          Priority          1

    queue tail-drop-thresholds
    --------------------------
    1     50[1] 60[2] 80[3] 100[4]
    queue thresh cos-map
    ----------------------------------------
    1     1       0 1
    1     2       2 3
    1     3       4
    1     4       6
    2     1       5 7
(text omitted)
```

The receive queue size ratio enables the administrator to set a ratio between the amount of traffic received by the strict-priority queue and the amount received by the normal queue. Currently, only two module types for the 6500 support altering this feature. They are the fabric-enabled 10/100 modules and the 10 Gigabit Ethernet modules. The port types for these modules are 1p1q0t and 1p1q8t, respectively. The following section covers input scheduling and congestion avoidance for these port types and discusses how to alter the receive queue size ratio.

Input Scheduling and Congestion Avoidance for 1p1q0t and 1p1q8t

In addition to the two port types 1p1q4t and 1q4t, two additional port types are available on other 6500 linecards, 1p1q0t and 1p1q8t. These two options are available to ports on the fabric-enabled 10/100 modules and the 10 Gigabit Ethernet modules, respectively. Mentioned earlier, the 1p1q0t port type, similar to the 1p1q4t, has a strict-priority queue and one normal queue. Unlike the 1p1q4t, however, the 1p1q0t port type has only a single nonconfigurable tail-drop threshold. The 10/100 fabric-enabled module has a nonblocking connection to the switch fabric. This implies there is less of an opportunity for congestion to occur on ingress, because contention for the switching fabric is reduced. As a result, these ports do not possess a configurable tail-drop threshold and start discarding traffic when the buffers reach 100-percent capacity.

The 1p1q8t port type on the 10 Gigabit modules offers an additional feature not available on any of the modules previously mentioned. Although it has two queues, both a strict-priority queue, and a configurable normal queue, this port type offers the option of configuring eight WRED thresholds as a congestion avoidance mechanism within the normal receive queue. The port ASIC available on the 10 Gigabit module makes WRED possible. WRED offers a more deterministic method of dropping lower-priority frames, and ensuring higher-priority flows are given preference, as frames accumulate within the queue. Refer to Chapter 2 for a more detailed description of WRED operation. Figure 8-6 shows WRED operation on 1p1q8t port types.

Figure 8-6   *WRED Operation for 1p1q8t Port Types*

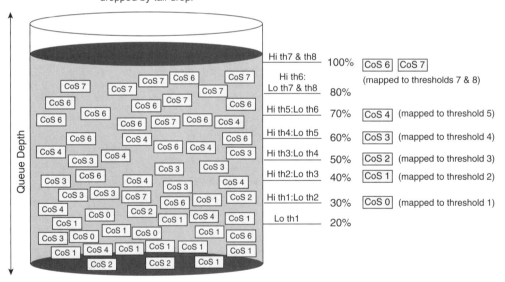

The 1p1q8t port type has eight instances of WRED, each instance having both a lower and an upper threshold. The lower threshold, also referred to as the *low-water mark*, ranges from 0 percent to 100 percent of the total normal queue size. The upper threshold, also referred to as the *high-water mark*, ranges from 1 percent to 100 percent of the total queue. When configuring the values, the lower threshold must be less than or equal to the higher threshold. The low-water mark enables the administrator to specify a lower bound, indicating the desire to randomly drop frames in times of congestion for a particular CoS mapped to that specific WRED range. The high-water mark, on the other hand, specifies at what percentage point during congestion it is permissible to tail drop all traffic with the appropriate CoS. During congestion, if the queue fills to a point that falls within a configured WRED range, frames with the applicable CoS are randomly dropped. The drop probability for those CoS values progressively increases as the queue fills, until the level of congestion reaches the upper limit of the range, at which point all frames with the corresponding CoS are tail dropped. WRED is discussed in further detail during the section on output scheduling. The following commands are used to configure the WRED thresholds for 1p1q8t port types:

```
(Hybrid)
set qos wred {1p1q8t} rx queue {queue#} {[thr1Lo:]thr1Hi [thr2Lo:]thr2Hi …
  [thr8Lo:]thr8Hi}
show qos info {runtime {mod/port}} | {config {mod/port} | {{port-type} rx}}
(Native)
wrr-queue random-detect {min-threshold} {queue#} {thr1% thr2% thr3% thr4% … thr8%}
wrr-queue random-detect {max-threshold} {queue#} {thr1% thr2% thr3% thr4% … thr8%}
show queueing interface tengigabitethernet {slot/port}
```

In Hybrid, you can configure all the thresholds with one command. Because there is only one normal queue, *queue#* is {**1**}. When configuring the threshold percentages, if a lower threshold is not explicitly configured, the lower bound defaults to zero. Therefore, if only a single value is specified for a threshold, that value is configured as the upper bound. The thresholds depicted in Figure 8-6 are configured as follows:

```
set qos wred 1p1q8t rx queue 1 20:30 30:40 40:50 50:60 60:70 70:80 80:100 80:100
```

In Native mode, the administrator uses two separate commands, one to configure all eight of the minimum thresholds for the various WRED classes and the other to configure the eight upper-bound thresholds. Again, in both instances the *queue#* is configured as {**1**}. Examples 8-7 and 8-8 demonstrate how to configure the receive queue WRED thresholds using Hybrid and Native modes, respectively.

Example 8-7   *Configuring Receive Queue WRED Thresholds for 1p1q8t in Hybrid Mode*

```
hybrid (enable) set qos wred 1p1q8t rx queue 1 20:35 30:45 40:55 50:65 60:75 70:85
  80:100 80:100
   WRED thresholds for queue 1 set to 20:35 and 30:45 and 40:55 and 50:65 and 60:75
  and 70:85 and
   80:100 and 80:100 on all WRED-capable 1p1q8t ports.
hybrid (enable) show qos info config 1p1q8t rx
(text omitted)
Rx WRED thresholds:
Queue #  Thresholds - percentage
-------  ----------------------------------------
1        20%:35% 30%:45% 40%:55% 50%:65% 60%:75% 70%:85% 80%:100% 80%:100%
(text omitted)
```

Example 8-8   *Configuring Receive Queue WRED Thresholds for 1p1q8t in Native Mode*

```
native(config-if)# rcv-queue random-detect min-threshold 1 20 30 40 50 60 70 80 80
native(config-if)# rcv-queue random-detect max-threshold 1 35 45 55 65 75 85 100 100
native# show queueing interface tenGigabitEthernet 8/1 | begin Receive
  Receive queues [type = 1p1q8t]:
    Queue Id    Scheduling  Num of thresholds
    ----------------------------------------
    queue random-detect-min-thresholds
    --------------------------------
       1     20[1] 30[2] 40[3] 50[4] 60[5] 70[6] 80[7] 80[8]
    queue random-detect-max-thresholds
    --------------------------------
       1     35[1] 45[2] 55[3] 65[4] 75[5] 85[6] 100[7] 100[8]
(text omitted)
```

After the WRED thresholds for the receive queue have been established, the CoS values are
then mapped to the desired threshold. The same configuration commands demonstrated at
the beginning of the section "Mapping CoS to Queues and Drop Thresholds" are applicable
in this situation. Unlike the previous examples, however, the number of available thresholds
has now increased to eight. Therefore, the valid values for the *thr #* parameter range from
1 to 8. Additionally, when configuring the commands in Hybrid, the *port-type* in this
instance is 1p1q8t. Finally, the configuration for priority queue mappings is identical to that
specified in the preceding section.

Configuring the Receive Queue Size Ratio

The 1p1q0t and 1p1q8t port types support configuring the receive queue size ratio for the
normal and strict-priority queues. By default, the normal queue is assigned 80 percent of
the total buffer space, and the strict-priority queue is provided the remaining 20 percent. To
alter and verify the percentage of memory allocated to the normal and priority queues, use
the following commands:

```
(Hybrid)
set qos rxq-ratio {1p1q0t | 1p1q8t} {queue1-ratio} {queue2-ratio}
show qos info {runtime {mod/port}} | {config {mod/port} | {{port-type} rx}}
(Native)
receive-queue queue-limit {normal-queue ratio} {priority-queue ratio}
show queueing interface {type num} [ | include  queue-limit ratios]
```

When configuring the command in Hybrid mode, *queue1-ratio* represents the percentage
of total buffer space assigned to the normal queue. *queue2-ratio* is the percentage assigned
to the strict-priority queue. Whether using Hybrid or Native mode, the values assigned to
the normal queue and the priority queue must add up to 100 percent, and both individual
values must be greater than zero. Prior to modifying default receive queue ratios, carefully
consider how a change will impact traffic behavior. Example 8-9 shows configuration of the
receive queue ratio size in Hybrid mode; Example 8-10 shows the same with Cisco IOS.

Example 8-9   *Configuring the Receive Queue Size Ratio in Hybrid Mode*

```
hybrid (enable) set qos rxq-ratio 1p1q0t 75 25
QoS rxq-ratio is set successfully.
hybrid (enable) show qos info config 1p1q0t rx
(text omitted)
Rx queue size ratio:
Queue #  Sizes - percentage
-------  -----------------------------------
1        75%
2        25%
```

Example 8-10   *Configuring the Receive Queue Size Ratio in Native Mode*

```
native(config-if)# rcv-queue queue-limit 75 25
  queue-limit configured on all 48 ports on slot 3.
native# show queueing interface fastEthernet 3/1 | include queue-limit
    queue-limit ratios:     75[queue 1]  25[queue 2]
```

Classification and Marking

Classification and marking on the Catalyst 6500 is performed by port ASICs and the PFC. Given the different capabilities, this section is broken down into the following topics:

- Port-Based Versus VLAN-Based QoS
- Classification Based on Destination MAC Address and VLAN
- Trust
- Classification and Marking Using ACLs and ACEs

In addition to the these listed topics, further attention is directed toward Cisco's *Modular QoS CLI* (MQC), which was introduced in Chapter 5, "Introduction to the Modular QoS Command-Line Interface." As before, numerous examples are provided demonstrating how these features are configured when operating in both Hybrid and Native modes.

Port-Based Versus VLAN-Based QoS

On the Catalyst 6500, QoS policies can be deployed at the individual port level or they can be applied on a per-VLAN basis. By default, all ports are configured for port-based QoS. This implies all classification policies, and marking and policing, configured for the port are only applicable to the port to which they are applied. Parameters are not shared by neighboring interfaces. On the contrary, VLAN-based QoS enables the administrator to apply all settings to all ports configured for a specific VLAN. VLAN-based QoS may be preferred in certain situations. When deploying voice in a campus environment, for example, consideration needs to be given to voice-control traffic. Although not as important as the actual voice frames, the control streams are responsible for establishing, maintaining, and terminating calls. Therefore, it is recommended to assign the control traffic a higher priority than normal user data. Because voice traffic is assigned to auxiliary VLANs, marking the control traffic is easily accomplished using VLAN-based QoS. You can use ACLs to identify the appropriate Layer 3 and 4 parameters, and then map them to the appropriate auxiliary VLAN. Additional instances when VLAN-based QoS can be used include when policing inter-VLAN traffic for specific VLANs and when establishing initial QoS policies for access layer devices with multiple VLANs. The latter scenario may be required, depending on the QoS capabilities of the access layer device. To alter the port policy to either port based or VLAN based, use the following commands:

```
(Hybrid)
set port qos {mod/port} {port-based | vlan-based}
(Native)
[no] mls qos vlan-based
```

NOTE   Linecards equipped with a DFC support only port-based policing. VLAN-based policing is currently not supported on DFCs. It will however, be supported on the DFC3, on a per-DFC3 basis.

If a port is configured for VLAN-based QoS, any ACLs applied at the port level are ignored. The opposite applies to ports configured for port-based QoS; ACLs applied at the VLAN level are ignored. As a result, it is vital to properly set the port to port-based or VLAN-based QoS in an effort to achieve the desired behavior. When configuring a port to be VLAN based in Cisco IOS, it is necessary to configure the port as a Layer 2 port. Therefore, prior to altering the interface policy, **switchport** must be entered while in interface configuration mode. The command **switchport** alters the port state from the default Layer 3 setting to Layer 2. By default, all ports on a 6500 with Cisco IOS are routed interfaces. The next two examples show how to successfully change a port's setting to VLAN based and how to verify the configuration.

Example 8-11   *Configuring a Port to VLAN Based in Hybrid Mode*

```
hybrid (enable) set port qos 5/30 vlan-based
QoS interface is set to vlan-based for ports 5/30
hybrid (enable) show qos info config 5/30
(text omitted)
Tx port type of port 5/30 : 2q2t
Rx port type of port 5/30 : 1q4t
Interface type: vlan-based
(text omitted)
```

Example 8-12   *Configuring a Port to VLAN Based in Native Mode*

```
native(config)# interface fastEthernet 6/35
native(config-if)# mls qos vlan-based
vlan-based mode is only for Layer 2 LAN interfaces.
native(config-if)# switchport
```

Example 8-12 *Configuring a Port to VLAN Based in Native Mode (Continued)*

```
native(config-if)# mls qos vlan-based
native# show mls qos | begin vlan-based
  QoS is vlan-based on the following interfaces:
    Gi1/1 Gi5/1 Fa6/1 Fa6/2 Fa6/34 Fa6/35
(text omitted)
```

Classification Based on Destination MAC Address and VLAN

A Catalyst 6500 without a PFC or an MSFC, but equipped with a Layer 2 switching engine, can classify and mark based on the destination MAC address and VLAN of an arriving frame. With this hardware configuration, the switching engine can support only Layer 2 CoS values. Therefore, this feature enables the administrator to map a specific CoS value to a host destination MAC address and VLAN pair. The following command is used to map the appropriate CoS (available in Hybrid only):

```
set qos mac-cos {dest MAC-addr} {dest VLAN} {CoS value}
show qos mac-cos {all | dest MAC-addr}
```

Unfortunately, this feature does not scale very well. Due to the vast number of MAC addresses in a given network, the configuration process could be administratively intensive and difficult to manage and maintain. If you include a PFC in the hardware profile of the switch, however, you can use the **set qos acl** command as an alternative to the preceding commands. The following example demonstrates how to map a CoS value to a destination MAC address and VLAN.

Example 8-13 *Mapping the CoS Value to a Destination MAC Address and VLAN*

```
hybrid (enable) set qos mac-cos 00-02-a5-07-83-0e 1 3
CoS 3 is assigned to 00-02-a5-07-83-0e vlan 1.
hybrid (enable) show qos mac-cos all
Number  VLAN  Dest MAC             CoS
......  ....  .................    ...
1       20    11-22-33-44-55-66    5
2       1     00-02-a5-07-83-0e    3
```

Trust

Trust is a concept covered in Chapter 2, in the section "Catalyst QoS Trust Concept." Trust is a classification method that enables the administrator to maintain a frame's CoS/ToS (*type of service*) settings. Upon ingress, the administrator can determine to further utilize the predetermined priority settings or can apply new settings to arriving frames on a port-by-port or VLAN basis. Trust is extremely important in determining a frame's behavior as it traverses the switch. The trust state of a given port determines how frames are classified, marked, and, as previously discussed, scheduled as they proceed from the ingress to egress port within the switch.

On the 6500, all ports by default are configured as untrusted. The exception to this is FlexWAN ports, which are trusted by default. For dot1q- and ISL-tagged frames arriving at an untrusted port, even if they possess a CoS or ToS setting greater than zero, those frames are reset with the default CoS configured for the respective port of entry. By default, this value is zero, but can be changed at the discretion of the administrator. To modify the default CoS setting for a port, use the following commands:

```
(Hybrid)
set port qos {mod/port} cos {CoS value}
show qos info {runtime | config} {mod/port}
(Native)
mls qos cos {CoS value}
show queueing interface {type num} [ | include Default COS]
```

The CoS setting derived from the port is then mapped to a corresponding internal DSCP value, which is used internally to determine the handling of the frame through the switch. For more detailed information, see the section titled "CoS-to-DSCP Mapping" in this chapter. (Refer to Table 8-12 for the default mapping tables within the Catalyst 6500.)

Similar to the Catalyst 3550, the 6500 is capable of trusting incoming frames based on their CoS, IP precedence, or DSCP values. Table 8-5 shows the trust states supported on the Catalyst 6500. The table correlates each module with the supported trust states.

Table 8-5   *Overview of Supported Trust States and Modules*

Module	Trust CoS	Trust IP Precedence	Trust DSCP
WS-X6024	Yes	No	No
WS-X6148	Yes	Yes	Yes
WS-X6224	Yes	No	No
WS-X6248	Yes	No	No
WS-X6316	Yes	Yes	Yes
WS-X6324	Yes	No	No
WS-X6348	Yes	No	No
WS-X6408	Yes	Yes	Yes
WS-X6408A	Yes	Yes	Yes
WS-X6416	Yes	Yes	Yes
WS-X6501	Yes	Yes	Yes
WS-X6502	Yes	Yes	Yes
WS-X6516	Yes	Yes	Yes
WS-X6524	Yes	Yes	Yes
WS-X6548	Yes	Yes	Yes
WS-X6816	Yes	Yes	Yes

trust-cos enables the administrator to trust the inbound CoS setting contained within the dot1q or ISL header. For all untagged frames or non-IP packets entering the switch, if a port is set to **trust-cos** all traffic entering the switch is set with the default CoS configured for the port. In addition, as mentioned in the preceding section, to take advantage of input scheduling on the 6500 the port must be configured to trust the inbound CoS. To enable a port to trust the inbound CoS, use the following commands:

```
(Hybrid)
set port qos {mod/port} trust {trust-cos}
show qos info {runtime | config} {mod/port}
(Native)
mls qos trust {cos}
show queueing interface {type num}
```

Under some circumstances, the administrator must perform additional configuration steps, beyond what is noted in the preceding commands. The WS-X6224/6248 and WS-X6324/6348 have a hardware restriction that prevents them from passing the learned CoS to the switching engine. Although the linecards recognize the arriving CoS, and use that value for input scheduling, when the frame header is passed to the switching engine for forwarding, the CoS value for the frame is not preserved, and as a result the CoS is rewritten to zero. Therefore, it is necessary to configure additional commands.

NOTE   The WS-X6148 linecard is not subject to the same hardware limitations as the WS-X6224/6248 and WS-X6324/6348. It is capable of trusting inbound CoS values without configuring additional commands. Also unlike the WS-X6224/6248 and Ws-X6324/6348, the WS-X6148 supports inbound trust for IP precedence and for DSCP values. At the time of writing, this support is found in CatOS Release 6.4(1) and subsequent 6.4 releases.

Example 8-14 shows the resulting message after setting the port to **trust-cos**. As described, the receive thresholds are enabled on the port. This allows inbound frames to utilize the ingress port scheduling. However, the port remains in the untrusted state. The example further includes the additional commands required to ensure the arriving CoS is sustained through the switch.

Example 8-14 *Enabling* **trust-cos** *on WS-X6224/6248 and WS-X6324/6348 in Hybrid Mode*

```
hybrid (enable) set port qos 6/1 trust trust-cos
Trust type trust-cos not supported on this port.
Receive thresholds are enabled on port 6/1.
Port  6/1 qos set to untrusted.
set qos acl {ip} {acl-name} {trust-cos} {any}
commit qos acl {acl-name}
set qos acl map {acl-name} {mod/port | vlan}
```

For the fabric-enabled 10/100 modules, it is not necessary to make additional configuration steps. In addition, the fabric-enabled 10/100 linecard is the only 10/100 card that supports port-based trust in Native mode. The default setting for all ports is untrusted, which can only be modified on Gigabit Ethernet and fabric-enabled 10/100 ports when running Cisco IOS. The same situation applies to ports configured for VLAN-based QoS.

trust-ipprec and **trust-dscp** instruct the switch to analyze the ToS field in the IP header of arriving packets. When configured, the IP precedence option accepts the three least significant bits in the precedence field within the ToS byte, whereas the DSCP option utilizes the 6 bits reserved for the codepoint value within the ToS byte. Configuring a port to trust the IP precedence or DSCP is accomplished as follows:

```
(Hybrid)
set port qos {mod/port} trust {trust-ipprec | trust-dscp}
show qos info {runtime | config} {mod/port}
(Native)
mls qos trust {ip-precedence | dscp}
show queueing interface {type num} [| include Trust state]
```

Modules with 1q4t port types, with the exception of Gigabit modules, do not support the IP precedence or DSCP trust option. This restriction applies to Catalyst 6500s running both Hybrid and Native modes. After the arriving frame or packet has been classified, using either the predetermined IP precedence or DSCP setting, that value is then used to derive the internal DSCP utilized by the switch. Once again, if the ingress port is configured to trust IP precedence, DSCP, or is instructed not to trust any Layer 2 or 3 priority settings (**untrusted**), the frame is passed directly to the switching engine. As a result, the arriving frame is not processed through the input scheduling and queuing mechanisms configured for the port. To revert a port to the default **untrusted** state, in Hybrid it is necessary to configure **set port qos** {*mod/port*} **trust untrusted**. In Native mode, the command is **no mls qos trust**.

NOTE   Regardless of the port trust state, each arriving frame is assigned a CoS value, which is forwarded to the switching engine within the D-bus header. If the incoming frame arrives on a dot1q or ISL trunk, the CoS value is derived from the priority of the marked frame. Otherwise, the default port CoS is assigned to the D-bus header. This applies to all traffic types.

The following examples demonstrate how to modify the trust state on Gigabit Ethernet and non-1q4t port types.

Example 8-15 *Altering the Default Trust State in Hybrid Mode*

```
hybrid (enable) set port qos 4/4 trust trust-cos
Port  4/4 qos set to trust-cos.
hybrid (enable) set port qos 4/5 trust trust-dscp
Port  4/5 qos set to trust-dscp.
hybrid (enable) show qos info config 4/4
QoS setting in NVRAM:
QoS is enabled
Policy Source of port 4/4: COPS
```

Example 8-15 *Altering the Default Trust State in Hybrid Mode (Continued)*

```
Tx port type of port 4/4 : 1p2q2t
Rx port type of port 4/4 : 1p1q4t
Interface type: port-based
ACL attached:
The qos trust type is set to trust-cos
(text omitted)
hybrid (enable) show qos info config 4/5
QoS setting in NVRAM:
QoS is enabled
Policy Source of port 4/5: COPS
Tx port type of port 4/5 : 1p2q2t
Rx port type of port 4/5 : 1p1q4t
Interface type: port-based
ACL attached:
The qos trust type is set to trust-dscp.
(text omitted)
```

Example 8-16 *Altering the Default Trust State in Native Mode (WS-X6548)*

```
native(config)# interface fastEthernet 3/12
native(config-if)# mls qos trust ip-precedence
native# show queueing interface fastEthernet 3/12 | include Trust state
  Trust state: trust IP Precedence
```

Examples 8-17 and 8-18 show how to configure a port back to its default untrusted state. The commands apply to all ports, regardless of interface port type.

Example 8-17 *Reverting to the Default Trust State in Hybrid Mode*

```
hybrid (enable) set port qos 4/4 trust untrusted
Port  4/4 qos set to untrusted.
hybrid (enable) show qos info config 4/4
QoS setting in NVRAM:
QoS is enabled
Policy Source of port 4/4: COPS
Tx port type of port 4/4 : 1p2q2t
Rx port type of port 4/4 : 1p1q4t
Interface type: port-based
ACL attached:
The qos trust type is set to untrusted.
(text omitted)
```

Example 8-18 *Reverting to the Default Trust State in Native Mode (WS-X6548)*

```
native(config)# interface fastEthernet 3/12
native(config-if)#no mls qos trust
native# show queueing interface fastEthernet 3/12
Interface FastEthernet3/12 queueing strategy:  Weighted Round-Robin
  Port QoS is enabled
  Port is untrusted
(text omitted)
```

Classification and Marking Using ACLs and ACEs

In addition to port trust states, the Catalyst 6500 utilizes ACLs to classify traffic flows, to enforce administratively defined QoS policies. Equipped with a PFC, the Catalyst 6500 can classify, and subsequently mark and police traffic, based on Layer 2, 3, and 4 characteristics. Policing is covered later in the policing section.

QoS ACL lookups are performed in hardware. The TCAM is the portion of memory responsible for storing all defined masks and ACL components for the switch. QoS ACLs are composed of individual ACEs. In turn, each ACE is composed of a pattern value and a mask value. The pattern value specifies the actual source and destination address, including any additional Layer 3- and 4-specified parameters. The mask in this case is defined as the portions of the pattern value that are specifically matched, or ignored.

Because the TCAM is a finite memory space, the number of configured masks and ACEs is also finite. For the Supervisor I Engine, the number of masks is limited to 2000. However, each mask can be shared among a maximum of eight ACEs. As a result, there are 16,000 possible supportable entries for the Supervisor I, which are shared among QoS and security ACLs. With a Supervisor II Engine the number of masks and entries increases. The Supervisor II supports 4000 different masks, and is still capable of associating 8 ACEs with 1 mask entry. Therefore, the number of entries increases to 32,000. Unlike the Supervisor I, however, these entries are dedicated to QoS.

Each supervisor engine can support up to 512 different ACL labels system wide. Labels are divided among QoS and security ACLs. ACL label resources are consumed based on ACL type and how they are applied. QoS ACLs can only be applied to a port/interface or VLAN. In either instance, the result is the use of one label. Prior to CatOS Software Release 6.3, 250 labels are reserved for QoS type ACLs. Software Release 6.3 and later increases the number of supported QoS ACLs from 250 to 500. For additional information regarding the TCAM, refer to the section "Catalyst 2950 and Catalyst 3550 Family of Switches QoS Architectural Overview" in Chapter 6.

Default ACLs

Aside from administratively defined ACLs, the Catalyst 6500 utilizes three default ACLs to ensure all ingress traffic is classified. These ACLs are applied to all ports/interfaces on the switch. Any traffic not matching a named ACL applied to a port or VLAN interface, matches one of the default ACLs. One ACL is reserved for IP traffic, designated with ethertype 0x800, another for IPX traffic, ethertype 0x8137 and 0x8138, and finally an ACL for all MAC traffic, which encompasses all other ethertype values, including AppleTalk, DECnet, Banyan VINES and, *Xerox Network Systems* (XNS). For all arriving frames, the ethertype value is used to determine which ACL is applied to the arriving frame. Each default ACL has only one ACE. Although the match criteria are not configurable, the default marking value can be altered. The exception to this rule applies to Catalyst 6500s equipped with a Supervisor II Engine. With a PFC2, it is not possible to the default IPX or MAC value.

This limitation does not impact IP traffic. By default, all traffic not matched by a named ACL is matched by one of the default ACLs and assigned an internal DSCP value of zero. Example 8-19 demonstrates how to modify the default DSCP value.

Example 8-19 *Modifying the Default Marking Value with a PFC2*

```
hybrid (enable) set qos acl default-action ip dscp 16 rx
IP ACL is set successfully.
hybrid (enable) show qos acl info default-action all
QoS default ACL on rx side:
set qos acl default-action
-------------------------
ip dscp 16
ipx
mac
(text omitted)
```

In Example 8-19 all ingress IP traffic to the 6500, which does not match a named ACL, is marked with a DSCP value of 16. Because the configuration in Example 8-19 was performed on a switch equipped with a PFC2, it was not possible to modify the DSCP values for IPX and MAC traffic. Example 8-20 shows the same procedures with a PFC1. In this instance, however, the default value for IPX and MAC traffic is modified.

Example 8-20 *Modifying the Default Marking Value with a PFC1*

```
hybrid (enable) set qos acl default-action mac dscp 8
QoS default-action MAC ACL is set successfully.
hybrid (enable) set qos acl default-action ipx dscp 32
QoS default-action IPX ACL is set successfully.
hybrid (enable) show qos acl info default all
QoS default ACL on rx side:
set qos acl default-action
-------------------------
ip dscp 0
ipx dscp 32
mac dscp 8
```

When running Cisco IOS, it is not possible to alter the default ACL marking parameters. The values for all traffic types are statically defined to zero. This is verified by performing a **show mls qos** {**ip** | **ipx** | **mac**} at the command line:

```
native# show mls qos ip
  QoS Summary [IP]:       (* - shared aggregates, Mod - switch module)
        Int Mod Dir  Class-map DSCP  AgId Trust FlId  AgForward-Pk  AgPoliced-Pk
-------------------------------------------------------------------------------
        All  1   -   Default   0     0*   No    0        8920394             0
native#
```

As shown in the preceding command output, a default class map is applied to all interfaces and marks all unmatched traffic with an internal DSCP value of zero. The same default behavior applies to all traffic types: IP, IPX, or MAC.

Defining and Configuring QoS ACLs in Hybrid Mode

As stated earlier, it is possible to classify and mark traffic on the Catalyst 6500 by applying administratively defined named ACLs. Each ACL contains one or more ACEs, which define the Layer 2, 3, and 4 parameters used to classify and subsequently mark or police network traffic. Similar to the default ACLs, the administrator has the option of configuring three ACL types: IP, IPX, or MAC. Each inbound frame is compared against the defined classification criteria specified in the ACEs. After a match has been established, the configured action is taken and no further ACEs are processed. Again, all traffic not matched by any of the named ACLs is matched by one of the default ACLs and marked with the associated default internal DSCP value. This section addresses configuring QoS ACLs in Hybrid mode, and then transitions to configuring ACLs with Native mode using class maps and policy maps.

Classification with ACLs in Hybrid mode is accomplished with the command **set qos acl** {**ip** | **ipx** | **mac**}. When performing classification utilizing IP ACLs, it is possible to classify traffic based on the following characteristics: Layer 3 source and destination address, Layer 3 precedence values, Layer 4 protocol IDs, Layer 4 TCP and UDP port numbers, Layer 4 *Internet Control Message Protocol* (ICMP) type and code values, and Layer 4 *Internet Group Management Protocol* (IGMP) message types. When configuring the various Layer 3 and 4 parameters, if a value or keyword is not specified for the protocol ID, port numbers, or message types, the PFC classifies all traffic matching the generic Layer 3 or 4 property indicated in the ACE. If an IP ACE is configured to match TCP or UDP traffic, for instance, if a particular port number or keyword is not specified, the ACE is matched against all TCP or UDP traffic, regardless of port. The same behavior applies to IP ACEs configured with the **icmp** or **igmp** keywords. If a particular message or code type is not indicated, all ICMP or IGMP traffic is matched. Additionally, if IGMP snooping is enabled on the switch, QoS does not support IGMP type traffic. Tables 8-6 through 8-8 identify the most common criteria used to classify IP traffic flows.

Table 8-6   *Layer 4 IP Protocol Criteria*

Protocol ID Keyword Value	Protocol ID Keyword Value	Protocol ID Keyword Value
AHP (51)	IGMP (2)	PCP (108)
EIGRP (88)	IGRP (9)	PIM (103)
ESP (50)	IP (0)	TCP (6)
GRE (47)	IpinIP (4)	UDP (17)
IGRP (9)	NOS (94)	**Protocol ID Range (0–255)**
ICMP (1)	OSPF (89)	

Table 8-7 *Layer 4 UDP Criteria*

Port Keyword Port	Port Keyword Port	Port Keyword Port	Port Keyword Port
Biff 512	Echo 7	RIP 520	Talk 517
Bootpc 68	Mobile-IP 434	SNMP 161	TFTP 69
Bootps 67	Name Server 42	SNMPtrap 162	Time 37
Discard 9	NetBIOS-DGM 138	SunRPC 111	Who 513
DNS 53	NetBIOS-NS 137	Syslog 514	XDMCP 177
DNSIX 195	NTP 123	TACACS 49	**Port range (0–65535)**

Table 8-8   *Layer 4 TCP Criteria*

Port Keyword Port	Port Keyword Port	Port Keyword Port	Port Keyword Port
BGP 179	FTP 21	LDP 515	Telnet 23
Chargen 19	FTP-Data 20	NNTP 119	Time 37
Daytime 13	Gopher 70	POP2 109	UUCP 540
Discard 9	Hostname 101	POP3 110	Whois 43
Domain 53	IRC 194	SMTP 25	WWW 80
Echo 7	Klogin 543	SunRPC 111	**Port range (0–65535)**
Finger 79	Kshell 544	TACACS 49	

Although not as granular as IP, IPX and MAC ACLs can classify traffic based on specific protocol numbers and ethertype values, as well as based on the source and destination network and host numbers. Administrators can identify particular IPX protocols based on keywords—(**ncp** (17), **rip** (1), **sap** (4), **spx** (5))—or a protocol number in the range from 0 to 19 or 21 to 255. MAC ACLs enable the administrator to identify traffic based on ethertype value, utilizing one of the keywords or values shown in Table 8-9. Once again, if a specific protocol or ethertype value is not included in the ACL configuration, the resulting behavior is to classify all IPX or MAC traffic based on the indicated network or node addresses.

Table 8-9 *MAC Classification Criteria*

Keyword Ethertype	Keyword Ethertype
AARP 0x80F3	DEC-Mumps 0x6009
Banyan-Vines-Echo 0x0baf	DEC-NetBIOS 0x8040
DEC-Amber 0x6008	DEC-Phase-IV 0x6003
DEC-DSM 0x8039	Ethertalk 0x809B
DEC-Diagnostic-Protocol 0x6005	XEROX-NS-IDP
DEC-LANBridge 0x8038	0x0600
DEC-LAT 0x6004	**Valid Configurable Ethertype Values** 0x809B,0x80F3
DEC-LAVC-SA 0x6007	0x6000–0x6009
DEC-MOP-Dump 0x6001	0x8038–0x8039
DEC-MOP-Remote-Console 0x6002	0x8040–0x8042
DEC-MSDOS 0x8041	0x0BAD,0x0BAF, 0x0600

For all ACL types, after the named ACLs have been configured, they are temporarily placed into an edit buffer within memory. As a result, if changes are made to an ACL, or a new ACL is created, it is necessary to commit the changes before they can be implemented. Committing the ACL copies the commands from the temporary edit buffer to the PFC in hardware. Commits are performed with the following command, **commit qos acl** {*ACL_name* | **all**}. Prior to committing any changes, it is possible to "roll back" any modifications without impacting the performance of currently operational ACLs. This eliminates any ACL alterations or additions present within the temporary edit buffer. This is accomplished with **rollback qos acl** {*ACL_name* | **all**}. When modifying default ACL parameters, it is not necessary to commit any changes. All changes take affect immediately. To verify whether an ACL has been committed to hardware, or if there are outstanding "not committed" changes, use **show qos acl editbuffer**. Refer to Example 8-23 in the "Classification and Marking in Hybrid Mode" section for a demonstration on configuring and applying QoS ACLs using Hybrid mode.

Class Maps and Policy Maps with Cisco IOS

With Cisco IOS, classification is performed utilizing Cisco's MQC, as described in Chapter 5. The modular CLI enables the administrator to classify all interesting traffic by defining named or numbered IOS ACLs and referencing them within class maps. Class maps are then applied to policy maps. Policy maps identify the actions performed on traffic corresponding to the predefined class maps, which are referenced within the policy map. Finally, the defined policies are then applied to the appropriate port or interface with the **service-policy** {**input** | **output**} command. For further information regarding the Cisco MQC, refer to Chapter 5.

Cisco IOS supports the classification of IP, IPX, and MAC type traffic. With Cisco IOS, both IP and IPX flows can be classified utilizing standard-numbered ACLs, extended-numbered ACLS, or named ACLs. For MAC layer traffic, network data is classified using named ACLs only.

NOTE   With Release 12.1(1)E and later, it is possible to classify IPX and MAC layer traffic. However, QoS support for IPX classification can be based on source network, and optionally destination network and node parameters. Classifying IPX type traffic based on socket numbers, source node, protocol, or service type is not supported.

When defining interesting traffic, you can configure multiple class maps. Potentially, one class map can be specified for each type of inbound traffic for a designated receiving interface. QoS on the Catalyst 6500 only supports one **match** statement when defining classification criteria. You can match traffic based on Layer 3 precedence values by using **match ip**, or administratively defined ACLs by using **match access-group**. All other class map options are not supported for QoS. The exception to this limitation is the **match protocol** option. With 12.1(13)E and later releases, **match protocol** can be used to support *network-based application recognition* (NBAR) on the Catalyst 6500 with an MSFC 2. At the time of writing, however, NBAR is implemented only in software. Refer to Chapter 9 for further details regarding NBAR support on the Catalyst 6500. After the traffic flows have been delineated, you can reference each class map within a policy map. You can assign only one policy map to each interface. For an example of configuring QoS policies using the MQC, refer to Example 8-24. Policy maps, like class maps, have certain configuration limitations. The following **class** {*class-name*} keywords are not supported under the QoS policy map configuration:

- **class** {*class-name*} **destination-address**
- **class** {*class-name*} **input-interface**
- **class** {*class-name*} **qos-group**
- **class** {*class-name*} **source-address**

Finally, remember when configuring QoS policies in Cisco IOS that the console does not immediately notify the administrator when an unsupported command is used. When the command is applied to the target interface using the **service-policy input** command, the administrator is notified of any discrepancies.

ACL-Based Classification and Marking in Hybrid Mode

Classification and marking are extremely important in determining how a frame is processed within the 6500, as well as for determining what preference it is given when forwarded on to the network. These actions determine the internal DSCP value chosen for a frame, which in turn translates to an egress DSCP and CoS value. After the classification parameters have been established, you must determine what action to apply to all traffic meeting those specifications. This section focuses on classification and marking in Hybrid mode, tying together all previously discussed topics. When a frame is received, it is forwarded out on the D-bus, where it is seen by all ports and the PFC. At the PFC, hardware-logic processes configured ACLs, which interact with port trust states to determine the proper classification or marking settings to derive the internal DSCP value.

Configuring classification and marking with QoS ACLs in Hybrid mode involves four supported rules. These rules are implemented using the following four keywords: **trust-cos**, **trust-ipprec**, **trust-dscp**, and **dscp**. Table 8-10 summarizes the corresponding behavior resulting from configuring one of the four ACE keywords and describes how each interacts with existing ingress port trust states.

Table 8-10   *Summary of Marking Rules in Hybrid Mode*

Port Trust State ACE Keyword	untrusted	trust-cos	trust-ipprec	trust-dscp
trust-cos	Port CoS value: default value (0)	Port CoS or CoS value of arriving frame	Port CoS or CoS value of arriving frame[1]	Port CoS or CoS value of arriving frame[1]
trust-ipprec	IP precedence value of arriving frame	IP precedence value of arriving frame	IP precedence value of arriving frame[1]	IP precedence value of arriving frame[1]
trust-dscp	DSCP value of arriving frame	DSCP value of arriving frame	DSCP value of arriving frame[1]	DSCP value of arriving frame[1]
dscp	DSCP value specified in ACE	Port CoS or CoS value of arriving frame[2]	IP precedence value of arriving frame[1]	DSCP value of arriving frame[1]

[1]Configuration settings do not apply to WS-X6224/6248 and WS-X6324/6348 series linecards.

[2]The internal DSCP value is derived from the DSCP value specified in the ACL for WS-X6224/6248 and WS-X6324/6348 series linecards.

As you can see in Table 8-10, when an ACE keyword is specified within a QoS ACL, the keyword overrides the port trust policy applied to the ingress interface or VLAN. The exception is when using the **dscp** keyword. Instead of always marking the frame header using the DSCP priority configured in the QoS ACE, the keyword operates in conjunction with the port trust state. If the ingress port is configured to trust the arriving CoS, IP precedence, or DSCP value, **dscp** instructs the switch to maintain the QoS setting derived from the ingress port's classification policy. If the ingress port trust is left at its default setting (**untrusted**), however, **dscp** marks the frame header with the value specified in the ACE. Other notable behavior includes configuring the **trust-cos** keyword within an ACE. **trust-cos** is not a recommended setting when the inbound port's trust policy is set to **untrusted**. This combination may result in unexpected behavior. Traffic arriving on an interface configured as **untrusted** is immediately labeled with the default port CoS setting, thus overwriting the existing CoS priority. The frame header is then forwarded directly to the switching engine. As a result, the value maintained by the **trust-cos** command, within the ACE, may not be the expected value. Therefore, when using the **trust-cos** keyword, it is recommended the port be configured for **trust-cos** as well.

NOTE   Because the WS-X6148 is not subject to the same hardware limitations as the WS-X6224/6248 and the WS-X6324/6348, all the marking rules provided in Table 8-10 apply.

Not all marking rules listed in the Table 8-10 apply to WS-X6224/6248 or WS-X6324/6348 linecards. As mentioned earlier, **trust-ipprec** and **trust-dscp** are not supported configurations at the port level for these modules. Also due to hardware limitations, the port ASIC for these linecards cannot preserve the inbound priority without the administrator entering additional commands. Therefore, if the desired action is to maintain the inbound CoS setting, a QoS ACL must be configured with the **trust-cos** keyword. Furthermore, as a result of the same port ASIC limitation, if the **dscp** keyword is specified rather than **trust-cos**, the arriving frame is marked based on the specified codepoint rather than the trusted inbound CoS priority.

Example 8-21 demonstrates how to configure a QoS ACL in Hybrid mode. In this example, a named ACL called VideoConf is created. For this ACL, the intent is to mark all traffic destined for TCP ports 1720, 1731, and 1503 with DSCP 26 and to maintain the classification established by the default port value for all other traffic. The TCP ports identified are control ports used in some video conferencing applications. Therefore, DSCP 26, equivalent to precedence 3, is applied to the matching traffic. In this instance, port 4/2 is assumed to be a trunk port.

Example 8-21 *Configuring and Applying an IP QoS ACL in Hybrid Mode*

```
hybrid (enable) set qos acl ip VideoConf dscp 26 tcp any any eq 1720
VideoConf editbuffer modified. Use 'commit' command to apply changes.
hybrid (enable) set qos acl ip VideoConf dscp 26 tcp any any eq 1731
VideoConf editbuffer modified. Use 'commit' command to apply changes.
hybrid (enable) set qos acl ip VideoConf dscp 26 tcp any any eq 1503
VideoConf editbuffer modified. Use 'commit' command to apply changes.
hybrid (enable) set qos acl ip VideoConf trust-cos ip any any
Warning: ACL trust-cos should only be used with ports that are also configured
with port trust=trust-cos.
VideoConf editbuffer modified. Use 'commit' command to apply changes.
```

After the ACL has been created, a message is sent to the console. It reminds the administrator to commit the changes to the PFC, removing them from the temporary edit buffer. Looking at the edit buffer, you can confirm the ACL has not yet been committed.

```
hybrid (enable) show qos acl editbuffer
ACL                              Type Status
-------------------------------- ---- ----------
VideoConf                        IP   Not Committed
hybrid (enable) commit qos acl VideoConf
QoS ACL 'VideoConf' successfully committed.
hybrid (enable) show qos acl editbuffer
ACL                              Type Status
-------------------------------- ---- ----------
VideoConf                        IP   Committed
```

After the ACL has been committed to hardware, you can verify the ACL configuration with the following command:

```
hybrid (enable) show qos acl info config VideoConf
 set qos acl ip VideoConf
 --------------------------------------------
```

Example 8-21   *Configuring and Applying an IP QoS ACL in Hybrid Mode (Continued)*

```
1. dscp 26 tcp any   any  eq 1720
2. dscp 26 tcp any   any  eq 1731
3. dscp 26 tcp any   any  eq 1503
4. trust-cos ip any  any
```

After verifying the ACL configuration, you can apply the ACL to the desired port or VLAN interface. This is accomplished by issuing the command **set qos acl map** {*ACL_name*} {{*mod/port*} | {*VLAN*}}. In the example, the ACL is mapped to a port. Recall that to successfully map the ACL to the desired port, the port must be set for port-based QoS. After the ACL has been successfully mapped to the desired port or interface, you can confirm the configuration with **show qos acl map** {**runtime** | **config**} {*ACL_name* | **all** |*mod/port*| *VLAN*}.

```
hybrid (enable) set qos acl map VideoConf 4/2
ACL VideoConf is successfully mapped to port 4/2.
hybrid (enable) show qos acl map config VideoConf
QoS ACL mappings on rx side:
ACL name                            Type Vlans
-----------------------------       ---- -------------------------------
VideoConf                           IP
ACL name                            Type Ports
-----------------------------       ---- -------------------------------
VideoConf                           IP 4/2
```

Finally, because the ACL has been created, committed to hardware, and applied to the desired port, it is possible to verify that the configured behavior is the desired behavior. The verification is based on the port's QoS configuration information. **show qos info** yields the following results:

```
hybrid (enable) show qos info config 4/2
QoS setting in NVRAM:
QoS is enabled
Policy Source of port 4/2: COPS
Tx port type of port 4/2 : 1p2q2t
Rx port type of port 4/2 : 1p1q4t
Interface type: port-based
ACL attached: VideoConf
The qos trust type is set to untrusted.
Default CoS = 2
(text omitted)
```

As displayed in the output, the port is configured for port-based QoS, and the QoS trust type is set to untrusted. Also the show command verifies that an ACL named VideoConf is attached to the port and that the default port CoS is 2. You may recognize behavior described in Table 8-10. Although all traffic arriving on port 4/2 is assigned the default CoS and forwarded directly to the PFC, because of the attached ACL and **dscp** keyword, all traffic destined to TCP ports 1720, 173, and 1503 are marked with DSCP 26. This behavior is attributed to the ingress port trust being set to untrusted. Furthermore, because the desire is to maintain the default CoS setting, it is necessary to configure the additional ACE with the **trust-cos** keyword. If the ACE is not included, all traffic not matching the first ACE is matched by the default IP ACL and assigned a DSCP value of zero.

ACL-Based Classification and Marking in Native Mode

The concepts for classification and marking with Native mode are similar to those discussed for Hybrid mode. In conjunction with the ACLs used to classify interesting traffic, however, Native mode incorporates the use of the MQC introduced in Chapter 5. As compared to operation in Hybrid mode, Native mode has its own set of rules for marking traffic. Table 8-11 summarizes these rules.

Table 8-11 *Summary of Marking Rules in Native Mode*

Port Trust State Policy Map Keyword	untrusted	trust cos	trust precedence	trust dscp
trust cos	Port CoS value: default value (0)	Port CoS or CoS value of arriving frame[1]	Port CoS or CoS value of arriving frame[1]	Port CoS or CoS value of arriving frame[1]
trust precedence	IP precedence value of arriving frame	IP precedence value of arriving frame[1]	IP precedence value of arriving frame[1]	IP precedence value of arriving frame[1]
trust dscp	DSCP value of arriving frame	DSCP value of arriving frame[1]	DSCP value of arriving frame[1]	DSCP value of arriving frame[1]
set ip precedence	Precedence value derived from value in policy map	Port CoS or CoS value of arriving frame[1]	IP precedence value of arriving frame[1]	DSCP value of arriving frame[1]
set ip dscp	DSCP value derived from value in policy map	Port CoS or CoS value of arriving frame[1]	IP precedence value of arriving frame[1]	DSCP value of arriving frame[1]

[1]Configuration settings do not apply to WS-X6224/6248 and WS-X6324/6348 series linecards.

Similar to the behavior in Hybrid mode, when the **trust** keyword is utilized in a policy map class, and subsequently applied to an interface with the **service-policy input** statement, the trust state of the policy map class supersedes the trust state specified at the interface. Also as specified in Table 8-11, it is not possible to configure the interface trust state for WS-X6224/6248 and WS-X6324/6348 linecards. On these linecards, all ports default to the nonconfigurable untrusted state. This behavior differs slightly from options available in Hybrid mode. Also **trust cos** is not available when using these series of modules in Native mode.

Prior to 12.1(12c)E1, marking was only possible through policing. Therefore, marking required the administrator to configure a policer, which did not police but just marked priority traffic and transmitted it. With the release of 12.1(12c)E1, **set ip precedence** and **set ip dscp** were made available as actions within a class, under the policy map configuration. Therefore, for traffic arriving on an untrusted interface, it became possible to set the

IP precedence or DSCP value for incoming frames. Again, similar to the behavior demonstrated in Hybrid mode with the ACE **dscp** keyword, **set ip precedence** and **set ip dscp**, when specified, do not supersede the configured port trust state. The PFC maintains the ingress CoS, IP precedence, or DSCP value, as long as the corresponding **mls qos trust** keyword is configured at the interface.

The following example demonstrates how to classify and subsequently mark traffic using Native mode. The same criteria used in the Hybrid examples is used here. Again, the intent is to mark all traffic destined for TCP ports 1720, 1731, and 1503 with a DSCP value of 26, whereas all other traffic is marked with the default CoS setting for the interface. The first step in the QoS policy creation is creating an ACL for all relevant traffic. When configured, the ACL is then mapped to an administratively defined class map. You can verify these configuration steps with the **show access-list** and **show class-map** commands.

Example 8-22 *Configuring and Applying a QoS Policy in Native Mode*

```
native(config)# access-list 110 remark Control traffic for Video Conferencing App
native(config)# access-list 110 permit tcp any any eq 1720
native(config)# access-list 110 permit tcp any any eq 1731
native(config)# access-list 110 permit tcp any any eq 1503
native(config)# class-map match-any Control-traffic
native(config-cmap)# match access-group 110
native# show access-list 110
Extended IP access list 110
    permit tcp any any eq 1720
    permit tcp any any eq 1731
    permit tcp any any eq 1503
native# show class-map Control-traffic
 Class Map match-any Control-traffic (id 12)
   Match access-group  110


```

When the desired traffic has been identified, and referenced in a class map, that class map is then mapped to a defined policy map. In this instance, the policy map name corresponds to a broader topic, which encompasses the traffic identified in the class map. This was done to demonstrate the modular aspect of the relationship between class maps and policy maps. The policy map name chosen is VideoConf. Because there are potentially different identifiable traffic streams, you can reference multiple class maps within one policy map. Each class map, in turn, may have its own marking parameter. For this example, the actual audio and video streams can be identified and placed within their own class map and marked appropriately. Therefore, the recommendation is to name the policy map something related to the class map, but in a broader sense. Depending on how the policies are formulated, for instance, the policy map may be named after a department or after an application (such as VideoConf). In this scenario, the goal is to mark all traffic destined for TCP ports 1720, 1731, and 1503 with DSCP 26. Therefore, the **set ip dscp** {*dscp value*} command is utilized within the policy map class, along with the desired value.

```
native(config)# policy-map VideoConf
native(config-pmap)# class Control-traffic
native(config-pmap-c)# set ip dscp 26
native# show policy-map VideoConf
```

continues

Example 8-22 *Configuring and Applying a QoS Policy in Native Mode (Continued)*

```
Policy Map VideoConf
  class  Control-traffic
    set ip dscp 26
```

After the policy map parameters have been established, you must apply the QoS policy to the appropriate interface to complete the process. Here, the desired interface is Gigabit 5/ 1, and the **service-policy input** {*name*} command is configured referencing policy map VideoConf.

```
native(config)# interface gigabitEthernet 5/1
native(config-if)# service-policy input VideoConf
native# show policy-map interface gigabitEthernet 5/1
 GigabitEthernet5/1
   service-policy input: VideoConf
     class-map: Control-traffic (match-any)
       0 packets, 0 bytes
       5 minute offered rate 0 bps, drop rate 0 bps
       match: access-group 110
 (text omitted)
native# show mls qos ip ingress
 QoS Summary [IP]:     (* - shared aggregates, Mod - switch module)
 Int           Mod Dir Cl-map DSCP AgId Trust FlId   AgForward-Pk    AgPoliced-Pk
 ----------------------------------------------------------------------------
 Gi5/1             1 I Control-t 26   3   No    0             0               0
 (text omitted)
native# show queueing interface gigabitEthernet 5/1
Interface GigabitEthernet5/1 queueing strategy:  Weighted Round-Robin
  Port QoS is enabled
  Port is untrusted
  Default COS is 2
 (text omitted)
```

Finally, after the appropriate steps for MQC have been completed, you can verify behavior. As demonstrated, **show policy-map interface** {*type num*} and **show mls qos ip ingress** detail the policy map class information. Specifically, the outputs include the ACL referenced in the class map and the DSCP value used to mark all conforming traffic. Based on the information in Table 8-11, and the output extracted from **show queueing interface** {*type num*}, note that the port is configured as untrusted. This implies all traffic matching the ACL is marked with DSCP 26. Recall that **set ip dscp** overrides interfaces with an untrusted port trust state. All remaining traffic is marked with the default CoS value of 2. As mentioned previously, this configuration is possible with Cisco IOS Release 12.1(12c)E1 and later. For earlier versions, it is necessary to configure a policer to mark all desired traffic. Policing is covered later in the chapter.

Mapping

After a frame header has been forwarded from the ingress port to the switching engine, and the appropriate priority value has been established, the PFC determines an internal DSCP value for the frame. This value is used to signify how a frame is handled while it traverses the switch, and ultimately how it is scheduled upon egress. A DSCP value is applied to all frames processed by the switching engine, regardless of traffic type. This behavior is also independent of the operating system. However, the manner for configuring the tables is different between Native mode and Hybrid mode. Table 8-12 shows the default mapping values used by the 6500.

Table 8-12   *Default Mapping Values*

CoS-to-DSCP Mapping	Precedence-to-DSCP Mapping	DSCP-to-CoS Mapping
CoS 0 = DSCP 0	IP precedence 0 = DSCP 0	DSCP 0–7 = CoS 0
CoS 1 = DSCP 8	IP precedence 1 = DSCP 8	DSCP 8–15 = CoS 1
CoS 2 = DSCP 16	IP precedence 2 = DSCP 16	DSCP 16–23 = CoS 2
CoS 3 = DSCP 24	IP precedence 3 = DSCP 24	DSCP 24–31 = CoS 3
CoS 4 = DSCP 32	IP precedence 4 = DSCP 32	DSCP 32–39 = CoS 4
CoS 5 = DSCP 40	IP precedence 5 = DSCP 40	DSCP 40–47 = CoS 5
CoS 6 = DSCP 48	IP precedence 6 = DSCP 48	DSCP 48–55 = CoS 6
CoS 7 = DSCP 56	IP precedence 7 = DSCP 56	DSCP 56–63 = CoS 7

The Catalyst 6500 determines the internal DSCP value based on the trust state specified either at the port or interface level, or based on the **trust** keyword or DSCP/IP precedence value specified in an ACL. The following sections detail how the internal DSCP values are derived from the appropriate sources and how internal DSCP values map to egress CoS. These topics are covered in the following order:

- CoS-to-DSCP Mapping
- Precedence-to-DSCP Mapping
- DSCP-to-CoS Mapping
- Policed DSCP-to-Mark Down Mapping

CoS-to-DSCP Mapping

If the ingress port or interface has been configured to **trust-cos**, the internal DSCP value is derived from the arriving CoS on the 802.1q or ISL trunk. Likewise, because an ACL or policy map class supersedes the port trust state, if they are configured to trust the incoming CoS value, the internal DSCP is again derived from the inbound CoS. One caveat to consider is traffic arriving on an untrusted port. Although incoming frames are marked with the default CoS setting configured for the port or interface, in this case the internal DSCP value is derived from the default ACL. By default, the default ACL applies a DSCP value of zero. As a result, if the desire is to maintain the CoS established by the default CoS value at the interface, it is necessary to use an ACL or policy map class to trust CoS, or modify the default DSCP value in the default ACL.

```
(Hybrid)
set qos cos-dscp-map {DSCP1 DSCP2 DSCP3 DSCP4 DSCP5 DSCP6 DSCP7 DSCP8}
show qos map config cos-dscp-map
(Native)
```

```
mls qos map cos-dscp {DSCP1 DSCP2 DSCP3 DSCP4 DSCP5 DSCP6 DSCP7 DSCP8}
show mls qos map [ | begin Cos-dscp map]
```

Table 8-12 shows the default mapping settings for the CoS-to-DSCP table. To modify and verify the default or modified mapping settings for the CoS-to-DSCP table, use the preceding commands. These commands enable an administrator to map one DSCP value to a CoS value. As a result, referencing the preceding commands, {*DSCP1*} maps to CoS 0 and {*DSCP2*} maps to CoS 1. This pattern applies to all DSCP values, concluding with {*DSCP8*}, which maps to CoS 7. Examples 8-23 and 8-24 demonstrate how to modify the default mapping values in both Hybrid and Native modes, respectively.

Example 8-23 *Modifying the CoS-to-DSCP Mapping Table in Hybrid Mode*

```
hybrid (enable) set qos cos-dscp-map 56 48 40 32 24 16 8 0
QoS cos-dscp-map set successfully.
hybrid (enable) show qos map config cos-dscp-map
CoS - DSCP map:
CoS    DSCP
---    ----
  0    56
  1    48
  2    40
  3    32
  4    24
  5    16
  6    8
  7    0
```

Example 8-24 *Modifying the CoS-to-DSCP Mapping Table in Native Mode*

```
native(config)# mls qos map cos-dscp 56 48 40 32 24 16 8 0
native# show mls qos map | begin Cos-dscp map
   Cos-dscp map:
        cos:   0  1  2  3  4  5  6  7
      ------------------------------------
       dscp:  56 48 40 32 24 16  8  0
(text omitted)
```

The values mapped in the preceding examples are not recommended settings. Instead, they demonstrate the capability of the CoS-to-DSCP mapping feature. It is normally not necessary to modify the CoS-to-DSCP mapping table from its defaults. If you do make alterations, however, carefully consider how the values are mapped and propagate the modifications across the entire network for consistency. Changes performed to this table impact the performance of the DSCP-to-CoS table, which needs to be considered. When configuring the mapping feature on WS-X6224/WS-X6248 and WS-X6324/WS-X6348 linecards, additional steps are required. In Hybrid, based on limitations previously discussed, a port configured to trust CoS sustains the inbound CoS setting by applying an ACE with the **trust-cos** keyword. The switch then derives the DSCP value from the CoS of the incoming tagged frame. With Native mode, trust is not a configurable option for these modules at the port or interface level. All ports default to untrusted. As a result, to maintain the local port CoS setting and use it to derive the internal DSCP, a policy map class must be configured and applied to the applicable interface. Otherwise, the value associated with the default ACL is utilized to obtain the internal DSCP value, which is statically defined as zero.

Precedence-to-DSCP Mapping

Similar to the CoS-to-DSCP mapping, internal DSCP values can also be derived from arriving IP precedence values. The default IP precedence-to-DSCP mapping is shown in Table 8-12. Frames arriving at ports or interfaces configured with the **trust-ipprec** or **trust ip-precedence** keywords obtain their internal DSCP value from the precedence of the ingress traffic. This same feature applies to ACLs and policy map classes. The feature is also available for WS-X6224/WS-6248 and WS-X6324/WS-X6348 modules. Because this configuration is not supported at the physical interface or port level for these linecards, using either Hybrid or Native modes, however, an ACL or a policy map class must be configured. The following commands enable the administrator to modify the default mappings and verify the configuration:

```
(Hybrid)
set qos ipprec-dscp-map {DSCP1} {DSCP2} {DSCP3} {DSCP4} {DSCP5} {DSCP6} {DSCP7}
  {DSCP8}
show qos maps config ipprec-dscp-map
(Native)
mls qos map ip-prec-dscp {DSCP1} {DSCP2} {DSCP3} {DSCP4} {DSCP5} {DSCP6} {DSCP7}
  {DSCP8}
show mls qos maps [ | begin IpPrec ]
```

As seen with CoS-to-DSCP mapping, {DSCP1} is associated with IP precedence 0 and {DSCP2} corresponds with IP precedence 1. The pattern then concludes with {DSCP8}, which maps to IP precedence 7. Examples 8-25 and 8-26 demonstrate how to alter the default IP precedence-to-DSCP mapping table and how to verify the configuration.

Example 8-25 *Modifying the IP Precedence-to-DSCP Mapping Table in Hybrid Mode*

```
hybrid (enable) set qos ipprec-dscp-map 56 48 40 32 24 16 8 0
QoS ipprec-dscp-map set successfully.
hybrid (enable) show qos maps config ipprec-dscp-map
IP-Precedence - DSCP map:
IP-Prec   DSCP
-------   ----
      0   56
      1   48
      2   40
      3   32
      4   24
      5   16
      6   8
      7   0
hybrid (enable)
```

Example 8-26 *Modifying the IP Precedence-to-DSCP Mapping Table in Native Mode*

```
native(config)# mls qos map ip-prec-dscp 56 48 40 32 24 16 8 0
native# show mls qos maps | begin IpPrec
   IpPrecedence-dscp map:
      ipprec:   0  1  2  3  4  5  6  7
      -----------------------------------
         dscp:  56 48 40 32 24 16  8  0
```

Once again, the values mapped in the preceding examples are not recommended settings. They demonstrate the capability of the IP precedence-to-DSCP mapping feature. The default settings are sufficient for most instances, unless specific requirements dictate otherwise. If the default settings are modified, however, it is imperative to maintain consistency across the entire network. One example where it may be necessary to modify the default map settings is when deploying voice in the campus. For voice streams, DSCP 26 is recommended for control traffic, whereas DSCP 46 is recommended for the actual voice packets. This is critical in environments where QoS policies are implemented using DSCP values. To demonstrate this scenario, consider the network in Figure 8-7.

The Catalyst 6500 in Figure 8-7 is trunked to a Layer 2 switch, which is trusting the incoming CoS set by the IP Phones. Also two laptops configured with IP Softphone are attached directly to the Catalyst 6500. IP Softphones are capable of marking voice packets with an IP precedence of 5. The router attached to the corporate WAN implements QoS using DSCP-based policies. In this case, to ensure the proper end-to-end handling for the voice traffic, it is necessary to alter the default values in the CoS-to-DSCP and IP precedence-to-DSCP mapping tables. For both tables, CoS 3 and IP precedence 3 are mapped to DSCP 26, and CoS 5 and IP precedence 5 are mapped to DSCP 46. Modifying the mapping tables to account for the voice traffic ensures the voice streams receive the appropriate service levels when forwarded to DSCP-capable devices.

Figure 8-7   *When to Change the Default Map Settings*

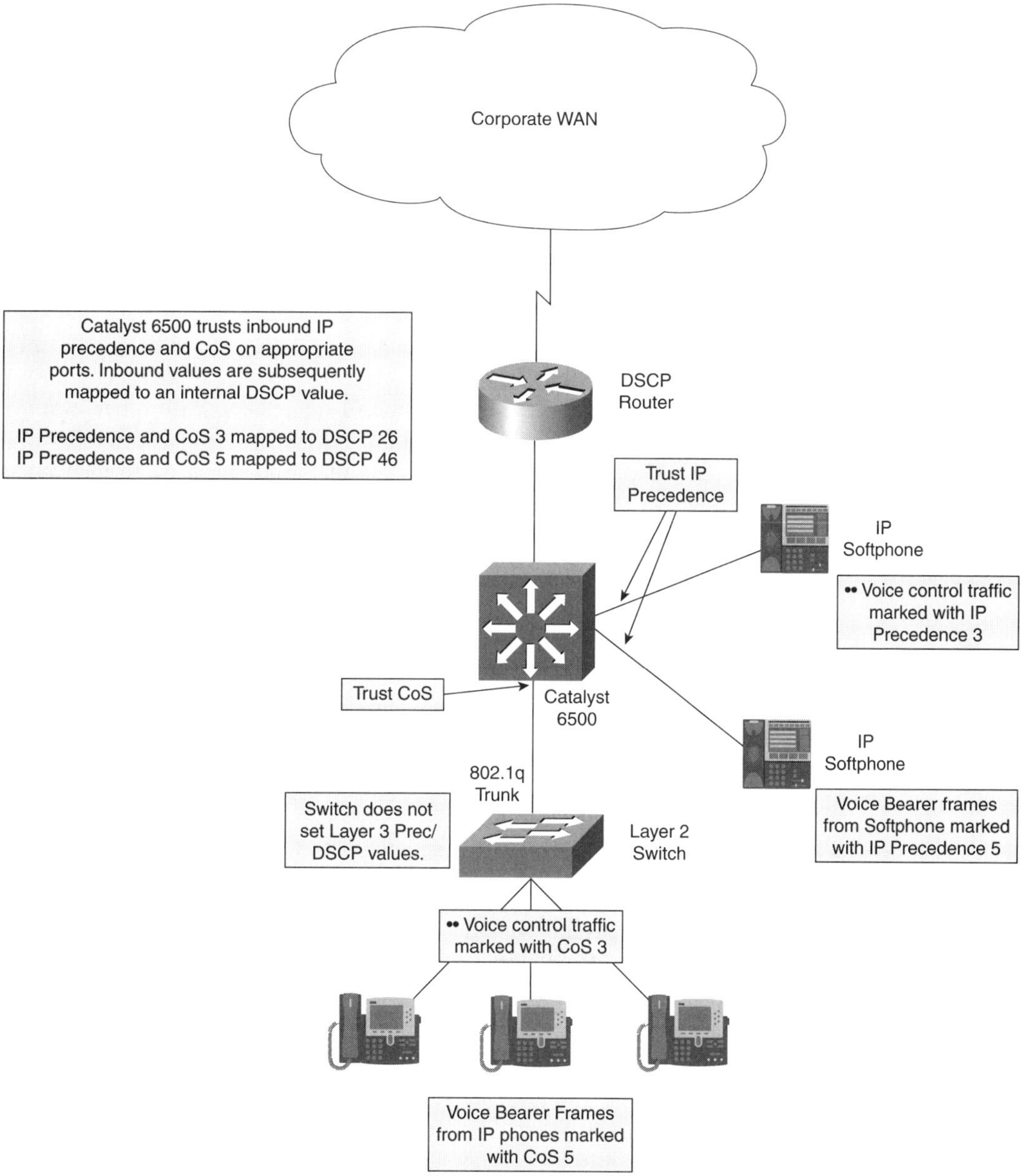

Catalyst 6500 trusts inbound IP precedence and CoS on appropriate ports. Inbound values are subsequently mapped to an internal DSCP value.

IP Precedence and CoS 3 mapped to DSCP 26
IP Precedence and CoS 5 mapped to DSCP 46

Corporate WAN

DSCP Router

Trust IP Precedence

IP Softphone

•• Voice control traffic marked with IP Precedence 3

Trust CoS

Catalyst 6500

IP Softphone

Voice Bearer frames from Softphone marked with IP Precedence 5

802.1q Trunk

Switch does not set Layer 3 Prec/ DSCP values.

Layer 2 Switch

•• Voice control traffic marked with CoS 3

Voice Bearer Frames from IP phones marked with CoS 5

Because the sources for the internal DSCP values have been determined, the discussion can now turn to how the internal DSCP values are mapped back into a frame upon egress.

DSCP-to-CoS Mapping

When the frame header is passed from the switching engine to the egress port or interface, the internal DSCP value is mapped back to a CoS value. The internal DSCP is also written to the ToS field of the Layer 3 IP header. The CoS value allows the frame to utilize the egress queue scheduling as it exits the switch. Output scheduling is covered in a later section. In addition to scheduling, if the outbound port is an ISL or 802.1q trunk, the CoS value is written into the trunk header and transmitted to the network. The CoS value is reflected in the user priority field. To modify and verify the configuration of the DSCP-to-CoS mapping table, use the following commands:

```
(Hybrid)
set qos dscp-cos-map {DSCP1 [DSCP2...DSCP64]}:{CoS}
show qos maps config dscp-cos-map
(Native)
mls qos map dscp-cos {DSCP1 [DSCP2 DSCP3 DSCP4 DSCP5 DSCP6 DSCP7 DSCP8]} to {CoS}
show mls qos map [ | begin Dscp-cos]
```

In Hybrid, a range of DSCP values can be mapped to a single CoS. If the intent is to map DSCP 24 through 35 to CoS 3, for example, the command can be configured as follows: **set qos dscp-cos-map 24-35:3**. Native mode does not permit the administrator to enter a range of values. A maximum of eight independent DSCP values can be specified per command. In addition, when entering individual DSCP values in Hybrid, you can enter multiple values; however, you must separate the values with commas. Native mode requires the DSCP values to be separated with spaces. The following two examples demonstrate how to configure the DSCP-to-CoS mapping table. They also demonstrate the differences in command syntax. Note that to demonstrate dependency, the following examples were configured to reflect the changes made to the CoS-to-DSCP mapping table in previous examples.

Example 8-27 *Modifying the DSCP-to-CoS Mapping Table in Hybrid Mode*

```
hybrid (enable) set qos dscp-cos-map 56-63:0
QoS dscp-cos-map set successfully.
hybrid (enable) set qos dscp-cos-map 48-55:1
QoS dscp-cos-map set successfully.
hybrid (enable) set qos dscp-cos-map 40-47:2
QoS dscp-cos-map set successfully.
hybrid (enable) set qos dscp-cos-map 32-39:3
QoS dscp-cos-map set successfully.
hybrid (enable) set qos dscp-cos-map 24-31:4
QoS dscp-cos-map set successfully.
hybrid (enable) set qos dscp-cos-map 16-23:5
QoS dscp-cos-map set successfully.
hybrid (enable) set qos dscp-cos-map 8-15:6
QoS dscp-cos-map set successfully.
hybrid (enable) set qos dscp-cos-map 0,2,4,6:7
QoS dscp-cos-map set successfully.
hybrid (enable) set qos dscp-cos-map 1,3,5,7:7
QoS dscp-cos-map set successfully.

hybrid (enable) show qos maps config dscp-cos-map
DSCP - CoS map:
DSCP                            CoS
```

Example 8-27 *Modifying the DSCP-to-CoS Mapping Table in Hybrid Mode (Continued)*

```
--------------------------------  ---
                            56-63  0
                            48-55  1
                            40-47  2
                            32-39  3
                            24-31  4
                            16-23  5
                             8-15  6
                              0-7  7
```

Example 8-28 *Modifying the DSCP-to-CoS Mapping Table in Native Mode*

```
native(config)# mls qos map dscp-cos 56 57 58 59 60 61 62 63 to 0
native(config)# mls qos map dscp-cos 48 49 50 51 52 53 54 55 to 1
native(config)# mls qos map dscp-cos 40 41 42 43 44 45 46 47 to 2
native(config)# mls qos map dscp-cos 32 33 34 35 36 37 38 39 to 3
native(config)# mls qos map dscp-cos 24 25 26 27 28 29 30 31 to 4
native(config)# mls qos map dscp-cos 16 17 18 19 20 21 22 23 to 5
native(config)# mls qos map dscp-cos 8 9 10 11 12 13 14 15 to 6
native(config)# mls qos map dscp-cos 0 1 2 3 4 5 6 7 to 7

native# show mls qos map | begin Dscp-cos
  Dscp-cos map:                           (dscp= d1d2)
     d1 :  d2 0  1  2  3  4  5  6  7  8  9
     -------------------------------------
      0 :     07 07 07 07 07 07 07 07 06 06
      1 :     06 06 06 06 06 06 05 05 05 05
      2 :     05 05 05 05 04 04 04 04 04 04
      3 :     04 04 03 03 03 03 03 03 03 03
      4 :     02 02 02 02 02 02 02 02 01 01
      5 :     01 01 01 01 01 01 00 00 00 00
      6 :     00 00 00 00
(text omitted)
```

Policed DSCP Mark-Down Mapping

The Catalyst 6500 has an additional feature that allows it to mark down DSCP values, based on internal policed DSCP mark-down tables. Contingent on configured policing parameters, instead of dropping out of profile frames, the mark-down table enables the administrator to define DSCP translations. This maps the previous internal DSCP value to another defined "marked-down" DSCP value for frames violating the configured policing contract. The PFC hardware version, either a PFC1 or PFC2, determines how many mark-down tables are available.

The Catalyst 6500 with a PFC1 only provides support for the single-rate policing function. As a result, the option of configuring the policed DSCP mark-down table for frames violating the normal traffic rate is available with the PFC1. On the other hand, the PFC2 provides an additional enhancement beyond what is available with the PFC1. The PFC2 can support a dual-rate policer. With the PFC2, two mark-down tables can be altered, a table for traffic violating the normal rate and streams violating the excess rate. Table 8-13 lists the default mapping values for both normal and excess rate policed DSCP mark-down tables.

Table 8-13 *Normal And Excess Rate Default Policed DSCP Mark-Down Values*

Internal DSCP	Mark-Down DSCP	Internal DSCP	Mark-Down DSCP	Internal DSCP	Mark-Down DSCP	Internal DSCP	Mark-Down DSCP
0	0	16	16	32	32	48	48
1	1	17	17	33	33	49	49
2	2	18	18	34	34	50	50
3	3	19	19	35	35	51	51
4	4	20	20	36	36	52	52
5	5	21	21	37	37	53	53
6	6	22	22	38	38	54	54
7	7	23	23	39	39	55	55
8	8	24	24	40	40	56	56
9	9	25	25	41	41	57	57
10	10	26	26	42	42	58	58
11	11	27	27	43	43	59	59
12	12	28	28	44	44	60	60
13	13	29	29	45	45	61	61
14	14	30	30	46	46	62	62
15	15	31	31	47	47	63	63

To alter how internal DSCP values are mapped to policed DSCP mark-down values, use the following commands:

```
(Hybrid)
set qos policed-dscp-map [excess-rate | normal-rate] {DSCP1 [DSCP2…DSCP64]}:{DSCP}
show qos maps config policed-dscp-map [excess-rate | normal-rate]
(Native)
mls qos map policed-dscp {max-burst | normal-burst} {DSCP1 [DSCP2 DSCP3 DSCP4 DSCP5
  DSCP6 DSCP7 DSCP8]} to {DSCP}
show mls qos map [ | begin Policed-dscp]
```

With the PFC2, the additional **excess-rate** and **normal-rate** keywords are available in Hybrid mode, and the **max-burst** and **normal-burst** keywords are available in Native mode. If neither of the keywords are specified, the configured DSCP mappings apply to the normal rate table. With the PFC1, the preceding keywords are not available.

When configuring the excess rate table on the PFC2, if changes have been made to the normal rate table, those alterations are independent from policies created for the excess rate table. This is attributed to the mark-down operation occurring after the frame has been processed through the policing function. Consider the scenario where a dual-rate policer is configured, and traffic streams violating the configured contract rates have their DSCP values marked down in both instances. If a frame violates only the normal traffic rate profile, it is marked down according to how the original internal DSCP value is mapped to other DSCP values in the normal rate table. When the same frame reaches the excess rate policer, it still possesses the original internal DSCP value. Therefore, if the frame exceeds the excess rate, the mark-down value is determined based on how the original DSCP value is mapped in the excess rate table. The following examples demonstrate how to modify and verify the policed DSCP tables in Hybrid and Native modes. Example 8-29 shows how to map DSCP 24 to DSCP 8 in the mark-down table in Hybrid, for a switch with a PFC1. Example 8-30 shows how to map DSCP 24 to DSCP 8 for the normal rate policer and DSCP 24 to DSCP 0 for the excess rate policer in Native mode.

Example 8-29 *Modifying the Policed DSCP Mark-Down Table in Hybrid Mode*

```
hybrid (enable) set qos policed-dscp-map 24:8
QoS policed-dscp-map set successfully.

hybrid (enable) show qos map config policed-dscp-map
DSCP - Policed DSCP map:
DSCP                                  Policed DSCP
--------------------------------      -----------
                              0   0
                              1   1
                              2   2
                              3   3
                              4   4
                              5   5
                              6   6
                              7   7
                           8,24   8
(text omitted)
```

Example 8-30 *Modifying the Policed DSCP Mark-Down Table in Native Mode*

```
native(config)# mls qos map policed-dscp normal-burst 24 to 8
native(config)# mls qos map policed-dscp max-burst 24 to 0

native# show mls qos map | begin Policed-dscp
  Normal Burst Policed-dscp map:                          (dscp= d1d2)
    d1 :  d2 0  1  2  3  4  5  6  7  8  9
    --------------------------------------
     0 :     00 01 02 03 04 05 06 07 08 09
     1 :     10 11 12 13 14 15 16 17 18 19
     2 :     20 21 22 23 08 25 26 27 28 29
     3 :     30 31 32 33 34 35 36 37 38 39
     4 :     40 41 42 43 44 45 46 47 48 49
     5 :     50 51 52 53 54 55 56 57 58 59
     6 :     60 61 62 63
  Maximum Burst Policed-dscp map:                         (dscp= d1d2)
```

Example 8-30 *Modifying the Policed DSCP Mark-Down Table in Native Mode (Continued)*

```
     d1 :  d2 0  1   2   3   4   5   6   7   8   9
     ----------------------------------------------
      0 :     00 01 02 03 04 05 06 07 08 09
      1 :     10 11 12 13 14 15 16 17 18 19
      2 :     20 21 22 23 00 25 26 27 28 29
      3 :     30 31 32 33 34 35 36 37 38 39
      4 :     40 41 42 43 44 45 46 47 48 49
      5 :     50 51 52 53 54 55 56 57 58 59
      6 :     60 61 62 63
(text omitted)
```

Policing

Policing is another feature available on the Catalyst 6500. Policing enables the administrator to control bandwidth utilization for certain applications. This guarantees the necessary bandwidth for voice and video and other mission-critical applications. Policing is performed in hardware on the PFC without impacting switch performance. Policing cannot occur on the 6500 platform without a PFC and is currently only supported for ingress traffic. The PFC version within the platform determines the extent of the policing functionality. The Catalyst 6500 offers both single-rate and two-rate policing.

The purpose of this section is to explain policing operation, as it pertains to the Catalyst 6500. It includes a discussion of microflow and aggregate policers, single-rate policing on the PFC1 and PFC2, and two-rate policing on the PFC2. Finally, the section includes numerous configuration examples and various show commands used to verify operation.

Microflow and Aggregate Policers

Two types of policers are available on the Catalyst 6500: microflow and aggregate policers.

Microflow policers limit the bandwidth consumed by individual flows on a port-by-port or interface basis. A flow is very specific and can be defined using Layer 3 source and destination addresses, Layer 4 protocol type, and Layer 4 source and destination port numbers. The bandwidth limitation is applied to each flow matching the criteria defined in the ACLs separately. The Catalyst 6500 can support up to 63 microflow policers.

Aggregate policers limit an aggregate of individual flows across multiple ports or interfaces, or on a single port or interface, to one specified rate. The shared aggregate policer polices all traffic to a configured rate for all ports to which the policer is applied. On the other hand, the interface aggregate policer polices all flows for each individual interface. Up to 1023 aggregate policers can be defined on the Catalyst 6500.

Consider the following example. Assume there is a microflow policer defined limiting the bandwidth consumption for certain IPTV streams to 1.5 Mbps. After the policer has been defined, it is applied to the appropriate interfaces, in this case ports 5/1 and 5/3. In this case, although one microflow policer has been defined and applied to the two separate ports, all IPTV traffic matching the configured criteria is limited to 1.5 Mbps per flow. Therefore, if one flow exists on port 5/1 and two flows exist on port 5/3, each flow is limited to 1.5 Mbps, for a combined total of 4.5 Mbps. Aggregate policers differ slightly. Consider the same situation, but now the configured policer is an aggregate policer. In this case, the combined inbound flows for port 5/1 and port 5/3 are considered and allocated a total of 1.5 Mbps. Any traffic exceeding this rate is classified as nonconforming and subsequently policed.

Figure 8-8   *Microflow Versus Aggregate Policer*

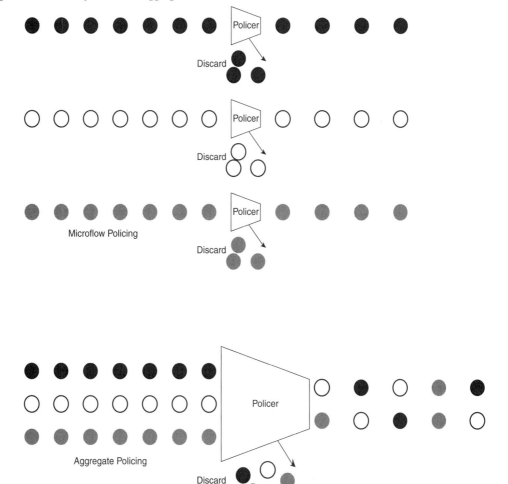

By default, microflow policing only impacts routed traffic. To police bridged traffic, **set qos bridged-microflow-policing enable** {*VLAN*} must be configured in Hybrid mode. The equivalent command for policing bridged traffic in Cisco IOS is **mls qos bridged**, which is configured under the VLAN interface.

Single-Rate Policing

Single-rate policing is supported with the PFC1 starting with Release 5.3(1) for Hybrid mode and Release 12.0(7)XE for Native mode. Release 6.1(1) for Hybrid mode and 12.1(5c)EX, and 12.1(8a)E for Native mode, introduced support for the PFC2. This is notable because the PFC2 incorporates an ASIC, allowing policing to occur at dual rates. The PFC2 offers the excess rate and burst configuration options as an additional enhancement. As a result, single-rate microflow and aggregate and two-rate aggregate policing are supported on the PFC2 with these minimum versions of code. This section focuses on the operation and configuration of the single-rate policer for Hybrid and Native modes.

The policing function on the Catalyst 6500 controls the data after it has completely entered a port and resides in the packet buffer. When the data arrives, it is compared to the QoS ACL entries configured. If the data stream matches an ACL entry that is mapped to a policer, the policer allocates one token for every data bit in the payload of the IP and IPX packets entering the switch. Sequentially, the policing function occurs after the internal DSCP value has been derived for the respective frame. If the data is not IP or IPX, the entire Layer 2 frame, as seen on the D-bus, is used by the policing counter. This includes the source and destination MAC addresses, as well as Layer 2 encapsulation, including packet padding and *cyclic redundancy check* (CRC) information. ISL and 802.1q encapsulation information is excluded. The size of the frame is important to consider when configuring the burst size. Ensure that enough tokens are available in the token bucket to sustain the maximum-sized frame processed by the policer.

NOTE   The ACLs for the policers are defined in the same manner as previously outlined. However, it is important to remember the effects the various trust keywords have on deriving the internal DSCP value. The trust keywords impact any policies defined in the policed DSCP tables.

After the switch has determined that the arriving frame meets the criteria defined in the QoS ACL, the next step is to establish whether the frame conforms or violates the configured contract. When configuring the policer, the administrator defines the type, name, rate, and burst depth.

The refresh interval, on the other hand, is already defined and fixed for the Catalyst 6500. The token bucket is refreshed every .25 ms, which equates to 4000 updates every second. The number of tokens placed into the token bucket during every interval depends on the configured contract rate. If enough tokens are present in the token bucket to accommodate an arriving frame, the data is considered conforming. As a result, no action is imposed on the frame, which is then forwarded to the egress port or interface. Because the frame was in profile, the policer is also charged the appropriate amount of tokens, equal to the size of the transmitted frame in bytes. If either policer, microflow or aggregate, determines a frame is out of profile, that frame is marked down or dropped according to the policy configured for that specific policer. If only a microflow policer is configured, the out-of-profile action is derived from the microflow policy. If only an aggregate policer is utilized, it specifies the out-of-profile action. If both policer types are defined, the most stringent decision is the one applied. The following list summarizes these rules:

- If the microflow policer returns an out-of-profile decision, mark or drop according to the microflow policing rule.

- If the aggregate policer returns an out-of-profile decision, mark or drop according to the aggregate policing rule.

- If either policer returns an out-of-profile decision, mark or drop according to the policing rule of the policer that returned the out-of-profile decision.

If both policers return an out-of-profile decision and the rule of either one is to drop, the packet is discarded; otherwise the packet is marked down and transmitted. The new DSCP value is taken from the policed DSCP mapping table. By default, frames are not marked down. They are mapped to the equivalent value. However, values can be modified by the administrator, and customized to meet specific network requirements. As demonstrated earlier, the mapping table is applied globally to the switch. For further information, refer to the section on mapping. Neither the microflow nor the aggregate policer is charged for the packet if either one returns a policing decision.

A Theoretical Example of Policing Behavior

As discussed, tokens in the token bucket are replenished at a regular fixed interval. The rate at which tokens are placed into the bucket is once every .25 ms. As a result, every second has 4000 refresh intervals. During every .25-ms interval, (.00025(s) * rate(bps)) tokens are placed into the bucket. If 10 Mbps is the configured rate, 2500 tokens are placed into the token bucket every .25 ms, assuming tokens need to be replaced. All tokens exceeding the capacity of the bucket are discarded. When selecting a burst size, it is important to ensure it is configured to be equal to or higher than the desired policing rate.

If you set the rate to 10 Mbps, an acceptable bucket depth, based solely on rate, is as follows:

$$10,000,000 \text{ (bps)} * .25 \text{ (ms)} = 2500, \text{ which you would round up to 3 kb}$$

However, packets that are transmitted through the network are never fixed in size; instead, they vary in length. The possibility exists that a maximum frame size (1518 bytes) can occur at any interval. Therefore, the burst size must be at least equal to the average or largest packet size. Consider the following example to demonstrate the behavior of the policer.

In this scenario

Time = .25 ms; therefore the following example represents 10 refresh cycles.

Assume there is a 100-Mbps interface, and the intent is to police all ingress traffic for the port down to 10 Mbps, and drop all traffic in excess of this rate. The bucket starts at full capacity, and the bucket depth is configured to 13 kb, which accounts for large packets arriving on the interface (1518 * 8 = 12144; rounded = 13000). This results in the following configuration:

```
set qos policer aggregate Test rate 10000 burst 13 drop
or
mls qos aggregate-policer Test 10000000 1625 violate-action drop
```

Table 8-14   *Operation of Aggregate Policer*

Time	Packet Size (Bytes)	Tokens Added*	Token Bucket Size (Bits)	Tokens Removed (Bits)	Final Bucket Size	
0	0	0	13000	0	13000	
1	751	0	13000	6008	6992	
2	600	2500	9492	4800	4692	
3	950	2500	7192	0	7192	<--policed
At t=3 No tokens are removed from the bucket, because there are not enough tokens to handle the entire packet. As a result, a packet arriving at t=3 is dropped due to policing.						
4	700	2500	9692	5600	4092	
5	830	2500	6592	0	6592	<--policed
At t=5 the ingress packet is dropped due to policing.						
6	1050	2500	9092	8400	692	
7	450	2500	3192	0	3192	<--policed
8	675	2500	5692	5400	292	
9	350	2500	2792	0	2792	<--policed
10	725	2500	5292	0	5292	<--policed

*Note No tokens are added at t=1 because the token bucket is at full capacity.

Due to the flow-control mechanisms utilized by TCP, the burst parameter setting based on the calculation demonstrated in the example is too low. The result is a "sawtooth" effect seen when TCP attempts to achieve line rate. The policer throttles the TCP stream by dropping frames, causing TCP to initialize its slow start mechanism. As a result, the average rate achieved by the TCP session is considerably lower than the configured rate for the policer. Therefore, when policing TCP streams, as an initial step, it is recommended to double the burst parameter (2 * burst) to effectively police at the configured rate. As described section "Burst Size" in Chapter 7, "Advanced QoS Features Available on the Catalyst 4000 IOS Family of Switches and the Catalyst G-L3 Family of Switches," if the round-trip time is known for a particular TCP stream, that value can be used to determine a burst value. Therefore, the preceding formula can be substituted with (2 * RTT * rate) to determine a baseline burst value. However, it is important to consider that policing is not designed or intended to be application-friendly. Policing either transmits a conforming frame, or polices based on the configured contract. The (2 * burst) or (2 * RTT * rate) recommendation is meant to be only a starting point. To obtain the desired results, you may have to further modify the burst parameter after observing the behavior of the traffic,

Configuring the Single-Rate Policer

To configure and verify single-rate policing in Hybrid and Native modes, use the following commands:

```
(Hybrid)
set qos policer {microflow | aggregate} {name} rate {rate} burst {burst} {policed-
dscp | drop}
show qos policer {config | runtime} {all | aggregate | microflow} [name]
show qos statistics { l3stats | {aggregate-policer [name]}}
```

```
(Native)
mls qos aggregate-policer {name} {rate} [{burst}] violate-action {drop | policed-
dscp-transmit | transmit}
police aggregate {name}
show mls qos aggregate-policer [name]
show mls qos ip {type num}
```

When the aggregate policer is configured in Native mode, the command is applied under the policy map class. The aggregate policer is referenced by configuring **police aggregate** {*name*}. The {*name*} parameter can be up to 31 characters long and is case sensitive. The policer name may include a–z, A–Z, 0–9, the dash character (-), the underscore character (_), and the period character (.). Policer names must start with an alphabetic character. They must also be unique across all microflow and aggregate policers. Keywords cannot be utilized from any command as a policer name.

The valid range for the rate and erate parameters is 32 kbps through 32 Gbps, for Hybrid. For Native mode, the maximum rate is 4 Gbps. To classify all traffic as out of profile, set the rate parameter to zero (0). Although the range is consistent, the values are inputted slightly different between operating systems. In Hybrid mode, rate is entered in kbps. As a result, if the desired rate were 1 Mbps, the configured value would be 1000. For Native mode the rate is configured in bps. Therefore, 1 Mbps is configured as 1000000. Table 8-15 lists some of the rate values and levels of granularity for the various ranges.

Table 8-15   *Rate Configuration Table*

Rate Range	Granularity	Rate Range	Granularity
1 to 1024 (1 Mbps)	32768 (32 kbps)	65537 to 131072 (128 Mbps)	4194304 (4 Mbps)
1025 to 2048 (2 Mbps)	65536 (64 kbps)	131073 to 262144 (256 Mbps)	8388608 (8 Mbps)
2049 to 4096 (4 Mbps)	131072 (128 kbps)	262145 to 524288 (512 Mbps)	16777216 (16 Mbps)

Table 8-15 *Rate Configuration Table (Continued)*

Rate Range	Granularity	Rate Range	Granularity
4097 to 8192 (8 Mbps)	262144 (256 kbps)	524289 to 1048576 (1 Gbps)	33554432 (32 Mbps)
8193 to 16384 (16 Mbps)	524288 (512 kbps)	1048577 to 2097152 (2 Gbps)	67108864 (64 Mbps)
16385 to 32768 (32 Mbps)	1048576 (1 Mbps)	2097153 to 4194304 (4 Gbps)	134217728 (128 Mbps)
32769 to 65536 (64 Mbps)	2097152 (2 Mbps)	4194305 to 8000000 (8 Gbps)	268435456 (256 Mbps)

Within each range, the hardware is configured with rate values that are multiples of the granularity values. The valid range for the burst parameters is 1 kb through 32 Mb. Again, the burst values are configured slightly different depending on the operating system. With Hybrid, burst is entered in *kilobits* (kb), whereas Native mode configures the burst in *bytes* (B). To maintain consistent QoS results, when applying a single policer to multiple ports, standardize the trust state across all affected ports.

Notice the previous commands do not include configuration for the microflow policer in Native mode. Unlike the aggregate policer, which is configured in global configuration mode, the microflow policer is entered using the MQC. To enable microflow policing in Native mode, **mls qos flow-policing** must be enabled in global configuration mode. By default, microflow policing is globally enabled in Native mode. You can verify this by issuing the command **show mls qos**. In addition to the microflow policer, it is also possible to configure a per-interface aggregate policer. Native mode offers the option of configuring two different aggregate policers. The previously defined aggregate policer behaves the same as the policer defined in Hybrid mode. The per-interface aggregate policer, on the other hand, applies to ingress traffic only on the port to which it is applied. Both the microflow and per-interface aggregate policers are configured under the policy map class using the following commands:

```
(Native IOS)
(Microflow Policer)
police flow {rate} [{burst}] [conform-action {drop | set-dscp-transmit {DSCP} | set-
  prec-transmit{prec} | transmit}] [exceed-action {drop | policed-dscp-transmit |
  transmit}]
(Aggregate Policer)
police {rate} [{burst}] [conform-action {drop | set-dscp-transmit {DSCP} | set-
  prec-transmit{prec} | transmit}] [exceed-action {drop | policed-dscp-transmit |
  transmit}]
```

As mentioned in the "Classification And Marking" section, prior to 12.1(12c)E1 **set ip precedence** and **set ip dscp** were not available options. As a result, to mark incoming traffic, a policer was required. Marking is accomplished using the **conform-action** option. Under this configuration option, it is possible to modify a frame's existing DSCP or IP precedence value. The frame is then forwarded to the appropriate egress port and scheduled according to the CoS derived from the new DSCP setting. The following examples demonstrate how to configure single-rate policing in both Hybrid and Native mode. The intent of these examples is to demonstrate policing lower-priority applications, ensuring sufficient bandwidth exists for mission-critical applications, particularly voice and video.

In the Hybrid mode example provided, an aggregate policer controls bandwidth consumption for web traffic. Web traffic is limited to 1 Mbps. All HTTP traffic exceeding the normal rate is dropped. Figure 8-9 shows the example configured in Hybrid mode. In the Native example, the same match criteria and limitations apply. In this instance, however, a microflow policer is used. Figure 8-10 shows the example configured for Native mode. To demonstrate the behavior of the different policers, a traffic generator is configured. The generator is attached via Fast Ethernet to the port to which the policer is applied. Three separate flows are created on the traffic generator, each destined for TCP port 80. In addition, each flow is set to generate packets at a rate of 2 Mbps, for a total of 6 Mbps.

Figure 8-9   *Single-Rate Aggregate Policer*

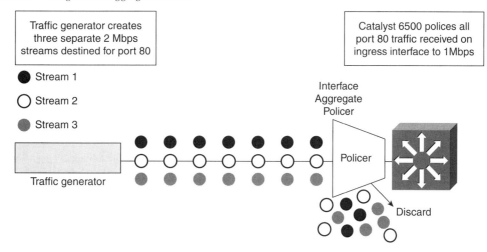

Example 8-31   *Configuring a Single-Rate Aggregate Policer in Hybrid Mode with a PFC2*

```
hybrid (enable) set qos policer aggregate HTTP-police rate 1000 burst 13 drop
QoS policer for aggregate HTTP-police updated successfully.
Rate is set to 992, erate is set to 992 burst is set to 13 and eburst is set to 13
   in hard
ware due to hardware granularity.
hybrid (enable) set qos acl ip HTTP-traffic dscp 0 aggregate HTTP-police tcp any any
   eq www
HTTP-traffic editbuffer modified. Use 'commit' command to apply changes.
hybrid (enable) commit qos acl HTTP-traffic
QoS ACL 'HTTP-traffic' successfully committed.
hybrid (enable) set qos acl map HTTP-traffic 5/10
ACL HTTP-traffic is successfully mapped to port 5/10.
```

continues

Example 8-31 *Configuring a Single-Rate Aggregate Policer in Hybrid Mode with a PFC2 (Continued)*

The first step is to define the policer with the appropriate parameters. Although 1 Mbps is the configured rate, the value is rounded down to the closest 32-kbps increment to conform to the hardware granularity for this particular range. Next, to account for the largest potential frame size (1518 bytes), the value 13000 is chosen for the burst. The policer is then applied to the appropriate ACL. When the ACL is applied to the desired port, it is necessary to verify configuration and performance.

```
hybrid (enable) show qos info config 5/10
QoS setting in NVRAM:
QoS is enabled
Policy Source of port 5/10: COPS
Tx port type of port 5/10 : 2q2t
Rx port type of port 5/10 : 1q4t
Interface type: port-based
ACL attached: HTTP-traffic
The qos trust type is set to untrusted.
Default CoS = 1
(text omitted)
```

Based on the **show qos info** output for port 5/10, it is confirmed the interface is set for port-based QoS. Also the ACL HTTP traffic has been applied. Further, note that the port has been left at the default untrusted state. As discussed in the previous sections, frames arriving on port 5/10 are marked with the port default CoS. Given this scenario, however, this value is overwritten. Remember, the internal DSCP value is derived from the default ACL, which equates to DSCP 0. Fortunately, because the port is untrusted, even if the default ACL DSCP value was modified, all traffic matching the ACL configured in the example is set to DSCP 0.

```
hybrid (enable) show qos policer config aggregate HTTP-police
QoS aggregate policers:
Aggregate name                      Avg. rate (kbps) Burst size (kb) Normal action
------------------------------- --------------- --------------- -------------
HTTP-police                                      1000              13 policed-dscp
                                Excess rate (kbps) Excess burst size (kb) Excess action
----------------- ----------------------- -------------
                                        1000                     13 drop
                                ACL attached
                                ------------------------------------
                                HTTP-traffic
```

show qos policer verifies the configuration for the defined policer HTTP-police. Notice that because the single-rate policer is configured on a Catalyst 6500 equipped with a PFC2, excess rate and burst are visible fields. Because the excess rate and burst are equal to the normal rate and burst, however, the excess policing feature is not invoked.

```
hybrid (enable) show qos statistics aggregate-policer HTTP-police
QoS aggregate-policer statistics:
Aggregate policer               Allowed packet Packets exceed Packets exceed
                                count          normal rate    excess rate
------------------------------- --------------- --------------- --------------
HTTP-police                               42768         208811         208811
```

Finally, reviewing **show qos statistics** for the aggregate policer reveals the desired performance. In total, 251,579 packets were forwarded to the port. This is confirmed by adding the total number of packets exceeding the excess rate (208,811) to the total number of packets conforming to the policing contract (42,768). When the percentage of conforming packets is computed (42,768 / 25,1579), it is evident the aggregate policer is operating as expected. Approximately, 1/6th of the total traffic conforms to the specified rate. The next example demonstrates the configuration and behavior of a microflow policer in Native mode.

Figure 8-10 *Single-Rate Microflow Policer*

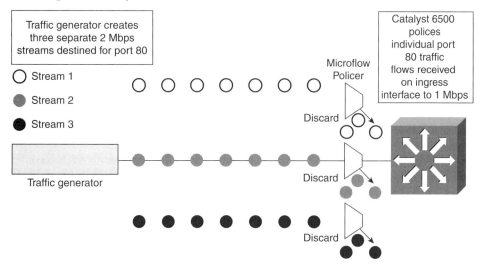

Example 8-32 *Configuring a Single-Rate Microflow Policer in Native Mode with a PFC2*

```
native(config)# mls qos flow-policing
native(config)# access-list 101 permit tcp any any eq www
native(config)# class-map HTTP-traffic
native(config-cmap)# match access-group 101
native(config)# policy-map HTTP-police
native(config-pmap)# class HTTP-traffic
native(config-pmap-c)# police flow 1000000 2000
```

After the interesting traffic has been defined, in addition to the class maps and policy maps, the results are applied to the appropriate interface with the command **service-policy input** {*name*}. At this point, the policer is now operational.

```
native# show mls qos ip fastEthernet 6/10
   [In] Policy map is HTTP-police   [Out] Default.
 QoS Summary [IP]:      (* - shared aggregates, Mod - switch module)
 Int            Mod Dir Cl-map DSCP AgId Trust FlId   AgForward-Pk   AgPoliced-Pk
 ----------------------------------------------------------------------------
 Fa6/10          1 I HTTP-traf  0    3*  dscp   2       682858                0
native# show mls ip detail
Displaying Netflow entries in Supervisor Earl
DstIP          SrcIP          Prot:SrcPort:DstPort  Src i/f:AdjPtr
 ----------------------------------------------------------------------------
 20.20.20.2     192.168.10.1   tcp :www    :www     0    : 0
 20.20.20.1     192.168.20.1   tcp :www    :www     0    : 0
 20.20.20.3     192.168.30.1   tcp :www    :www     0    : 0
```

continues

Example 8-32 *Configuring a Single-Rate Microflow Policer in Native Mode with a PFC2 (Continued)*

```
Pkts        Bytes       Age   LastSeen  Attributes
-------------------------------------------------------
62605       30426030    273   15:07:31  L3 - Dynamic
62675       30460050    273   15:07:31  L2 - Dynamic
62677       30461022    273   15:07:31  L2 - Dynamic
    QoS     Police Count Threshold   Leak      Drop Bucket  Use-Tbl Use-Enable
-----------+------------+---------+----------+----+--------+-------+----------+
    0x0       60278         0          0       NO   1798      NO       NO
    0x0       60207         0          0       NO   1857      NO       NO
    0x0       60206         0          0       NO   1640      NO       NO
```

Two-Rate Policing

The PFC2 provides additional policing enhancements beyond the capabilities of the PFC1. The PFC2 is capable of aggregate policing at dual rates. Dual-rate aggregate policing was introduced for the Catalyst 6500 in CatOS Software Release 6.1(1) and in Cisco IOS Release 12.1(8a)E. In addition to the traditional normal rate and normal burst size, the PFC2 introduces an excess rate and an excess burst for the policer. With this configuration, the drop indication applies to the excess rate, as opposed to the normal rate. Packets exceeding the normal rate are always marked down, unless they also exceed the excess rate. If they exceed the excess rate, the packets are either marked down or dropped, depending on the administratively defined policy. Figure 8-11 shows the operation of the two-rate policer.

Figure 8-11 *Two-Rate Policer*

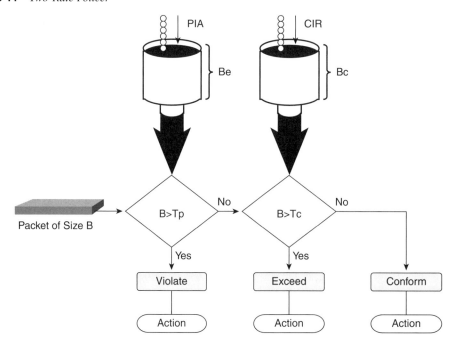

To complement the policing enhancements offered by the PFC2, there are now two policed DSCP map tables corresponding to each rate for marking down out-of-profile packets, as demonstrated in the previous mapping section. Operation of the two-rate policer on the Catalyst 6500 is analogous to the "two-rate three-color marker" described in IETF RFC 2698. As depicted in Figure 8-11, the two-rate policer adds a second bucket to the operation. Similar to the single-rate policer, both buckets use a token bucket mechanism; however, each bucket operates independently of the other. The following commands are used to configure and verify operation for the two-rate policer on the Catalyst 6500 with a PFC2:

```
(Hybrid)
set qos policer aggregate {name} rate {rate normal} policed-dscp erate {rate excess}
   {policed-dscp | drop} burst {burst normal} eburst {burst excess}
show qos policer {config | runtime} {{aggregate [name]} | all}
show qos statistics { l3stats | {aggregate-policer [name]}}
                64
(Native)
mls qos aggregate-policer {name} {rate CIR} [burst CIR] [burst PIR] pir {rate PIR}
   [[conform-action {drop | set-dscp-transmit {DSCP} | set-prec-transmit {prec} |
   transmit}] [exceed-action{drop | policed-dscp-transmit | transmit}] [violate-action
   {drop | policed-dscp-transmit |transmit}]]
police aggregate {name}
police {rate CIR} [[burst CIR] [burst PIR]] pir {rate PIR} [[conform-action {drop |
   set-dscp-transmit {DSCP} | set-prec-transmit {prec} | transmit}] [exceed-action {
   drop | set-dscp-transmit {DSCP} | set-prec-transmit {prec} | policed-dscp-transmit |
   transmit}] [violate-action {drop | policed-dscp-transmit | transmit}]]
show mls qos
show mls qos aggregate-policer [name]
show mls qos ip {type num}
```

For Native mode, two aggregate policers are depicted. Recall from configuring the single-rate policer, **mls qos aggregate-policer**, when applied to multiple ports through a policy map class, polices all ports to the specified rate. The alternative aggregate policer polices traffic to the configured rate on a per-port basis. Within either aggregate policer, the normal rate, or *committed information rate* (CIR), determines how many tokens are placed in the bucket every .25 ms. The excess rate, or *peak information rate* (PIR), determines how many tokens are placed into the excess bucket based on the same frequency. Both token buckets operate independently of each other.

Unlike the single-rate policer, which offers two policing actions, the two-rate policer provides support for a third policing action. These three policing actions correspond to the green, yellow, and red transactions detailed in RFC 2698.

The first policing action matches all traffic conforming to the normal and excess policing rates. Because the packets conform to both rates, no action is required from the switch. In Hybrid, the switch maintains the existing QoS parameters assigned to the packet, which is forwarded to the egress scheduler. In Native mode, the option exists to transmit the conforming packet, assign a new IP precedence or DSCP value, or drop the packet. If the **drop** keyword is specified for the **conform-action**, the **exceed-action** and **violate-action** are automatically configured to **drop**.

The second policing action adheres to traffic exceeding the normal rate, but conforming to the excess rate. In Hybrid mode, packets exceeding the normal rate, but conforming to the excess, rate are marked down based on the normal rate policed DSCP table. In Native mode, the administrator can instruct the policing logic to drop, mark down, or forward traffic matching the criteria for the second policing action. In addition, in Native mode, the per-port aggregate policer also allows a new DSCP or IP precedence value to be assigned. The **drop** keyword is not available in Hybrid for traffic conforming to the excess rate, but violating the normal rate. In Native mode, however, if the **drop** keyword is specified, the resulting behavior can be compared to the single-rate policer.

The third policing action defines the policy applied to all traffic violating the normal and excess rates. For Hybrid and Native modes, packets can either be dropped or marked and forwarded with a policed DSCP value. In addition, Native mode provides the **transmit** keyword as an option for violating traffic. When defining the policing policies for the three different policing levels, subsequent policing policies cannot be less stringent than previously defined policies. If the **policed-dscp-transmit** keyword is specified for the **exceed-action**, for example, **transmit** cannot be specified for the **violate-action**. The configured action must be equal or more severe.

With the release of CatOS 7.2 and later versions, the **eburst** parameter is configured independently of the **burst** parameter. This provides additional autonomy when configuring the **burst** parameters. Prior to the 7.2 release, the administrator is limited to only configuring the **burst** option. The **eburst** value is derived from the **burst** value. The **burst** and **eburst** values define the bucket depth for the respective token buckets. The two token buckets, controlled by the policing ASIC on the PFC, operate independently of each other. Tokens configured for the normal bucket are only allocated to packets conforming to the normal rate, whereas tokens configured for the excess bucket are only allocated to packets conforming to the excess rate. Tokens from the two buckets cannot be combined to service a packet. Enough tokens must be present in either bucket to service an entire packet. If the optional **eburst** value is not explicitly configured, the burst size is set to the same value for both normal and excess rate policers.

When configuring the two-rate policer, ensure the configured burst values are at least equal to the average or largest serviced packet size. In addition, set the excess rate value to be greater than or equal to the normal rate. If the two policing rates are configured equally, the resulting behavior is a single-rate policer. In this situation, although there are two separate token buckets, one for normal rate and the other for excess rate, both buckets are charged for a successfully transmitted packet. Therefore, if a packet arrives, which does not exceed the normal rate, and the normal rate equals the excess rate, tokens amounting to the size of the packet are depleted from both buckets. The following examples demonstrate configuring an aggregate two-rate policer in Hybrid and Native modes.

Example 8-33 *Configuring an Aggregate Two-Rate Policer in Hybrid Mode*

```
hybrid (enable) set qos policer aggregate HTTP-police rate 1000 policed-dscp erate
  2000 drop burst 13 eburst 13
QoS policer for aggregate HTTP-police updated successfully.
Rate is set to 992, erate is set to 1984 burst is set to 13 and eburst is set to 13
  in hardware due to hardware granularity.
```

Example 8-33 *Configuring an Aggregate Two-Rate Policer in Hybrid Mode (Continued)*

```
hybrid (enable) set qos acl ip HTTP-traffic dscp 0 aggregate HTTP-police tcp any any
    eq www
HTTP-traffic editbuffer modified. Use 'commit' command to apply changes.
hybrid (enable) commit qos acl HTTP-traffic
QoS ACL 'HTTP-traffic' successfully committed.
hybrid (enable) set qos acl map HTTP-traffic 5/10
ACL HTTP-traffic is successfully mapped to port 5/10.
hybrid (enable) show qos info config 5/10
QoS setting in NVRAM:
QoS is enabled
Policy Source of port 5/10: COPS
Tx port type of port 5/10 : 2q2t
Rx port type of port 5/10 : 1q4t
Interface type: port-based
ACL attached: HTTP-traffic
The qos trust type is set to untrusted.
Default CoS = 1
(text omitted)

hybrid (enable) show qos policer config aggregate HTTP-police
QoS aggregate policers:
Aggregate name                       Avg. rate (kbps) Burst size (kb) Normal action
------------------------------- ---------------- --------------- -------------
HTTP-police                                      1000             13 policed-dscp
                                Excess rate (kbps) Excess burst size (kb) Excess action
                                ---------------- ---------------------- -------------
                                                 2000                   13 drop
                                ACL attached
                                -----------------------------------
                                HTTP-traffic
hybrid (enable) show qos statistics l3stats
Packets dropped due to policing:         212586
IP packets with ToS changed:               1276
IP packets with CoS changed:             150636
Non-IP packets with CoS changed:              0
hybrid (enable) show qos statistics aggregate-policer HTTP-police
QoS aggregate-policer statistics:
Aggregate policer               Allowed packet Packets exceed Packets exceed
                                count          normal rate    excess rate
------------------------------- -------------- -------------- --------------
HTTP-police                         109443         205768         212586
```

Example 8-34 *Configuring an Aggregate Two-Rate Policer in Native Mode*

```
native(config)# access-list 101 permit tcp any any eq www
native(config)# class-map HTTP-traffic
native(config-cmap)# match access-group 101
native(config)# policy-map HTTP-police
native(config-pmap)# class HTTP-traffic
native(config-pmap-c)# police 1000000 2000 2000 pir 2000000 conform-action transmit
  exceed-action policed-dscp-transmit violate-action drop
native# show mls qos
```

Example 8-34 *Configuring an Aggregate Two-Rate Policer in Native Mode (Continued)*

```
  QoS is enabled globally
  Microflow policing is enabled globally
(text omitted)
----- Module [1] -----
  QoS global counters:
    Total packets: 291876
    IP shortcut packets: 0
    Packets dropped by policing: 297504
    IP packets with TOS changed by policing: 151
    IP packets with COS changed by policing: 282786
    Non-IP packets with COS changed by policing: 0
native# show mls qos ip fastEthernet 6/10
  [In] Policy map is HTTP-police   [Out] Default.
 QoS Summary [IP]:      (* - shared aggregates, Mod - switch module)
 Int           Mod Dir Cl-map DSCP AgId Trust FlId  AgForward-Pk  AgPoliced-Pk
 ----------------------------------------------------------------------------
 Fa6/10          1 I HTTP-traf  0    2   dscp   0        153203        297504
```

Congestion Management and Congestion Avoidance

After a frame has been classified, processed through all the applicable QoS policies, and a forwarding decision has been made, the frame is then forwarded to the appropriate egress queue. At the transmit interface, the Catalyst 6500 employs congestion management and congestion avoidance features to ensure priority traffic has precedence when accessing the network during periods of link oversubscription. Deeper buffers and more complex queuing mechanisms are normally found at egress interfaces. This is because during peak traffic periods congestion is more common at these points. Congestion within the campus LAN is attributed to link-speed mismatches and to aggregation points within the network. Although input scheduling ensures certain critical traffic is given priority to the switch bus or fabric, congestion upon ingress is not a common occurrence and does not provide guarantees to traffic exiting the switch. Because it is more common to have either a single Gigabit Ethernet connection flowing downstream to a single Fast Ethernet connection, or 24 to 48 Fast Ethernet connections flowing upstream to a single Gigabit Ethernet connection, it is imperative to ensure mission-critical applications and voice traffic are guaranteed access to the network at these points, minimizing the end-to-end latency and jitter. For these examples, the switch backplane does not serve as a bottleneck for the network traffic; instead, the bottleneck is the outbound interface. As a result, it is more efficient and critical to properly deploy congestion management and congestion avoidance techniques at the egress interface. Table 8-16 summarizes some of the egress congestion management and congestion avoidance port capabilities.

Table 8-16 *Congestion Management and Avoidance Mechanisms per Module*

Module	Transmit Ports	Supports WRED	Priority Queue	Number of WRR Queues
WS-X6024	2q2t	No	No	2
WS-X6148	2q2t	No	No	2
WS-X6224	2q2t	No	No	2
WS-X6248	2q2t	No	No	2
WS-X6316	1p2q2t	Yes	Yes	2
WS-X6324	2q2t	No	No	2
WS-X6348	2q2t	No	No	2
WS-X6408	2q2t	No	No	2
WS-X6408A	1p2q2t	Yes	Yes	2
WS-X6416	1p2q2t	Yes	Yes	2
WS-X6501	1p2q1t	Yes	Yes	2
WS-X6502	1p2q1t	Yes	Yes	2
WS-X6516	1p2q2t	Yes	Yes	2
WS-X6524	1p3q1t	Yes	Yes	3
WS-X6548	1p3q1t	Yes	Yes	3
WS-X6816	1p2q2t	Yes	Yes	2

Congestion management on the 6500 involves associating different CoS levels with the available transmit queues on the egress port. It also pertains to how the various transmit queues are scheduled and the frequency they are serviced. Figure 8-2 depicts the various congestion management and congestion avoidance features available at the output port. The Catalyst 6500 utilizes *weighted round-robin* (WRR) as an output scheduling mechanism between the various queues. Congestion avoidance allows the switch to monitor and manage the buffer utilization within the queue. The Catalyst 6500 implements two congestion avoidance mechanisms, tail drop and WRED.

The purpose of this section is to cover the various congestion management and congestion avoidance techniques available within the Catalyst 6500. Congestion management focuses on mapping CoS values to transmit queues and thresholds, configuring output queue scheduling WRR weighting factors, and configuring the transmit queue size ratio. The section concludes with congestion avoidance strategies, including configuring tail-drop thresholds for transmit queues and configuring WRED thresholds for transmit queues. Throughout the discussion, examples are provided demonstrating the necessary configuration steps and behavior for Hybrid and Native modes.

Congestion Management

As was the case with the input queues and scheduling, output scheduling and congestion management is accomplished using individual port ASICs. Also similar to input scheduling, the Catalyst 6500 utilizes CoS values to determine which transmit queue a departing frame is assigned. As demonstrated in the mapping section, the egress CoS value is derived from the internal DSCP value. In addition, at the same time the DSCP is mapped to the CoS, the ToS field in the IP header is rewritten with the internal DSCP value. As a result, upon egress the QoS setting is sustained in the Layer 2 trunk header and the Layer 3 IP packet header.

Refer back to Table 8-2, which depicts the transmit queue capabilities of the different linecards available on the Catalyst 6500. Many of the earlier 10/100 and Gigabit modules have two transmit queues, with two configurable thresholds assigned to each queue. This configuration is denoted as 2q2t. More recent Gigabit linecards incorporate an additional strict-priority queue. This queue preemptively services all frames marked with CoS 5 by default. As long as the priority queue is void of packets, the lower queues are serviced. Therefore, by default all voice traffic is sent to the priority queue and given preference over traffic in the other queues. The addition of the priority queue, in this instance, changes the transmit port type to 1p2q2t. For newer 10/100 and 100-Mb modules, the queue structure differs slightly. These cards have four queues, one strict-priority queue and three normal queues. In this instance, however, each queue only utilizes one WRED threshold. This port type is represented by 1p3q1t. Finally, the 10 Gigabit linecards offer yet another transmit port type. Specified as 1p2q1t, these port types support strict-priority queuing and two normal queues, each with one WRED threshold.

Mapping CoS Values to Transmit Queues and Thresholds

After the linecard queuing structure has been determined, it is possible to modify how the CoS values are mapped to the various queues. Table 8-17 displays the default CoS distribution across the various transmit queues.

NOTE   To verify the queuing capabilities of a specific port or interface, issue the **show port capabilities** {*mod* [*/port*]} in Hybrid or **show interface capabilities** [**module** {*mod#*}] in Native mode.

Table 8-17   *Default CoS Queue Assignments for Egress Port Types*

CoS Values	Transmit Queue
Default Queue Assignments:	
2q2t Port Types	
0–1	1 Threshold 1
2–3	1 Threshold 2

Table 8-17 *Default CoS Queue Assignments for Egress Port Types (Continued)*

4–5	2 Threshold 1
6–7	2 Threshold 2
Default Queue Assignments: **1p2q2t and 1p2q1t Port Types**	
0–1	1 Threshold 1
2–3	1 Threshold 2
4,6	2 Threshold 1
7	2 Threshold 2
5	3
Default Queue Assignments: **1p3q1t Port Types**	
0–1	1
2–4	2
6–7	3
5	4

As mentioned, the CoS values mapped to the various queues are derived from the internal DSCP values used as the frame traverses the switch. The DSCP value, in turn, originates from the classification policy assigned to the ingress port. As a result, it is imperative to carefully consider any ingress QoS policies, because they ultimately impact how the frame is processed upon egress. To modify which queue a particular CoS is mapped to and verify those changes, use the following commands:

```
(Hybrid)
set qos map {port-type} tx {queue#} {thr #} cos {cos-list}
show qos info config {port-type} tx
(Native)
wrr-queue cos-map {queue#} {thr #} {CoS1 [CoS2] [CoS3] [CoS4] [CoS5] [CoS6] [CoS7]
  [CoS8]}
show queueing interface {type num} [ | begin queue thresh]
```

NOTE As you may recall from the input scheduling section, modifying the ingress CoS mapping characteristics for 1q4t port types affects the CoS mappings for 2q2t port types. The opposite also holds true when modifying the 2q2t port types.

In Hybrid, when modifying the ingress and egress queue mappings, the configuration changes apply to all ports associated with the designated port type. Therefore, if you modify the CoS assignments for 1p2q2t port types, all modules with this transmit capability inherit the specified parameters. Examples 8-35 and 8-36 demonstrate altering the default CoS assignments and then validating the changes made.

Example 8-35 *Mapping CoS Value to Transmit Queue and Threshold in Hybrid Mode*

```
hybrid (enable) set qos map 2q2t tx 2 1 cos 3
QoS tx priority queue and threshold mapped to cos successfully.

hybrid (enable) show qos info config 2q2t tx
QoS setting in NVRAM for 2q2t transmit:
QoS is enabled
Queue and Threshold Mapping for 2q2t (tx):
Queue Threshold CoS
----- --------- ---------------
1     1         0 1
1     2         2
2     1         3 4 5
2     2         6 7
(text omitted)
**Note:  Receive queue configuration matches transmit queue.

hybrid (enable) show qos info config 1q4t rx
QoS setting in NVRAM for 1q4t receive:
QoS is enabled
Queue and Threshold Mapping for 1q4t (rx):
Queue Threshold CoS
----- --------- ---------------
1     1         0 1
1     2         2
1     3         3 4 5
1     4         6 7
 (text omitted)
```

The preceding example represents the recommended configuration for ports without a priority queue in a voice-deployed environment. With no strict-priority queue, frames with CoS 5 remain mapped to the second queue and first threshold. In this instance, frames marked with CoS 3 are mapped to the same queue and threshold as frames marked with CoS 4 and 5. Depending on the traffic levels, this configuration affords frames marked with CoS 5 the least amount of potential delay, jitter, and drop probability (because traffic in the second, or high, queue is scheduled more frequently than traffic in the lower queue). This ensures that frames with low delay tolerances are expedited, whereas traffic in the lower queue is buffered. Also as depicted in the example, the CoS mapping parameters for 2q2t port types are duplicated for 1q4t port types on the receive side.

Example 8-36 *Mapping CoS Value to Transmit Queue and Threshold in Native Mode*

```
native(config-if)# wrr-queue cos-map 2 1 3
  cos-map configured on:  Gi2/1 Gi2/2 Gi2/3 Gi2/4 Gi2/5 Gi2/6 Gi2/7 Gi2/8
native(config-if)# wrr-queue cos-map 2 2 6
  cos-map configured on:  Gi2/1 Gi2/2 Gi2/3 Gi2/4 Gi2/5 Gi2/6 Gi2/7 Gi2/8

native# show queueing interface gigabitEthernet 2/1 | begin queue thresh
    queue thresh cos-map
    ---------------------------------------
    1    1      0 1
    1    2      2
    2    1      3 4
    2    2      6 7
    3    1      5
(text omitted)
```

As noted earlier in the chapter, when you configure QoS on the Catalyst 6500, the ASICs are being programmed directly. Therefore, when ports and interfaces share the same ASIC, they inherit or share QoS configuration parameters. Example 8-36 demonstrates this behavior. Also the strict-priority queue is depicted directly above. By default, frames marked with CoS 5 are mapped to the strict-priority queue. To map other CoS values to the strict-priority queue, utilize **priority-queue cos-map 1** {*CoS*} for Native mode and **set qos map** {*port type*} **tx** {*queue#*} {*thr#*} **cos** {*CoS*} when running Hybrid. In Hybrid, queues are numbered starting with the lowest-priority queue and ending with the highest-priority queue. As an example, there are three available queues for 1p2q2t port types. The first queue represents the lowest standard priority queue available and offers the least amount of insurance for network traffic. However, queue three in this case is the strict-priority queue, and as a result offers a low drop probability and minimal delay during periods of congestion. After the CoS values have been mapped to a corresponding queue and threshold, it is important to analyze the scheduling between the different queues. This analysis ensures high-priority and mission-critical traffic is receiving sufficient bandwidth during periods of congestion.

Configuring Output Queue Scheduling WRR Weighting Factors

Covered in Chapter 2, WRR is a scheduling mechanism used to determine the frequency with which certain queues are serviced. Unlike round-robin, which offers each participating queue equal access to the allocated bandwidth, WRR enables the administrator to assign a weighting factor allowing queues to utilize a greater share of the bandwidth. If a queue has a higher weight, it is permitted to transmit more frames onto the network. Hence, it is serviced more frequently than other queues. With the exception of the strict-priority queue, all port transmit queues participate in the WRR scheduling process. Figure 8-12 shows the WRR operation among multiple queues.

Figure 8-12 *Output Scheduling Using WRR*

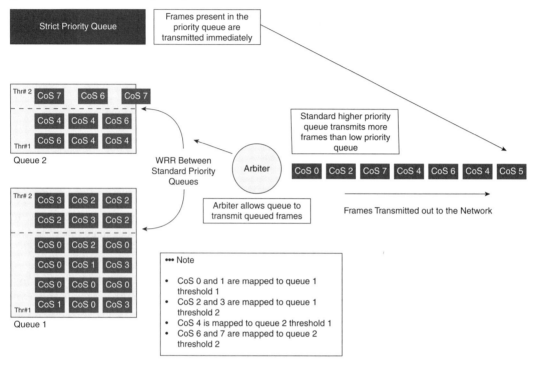

NOTE	Remember that WRR and other scheduling mechanisms only affect traffic when congestion is experienced on a port. Also WRR does not rate limit traffic during periods of congestion. If only low-priority traffic is present in the egress queue, even during congestion, it is permitted full access to the available bandwidth.

As depicted in the figure, the strict-priority queue on the Catalyst 6500 does not participate in WRR scheduling. When a frame enters the strict-priority queue, the queue is immediately given access to the network. The switch checks the priority queue after each frame is transmitted from a standard-priority queue. The remaining lower-priority standard queues are not permitted to transmit until the strict-priority queue is void of any traffic. When that occurs, the remaining queues are permitted to transmit, and are scheduled in the specified WRR fashion. Because the lower-priority queues service the lower-priority traffic, when assigning weights ensure the higher-priority queues always receive a higher weighting factor. This measure guarantees more critical traffic receives preferential treatment. The following commands enable the administrator to assign different weighting factors to the various queues and to confirm the configuration:

```
(Hybrid)
set qos wrr {port-type} {queue1 val} {queue2 val}…{queueN val}
show qos info config {port-type} tx
(Native)
wrr-queue bandwidth {queue1 val} {queue2 val}…{queueN val}
show queueing interface {type num}
```

To determine the bandwidth allotted for a particular queue, use the same formula introduced in Chapter 7:

$$(W/S) * B = n$$

W represents the weight of the queue in question. This value is divided by the sum of all weights (*S*) for the various transmit queues assigned to this interface. Finally, that value is multiplied by the total bandwidth (*B*) accessible to the port. The result (*n*) is the total available bandwidth for this transmit queue. By default, the weights assigned to the standard-priority queues for ports with two transmit queues are 100 for the low priority standard queue and 255 for the high-priority standard queue. This implies the lower-priority queue is permitted approximately 30 percent of the bandwidth, whereas the higher-priority queue receives the remainder during periods of congestion. For interfaces with three transmit queues, the default values are 100, 150, and 200. This equates to 22 percent, 33 percent, and approximately 45 percent for the low-, medium-, and high-priority queues, respectively. Examples 8-37 and 8-38 show how to modify the default round-robin weighting factors for the various transmit queues.

Example 8-37 *Configuring WRR Scheduling Values in Hybrid Mode*

```
hybrid (enable) set qos wrr 1p2q2t 85 255
QoS wrr ratio is set successfully.

hybrid (enable) show qos info config 1p2q2t tx
QoS setting in NVRAM for 1p2q2t transmit:
QoS is enabled
(text omitted)
WRR Configuration of ports with 1p2q2t:
Queue #  Ratios
-------  ------------------------------------
1         85
2         255
```

Example 8-38 *Configuring WRR Scheduling Values in Native Mode*

```
native(config-if)# wrr-queue bandwidth 70 125 255
  bandwidth configured on all 48 ports on slot 3.

native# show queueing interface fastEthernet 3/1
Interface FastEthernet3/1 queueing strategy:  Weighted Round-Robin
  Port QoS is enabled
  Trust state: trust IP Precedence
  Default COS is 0
  Transmit queues [type = 1p3q1t]:
    Queue Id    Scheduling  Num of thresholds
    -----------------------------------------
       1          WRR                1
```

Example 8-38 *Configuring WRR Scheduling Values in Native Mode (Continued)*

```
        2          WRR              1
        3          WRR              1
        4          Priority         1
    WRR bandwidth ratios:   70[queue 1] 125[queue 2] 255[queue 3]
(text omitted)
```

Configuring the Transmit Queue Size Ratio

Like the receive queue ratio, the transmit queue ratio enables the administrator to define the maximum amount of memory a queue is permitted to occupy for buffering egress traffic. The queues can be tailored to meet the requirements of the specific flows traversing the port. If multiple queues are available on an egress port, each queue must share the total amount of buffer space with the other queues. When allocating space for the various queues in Hybrid, the values are expressed as percentages. As a result, the sum of these percentages must amount to 100 percent of the total available buffer space. In Native mode, the values are relative weights. Each queue is assigned a weighting factor, which can be used to calculate the approximate percentage assigned to the particular transmit queue. For example, by default each 10/100 port on a WS-X6348 or WS-X6148 linecard shares 112 KB among all queues for outbound traffic. Gigabit Ethernet ports share 439 KB of memory among all queues. To modify the percentage of buffer space or weights assigned to the various transmit queues, use the following commands:

```
(Hybrid)
set qos txq-ratio {port-type} {queue1} {queue2}…{queueN}
show qos info config {port-type}
(Native IOS)
wrr-queue queue-limit {low-priority queue} {high-priority queue}
show queueing interface {type num}
```

Table 8-18 depicts the default transmit queue ratio settings for 2q2t, 1p2q2t, and 1p2q1t port types.

Table 8-18 *Default Transmit Queue Ration Settings*

Port Type	Standard Low-Priority Queue	Standard High-Priority Queue	Strict-Priority Queue
2q2t (Hybrid)	80	20	N/A
2q2t (Native)	70	30	N/A
1p2q2t*	70	15	15
1p2q1t*	50	30	20

*Values apply to queues for both Hybrid and Native modes.

(Values assigned to queues in Hybrid mode are expressed as percentages. Values assigned to queues in Native mode are expressed as weights.)

As shown in Table 8-18, a considerable portion of the buffer is assigned to the standard low-priority queue, because the higher-priority queues receive more access to the available bandwidth, which is determined by the WRR weighting factors. Because minimizing the total end-to-end delay is critical for real-time applications and voice, the higher-priority queues need to be serviced more frequently. As a result, they do not require as much buffer space, because buffering introduces additional delay and jitter. For low-priority queues, enough buffer space must be allocated to ensure low-priority outbound frames are accommodated with minimal to no drops, allowing sufficient time to service the higher-priority queues. When configuring the transmit queue ratio in Hybrid, the command line enables the administrator to configure all queues, including the strict-priority queue. For Native IOS, it is only possible to explicitly define the weights for the standard low- and high-priority queues. For 1p2q2t port types, the strict-priority queue must be configured to match the value for the standard high-priority queue. This requirement applies to switches operating in Hybrid mode and Native IOS. Although in Hybrid the administrator can configure different percentages for the strict-priority and the standard high-priority queue, the switch still programs the values to be equal. This behavior is a hardware limitation applicable to 1p2q2t port types. The following examples demonstrate how to configure the transmit queue ratio for the applicable port types in Hybrid and Cisco IOS.

Example 8-39 *Configuring the Transmit Queue Ratio in Hybrid Mode*

```
hybrid (enable) set qos txq-ratio 1p2q2t 60 20 20
QoS txq-ratio is set successfully.

hybrid (enable) show qos info config 1p2q2t tx
QoS setting in NVRAM for 1p2q2t transmit:
QoS is enabled
(text omitted)
Tx queue size ratio:
Queue #  Sizes - percentage
-------  ------------------------------------
1        60%
2        20%
3        20%
```

Example 8-40 *Configuring the Transmit Queue Ratio in Native Mode*

```
native(config-if)# wrr-queue queue-limit 60 25

native# show queueing interface tenGigabitEthernet 8/1
Interface TenGigabitEthernet8/1 queueing strategy:  Weighted Round-Robin
  Port QoS is enabled
(text omitted)
    queue-limit ratios:     60[queue 1]  25[queue 2]
```

Congestion Avoidance

Congestion avoidance involves proactively managing queues. The purpose is to avoid buffer exhaustion, and subsequently tail-dropping frames. The Catalyst 6500 offers *Weigthed Random Early Detection* (WRED) as a congestion avoidance mechanism. Table 8-16 lists the various linecards supporting WRED. WRED operation is very similar to *Random Early Detection* (RED). It utilizes configured thresholds to determine when to randomly drop frames in a queue. Unlike RED, however, WRED is QoS aware. It uses the CoS values assigned to the various frames to determine which frames to randomly drop. WRED is most efficient in instances where multiple TCP streams are traversing the same port. WRED exploits TCP's windowing mechanism to avert congestion. WRED also helps prevent a phenomenon called global synchronization. Speaking in broad terms, *global synchronization* is a side effect of tail drop, where all TCP flows reduce, and subsequently increase, their window size at the same time. A detailed discussion regarding global synchronization is beyond the scope of this text. For more information regarding the operation of WRED, refer to Chapter 2.

One other queue management technique the Catalyst 6500 employs is assigning tail-drop thresholds to the available transmit queues. This enables the administrator to assign maximum high-level marks within the queue for specified marked frames. When CoS values are mapped to a specific queue and threshold, as demonstrated earlier, if the amount of frames exceeds the maximum specified threshold level, all subsequent frames queued for transmission are tail dropped.

Configuring Tail-Drop Thresholds for Transmit Queues

The commands utilized for configuring the tail-drop thresholds for the receive queues are the same for transmit queues.

```
(Hybrid)
set qos drop-threshold {port-type} tx queue {queue#} {thr1} {thr2}...{thrN}
show qos info config {port-type} tx
(Native)
wrr-queue threshold {queue#} {thr1} {thr2}...{thrN}
show queueing interface {type num} [ | begin queue tail-drop]
```

Currently, only 2q2t port types provide configurable tail-drop thresholds. Table 8-19 lists the default threshold values.

Table 8-19   *Default Tail-Drop Thresholds for 2q2t Port Types*

Standard Low-Priority Queue	Standard High-Priority Queue
Threshold 2: 100% capacity	Threshold 2: 100% capacity
Threshold 1: 80% capacity	Threshold 1: 80% capacity

The transmit queue ratio defines the amount of memory allocated to each queue. The tail-drop thresholds define the maximum levels within the allotted space for frames marked with a particular CoS. Using the default values, consider frames with CoS values mapped to the first threshold in the low-priority queue. When the available buffer reaches 80-percent capacity, all subsequent frames mapped to this threshold are tail dropped. The same applies to frames mapped to the second threshold. As soon as the queue reaches 100-percent capacity, all consecutive frames mapped to this queue are tail dropped. In addition to 2q2t type interfaces, strict-priority queues utilize tail drop to manage the queue. However, the thresholds for the strict queue are nonconfigurable. The level is fixed at 100-percent capacity. Examples 8-41 and 8-42 demonstrate configuring and verifying the tail-drop thresholds for 2q2t type ports.

Example 8-41   *Configuring Transmit Queue Tail-Drop Thresholds in Hybrid*

```
hybrid (enable) set qos drop-threshold 2q2t tx queue 1 65 100
Transmit drop thresholds for queue 1 set at 65% 100% .
hybrid (enable) set qos drop-threshold 2q2t tx queue 2 85 100
Transmit drop thresholds for queue 2 set at 85% 100% .
hybrid (enable) show qos info config 2q2t tx
QoS setting in NVRAM for 2q2t transmit:
QoS is enabled
(text omitted)
Tx drop thresholds:
Queue #  Thresholds - percentage
-------  ------------------------------------
1        65% 100%
2        85% 100%
```

Example 8-42   *Configuring Transmit Queue Tail-Drop Thresholds in Native Mode*

```
native(config-if)# wrr-queue threshold 1 65 100
  threshold configured on:  Gi8/1 Gi8/2 Gi8/3 Gi8/4 Gi8/5 Gi8/6 Gi8/7 Gi8/8
native(config-if)# wrr-queue threshold 2 85 100
  threshold configured on:  Gi8/1 Gi8/2 Gi8/3 Gi8/4 Gi8/5 Gi8/6 Gi8/7 Gi8/8
native# show queueing interface gigabitEthernet 8/1
Interface GigabitEthernet8/1 queueing strategy:  Weighted Round-Robin
  Port QoS is enabled
  Port is untrusted
  Default COS is 0
  Transmit queues [type = 2q2t]:
(text omitted)
queue tail-drop-thresholds
  -------------------------
1    65[1] 100[2]
2    85[1] 100[2]
```

One limitation expressed earlier regarding tail drop is its interaction with TCP flows. Tail drop is not conducive to TCP traffic, because it could potentially drop multiple frames from numerous TCP streams, which could lead to global synchronization. The result of this behavior is suboptimal bandwidth utilization. WRED attempts to address this issue.

Configuring WRED Thresholds for Transmit Queues

WRED consists of two different thresholds. In addition to a maximum tail-drop threshold, this congestion avoidance mechanism enables the administrator to configure a lower threshold. The lower threshold specifies the level to initiate randomly dropping specified frames. Frames are not dropped if buffer utilization is below the lower bound. When the buffer usage for the queue reaches the specified lower threshold, it starts dropping frames marked with the CoS mapped to the particular threshold. As the buffer continues to fill, the drop rate increases at a linear rate, until it reaches the maximum defined threshold. When the maximum level is attained, all additional frames assigned to the queue and WRED threshold are tail dropped. The following commands configure the WRED thresholds for the designated queues:

```
(Hybrid)
set qos wred {port-type} tx queue {[thr1Lo:]thr1Hi [[thr2Lo:]thr2Hi]}
show qos info config {port-type} tx
(Native)
wrr-queue random-detect min-threshold {queue#} {thr1} [{thr2}]
wrr-queue random-detect max-threshold {queue#} {thr1} [{thr2}]
show queueing interface {type num} [ | begin random-detect]
```

Because UDP streams do not incorporate any flow-control mechanisms, WRED has very little effect on this type of traffic. The default WRED thresholds assigned to 1p2q2t type interfaces are depicted in the table.

Table 8-20 *Default WRED Thresholds for 1p2q2t Standard Queues*

Standard Low-Priority Queue	Standard High-Priority Queue
Threshold 2 Low: 70 High: 100	Threshold 2 Low: 70 High: 100
Threshold 1 Low: 40 High: 70	Threshold 1 Low: 40 High: 70

For 1p2q1t and 1p3q1t port types, 70 percent is the default minimum threshold, and 100 percent is the default maximum threshold for each queue. When configuring the WRED thresholds, the high value cannot be lower than the low value. However, the two values can be equal. By configuring the high and low values to be equal, you create a tail-drop threshold. This tail-drop threshold may be useful, for reasons previously mentioned, if the traffic mapped to a queue and threshold is composed solely of UDP type traffic. Again, the priority queue defaults to a nonconfigurable 100-percent tail-drop threshold. The following examples show how to configure the WRED thresholds for the applicable queues.

Example 8-43 *Configuring WRED Transmit Queue Thresholds in Hybrid Mode*

```
hybrid (enable) set qos wred 1p2q2t tx queue 1 65:85 80:100
WRED thresholds for queue 1 set to 65:85 and 80:100 on all WRED-capable 1p2q2t ports.
hybrid (enable) set qos wred 1p2q2t tx queue 2 70:90 80:100
WRED thresholds for queue 2 set to 70:90 and 80:100 on all WRED-capable 1p2q2t ports.

hybrid (enable) show qos info config 1p2q2t tx
QoS setting in NVRAM for 1p2q2t transmit:
QoS is enabled
(text omitted)
Tx WRED thresholds:
Queue #  Thresholds - percentage
-------  -------------------------------------------
1        65%:85% 80%:100%
2        70%:90% 80%:100%
```

Example 8-44 *Configuring WRED Transmit Queue Thresholds in Native Mode*

```
native(config-if)# wrr-queue random-detect min-threshold 1 75
  WRED_threshold configured on all 48 ports on slot 3.
native(config-if)# wrr-queue random-detect min-threshold 2 75
  WRED_threshold configured on all 48 ports on slot 3.
native(config-if)# wrr-queue random-detect min-threshold 3 80
  WRED_threshold configured on all 48 ports on slot 3.

native# show queueing interface fastEthernet 3/1
Interface FastEthernet3/1 queueing strategy:  Weighted Round-Robin
  Port QoS is enabled
  Trust state: trust IP Precedence
  Default COS is 0
  Transmit queues [type = 1p3q1t]:
(text omitted)
    queue random-detect-min-thresholds
    ---------------------------------
       1    75[1]
       2    75[1]
       3    80[1]
```

Automatic QoS

Auto-QoS facilitates the QoS configuration process for the Catalyst 6500. At the time of writing, Auto-QoS is available with CatOS Software Release 7.5. Auto-QoS assists the administrator in configuring classification, congestion management, mapping, and congestion avoidance. The Auto-QoS feature on the Catalyst 6500 is divided into two components. Global Auto-QoS provides recommended QoS parameters on a switch-wide basis, whereas port-specific Auto-QoS configures parameters on a per-interface basis. With CatOS Release 7.5, Auto-QoS commands are specifically focused on voice-related applications. However, future software releases will provide additional functionality and capabilities.

NOTE   At the time of writing, Auto-QoS is not available in Cisco IOS for the Catalyst 6500. However, there are plans to integrate the feature in future Cisco IOS releases.

Global Auto-QoS

The global Auto-QoS command focuses on QoS parameters affecting the entire switch. To enable global Auto-QoS, enter the following command in enable mode on the supervisor:

```
set qos autoqos
```

When you enter the preceding command, any QoS commands previously configured are modified. Therefore, you should enable any Auto-QoS commands prior to manually altering the switch QoS properties. **set qos autoqos** first enables QoS on the switch, if it is not already enabled. The global Auto-QoS command does not alter any default QoS configurations applied at the port level. Because congestion management, congestion avoidance, and CoS-to-queue mappings depend on port types rather than specific ports, commands related to these mechanisms are incorporated into the global Auto-QoS command. Refer to Table 8-2 for a detailed list of the various modules and the corresponding port types, and review the section "Catalyst Feature Overview" in Chapter 3, which provides additional information on port type nomenclature. Tables 8-21 and 8-22 list the resulting commands executed when configuring global Auto-QoS.

Table 8-21 *Added Global Auto-QoS Configuration Commands*

* **set qos enable**
set qos policy-source local
set qos acl default-action ip dscp 0
set qos ipprec-dscp-map 0 10 18 24 34 46 48 56
set qos cos-dscp-map 0 10 18 24 34 46 48 56
set qos dscp-cos-map 0-7:0 8-15:1 16-23:2 24-31:3 32-39:4 40-47:5 48-55:6 56-63:7
** **set qos policed-dscp-map 26:0**
** **set qos policed-dscp-map 46:0**

*Command is enabled on the switch if it was not previously enabled.

**All normal and excess rate policed DSCP map values are configured for default values. The exception is DSCP 26 and DSCP 46.

Table 8-22 *Added Global Auto-QoS Port Type Configuration Commands*

2q2t/1q4t
set qos map 2q2t tx queue 2 2 cos 5,6,7
set qos map 2q2t tx queue 2 1 cos 1,2,3,4
set qos map 2q2t tx queue 1 1 cos 0
set qos drop-threshold 2q2t tx queue 1 100 100
set qos drop-threshold 2q2t tx queue 2 80 100
set qos drop-threshold 1q4t rx queue 1 50 60 80 100
set qos txq-ratio 2q2t 80 20
set qos wrr 2q2t 100 255
1p3q1t/1p1q0t
set qos map 1p3q1t tx 1 1 cos 0
set qos map 1p3q1t tx 2 1 cos 1,2
set qos map 1p3q1t tx 3 1 cos 3,4

Table 8-22   *Added Global Auto-QoS Port Type Configuration Commands (Continued)*

set qos map 1p3q1t tx 3 0 cos 6,7
set qos map 1p3q1t tx 4 cos 5
set qos wrr 1p3q1t 20 100 200
set qos wred 1p3q1t queue 1 70:100
set qos wred 1p3q1t queue 2 70:100
set qos wred 1p3q1t queue 3 70:90
set qos map 1p1q0t rx 1 cos 0,1,2,3,4
set qos map 1p1q0t rx 2 cos 5,6,7
set qos rxq-ratio 1p1q0t 80 20
1p2q2t/1p1q4t
set qos map 1p2q2t tx 1 2 cos 0
set qos map 1p2q2t tx 2 1 cos 1,2,3,4
set qos map 1p2q2t tx 2 2 cos 6,7
set qos map 1p2q2t tx 3 cos 5
set qos txq-ratio 1p2q2t 75 15 15
set qos wrr 1p2q2t 50 255
set qos wred 1p2q2t queue 1 1 40:70
set qos wred 1p2q2t queue 1 2 70:100
set qos wred 1p2q2t queue 2 1 40:70
set qos wred 1p2q2t queue 2 2 70:100
set qos map 1p1q4t rx 1 1 cos 0
set qos map 1p1q4t rx 1 3 cos 1,2,3,4
set qos map 1p1q4t rx 1 4 cos 6,7
set qos map 1p1q4t rx 2 cos 5
set qos rxq-ratio 1p1q4t 50 255
set qos drop-threshold 1p1q4t rx queue 1 50 60 80 100
1p2q1t/1p1q8t
set qos map 1p2q1t tx 1 1 cos 0
set qos map 1p2q1t tx 2 1 cos 1,2,3,4
set qos map 1p2q1t tx 2 cos 6,7
set qos map 1p2q1t tx 3 cos 5

continues

Table 8-22 *Added Global Auto-QoS Port Type Configuration Commands (Continued)*

set qos txq-ratio 1p2q1t 75 15 15
set qos wrr 1p2q1t 50 255
set qos wred 1p2q1t queue 1 70:100
set qos wred 1p2q1t queue 2 70:100
set qos map 1p1q8t rx 1 1 cos 0
set qos map 1p1q8t rx 1 5 cos 1,2
set qos map 1p1q8t rx 1 8 cos 3,4
set qos map 1p1q8t rx 2 cos 5,6,7
set qos wred 1p1q8t queue 1 1 40:70
set qos wred 1p1q8t queue 1 5 60:90
set qos wred 1p1q8t queue 1 8 70:100
set qos rxq-ratio 1p1q8t 80 20

Port-Specific Auto-QoS

The port-specific Auto-QoS functions define, in one of two ways, the classification method used for traffic ingress to a specific port. One way involves specifying the type of device attached to the port, either a Cisco IP Phone or Cisco IP Softphone. The other method requires specifying the trust state for a particular port, either trust DSCP or trust CoS. Configuring port-specific Auto-QoS also assigns extended trust capabilities and CoS assignments to attached IP Phones using *Cisco Discovery Protocol* (CDP) version 2. If CDP version 2 is not enabled, the information cannot be communicated to an attached Cisco IP Phone. Refer to the section "Voice VLANs and Extended Trust" in Chapter 2 for additional information on CDP and extended port-based QoS capabilities. A PFC is a prerequisite for using either the trust DSCP or IP Softphone Auto-QoS option. To configure port-specific Auto-QoS, use one of the following commands:

```
set port qos {mod/port} autoqos voip ciscoipphone
set port qos {mod/port} autoqos voip ciscosoftphone
set port qos {mod/port} autoqos trust dscp
set port qos {mod/port} autoqos trust cos
```

The "Classification and Marking" section within this chapter discusses trust and internal DSCP in further detail. The **trust dscp** and **trust cos** classification keywords are used to classify all traffic based on arriving DSCP or CoS values. You can use the **cos** keyword for trusted uplink ports attached to devices capable of only modifying the trunk header of an Ethernet frame. This ensures previously assigned CoS values are honored at the arriving switch port, and subsequently mapped to a corresponding internal DSCP value. You can use the **dscp** keyword for uplink ports attached to devices capable of altering the DSCP field in the IP header. This capability is relevant, for instance, when connecting to a 3550, another

6500, or even a router. A PFC is required to use the **dscp** keyword. Table 8-21 depicts the CoS-to-DSCP and IP precedence-to-DSCP mapping values if the global Auto-QoS command is executed; Table 8-12 shows the default assigned mapping values.

The **voip ciscoipphone** and **voip ciscosoftphone** keywords simplify the process of configuring voice-specific QoS on a port. The **ciscoipphone** option configures the ingress port to trust the control and voice-bearer traffic received from an IP Phone. By default, this traffic is marked by the phone with CoS 3 and CoS 5, respectively. As mentioned previously, if CDP is enabled and the port terminates into a Cisco IP Phone, additional QoS capabilities are extended to support devices attached to a switchport on the phone. For additional information regarding the Cisco IP Phone, refer to the section "The Cisco IP Phone" in Chapter 2. The **ciscosoftphone** option configures an ingress port to trust voice traffic generated by the Cisco Softphone application. The Softphone application properly marks the control and voice traffic within the IP header. As a result, ACLs trusting the ingress DSCP values are configured for the port (and, based on worst-case performance parameters, policers are configured to regulate control and voice traffic generated by the application). A PFC is required for configuring the **ciscosoftphone** keyword.

As discussed in the "Trust" section within this chapter, the WS-X6224/6248 and WS-X6324/6348 have certain hardware limitations that prevent them from supporting certain trust states on a port. As a result, additional intelligence has been added to the port-based Auto-QoS command to account for this limitation. For 1q4t/2q2t port types, when the **trust cos**, **trust dscp**, or **voip ciscoipphone** keywords are used, additional commands and ACLs are configured to support the configured feature. When specifying **trust cos** or **voip ciscoipphone**, the following additional commands are added for the port configuration:

```
set port qos {mod/port} trust trust-cos
set qos acl map ACL_IP-PHONES {mod/port}
set qos acl ip ACL_IP-PHONES trust-cos ip any  any
commit qos acl ACL_IP-PHONES
```

When specifying the **trust dscp** keyword, the following commands are added to complete the port configuration:

```
set port qos {mod/port} trust untrusted
set qos acl map ACL_IP-TRUSTDSCP {mod/port}
set qos acl ip ACL_IP-TRUSTDSCP trust-dscp ip any  any
commit qos acl ACL_IP-TRUSTDSCP
```

NOTE   The WS-X6148 module is capable of supporting **trust-cos**, **trust-dscp**, and **trust-ipprec**. However, this capabilitiy is integrated in 6.4, and was not included in CatOS Release 7.5.

Tables 8-23 through 8-26 depict the executed commands when configuring port-specific Auto-QoS.

Table 8-23 *Port-Specific Auto-Qos Commands for the* **ciscoipphone** *Keyword*

set port qos {*mod/port*} **policy-source local**
set port qos {*mod/port*} **port-based**
set port qos {*mod/port*} **cos 0**
set port qos {*mod/port*} **cos-ext 0**
set port qos {*mod/port*} **trust-ext untrusted**
set port qos {*mod/port*} **trust-device ciscoipphone**
* **set port qos** {*mod/port*} **trust trust-cos**

*Enables receive queue thresholds for 1q4t port types. Additional commands are added for 1q4t/2q2t port types.

Table 8-24 *Port-Specific Auto-QoS Commands for the* **ciscosoftphone** *Keyword*

set port qos {*mod/port*} **policy-source local**
set port qos {*mod/port*} **port-based**
set port qos {*mod/port*} **cos 0**
set port qos {*mod/port*} **cos-ext 0**
set port qos {*mod/port*} **trust-ext untrusted**
set port qos {*mod/port*} **trust-device none**
set port qos {*mod/port*} **trust untrusted**
set qos policer aggregate POLICE_SOFTPHONE-DSCP46-mod-port rate 320 burst 20 policed-dscp
set qos policer aggregate POLICE_SOFTPHONE-DSCP24-mod-port rate 32 burst 8 policed-dscp
set qos acl ip ACL_IP-SOFTPHONE-mod-port trust-dscp aggregate POLICE_SOFTPHONE-DSCP46-mod-port any dscp-field 46
set qos acl ip ACL_IP-SOFTPHONE-mod-port trust-dscp aggregate POLICE_SOFTPHONE-DSCP24-mod-port any dscp-field 24
commit qos acl ACL_IP-SOFTPHONE-mod-port
set qos acl map ACL_IP-SOFTPHONE-mod-port mod/port

Table 8-25 *Port Specific Auto-QoS for Trust DSCP*

set port qos {*mod/port*} **policy-source local**
set port qos {*mod/port*} **port-based**

Table 8-25   *Port Specific Auto-QoS for Trust DSCP (Continued)*

set port qos {*mod/port*} **cos 0**
set port qos {*mod/port*} **cos-ext 0**
set port qos {*mod/port*} **trust-ext untrusted**
set port qos {*mod/port*} **trust-device none**
* **set port qos** {*mod/port*} **trust trust-dscp**

*Command not executed for modules with 2q2t and 1q4t port types. Additional commands are added for 1q4t/ 2q2t port types.

Table 8-26   *Port-Specific Auto-QoS for Trust CoS*

set port qos {*mod/port*} **policy-source local**
set port qos {*mod/port*} **port-based**
set port qos {*mod/port*} **cos 0**
set port qos {*mod/port*} **cos-ext 0**
set port qos {*mod/port*} **trust-ext untrusted**
set port qos {*mod/port*} **trust-device none**
* **set port qos** {*mod/port*} **trust trust-cos**

*Enables receive queue thresholds for 1q4t port types. Additional commands are added for 1q4t/2q2t port types.

As demonstrated throughout the chapter, the Catalyst 6500 has a vast array of QoS capabilities. Auto-QoS expedites the configuration of these available QoS features and ensures critical applications, particularly voice traffic, are properly serviced on a switch-wide and per-port basis.

Summary

The Catalyst 6500 Family of switches offers the administrator wide-ranging flexibility for deploying QoS in the campus environment. The Catalyst 6500 series is fully capable of supporting the demands of today's converged campus networks. Given the versatility and broad range of QoS mechanisms of the Catalyst 6500s, you can position these devices at all layers of the campus topology. In addition, because the QoS functions are performed in hardware, the application of QoS policies results in no additional impact to the packet-forwarding rate. The following list summarizes the features and capabilities available on the Catalyst 6500 series devices:

- Includes QoS support for both Hybrid and Cisco IOS.
- Supports input scheduling based on trusted CoS.

- Offers input strict-priority queuing for expeditious handling of voice traffic on specific linecards.

- Classifies traffic based on CoS, IP precedence, and DSCP values.

- Performs classification and marking based on Layer 2, 3, and 4 defined ACLs.

- Supports up to 63 ingress microflow and 1023 ingress aggregate policers. At the time of this writing, egress policing is not supported.

- Provides single-rate policing and dual-rate policing capabilities, depending on PFC revision.

- Accomplishes complex egress congestion avoidance and congestion management techniques, including WRED, egress strict-priority queuing, and WRR scheduling.

- Automated QoS to facilitate the configuration process to support voice and other mission critical data on the network.

This chapter focused on the QoS capabilities of the supervisor engine, the PFC, and the various linecards. Chapter 9 further details the QoS functionality of the Catalyst 6500 family, by discussing the QoS features available when a FlexWAN and MSFC are incorporated into the switch.

CHAPTER 9

QoS Support on the Catalyst 6500 MSFC and FlexWAN

Chapter 8, "QoS Support on the Catalyst 6500," detailed the Catalyst 6500's *quality of service* (QoS) capabilities from a campus LAN perspective. Moreover, the chapter further detailed the QoS capabilities by describing the architecture and behavior of the individual port *application-specific integrated circuits* (ASICs) and the *Policy Feature Card* (PFC) on the Catalyst 6500. As discussed in Chapter 8, when equipped with specific linecards and a PFC, the Catalyst 6500 is highly versatile and offers many QoS mechanisms. These features help maintain the end-to-end QoS policies enforced in the LAN environment, ensuring the timely delivery of mission-critical applications.

This chapter focuses on the QoS mechanisms available on the *Multilayer Switch Feature Card* (MSFC) and FlexWAN. The MSFC and FlexWAN extend the 6500's QoS capabilities to the *metropolitan-area network* (MAN) and *wide-area network* (WAN). The intended use of the MSFC forwarding engine is strictly for switching packets that are not hardware switched by the PFC. Examples of software-switched traffic processed by the MSFC include packet flows requiring *Network Address Translation* (NAT), encryption, policy routing, and broadcast forwarding in specific software versions. The FlexWAN module, designated as part number WS-X6182, enables WAN capabilities on the Catalyst 6500. Integrating the MSFC and FlexWAN module into a Catalyst 6500 enables the administrator to consolidate QoS policies for WAN and LAN routers within one platform, simplifying the configuration process. This integration also offers the possibility for end-to-end QoS deployment, sustaining service levels for mission-critical applications across the entire network without the use of external routers, multiple platforms, and multiple versions of Cisco IOS.

The FlexWAN and MSFC employ IOS-based QoS concepts introduced in Chapter 2, "End-to-End QoS: Quality of Service at Layer 3 and Layer 2." This chapter discusses how the FlexWAN and MSFC support QoS features, and includes information on the following topics:

- MSFC and FlexWAN Architectural Overview
- QoS Support on the MSFC and FlexWAN
- Classification
- Marking
- Policing and Shaping
- Congestion Management and Scheduling

- Congestion Avoidance
- Summary

This chapter focuses on these QoS features available to software-switched traffic on the Catalyst 6500 and FlexWAN traffic flows. It also discusses the mechanisms used to ensure reliable delivery of traffic throughout the entire network via the use of the FlexWAN and MSFC. Prior to reading Chapter 9, it is strongly recommended to review Chapter 2 and Chapter 5, "Introduction to the Modular QoS Command-Line Interface," to obtain the appropriate background.

MSFC and FlexWAN Architectural Overview

This section expands on some of the concepts presented in Chapter 8 within the section titled "Catalyst 6500 Architectural Overview." As discussed in Chapter 8, the MSFC, in conjunction with the PFC, is responsible for Layer 3 forwarding within the Catalyst 6500. With a Supervisor I Engine, the first packet in a flow is software switched by the MSFC. When the first packet is forwarded, the forwarding decision made by the MSFC is also programmed into hardware ASICs on the supervisor engine. This process is referred to as hardware-based *multilayer switching* (MLS). When the initial packet is forwarded in software by the MSFC, and the MLS flow is completed in hardware, all subsequent packets are switched by the PFC. With a Supervisor II Engine, the MSFC is not primarily responsible for forwarding packets. The MSFC builds the Layer 3 forwarding information, which is passed via an out-of-band channel to the PFC on the supervisor engine. The MSFC builds a *Cisco Express Forwarding* (CEF) table, which is copied directly into hardware on the PFC. Copying the CEF table to the PFC permits all forwarding decisions to be made in hardware. In the event an entry does not exist in the PFC for an arriving packet, it is then software switched by the MSFC. The switching process on the Supervisor II Engine is referred to as *CEF-based Layer 3 switching*.

NOTE   For additional information on MLS-based switching on the Supervisor I Engine, refer to the following technical document at Cisco.com:

"Configuring IP Unicast Layer 3 Switching on Supervisor Engine I"

For additional information on CEF-based switching on the Supervisor II Engine, refer to the following technical document at Cisco.com:

"Configuring CEF for PFC2"

In addition to building the Layer 3 forwarding information, the MSFC is also responsible for applying configurations to the FlexWAN module. In addition, the MSFC switches and encapsulates non-IP traffic for both ingress and egress packets traversing the FlexWAN.

The FlexWAN module binds to the active or designated MSFC within the 6500. As stated in the introduction, the FlexWAN extends the Catalyst 6500's reachability to the MAN and WAN. The FlexWAN is a single-slot module that can be integrated into the Catalyst 6500. The physical appearance of the FlexWAN module can be compared to a *Versatile Interface Processor* (VIP) for a 7500. Similar to the VIP, the FlexWAN has two bays, which accommodate two modular WAN port adapters. From the MSFC, the FlexWAN port adapters are configured identically to the way Cisco 7200 or 7500 port adapters are configured. The FlexWAN contains two VIPs capable of supporting one port adapter for each VIP. The FlexWAN port adapters are configurable strictly from the MSFC and not recognized by the switch in Hybrid mode. If running the Cisco Native IOS, the FlexWAN module interfaces are configured from the command line similar to any other available interface. Table 9-3 depicts the 7200/7500 WAN port adapters supported by the FlexWAN.

Unlike the VIP, which only incorporates a single processor and memory to control both bays, the FlexWAN module is comprised of two VIPs. Therefore, the FlexWAN module services the two installed port adapters with a dedicated processor and memory for each bay. Each processor performs the encapsulation and QoS functions independently for its assigned slot. Also the MSFC communicates with each processor on the FlexWAN independently through the *Ethernet out-of-band channel* (EOBC). However, only system control information is exchanged via the EOBC. Routing and forwarding decisions are still maintained by the MSFC and central PFC. As a result, the FlexWAN uses the central *data bus* (D-bus) and *results bus* (R-bus) for forwarding and receiving data packets. This even applies for packets being forwarded out a different subinterface on the same port adapter. The D-bus, R-bus, and EOBC are introduced in Chapter 8.

For more detailed information regarding the architecture of the Catalyst 6500, consult the following technical document at Cisco.com:

"Catalyst 6000 and 6500 Series Architecture"

Hardware and Software Requirements

As described in Chapter 8, the administrator has two software options available to support operations on the Catalyst 6500. The first option requires the administrator to load two separate software versions. One version supports the supervisor module, and the other version supports the MSFC. This configuration is referred to as *Hybrid mode*. The alternative arrangement requires only one version of software to be positioned on the platform. This one version sustains both the supervisor and the MSFC. This version of software is referred to as *Cisco Native IOS*.

For additional information on naming conventions and differentiating the various software versions for the Catalyst 6500, refer to the section titled "Identifying the Catalyst Software" in Chapter 8.

The MSFC is supported in both Native IOS and Hybrid. The only hardware requirement for supporting an MSFC is that the supervisor engine must incorporate a PFC. Table 9-1 depicts the minimum versions of software required for both Native IOS and Hybrid to support an MSFC with the respective supervisor engine.

Table 9-1   *Minimum Software Versions for MSFC Support*

	Sup I MSFC I	Sup I MSFC II	Sup II MSFC II
Native IOS	12.0(7)XE	12.1(2)E	12.1(8a)E
Hybrid	CatOS: 5.3(1)CSX Cisco IOS: 12.0(3)XE1	CatOS: 5.4(3) Cisco IOS: 12.1(2)E	CatOS: 6.1(1) Cisco IOS: 12.1(3a)E1

The FlexWAN requires both a PFC and an MSFC to be installed within the 6500. As stated previously, the FlexWAN is associated with the designated MSFC. In the presence of a redundant MSFC configuration, the FlexWAN interfaces appear only on the designated MSFC. As a result, a failover to the backup MSFC must occur for the FlexWAN interfaces to appear on the redundant MSFC. When the interfaces are available on the alternate MSFC, they can be configured and saved to memory. If a failover occurs in the future, the saved configuration on the redundant MSFC is used. Similar to the MSFC, the FlexWAN module is supported in either Hybrid or Native IOS. Table 9-2 provides the minimum software versions for both Native IOS and Hybrid to support the FlexWAN module.

Table 9-2   *Minimum Software Versions for FlexWAN Support*

	Sup IA MSFC I with FlexWAN	Sup IA MSFC II with FlexWAN	Sup II MSFC II with FlexWAN
Native IOS	12.1(5a)E1	12.1(5a)E1	12.1(8a)E
Hybrid	CatOS: 5.4(2) Cisco IOS: 12.1(1)EX1 and 12.1(1)E	CatOS: 5.4(2) Cisco IOS: 12.1(2)E	CatOS: 6.1(1) Cisco IOS: 12.1(3a)E1

When selecting software to support the FlexWAN module, it is necessary to choose a version with a "v" listed in the feature set field. This is identical to the requirement for supporting a VIP on a 7500. If the intent is to load the Enterprise feature set with support for *Secure Shell* (SSH), Triple Data Encryption Standard (3DES), and the FlexWAN module, the feature set field would appear as jk2sv. This requirement applies to IOS versions released prior to 12.1(5a)E. For 12.1(5a)E and all subsequent releases, FlexWAN support is incorporated into each software version. The exception to this rule begins with IOS Release 12.1(13)E. Starting with this software release, the "LAN-only" feature set is introduced. This specific feature set does not incorporate support for the FlexWAN module. However, this exception only applies to Native IOS; the Hybrid Software version maintains support for the FlexWAN module.

The FlexWAN module supports numerous 7200/7500 WAN port adapters in the individual bays. This support allows for the integration of existing available hardware. However, the FlexWAN does not support LAN port adapters, double-wide port adapters, or service modules, such as the VPN accelerator module. Double-wide port adapters are not supported due to the availability of separate processors for each bay. Table 9-3 shows which 7200/7500 WAN port adapters are supported with the FlexWAN module.

Table 9-3 *Supported 7200/7500 WAN Port Adapters*

T1/E1	T3/E3	HSSI	ATM	Packetover SONET
PA-4T+	PA-T3	PA-H	PA-A3-T3	PA-POS-OC3MM
PA-8T-V35	PA-2T3	PA-2H	PA-A3-E3	PA-POS-OC2SMI
PA-8T-X21	PA-T3+		PA-A3-OC3MM	PA-POS-OC3SML
PA-8T-232	PA-2T3+		PA-A3-OC3SMI	
PA-MC-4T1	PA-E3		PA-A3-OC3SML	
PA-MC-8T1	PA-2E3		PA-T1-IMA	
PA-MC-8TE1+	PA-MC-T3			
PA-MC-8E1/120	PA-MC-2T3+			
PA-MC-STM-1	PA-MC-E3			

QoS Support on the MSFC and FlexWAN

The MSFC and FlexWAN offer a broad range of QoS mechanisms. The QoS support on the MSFC and FlexWAN are derived from the distributed QoS support for a VIP, available on the 7500. Therefore, the MSFC and FlexWAN provide intelligent distributed QoS services, which allow QoS policies to be extended across the MAN and WAN.

The QoS features available for the MSFC and FlexWAN are primarily configured using the *Modular QoS command-line interface* (MQC), introduced in chapter 5. The MQC enables the administrator to classify traffic, define policies, and apply those policies in a systematic modular fashion. For a more detailed discussion regarding the MQC, refer to Chapter 5.

When a WAN packet arrives or departs a FlexWAN interface, the FlexWAN is responsible for applying its own QoS mechanisms to that packet. When the packet is received on the WAN interface, any configured ingress QoS policies defined on the interface are applied to the packet. The same behavior applies to egress packets. When the forwarding decision has been made and the packet is encapsulated with the appropriate WAN header, any egress QoS policies defined on the interface are applied to the packet, which is then queued for transmission. This behavior is particularly true for policing functions on the FlexWAN. The FlexWAN is responsible for policing traffic streams on its interfaces, due to the potential discrepancies that may result from the variation in header length between a WAN and

Ethernet frame. Although the PFC does not perform any policing or QoS services for the WAN traffic, it does switch WAN traffic at Layer 3. However, the PFC does not modify the Layer 3 *type of service* (ToS) field when processing these packets.

Aside from the FlexWAN performing its own set of QoS functions, there are other things to consider when deploying QoS on a 6500 with an MSFC and FlexWAN. When a frame is sent either to the MSFC or FlexWAN, the Layer 2 CoS settings applied to that frame are not maintained. By default, a 6500 equipped with a PFC I sets the CoS to zero if the frame is processed and forwarded from the MSFC or the FlexWAN. With a PFC II, CoS is derived from the precedence value in the IP header. This feature is not configurable. For IP and IPX packets, the MSFC is not normally involved in the forwarding process. Therefore, careful consideration must be given when applying QoS policies to the MSFC and FlexWAN so that the outcome results in the desired behavior. The QoS policies discussed in this chapter center on the FlexWAN module. Although the MSFC is required for configuring the FlexWAN module, it is not possible to run many of the mechanisms discussed without a FlexWAN module. The exception to this is *network-based application recognition* (NBAR). With Cisco IOS Release 12.1(13)E, software-assisted NBAR is supported without a FlexWAN module. At the time of this writing, hardware-assisted NBAR is not yet supported.

Classification

Classification is the first step in applying QoS policies within a network. If traffic is not classified, policies cannot be applied. Classification categorizes network traffic and assigns those categories to different classes of service. When the traffic is classified, QoS mechanisms are used to maintain the appropriate service levels for a particular category or class. Voice traffic, for example, is extremely vulnerable to delays in the network, and as a result requires expeditious handling on an end-to-end basis. Contrary to the voice traffic, HTTP or web-based traffic is not significantly impacted by delays or drops experienced in the network. Therefore, based on the diverse handling requirements, it is necessary to classify these types of traffic differently. When all traffic is assigned to the appropriate class, mechanisms, such as Low Latency Queuing (LLQ) for voice or *Class-Based Weighted Fair Queuing* (CBWFQ) and marking for web-based applications, are applied to accommodate the required service levels.

There are several ways to implement classification. One method is to classify all traffic traveling through a specific interface. However, this is primarily for situations where a homogenous mixture of traffic is present. For those instances, all traffic departing or leaving a particular interface should be provided the same service level. However, this type of classification policy is more the exception than the norm. If the previous policy is applied to an interface where there is a heterogeneous mixture of traffic, any benefits obtained from deploying QoS are negated. This QoS negation results because no distinctions are being made between the different assigned priority levels for the various traffic flows.

Another classification method is to use standard and extended access lists. *Access-control lists* (ACLs) match addressing information, protocol IDs, or Layer 4 port numbers. When configuring ACLs, however, prior knowledge of the actual applications and protocols operating on the network is necessary. Matching values previously specified in the ToS field of the IP header, either IP precedence or *differentiated services codepoint* (DSCP), is yet another classification method. This allows forwarding decisions and policies to be applied based on predetermined values assigned at either the access or distribution layers of the network.

One other classification mechanism implemented on the Catalyst 6500 for the FlexWAN and MSFC is *distributed network-based application recognition* (dNBAR). dNBAR, through the use of *packet description language modules* (PDLMs), recognizes and classifies a wide range of IP-based applications, as well as HTTP traffic found on networks. Not only does dNBAR recognize applications using static port assignments, it is capable of classifying applications that utilize dynamic port assignments, as well as classifying HTTP traffic based on subport characteristics. dNBAR was initially only supported on the Catalyst 6500 with a FlexWAN module with Software Release 12.1(6)E. However, Cisco IOS Software Release 12.1(13)E expanded NBAR support to include LAN interfaces and does not require a FlexWAN module. NBAR is supported only with the MSFC II. This section briefly describes NBAR and demonstrates how NBAR may be deployed on the Catalyst 6500.

NOTE	PDLMs provide the necessary information to the NBAR inspection process, allowing NBAR to recognize the various applications. PDLMs can be loaded into Flash, and do not require downtime for the system. As new PDLMs become available, they can be loaded on the Catalyst 6500 for additional protocol support. PDLMs are only available through Cisco.
	For a current list of protocols supported by NBAR at the time of this writing, refer to the following document at Cisco.com:
	"Cisco IOS Software Release 12.2T Network-Based Application Recognition"
	Or download PDLMs directly from the following website:
	www.cisco.com/cgi-bin/tablebuild.pl/pdlm

NBAR Protocol Discovery

The first step in being able to classify network traffic is to actually know what protocols and applications are running on the network. This knowledge enables administrators to prioritize business-critical information and applications over less-important applications. Unfortunately, to configure ACLs to classify network traffic you must have prior knowledge of the network applications, as well as their associated protocol or port numbers. One option for discovering the protocols currently traversing an interface within the network is using NBAR protocol discovery. NBAR is capable of recognizing any protocol included within the PDLM file. Protocol discovery is applied to the desired interface or group of interfaces using the following command at each intended interface:

```
ip nbar protocol-discovery
```

When protocol discovery is applied to the interface, statistics are gathered depicting the active protocols traversing the interface. To view the results of the protocol discovery process, use the following command:

```
show ip nbar protocol-discovery [interface type num]
```

Example 9-1 demonstrates the behavior of the NBAR protocol discovery process.

Example 9-1 *Configuring and Verifying NBAR Protocol Discovery*

```
MSFC#configure terminal
MSFC(config)#interface serial 3/1/0
MSFC(config-if)#ip nbar protocol-discovery
MSFC#show ip nbar protocol-discovery interface serial 3/0/0

 Serial3/0/0
                            Input                   Output
    Protocol                Packet Count            Packet Count
                            Byte Count              Byte Count
                            30 second bit rate (bps) 30 second bit rate (bps)
    ------------------------ ------------------------ ------------------------
    fasttrack               1142                    25636899
                            53674                   7691069400
                            0                       1988000
    secure-http             2227281                 32046128
                            104682300               6409225600
                            27000                   1657000
    ssh                     209780                  22432288
                            9859648                 5608071500
                            0                       1449000
    realaudio               19227675                217434
                            4806918750              10219398
                            1242000                 2000
    ntp                     2990024                 6409226
                            140531614               961383900
                            38000                   249000
    icmp                    36144                   102
                            2170488                 10608
                            0                       0
    eigrp                   19540                   9724
                            1242576                 620451
                            0                       0
    bgp                     812                     406
                            39788                   17864
                            0                       0
 (text omitted)
    Total                   5702157                 140751114
                            268799486               34224484573
                            67000                   6585000
```

NBAR Classification

For low-speed serial connections, it is essential to ensure critical applications are given precedence to the available bandwidth. You can use NBAR protocol discovery to discover what applications are utilizing network resources, as well as roughly estimate the bandwidth consumption of those protocols. You can use this information to determine effective policies to sustain end-to-end service levels.

In the preceding **show ip nbar protocol-discovery** output, for example, NBAR recognizes Fasttrack as one of the applications utilizing considerable bandwidth on this connection. Fasttrack is a protocol used for peer-to-peer applications, such as Kazaa and Grokster. In this example, protocols matching these descriptions are not mission-critical and are deemed low-priority. To restrict the bandwidth used by the protocols matching these descriptions, the following example uses a policer. As a result, access to the available bandwidth is restricted for these applications. The policer is configured using the MQC and is verified using **show policy-map interface** {*type num*}.

Example 9-2   *Configuring Distributed NBAR Classification and Verifying Configuration*

```
MSFC#configure terminal
MSFC(config)# class-map match-all Fasttrack
MSFC(config-cmap)#match protocol fasttrack
MSFC(config)#policy-map Non-critical-apps
MSFC(config-pmap)#class Fasttrack
MSFC(config-pmap-c)#police 128000 1500 1500 conform-action set-prec-transmit 0
exceed-action drop
MSFC#show policy-map interface serial 3/0/0
 Serial3/0/0
  service-policy output: Non-critical-apps
    class-map: Fasttrack (match-all)
      190667 packets, 57200100 bytes
      30 second offered rate 1345000 bps, drop rate 10000 bps
      match: protocol fasttrack
      police:
        128000 bps, 1500 limit, 1500 extended limit
        conformed 18263 packets, 5478900 bytes; action: set-prec-transmit 0
        exceeded 5 packets, 1500 bytes; action: drop
        violated 76902 packets, 23070600 bytes; action: drop
        conformed 129000 bps, exceed 0 bps violate 548000 bps
    class-map: class-default (match-any)
      640676 packets, 143760844 bytes
      30 second offered rate 3387000 bps, drop rate 0 bps
      match: any
        640676 packets, 143760844 bytes
        30 second rate 3387000 bps
```

In the preceding configuration, NBAR classifies Fasttrack traffic. The **match protocol** statement enables the administrator to specify one of the protocols recognized by NBAR as match criteria. In the example, the **fasttrack** keyword is selected. Although it is not depicted, multiple protocols may be specified as match criteria. Also if multiple protocols are listed, the class map may be configured to match all conditions, or any one of the conditions configured by selecting either the **match-any** or **match-all** keyword. The example demonstrates the **match-all** keyword. Within the policy map **fasttrack**, the MSFC polices traffic to limit the utilized bandwidth for these protocols. Additionally, the MSFC marks packets conforming to the policing contract with an IP precedence value of zero. This provides only Best Effort delivery for these packets and ensures the MSFC does not favor these packets over more mission-critical applications when competing for bandwidth on congested interfaces.

As demonstrated in the preceding example, NBAR is not an all-encompassing QoS mechanism. Rather, it is a classification tool used for classifying IP-based traffic. NBAR works in conjunction with other available QoS tools such as policing. Another mechanism NBAR operates with is class-based marking. The following section discusses class-based marking for the MSFC and FlexWAN module.

Marking

The purpose of marking is to assign different priority levels to various traffic flows. It allows downstream devices to differentiate higher-priority traffic from lower-priority traffic and perform predefined policies based on assigned precedence values or specific bits set within the particular header. The FlexWAN module is capable of marking traffic using class-based marking, *committed access rate* (CAR), or class-based policing to identify various traffic streams. Class-based marking enables the administrator to specify the IP precedence or DSCP values within the IP header, assign incoming packets to a local QoS group, or set MPLS experimental bits. CAR and class-based policing can be configured to solely mark traffic matched by the configured classification criteria. Instead of discarding violating packets, the packets are marked down and forwarded. This section explains class-based marking, CAR, and class-based policing as marking mechanisms and how they are configured on the FlexWAN module.

Class-Based Marking

Class-based marking is a mechanism used to identify and mark various traffic flows in the network. Different devices then use these set values to prioritize traffic when congestion is experienced in the network. The administrator assigns values to the various traffic flows, based on specific classification criteria. When the individual flows or groups of flows are assigned the appropriate marking parameters, devices in the network are able to act on those packets based on their assigned marking. This action allows downstream devices to differentiate among the various high- and low-priority protocols and applications, and deterministically drop or forward packets to maintain defined service levels. When configuring class-based marking on the FlexWAN module, you have three possible marking options. The following command syntax shows the three available options:

```
set {{ip {dscp {dscp} | precedence {prec}}} | {qos-group {group#}} | {mpls experimental
   {exp}}}
```

One option is to assign a value to the ToS field. The administrator assigns either an IP precedence or DSCP value within the IP header. The second option is to assign the traffic to a QoS group. This provides additional granularity beyond the 64 possible DSCP values. **set qos-group** can be used in networks that have a significant number of different classes of traffic, and can scale up to 100 different assigned values. Because QoS groups are assigned to ingress traffic, the FlexWAN module uses the QoS group value to prioritize traffic for transmission. Finally, the FlexWAN module also supports **set mpls experimental** for egress traffic. Often, packets are marked based on IP precedence or DSCP values. DSCP is the recommended alternative if all devices in the network support DSCP. DSCP provides substantially more granularity than IP precedence, permitting up to 64 different service levels to be defined. Example 9-3 through Example 9-6 demonstrate and explain the various steps of configuring class-based marking on the FlexWAN module, including the following:

- Defining classes and grouping application by class (Example 9-3)

- Configuring policies based on essential and nonessential traffic (Example 9-4)

- Implementing the service policy statement (Example 9-5)

- Verifying that the configuration appears as intended (Example 9-6)

Example 9-3 *Configuring Distributed Class-Based Marking on the FlexWAN Module*

```
MSFC#configure terminal
MSFC(config)#class-map match-any Non-essential
MSFC(config-cmap)#match protocol http
MSFC(config-cmap)#match protocol fasttrack
MSFC(config)#class-map match-any Low-Priority
MSFC(config-cmap)#match protocol smtp
MSFC(config-cmap)#match protocol secure-http
MSFC(config)#class-map match-any Business-essential
MSFC(config-cmap)#match protocol sqlnet
MSFC(config-cmap)#match protocol sqlserver
MSFC(config)#class-map match-any Video-preso
MSFC(config-cmap)#match protocol netshow
```

The first step in configuring class-based marking is to define the various classes and group the related applications and protocols into those classes. In this example, the classes are defined based on the impact they have on business functions. Applications using the Fasttrack protocol and normal web-based traffic are considered nonessential, and as a result are placed in the appropriate class. Mail traffic and secure web traffic, although not considered business-critical, are placed in a higher category than the nonessential elements. Applications essential to the business are placed in an even higher category. Because database traffic is time-sensitive, it is critical that any database components receive preferential treatment over other less-important protocols and applications. Finally, a separate category has been configured for the video applications. When the traffic has been classified, the policies are configured.

Example 9-4 *Configuring Essential and Nonessential Traffic*

```
MSFC#configure terminal
MSFC(config)#policy-map CB-Marking
MSFC(config-pmap)#class Non-essential
MSFC(config-pmap-c)# police 256000 1500 1500 conform-action set-dscp-transmit 0
  exceed-action drop
MSFC(config-pmap-c)#class Low-Priority
MSFC(config-pmap-c)#set ip dscp 8
MSFC(config-pmap-c)#class Business-essential
MSFC(config-pmap-c)#set ip dscp 16
MSFC(config-pmap-c)#class Video-preso
MSFC(config-pmap-c)#set ip dscp 24
```

In addition to marking the "nonessential" traffic with DSCP 0, the traffic is also being policed to 256 kbps. Therefore, not only is the nonessential traffic dropped first during periods of congestion, the bandwidth is also limited, allowing more availability to other protocols and applications, such as voice. When the policies are defined, the configured policy map is applied to the interface with the desired **service-policy** statement.

Example 9-5 *Configuring the **service-policy** Statement*

```
MSFC(config)#interface serial 3/0/0
MSFC(config-if)#service-policy input CB-Marking
MSFC(config-if)#end
```

After all the configuration steps have been taken, you can verify the configuration and performance with **show policy-map interface** {*type num*}.

Example 9-6 *Verifying the Configuration*

```
MSFC#show policy-map interface serial 3/0/0
 Serial3/0/0
  service-policy input: CB-Marking
    class-map: Non-essential (match-any)
      198987 packets, 61685950 bytes
      30 second offered rate 1233000 bps, drop rate 925000 bps
      match: protocol http
        119392 packets, 41787200 bytes
        30 second rate 834000 bps
      match: protocol fasttrack
        79595 packets, 19898750 bytes
        30 second rate 395000 bps
      police:
        256000 bps, 1500 limit, 1500 extended limit
        conformed 49311 packets, 12694050 bytes; action: set-dscp-transmit 0
        exceeded 8 packets, 2600 bytes; action: drop
        violated 149668 packets, 48989300 bytes; action: drop
        conformed 252000 bps, exceed 0 bps violate 978000 bps
    class-map: Low-Priority (match-any)
      129343 packets, 35071825 bytes
      30 second offered rate 699000 bps, drop rate 0 bps
      match: protocol smtp
```

Example 9-6   *Verifying the Configuration (Continued)*

```
                    39798 packets, 5969700 bytes
                    30 second rate 118000 bps
                 match: protocol secure-http
                    89545 packets, 29102125 bytes
                    30 second rate 580000 bps
                 set:
                    ip dscp 8
              class-map: Business-essential (match-any)
                 139292 packets, 23878575 bytes
                 30 second offered rate 476000 bps, drop rate 0 bps
                 match: protocol sqlnet
                    79595 packets, 17908875 bytes
                    30 second rate 355000 bps
                 match: protocol sqlserver
                    59697 packets, 5969700 bytes
                    30 second rate 118000 bps
                 set:
                    ip dscp 16
              class-map: Video-preso (match-any)
                 159189 packets, 55716150 bytes
                 30 second offered rate 1113000 bps, drop rate 0 bps
                 match: protocol netshow
                    159189 packets, 55716150 bytes
                    30 second rate 1113000 bps
                 set:
                    ip dscp 24
              class-map: class-default (match-any)
                 176 packets, 11174 bytes
                 30 second offered rate 0 bps, drop rate 0 bps
                 match: any
                    176 packets, 11174 bytes
                    30 second rate 0 bps
```

Marking Using Committed Access Rate (CAR)

CAR is a legacy QoS mechanism and is not generally recommended for new deployments.
For the sake of completeness, an explanation of CAR's configuration and functionality is
included in this chapter. Although CAR is primarily used as a policing mechanism, you can
also use CAR to mark traffic. CAR is configured to match traffic using an ACL, a pre-estab-
lished DSCP value, a QoS group, or CAR matches all ingress or egress traffic traversing an
interface, based on the direction the command is applied. The following command applies
CAR to the desired interface:

```
rate-limit {input | output} [[access-group[rate-limit] list #] | [qos-group
   group#>] | [dscp dscp]] {rate} {normal burst} {excess burst} conform-action
   {conform-action} exceed-action {exceed-action}
```

The **rate-limit** command is applied to a specific interface and configured in interface
configuration mode. The required **input** or **output** option specifies the direction the **rate-
limit** command is applied, relative to the traffic flow. The next set of options allows traffic

to be matched against a predetermined list or assigned value. The specified rate is measured in bits per seconds, and the burst values are measured in bytes. The **conform-action** and **exceed-action** determine what actions are taken for conforming and nonconforming packets, respectively. The following output displays the configurable actions. The keywords shown are available for both **conform-action** and **exceed-action**.

Example 9-7 *Configurable Options for the **rate-limit** Command*

```
MSFC(config-if)#rate-limit input 1000000 187500 375000 conform-action ?
  continue              scan other rate limits
  drop                  drop packet
  set-dscp-continue     set dscp, scan other rate limits
  set-dscp-transmit     set dscp and send it
  set-prec-continue     rewrite packet precedence, scan other rate limits
  set-prec-transmit     rewrite packet precedence and send it
  set-qos-continue      set qos-group, scan other rate limits
  set-qos-transmit      set qos-group and send it
  transmit              transmit packet
```

If the intent is to use CAR to mark packets, as opposed to police, the **drop** keyword is not used. Instead, a set action is specified to modify the ToS field in the IP header, or set the local QoS group value for a packet. The **transmit** keyword is yet another option, which allows a packet to be forwarded without modifying any existing settings. One additional feature with CAR is the flexibility to configure multiple **rate-limit** statements on the same interface. By using the **continue** keyword, independently or within a set action, packets can be processed through multiple **rate-limit** statements until a match is found. In the event a match is not found, the default action is to transmit. Therefore, in the absence of a match, the packet is just forwarded. Example 9-8 demonstrates configuring CAR to mark traffic. In the example, an extended ACL is configured specifying the traffic to be considered. In this instance, secure web traffic is being forwarded to the serial interface noted in the example. However, the traffic is not marked with a value that conforms to the QoS policy in place. The intent is to mark all secure web traffic conforming to the configured 1-Mbps rate with DSCP 8. Any traffic exceeding this rate is marked with DSCP 0.

Example 9-8 *Marking Secure Web Traffic with CAR*

```
MSFC#configure terminal
MSFC(config)#access-list 101 permit tcp any any eq 443
MSFC(config)#interface serial 3/0/0
MSFC(config-if)#rate-limit input access-group 101 1000000 187500 375000 conform-
action set-dscp-transmit 8 exceed-action set-dscp-transmit 0
MSFC(config-if)#end

MSFC#show interface serial 3/0/0 rate-limit
Serial3/0/0
  Input
    matches: access-group 101
      params:  1000000 bps, 187500 limit, 375000 extended limit
      conformed 115046 packets, 46018400 bytes; action: set-dscp-transmit 8
      exceeded 56927 packets, 22770800 bytes; action: set-dscp-transmit 0
      last packet: 4ms ago, current burst: 281100 bytes
      last cleared 00:06:12 ago, conformed 988000 bps, exceeded 489000 bps
```

The output verifies traffic conforming to the configured contract is marked with DSCP 8, whereas traffic violating the contract is marked with DSCP 0. The following section demonstrates using the class-based policer to accomplish the same results provided in Example 9-8.

Marking Using a Class-Based Policer

Similar to CAR, but preferred for new deployments, the class-based policer marks traffic without enforcing any policing actions. However, the class-based policer has three different actions it enforces on traffic. Like CAR, it has a conform- and an exceed-action, however the class-based policer also has a third action, violate. The violate-action applies an additional set of actions to traffic violating the configured rate and exceeding the assigned conform and excess burst values. Class-based policer operation is discussed in further detail in the "Policing and Shaping" section of this chapter.

Example 9-9   *Configuring the Distributed Class-Based Policer for Marking*

```
MSFC#configure terminal
MSFC(config)#class-map match-all Secure-Web
MSFC(config-cmap)#match protocol secure-http
MSFC(config)#policy-map Marking-policy
MSFC(config-pmap)#class Secure-Web
MSFC(config-pmap-c)#police 1000000 1500 1500 conform-action set-dscp-transmit 1
exceed-action set-dscp-transmit 0 violate-action set-dscp-transmit 0
MSFC(config)#interface serial 3/0/0
MSFC(config-if)#service-policy input Marking-policy
MSFC(config-if)#end
MSFC#show policy-map interface serial 3/0/0
 Serial3/0/0
  service-policy input: Marking-policy
    class-map: Secure-Web (match-all)
      89929 packets, 35971600 bytes
      30 second offered rate 1497000 bps, drop rate 0 bps
      match: protocol secure-http
      police:
        1000000 bps, 1500 limit, 1500 extended limit
        conformed 59733 packets, 23893200 bytes; action: set-dscp-transmit 1
        exceeded 41 packets, 16400 bytes; action: set-dscp-transmit 0
        violated 30155 packets, 12062000 bytes; action: set-dscp-transmit 0
        conformed 994000 bps, exceed 0 bps violate 500000 bps
    class-map: class-default (match-any)
      91 packets, 5764 bytes
      30 second offered rate 0 bps, drop rate 0 bps
      match: any
        91 packets, 5764 bytes
        30 second rate 0 bps
```

Similar to classification, marking is not a mechanism used independently. As demonstrated in one of the previous examples, NBAR can be a classification method used in conjunction with class-based marking. However, the important aspect of marking is it also allows other devices in the network to be able to differentiate between critical and noncritical traffic, based on the marking values. When the values are determined, different policies can be applied to the traffic, including Priority Queuing, policing, or shaping. The following section discusses policing and shaping on the FlexWAN module.

Policing and Shaping

Chapter 2 introduced policing and shaping. As discussed, both features use a token bucket mechanism for operation. Based on the token bucket analogy, when there are enough tokens available in the bucket to service an entire arriving packet, the packet is permitted to proceed. However, there is a difference between how the policer and shaper function. The shaper adapts to bursty traffic. The shaper allocates a finite amount of buffer space to accommodate burstiness. This prevents traffic exceeding the average rate from being dropped and allows packets to wait in a buffer until a sufficient amount of tokens are available to service the entire packet. The end result of the shaper is it smoothes traffic spikes down to the average configured rate. However, although shaping utilizes buffers to prevent excessive drops, the buffering process introduces latency, which adversely impacts delay-sensitive applications. As mentioned in Chapter 2, shaping is one way to prevent higher-speed interfaces from overrunning potentially lower-speed downstream interfaces. (The example used is in a Frame Relay environment.) Before deploying a shaper in a converged environment, however, you should fully understand the effects it has on traffic in the network.

Although policing uses the same token bucket scheme, policing does not buffer traffic. As a result, when the available tokens are exhausted, packets are dropped, instead of being buffered. It is also possible to drop packets using a shaper. However, packets are only dropped when the buffer space is depleted. When deploying policers and shapers in the network, the recommendation is to shape on the upstream interface and police on the downstream interface. A situation where this is practiced is when end customers connect to a service provider. The end customer does not want the service provider to determine what traffic is going to be randomly dropped. Therefore, the customer configures a shaper to conform to the policing contract configured on the service provider's receiving interface. This permits the customer to prioritize and deterministically drop traffic during periods of congestion, to ensure all mission-critical traffic is not dropped in the service provider's network. The FlexWAN module implements two types of policers: CAR and the class-based policer. The "Marking" section of this chapter demonstrated how CAR and class-based policing could be used to mark traffic. The following two sections discuss how these mechanisms are utilized as policers. This section concludes with deploying distributed traffic shaping on the FlexWAN.

Figure 9-1   *Policing and Shaping in the Network*

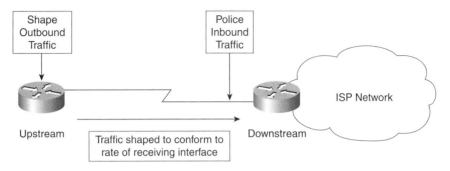

NOTE   This section does not provide an in-depth exhausted discussion on the various policing and shaping techniques. It is meant to provide a fundamental overview regarding the operation of the various mechanisms, as well as provide examples and instances where the various functions can be applied. For a more thorough discussion regarding policing and shaping, refer to Chapter 2 or refer to the following document at Cisco.com:

"Policing and Shaping Overview"

Committed Access Rate (CAR)

Prior to class-based policing and the release of the Cisco MQC, CAR was the preferred method for policing traffic. CAR does not allocate buffer space for queuing oversubscribed packets, nor does CAR guarantee minimum amounts of bandwidth for applications. The purpose of CAR, like most policers, is to limit access to the available bandwidth. This enables administrators, through designing specific policies, to ensure lower-priority applications do not starve out mission-critical applications. This facilitates network traffic flowing more deterministically through the network. The command syntax displayed previously in Example 9-8 is used to configure CAR as a policing mechanism:

```
rate-limit {input | output} [[access-group[rate-limit] list #] | [qos-group group#] |
   [dscp dscp]] {rate} {normal burst} {excess burst} conform-action {conform-action}
   exceed-action{exceed-action}
```

CAR works using a token bucket mechanism. The committed rate, measured in bits per second, defines the token arrival rate. As long as there are sufficient tokens available to service an entire packet, traffic flows through the policer. When the tokens are depleted, or there aren't enough available to accommodate an entire packet, that packet and possibly subsequent packets are dropped. The token bucket depth is defined by the burst parameters. CAR defines a *committed burst* (Bc) and an *excess burst* (Be). When defining the burst values, in order to use the excess burst capability, the Be value must be greater than Bc. If

Be equals Bc, excess burst is not defined, and there are no additional tokens available when the Bc bucket is depleted. Also it is not possible to configure the Be value to be less than Bc. In the event this does occur, Cisco IOS sets the Be equal to Bc. The burst values are measured in bytes.

Table 9-4 demonstrates CAR's operational behavior however; a few assumptions have been made. For demonstration purposes, token replenishment does not occur. Also all packets in the table arrived at the same instance on the receiving interface. Packet size is fixed at 250 bytes per packet. Finally, the values for the rate, committed burst, and excess burst are 8000 bits per second, 1500 bytes, and 3000 bytes, respectively.

NOTE
For Table 9-4, the Be value is configured for 3000 bytes. When configuring the Be parameter for CAR, it is necessary to consider the Bc value. The configured Be value is actually the sum of the Bc and Be. Therefore, for Table 9-4, although the configured Be is 3000 bytes, only 1500 additional bytes are available for the Be bucket.

Table 9-4   *CAR Operation (Actual and Compounded Debt)*

Time	Packet Size	Actual Debt (ai)	Compounded Debt (Dc)	
0	0	0	0	<-- Committed burst bucket depleted.
1	250	250	250	
2	250	500	750	
3	250	750	1500	
4	250	1000	**2500**	<-- Packet dropped. (Dc exceeds Be.)
4		750	0	<-- Tokens not removed from excess burst bucket.
5	250	1000	1000	
6	250	1250	**2250**	<-- Packet dropped. (Dc exceeds Be.)
6		1000	0	
7	250	1250	1250	
8	250	1500	**2750**	<-- Packet dropped. (Dc exceeds Be.)

Table 9-4   *CAR Operation (Actual and Compounded Debt) (Continued)*

Time	Packet Size	Actual Debt (ai)	Compounded Debt (Dc)	
8		1250	0	
9	250	1500	1500	<-- Packet transmitted.

After Time 9, all subsequent packets experience a tail-drop scenario (ai > Dc), until the bucket is replenished with tokens.

The table demonstrates the interaction between actual and compounded debt. As conforming packets are processed by the CAR mechanism, the actual and compounded debt values accrue. When a packet causes the compounded debt value to exceed the excess burst, that packet is dropped. Because the packet is discarded, however, no tokens are removed from the bucket and the compounded debt is reset to zero.

Example 9-10   *Configuring Distributed CAR for Ingress Traffic Flows*

```
MSFC#configure terminal
MSFC(config)#access-list 110 remark Non-essential traffic
MSFC(config)#access-list 110 permit tcp any eq 1214 any
MSFC(config)#access-list 110 permit tcp any e 80 any
MSFC(config)#access-list 111 remark Low-priority traffic
MSFC(config)#access-list 111 permit tcp any eq 25 any
MSFC(config)#access-list 111 permit tcp any eq 443 any
MSFC(config)#access-list 112 remark Mission-Critical traffic
MSFC(config)#access-list 112 permit tcp any eq 1521 any
MSFC(config)#access-list 112 permit tcp any eq 1433 any
MSFC(config)#access-list 113 remark Video-applications
MSFC(config)#access-list 113 permit tcp any eq 1755 any
MSFC(config)#access-list 114 permit ip any any
MSFC(config)#interface serial 3/0/0
MSFC(config-if)#rate-limit input access-group 110 344000 65625 131250 conform-
action set-dscp-transmit 0 exceed-action continue
MSFC(config-if)#rate-limit input access-group 111 400000 75000 150000 conform-
   action set-dscp-transmit 6 exceed-action continue
MSFC(config-if)#rate-limit input access-group 112 400000 75000 150000 conform-
   action set-dscp-transmit 16 exceed-action continue
MSFC(config-if)#rate-limit input access-group 113 1000000 187500 375000 conform-
   action set-dscp-transmit 26 exceed-action continue
MSFC(config-if)#rate-limit input access-group 114 4000000 750000 1500000 conform-
   action drop exceed-action drop
MSFC(config-if)#end

MSFC#show interface serial 3/0/0 rate-limit
Serial3/0/0
  Input
    matches: access-group 110
```

continues

Example 9-10 *Configuring Distributed CAR for Ingress Traffic Flows (Continued)*

```
      params:  344000 bps, 65625 limit, 131250 extended limit
      conformed 294270 packets, 80617800 bytes; action: set-dscp-transmit 0
      exceeded 641561 packets, 209489650 bytes; action: continue
      last packet: 4ms ago, current burst: 131010 bytes
      last cleared 00:31:56 ago, conformed 336000 bps, exceeded 874000 bps
    matches: access-group 111
      params:  400000 bps, 75000 limit, 150000 extended limit
      conformed 315610 packets, 93739250 bytes; action: set-dscp-transmit 6
      exceeded 529878 packets, 197663700 bytes; action: continue
      last packet: 4ms ago, current burst: 149850 bytes
      last cleared 00:31:56 ago, conformed 391000 bps, exceeded 825000 bps
    matches: access-group 112
      params:  400000 bps, 75000 limit, 150000 extended limit
      conformed 550546 packets, 93677725 bytes; action: set-dscp-transmit 16
      exceeded 104531 packets, 18620850 bytes; action: continue
      last packet: 1ms ago, current burst: 88350 bytes
      last cleared 00:31:56 ago, conformed 391000 bps, exceeded 77000 bps
    matches: access-group 113
      params:  1000000 bps, 187500 limit, 375000 extended limit
      conformed 658258 packets, 230390300 bytes; action: set-dscp-transmit 26
      exceeded 0 packets, 0 bytes; action: continue
      last packet: 4ms ago, current burst: 250 bytes
      last cleared 00:31:58 ago, conformed 960000 bps, exceeded 0 bps
    matches: access-group 114
      params:  4000000 bps, 750000 limit, 1500000 extended limit
      conformed 1276414 packets, 425802136 bytes; action: drop
      exceeded 0 packets, 0 bytes; action: drop
      last packet: 4ms ago, current burst: 400 bytes
      last cleared 00:31:58 ago, conformed 1775000 bps, exceeded 0 bps
```

Class-Based Policer

The class-based policer is an alternative policing mechanism available for the FlexWAN module. Because of the development of the MQC, the class-based policer is the recommended policer for newer deployments. Similar to CAR, the class-based policer uses a token bucket mechanism to perform the policing action. Compared to CAR, however, the class-based policer is more versatile and actually employs the use of two token buckets rather than one. The two token buckets for the class-based policer represent the *committed burst size* (CBS) and the *excess burst size* (EBS). The committed information rate is responsible for defining how the rate tokens are replenished in both token buckets. As a result of using the additional token bucket, the class-based policer offers three possible policing actions. These three actions are modeled after the behavior described in RFC 2697, which discusses the single-rate three-color policer. The various available actions—conform, exceed, and violate—represent the three different colors green, yellow, and red, respectively.

The class-based policer is configured using the MQC. The policing parameters are configured under the policy map class using the following command:

```
police {rate} [normal burst] [excess burst] conform-action {conform-action} [exceed-
action {exceed-action}] [violate-action {violate-action}]
```

Figure 9-2   *Class-Based Policer*

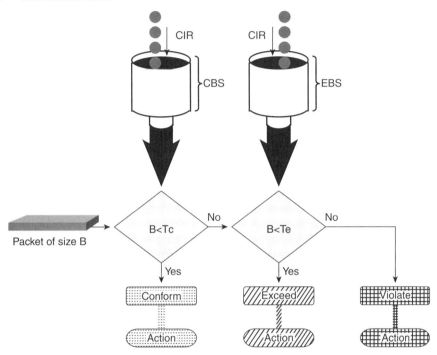

The rate is measured in bits per second, and the optional burst parameters are measured in bytes. Five options are available for the conform-action; **drop**, **transmit**, **set-dscp-transmit**, **set-prec-transmit**, and **set-qos-transmit**. These same options are available for the exceed-action and violate-action as well. All packets conforming to the configured committed information rate are forwarded based on the forward action. When a packet is forwarded, the number of tokens equal to the size of the packet is removed from the Bc bucket. If a packet exceeds the committed information rate, meaning, there are not enough tokens in the Bc bucket to service the entire packet, the exceed-action is enforced. When a packet is forwarded based on the exceed-action, the appropriate amount of tokens are depleted from the Be bucket. Finally, if a packet exceeds the configured rate and there are not enough tokens available in the Be bucket to accommodate the entire packet, the packet violates the configured contract. As a result, the violate-action is enforced. This may result in marking down the packet's DSCP value or just dropping the violating packet. You can also configure the class-based policer to emulate a single-bucket CAR implementation. By only configuring the conform-action and exceed-action, the class-based policer will behave based on a single-bucket policing mechanism. If the violate-action is not specified in the configuration, the Be bucket is not configured, and therefore not used. Also specifying the **drop** keyword as the preferred action at any point results in all subsequent actions being configured to drop. Example 9-11 shows a class-based policer configuration and how to verify the behavior.

Example 9-11 *Configuring and Verifying Distributed Class-Based Policing*

```
MSFC(config)#class-map match-any Non-essential
MSFC(config-cmap)#match protocol http
MSFC(config-cmap)#match protocol fasttrack
MSFC(config)#class-map match-any Low-Priority
MSFC(config-cmap)#match protocol smtp
MSFC(config-cmap)#match protocol secure-http
MSFC(config)#class-map match-any Business-essential
MSFC(config-cmap)#match protocol sqlnet
MSFC(config-cmap)#match protocol sqlserver
MSFC(config)#class-map match-any Video-preso
MSFC(config-cmap)#match protocol netshow
MSFC(config-cmap)#exit
MSFC(config)#policy-map CB-Policing
MSFC(config-pmap)#class Non-essential
MSFC(config-pmap-c)#police 344000 65625 65625 conform-action set-dscp-transmit 0
  exceed-action drop
MSFC(config-pmap-c)#exit
MSFC(config-pmap)#class Low-Priority
MSFC(config-pmap-c)#police 400000 75000 75000 conform-action set-dscp-transmit 6
  exceed-action set-dscp-transmit 0 violate-action drop
MSFC(config-pmap-c)#exit
MSFC(config-pmap)#class Business-essential
MSFC(config-pmap-c)#police 400000 75000 75000 conform-action set-dscp-transmit 16
  exceed-action set-dscp-transmit 8 violate-action drop
MSFC(config-pmap-c)#exit
MSFC(config-pmap)#class Video-preso
MSFC(config-pmap-c)#police 1000000 187500 187500 conform-action set-dscp-transmit
26 exceed-action set-dscp-transmit 18 violate-action drop
MSFC(config-pmap-c)#exit
MSFC(config-pmap)#exit
MSFC(config)#interface serial 3/0/0
MSFC(config-if)#service-policy input CB-Policing
MSFC(config-if)#end

MSFC#show policy-map interface serial 3/0/0
 Serial3/0/0
 service-policy input: CB-Policing
   class-map: Non-essential (match-any)
     475684 packets, 147459900 bytes
     30 second offered rate 1230000 bps, drop rate 650000 bps
     match: protocol http
       285389 packets, 99886150 bytes
       30 second rate 833000 bps
     match: protocol fasttrack
       190295 packets, 47573750 bytes
       30 second rate 395000 bps
     police:
       344000 bps, 65625 limit, 65625 extended limit
       conformed 151166 packets, 41049400 bytes; action: set-dscp-transmit 0
```

Example 9-11 *Configuring and Verifying Distributed Class-Based Policing (Continued)*

```
          exceeded 405 packets, 130850 bytes; action: drop
          violated 324112 packets, 106279300 bytes; action: drop
          conformed 341000 bps, exceed 0 bps violate 887000 bps
      class-map: Low-Priority (match-any)
        394109 packets, 132133750 bytes
        30 second offered rate 707000 bps, drop rate 226000 bps
        match: protocol smtp
          95140 packets, 14271000 bytes
          30 second rate 117000 bps
        match: protocol secure-http
          298969 packets, 117862750 bytes
          30 second rate 587000 bps
        police:
          400000 bps, 75000 limit, 75000 extended limit
          conformed 178233 packets, 48220925 bytes; action: set-dscp-transmit 6
          exceeded 439 packets, 149825 bytes; action: set-dscp-transmit 0
          violated 218631 packets, 84629025 bytes; action: drop
          conformed 396000 bps, exceed 0 bps violate 309000 bps
      class-map: Business-essential (match-any)
        332979 packets, 57081025 bytes
        30 second offered rate 475000 bps, drop rate 54000 bps
        match: protocol sqlnet
          190265 packets, 42809625 bytes
          30 second rate 356000 bps
        match: protocol sqlserver
          142714 packets, 14271400 bytes
          30 second rate 117000 bps
        police:
          400000 bps, 75000 limit, 75000 extended limit
          conformed 281382 packets, 48220450 bytes; action: set-dscp-transmit 16
          exceeded 802 packets, 149950 bytes; action: set-dscp-transmit 8
          violated 54235 packets, 9300375 bytes; action: drop
          conformed 396000 bps, exceed 0 bps violate 76000 bps
      class-map: Video-preso (match-any)
        316766 packets, 110868100 bytes
        30 second offered rate 1107000 bps, drop rate 79000 bps
        match: protocol netshow
          316766 packets, 110868100 bytes
          30 second rate 1107000 bps
        police:
          1000000 bps, 187500 limit, 187500 extended limit
          conformed 316429 packets, 110750150 bytes; action: set-dscp-transmit 26
          exceeded 535 packets, 187250 bytes; action: set-dscp-transmit 18
          violated 3734 packets, 1306900 bytes; action: drop
          conformed 992000 bps, exceed 0 bps violate 112000 bps
      class-map: class-default (match-any)
        95643 packets, 19061418 bytes
        30 second offered rate 157000 bps, drop rate 0 bps
        match: any
          95643 packets, 19061418 bytes
          30 second rate 157000 bps
```

Distributed Traffic Shaping

Traffic shaping is a mechanism that regulates the amount of traffic leaving a particular interface. Contrary to the policer, the traffic-shaping mechanism allocates buffers to accommodate traffic exceeding the committed information rate. Buffering allows the traffic shaper to tolerate short bursts in traffic, which are regulated and subsequently transmitted at the committed rate. Shaping is commonly found in Frame Relay environments, or on interfaces peering to a service provider. Due to potential speed mismatches within a Frame Relay cloud, traffic shaping is implemented to ensure downstream interfaces are not overwhelmed with traffic. Traffic shaping prevents bottlenecks and congestion from occurring within the network. In the case of service providers, they provide their customers with specific service-level contracts. Frequently, service providers strictly enforce these contracts by policing traffic transmitted toward the provider cloud. Shaping can be applied in this instance to ensure network traffic conforms to the provider's policies. This enables the end user to deterministically prioritize their traffic and ensure mission-critical applications are not left to the discretion of the provider. The FlexWAN module supports *distributed traffic shaping* (DTS). DTS is configured using the MQC and applied under the policy map class using the following command:

```
shape {average | peak} {rate} [normal burst] [excess burst]
```

Rate is expressed in bits per second and represents the average transmission rate for egress traffic. Normal burst (Bc) and excess burst (Be) are expressed in bits and represent the number of bits transmitted per time interval (Bc/rate). When the **average** keyword is specified, a total of Bc is transmitted per time interval. If the **peak** keyword is specified, (Bc + Be) is transmitted per time interval. When establishing burst values, increasing Bc increases the time between transmissions. This negatively impacts latency for time-sensitive applications if the shaping mechanism is applied to the physical interface. When configuring shaping using the MQC, if voice traffic is present, it is normally assigned to the LLQ. When assigned to the strict-priority LLQ, voice traffic present in the queue is immediately serviced ahead of other traffic. Therefore, voice streams are not affected by shaping imposed on the other configured queues. If shaping is applied to a physical interface, however, Bc and its effect on network traffic must be carefully considered, particularly if voice traffic traverses the same interface.

In addition to the previous **shape** command, DTS provides mechanisms specific to Frame Relay environments. When congestion is experienced within a Frame Relay cloud, switches within the cloud send congestion notifications—*forward-explicit congestion notifications* (FECNs) and *backward-explicit congestion notifications* (BECNs)—to the end devices. These congestion notifications inform the devices along the transmission path that congestion has occurred and transmission rates should be throttled. The first command listed instructs the receiving interface to send BECNs back to the transmitting device once a FECN is received from the network. The second command specifies what transmission rate the interface should adjust to in the event congestion is detected. Both commands are configured using the MQC and applied under the policy map class:

```
shape fecn-adapt
shape adaptive {rate}
```

NOTE   Frame Relay operation is beyond the scope of this book. For more information regarding Frame Relay, refer to the Frame Relay technology overview document at Cisco.com.

The following example demonstrates how to configure DTS on the FlexWAN module. In this example, all traffic on serial 3/0/2 is shaped down to 2.4 Mbps. This example shows the upstream transmitting and downstream receiving interfaces and the shaping mechanism operation. Figure 9-3 depicts how these devices are connected.

Figure 9-3   *Distributed Traffic Shaping*

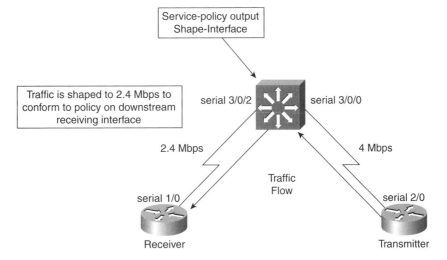

Example 9-12   *Configuring and Verifying Distributed Traffic Shaping*

```
MSFC#configure terminal
MSFC(config)#access-list 150 permit ip any any
MSFC(config)#class-map All-traffic
MSFC(config-cmap)#match access-group 150
MSFC(config-cmap)#policy-map Shape-Interface
MSFC(config-pmap)#class All-traffic
MSFC(config-pmap-c)#shape average 24000000
MSFC(config)#interface serial 3/0/2
MSFC(config-if)#service-policy output Shape-Interface
MSFC(config-if)#end
Transmitting#show interfaces serial2/0
Serial2/0 is up, line protocol is up
  Hardware is M4T
  Internet address is 192.168.50.2/30
  MTU 1500 bytes, BW 4000 Kbit, DLY 20000 usec,
     reliability 255/255, txload 255/255, rxload 26/255
  Encapsulation HDLC, crc 16, loopback not set
  Keepalive set (10 sec)
```

continues

Example 9-12 *Configuring and Verifying Distributed Traffic Shaping (Continued)*

```
    Last input 00:00:00, output 00:00:00, output hang never
    Last clearing of "show interface" counters 00:22:09
    Queueing strategy: fifo
    Output queue 0/40, 0 drops; input queue 0/75, 0 drops
    30 second input rate 53000 bits/sec, 152 packets/sec
    30 second output rate 2564000 bits/sec, 1320 packets/sec
       199706 packets input, 8838730 bytes, 0 no buffer
       Received 155 broadcasts, 0 runts, 0 giants, 0 throttles
       0 input errors, 0 CRC, 0 frame, 0 overrun, 0 ignored, 0 abort
       1709676 packets output, 417003428 bytes, 0 underruns
       0 output errors, 0 collisions, 0 interface resets
       0 output buffer failures, 0 output buffers swapped out
       0 carrier transitions     DCD=up  DSR=up  DTR=up  RTS=up  CTS=up

MSFC#show policy-map interface serial3/0/2
 Serial3/0/2
  service-policy output: Shape-Interface
    class-map: All-traffic (match-all)
       1374692 packets, 333637211 bytes
       30 second offered rate 2587000 bps, drop rate 51000 bps
       match: access-group 150
       queue size 134, queue limit 500
       packets output 1320791, packet drops 53898
       tail/random drops 53898, no buffer drops 0, other drops 0
       shape: cir 2400000,  Bc 9600,  Be 9600
         output bytes 312025836, shape rate 2419000 bps
       fair-queue: per-flow queue limit 125
    class-map: class-default (match-any)
       0 packets, 0 bytes
       30 second offered rate 0 bps, drop rate 0 bps
       match: any
         0 packets, 0 bytes
         30 second rate 0 bps
Downstream#show interfaces serial1/0
Serial1/0 is up, line protocol is up
  Hardware is M4T
  Internet address is 192.168.60.2/30
  MTU 1500 bytes, BW 4000 Kbit, DLY 20000 usec,
     reliability 255/255, txload 3/255, rxload 152/255
  Encapsulation HDLC, crc 16, loopback not set
  Keepalive set (10 sec)
  Last input 00:00:00, output 00:00:00, output hang never
  Last clearing of "show interface" counters 00:07:35
  Queueing strategy: fifo
  Output queue 0/40, 0 drops; input queue 39/75, 0 drops
  30 second input rate 2397000 bits/sec, 1269 packets/sec
  30 second output rate 55000 bits/sec, 154 packets/sec
     577710 packets input, 136495374 bytes, 0 no buffer
     Received 53 broadcasts, 0 runts, 0 giants, 0 throttles
     0 input errors, 0 CRC, 0 frame, 0 overrun, 0 ignored, 0 abort
     69483 packets output, 3082383 bytes, 0 underruns
     0 output errors, 0 collisions, 0 interface resets
     0 output buffer failures, 0 output buffers swapped out
     0 carrier transitions     DCD=up  DSR=up  DTR=up  RTS=up  CTS=up
```

Congestion Management and Scheduling

Discussed in Chapter 2, congestion management is a technique used to manage traffic flows at points of congestion within the network. The congestion management process involves the following three steps:

1 Creating different queues to accommodate network traffic

2 Assigning packets to the various queues based on predefined characteristics

3 Scheduling between the various queues to provide queued packets access to the available bandwidth when congestion has occurred on the link

This section discusses the various congestion management mechanisms supported on the FlexWAN module. They include *distributed Weighted Fair Queuing* (dWFQ), *distributed Class-Based Weighted Fair Queuing* (dCBWFQ), and *distributed Low Latency Queuing* (dLLQ). Examples are provided in the section demonstrating the necessary configuration steps, as well as show commands to verify functionality.

Distributed Weighted Fair Queuing

Distributed Weighted Fair Queuing (dWFQ) is a congestion management mechanism that operates on the FlexWAN's VIPs and provides fair treatment for outbound flows on congested interfaces. WFQ is enabled by default on all interfaces operating at 2.048 Mbps and less. WFQ protects low-bandwidth traffic flows by ensuring high volume conversations do not monopolize the available bandwidth. The mechanism works by assigning each traffic flow to its own queue. A flow is defined as packets possessing the same source IP address, destination IP address, source TCP or UDP port, destination TCP or UDP port, protocol ID, and type of service value. Once a packet is assigned to a queue, the WFQ mechanism services each queue ensuring each queue receives a fair share of the available bandwidth, based on the assigned weight for that flow.

WFQ uses packet size and arrival time in conjunction with a weighting factor to permit access to the bandwidth. WFQ is QoS aware. If a packet arrives with a high precedence value, the weight assigned to the packet will be low. Therefore, the higher the precedence value the lower the weight. The lower weight translates to faster de-queuing and transmission time, which translates to more access to the available bandwidth. dWFQ for a VIP or FlexWAN is configured on the physical WAN interface. dWFQ operates the same as WFQ, with the exception weight is not assigned to a packet when executed in a distributed fashion on one of the VIPs of the FlexWAN module. All traffic flows are provided equal access to the available bandwidth. However, low bandwidth flows are still protected from being starved by high bandwidth conversations. The following commands configure flow-based dWFQ on the target interface. The subsequent **show** commands allow the administrator to verify the configuration and monitor the statistics for the applicable interface.

```
fair-queue
fair-queue [[aggregate-limit {# packets}] | [individual-limit {# packets}]]
show queueing fair [interface {type num}]
show interface {type num}
```

The command **fair-queue** enables flow-based dWFQ for the configured interface. After dWFQ is enabled on the interface, the optional **aggregate-limit** keyword in conjunction with the **fair-queue** command is used to specify the maximum number of packets that may be present between all queues. Exceeding this value results in enforcement of the individual queue limits and possible discard for subsequent arriving packets needing to be queued. The optional **individual-limit** keyword specifies the maximum number of packets that can be queued for an individual flow queue. If the number of packets queued for a per flow queue increases above the number specified by the **individual-limit** keyword, all subsequent arriving packets are dropped. Despite the enforcement of the aggregate and individual limits, packets already placed in the queue are not discarded. It is not recommended to alter the **aggregate-limit** or **individual-limit** values from their default settings. Before deciding to change the values from their defaults, carefully consider how these changes will impact network and traffic performance.

dWFQ's benefit is its relative ease to implement. dWFQ functions independently of access-lists or the MQC. Although WFQ provides fair access to the available bandwidth, it does not provide specific bandwidth guarantees for the various queues or classes during periods of congestion. The next section describes class-based weighted fair queuing and its benefits.

Distributed Class-Based Weighted Fair Queuing

CBWFQ is the most widely recognized QoS mechanism deployed today. CBWFQ enhances the functionality available with WFQ.

CBWFQ provides scalable fair treatment of traffic on a class-by-class basis. However, CBWFQ also assigns minimum bandwidth guarantees to classes of traffic, to ensure bandwidth is available for critical applications. The minimum bandwidth assigned to a class is expressed as a percentage or a rate, expressed in kilobits per second. This number guarantees a class a minimum level of bandwidth in the event congestion is experienced on the interface, and assigns a weight to all packets matching the criteria of the given class. This weight denotes the frequency a class is serviced during periods of congestion, ensuring the fair treatment of all traffic according to the configured policy. Because the weight assigned to a class is a percentage based on the total available bandwidth for the assigned interface, it is essential to ensure the bandwidth statement for the interface properly depicts what is available. Any remaining bandwidth not assigned to one of the configured classes is allocated to the default class. By default, the sum of all bandwidth assigned to the various classes cannot exceed 75 percent of the total available bandwidth provisioned for an interface. The remaining 25 percent provides minimum bandwidth guarantees for Best Effort, overhead, and network control traffic. Use the following command to assign a minimum bandwidth to a class:

```
bandwidth {{rate} | percent {percentage}}
```

CAUTION   You can alter the 75 percent maximum bandwidth guarantee allocated for all configured classes by using the interface command **max-reserved-bandwidth** [*percent*]. However, before modifying this value, careful consideration must be given to ensure the configured classes do not consume the available bandwidth, starving overhead and critical network control traffic.

CBWFQ is configured using the MQC. The minimum bandwidth guarantee assigned to the appropriate class is configured under the policy-map class. For all administratively defined classes, a minimum bandwidth must be assigned to the applicable class before fair queuing is enabled. The exception to this behavior is the default class. A minimum bandwidth guarantee is not required to configure flow-based WFQ for the default class. Fair-queuing is configured for a specific class using the command **fair-queue** [**queue-limit** {*queue #*}]. The **queue-limit** keyword associated with the **fair-queue** command specifies the maximum number of possible per-flow queues for the configured class. Optionally, the command **queue-limit** {*packets*}, also configured under the policy-map class, specifies the maximum number of packets that can be queued for the associated class. If the number of packets queued for the class increases above the number specified by the **queue-limit** command, all subsequent packets are tail-dropped. Example 9-9 demonstrates configuring flow-based WFQ for the default class called "class-default." The default class matches any packets not matched by the classification criteria specified in the configured class-maps. Configuring flow-based WFQ for the default class allows queues within the class to fairly share the available bandwidth.

Unlike policing and shaping, the minimum bandwidth guarantees configured for CBWFQ do not represent a maximum upper-bound limit. If a particular class is not transmitting, or fully utilizing the minimum allocated bandwidth, that bandwidth is available to the other classes, allowing them to transmit above their minimum guarantees. Example 9-13 demonstrates configuring and verifying CBWFQ behavior.

Example 9-13   *Configuring Distributed WFQ*

```
MSFC#configure terminal
MSFC(config)#class-map match-any Low-Priority
MSFC(config-cmap)#match protocol smtp
MSFC(config-cmap)#match protocol secure-http
MSFC(config)#class-map match-any Business-essential
MSFC(config-cmap)#match protocol sqlnet
MSFC(config-cmap)#match protocol sqlserver
MSFC(config)#class-map match-any Video-preso
MSFC(config-cmap)#match protocol netshow
MSFC(config-cmap)#exit
MSFC(config)#policy-map dCBWFQ
MSFC(config-pmap)#class Low-Priority
MSFC(config-pmap-c)#bandwidth 400
MSFC(config-pmap-c)#fair-queue
MSFC(config-pmap-c)#exit
MSFC(config-pmap)#class Business-essential
MSFC(config-pmap-c)#bandwidth 400
MSFC(config-pmap-c)#fair-queue
MSFC(config-pmap-c)#class Video-preso
MSFC(config-pmap-c)#bandwidth 1000
```

continues

Example 9-13 *Configuring Distributed WFQ (Continued)*

```
MSFC(config-pmap-c)#fair-queue
MSFC(config-pmap)#class class-default
MSFC(config-pmap-c)#fair-queue
MSFC(config-pmap-c)#exit
MSFC(config-pmap)#exit
MSFC(config)#interface serial 3/0/2
MSFC(config-if)#service-policy output dCBWFQ
MSFC(config-if)#end

MSFC#show interfaces serial 3/0/2
Serial3/0/2 is up, line protocol is up
  Hardware is Serial
  Internet address is 192.168.60.1/30
  MTU 1500 bytes, BW 4000 Kbit, DLY 20000 usec,
     reliability 255/255, txload 165/255, rxload 1/255
  Encapsulation HDLC, crc 16, loopback not set
  Keepalive set (10 sec)
  Last input 00:00:03, output 00:00:01, output hang never
  Last clearing of "show interface" counters 11:15:58
  Input queue: 0/75/0/0 (size/max/drops/flushes); Total output drops: 0
  Queueing strategy: VIP-based fair queuing
  Output queue :0/40 (size/max)
  30 second input rate 1000 bits/sec, 3 packets/sec
  30 second output rate 2653000 bits/sec, 1271 packets/sec
     94583 packets input, 5754020 bytes, 0 no buffer
     Received 0 broadcasts, 0 runts, 0 giants, 0 throttles
     0 input errors, 0 CRC, 0 frame, 0 overrun, 0 ignored, 0 abort
     44615858 packets output, 2920117041 bytes, 0 underruns
     0 output errors, 0 collisions, 0 interface resets
     0 output buffer failures, 0 output buffers swapped out
     0 carrier transitions
     RTS up, CTS up, DTR up, DCD up, DSR up

MSFC#show policy-map interface serial 3/0/2
 Serial3/0/2
  service-policy output: dCBWFQ
    class-map: Low-Priority (match-any)
      104897 packets, 26826925 bytes
      30 second offered rate 374000 bps, drop rate 0 bps
      match: protocol smtp
        41512 packets, 6226800 bytes
        30 second rate 97000 bps
      match: protocol secure-http
        63385 packets, 20600125 bytes
        30 second rate 274000 bps
      queue size 0, queue limit 100
      packets output 105295, packet drops 0
      tail/random drops 0, no buffer drops 0, other drops 0
      bandwidth: kbps 400, weight 10
      fair-queue: per-flow queue limit 25
    class-map: Business-essential (match-any)
      147389 packets, 26827900 bytes
      30 second offered rate 374000 bps, drop rate 0 bps
      match: protocol sqlnet
```

Example 9-13 *Configuring Distributed WFQ (Continued)*

```
                96712 packets, 21760200 bytes
                30 second rate 278000 bps
            match: protocol sqlserver
                50677 packets, 5067700 bytes
                30 second rate 94000 bps
            queue size 0, queue limit 100
            packets output 147934, packet drops 0
            tail/random drops 0, no buffer drops 0, other drops 0
            bandwidth: kbps 400, weight 10
            fair-queue: per-flow queue limit 25
        class-map: Video-preso (match-any)
            191646 packets, 67076100 bytes
            30 second offered rate 937000 bps, drop rate 0 bps
            match: protocol netshow
                191646 packets, 67076100 bytes
                30 second rate 937000 bps
            queue size 0, queue limit 250
            packets output 192407, packet drops 0
            tail/random drops 0, no buffer drops 0, other drops 0
            bandwidth: kbps 1000, weight 25
            fair-queue: per-flow queue limit 62
        class-map: class-default (match-any)
            138172 packets, 33814224 bytes
            30 second offered rate 472000 bps, drop rate 0 bps
            match: any
                138172 packets, 33814224 bytes
                30 second rate 472000 bps
            queue size 0, queue limit 550
            packets output 138803, packet drops 0
            tail/random drops 0, no buffer drops 0, other drops 0
            fair-queue: per-flow queue limit 137
MSFC#show queueing fair interface serial 3/0/2
Current fair queue configuration:
 Serial3/0/2 queue size 0
        pkts output 1002701, wfq drops 0, nobuffer drops 0
 WFQ: aggregate queue limit 1000 max available buffers 1000
        Class 0: weight 55 limit 550 qsize 0 pkts output 235046 drops 0
        Class 2: weight 25 limit 250 qsize 0 pkts output 326801 drops 0
        Class 8: weight 10 limit 100 qsize 0 pkts output 180851 drops 0
        Class 11: weight 10 limit 100 qsize 0 pkts output 260001 drops 0
```

NOTE   The FlexWAN module supports configuring dCBWFQ on a per-VC basis. This is supported for *available bit rate* (ABR) and *variable bit rate* (VBR) classes of service. *Unspecified bit rate* (UBR) and UBR+ do not provided bandwidth guarantees. dCBWFQ are configured using the MQC. As a result, service policies are applied to individual *virtual circuits* (VCs) and individual members of a VC bundle. To implement flow-based WFQ on a per-VC basis, the default class is configured for **fair-queue** under the policy map. So long as traffic is not matched by other classification criteria, the traffic defaults to the default class where flow-based WFQ is applied. For additional information on IP-to-ATM CoS, refer to the following technical document available at Cisco.com:

"Configuring IP to ATM Class of Service"

Distributed Low Latency Queuing

Although WFQ protects low-bandwidth traffic, such as voice, from being starved of network resources during periods of congestion, WFQ cannot guarantee consistent delay variations between packets. Although delay can affect overall voice quality, as long as the delay is consistent the end user might not notice a difference in service. However, variation in arrival time between voice packets, referred to as *jitter*, can quickly degrade the performance of voice quality. dLLQ is specifically targeted for voice traffic. LLQ assigns a strict-priority queue for voice traffic. The benefit of the priority queue is that instead of waiting for the scheduler to service the various other queues, the strict-priority queue is provided immediate access to the transmission media. Traffic in the strict-priority queue is immediately forwarded regardless of congestion on the interface. When a packet is placed in the strict-priority queue, the scheduler immediately services that packet. Example 9-14 demonstrates configuring dLLQ on the FlexWAN module.

Example 9-14 *Configuring and Verifying dLLQ*

```
MSFC#configure terminal
MSFC(config)#ip access-list extended Voice-Control
MSFC(config-ext-nacl)#remark Permit Voice Control Traffic
MSFC(config-ext-nacl)#permit tcp 192.168.20.0 0.0.0.255 host 192.168.60.2 eq 2000
MSFC(config-ext-nacl)#permit tcp 192.168.40.0 0.0.0.255 host 192.168.60.2 eq 2748
MSFC(config-ext-nacl)#permit udp 192.168.20.0 0.0.0.255 host 192.168.60.2 eq tftp
MSFC(config)#class-map Voice-Control
MSFC(config-cmap)#match access-group name Voice-Control
MSFC(config)#ip access-list extended Voice-traffic
MSFC(config-ext-nacl)#remark Permit Phones to Phone Communication
MSFC(config-ext-nacl)#permit udp 192.168.20.0 0.0.0.255 192.168.70.0 0.0.0.255
  range 16384 32767
MSFC(config-ext-nacl)#permit udp 192.168.40.0 0.0.0.255 192.168.70.0 0.0.0.255
  range 16384 32767
MSFC(config)#class-map Voice-traffic
MSFC(config-cmap)#match access-group name Voice-traffic
MSFC(config)#access-list 101 permit tcp any any eq 443
MSFC(config)#class-map match-all Secure-HTTP
MSFC(config-cmap)#match access-group 101
MSFC(config-cmap)#class-map match-any Business-essential
MSFC(config-cmap)#match protocol sqlnet
MSFC(config-cmap)#match protocol sqlserver
MSFC(config)#policy-map LLQ-Policy
MSFC(config-pmap)#class Voice-Control
MSFC(config-pmap-c)#set ip dscp 26
MSFC(config-pmap-c)#bandwidth percent 20
MSFC(config-pmap-c)#class Business-essential
MSFC(config-pmap-c)#bandwidth percent 20
MSFC(config-pmap-c)#class Secure-HTTP
MSFC(config-pmap-c)#bandwidth percent 20
MSFC(config-pmap-c)#class Voice-traffic
```

Example 9-14 *Configuring and Verifying dLLQ (Continued)*

```
MSFC(config-pmap-c)#set ip dscp ef
MSFC(config-pmap-c)#priority 500 1500
MSFC(config)#interface serial 3/0/2
MSFC(config-if)#service-policy output LLQ-Policy
MSFC#(config)end

MSFC#show policy-map interface serial 3/0/2
 Serial3/0/2
  service-policy output: LLQ-Policy
    queue stats for all priority classes:
      queue size 0, queue limit 250
      packets output 71195, packet drops 0
      tail/random drops 0, no buffer drops 0, other drops 0
    class-map: Business-essential (match-any)
      124590 packets, 21358250 bytes
      30 second offered rate 452000 bps, drop rate 0 bps
      match: protocol sqlnet
        71194 packets, 16018650 bytes
        30 second rate 339000 bps
      match: protocol sqlserver
        53396 packets, 5339600 bytes
        30 second rate 113000 bps
      queue size 0, queue limit 50
      packets output 124591, packet drops 0
      tail/random drops 0, no buffer drops 0, other drops 0
      bandwidth: 20%, kbps 400
    class-map: Voice-Control (match-any)
      71195 packets, 6229550 bytes
      30 second offered rate 131000 bps, drop rate 0 bps
      match: access-group 120
        71195 packets, 6229550 bytes
        30 second rate 131000 bps
      queue size 0, queue limit 50
      packets output 73149, packet drops 0
      tail/random drops 0, no buffer drops 0, other drops 0
      bandwidth: 20%, kbps 400
      set:
        ip dscp 26
    class-map: Secure-HTTP (match-all)
      167307 packets, 66922800 bytes
      30 second offered rate 1419000 bps, drop rate 93000 bps
      match: access-group 101
      queue size 48, queue limit 50
      packets output 109971, packet drops 61929
      tail/random drops 61929, no buffer drops 0, other drops 0
      bandwidth: 20%, kbps 400
    class-map: Voice-traffic (match-any)
      71195 packets, 14239000 bytes
      30 second offered rate 301000 bps, drop rate 0 bps
      match: access-group 121
        71195 packets, 14239000 bytes
        30 second rate 301000 bps
```

continues

Example 9-14 *Configuring and Verifying dLLQ (Continued)*

```
        Priority: kbps 500, burst bytes 1500, b/w exceed drops: 0
        set:
          ip dscp 46
    class-map: class-default (match-any)
      77 packets, 4928 bytes
      30 second offered rate 0 bps, drop rate 0 bps
      match: any
        77 packets, 4928 bytes
        30 second rate 0 bps
      queue size 0, queue limit 100
      packets output 121, packet drops 0
      tail/random drops 0, no buffer drops 0, other drops 0
```

Congestion Avoidance

The purpose of congestion avoidance is to avoid congestion from occurring at bottlenecks within the network. This avoidance is accomplished by proactively managing transmit queues. Congestion avoidance mechanisms are specifically targeted for TCP-based applications. TCP uses flow-control mechanisms to manage established communication sessions. As a result, drops in the network impact TCP sessions; drops are indicators of congestion. Unfortunately, UDP traffic does not employ any flow-control mechanisms at the protocol level; therefore traffic is not throttled as a result of a dropped packet.

The FlexWAN module employs *distributed Weighted Random Early Detection* (dWRED) as a congestion avoidance mechanism for port adapter interfaces. The mechanism's weighting factor enables the administrator to determine the probability a packet is dropped based on its assigned IP precedence or DSCP value. The following section discusses dWRED operation on the FlexWAN module.

Distributed Weighted Random Early Detection

dWRED attempts to alleviate congestion within a network. dWRED accomplishes this by proactively monitoring transmit queues. As traffic accumulates in the queues, dWRED randomly discards packets to prevent congestion from occurring. dWRED monitors the average length of a transmit queue. Within the queue are established minimum and maximum thresholds associated with the various IP precedence and DSCP values. As long as the average queue length for a queue remains below the minimum WRED threshold, the packet is queued for transmission. If the average queue length exceeds the minimum threshold, however, the packet is potentially discarded. Whether the packet is discarded depends on the IP precedence or DSCP value for the packet. The higher the assigned IP precedence or DSCP value, the lower the chances for packet discard. When the packet exceeds both the minimum and maximum thresholds, all packets are dropped. The following commands configure dWRED for a particular class using the MQC:

```
random-detect {dscp-based | precedence-based}
random-detect exponential-weighting-constant {exponent#}
random-detect {{dscp {dscp}} | {precedence{prec}}} {min thr} {max thr} {mark
   probability}
```

The first **random-detect** command specifies whether random-detect uses IP precedence or DSCP values. Note that when the DSCP-based or precedence-based method is chosen, all configured classes must use the same method. The exponential weighting factor is a configurable value and affects how WRED calculates the average queue size. The higher the weighting values, the less susceptible WRED is to variations in the queue size. As a result, if the value is set too high, WRED may react slower to signs of congestion, and fail to police the queue. For smaller weighting values, WRED responds to changes in the queue size. If the weighting value is set too low, however, packets may be dropped too frequently. It is not recommended to alter the exponential weighting factor, because of the dramatic impact it may have on performance. Finally, the DSCP or IP precedence values are mapped to a minimum and maximum threshold, measured in packets. In addition, each precedence value or DSCP value is assigned a mark probability. The *mark probability* is a denominator that specifies how many packets are dropped when the maximum threshold is attained. If the value is 25, for example, at the maximum threshold 1 out of every 25 packets is dropped. As the average queue size exceeds the minimum threshold, the drop rate is linear with respect to the mark probability. As a result, as the queue size increases, the probability linearly increases for packets to be discarded. This occurs until the maximum threshold is exceeded and all packets mapped to that threshold are dropped. Example 9-15 demonstrates configuring dWRED and verifying the behavior.

Example 9-15 *Configuring dWRED on the FlexWAN Module*

```
MSFC#configure terminal
MSFC(config)#class-map match-any Low-Priority
MSFC(config-cmap)#match protocol smtp
MSFC(config-cmap)#match protocol secure-http
MSFC(config)#class-map match-any Business-essential
MSFC(config-cmap)#match protocol sqlnet
MSFC(config-cmap)#match protocol sqlserver
MSFC(config)#class-map match-any Video-preso
MSFC(config-cmap)#match protocol netshow
MSFC(config-cmap)#exit
MSFC(config)#policy-map dCBWFQ
MSFC(config-pmap)#class Low-Priority
MSFC(config-pmap-c)#bandwidth 400
MSFC(config-pmap-c)#fair-queue
MSFC(config-pmap-c)#random-detect dscp-based
MSFC(config-pmap-c)#exit
MSFC(config-pmap)#class Business-essential
MSFC(config-pmap-c)#bandwidth 400
MSFC(config-pmap-c)#fair-queue
MSFC(config-pmap-c)#random-detect dscp-based
MSFC(config-pmap-c)#class Video-preso
MSFC(config-pmap-c)#bandwidth 1000
MSFC(config-pmap-c)#fair-queue
MSFC(config-pmap-c)#random-detect dscp-based
```

continues

Example 9-15 *Configuring dWRED on the FlexWAN Module (Continued)*

```
MSFC(config-pmap)#class class-default
MSFC(config-pmap-c)#fair-queue
MSFC(config-pmap-c)#random-detect dscp-based
MSFC(config-pmap-c)#random-detect dscp 0 20 100 25
MSFC(config-pmap-c)#random-detect dscp 8 75 250 100
MSFC(config-pmap-c)#exit
MSFC(config-pmap)#exit
MSFC(config)#interface serial 3/0/2
MSFC(config-if)#service-policy output dCBWFQ
MSFC(config-if)#end

MSFC#show policy-map interface serial 3/0/2
 Serial3/0/2
  service-policy output: dCBWFQ
    class-map: Low-Priority (match-any)
      2547111 packets, 645072400 bytes
      30 second offered rate 370000 bps, drop rate 0 bps
      match: protocol smtp
        1044221 packets, 156633150 bytes
        30 second rate 69000 bps
      match: protocol secure-http
        1502890 packets, 488439250 bytes
        30 second rate 298000 bps
      queue size 0, queue limit 100
      packets output 2559341, packet drops 0
      tail/random drops 0, no buffer drops 0, other drops 0
      bandwidth: kbps 400, weight 10
      fair-queue: per-flow queue limit 25
      random-detect:
        Exp-weight-constant: 9 (1/512)
        Mean queue depth: 0
        Class Random      Tail   Minimum   Maximum    Mark      Output
              drop        drop threshold threshold probability  packets
        0         0         0        25        50      1/10      117590
    class-map: Video-preso (match-any)
      4607686 packets, 1612690100 bytes
      30 second offered rate 923000 bps, drop rate 0 bps
      match: protocol netshow
        4607687 packets, 1612690450 bytes
        30 second rate 923000 bps
      queue size 0, queue limit 250
      packets output 4629910, packet drops 0
      tail/random drops 0, no buffer drops 0, other drops 0
      bandwidth: kbps 1000, weight 25
      fair-queue: per-flow queue limit 62
      random-detect:
        Exp-weight-constant: 9 (1/512)
        Mean queue depth: 0
        Class Random      Tail   Minimum   Maximum    Mark      Output
              drop        drop threshold threshold probability  packets
        26        0         0       108       125      1/10      130443
    class-map: Business-essential (match-any)
```

Example 9-15 *Configuring dWRED on the FlexWAN Module (Continued)*

```
        2375525 packets, 408280000 bytes
        30 second offered rate 370000 bps, drop rate 0 bps
        match: protocol sqlnet
          1365820 packets, 307309500 bytes
          30 second rate 277000 bps
        match: protocol sqlserver
          1009705 packets, 100970500 bytes
          30 second rate 92000 bps
        queue size 0, queue limit 350
        packets output 2389714, packet drops 0
        tail/random drops 0, no buffer drops 0, other drops 0
        queue-limit 350
        bandwidth: kbps 400, weight 10
        fair-queue: per-flow queue limit 87
        random-detect:
          Exp-weight-constant: 9 (1/512)
          Mean queue depth: 0
          Class Random      Tail   Minimum   Maximum     Mark      Output
                drop        drop threshold threshold  probability  packets
          16      0           0        31        50      1/10      116425
      class-map: class-default (match-any)
        3304694 packets, 813059382 bytes
        30 second offered rate 464000 bps, drop rate 0 bps
        match: any
          3304694 packets, 813059382 bytes
          30 second rate 464000 bps
        queue size 0, queue limit 550
        packets output 3325430, packet drops 0
        tail/random drops 0, no buffer drops 0, other drops 0
        fair-queue: per-flow queue limit 137
        random-detect:
          Exp-weight-constant: 9 (1/512)
          Mean queue depth: 0
          Class Random      Tail   Minimum   Maximum     Mark      Output
                drop        drop threshold threshold  probability  packets
          0       0           0        20       100      1/25       88946
          8       0           0        75       250      1/100          0
```

WRED is specifically targeted for TCP-based applications. When a dropped packet is detected, the TCP sender initiates TCP's "slow start" mechanism. This enables the sender to gradually increase its transmission rate. The random dropping of packets for TCP flows alleviates the possibility for global synchronization to occur. Unfortunately, WRED has little effect on applications that do not employ flow-control mechanisms. Therefore, for classes composed primarily of UDP traffic, WRED has little effect.

Summary

This chapter focused specifically on QoS performance and configuration for the MSFC and FlexWAN module. As demonstrated in the examples, QoS on the MSFC and FlexWAN is configured using the MQC, introduced in Chapter 5. The majority of the features available for the FlexWAN module and the MSFC are based on the QoS features supported on the 7500 with a VIP. In addition, the FlexWAN module and the MSFC extend the 6500's reachability to the MAN and WAN environments. Their integration allows for ease of configuration and management, as well as the capability to extend QoS support across the enterprise. This versatility ensures the appropriate service levels are maintained for mission-critical applications and protocols on an end-to-end basis. This chapter covered the following QoS concepts:

- Classification using dNBAR and NBAR protocol discovery.

- Marking using CAR, class-based policing, and the class-based marker.

- Policing and shaping functions on the FlexWAN module. The chapter demonstrated CAR and the class-based policing behavior, as well as DTS.

- Congestion management mechanisms available on the FlexWAN module. This discussion covered dWFQ, dCBWFQ, and dLLQ.

- Congestion avoidance mechanisms, particularly dWRED.

End-to-End QoS Case Studies

Earlier chapters of this book focused on specific product lines of Catalyst switches and provided examples based on those product lines. This chapter reviews several common *quality of service* (QoS) features by applying these features to a sample campus network design scaled to six switches. The campus network design characterizes a common campus topology but represents the core, distribution, and access layer using only two switches at each layer. The campus network topology uses various families of Catalyst switches to form a multiplatform design. The campus network design and topology exaggerate the use of QoS features for the purpose of providing examples and leans toward a classification model of trusting access layer ports. Furthermore, some of the configurations in this chapter are similar to those generated by Auto-QoS. Because at time of publication Auto-QoS was not widely available on all platforms, Auto-QoS discussions are not included in this chapter.

The sample network design includes the following QoS features:

- Input scheduling
- Classification based on trust configuration
- ACL-based classification
- Marking using policy maps
- Rate and markdown policing
- Individual policing
- Congestion management
- Congestion avoidance

This chapter applies these QoS features to the sample campus network topology in Figure 10-1 for review of an end-to-end QoS configuration. This chapter explains the network design and topology shown in Figure 10-1, describes each of the network layers and the QoS configuration, and summarizes the applications for common QoS features. At the conclusion of this chapter, you will understand how to apply common QoS features to a campus network design and topology.

Chapter Prerequisites and Material Presentation

This chapter assumes the reader has read through all the material in the previous chapters and grasps the basic understanding of all the QoS fundamentals presented in earlier chapters. This chapter presents material from an overview perspective. The chapter does not discuss command-line parameters or configuration specifics. Instead, this chapter presents a sample configuration and then discusses it. The reader should know how to relate the QoS configuration discussions to the sample configurations. The end goal of the chapter is to give the reader an understanding and overview of an end-to-end QoS design and topology.

Furthermore, this chapter refers to applications such as file sharing and databases. In many examples, *access-control lists* (ACLs) define these applications using TCP and UDP port assignments. The ACLs in the examples are not true representations of the necessary ACLs to profile the applications. Instead, the examples include the ACLs for completeness of the *command-line interface* (CLI) syntax.

The material presented in this chapter begins with the access layer and moves to the core. Because the classification begins in the access layer, the explanations begin there as well. To facilitate an easier understanding of the sample configuration presented, the configurations do not illustrate repeated identical interface configurations or infrastructure-related materials, such as spanning-tree parameters, IP routing protocols, and VLAN databases.

Multiplatform Campus Network Design and Topology

Figure 10-1 shows the campus network topology this chapter uses for sample configurations. The principle of the campus network design is to apply QoS features to support multiple *classes of service* among different classes of users and applications. To illustrate a sample campus network topology, the campus network design mimics a university campus consisting of multiple buildings. Each building uses two distribution layer switches to aggregate access layer switches that connect individual workstations and IP Phones in multiple wiring closets per floor of each building. The core aggregates each building by interconnecting the distribution layer switches. In addition to providing aggregation, the core also offers redundant Internet connectivity with firewall filtering, *virtual private networking* (VPN) services, and IP connectivity to iSCSI routers that interconnect a Cisco Multilayer Director and Fabric Switches (MDS) Fibre Channel *storage-area network* (SAN). A core server farm supplies global enterprise services such as e-mail, file storage, web services, and applications.

In the core, one of the Catalyst 6500 switches uses Native IOS Software; the other Catalyst 6500 switch uses Hybrid Software. Chapter 8, "QoS Support on the Catalyst 6500," discusses the differences between Native and Hybrid Software. The topology uses different software for illustration purposes; most campus designs keep the software versions consistent.

Figure 10-1 *Sample Multiplatform Campus Network Topology*

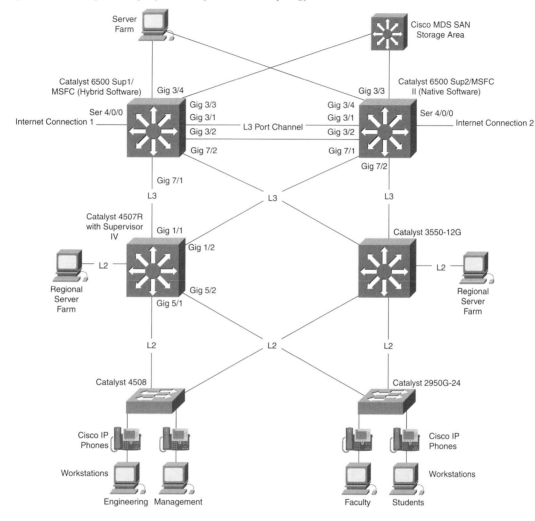

Catalyst 4507R and 3550-12G switches create the distribution layer. The distribution layer aggregates access layer switches in buildings throughout the campus network. These switches also connect regional server farms for the purpose of providing services on a per-building basis. Such services include web caching, authentication, and file services. The distribution layer uses Layer 3 connections to the core with Layer 2 connections to the access layer. As a result, the distribution layer switches route between local IP subnets. The core switches advertise default routes to the distribution layer so that the distribution layer can route to other IP subnets residing in other buildings. It is not necessary for the distribution layer to contain all the campus routes in its routing table.

Catalyst 2950 and 4506 switches comprise the wiring closet. These switches have redundant connections to the distribution layer via Layer 2 connections. The switches do not use the *Spanning Tree Protocol* (STP) for link redundancy; instead, these switches use *Hot Standby Router Protocol* (HSRP) for link redundancy. The design achieves link redundancy without the use of STP by designing each access layer switch with unique VLANs. Because there is no trunk between the distribution switches to carry the VLAN traffic between distribution switches, using unique VLANs per access layer results in these VLANs existing only on a single port per distribution switch. As a result, any respective VLAN interface moves to the down state during a link failure between the distribution and access layer. Consider the case when HSRP is in the active state for a VLAN on the Catalyst 4507R switch, and a link failure occurs between the Catalyst 4507R switch and the Catalyst 4506 switch. The VLAN interfaces associated with the link failure move to the down state because the only interface associated with the VLAN interface is no longer in the line protocol up state. Switches move VLAN interfaces to the down state when no ports in the VLAN are in the line protocol up state to prevent routing black holes. After the VLAN interface moves to the down state on the Catalyst 4507R switch, the HSRP peer on the Catalyst 3550-12G switch assumes full responsibility for routing traffic because it no longer hears HSRP hellos from the neighbor peer and therefore becomes the active HSRP router.

Although this design does not use STP for redundancy, STP is still utilized to prevent Layer 2 loops and broadcast storm that are caused by incorrect cabling, faulty hardware, or software defects. This design uses STP features such as Portfast and Trunkfast to expedite convergence; consult the Cisco website for more details on these features. An alternative to this wiring closet design is to use STP for redundancy. Although the STP method is currently the most popular, the current design trend is to use the method previously described.

For additional information on HSRP, refer to the following technical documents at Cisco.com:

> "Using HSRP for Fault Tolerate IP Routing"
> "HSRP Technical Tips"

Each access layer switch uses a least two VLANs, one for data and another for voice. The access layer connects various types of users in the campus. In this example, the campus network classifies traffic on access layer switches based on the following predefined types of users:

- Faculty
- Students
- Engineering
- Management

Access Layer Switches

The access layer switches connect individual workstations and IP Phones of various user types. In this example, the switches used for access layer switches are the Catalyst 2950G-24 and Catalyst 4506 switch. The next sections explore a sample QoS configuration for the Catalyst 2950G-24. Following the discussion of the QoS configuration for the Catalyst 2950G-24 is a discussion for the QoS configuration of the Catalyst 4506.

In brief, the next two sections discuss the following QoS features applied on access layer switches:

- Trust Cisco IP Phone
- Untagged packet classification
- Ingress port policing
- Congestion management
- Weighted round-robin
- Strict-priority queuing
- Egress CoS-to-transmit queue mapping

Catalyst 2950G-24

Example 10-1 illustrates the sample configuration applied to Figure 10-1.

Example 10-1 *Catalyst 2950 Sample Configuration for Figure 10-1*

```
Switch-2950#show running-config
Building configuration...
Current configuration : 2304 bytes
!
version 12.1
(text deleted)
!
!
wrr-queue bandwidth 10 40 30 20
wrr-queue cos-map 1 0 1
wrr-queue cos-map 2 2 3
wrr-queue cos-map 3 4
wrr-queue cos-map 4 5 6 7
!
class-map match-all Faculty_Profile
  match access-group 100
class-map match-all Student_Profile
  match access-group 101
!
!
policy-map STUDENT
  class Student_Profile
    police 4000000 16384 exceed-action drop
```

continues

Example 10-1 *Catalyst 2950 Sample Configuration for Figure 10-1*

```
policy-map FACULTY
  class Faculty_Profile
    police 1000000 8192 exceed-action drop
    set ip dscp 0
!
(text deleted)
!
!
interface FastEthernet0/1
 switchport access vlan 2
 switchport voice vlan 700
 no ip address
 service-policy input FACULTY
 mls qos trust device cisco-phone
 spanning-tree portfast trunk
!
(text deleted)
!
interface FastEthernet0/13
 switchport access vlan 3
 no ip address
 service-policy input STUDENT
 mls qos cos 1
 mls qos cos override
 spanning-tree portfast
!
(text deleted)
!
interface GigabitEthernet0/1
 switchport mode trunk
 switchport trunk encap dot1q
 no ip address
 mls qos trust dscp
!
interface GigabitEthernet0/2
 switchport mode trunk
 switchport trunk encap dot1q
 no ip address
 mls qos trust dscp
!
(text deleted)
!
access-list 100 permit tcp any any eq 25000
access-list 100 permit udp any any eq 25000
access-list 101 permit ip any any
!
(text deleted)
!
end
```

For classification, the Catalyst 2950 switch uses two different classification models based on the front-panel port. The campus faculty and administrators use interfaces 1 through 12 for Cisco IP Phones and workstations. Ports 13 through 24 connect directly to student buildings, labs, and offices. Generally, network designs apply classification models on a per-interface basis. However, alternative methods of classification exist, such as using ACLs and policy maps where classification models utilize Layer 3 and 4 ingress packet information rather than the front panel.

The interfaces designated for faculty workstations and Cisco IP Phones use the trust DSCP based on the connected Cisco IP Phone method for classification. The switch trusts DSCP on ingress packets based on whether the interface learns that a Cisco IP Phone is connected. The switch learns of attached Cisco IP Phones via the *Cisco Discovery Protocol* (CDP). For switch interfaces that do not learn of an attached Cisco IP Phone, the switch classifies all ingress frames with a CoS value of zero. These switches map the classified CoS or *differentiated services codepoint* (DSCP) value to internal DSCP, which determines the policing, scheduling, and queuing behavior in packet processing.

Furthermore, the interface configuration consists of the default extended trust parameters. The default parameters inform the Cisco IP Phone to rewrite all incoming CoS values to zero for any ingress packets into the PC port of the phone. For more information regarding these classification techniques, refer to Chapter 2, "End-to-End QoS: Quality of Service at Layer 3 and Layer 2," and Chapter 3, "Overview of QoS Support on Catalyst Platforms and Exploring QoS on the Catalyst 2900XL, 3500XL, and Catalyst 4000 CatOS Family of Switches."

For interfaces designated for student use, the switch classifies ingress packets with the default port CoS of zero because of the default classification configuration of the Catalyst 2950G-24 switch. By default, the Catalyst 2950 Family of switches uses the untrusted configuration for all interfaces. The command **mls qos cos override** configures the switch to also classify 802.1q tagged frames with the default port CoS of zero. As a result, the interface classification state is untrusted for both 802.1q tagged and untagged frames.

To prevent the faculty workstations from consuming excessive bandwidth for file-sharing applications, the switch polices all traffic for file-sharing applications to 1 Mbps on ingress per port using the FACULTY policy map. The configuration uses ACL 100 to define file-sharing traffic. The policy map action reclassifies and marks all traffic matching the file-sharing class to a DSCP value of zero. This reclassification ensures the switch does not schedule or queue packets for file-sharing applications before any other higher-priority data traffic.

For student workstations, the STUDENT policy map limits the total traffic ingress per port to 4 Mbps. The policy map does not take into account any traffic profile; instead, the policy map restricts bandwidth for all traffic.

For congestion management, the switch uses *weighted round-robin* (WRR) with custom bandwidth configurations rather than strict-priority queuing. Because the Catalyst 2950 switch uses four transmit queues and the WRR parameters are global, each queue, 1 through 4, receives the following global bandwidth assignments: 10 percent, 40 percent, 30 percent, and 20 percent. In this manner, the lower-priority queues receive the lowest scheduling bandwidth while queues 2 and 3 receive higher bandwidth. Queue 4 is the highest-priority queue; however, most traffic in the network occupies lower queues and assigning a large WRR bandwidth value to queue 4 is unnecessary. Furthermore, the CoS-to-transmit queue mapping configuration places traffic for CoS 5 into queue 4. The default configuration is to place CoS 5 traffic into queue 3. Because voice traffic from Cisco IP Phones has a CoS value of 5 by default, placing voice traffic in queue 4 yields better performance because WRR services queue 4 before other queues.

Catalyst 4506

Example 10-2 shows the Catalyst 4506 sample configuration applied to Figure 10-1. In this example, the Catalyst 4506 is populated with a Supervisor III Engine.

Example 10-2 *Catalyst 4506 Sample Configuration for Figure 10-1*

```
Switch-4506#show running-config
Building configuration...
Current configuration : 4658 bytes
!
version 12.1
(text deleted)
!
qos
(text deleted)
!
!
class-map match-all Management_Profile
  match access-group 101
class-map match-all Engineering_Profile
  match access-group 100
!
!
policy-map MANAGEMENT
  class Management_Profile
    police 1 mbps 16000 byte conform-action transmit exceed-action drop
policy-map ENGINEERING
  class Engineering_Profile
    police 5 mbps 1600 byte conform-action transmit exceed-action drop
!
(text deleted)
!
interface GigabitEthernet1/1
 switchport mode trunk
 switchport encap dot1q
 qos trust dscp
 tx-queue 1
   bandwidth 400 mbps
 tx-queue 2
   bandwidth 200 mbps
 tx-queue 3
```

Example 10-2 *Catalyst 4506 Sample Configuration for Figure 10-1*

```
   bandwidth 200 mbps
   priority high
 tx-queue 4
   bandwidth 200 mbps
 !
interface GigabitEthernet1/2
 switchport mode trunk
 switchport encap dot1q
qos trust dscp
 tx-queue 1
   bandwidth 400 mbps
 tx-queue 2
   bandwidth 200 mbps
 tx-queue 3
   bandwidth 200 mbps
   priority high
 tx-queue 4
   bandwidth 200 mbps
 !
(text deleted)
 !
interface FastEthernet6/1
 description Engineering
 switchport access vlan 4
 switchport voice vlan 701
 qos trust dscp
 service-policy input ENGINEERING
 tx-queue 3
   priority high
 spanning-tree portfast
 !
(text deleted)
 !
interface FastEthernet6/25
 switchport access vlan 5
 switchport voice vlan 701
 qos trust dscp
 service-policy input MANAGEMENT
 tx-queue 3
   priority high
 spanning-tree portfast
 !
(text deleted)
 !
access-list 100 permit tcp any any range 25000 30000
access-list 100 permit udp any any range 25000 30000
access-list 101 deny   ip any 10.0.0.0 0.255.255.255
access-list 101 permit ip any any
 !
(text deleted)
 !
end
```

As with the Catalyst 2950 switch, the Catalyst 4506 switch uses two different classification models based on the front-panel port. The campus engineering staff uses interfaces 1 through 24 for Cisco IP Phones and workstations. The campus management staff connects to interfaces 25 through 48.

The interfaces designated for either engineering or management employ the trust DSCP classification method. The switch just trusts the DSCP value of all ingress frames. As a result, the switch maps any packet's ingress DSCP directly to the internal DSCP value. Furthermore, the interface configuration consists of the default extended trust parameters. The default parameters inform the Cisco IP Phone to rewrite all incoming CoS values to zero for any ingress packets into the PC port of the phone.

For interfaces designed for use by the engineering staff, the switch polices all file-sharing and web-gaming traffic to 5 Mbps on ingress. The ENGINEERING policy map defines this behavior. The class map Engineering_Profile maps the ACL that defines the file-sharing and web-gaming traffic profile to the policy map.

For interfaces used by the management staff, the switch polices all Internet-bound traffic to 1 Mbps. The campus network connects to the Internet via two T3s(45 Mbps). Limiting the Internet-bound traffic for these ports to 1 Mbps is sufficient. The MANAGEMENT policy map defines this behavior. The class map Management_Profile maps the ACL that defines the file-sharing and web-gaming traffic profile to the policy map. The ACL defines Internet-bound traffic by noting which destination IP addresses are internal. All internal IP addressing in the campus network resides on the 10.0.0.0/8 subnet.

For congestion management on the Gigabit Ethernet interfaces uplinked to the core, the switch uses WRR and Priority Queuing on a per-interface basis. The Catalyst 4506 switch uses four transmit queues per interface. For interfaces connecting the management and engineering workstations and IP Phones, the switch applies strict priority to queue 3 while implementing the default behavior of WRR sharing per queue. Each queue receives 250 Mbps as a share value by default. In conjunction with the strict-priority queuing, the switch transmits traffic out of queue 3 before servicing any other queue up until the share value of 250 Mbps. On the Catalyst 4000 Family of switches, queue 3 is the only queue available for strict-priority scheduling. By default, IP Phone voice traffic with CoS values 5 and DSCP values of 46 occupy queue 3 on egress. As a result, no mapping of voice traffic is necessary by default in this example.

For the uplinks connecting to the distribution layer, the congestion management differs slightly. Although queue 3 is a strict-priority queue, the queue only receives a share value of 200 Mbps. Queues 1, 2, and 4 receive 400 Mbps, 200 Mbps, and 200 Mbps as share values, respectively. As a result, egress scheduling is slightly different per queue than the default configuration. The principle behind the alternate scheduling configuration is that the higher-priority queues do not need more than 200 Mbps.

Distribution Layer

The distribution layer switches dual connect access layer switches via Gigabit Ethernet interfaces. The distribution layer switches used in this example are the Catalyst 4507R and the Catalyst 3550-12G switches. The next two sections explores a sample QoS configuration for both of these switches.

In brief, the next two sections discuss the following QoS features applied on distribution layer switches:

- Trust DSCP classification
- Reclassification using policy maps
- WRR
- Strict-priority queuing

Catalyst 3550-12G

Example 10-3 illustrates the Catalyst 3550-12G sample configuration applied to Figure 10-1.

Example 10-3 *Catalyst 3550-12G Sample Configuration for Figure 10-1*

```
Switch-3550#show running-config
Building configuration...
Current configuration : 3460 bytes
!
version 12.1
(text deleted)
!
mls qos
!
class-map match-all VOIP
  match access-group 100
class-map match-all Database_iSCSI
  match access-group 102
class-map match-all Other
  match any
class-map match-all VIDEO
  match access-group 101
!
!
policy-map RECLASSIFY
  class VOIP
    trust dscp
  class VIDEO
    set ip dscp 34
  class Database_iSCSI
    set ip dscp 25
  class Other
    set ip dscp 0
!
```

continues

Example 10-3 *Catalyst 3550-12G Sample Configuration for Figure 10-1 (Continued)*

```
(text deleted)
!
interface GigabitEthernet0/1
 no switchport
 ip address 10.2.2.1 255.255.255.252
 wrr-queue bandwidth 400 200 250 100
 wrr-queue cos-map 4 5
 priority-queue out
!
interface GigabitEthernet0/2
 no switchport
 ip address 10.2.2.5 255.255.255.252
 wrr-queue bandwidth 400 200 250 100
 wrr-queue cos-map 4 5
 priority-queue out
!
interface GigabitEthernet0/3
 switchport trunk encapsulation dot1q
 switchport trunk allowed vlan 2,3,700,1002-1005
 switchport mode trunk
 no ip address
 wrr-queue bandwidth 400 200 250 100
 wrr-queue cos-map 4 5
 service-policy input RECLASSIFY
 priority-queue out
!
interface GigabitEthernet0/4
 switchport trunk encapsulation dot1q
 switchport trunk allowed vlan 4,5,701,1002-1005
 switchport mode trunk
 no ip address
 wrr-queue bandwidth 400 200 250 100
 wrr-queue cos-map 4 5
 service-policy input RECLASSIFY
 priority-queue out
!
interface GigabitEthernet0/5
 switchport access vlan 201
  no ip address
 wrr-queue bandwidth 400 200 250 100
 wrr-queue cos-map 4 5
 service-policy input RECLASSIFY
 priority-queue out
(text deleted)
!
interface Vlan2
 ip address 10.0.2.3 255.255.255.0
 no ip redirects
 standby 2 ip 10.0.2.1
 standby 2 priority 100
 standby 2 preempt
 !
```

Example 10-3 *Catalyst 3550-12G Sample Configuration for Figure 10-1 (Continued)*

```
(text deleted)
!
access-list 100 permit ip 10.200.0.0 0.0.255.255 10.200.0.0 0.0.255.255
access-list 101 permit tcp 10.0.0.0 0.255.255.255 10.0.0.0 0.255.255.255 range 25000
  25999
access-list 101 permit udp 10.0.0.0 0.255.255.255 10.0.0.0 0.255.255.255 range 25000
  25999
access-list 102 permit tcp 10.0.0.0 0.255.255.255 10.0.0.0 0.255.255.255 eq 3260
!
(text deleted)
!
end
```

In the access layer, the switches defined two levels of service. The switches classified traffic from IP Phones as trusted, and the switch classified all other traffic with a CoS value of zero. The campus network design reclassifies traffic from the access layer and defines multiple levels of service.

The RECLASSIFY policy map reclassifies traffic into four categories: VOIP, VIDEO, Database_iSCSI, and Other. The *Voice over IP* (VoIP) traffic represents any traffic to and from Cisco IP Phones and their respective servers. These servers include the Cisco Call Manager and Unity servers. Because the access layer preserved the classification applied by the individual IP Phones, the RECLASSIFY policy map just trusts DSCP for any frames traversing the voice VLANs. ACL 100 defines the IP subnets that define the voice VLANs. This method actually provides multiple levels of services because the signaling and voice frames to and from IP Phones use different DSCP values.

The VIDEO class map defines traffic for video and voice applications. ACL 101 defines the applications by TCP and UDP ports numbers. This example uses arbitrary port numbers for brevity in the configuration. The policy map classifies traffic for the VIDEO class map with a DSCP value of 34. This value is less than the Cisco IP Phone packet default DSCP value of 46.

The Database_iSCSI class map characterizes traffic for database applications and traffic that matches protocol ports used by the iSCSI protocol in ACL 102. As with any ACL in this chapter, ACL 102 is not a complete representation of an ACL that would define all database and iSCSI traffic. The policy map classifies traffic for this class map with a DSCP value of 25. Finally, the policy map classifies all traffic that does not match any other profile to a DSCP value of 0. This configuration step is for illustration purpose because the ingress port is untrusted, traffic not matching any of the reclassification uses an internal DSCP value of 0, nonetheless.

For congestion management, the switch uses WRR with custom bandwidth configurations and a strict-priority queue designation on all interfaces connecting to other switches. The Catalyst 3550 Family of switches uses four transmit queues. In this example, each queue, 1 through 4, receives the following interface WRR bandwidth assignments: 400, 200, 250, and 100, respectively. The configuration of the WRR bandwidth is a relative value and not a bandwidth parameter in bits per second. Because the sum of the bandwidth assignments is 1000 and each interface is 1 Gbps, the values represent bandwidth weights that map directly to megabits per second. Queue 4 is the highest-priority queue; however, most traffic in the network resides in lower queues and configuring a large WRR bandwidth value to queue 4 is unnecessary. In addition, the CoS-to-transmit queue mapping places egress traffic for CoS 5 into queue 4 rather than queue 3, the default configuration, because voice traffic uses CoS value 5 by default. Furthermore, queue 4 is a priority queue. Using the priority queue configuration forces the switch to service queue 4 before servicing any other queue.

Catalyst 4507R

Example 10-4 shows the Catalyst 4507R sample configuration applied to Figure 10-1.

Example 10-4   *Catalyst 4507R Sample Configuration for Figure 10-1*

```
Switch#show running-config
Building configuration...
Current configuration : 4241 bytes
!
version 12.1
(text deleted)
!
qos
(text deleted)
!
!
class-map match-all VOIP
  match access-group 100
class-map match-all Database_iSCSI
  match access-group 102
class-map match-all Other
  match any
class-map match-all VIDEO
  match access-group 101
!
!
policy-map RECLASSIFY
  class VOIP
    trust dscp
  class VIDEO
    set ip dscp 34
  class Database_iSCSI
    set ip dscp 25
  class Other
    set ip dscp 0
!
!
(text deleted)
!
interface GigabitEthernet1/1
 no switchport
```

Example 10-4 *Catalyst 4507R Sample Configuration for Figure 10-1 (Continued)*

```
 ip address 10.2.1.1 255.255.255.252
 qos trust dscp
 tx-queue 1
   bandwidth 400 mbps
 tx-queue 3
   bandwidth 200 mbps
   priority high
 tx-queue 4
   bandwidth 150 mbps
 !
 interface GigabitEthernet1/2
 no switchport
 ip address 10.2.1.5 255.255.255.252
 qos trust dscp
 tx-queue 1
   bandwidth 400 mbps
 tx-queue 3
   bandwidth 200 mbps
   priority high
 tx-queue 4
   bandwidth 150 mbps
 !
 interface GigabitEthernet 2/1
 switchport access vlan 201
 service-policy input RECLASSIFY
 tx-queue 3
   priority high
 spanning-tree portfast
 (text deleted)
 !
 interface GigabitEthernet5/1
 switchport trunk encapsulation dot1q
 switchport trunk allowed vlan 2,3,700
 switchport mode trunk
 service-policy input RECLASSIFY
 tx-queue 3
   priority high
 !
 interface GigabitEthernet5/2
 switchport trunk encapsulation dot1q
 switchport trunk allowed vlan 4,5,701
 switchport mode trunk
 service-policy input RECLASSIFY
 tx-queue 3
   priority high
 !
 (text deleted)
 !
 interface Vlan2
 ip address 10.0.2.2 255.255.255.0
 no ip redirects
 shutdown
```

continues

Example 10-4 *Catalyst 4507R Sample Configuration for Figure 10-1 (Continued)*

```
 standby 2 ip 10.0.2.1
 standby 2 priority 150
 standby 2 preempt
!
(text deleted)
!
!
access-list 100 permit ip 10.200.0.0 0.0.255.255 10.200.0.0 0.0.255.255
access-list 101 permit tcp 10.0.0.0 0.255.255.255 10.0.0.0 0.255.255.255 range 25000
  25999
access-list 101 permit udp 10.0.0.0 0.255.255.255 10.0.0.0 0.255.255.255 range 25000
  25999
access-list 102 permit tcp 10.0.0.0 0.255.255.255 10.0.0.0 0.255.255.255 eq 3260
!
(text deleted)
!
end
```

As with the Catalyst 3550-12G in the distribution layer, the Catalyst 4507R reclassifies all ingress traffic from access layer switches. The fundamental QoS configurations between the Catalyst 3550-12G switch and the Catalyst 4507R switch are identical; however, there are a few configuration syntax and operational differences in congestion management between the two families of switches.

With regard to congestion management, the WRR bandwidth parameters configure per transmit queue. The default bandwidth parameter is 250 Mbps. Furthermore, transmit queue 3, not queue 4 as with the Catalyst 3550 Family of switches, is designated as the priority queue. As a result, a CoS-to-transmit queue configuration is not necessary because the default CoS-to-transmit queue mapping places voice traffic from Cisco IP Phones into queue 3. Other than these few syntax and operational differences, both the Catalyst 3550-12 and Catalyst 4507R behave identically using these distribution layer configurations.

Core Layer

The core layer switches dual connect distribution switches via Gigabit Ethernet interfaces. The switch used in this example for core layer switches is the Catalyst 6500. Each Catalyst 6500 operates using different software. One switch uses Hybrid Software; the other switch uses Native IOS. The next two sections explore a sample QoS configuration applied identically to both these switches.

In brief, the next two sections discuss the following QoS features applied on distribution layer switches:

- Trust DSCP classification
- Reclassification using policy maps

- Policing to mark down traffic
- WRR
- Strict-priority queuing
- WRED congestion avoidance
- Transmit queue size manipulation

Catalyst 6500 Hybrid OS

Example 10-5 shows the Catalyst 6500 Hybrid OS sample configuration applied to Figure 10-1.

Example 10-5 *Catalyst 6500 CatOS Sample Configuration for Figure 10-1*

```
6k-Hybrid> (enable) show config
This command shows non-default configurations only.
Use 'show config all' to show both default and non-default configurations.
..............
(text deleted)
begin
!
# ***** NON-DEFAULT CONFIGURATION *****
!
!
(text deleted)
!
#qos
set qos enable
set qos wrr 1p2q2t 30 70
set qos txq-ratio 1p2q2t 60 20 20
set qos wred 1p2q2t tx queue 1 50:75 70:100
set qos wred 1p2q2t tx queue 2 60:80 75:100
set qos ipprec-dscp-map 0 8 16 26 34 46 48 56
set qos cos-dscp-map 0 8 16 26 34 46 48 56
set qos policed-dscp-map 0:0
set qos policed-dscp-map 1:1
set qos policed-dscp-map 2:2
set qos policed-dscp-map 3:3
set qos policed-dscp-map 4:4
set qos policed-dscp-map 5:5
set qos policed-dscp-map 6:6
set qos policed-dscp-map 7:7
set qos policed-dscp-map 8:8
set qos policed-dscp-map 9:9
set qos policed-dscp-map 10:10
set qos policed-dscp-map 11:11
set qos policed-dscp-map 12:12
set qos policed-dscp-map 13:13
set qos policed-dscp-map 14:14
set qos policed-dscp-map 15,25:0
set qos policed-dscp-map 16:16
set qos policed-dscp-map 17:17
```

continues

Example 10-5 *Catalyst 6500 CatOS Sample Configuration for Figure 10-1 (Continued)*

```
set qos policed-dscp-map 18:18
set qos policed-dscp-map 19:19
set qos policed-dscp-map 20:20
set qos policed-dscp-map 21:21
set qos policed-dscp-map 22:22
set qos policed-dscp-map 23:23
set qos policed-dscp-map 24:24
set qos policed-dscp-map 26:26
set qos policed-dscp-map 27:27
set qos policed-dscp-map 28:28
set qos policed-dscp-map 29:29
set qos policed-dscp-map 30:30
set qos policed-dscp-map 31:31
set qos policed-dscp-map 32:32
set qos policed-dscp-map 33:33
set qos policed-dscp-map 34:34
set qos policed-dscp-map 35:35
set qos policed-dscp-map 36:36
set qos policed-dscp-map 37:37
set qos policed-dscp-map 38:38
set qos policed-dscp-map 39:39
set qos policed-dscp-map 40:40
set qos policed-dscp-map 41:41
set qos policed-dscp-map 42:42
set qos policed-dscp-map 43:43
set qos policed-dscp-map 44:44
set qos policed-dscp-map 45:45
set qos policed-dscp-map 46:46
set qos policed-dscp-map 47:47
set qos policed-dscp-map 48:48
set qos policed-dscp-map 49:49
set qos policed-dscp-map 50:50
set qos policed-dscp-map 51:51
set qos policed-dscp-map 52:52
set qos policed-dscp-map 53:53
set qos policed-dscp-map 54:54
set qos policed-dscp-map 55:55
set qos policed-dscp-map 56:56
set qos policed-dscp-map 57:57
set qos policed-dscp-map 58:58
set qos policed-dscp-map 59:59
set qos policed-dscp-map 60:60
set qos policed-dscp-map 61:61
set qos policed-dscp-map 62:62
set qos policed-dscp-map 63:63
set qos policer microflow iSCSI_mark_down rate 100000 burst 32000 policed-dscp
clear qos acl all
#VTC-Server
set qos acl ip VTC-Server trust-ipprec ip any  any
#iSCSI-Traffic_1
set qos acl ip iSCSI-Traffic_1 trust-dscp microflow iSCSI_mark_down tcp 10.0.0.0
  255.0.0.0 10.0.0.0 255.0.0.0 eq 3260
```

Example 10-5 *Catalyst 6500 CatOS Sample Configuration for Figure 10-1 (Continued)*

```
#iSCSI-Traffic_2
set qos acl ip iSCSI-Traffic_2 dscp 25 tcp 10.0.0.0 255.0.0.0 eq 3260 10.0.0.0
255.0.0.0
#
commit qos acl all
!
(text deleted)
!
#module 3 : 16-port 1000BaseX Ethernet
set module name    3
set vlan 100  3/1-2
set vlan 101  3/4
set vlan 102  3/5
set vlan 600  3/3
(text deleted)
set port qos 3/1-2,3/4-16 trust trust-dscp
set qos acl map iSCSI-Traffic_1 3/1
set qos acl map iSCSI-Traffic_1 3/2
set qos acl map iSCSI-Traffic_2 3/3
(text deleted)
set port channel 3/1-2 mode desirable silent
!
#module 4 : 0-port FlexWAN Module
!
#module 5 : 0-port Switch Fabric Module
!
(text deleted)
!
#module 7 : 16-port 1000BaseX Ethernet
set module name    7
set vlan 1071 7/1
set vlan 1072 7/2
(text deleted)
set port qos 7/1-16 trust trust-dscp
set qos acl map iSCSI-Traffic_1 7/1
set qos acl map iSCSI-Traffic_1 7/2
(text deleted)
!
end
```

The distribution layer classifies traffic into multiple levels depending on the protocol and application. It is not necessarily for the core switch to reclassify traffic from the distribution layer. As a result, all interfaces that connect to other switches just classify traffic based on the trust DSCP classification mechanism. The core switches connect to other switches using interfaces on module three.

Furthermore, the global server farms consist of Cisco Call Manager and Unity servers. The servers in the global farm have the DSCP values, IP precedence, and CoS values administered securely and correctly. Using the trust DSCP classification mechanism is sufficient for these interfaces as well. The core switches use module seven for connecting the global servers farm.

The SAN, which connects to the core switches on module seven port one, does not mark traffic on egress. As a result, the core switches classify the traffic using an ACL. The goal of the ACL is to mark only traffic for iSCSI packet flows. As a result, the iSCSI-Traffic_2 policy ACL defines traffic from the iSCSI SAN for classification. The SAN network connects to port 3/3, and hence, the **set qos acl map iSCSI-Traffic_2 3/3** configuration command. The switch treats all other ingress traffic on this port as untrusted.

Furthermore, the core switches use an ingress microflow policer, iSCSI_mark_down, on all ports connecting to other switches to mark down iSCSI traffic exceeding 100 Mbps. This policer prevents any building in the campus from overloading the egress transmit on the interface connecting to the SAN network. The iSCSI protocol uses TCP as the transport; therefore, the out-of-order packets that may result for different scheduling of frames over the policing rate are not an issue. Because the distribution layer marks iSCSI frames with a DSCP value of 25, the policed DSCP mapping table configuration forces the switch to mark down frames above the policing with a DSCP value of 25 to 0.

In terms of congestion management and avoidance, all Catalyst 6500 switch ports in this design utilize one priority eqress queue and two standard eqress queues, each with two configurable *Weighted Random Early Detection* (WRED)-drop thresholds (1p2q2t). Because of the priority queue designation, the switch services all traffic in the priority before servicing the standard queues. The switches service the standard queues using WRR.

The configuration applies bandwidth values of 30 and 70 for each of the standard queues, respectively. The priority queue does not use a bandwidth designation because the switch services that queue whenever traffic exists in the queue regardless of WRR scheduling. The bandwidth values use weights between 1 and 255 for bandwidth assignment. In this example, queue 1 receives 30 percent of the bandwidth and queue 2 receives 70 percent of the bandwidth.

The switches assign the transmit queue size for the egress queues, 1 through 3, as 60 percent, 20 percent, and 20 percent, respectively. Transmit queue 3 represents the strict-priority queue. Higher-priority queues generally do not have a large amount to transmit. Furthermore, queuing large amounts of high-priority traffic is generally unnecessary due to the time-sensitive nature of higher-priority traffic.

In terms of congestion avoidance, the Catalyst 6500s use WRED. Each transmit queue uses two threshold values. The threshold values are not the same for each transmit queue. For transmit queue 1, the first threshold uses a minimum value of 50 percent and a maximum value of 75 percent; the second threshold uses 70 percent and 100 percent, respectively. In this manner, queue 1 has two thresholds at which to randomly and totally drop frames.

This example uses the default CoS-to-egress queue mapping. In addition, all other QoS mapping tables also use the default configuration.

Catalyst 6500 Hybrid MSFC

Example 10-6 illustrates the Catalyst 6500 Hybrid *Multilayer Switch Feature Card* (MSFC) sample configuration applied to Figure 10-1.

Example 10-6 *Catalyst 6500 MSFC Sample Configuration for Figure 10-1*

```
C6k-Hybrid-MSFC#show running-config
Building configuration...
Current configuration : 8949 bytes
!
version 12.1
!
(text deleted)
!
class-map match-any Internet-traffic
  match any
!
!
policy-map Shape-Internet
  class Internet-traffic
    shape average 45000000 180000 180000
!
(text deleted)
!
interface Serial4/0/0
 bandwidth 45000
 no ip address
service-policy output Shape-Internet
 dsu bandwidth 44210
 framing c-bit
 cablelength 10
 !
(text deleted)
end
```

The campus network design uses redundant Internet connections. A FlexWAN module in the Catalyst 6500s connects the Internet directly to T3s. To drop excess traffic transmitted on the interface, the FlexWAN uses a shaper. The policy map uses a class map that matches all traffic to shape the egress traffic out the serial interface to 45 Mbps. In this example, the shaper uses a committed burst rate of 180 kbps and an excess burst rate of 180 kpbs.

Catalyst 6500 Native IOS

Example 10-7 shows the Catalyst 6500 Native IOS sample configuration applied to Figure 10-1.

Example 10-7 *Catalyst 6500 Native IOS Sample Configuration for Figure 10-1*

```
C6k-Native#show running-config
Building configuration...
Current configuration : 11129 bytes
!
version 12.1
(text deleted)
!
!
class-map match-all iSCSI-Traffic_1
  match access-group 151
class-map match-all iSCSI-Traffic_2
  match access-group 152
!
!
policy-map Mark_DSCP_iSCSI
  class iSCSI-Traffic_2
    set ip dscp 25
policy-map iSCSI_mark_down
  class iSCSI-Traffic_1
      police 96000 32000 32000 conform-action transmit exceed-action policed-dscp-
transmit
!
(text deleted)
!
mls qos map policed-dscp normal-burst 25 to 0
mls qos map ip-prec-dscp 0 8 16 26 34 46 48 56
mls qos map cos-dscp-map 0 8 16 26 34 46 48 56
mls qos
!
(text deleted)
!
interface Port-channel1
 description Port-Channel (G3/1 G3/2) to Core(Hybrid) 6500
 ip address 10.0.0.2 255.255.255.252
 mls qos trust dscp
 service-policy input iSCSI_mark_down
!
(text deleted)
!
interface GigabitEthernet3/1
 no ip address
 wrr-queue queue-limit 60 20
 wrr-queue random-detect min-threshold 1 50 70
 wrr-queue random-detect min-threshold 2 60 75
 wrr-queue random-detect max-threshold 1 75 100
 wrr-queue random-detect max-threshold 2 80 100
 mls qos trust dscp
 channel-group 1 mode desirable
!
interface GigabitEthernet3/2
 no ip address
 wrr-queue queue-limit 60 20
```

Example 10-7 *Catalyst 6500 Native IOS Sample Configuration for Figure 10-1*

```
 wrr-queue random-detect min-threshold 1 50 70
 wrr-queue random-detect min-threshold 2 60 75
 wrr-queue random-detect max-threshold 1 75 100
 wrr-queue random-detect max-threshold 2 80 100
 mls qos trust dscp
 channel-group 1 mode desirable
!
interface GigabitEthernet3/3
 description Gigabit Connection to SAN
 switch access vlan 600
 wrr-queue queue-limit 60 20
 wrr-queue random-detect min-threshold 1 50 70
 wrr-queue random-detect min-threshold 2 60 75
 wrr-queue random-detect max-threshold 1 75 100
 wrr-queue random-detect max-threshold 2 80 100
 service-policy input Mark_DSCP_iSCSI
 mls qos trust dscp
!
(text deleted)
!
interface Serial4/0/0
 no ip address
 rate-limit output 45000000 8437500 16875000 conform-action transmit exceed-action
drop
 shutdown
 dsu bandwidth 44210
 framing c-bit
 cablelength 10
!
(text deleted)
!
interface GigabitEthernet7/1
 ip address 10.2.1.6 255.255.255.252
 service-policy input iSCSI_mark_down
 mls qos trust dscp
!
interface GigabitEthernet7/2
 ip address 10.2.2.6 255.255.255.252
 service-policy input iSCSI_mark_down
 mls qos trust dscp
!
(text deleted)
!
access-list 101 permit ip any any
access-list 151 permit tcp 10.0.0.0 0.255.255.255 10.0.0.0 0.255.255.255 eq 3620
access-list 152 permit tcp 10.0.0.0 0.255.255.255 eq 3620 10.0.0.0 0.255.255.255
!
(text deleted)
!
end
```

Although the configuration syntax differs, the Native IOS QoS features used in Example 10-7 are identical to the Hybrid CatOS and MSFC IOS configurations from Examples 10-5 and 10-6. The Native IOS configuration models the CLI from the Catalyst 3550 and Catalyst 4500 Family of switches. Because both the Catalyst 6500s in Figure 10-1 use identical line modules, both switches operate identically in all aspects of QoS.

Summary

This chapter reviewed some of the common QoS features applied to a sample campus network topology. Many alternative configurations exist for campus network designs; however, this chapter evaluated the common features in application. Although not explicitly stated, this chapter highlighted the following QoS principles:

- As evident from the configurations, understanding packet flow and traffic profile is essential to building any Campus QoS design and topology.

- Classification on access layer switch interfaces is viable using policy maps with ACLs or trusting based on an attached Cisco IP Phone.

- Deploy reclassification and marking as needed throughout the campus to differentiate service in more levels than possible with access layer switches.

- Use policers to restrict unwanted traffic flows such as Internet gaming and file sharing.

- Deploying WAN interfaces on Catalyst switches eases configuration and provides for additional QoS features.

- Use a method of Priority Queuing when scheduling voice packets from transmit queues.

- Carefully administer QoS maps to maintain desired queuing and scheduling behavior.

- Use congestion avoidance techniques on any interface where congestion is common.

INDEX

Numerics

A

B

M

N

O

P